ABOUT THE AUTHOR

Callista Bowright is the pen name of two people. Alicia Wright and Stella Bowling. Although both had equal input Stella was the creative writer.

Alicia came from two up, two down beginnings in Lancashire. Stella came from wealth, a private education, and a sheltered existence. Their lives collided, dramatically, one September day and this novel was born.

Alicia lives in Norfolk, and her company has become the success it is due to her business acumen and tough glamour. She has five children and many grandchildren.

Stella lives a hippy life in rural Suffolk. She is, at 78, only recently retired. She has two remaining daughters - but four children and a wealth of grandchildren and great grandchildren in Europe and Canada. She lives with her much loved grandson, whom she had raised, since his mother's tragic death in 2012.

Cover design by Petra Lemonnier

THE SIXTH
OF SEPTEMBER

CALLISTA BOWRIGHT

authorHOUSE®

AuthorHouse™ UK
1663 Liberty Drive
Bloomington, IN 47403 USA
www.authorhouse.co.uk
Phone: 0800 047 8203 (Domestic TFN)
*   +44 1908 723714 (International)*

Cover design by Petra Lemonnier

Published by AuthorHouse 06/11/2019

ISBN: 978-1-7283-8515-0 (sc)
ISBN: 978-1-7283-8514-3 (hc)
ISBN: 978-1-7283-8513-6 (e)

Print information available on the last page.

This book is printed on acid-free paper.

CONTENTS

OLIVIA CHILDHOOD, ONE

Her earliest memories were of riding her tricycle along a wide driveway in the town in Lancashire where she was born; she was three or four years old. A gregarious, sunny child with blonde hair, she was already showing the early signs of her future beauty. Her snub nose and her arms were smothered in freckles. Life was happy then. She played with her older brother, Paul, in the large garden, with the neighbour's children shrieking with delight and arguing as children always do. The streets were safe for a young child then. The neighbour would send her up to the shop with a basket and a list of items that a child her age could easily carry. The shopkeeper would pack the little basket and send Olivia home, where the neighbour always gave her ninepence for her trouble. Olivia kept the threepenny piece but promptly gave sixpence to her mother. "I'll put this away for you, love," her mother would say. Little did Olivia realise that the sixpence would disappear into their gas meter.

From that age until Olivia was 10, life was comparatively normal. Her father—she called him that until later, when she started to call him "the sperm donor", a name she used for the rest of his life—was a cold, stern, forbidding presence, but he had not then shown his dark and terrible depths.

Her mother, Minnie, was a beautiful woman, with the pale, fine hair that Olivia had inherited and the lovely bone structure that was to distinguish Olivia from then on. One of Olivia's earliest memories was of standing next to her mother at the kitchen sink, where her mother was peeling a potato with the help of a stand. Her mother could only use one hand, as the other one was in plaster. She worked at a factory nearby, and a man had smashed her wrist with a shovel. Her mother had had an operation in which bone had been removed from her hip and grafted into her shattered wrist. She had been deemed disabled and received a pension. Olivia remembered her mother as the most beautiful woman she had ever known, with her grey eyes, and delicate snub nose. She was tall and slender, and she had perfect poise and an ability to radiate confidence. Every Saturday, without fail, Minnie went to the hairdressers and returned with her long, lovely hair dressed to perfection. Olivia always remembered her mother smelling quite heavenly after these visits, with all the hair spray and other products that had been used to tease her hair into mounds like blonde clouds. Olivia remembered, too, the dangly diamanté earrings her mother hung from her ears, which caught the light and sparkled like stars whenever Minnie moved her head. Olivia wanted to look like that. She made herself a promise at a very early age that one day she would have hair like that, jewellery like that, make-up exquisitely applied as her mother did, and that she would have the same poise and confidence.

When the adults all came back from the Saturday night outing to the pub—a lot of family and friends went—it would be about eleven to twelve at night, and Minnie would go upstairs and kiss the children goodnight. Then, from downstairs, Olivia would hear the piano being played and voices singing. The one voice that stood out was her mother's clear, sharp, beautiful soprano. She would sing Olivia's favourite "Vilia, the Witch of the Wood" and old Irish songs that everyone knew and loved. "Paddy McGinty's Goat" was often trotted out, and everyone would join in and laughed at the humorous verses.

Minnie was a beautiful, talented woman, and she had depths that Olivia was to discover as she grew up. She was a nationally famous medium, a healer, a transmedium, and she used and taught meditation. She would do readings and ask people to put whatever they deemed suitable in the box at the door. She became very famous; she established a spiritualist church in Stafford which was affiliated to the Spiritualist National Union. She was also linked to the Arthur Findlay College Stansted Hall. Olivia knew nothing of her mother's powers at first; her mother was waiting for signs of the blossoming of the powers she suspected her daughter possessed and which she would nurture. Later on Olivia was to learn the Seven Principles of Modern Spiritualism:

> The fatherhood of God,
> The brotherhood of man,
> Communion of spirits and the ministry of angels,
> Continuous existence of the human soul,
> Personal responsibility,

Compensation and retribution hereafter for all good and evil
deeds done on earth,
Eternal progress open to every human soul.

Minnie drilled her in this, and these formed Olivia's beliefs.
She slowly grew to have the same powers as her mother
possessed. But at this early age she lived in ignorance of her
mother's talents and gifts, of the future that lay ahead for her,
and the way these powers would affect her in her coming life.
In the last fifteen years of Minnie's life, she was devoted to
the Spiritualist National Union, the headquarters of which was
Stansted Hall—this is the Vatican of this religion. Workshops,
classes, and readings took place there regularly. At the Arthur
Findlay College next to Stansted Hall, mediums were trained.
There were workshops on fakes and trickery to alert those
with a serious belief to the possible fraudulent practices
that abounded. No aspiring medium could be affiliated to
the Spiritualist National Union without a certificate in many
disciplines and studies. They studied and were trained in
mediumship, speaking, demonstrations, and healing. Minnie
was adept and highly qualified and experienced in all these
things. She was well known and respected, and after she died,
a tree and a plaque were placed outside the church in her
memory.

Olivia's mother was a remarkable woman in many ways. At
the time, Olivia knew of her beauty and her singing voice; later
she would learn what a unique woman she really was. She
went with her mother to witness a healing by transmediumship.
The subject was a man who had serious cancer and had only
six months to live. He realised that he could not be cured but

wanted simply to live out the end of his life free of pain and in peace. He was resigned to the outcome and told everyone that he would see them all after. Olivia sat expectantly, unafraid, and with perfect trust in what was going to unfold. She watched, awestruck, as her mother's outline changed, and in front of them all she became a stooped, very aged man. He was obviously Chinese, and he wore what seemed to Olivia to be a garment from a time long ago, a purple silk robe. He had a long black pigtail going down his back. Minnie had done a complete physical transformation! Her eyes became slanted, and she appeared to be slender and about 5 feet and 5 inches in height. This person moved with tiny, shuffling steps, and when he came around behind the chair of the sick subject, he spoke in a quavering pidgin English. During the session he continually spoke to what seemed to be a throng of other spirits around him in order to gain the power needed to accomplish his healing. He would speak to the spirit surrounding him and, at the same time, to the people in the room, explaining that the man was receiving energy to continue living longer and without suffering. He held his hands about six inches away from the sufferer's shoulders, healing not his physical but his ethereal body. He held his hands over the man's chest, kidneys, and heart, still continuing to converse with the other spirits around him as if it were a teaching session. This very, very old man seemed to Olivia to embody pure spirit, pure love, and a tremendous store of knowledge. He remained in this position for just over ten minutes. Before the healing began, the sufferer had been hunched up in pain, grey, and quite obviously suffering. Now Olivia saw colour return to his face. His clenched hands opened and relaxed onto his lap. There was a palpable change.

The old man was now clearly exhausted. He bowed his head and spoke to the spirits around him. Then, still with a bowed head, he shuffled towards each person in the room individually and thanked them. He addressed the patient's wife and thanked her as "a team member". Then he shuffled up to Olivia, eyes closed, and placed his hand on her head. His eyes opened, and Olivia saw that they were the oriental, slanted, rheumy eyes of an ancient mandarin, not those of her mother.

"My medium's child, you have gifts. Use them." It was an order, not a request. The elderly man thanked everyone around him for the energy they had released to enable him to perform the healing. Then he turned, shuffled towards the wall, stood facing it, and his whole body jerked. Minnie was back again. Throughout it all she had remembered nothing. She had stepped aside, away from her body, as if she had gone to sleep and been bathed in warmth somewhere safe. Not for one second was Olivia concerned for her mother's safety, nor was she shaken by the events she'd witnessed. To her it seemed natural, inevitable. The sick man, Gary, lived not for the six months given to him but a full two years longer. He continued to work in a supermarket, and he lived peacefully and free from pain. One night he went to sleep and did not wake again. His wishes had been fulfilled.

Minnie healed very many people in this fashion, and she passed on her gifts to Olivia. She was a strong influence on her daughter's life and a memorable one.

Olivia remembered being 6 and coming downstairs to the strains of Jimmy Brown on the radio. She heard the squalling of something like a kitten. There in a crib was a very small, very red-faced baby. Her mother was lying in a bed nearby, and she smiled at Olivia. "This is your new baby brother," she told her. Olivia did not then know that some four or five years later she would have another sister and that she would eventually have to bring them both up by herself.

At some point they moved to a small two-up-and-two-down terraced house. As her brother Wayne became a toddler, Olivia's mother inherited a house from her aunt Minnie. Olivia's mother had been named after the aunt. Although it was a smaller house, it made sense to move into it. There would be no mortgage or rent to pay, which would free up much-needed money for the necessities of life which children created. For a child used to a spacious house, this was a dark, cramped place. There was no large garden to play in, it was on a main road, and there was only a tiny backyard, which contained a coal shed and a long-drop toilet. There was a tiny kitchen, which was really just an extension full of old fashioned, sixties-style furniture, and no bathroom. The house was dark, so very dark. There was a cellar, which Olivia hated. As she stood at the top of the cellar steps, she could smell the dank, musty smell of decay, age, and dust. The gas and electricity meters were in this grim, unpleasant place, and Olivia was often sent down to insert money in them both. She tried to get this chore over as swiftly as possible so that she could escape the dark and the putrid stench. The house had only two bedrooms. The one at the right of the top of the stairs was her parents' room; all the children would share the one on the left. As you entered the house, everything was to the right. There was a door on the right leading into a room that Olivia's mother tried to keep for "best"—for visitors. Past that was the staircase, with a red carpet strip running up the middle. Then there was a door opposite which led into the everyday room. This had a square of carpet surrounded by lino. Off this room was the kitchen, where you could barely have swung a very tiny cat. Because there was only the outside toilet, at night everyone in the house used a bucket in the middle of the landing. Olivia frequently had to empty this foul-smelling bucket into the toilet outside, struggling with its weight and hating every moment of this chore.

Olivia did not realise when they moved to this smaller house that her mother was pregnant. Her brother, Wayne, was about 3 then. Olivia was by then old enough to recognise what was occurring and was able to discuss with her mother the imminent arrival of another sibling. One morning when Olivia went downstairs, she was aware that things were happening. During the night she had heard voices. Her grandmother had arrived, and she was instructing the sperm donor to put on his coat and go out and get the midwife. Olivia's mother had been confined to strict rest for the weeks preceding the birth, as she suffered from very high blood pressure. The front room had been turned into a bedroom already to allow this rest. Olivia's mother was not to excite herself in any way. She had been told not to watch horror films on the television but instead to lie quietly, reading poetry or something calming and bland. When Olivia reached the bottom of the stairs, her grandmother was gently bossing the sperm donor, getting him to make himself useful.

Olivia went into the front room. Her mother lay propped up by pillows, pale and looking exhausted. Her body was still very swollen. She smiled at Olivia. In the corner of the room was a Moses basket on a stand. "Go and look at your new sister." Olivia was told later that she'd walked to the basket, looked down into it, turned very red, and simply turned and walked away. Olivia did remember looking down at the baby but little else. Indeed, she had few recollections of her sister, Grace, for some time—except that later her sister would refuse to use the dreaded upstairs bucket while also being terrified to go out in the darkness to use the long drop. Olivia would go with her, and her sister would hold her tightly around her neck with her skinny arms and sob. Until she was fifteen Olivia shared a bed with Grace.

The sperm donor had a friend called Stanley, an elderly chap. He liked Olivia to come with the sperm donor to visit him. Olivia was always bored stiff by these visits, but she behaved herself and sat quietly whilst the adults talked, smoked, and drank tea or beer. When Stanley died, he left £1,000 to the sperm donor. This enabled him to put a deposit on a very different house.

It was about two years before Olivia's parents split up that they moved to a large Victorian house that she loved. It had three storeys, four cellars, a huge bathroom, and an attic. Her favourite room was the bathroom—it was so large and had a washbasin covered in painted roses. Red roses twined around the old, cream-embellished china with green connecting stems. She would run her fingers over the flowers and imagine them twining around the door of a cottage far out in the remote countryside. There was a huge, dusty attic full of old treasures, including a splendid old rocking horse with a long mane and tail and faded, scratched dappled paint, large compelling eyes, and flared nostrils lined with black. Olivia spent hours on his back, talking to him and stroking his long coarse mane as she sang softly to herself: "I had a little pony; | His name was dapple grey. | I lent him to a lady | To ride a mile away. | She whipped him and she lashed him; | She rode him through the mire. | I would not lend my pony now | For any lady's hire." And she laid her blonde head against the horse's mane and rocked and rocked, and rocked.

One day the sperm donor came home with a young girl who, he told Olivia's mother, was homeless and without parental support. The girl's name was June. She was a washy blonde, with a sallow, dirty skin and almost colourless eyes. She was thin and unhealthy looking, and Olivia disliked her at first sight. "Where is she going to sleep?" Olivia's mother asked. "We haven't the room for another body here." She did not look at all pleased. Olivia's dislike of June increased a great deal when she found out that she was to share her single bed. The sperm donor insisted that June must have some kind of home. They couldn't turn her out to walk the streets; she was a poor, unfortunate, needy being, and somehow, he was obliged to solve her problems. Olivia thought that they already had a large enough family to house and support. She did not think that they should be forced to take on this person, particularly since Olivia's bedroom was no longer hers. She felt robbed and exposed. She could not change her views of this girl, and her dislike of June increased daily.

Then Olivia's maternal grandfather died. Her grandmother, who had loved him deeply, was distraught. She moved into the house which was already bursting at the seams. Olivia was very fond of her grandmother, and she welcomed her presence. Minnie was also glad of her mother's help, to watch the younger children while she worked or when she tried to get some rest after working and then doing a great deal of housework. Olivia welcomed her grandmother's company, her kindness, and her love. But, slowly, there was a change, which worried and upset Olivia. Her once-calm grandmother was becoming unpredictable and sullen. Her temper was uncertain, and she began to exhibit behaviours never seen before. In later years Olivia realised that her grandmother was becoming unstable due to the severe grief she was trying to cope with after her husband's death. But at that time she had no idea of that kind of thing, and it alarmed and frightened her greatly.

One day Olivia was playing outside in the road that ran behind the house. Her grandmother was looking after the younger siblings whilst Minnie was out. Suddenly Olivia's grandmother strode out, went up to Olivia, and slapped her hard across her face. Olivia was shocked and hurt. She did not understand why this had happened. What had she done? Her grandmother ranted at her and told her she should have been watching her small sister, Grace. Olivia was confused, as she had not been told to do this; it was not her task. Her grandmother was angry. The baby had crawled into the fireplace and grabbed a bar of the electric fire, which had broken off. It was fortunate that the fire had been switched off when this had occurred. It became clear to Olivia that she was being punished for her grandmother's negligence and that there had been words between Minnie and her mother.

Some weeks later, while going upstairs, Olivia heard her grandmother sobbing in her bedroom. Olivia went in and put her arms around her grandmother. It distressed her to see her so upset, and she imagined it must be because of her grandfather's recent death.

"Don't cry. Is it because you're sad about Granddad?"

Her grandmother wiped tears from her face with a handkerchief. She shook her head. "No, my love, it's that June; we've just had a big argument. I can't stand the little bitch. I shall have to find somewhere else to live. It's getting me down." Her grandmother was very distressed, and this angered Olivia. She set out for her own bedroom, where she knew June was. She pushed the door open and faced the girl.

"You can just get out of our house! You've upset my gran. She's crying her eyes out. We don't want you here! You're just trouble. I don't want you in my bed—not even inside my bedroom. Get out—just get out!" Olivia slammed the door and went downstairs. She was shaking with anger. She hoped the hated June would disappear and leave them all in peace. She did not go, much to Olivia's bitter disappointment.

The following morning, her mother returned from work at half past six; Olivia was asleep. Her mother entered her room, pulled back the bedclothes, and delivered several hard, stinging, painful blows to Olivia's legs. Olivia jumped up, crying out with pain. She could not understand what was happening. First her grandmother had hit her out in the street; now her own mother had assaulted her in this manner! Why? What had she done? She was soon to find out. June had gone crying to the sperm donor and reported Olivia's verbal attack on her. Olivia defended her action, explaining how she had found her grandmother sobbing and what her grandmother had told her. But her grandmother had denied every word of the truth, and Olivia was treated like a criminal and a liar. Her faith in adults took a steep and traumatic dive. And the hated June had not gone.

Then there was another significant change in the family's dynamics. Another man appeared in Olivia's grandmother's life. Her grandmother's moods softened; her depression and bitterness disappeared. Olivia was happy at this; her grandmother had started to make her life very unpleasant, and now she was almost back to being the person Olivia loved very deeply.

Then her parents' seventeenth wedding anniversary came around. There was a party for family and friends, with food, a large cake, alcoholic drinks of all sorts, and copious amounts of strong tea. What transpired at this party Olivia would never know—but two days later the hated June was kicked out unceremoniously, weeping and pleading. Olivia was not at all sorry to see her go, she had caused more than enough inconvenience and trouble to them all.

The sperm donor tried to convince Minnie to take the girl back. He pleaded and wheedled, but Minnie was adamant. "No. I'm not having that girl in my house again—ever. If you want her here, then it's her or me."

Three days later the sperm donor brought June back with him. "I found her down by the canal, Minnie. She was crying, breaking her heart. She's got nobody, no family; no one wants the kid. She can't sleep in the street, for God's sake."

So June returned to the house, and the tension slowly grew. Olivia later learnt that her mother had already planned her escape and had been sneaking her clothes and possessions out of the house, leaving them with a friend after this. The scene for Olivia's future was being set, action by action.

One day Olivia came downstairs for breakfast and could not see her mother or hear her voice, as she usually did at this time of day. Searching for her, Olivia found six envelopes on the big dresser. On two her name was written in her mother's hand. On opening the first one, Olivia found two crisp pound notes. She was ecstatic, thinking to herself that it must be Christmas and she hadn't noticed its arrival—but the second envelope shattered her small world. In it was a letter from her mother telling her that she was leaving, as she could no longer take the marriage she was in. But she would soon be back for all of them; it was just a matter of weeks, the letter assured the sad little girl. Olivia stood shaking and crying; she felt so terribly alone. Her beloved mother was gone. She had said she would be back in a few weeks—but how many was that? Just then the sperm donor came in. He saw Olivia sobbing.

"For Christ's sake, what are you snivelling about now?" he demanded angrily.

"Mum's gone, my mum's gone ..." Olivia continued to sob.

"What the hell are you talking about, girl?"

"There's an envelope for you in the living room," Olivia told him. He went down, picked up the letter, opened it, and read it.

"Bloody hell! What am I supposed to have done this time?" HIs face was dark. "Go on." He tossed his head in the direction of the door. "Get to school." Olivia had to leave and go to school, shattered, shocked, numb, and not knowing what was to happen to her and her siblings.

It was her eleventh birthday just a little later, and she didn't want to celebrate or even acknowledge the occasion. It was the last time she would receive cards and presents, the last real, normal birthday she would have for many years. Later on Olivia would learn that the one she called the sperm donor had regularly and violently beaten her beloved mother. Olivia's small world became suddenly black and cold and frightening. She clung to the promise of her mother's return as the only beacon in her darkness and misery. She had begun to discover for herself the unpleasant reality of the man who had fathered her. When he had her alone in the kitchen, away from her mother he would spend great lengths of time ranting at her and lecturing her on what he considered her unacceptable behaviour. Once he had snarled on at her and had begun to jab his finger into her face, closer and closer, until his nail had cut her cheek and made it bleed. When her mother asked her what had happened, Olivia had told her of the man's actions; her mother had tackled him about the incident, and Olivia had learnt her first lesson of the duplicity and cruelty of men. He denied the whole matter, and Olivia was left dazed and hurt. Her trust had suffered a blow, and it gradually diminished as her life unfolded into shadowy horror.

Olivia realised that this man who had appeared as a normal, friendly, run-of-the-mill guy to all and sundry was a two-faced, secretive, hypocritical tyrant. Olivia remembered it well. Her mother had left two days before her eleventh birthday, and from that day until her sixteenth birthday her life became a living hell. From that day on, she replaced her mother. She cleaned the house, cooked, and struggled to care for, feed, and keep clean her brother and sister whilst attending school. And every day she came home to a beating. The sperm donor abused her verbally as well, calling her a rat, a slag, a prostitute, and no better than that cow who had left him.

Later Olivia discovered that her mother had left to try and establish a home for her children when she could no longer stand the constant verbal and physical abuse inflicted on her. She had left with a man she'd met in the factory, a man she was honest enough to tell she didn't really love him but who loved her deeply. He had determined to help her find a home after she had escaped the brutal life she was enduring. When Olivia was 16, this kindly man became her father, the only one she had looked on as worthy of that name, and a more caring, compassionate, and loving man Olivia had yet to find. But that was still in the future for her—the present still had to be endured, in all its terrible reality.

Olivia and her siblings were suffering the loss and confusion that their mother's leaving had wrought. Olivia had to endure the presence in the house, and her sperm donor's bed, of the 17-year-old tarty imbecile. June imagined she had taken over the role of Minnie and lorded it over the children. They ignored her attempts to domineer and control them. As she had disappeared from Olivia's bed immediately, Olivia assumed that she was sleeping with the sperm donor. Olivia made great efforts to ensure that her younger siblings were kept as clean and as smart as her mother would have kept them. She dressed them and did their hair meticulously. June tried to interfere with everything, but Olivia ignored her. Then June tried to boss around the youngest children, but they ignored her. Her biggest mistake was to try to foist herself on Olivia. Even at this young age, Olivia was a strong, determined person who would not tolerate bullying and interference.

When June began barking out orders, Olivia simply looked at her with a keen stare. "Who the hell d'you think you're talking to? Don't you talk to me like that. You're not wanted here. Just leave us well alone, or get out—go on—out of that door." And June realised that this was one area she should not meddle in. Olivia told her siblings to go and do something else if June gave them orders. She tried in every way she possibly could to make June feel unwanted—as she indeed was.

As well as suffering this terrible change, Olivia had to move to the high school and desperately needed her mother's love and guidance in this step in her life. She had no friends and no mother; she was totally isolated. She had to run from school to tackle the piles of laundry, ironing, cooking, and cleaning that five people required. She was often exhausted, and one day the sperm donor caught her, slumped and aching, on a chair. That was the first time he dragged her by her hair, punched her, threw her against the wall, and then kicked her mercilessly for almost fifteen minutes. As she crawled to her feet, dazed and bleeding, he sneered at her. "Now try sitting down again."

This was to be the pattern of Olivia's misery for the next four years. She was to learn the worst of tortures he had devised for her—the one she feared most was beatings with the buckle end of his belt. On one particularly awful occasion, Olivia was ten minutes late home from school. It was a Monday, one of the days on which the sperm donor would go out drinking at lunchtime. He drank on Fridays, Saturdays, Sundays, and Mondays. Then he worked nights on Mondays, Tuesdays, Wednesdays, and Thursdays. Whilst drunk, he would brag about his army service, about how he had fought the Viet Cong. He had been a medic, a trained nurse. He'd been lying in the jungle, with snakes crawling all over him, knowing he had to keep quiet and escape the ruthless enemy. He had contracted malaria. The tales went on and on. In later years Olivia's mother told her that he had been nothing in the army—just a mere tick-tock, a basic soldier. He had a mass of spots on his back, which he attributed to his "jungle trauma". He expected Olivia to pour Dettol onto them and then scrub his back vigorously. In truth, this was simply acne—but the sperm donor had to have something more exotic than that.

On this day Olivia had been held up by her teacher. She had pleaded to be released, as she was terrified of being late arriving home. She had about two miles to walk and only thirty-five minutes to walk it in. She ran as fast as she could, but the time that the teacher had kept her made her ten minutes late. As she came up the road, she saw the look on the sperm donor's face—one of black anger, almost of murder. Olivia knew that she would suffer a beating for this.

She walked into the tiny courtyard, which had a path only a foot long. She was terrified and tried to explain her lateness. She could barely form the words. "Th-the t-t-t-teacher k-kept me—I tried—I-I'm s-s-sorry—" She stammered and wrestled with the words.

He glared at her. He spoke coldly and angrily, and very slowly. "Get. In. The. House. Now!"

Olivia was resigned to her coming fate. She knew she could not avoid a beating. As she went into the hall, he grabbed her by the back of her neck and threw her down, very hard, onto the settee. It was one of the old cottage types, with wooden arms and a wooden back. On other occasions, the sperm donor had tried to break Olivia's back by forcibly bending her over the wooden bars at the back.

Olivia was aware that she needed quite desperately to urinate. The sperm donor wrapped the soft end of his belt around his wrist. This left a good ten inches with the buckle on the end of it, and he swung this above his head and brought it down very hard, not caring where the blows landed or what injuries he inflicted on the helpless child. Her body was covered from top to ankles in huge, red welts that would turn black and blue very soon. Olivia was in terrible pain and fear. Halfway through this merciless cruelty, she could no longer hold her bladder in control. She screamed out, "Stop, stop—oh, please stop!" But the urine came in a hot, wet stream, all over her, and where her body was wet, the blows raining down stung even more. The beating continued for twenty minutes, and at the end of it, Olivia thought, *I know now just what slaves went through when they were beaten.*

By now Olivia had no more breath or strength to scream any longer. She lay, taking the blows, unable to react. Then, his anger spent, or exhausted from that anger and from the physical exertion, the sperm donor lifted Olivia up by the front of her jumper and threw her towards the door. She landed heavily and limply, like a rag doll. He went up to her and kicked her in her stomach; he was wearing his heavy working boots.

"Get upstairs. Go on, get upstairs, and clean yourself up." Olivia knew that she must get up there as quickly as she could. The devil was behind her, but her weak, little body had nothing left. She could not drag herself up the stairs, however hard she tried to. Her whole body smarted and ached with pain. Her neck and throat, her shoulders, her back, her breasts, her stomach, her buttocks, thighs and legs—all were a mass of fiery pain. It was the worst agony she had yet faced. At last she found the strength to drag herself along. She crawled up the last few steps and staggered into the partitioned-off bathroom. She stripped all her clothes off and looked at herself in the mirror. It was like looking at someone else. She did not recognise this mass of swollen, bruised flesh. Who was this person? Her brain had cut off, unable to cope with any more torment. The shock gripped her and paralysed her. She held onto the basin, swaying, and begged God to let her die, just die; she could not take any more. She remained there, looking at this stranger who faced her from the mirror, and then she heard him screaming from the bottom of the stairs. She shuddered and closed her eyes.

"Get yourself down here, my lady! The kids'll be back from school soon, and they'll need feeding. If the food's not on the table when they get here, you'll think that was just playtime."

Where Olivia found the strength to wash her aching body and to dress, she would never know, but find it she did, and she went down as fast as she could force herself to. She had no real cooking to do. The sperm donor would not spend money feeding his children on real and nourishing food. They fed on powdered potato and powdered soups, which Olivia merely reconstituted with boiling water. The sperm donor then made up their insufficient diet by giving them vitamin tablets. This ensured that they survived in a reasonable fashion, and nobody outside that home knew the extent of the deprivation and cruelty that existed within. All of them were stick-thin. At 15 years of age Olivia was barely 7 stone in weight.

That night Olivia sat on the bed, still aching, burning, and smarting. This was the worst beating she had ever taken, and now, in her young, tender mind, there crept the terrible realisation that her mother was never coming back. She did not know then that her mother had been fighting endlessly to get her children back. The younger ones would go for short visits but would soon be back. The welfare officer would be sent to check the home and the children, but this was of no avail. On the days that these inspections were due, the sperm donor would make very sure that he was sober. He would stay up all night cleaning the house from top to bottom, and the children would be threatened to never, ever breathe a word of the reality of their terror and hardship.

The visiting officer would question them. "Are you happy here? Is everything all right with your life with your father? If you had the option, would you rather live with your mother?"

The replies were predictable. The children were terrified. They would not tell the truth.

Olivia sat there thinking of all this. She was at the end of her small tether, her ability to endure. She went to the chest of drawers and took out a pile of medication that had accumulated over the years when her mother and grandmother had been there. She spread the tablets out over her bedcover and got a glass of water. She scooped up a handful of them, and raised

21

them to her mouth. Just then, her small sister, who was asleep in the bed beside her, stirred and mumbled in her sleep. Olivia was shocked into reality. If she did this and died, she would be released from this agonising hell—but who would care for her siblings? Who would protect them from his violence, shield them from the blows? For a second Olivia sat, frozen in time, the handful of tablets halfway to her mouth and the glass of water in her other hand. Then she put them all back in the bag, put the bag back in the drawer, and slid back down into her bed. She must fight on—for her brothers and sister. Life was not always about oneself, even when one was suffering terribly. Olivia was small, weak, and beaten down, but she was also unselfish, caring, and very brave. She slept. The wheels of destiny moved silently and unerringly; her future, and her character, were slipping into their places.

They had by now moved again to a smaller house, and Olivia was once more required to share a bed with her sister, who was barely 3 at this time. Her sister would all too frequently wet the bed, so Olivia would get up at six in the morning, wash down her sister, wash the sheets and hang them on the line, and turn the mattress, working desperately against the time when the dreaded sperm donor would return from night shift. Had he found her tiny sister wet and the bed wet too, he would have spanked her hard with his hand—as he already had before— and then throw her against the wall, this little girl of not yet 3 years. Olivia had learnt that she must protect her small brother and sister from his sudden outbursts and violence by physically placing herself between them. If she could say something that would annoy him, she could gain his attention, and she would take the beatings intended for these two small, innocent beings.

Once he had beaten Olivia so hard that he had broken her collarbone. As she always had to, she covered up the bruising and struggled through the pain and misery. One day at school, a friend of Olivia's, a spoilt child called Karen who came from a wealthy family, said, "Let's not go back into school; let's go to my house. Mum won't mind." Olivia agreed. Karen's house was nearer her home than the school was; she wouldn't have far to go to be there in time. She was beginning to get a little bit braver now. They went to Karen's home. Her mother was rather lax; she indulged her daughter and would happily have told the school that Karen had a headache to excuse any absence. The girls went into the back room and put on the record player. Then a sad song came on, and Olivia burst into tears.

Karen looked at her in alarm. "Whatever's the matter, Livvy? What are you crying for, you daft cow?"

Then it all came out in a torrent of revelation, and relief. Olivia told Karen what was happening: the misery, the beatings, the cruelty, the deprivation, the fear.

Karen looked at her in disbelief and horror. "Well, it shouldn't be happening! Let's go and tell my mum about it—let's see what she can do about it."

"No, no—you can't—you mustn't!" Olivia was terrified, wishing she hadn't broken down like that.

"Yes, we will. Come on; I'm going to tell Mum." Karen almost ran to the kitchen, where her mother was preparing something that to Olivia's eyes and nostrils seemed to be a dream feast. Karen recounted, word for word, what Olivia had told her. Karen's mother asked Olivia if it was really true. Olivia told her that it was and repeated the sad story. Karen's mother went out of the room, quickly and determinedly. This was a rich family. They

23

had one of the things that only the posh families had then—a telephone. She rang the police. Olivia's heart sank at the very sound of the word *police*. When they arrived, Olivia changed her mind, and her heart rose with relief. At last somebody would surely rescue her and her brother and sister from their hell. The large, sullen policeman listened to the story that Olivia told him. The look on his face was very difficult to read. He then said, "OK, get in the car." When the car started, Olivia presumed they were going to the police station so he could take a formal statement. This wasn't the case—he took her back to her house and stood her before her tormentor. *At last!* Olivia thought. *This man will stand up for us.*

The policeman looked at Olivia and then at the sperm donor. "If I were you, sir, I'd keep this one under control," he said brusquely. The policeman turned to leave.

Olivia's world collapsed. She tried to blurt out, "Help me—help us!" but nothing came out of her mouth. After that there was silence. The expected beating came eventually. There was no escape. Olivia learnt that she must keep her mouth firmly closed and trust nobody—even those who were supposed to protect her.

On Saturday nights the sperm donor brought back fish and chips, which Olivia and her brother were forced to eat sitting in the kitchen. The sperm donor would have already been drinking, and the two children ate as fast as they could to try and escape as quickly as possible. But for Olivia there was always a beating. Later in her life she realised that he was not only beating her but her mother, who she resembled strongly. In his sick mind, Olivia and her mother were one and the same.

Over five years the violence continued. He dragged her out of the top bunk bed she shared with her young sister and threw her down the stairs and through a glass door. He slung her against the wooden-barred back of a settee and pushed her hard up against it to try and break her back. For Olivia there was no respite—this was her life. Despair, loneliness, confusion, depression, and pain filled the days of her young life. She daydreamed of her beautiful mother and her soft voice and the touch of her hand. She was a shabby girl with dirty, ill-fitting clothes. She was aware that she smelt bad, as she was not allowed many baths or any luxuries like deodorant. In her darkest times she dreamt of a life where she had more than one bathroom, toiletries overflowing them, cupboards full of clothes and shoes, a wonderful kitchen filled with food, a huge living room with deep, soft comfortable furniture, a bed so large she would almost be lost in it—and above all, a man. The man would be kind, gentle, loving, caring, and protective. He would have strong arms into which she could run and be sheltered from fear and violence and ... These were just dreams, but they were all she had.

Olivia would sit at the back of her classroom, always trying to avoid being seen too much and attempting to cover up the constant bruising, welts, and marks on her body. Nearly every day she was assaulted, early in the morning before she left for school. By now her siblings were able to get themselves up and dressed, so Olivia would stay in bed until ten minutes before the sperm donor arrived from work. She was able to dress hurriedly and be downstairs by the time he came into the kitchen. But on those mornings when she didn't quite make it, and he found her still in bed, he would drag her out and kick her in the back of her head with his heel. With all the other beatings she constantly endured, it was almost impossible to totally conceal the results. On this particular morning, Olivia had been kicked in the head and also behind her ears, causing bad bruising. She sat at the back of the class as usual that day; it was about eleven in the morning. Her soft, lovely blonde hair was very long, as she had never been to a hairdresser since her mother's departure. She had combed her hair back behind her ears, as it would otherwise fall onto her work and irritate her. Next to her sat her friend Julie. Just as Olivia brushed her hair behind her ear, Julie turned and saw the rim of Olivia's ear—it was black.

Julie's eyes went wide with shock. She stared at Olivia. "What on earth have you done, Livvy!"

Olivia hesitated. She had made one mistake and told somebody of her plight—and nothing had been done to help. All it had brought was retribution and more horror. She did not want to say anything, but Julie could see that things were very wrong, so she gently pushed, and pushed, and pushed. Then it all came pouring out—the indoctrination, the terrifying beatings, not being allowed anything that normal teenagers were allowed, like boyfriends, or makeup, or decent clothes. She pointed out the ugly, ill-fitting winkle-picker shoes that deformed her feet. Olivia sat weeping as she told her friend this dreadful secret. She told how she dared not tell anyone, as she was so afraid that the sperm donor would actually kill her; he had already once tried to strangle her.

Julie looked at Olivia in pity. She took Olivia's hand. "You can't live like this, Livvy; you've got to tell someone." Olivia told Julie that she trusted nobody, that she had once told the police, and they had just dumped her back at her home, leaving her to the mercies of the violent sperm donor. Who could she possibly trust now?

At this point they split up to go to different classes for different subjects; Olivia picked up her bag and left. As she settled down in the next class, Olivia looked up and saw that someone was whispering to the teacher. The teacher looked up at Olivia.

"Olivia, would you go to the headmaster's office, please?" Olivia realised then that Julie had told someone.

Olivia followed the teacher who led her silently to the headmaster's office. Outside she stopped. "Olivia, we've heard from Julie what's been going on. You must tell the headmaster the same truths."

"I can't!"

"You must! You must be very brave. It's the only way we can help you. Tell him the lot—in detail—and we can put a stop to it. Trust us." She laid her hand gently on Olivia's shaking arm. They went in, and Olivia sat down in the chair next to the headmaster's desk.

"Olivia is this true—what Julie and your teacher have told me?" He looked at her keenly. This was a teacher of the old school, not someone you could lie to.

Olivia looked at him squarely, straight in his face, and said, "Yes, it's all true."

"Right, tell me what's been going on." And Olivia told him. It took her about twenty-five minutes to tell them all that had happened to her in those terrible, traumatic, sad years.

The headmaster listened in silence. Then he sat back and drew in a deep breath. If you have been beaten as you say you have, then you will have bruises and scars. Will we find any?"

"Yes, you will."

"We will have to examine you for evidence. I'm sure you understand this." Seeing the horror on the girl's face, he held up his hand reassuringly. "The assistant headmistress will be present. We just need to back up this case with strong evidence. Go across the corridor into the medical room, strip to your bra and pants, and cover your top with your blouse. We won't cause you any distress. We just do need to see this indisputable evidence. Is this all right with you?"

"Yes." Olivia went to the room. She stripped to her underwear and rolled her blouse into a tube, which she held across her breasts. She stood with her back to the door.

The door opened. Olivia heard the slight gasp of horror from the assistant headmistress as she saw it all—all the story laid out in its awful, ingrained viciousness. The assistant head asked, "Is it all right for the headmaster to come in now?"

Olivia was staring out of the window. She was embarrassed, trying not to be there. She wanted this help but resented what it was subjecting her to. Then she heard the headmaster cough. He said, "Olivia, please could you turn round?"

Instantly Olivia was back with her tormentor. Fear bubbled hotly through her body. She dropped her head and turned. The shock on their faces was intense. They stared, horrified, at her bruises, belt marks, and cuts. They examined her and noted the dip in her collar bone where the broken bone had been untreated. All she had said was too, too true. They listened to her faltering account of all she was expected to do—of her protection of her small brother and sister, her exhaustion after her school day, her constant fears and stresses. They listened in silence. The headmaster's face was growing red with anger. Then he strode out of the room.

The headmistress looked at Olivia with deep sympathy in her eyes. "Are you all right?"

"Yes, I'm OK." Olivia was conditioned to say this. She was not used to anyone asking her genuine questions, or putting their arms around her, or listening to her and really reacting. The headmistress told her to get dressed and then go back to the headmaster's office. Olivia dressed and went there. Both heads were waiting for her.

The headmaster looked up at her with great pity in his eyes. "I'm going to drive over to your house and sort this, Olivia."

"No—please, no! Don't do that, please. He'll kill me—you just don't know what—" She sobbed desperately.

"Don't worry, Olivia. When I've finished with him, he'll never lay another finger on you again. Trust me."

"You won't find him—he's on nights."

"Trust me, Olivia. I'll find him."

Later, the headmaster got into his car and drove to Olivia's home, where he confronted the sperm donor. After the headmaster had left and Olivia was alone with the sperm donor, they just looked at each other, both knowing what had happened. For two weeks he did not touch her. Some kind of hope began to grow in her that her misery was over. Two weeks later he changed all this; he beat and kicked her for nearly three hours. Finally he grabbed a large bronze ornamental cross, and holding it up, he swore never to touch his daughter again. Then he threw the cross at her; it grazed her face and left a permanent mark on her temple.

His promise did not last. When Olivia was 15 he took her and her brother and sister on holiday to Morecambe. Her oldest brother, Paul, had by this time joined the navy, in an attempt to escape the misery of their home life. The sperm donor took the younger two out with him daily, but Olivia was locked in the chalet, alone and miserable. All she had to look forward to was the nightly beatings he inflicted on her.

On the Saturday night, he got drunk and returned staggering and mumbling. Olivia was in bed, on her period; he pulled back the covers. "Get out!" he snapped. She obediently climbed out and stood shaking, with her arms around her body protectively. He threw her up against the wall and began to pull off her nightdress; she tried to protect her modesty with her arms and huddled down, but he made her remove her knickers. "Get rid of this," he growled and pointed at her sanitary towel and belt. Reluctantly she removed them and stood trembling and terrified, with blood trickling down her thighs and legs. He smashed his fist into her once, twice, and endlessly. When he stopped for breath he told her, "Stand against the wall, facing me, and do not move"!

Olivia obediently stood with her back against the wall, naked and terrified, with a pool of blood gathering around her foot. Every time she tried to cover herself and protect her modesty, he would get up from the chair he was sitting on, stare at her with unblinking eyes, and beat her again. When he was satiated, she ran into the bathroom to clean herself up. She was obliged to walk through the living room of the small chalet to get to her bedroom, and as she passed the door of his bedroom, he called her in. She went in reluctantly to where he lay on the bed. He threw back the covers, and she saw that he was naked. He pointed to the bed. "Get in," he said softly. Olivia was terrified; she knew vaguely what was going to happen. She was a virgin. For a second she was paralysed with terror, unable to move or speak or even think. She suddenly came to and fled to her own bedroom, where her terror gave her the strength to drag the heavy dressing table across the door. Panting, she leaned on it, dreading every sound. She stayed with her back to it for hours, while he pounded on the door and ordered her to obey him. Finally he went, and silence fell. As dawn streaked the sky with red, she fell asleep from sheer exhaustion. These episodes were to continue; he would strip her naked, and she would plead with him not to do what she knew was wrong and terrible. She would keep pleading and talking in order to distract him, and he would finally beat her to silence her. Olivia had reached the stage where she would whisper to herself, in the extremes of misery, "Kill me—take me!" Her lifelong attitudes towards and hang-ups over sex were all instilled in Olivia by these experiences.

There was throughout all this misery and darkness one person, one man, who Olivia had learnt to trust. After all the family turmoil of the seventeenth anniversary party and the rifts caused by the presence of June, things had settled down for a short while. One day Olivia had come home from school and climbed the stone steps to the kitchen. She'd greeted her parents and then stopped. Sitting in the chair that her beloved grandfather had always occupied was a small elderly man with thick, wavy, dark hair, bushy eyebrows, glasses, and a pleasant smile. He was holding a cup of tea. Olivia stood staring at him, curious and unsmiling. He looked back at her, smiling. Minnie said, "Olivia, let me introduce you to your grandad."

Immediately Olivia was shocked and angry. This was not her beloved grandad. How could anyone replace him? She immediately resented this interloper who was claiming to be her dead grandfather. Again the man smiled warmly, but Olivia's expression did not change. She just glared. "No, you're not. You're not my grandad."

The adults all smiled and exchanged looks. Minnie put her arm around Olivia. "This is your dad's dad, love. I know you haven't met yet, but he is related to you." Olivia nodded at the stranger and then asked if she could change and go out to play. Minnie understood perfectly the child's confusion.

Olivia and this new relative did not see each other again for at least two years. Then, after her parents had split up, Olivia was cleaning the kitchen one day while the sperm donor was lounging around. There was a knock on the back door, and the sperm donor actually got up to open it. He'd obviously known that someone was coming. It was the new grandad. Olivia found out that he was called Edward and that she really liked him. Slowly, but very surely, he worked his way into her untrusting and traumatised heart. Although Edward did not witness any physical violence, he could see the shabby clothing and shoes the children wore, see how thin and pale they were, see how afraid of his son they all were. Although he had several grandchildren in that family, it soon became clear that Olivia was the favourite. Edward came to tea often, but soon he was asking Olivia to go to the next town on Sundays to have tea with him. She would board the bus and travel there. Edward would meet her in the town centre and walk her to his tiny, neat, cosy home. But before he did, he would always take her around the market and buy her something. It would be nothing exceptional, just some small treasure, although once he had bought her a cardigan, brown with stripes. To Olivia, who had had nothing new for two years, it was fantastic. She felt like the bee's knees wearing it.

Back at Edward's house, tea would be ready. It was always sandwiches, usually made with tinned red salmon, which Olivia loved, and cucumber on white bread, Mr. Kipling cakes—these Olivia really loved—and strong black tea to wash it all down. After her unending diet of dehydrated soup and potato, this was a feast, and she could relax to eat it. By now Olivia had fallen victim to the habit of smoking, which she tried vigorously to hide, especially from the sperm donor. Edward smoked the untipped, exceedingly strong Senior Service cigarettes. He would light one up, take a few puffs on it, put it out, and then go into the kitchen to finish preparing or bring in the tea. While he was out there, Olivia would quickly light up the discarded cigarette and take a few hasty drags on it. On this particular day she was drawing on the half cigarette when Edward came in from the kitchen with a plate of salmon sandwiches in one hand and a dish of cucumber in the other. He stood in the doorway looking at Olivia, put the sandwiches on the table, and sat down. Clasping his hands underneath his chin—a habit Olivia was to copy in later life—he looked at her again.

"How long have you been smoking, then?" he asked her quietly. Olivia's colour drained. If the sperm donor were to find out, it would mean terrible punishment for her. Edward must have seen her reaction.

"Not long, Grandad. I only have a few puffs now and then."

"Well, go on. Light it back up, then." Olivia was used to mistrusting, to being tricked, to having to second-guess the sperm donor. Was this just a trick to catch her out again?

Edward looked at her, half smiling. "It's all right, my love. You smoke if you want to."

Olivia was used to obeying, so she relit the cigarette and took a few puffs on it. It was very strong. She handed it back to Edward. "I can't smoke any more, Grandad."

Edward took it from her, smiling. He had a couple of pulls himself; then he put it out. "Shall we eat then, my love?"

Olivia still hesitated. "Are you going to tell him?"

"You can trust me, love. Whenever you want a smoke, you can just come here and light up. Just trust me." And Olivia knew then, instinctively, that she could trust him.

A few weeks later, Edward came to Olivia's home for dinner. The sperm donor had sent her out to buy those thin, spare minute chops. Like tracing paper, but with a small amount of real meat on them, they were nothing like the desiccated rubbish they usually lived on. It was just to impress Edward and to fool him into thinking that this was the norm. Sometimes Edward would go with the sperm donor for a drink and stay overnight. Edward would watch Olivia, see the fear in her face, and listen to the barked orders from his son to the wretched girl. From the kitchen Olivia could hear them. One day Edward said, "I'm going to tell you something, Albert—and you might not like it."

Christ, thought Olivia. *He's going to tell him about me smoking.* She froze.

"If you have a dog," Edward began, "and you keep it chained up in the backyard for two years, and one day you forget to close the gate, and that dog slips it leash, it'll run away, and you'll never see it again."

Albert, the sperm donor, was silent for minutes. Then he said, tersely, "Well, if I had a dog tied up in the backyard, it'd be because I didn't want it anyway." In that second Olivia knew just how little the man who had fathered her cared for her. She knew that the sperm donor didn't want her—but he also didn't want her mother, who desperately wanted her, to have her either. He knew exactly just what he was doing to both of them. She was being used to hurt her mother. She was just a weapon—worthless. The feeling that she wanted to die, just die, washed over her again. The physical and psychological torment were winning.

This small, pleasant man whom Olivia had snubbed at their first meeting was becoming her closest friend and ally. Nothing was ever discussed, he did not pressure Olivia for facts or details, but Olivia knew that Edward knew, and Edward knew that Olivia knew that he knew. He was powerless to help Olivia as he would have wanted to—and she realised this. But there was always an unspoken bond that made Olivia Edward's favourite. Always they shared the salmon sandwiches, and the cakes, and the strong tea and even stronger cigarettes, and the trips around the market. Olivia treasured two presents from these trips—her striped cardigan, and a radio and tape player, a "boom box", the must-have for teens of the day. It cost Edward a lot of money, and Olivia appreciated it so very much. It had been given to her by someone who actually cared for her and about her.

Later, just before Olivia left her captivity, she went to see Edward. He told her he wanted to know his first great-grandchild. Olivia promised that she would bring her; even then she already knew she would have a girl. But it was not to be, and Olivia never lost the guilt she felt at letting him down. He had been a bright star in her darkness, a comfort in the misery of her ordeal. She would always love him.

At this point in Olivia's life something occurred that revealed to her that she was no ordinary child. She had from time to time had dreams that showed her certain things that were going to happen to people in their lives. Every time this happened, these dreams were proved to be uncannily accurate. Olivia kept the knowledge to herself, half afraid of this disturbing ability, although she realised that she'd inherited this gift from Minnie. That summer the school was abuzz with excitement, as there was to be a trip to Spain for the teenage pupils whose parents could afford to send them. Travel, even as far afield as Europe, was uncommon in those days, and it was a talking point daily. Olivia watched the other girls talking of the new clothes they had been bought, their passports, and the plane trip they were to take. She felt very isolated. There would be no travel anywhere for her, no escape from her prison and the misery of her daily existence. One night she fell asleep exhausted after a day at school, housework, the care of her siblings, and the inevitable beating. Suddenly she was in an aeroplane. She stood in the middle of the gangway, watching her school friends chattering and laughing excitedly. She saw the hostesses pushing trollies of food and drink up and down. Below her, as she gazed out of the window, she saw clouds like a great ice field, stretching out as far as she could see. Huge, wispy streaks of cloud passed as the aircraft pushed through them. She had never been up in a plane and had had no idea what it would be like to fly above clouds and through them; this was a revelation to her. Suddenly the noise of the aircraft ceased, and Olivia was on the ground, looking upwards at the great silver giant as it streaked above what was clearly the sea. As she watched, it began to tilt forwards and fall downwards at a great speed towards the water. Olivia was horrified. She knew something terrible was about to happen, and she could do nothing to warn her friends of the impending tragedy. As she watched, gasping and clenching her fists, the plane hit the water and broke into two pieces. And then Olivia was in the water with her friends. She heard them screaming and reached out to try and help them, but she could do nothing. She saw and felt the terror on their faces as, strapped to their seats or flung across the aisles and tangled in the broken seats, they struggled to escape the dark, cold water that was dragging them down relentlessly. Olivia could feel the suction of the aircraft fuselage; she saw and felt it dragging them all down. The air was being pulled from her lungs, and she experienced the pain and the terror. She fought and struggled desperately; then she was pulling away from them. Away and into space, and that part of her that was with the victims in the crash was being pulled back into her body, while their pathetic cries and pleading were still with her. She woke and lay trembling and sobbing. She must do something. She knew that this was not just a bad dream; it really was going to happen, and she must prevent it.

The next day, as soon as she reached the school, she made for the headmaster's office. Outside his door was a box with a glass window fastened to the wall. Any pupil desiring to go in would knock and, if a green light showed, would enter the sanctum. But if the light was red, then the student would have to remain outside in the corridor until the light turned green; this often meant a long wait. Olivia raced towards the door and knocked urgently. The light in the box turned red. She ignored it, pushed the door open, and walked in. The headmaster, Mr Aloysius Broadbent, was a large, corpulent man with a bald head skimmed by a sprinkling of ginger fluff. He had watery, colourless eyes, almost no lips, and a huge set of chins. The chins had an existence of their own and followed each movement of his head like a chorus of well-drilled servants. He sat back in his chair and glared at Olivia. "Did you not see the red light, girl? Get out of my office—now!"

Olivia lunged forward and placed her hands on his desk. "I must talk to you! You have to stop them going to Spain. I had this dream—I saw them all dying and drowning and screaming. The plane's going to crash. I was there! I know—please listen to me. You've got to stop them going, or they'll all die—please Mr. Broadbent!"

He leaned forward. His face was very angry. "Get out of my office girl. Are you mad? Get to your classroom and stop this stupid insanity."

Olivia was sobbing. Tears were pouring down her face. She threw herself across the desk and grabbed Mr Broadbent's hands desperately.

"I saw them—they were drowning. I couldn't help them, but you can. You must stop them going! Oh, please, I did see them in this dream. It was real—not just a dream—you have to believe me—oh, please! They'll all die if you won't stop them going on that plane." By now Olivia was shaking and gasping as the tears washed down her face and onto her school shirt. She wiped her face with the sleeve of her jumper.

The headmaster gritted his teeth and breathed deeply. "Out—out, girl! Go to your class. I do not want a repetition of this scene—ever!" He got up from his chair, grabbed the weeping girl by her arm, and steered her none too gently to the door and out of it. Olivia was desperate. She ran to her class and tried to explain the dream and the danger to her class teacher but was told tersely and coldly to sit down and behave. Her fellow pupils sneaked furtive glances at her, and she was the subject of much gossip for some while. But Olivia knew that she was right; she had not dreamt but positively lived what had occurred. She tried to forget what was going around constantly in her head but the feelings and the screams and the horror persisted. Weeks later, the school trip commenced. The coach left the school, carrying its cargo of excited, chattering girls. Olivia watched them go, and the cold, electric chill of premonition ran down her spine. She returned from school and carried on with her backbreaking round of chores and childcare, trying to forget the pictures in her head. But when she went out to get the washing off the line she heard her neighbours gossiping.

"Went down over the sea, they said, all of them kids killed. Didn't stand a chance."

"Yes, isn't it awful? Heard that it broke in half or something like that."

"Well, I suppose the only good thing—if there was one—was that they must have all been dead when they hit the water."

But Olivia knew they hadn't been; she had heard their frantic screams in her head.

When school reopened and she met Mr Broadbent for the first time, she stood in the middle of the corridor with her arms around herself and stared at him keenly. He dropped his eyes and turned his head away from her gaze as he passed her. Nothing was ever said from that day on. But Olivia knew then that she possessed a power and a gift that would be a force in her life.

In November, Olivia was 15 years old. Edward had paid for her to attend a private college—it must have cost him a great deal, Olivia thought—where she was taught shorthand, typing, commerce, and all the secretarial skills she would need to get herself a good, secure job. Olivia excelled at this course and, when she left, soon got herself a position at a pharmaceuticals company. She stood out for the worst of reasons. Her clothes were shabby, outdated, and ill-fitting. Her one pair of winkle-picker shoes still hurt and deformed her growing feet. She was painfully aware, as she had been at school, that she did not smell at all pleasant. She was only allowed one bath a week, with evil-smelling carbolic soap, and had no deodorant, powder, perfume, or cream to make her feel fresh and confident.

At work she met a boy that she liked. He was called Kevin, and they arranged to meet. Olivia was fearful and excited in the same breath. If the dreaded sperm donor were to even hear a whisper, she would be punished unremittingly. Taking her courage in both hands, she faced the sperm donor and told him she had to go to meet a friend from work who had a book she needed for the current project. He was silent for a moment and then grudgingly said, "Off you go, then, but be back here in fifteen minutes. Not one minute longer!"

Olivia knew what would befall if she were late. She left the house and ran as fast as her painful feet in her worn shoes would allow her to. With a pounding heart, she threaded her way through the maze of back streets. In the distance she saw Kevin and smiled. He returned her smile, but immediately his smile faded, and she saw he was looking behind her. Turning, she saw the sperm donor bearing down on them and she shuddered. He walked up to Kevin and pushed his face into the boy's face. "You!" he said threateningly. "You get off home now, or I'll knock you stupid."

He turned to Olivia. "And *you* get back home. I'll deal with you later."

He walked towards the working men's club, where Olivia knew he would drink heavily. She also knew that she would be beaten or raped or both—or even killed. He had broken almost every bone in her small body and perforated her eardrum, and none of these injuries had ever been treated. In that second she knew she must go. She had to seek help—find her mother— end this nightmare. She ran to the home of a cousin whom she had not seen or spoken to for over three years. The girl listened to Olivia as she hesitatingly told her dreadful tale. The two of them wept and embraced.

For four years Olivia had been obliged to lie to the welfare officer who visited them at her mother's request, as a word of the truth would have earned her a terrible beating. Olivia had been given the phone number of her mother's mother-in-law, and she sneaked conspiratorially with her cousin to the public telephone box—there were no in-house telephones then. The mother-in-law told her, "Call this number tomorrow night, and

41

I'll have your mother here." The next night they crept through the alleyways again, dreading the possibility of being caught by Olivia's tormentor. With shaking hands, Olivia dialled the number and inserted the coins. Then she heard that voice—that angel's voice—the voice of her mother. Olivia wept as she poured out her grief to her mother and her cousin fed coins into the telephone box. Olivia told of her ordeal and of how she needed and loved and wanted her mother. Her mother told her she would pay for her ticket to reach her, and the cousins returned, determined that Olivia should escape.

They were frightened, as friends had informed them that the sperm donor had been knocking on doors and demanding information. Her cousin's parents told her cheerfully that if he were to knock on their door he would receive a very swift kick in the gonads. The next day Olivia and her cousin sneaked anxiously to the railway station and hid in the toilets after Olivia had collected her prepaid ticket. They remained there until the train snorted in. Her cousin sobbed, hugged her, and waved her goodbye as the train steamed out. Even on the train Olivia was afraid that her tormentor would appear to drag her back to her hell. At last they squealed to a stop, and Olivia alighted onto the platform. Not very far away she saw the figure she had dreamed of for those terrible years—her mother. She ran into her waiting arms, sobbing. The love flowed into her from her mother's body, and she wanted to die with relief and happiness. "Mum," she whispered. "My mum."

She had escaped him. She was free. She swore from that moment that no man would ever lay a hand on her again—if one did, she would kill him.

OLIVIA, TWO

Olivia's mother took her to a car, where her stepfather sat waiting. He spoke to her in a soft, friendly voice. She almost immediately felt that this man could be trusted, but she would need time before she allowed him completely into her life. The warm, clean, friendly house was the first place where she ever experienced family and love. It was about half past eight in the evening when they arrived. A young girl was babysitting with the siblings that Olivia had not yet met. Her other younger siblings had never been allowed to speak about family matters when they returned after their visits to Minnie and the new father, so Olivia had not heard about the new additions. It was a great surprise to her. Her mother introduced the girl who sat on the settee, watching television, as the daughter of a friend, who was looking after the two boys. Seeing the puzzled look on Olivia's face she said, "You do know about your two brothers?"

"No—nothing."

"You have two brothers: Jack, he's 3, and Gregory, he's 18 months."

Olivia felt the tears running down her face. Her mother paid and packed off the babysitter quite quickly. She turned to Olivia. "Do you want to see the boys, love? They're asleep upstairs." Olivia nodded her head. They went upstairs and into the room the boys shared. There, in the bed, was the 3-year old, with thick, curly, dark hair spread on the pillow. Olivia leaned down to look closely. Then she went to the cot, where she saw an angelic blonde baby, lying with his arm above his head. He was dressed in a yellow Babygro and clutching a white teddy bear. Olivia fell in love with the blonde angel at first sight. She wanted to pick both boys up and cuddle them tightly. She explained to her mother that her siblings had been forbidden to tell her anything. She had not known about these two new family members.

They sat her at the kitchen table and fed her with bacon and eggs and hunks of white, crusty bread smothered in butter. She finished her mug of hot, sweet tea and gazed at her mother. Her mother smiled, and the smile made tears roll down Olivia's cheeks. Minnie walked to her and opened her arms. "Come here, my love, and let's get you a nice bath. You're tired out."

They went up to the spotless bathroom, with its white china suite and what seemed to Olivia to be a mountain of clean towels. Bottle after bottle of coloured toiletries stood on shelves. Her mother ran a deep, hot bath and filled it with sweet-smelling bubbles. She took the ragged, evil smelling clothes off Olivia and immediately saw the bruises, cuts, and welts on her child's body. Her hand went to her mouth. "Oh my dear God! What has he done to you, my love?"

Sobbing, Olivia attempted to explain, but her mother silenced her gently. "You're too tired, my love. We'll sort this all out tomorrow."

After a long soak in the fragrant water and her mother's washing of her long, golden hair, Olivia snuggled into the huge towel her mother held out. Minnie enfolded Olivia and held her close for a long time. "It's over now, my sweetheart. Nobody's going to harm you again—ever." Wearing a warm, clean, soft nightdress that was her mother's, Olivia was tucked into a bed that had soft, sweet sheets and warm blankets that seemed to welcome her. Her mother rocked her in her arms gently and kissed her pale-golden hair. As Olivia fell asleep, her last thought was, *I'm home—home—home.*

Over the next few days, she poured out her story to her mother and her stepfather, to whom she was slowly growing attached. The two of them listened in sombre silence as she described all the misery and horror of her existence with the sperm donor, her desperate worry for her sister and brother left behind, for whom she felt so much responsibility, and her fears that her hated tormentor would come to this haven and force her to leave. Her mother and stepfather continually reassured her that they would not allow any more harm to befall her, but Olivia's fear of the black presence who had taken away her childhood was overwhelming.

The day after she had found safety and love with her mother and her stepfather, Olivia, dressed in clothes loaned by the neighbour's daughter, went to town in the car with them. They went from shop to shop, and Olivia excitedly tried on and chose dresses, skirts, blouses, jumpers, coats, scarves, gloves, beautiful lacy bras and panties, cosmetics, and a little make-up. She was enthralled by the experience. Once back home, she modelled her new wardrobe, swirling around with one hand on her hip and her head arched to one side like a professional catwalk model. Her mother and stepfather laughed and applauded. Olivia took them upstairs, with her mother's help, and hung them proudly in the wardrobe and folded them into the drawers. Then she carefully dressed in her new underwear, a pair of dark-tan tights, a pleated woollen skirt, and a deep-blue blouse. She tied velvet ribbons into her blonde plaits, sprayed herself with perfume, applied a little eyeshadow and lipstick, and then fastened around her wrist the lovely silver bracelet that her mother and stepfather had given to her. Last of all, she slid her feet into one of the four pairs of shoes she had been given. These were black leather, shiny and supple, with silver buckles, and they hugged her feet like an embrace. She looked at herself in the mirror. "This," Olivia said to her reflection, "is how I will always be. I will always have what I want and live as I want to."

She went down to the smell of beef and vegetable casserole and the gentle murmuring and laughter of her new family in the warm, loving place that enfolded her.

In the next few days, Olivia sat with her mother, telling her urgently of the conditions in the house she had escaped. She described the deprivation, squalor, verbal abuse, neglect, and the terrible beatings, with broken bones, bruises, and cuts. And then there was the thing that she could only whisper—the times when he had stripped her and she had feared she would be raped. Her mother cried with her and held her close, attempting to comfort her. Olivia's worst fear was for her siblings who were still imprisoned in the grim nightmare. Her mother told her they would be coming to her for Easter (it was then April). She had managed, on the last custody hearing, to gain access to Wayne and Grace and for almost the last year she had had regular access, having them for a week or two, depending on which school holiday it was.

"So you don't have to worry, my love," she said, smiling.

Five days later, Olivia and her mother set off on the bus for town. Olivia imagined that they were going shopping. She loved to wander around choosing vegetables, meat, fish, and especially fruit, as she had seen little fresh food in her four years of misery. On the bus, her mother informed her gently, "My love, I'm taking you to a solicitor, to explain what you've told me. You don't need to be frightened. He'll only want to help you."

Her mother must have phoned and arranged this without Olivia's knowledge. They arrived at the office and sat in comfortable chairs in the imposing office. Her mother put her hand gently over Olivia's hand. "I know this is going to be hard for you, my love, because of all the things you'll have to tell them. But I'll be there with you, and if you want to stop, just look at me."

At last the smiling receptionist ushered them into the office of a Mr Spencer. Olivia was nervous; her heart was pounding, and her mouth was very dry. Mr Spencer indicated two seats for her and her mother to sit on. He spoke in a quiet, kindly voice. Falteringly, Olivia began her account of those four years. As it all poured out, like poison flushed from a wound, her voice grew stronger and more even. Mr Spencer wrote quickly and efficiently, pausing only to ask a question now and then. At the end, he had written over twenty foolscap sheets concerning four years of Olivia's life. The solicitor sat back. "Now, Olivia, I would like you to let us take some photographs of your body and your injuries."

Seeing the fear and alarm in the girl's eyes, he leaned forward, raising a reassuring hand. "It will be a lady photographer, an official photographer, and your mother will be with you all the time. We will only take pictures necessary for evidence."

In the small room to which she and her mother were taken, Olivia stripped to her underwear. The photographer assured her kindly that nothing degrading or distressing would occur or be allowed. Olivia did not feel distressed. Rather, she felt suddenly strong and determined. She would stand there and let the photos tell her story and convict the sperm donor. No man would harm or intimidate her ever again.

Two weeks later, her mother and stepfather went to pick her two siblings up for Easter. The sperm donor could not prevent this, as a court order had been made. Olivia was left in charge of her two newly found young brothers. She watched the car leaving the drive and disappearing into the distance. She silently wished them a safe journey and anticipated the arrival of her much-missed brother and sister. At last they were there, climbing out of the car, bewildered and confused. Olivia gathered them into her arms and kissed them. They did not respond; they had never been shown love or overt affection and did not know what to do. Olivia held them tightly. "You're free," she said to them. They were bewildered and stared at her silently.

"You're not going back, ever. This is your home now, with Mum and Dad"—for she had soon felt confident and secure enough to call this gentle, kind man by that name. It was a name she had longed to use for so very long. She saw her small brother's shoulders slump as if a huge weight had been lifted from them. They, too, got the bath in hot, soapy water, the fluffy towels, the clean and comfortable beds, and the trips to town for everything they had missed during their tiny lives. Olivia was happy. They were all home now, home with parents who loved and cared for them. Still the shadowy, feared spectre of the sperm donor haunted her. But Olivia told herself that he would not defeat her and taint her life. No man would. She *would* succeed in life and attain her dreams.

At last the day came when Olivia and her mother and new father were to go to court - hopefully to get custody of all three children given to her mother. The traumatic time Olivia had spent in the solicitor's office would now bear fruit. They drove to Liverpool and Olivia was fascinated by the large city. Her stepfather pointed out the famous Liver birds on top of the main court building where the case was to be heard and they climbed the imposing steps and went into the large, echoing entrance hall.

Olivia sat outside the courtroom on the polished wooden bench, nervously waiting to be called to give witness. She heard a distant murmur of voices and the click-clack of heels as suited court clerks hurried by. Then her mother came out. *I have to go in there and give evidence*, Olivia thought anxiously. She rose slowly. Her mother came to her with open arms and a big, ecstatic smile. "I've got custody of both of them!" she declared, and she hugged Olivia closely. "You don't have to go in there or say anything my love - it's all over." They cried and laughed and then bundled into the car, feeling joy and overwhelming relief that it was all over. Olivia's stepfather stood quietly smiling. The love in his eyes for his wife and her children was so very clear. Olivia's dreams were slowly coming true.

The sperm donor hadn't given up, as Olivia had feared he would not. He sent the police round to collect the two youngest children, but custody had been given to their mother, and the police apologised and left. They must have told the sperm donor that there was a teenage girl in the house too, because a week later he arrived in a white van. Olivia was upstairs, preparing for her first date with the boy she was later to marry. Her mother had bought her a lovely new blue dress, with a swirling skirt and a tight-fitting bodice, jewellery to enhance it, and low-heeled shoes with diamanté bows on the fronts. Her boyfriend was planning to take her to a nightclub in the next town to see the comedian, Charlie Brown, and Olivia was equally delirious with excitement and nervous. It was the first time that she had ever dressed as a normal teenager, been going out on a date with a boy, and going to a show! It was unbelievable, the change from caterpillar to butterfly in such a very short time.

She sat on the bed with her hair in rollers, whilst her mother helped her apply make-up to a face that was becoming more beautiful by the week. They heard Olivia's new dad shout at Minnie from the bottom of the stairs. For the first time Olivia heard an emotion that was very rare in his voice—anger. Her mother looked puzzled and said to her daughter, "I'll be back in a jiffy, honey."

Olivia heard the murmuring of voices in the hallway. Suddenly her bedroom door opened, and her mother stood there. She was not smiling. She came, sat on the bed, and put her arm around Olivia.

"I need you to be strong, love." Olivia froze.

"He's downstairs."

Olivia was terrified—her worst nightmare was unfolding. He had found her and her safe haven.

Her mother stroked her face gently. "He wants to see you and speak to you. I can't stop him, but he can't touch you or make you do anything. You're sixteen now."

But, thought Olivia, *he will kill me now. I am in danger. Oh please, let this be a bad dream.*

Her mother spoke quietly "Walk with him down the lane—"

"But—" Olivia was shaking—"he'll take me away, hurt me!"

"No. Walk down the lane in front of the house, and stay within sight of the kitchen window. I'll be watching everything." Her mother started to remove the rollers from Olivia's hair and then brushed it out. If that man was going to see his daughter, he would see her well dressed, clean, fragrant, and beautiful, as she had been from the first.

Slowly Olivia descended the stairs. There in the hall was the hated sperm donor. She hadn't seen him for three months, but her fear and loathing welled up immediately.

"I only want to talk to you," he said. "Let's go outside." He opened the front door and Olivia reluctantly followed him. She saw the white van parked near the house. *He will push me into that van and drive away with me. They will try to save me, but he will kill me—beat me to death, strangle me.* At that moment he did try to steer her towards the van by holding her elbow.

Inside her, strength and determination and power surged. She remembered that her mother was at the window, watching. "No," she said firmly. "We'll go up the lane." She set off quickly so that he was forced to follow her. As soon as she knew she was out of her mother's sight, she swiftly turned and walked back towards the house. She continued to do this, to ensure her mother's protective gaze.

As they walked, he pleaded with her to return. "I'll never lay a hand on you again, I promise. You can have boyfriends and go out and wear make-up and do what you want—just come back with me. I'll change, you'll see …" He babbled on.

She stopped near the garden gate and turned to him. "I'm never coming back to live with you—ever—and I don't want to see you again! You're not my father. My father is here, with all my family. You never were a father. You're just"—she paused and clenched her fists—"just a sperm donor and nothing else."

Then he began to cry and continue to plead with her. Olivia was surprised, for she had never seen a man cry, ever—and especially not this man. For a second she felt a pang of pity for this shabby, unshaven, hunched human, but her instinct for survival kicked in rapidly.

"I'm going in now." She walked up to the front door. "I don't want to see you again—ever." She walked into the house, closed the door, and ran to her mother's arms. They looked out of the kitchen window. He stood there, wiping his tears with the back of his hand and gazing at the door into which his daughter had disappeared. Then he slowly turned, climbed into the white van, and drove away, out of Olivia's sight and, she thought, her life. But there would be further meetings.

Childhood was nearly passed. The adult world beckoned Olivia.

OLIVIA, THREE

Olivia stood in front of the long mirror. She was delighted with what she saw: the lovely blue dress; the stockings; the new shoes; the jewellery; the soft, clean, curly hair; and the make-up her mother had applied. She lifted her arm and smelt the perfume on her wrist. She twirled around and looked over her shoulder to see that every aspect of her was pleasing. After years of imprisonment in which her only escape had been to attend school or deliver her siblings there, she was being allowed to go out with her young man to attend the Charlie Williams show. Olivia felt grown up. She felt trusted and triumphant and beautiful. She also felt a tiny frisson of danger; she was a virgin, unused to boys and the dark adolescent sex scene she imagined to be a source of wonder and excitement.

The evening was a success. Olivia loved the show and the laughter and happiness around her. She and Brian walked home afterwards, and a little way before they turned into her road, Brian stopped under a lamp post and pulled her to him. He pushed his mouth down onto hers in a fierce kiss. Olivia froze; immediately she was back with the hated sperm donor, and something terrible was about to happen. Brian's hands wandered down to Olivia's breasts, and he fondled them. She was terrified; she had no idea what was happening or about to happen. Her knowledge of the facts of life, sex, and procreation was sketchy and totally weird. She imagined that women came into season as dogs did and were mounted and mated in the same manner.

At this point Brian realised that Olivia was uncomfortable. He stopped, took her hand, and walked her home without any comment. He kissed her goodnight warmly and thanked her for a good evening in return for her thanking him. Olivia liked him. They continued dating regularly. Some six weeks afterwards, they were alone in the front room on the sofa. Olivia's mother was at work, and the inevitable unwound. Brian kissed and embraced Olivia, and feelings rose. She whispered shyly in his ear, "I'm a virgin; please go carefully and slowly with me."

It was not the romantic, passionately beautiful experience of deflowering that Olivia had expected. Brian was experienced; this wasn't his first time, she thought. He knew exactly what he was doing and did it well, in her inexperienced view. Although she was shaking with fear and memories, she managed to put her arms around him. He carefully entered her with a gentleness that reassured her that it was going to be all that she hoped it would be. She winced.

"Sorry," he mumbled. He pulled out and kissed her, missing her mouth and planting his lips on her ear. He tried again to enter her, and she winced again but pulled him into her body. He groaned as he moved faster, gasping and crying out as he climaxed and rolled away from her.

Olivia thought, *This is not what I thought it would be*. Brian cleaned himself up and then lay beside her, stroking her hair.

She did not feel the wonderful thrill and glow she had been led to imagine she would, but there *was* a faint feeling of being closer, somehow, to this boy, of belonging to him in a very special way. They continued to explore sex as the relationship developed, but it remained on a basic, predictable level.

Olivia had obtained employment at a garage, working with her mother. She had been unable to get a job in an office but was not disappointed at this, as she had only unpleasant memories of her lonely, unhappy time at the pharmaceuticals company, aware of her body odour, her shabby clothes and shoes, her lack of cosmetics and perfumes and—worst of all—aware of the scathing, sneering, contemptuous glances of her fellow workers. She had known that she was prettier than many of those girls but had also known that she was inferior, different, unwanted.

When a vacancy arose for someone to work the 7.30 to 3.00 shift six days a week to fit in with her mother's shifts, Olivia jumped at the chance. On handover, Olivia and her mother would check the readings on the petrol pumps, check stock and oil, and log all the various things that had to be recorded. This would take about half an hour, and then Olivia would go home and tackle the tasks her mother had set her to help keep the large household running smoothly. Her stepfather worked in a factory directly behind the house. Olivia would prepare the vegetables and keep an eye on her siblings, and he would cook whatever her mother had left ready. After Olivia had helped to put her siblings to bed in the evenings, she would go out to meet Brian.

They ran smoothly as a family. Olivia began to feel grounded and secure for the first time in her adolescent life. It was decided by Brian and Olivia that they would become engaged on Olivia's seventeenth birthday—they were in love. They would wait three years before marrying; they would live off one wage and save the other. They were confident of this love and of their plans for the future. Brian had bought her a small second-hand engagement ring. It was a solitaire diamond set in platinum, and Olivia was very proud of it. This was her visible sign of the love that a man carried for her, a man who valued and loved and treasured her. A party for the engagement had been planned on her birthday, and Olivia's mother had gladly agreed to a buffet meal. She was happy with the couple's plans for a three-year wait until they married. Brian had a large family. His parents and siblings were immensely fond of Olivia and equally happy about the engagement and the couple's plans.

A week before the party, Olivia got out of bed to get ready for work feeling very nauseous and dizzy. She sat on the edge of the bed until the feelings passed and tried to forget them, as nothing else seemed to be wrong with her. The party went off in style; it was a huge success. But the following morning, Olivia awoke to more nausea and unsteadiness. She managed to force down her cereal and went outside, where her stepfather was warming up the car engine. If he was not on shift, he would run Olivia to work. As she walked down the garden pathway, she suddenly vomited her breakfast forcibly over the flowerbed. She climbed shakily into the car, aware of her stepfather glancing at her curiously. About a week later she realised that her expected period had not arrived; in fact, she couldn't remember when her last period had been. She made an appointment with her doctor without saying a word to her parents or to Brian. She had to take a specimen of urine with her and would have to wait four days for a result. In the evening, she and Brian sat together in the living room alone.

"I had to go to the doctor today," Olivia began.

"Why? Are you OK?" Brian looked mildly concerned.

"I keep being sick—every morning. I think I may be pregnant." He was silent for a while as he took in the information. Olivia knew that there was no need for concern on her part. She knew that this was just an inevitable part of their relationship and that Brian would stand by her and take it in his stride. He put his arm around her. "Well, it looks like we won't be saving up for a house then, eh? We'd better get married right away."

And so Olivia's future was written without her even knowing it. She loved this boy, she told herself. She loved him, and so this must be what love was. But deep in her heart there was confusion and fear, and a sense that this was not what she had sought.

They kept the news to themselves for three days and then, on the way to Brian's parents' house, he said, "We've got to tell them."

"But I won't get the results from the doctor until tomorrow," Olivia said. "Shouldn't we wait?"

"Nah," said Brian. "Might as well tell them now and get it over." Olivia's heart thumped, and she felt that it would leap out of her chest. She noticed that her hands were shaking almost uncontrollably. It was as if she had committed some crime, not conceived a child outside of marriage.

At his parents' home they sat together on the sofa, holding hands. Brian's mother sat on the end of the sofa, and his father sat in his large, comfortable recliner opposite them. Olivia and Brian spent an hour nudging each other and whispering, each wanting the other to break the news.

"You tell them; they're your parents," Olivia whispered. "Or you can tell mine."

Brian took a deep breath and leaned forward. "Dad, Mum, I've got something to tell you." He took another deep breath. "Olivia's pregnant."

There was a silence that seemed to last for hours. Then Brian's father burst out laughing—happy, hearty laughter. His mother had already started to organise turning the dining room into a bedsitter for the soon-to-be newlyweds, and now she began talking excitedly and enthusiastically. There was complete and utter acceptance of the news, no word of reproof or anger. Olivia sat listening—listening as her future was mapped out and arranged for her by others. It was done lovingly, but Olivia felt her life slipping from her control. She had to trust this boy she was about to commit her life to. She closed her eyes as nausea gripped her and hoped fervently that her trust would not be broken.

They went back to Olivia's home and her parents. All the way there Olivia was silent; her heart was again thumping furiously. Brian squeezed her hand comfortingly as they went in. Her mother sat reading the newspaper.

Olivia spoke. "Mum—" The paper remained in place.

"Mum—I—I think I'm pregnant."

Still the paper did not stir.

"Don't tell me something I already know," her mother said quietly and firmly, and the newspaper remained there, shutting Olivia out. For four days she didn't speak a word to Olivia. Handing over on shifts at the petrol station became a nightmare. In the end, Olivia had to resort to writing everything down. It was a brief unhappy time, but soon her mother was excitedly telling everyone that she was about to become a grandmother and her love was in evidence once more, to Olivia's relief.

This was the time when to be a single parent was on a level with being a murderer. Curtains twitched as the guilty, soiled mother pushed past with the pram containing the bastard child. Many young girls were forced to hand over their beloved children to cold, uncaring local authority workers, to be adopted and to disappear forever from their mothers' lives, mourned and missed on both sides. Olivia's mother told her that she could stay at home and have her baby. Minnie would protect her from the hypocritical moral indignation of society.

Olivia said, "We're already engaged, Mum. It doesn't matter; we're getting married."

"Don't get married just for that reason, love, it's a bad decision."

"We made this baby, so I'm going to get married and give it a name."

"Just be sure, love. Don't ruin your entire life by—" She stopped.

"It's OK, Mum, we've decided. Don't worry. I've made up my mind."

Olivia had applied to join the Queen Alexandra's Royal Army Nursing Corps a little while before this, and the papers for her joining had arrived that day for her mother to sign. Her mother looked at them sadly. Then she tore them up and threw them in the kitchen bin. "You won't be needing these now. Pity."

Yes, thought Olivia, *a great pity. That would have been my future, my career, my life. But this is the path that I have chosen and the path that I must tread. I have given my heart to this boy. I love him—at least I think this is love.* And so she went to wed her first love.

Olivia and her mother went to buy her wedding dress. Olivia was a tiny thing of barely 7 1/2 stone. She had a 38-inch bust and an 18-inch waist. With her grey eyes and pale-blonde hair, she was a beauty who turned heads. Finding a dress to fit her was a daunting task. Finally they found a cream dress in Mothercare with a strategically placed frill which covered her emerging bump, and a light-blue floppy hat to match. Olivia and Brian were very proud that they had paid for the registry office wedding and the reception themselves. It was a tremendous success. The families and friends had a memorable time. They held a whip round at the end of the reception to enable the couple to spend one night of luxury in a local five-star hotel.

Too quickly it was all over, and they were installed in the one-room bedsitter in Brian's parents' home. They had a convertible settee to sleep on; it was hard and very uncomfortable. For Olivia and her pregnant, changing body it was torture. The room was next to the family kitchen, so there was little quiet and peace for them. Every Saturday morning Brian's mother was up and awake at six to begin the family wash. The noise and steam invaded their privacy. Before this, Brian and Olivia had not been together alone and naked. Olivia felt awkward and aware of the bulk of the growing baby. She had wanted this to be romantic, like the scene she had dreamt of, where Brian was overwhelmed with her beauty, took her in his arms, and carried her to a great, soft bed and made love to her whilst choirs sang in their heads. In reality she stood uncomfortably, embarrassed to remove her underwear and expose the swollen belly and huge breasts that she found so grotesque. Brian was not repelled by them, but he, too, was slightly lost at stripping and standing naked before his new wife. Olivia told herself that she loved this boy and that when things were normal—although she was uncertain as to what normal was—she would feel a surge of love for him. She found herself increasingly uncertain as to what love actually was but told herself that pregnancy was affecting her thought processes—for now.

Olivia's labour began early one gloomy morning, and she was admitted to hospital. Fathers were not yet considered to be part of the process at that time, and Olivia was left, at 17 years of age, to cope on her own. The midwife assigned to her was a grim, harsh woman whose disapproval of Olivia's young age was not hidden. Olivia struggled and suffered for the eighteen hours of her ordeal. After the birth, the staff struggled to dislodge the retained placenta by breaking capsules of muscle relaxants underneath Olivia's nose and forcing her knees up to her shoulders whilst tugging on the umbilical cord. Olivia was exhausted and shivering. Finally a doctor was called, and he strode into the delivery room without a word of greeting to anyone. He was very obviously upset at being called to the delivery room; he was wearing his pyjamas under his white coat. He pushed what seemed to be his entire arm up into Olivia's womb and proceeded to drag the stuck afterbirth away. Olivia screamed and bit and scratched. She had been cut roughly to allow the baby's head through, and the episiotomy was unstitched and agonising. Finally, mercifully, they anaesthetised her. When she emerged from sleep, she found herself in a side room with a bag of blood dripping slowly into her arm. She lay there sore, tired, and wondering vaguely what had happened to her. The Asian doctor who had performed the rough procedure on her came in. He checked the blood drip and her charts and then came to the bedside. He told her that she had lost almost half the blood level of her body and had had to have over one hundred stitches inserted inside and outside her womb. Olivia listened, tired and disinterested, willing the man to go away. At last he did.

She dozed but then stirred as a nurse came in holding a small, tightly wrapped bundle. "You awake, love? Here's your daughter. Look, she's lovely."

Olivia struggled up and turned to look at the tiny baby in the blanket. She had masses of dark hair and a tiny turned-up nose. Olivia thought that she was the most beautiful thing she had ever seen. She took her from the nurse and gazed down at her. The tiny hands waved and worked towards her small mouth. Olivia felt such a surge of hot, protective love that tears rolled down her face.

"There, there, my love. You're tired. You've had a really rough time. She was a good size, 7 pounds and 2 ounces. Your husband has just arrived with your mum. He'll be in soon."

The nurse left, and Olivia held the small baby closely, inhaling the sweet smell of her skin and brushing her tiny face with her finger. Brian came in quietly and stood hesitantly at the door.

"Hello, love. Are you OK? They said you had a bad birth." He stopped, went to the bed, and looked at his daughter.

"Oh my, she's sweet! So pretty, just like you. Here, let me hold my girl."

He lifted her out of Olivia's arms and rocked her gently. He turned to Olivia. "I really like the name Elizabeth. Do you like it, love?"

"Yes." Olivia smiled wearily. "Yes, I like it very much. Elizabeth—Beth."

Brian rocked the baby and spoke softly to the little thing. "Yes, Beth, little Beth. My little lovely." He walked around with the tiny bundle, smiling and talking to his daughter. Then he went back to the bed. "Your mum's out there, love. She'll want to see you if you—"

But Olivia was asleep. Brian kissed her softly on her cheek and then went to look for a nurse to hand Beth to. The night came whispering down and the hospital sounds continued faintly around her, but Olivia slept deeply and soundly. She had made another step on her journey. She was a mother although still almost a child herself.

Olivia and Brian had, by this time, got a two-bedroomed flat, which consisted of a living room, a kitchen, a bathroom, a bedroom, and a small box room—perfect for them and a baby. Olivia was beginning to get the measure of Brian. He was, in short, rather lazy. He would come home from work and just flop down on the settee, without changing his clothes or even washing. He rarely lifted a finger to help Olivia, and she was obliged to look after the baby and do everything in the house herself. Slowly, slowly her dream of love was unravelling; the reality was so very different. The romance had never happened. The lovemaking became almost routine, but still she responded, hoping that her dream would awaken some honeyed evening. Nine months later she was pregnant again. Her mother-in-law proved a godsend, helping tutor her in the skills of motherhood. Olivia was so young and inexperienced and had one tiny baby to cope with, another on the way, and a husband who did little else in the home except recline on the settee and use her body for his sexual needs as often as he possibly could. He earned his pay and was a hard worker, providing for his family, but Olivia knew the glitter and excitement of the first days was rapidly going. She knew it when he fumbled for her in bed and took his pleasures without regard to her needs, finishing quickly and falling asleep, leaving her awake and wretched in the darkness. He would go out twice a week to the local pub, Olivia unable to go with him because of the baby. He often he returned very late, smelling of drink, and she slowly began to suspect that he did not just drink and chat during his absences.

Her second child, another girl, was again born with complications and a retained placenta. She was a cherubic-looking child, weighing in at 6 pounds and 12 ounces, with a mop of blonde hair. They called her Tanya, and Brian was briefly attentive after the birth. Olivia was unwell when she got home with the new baby. She knew that something was not right inside her body. She went to her doctor again and again, telling him that she felt that something was amiss, but he dismissed her fears and sent her away. She woke up one morning to find blood everywhere; pouring out of her. She staggered to her neighbour at seven in the morning and knocked desperately at their door to borrow the phone and call her doctor. When he arrived, he told her to get into bed and stay there until the ambulance arrived. She was rushed into hospital, where an emergency D and C was performed. The surgeon came to check on her afterwards. "You're lucky to be here," he informed her. "Half an hour more and your heart would have stopped beating through blood loss." Olivia recovered from this setback and threw herself into raising her young children. She tried to rekindle some sort of life into her relationship with Brian. The spark was dying; her dream was sliding out of reach. This was not what she had expected or wanted. She had given her heart to this boy—this man—and her heart was slowly being crushed and killed by his indifference and selfishness.

Brian's job at the garage came to an end, and he went to work with Olivia's stepfather at the factory. This, too, soon ended, as many were made redundant. Then Brian found a post as a milkman. From the first weeks of this job Olivia could date the signs of the disintegration of their relationship. Indifference became neglect, and for the first time in their life together, Olivia was rejected. Wanting Brian's lovemaking, she reached out to him, and he rolled coldly away. He made increasingly unbelievable excuses for his long absences, for the later and later hours he apparently spent at his local pub, and for the faint smells of skin and body and nearness that she picked up so often. There were other subtle, indescribable nuances that she could only experience but not describe. She knew he was a cheat and an adulterer.

Within the year, Brian decided that he was going to join the army, much against the wishes of his parents. He enlisted in the Royal Artillery, and he and Olivia gave up their house and moved in with his sister. His sister had become pregnant while still at school, but the putative father had not stayed. She had met a man who moved in with her; he was good to her and to her small daughter, but he was not, Olivia discovered, a nice person. He soon began cornering Olivia in the kitchen and hallway and attempting to fondle her breasts and kiss her. She was not going to tolerate this. She quickly packed her belongings and took herself and the two tiny girls to her mother's house, as Brian was doing his basic training in Sutton Coldfield. This move was not the best Olivia had made. Very soon she fell out with her mother. She quickly moved in with her mother-in-law. This proved to be a happy, relaxed time for her, as Brian's mother was an accepting, cheerful woman, and the two small girls were just another source of joy to her and her husband. Brian and Olivia moved to married quarters in Hampshire a few months later, and from there to Germany, where Brian was stationed for almost eight years. There another girl, Sally, was born to them. It was a huge disappointment to Brian, who desperately wanted a son. She was another blonde, pretty girl, like a china doll.

Then, at last, Olivia gave birth to a boy, who weighed in at 8 pounds and 12 ounces. The umbilical cord was wound around his neck twice; he was blue and took time to start breathing, but then he took his first breath and bellowed heartily. When he was put into Olivia's arms and she saw his faint fuzz of golden hair, she felt overwhelming love yet again.

Then Olivia's life was shattered.

Wayne, her youngest brother by the sperm donor, had been her favourite child. He was like her own child, because when Olivia's mother had left—and Olivia never, ever, held any grudge against her mother for this—Olivia had become a mother to her siblings. A mother should never have favourites, but Olivia had a special place, a special love, for Wayne. She had so often taken the blows intended for him. Once when Wayne returned from school, the sperm donor had told him to change out of his school uniform and into his jeans. Wayne had come down in a pair of corduroys, and the sperm donor had flung him onto the settee and begun to punch and beat him mercilessly. Olivia had just then returned from school. Seeing what was happening, she'd flung her school bag onto the ground and thrown herself between her brother and his tormentor. "Run, Wayne. Go upstairs—run!" she'd shouted as blows rained down on her. She had loved the small, sweet boy, and she would have withstood the legions of hell to protect him. Wayne grew into a tall, handsome, fit young man. He had shoulder-length blond hair and the most compelling deep-brown eyes. He had a character to match his looks. He was admired and respected by all who met him. He was kind, helpful, unselfish, and a lover of justice who would not tolerate bullies or tyrants. He had grown into a wonderful adult. He seemed to have survived the worst that his childhood had thrown at him. He and Olivia were very close because they shared a terrible past. The song that held them closely together was "Bridge Over Troubled Water". When Olivia and her siblings were enduring their terrible childhood, her older brother, Paul, and Wayne, the baby, would wait until the sperm donor had left the house. They would sit each side of Olivia and stroke her shoulders gently, to show their concern and love for her, and they would play that song. In later life, when times were fragile and traumatic, Wayne and Olivia would hold each other close and sing along with the words that held so much meaning to them.

After Wayne and his brothers were reunited with their mother and her new husband, Wayne lived a normal life and seemed to be recovering. After Olivia married, she did not see her brother often, but she felt that he had been able to cope with his past and put it well behind him.

Wayne's private life was, indeed, troubled. He had got his girlfriend pregnant, and he confided in Olivia that he had also impregnated another girl. They had sat and talked about it for over an hour, but Olivia had felt that Wayne had already made up his mind. He married a pretty, Irish girl, but the marriage only lasted six weeks. The girl had moved in with Wayne and his mother, but this proved a disastrous mistake, and the girl quickly moved back with her own mother. She eventually gave birth to a daughter, and the other girl soon after this presented Wayne with a son. He had much input into the lives of his children, and he loved them dearly.

Wayne bought himself a house, of which he was very proud. He asked Olivia to come and see it. She was very proud of what he had achieved and said so, but Wayne seemed unhappy.

"You don't really like it, do you?" he told her, looking downcast.

"Of course I do, love. It's great. You've really done well." The house was ordinary, nothing remarkable, but Wayne had had got his foot on the property ladder, and Olivia was pleased for him. But he was not convinced. He really seemed to believe that Olivia did not like or appreciate his house.

One day Wayne and Olivia were sitting outside her mother's home, having a cigarette together. It was a beautiful summer's day, and they were on the patio, in two garden chairs with comfortable cushions. The patio overlooked a large lawn with rose borders and laurel trees, which gave them privacy from the neighbours. Wayne said to her, "I might have to go away for a bit. If I have to go away, just know I'll be all right."
"What's the matter with you? You're not going anywhere." Olivia looked at him, puzzled.
"I might be going away for a long time, and you might not hear from me, but just know I will be OK."
"Wayne, you can't go away. If you're in trouble and you need to go anywhere, then come and stay with me in Germany."
Wayne just stopped then. He cut off completely. Olivia did not see the significance of this strange exchange until it was too late.

When Olivia's husband was posted to Germany, it was a big wrench for her. The army became her family. One morning, three days before Olivia's birthday, Brian had suggested that they go back to England for a week. They were able to do this, so they were making preparations for their return. Olivia went to put the kettle on for a cup of tea for them both. The flat was three floors up, and looking out of the window as she waited for the kettle to boil, Olivia saw a car draw up and an officer get out. This was unusual, as officers usually stayed well inside their own quarters. Olivia watched him idly as she prepared the tea, and she noticed that he was walking towards the block she lived in. Then there was a knock on the door. Brian opened it, and Olivia heard the officer say, "I need you to step outside for just a moment."

Olivia thought that Brian might be in some kind of trouble, but soon Brian returned. He took Olivia by her arm and led her into the living room. There he sat her down on the settee. He looked at her with a worried expression. "I need to tell you. Something bad's happened."

"Something bad? Well, what? Tell me." Instantly Olivia thought of her mother.

"Well, I don't know exactly what's happened, but it's just … well … bad."

"Bad, you know what bad is—tell me, for God's sake!"

Brian hesitated. "It's one of your brothers—he's dead." Brian went to the flat below, to use their phone to try and get some information. Olivia sat hunched, praying to God not to let it be Wayne. She didn't want it to be any one of her four brothers, but Wayne—no, not him! He was her angel. He had come through their nightmare with her, not unscathed, but he had grown. He was everyone's hero. A golden boy. Loved. Respected. Then Brian was back, and he looked at her, stricken.

"It's Wayne," he said. Olivia sat frozen. A tidal wave of pain, disbelief, and horror swept over her. She could not function. Wayne, her baby brother! No, no—it could not be true!

"Come on." Brian took her arm. "We must get the kids and our stuff together and get back to England."

"No." Olivia was unable to move. "No, Wayne's strong. Wayne can't die." She sat, staring at the wall.

"Come on, Livvy, we have to get going. We have to see to the kids."

Olivia went to the bedroom and was trying to get a suitcase out of the wardrobe, when she fell, into the wardrobe. She lay there, unable to move. Brian swiftly got her out and lifted her up onto the bed. Then he did all the packing and got the children ready to leave. Olivia remembered nothing of the car journey to the ferry or how the tickets were obtained. It was a dream, a terrible dream. They had a four-berth cabin. Brian slept with one child, Olivia with another, and the other children had a bunk apiece. Olivia got up in the night and wandered around the pitching, rolling deck, holding onto the rail and thinking. *This is just a ruse. When I get to Mum's he'll be there, and he'll say he just did it to get me back.* And then, she thought, he would put his strong, muscular arms around her and hold her tightly. Yes, that was it. It was just a ploy to get her back to England.

They docked and drove to her mother's house. When the door opened and Olivia saw her stepfather's face, she knew it was all too real. Immediately Olivia's tears coursed down her face, her heart raced, and she felt as if it would burst. For a full week her heart beat abnormally; she felt panicky, terrified, as if she really would die. Her mother was lying on the bed, Olivia did not know how the poor woman was managing to keep her sanity. Olivia listened as she told her the circumstances of Wayne's death, and she was overcome with grief, guilt, and despair. Why had she not been there to protect her family? Why had she not been able to prevent Wayne from taking this step? Why had she not foreseen this? She just wanted to take him in her arms and keep away whatever had threatened him, driven him to this terrible end. Her mother told her that Wayne's partner had come to her house and told her that she was suffering really bad headaches. Minnie had given her a pack of almost one hundred strong painkillers. Wayne and the partner had gone out the night before the tragedy and had a few drinks. The stories of the witnesses differed. One said he was very drunk and that there had been words between the pair. Another said that he had been happy and laid back, and that he had a good, relaxed evening. They returned home and the partner went to bed.

Wayne appeared to have stayed downstairs in the kitchen and prepared his partner's sandwiches to take to work with her the next day. He then took about seventy-five of the painkillers, lay down on the settee, and drifted away. He had left a note, in which he asked that his daughter be told that he was not a coward. Wayne's partner had found him in the morning and had called an ambulance. The paramedics had managed to get a very faint heartbeat, but Wayne had died almost immediately.

Olivia sat beside her mother on the bed, listening to the story of her baby brother's death. She hunched up and put her arms around her body, sobbing, as if her very soul would wash out of her body. "Oh God, why wasn't I here to hold him, to keep away whatever it was that made him do this? I should have protected him. I failed him. Oh Wayne, my darling boy." She had protected him all that time, taken all those beatings, fought to save him from being affected until he could grow and overcome their terrible past. But the one time—the one time—she had not been there. She had failed him. She rocked in agony. The tears fell unchecked, burning her face. The day slipped away. They cried, made tea and held each other's hands. They walked around restlessly, hugged, and then cried again. The hurt in the house was palpable. Olivia just wanted to sleep and not wake up. Her own grief was unendurable, but to see her mother's searing pain was almost too much to bear.

They went to the mortuary to see Wayne's body. He was draped in a purple cloth with a gold cross on it; his eyes were half closed. Olivia remembered that he had always slept with his eyes half closed, and she laughed. "Wake up, you silly bugger—" Then she stopped, remembering why they were there. She touched his face; it was cold, so cold. And then she realised that Wayne was gone. His physical body was no longer functioning. Her darling, strong, much-loved hero of a man—her golden boy—was dead. He had been unable to cope with the past. He had internalised the cruelty, the degradation, the fear, and the pain, and he had been unable to take any more. Instead of going to Olivia, who would have helped him, or sought help, he had simply lain down, listening to their song, and drifted away to a place where those black memories could never touch him again, a place of peace, warmth, and forgetfulness.

Olivia was not a person to ever actively hate anyone. Hate was a strong word. Hate could turn back on the hater and inflict damage. But at that moment she hated the sperm donor. She hated him with a cold, unrelenting hate that would never cease. Years later he would be in a wheelchair, blind and with agonising pain in his spine, but Olivia would have no pity for him. She would wish him only more pain and misery—and, as a final and painful end for him—that he would burn in the unending fires of hell for eternity and suffer what he had inflicted on his helpless children.

Of all the agonies that Olivia suffered in her life, Wayne's death was the worst she was ever to know. The loss of a child leaves you with an inner loneliness that can never be filled. Wayne was like her child, and her very soul had been torn out when he died.

In the following days, Olivia had to arrange the funeral. She had to try and comfort her distraught mother. She had to prevent her, at one point, from banging her head against the wall in her grief. At the cremation, Olivia stood with her family, numb, almost unable to take in what was occurring. They played "Morning has Broken". This had been played at morning assembly when Wayne was at school, and he had loved it. Olivia wept silently. At last the service was nearly over, and then there was the committal. The curtains began to close around the coffin as it slid away. Olivia's sobs increased. She cried out and put her hand forward as if to bring it back again. Her older brother, Paul, told her to stop before she became hysterical. Olivia told him that she was beyond that. She was in a world where emotions were overwhelming and not possible to know, unless you were in the land of those who have lost a child, a part of themselves. Her brother put his arm around Olivia, as he had done so often when they were frightened, tormented children. Olivia could not look at his face. He had the same brown eyes as Wayne had. Afterwards they all went to the pub, where Olivia got very, very drunk. Somebody put "He Ain't Heavy, He's My Brother" on the jukebox, and she sank to her knees. *Oh God*, she thought. *I'd carry him on my back for the rest of my life if I could only see him again, hear his voice, hold his hand.*

After that she dreaded going to sleep. There was always the morning, and the brief second when the world was normal— until she remembered, and life was dark. She slept one night and had a very strange experience. It was not a dream; it was too real. She was walking through a park. On her left were tall bushes; she could see through the branches, and she kept looking to find a way through them. Nearby she could see benches, all apparently empty. Then she saw him, Wayne, sitting on one of the benches. She searched frenziedly for a gap in the trees. At last she found one, struggled through it, and ran to him. She sat down beside him and snuggled into him. He put his arms around her. There was not one word spoken, and she cried with sheer joy. They sat, arms around one another, all night long. Wayne stroked her face wordlessly, and she knew that he loved her and that he was sorry for the pain he had caused her. The bond that love forges held them as the night passed. Olivia did not want to wake up. She knew that if she did he would be gone, but when she did wake and lay sobbing, it was with the knowledge that he was not gone. He was with her always. She would never hold him again, never breeze into his house saying, "Put kettle on, kid." But she knew, without any shadows of darkness and despair, that he was with her forever and that she would see him again one day.

Olivia caught Brian out in his first affair—the first of very many—whilst they were still in Hampshire. Later she would say of him, "If it had a pulse, he would fuck it". That became the pattern of their life from then on. She raised the children, and he slept with every woman who crossed his path. They had been married for almost thirteen years. Olivia discovered that affair with a woman named Muriel, and a heated row followed. Olivia did not really want to end her marriage over one incident. She was hurt and very angry, but she decided to forgive him and move on. She had no wish to be a single mother or for her children to be raised without a proper family. She knew enough about dysfunctional, incomplete families, and she was not anxious to see her children pulled from one to another because of one happening. But many other affairs followed. Olivia turned a blind eye and tried to hold her family together. Then Brian started an affair with an Irish woman called Bridget, who had a Canadian husband. He begged once more for her forgiveness, promising to leave Bridget, and cut all ties. But Olivia discovered that he was still going back to see this woman, and a blazing row followed.

Olivia had been diagnosed with a breast lump, and she had to have strong antibiotic injections, which were very painful and left her breast and arm numb. They operated to pack the breast, and she came round from the anaesthetic to find her breast engorged, agonisingly painful, and black. The following day she left the clinic, and that was when she found out that Brian was seeing this Irish woman a great deal, despite all his promises. Olivia had had her fill of Brian and his affairs. She decided that their marriage was going to end. They packed and drove to the ferry to go back to England. All the way there, and it was a long journey, Brian begged and tried to persuade Olivia to stay with him.

They arrived at Olivia's mother's house and settled there with the children. Olivia did not want him there. She had to sleep on the settee, as she was not going to sleep with Brian. Night after night, as she tried to sleep, Brian walked up and down in the room, trying to make her listen to him. After five nights of this, Olivia's mother took her to one side. She held out her clenched hand and dropped a large yellow pill into Olivia's hand. "Here, love, take this tonight, and I'll sit downstairs near you."

"What is it.?"

"They gave it to me to help me sleep after an operation a few years ago. You need a good sleep. He's been keeping you up every night since you got back. You need your sleep. This'll knock you out." And it did. Olivia slept like one dead.

A few days later, Brian moved out and went to live with his parents. And so, after eight years in Germany, Olivia headed home to England and her mother's home, with four suitcases and four children. She had trusted her heart to the wrong man. Love was just out of sight, around the next corner, waiting somewhere for her. Next time she would get it right.

OLIVIA, FOUR

Olivia moved in with her mother. The house was crowded, as her two half-brothers and her sister, Grace, lived there. The children slept in two of the rooms, Olivia's parents in another, and Olivia and Grace slept in the living room, one on the sofa and the other in a sleeping bag on the floor. It was a crowded and noisy environment, but for now it was home. At the weekends Olivia and Grace would go out together to local nightclubs. Their mother would babysit Olivia's four children, while they dressed up and applied make-up to feel good. Their outings were pretty innocent. They didn't parade themselves like tarts but sat on bar stools with crossed legs, skirts covering those legs, and demure smiles and glances from beneath artistically made up eyelids. They attracted men who wanted to dance with them, and both had been walked home and left on the doorstep after lingering kisses and fumbling attempts to grope their bodies, which was quickly discouraged.

One evening Olivia met a man called Peter Rutter. He was not terribly tall—Olivia much preferred tall men—but dark and good-looking in an almost menacing way. Olivia was surprised to learn that he was in the police force, as she had always believed that there was a strict height code for policemen. He told her he was 27, which was a relief for Olivia, as she was now 28 and was growing slightly weary of the younger men who crowded around her. She had to admit to herself that she seemed to be attracted to younger men; however, she was a little afraid of being labelled for her preferences.

The romance developed. Olivia was now living in a council house of her own with her children and Grace. Peter moved in with them shortly after. Olivia soon discovered that he was a very crooked policeman, one who was into every illegal aspect of his job. He was a thief and a liar and someone who was happy to practice violence on those on remand or arrested. He was quite happy to negotiate with any crook, and there was more stolen property in Olivia's house than she cared to think about. He did not like the fact that Olivia's first husband visited the house to see his children and, for some reason, nicknamed him Rambo. Olivia fell out with Peter regularly during their eleven-year relationship and threw him out on several occasions. She caught him out in lies—the first one being that he'd actually been only 22 when they met. She began to have deep suspicions about his behaviour as a police officer when an investigation was begun by the force into aspects of the local police. There were serious accusations of extreme violence and corruption, and Peter began talking of moving down to East Anglia. Olivia knew deep inside her that he was involved and began to hear the alarm bells ringing in her head. She knew that he was not the man for her, not the man she wanted in her life, not the man she really loved. But she had brought him into her house, and her children had grown to love him. She had shown acceptance of him in her life. She had better try to make this relationship work, she told herself—but she knew that she could never willingly give her heart to a man like this.

For three years Peter worked on her relentlessly, trying to persuade her to have his child. "I'm bringing up four of yours, after all—it's only fair if I have at least one of my own, isn't it, love?" And he endlessly pressured her to get married. Olivia resisted for a long time, but the steady drip, drip of his voice wore her down, and finally she agreed that they would try for a baby. In those days you took a specimen to the chemist and, hours later, knew the result. Peter took the sample and returned for the outcome. He opened the door. There was a triumphant smile on his face. "Well, you'll have to marry me now, won't you? You're pregnant."
Olivia heard the clanging of the cell door shutting behind her.

Her fifth child, a lovely little girl they called Cheryl, had a very traumatic birth. This was when Olivia realised, quite definitely, that she possessed strange and almost frightening powers. Because of the previous medical problems she had encountered giving birth to her other children, Olivia was again in a serious situation. Senior obstetric staff crowded the delivery room. The midwife had told Olivia, very sternly, that she must not, on any account, push the baby, as the head was jammed inside the womb due to a seriously scarred cervix.
Olivia was almost obliged to push, but she fought the urge in order to protect her unborn child. She was very tired and felt herself drifting away gently and painlessly. There, in front of her, she saw an aunt who had died some years before. Her aunt was standing in what seemed to be a white wall that was not solid; it was soft like a cloud, enveloping both of them at the

same time. Her aunt reached her hand towards Olivia and took her hands. "Come with me, my love." She smiled, and Olivia went with her through the whiteness. What happened there Olivia would never remember, but suddenly she was back in the hospital bed again, and her aunt was telling her that she must push the child out naturally, that all would be well with them both; her daughter would be safe. Olivia felt herself drifting back into her body again, and there were the doctors and midwives, still talking quietly in the corner of the delivery room. Suddenly Olivia felt the urge to push, and she did so as noiselessly as she could, trying not to let her expression signal what she was doing. She pushed desperately, trying to bring this little girl into the world against the odds. Just then the midwife turned towards her and pulled back the sheet covering her.

"Oh my goodness, she's pushing! Stop, Mrs Rutter—stop right away!"

But it was too late. The head had crowned, and Olivia continued to grunt and strain as she felt the baby emerge. The staff rushed the child away to the resuscitation pad, and Olivia asked, "Will she be OK?"

"She's looking good," the midwife said. Then she turned back. "How did you know it was a girl?"

"From the same person who told me to push and get her out naturally." Olivia smiled.

When the tiny girl was cradled in her arms, she knew two things. She had allowed herself to give her heart and her body to yet another man who was not the man she wanted or needed or was destined to be with; and she had inside her powers that were terrifying yet wonderful.

When Cheryl was about 4 months old, Olivia rang a solicitor and asked how she could change her surname by deed poll. He was very helpful. He told her that she could pay out a lot of money and go through the full legal procedure, or she could simply inform those who issued her utility and other bills that her surname was now Rutter. This was perfectly legal and acceptable and a damned sight cheaper. So Olivia did this, and she phoned Peter at work and told him she had done it. When the first bills arrived with Mr and Mrs Peter Rutter on the envelope, Olivia said, "There you are. Now I don't have to marry you. I've changed my name." She did not, whatever happened, want to marry this man, and she hoped this would solve her dilemma. But the relentless pressure from both sides of the family continued; so did the steady insistence of Peter. This family pressure had been growing for several years, and Olivia had been able to fight it off, but now she had to give in. She had serious doubts about the man to whom she was committing herself and her life. She knew that her heart was going to be broken, but she was pulled into the situation with the inevitability of a maelstrom, tugged deep into a life she did not want. The ceremony took place in the same registry office in which she and Brian had been married, and she felt a chill of despair as she went through the motions and attempted to look happy.

Olivia had found a talent for business. She had started work in a local beauty salon whilst still young and had developed two things—a love of the beauty business and a burning desire to own not just a salon but a chain of them, an empire of her own. She was promoted, place by place, until she rose to be manager of the salon. Along the way she attended college and studied every aspect of the beauty world. She also took higher courses in business management, and in later years obtained a very good degree in business studies. She also went abroad and investigated the latest innovations in hair, skin, and nail technology. She bought out the salon and then opened several others. In later years she established her dreams of empire when she named her project Diamond Lady and sold franchises which spread over England. For now she owned two salons and had a reasonably good return. Her tenancy in army married quarters had earned her points, as well as the years in her council house in the North, and this enabled her to buy her first property up there.

When Peter eventually did get his transfer to the East Anglian force, Olivia had barely five days to drive down there and find a house for them all to move into. She found one that surpassed all her dreams. It was very unusual, two houses knocked into one huge, rambling home with endless corridors, a large downstairs toilet, and two separate kitchens, both of which were spacious and bright. There were five bedrooms and three storeys, with a bathroom on each of the two top floors. As if this was not enough to enthral Olivia and the children, there was also a huge garden, containing a large, old oak tree with a swing attached to one of its immense branches by a thick rope. The children were ecstatic when they first saw it and the twisting pathways and the summer house at the bottom.

In the October, Olivia and Peter went to Turkey for a holiday. The marriage was not just rocky, it was a total disaster, and this holiday, which brought them in close proximity to each other, resulted in furious arguments and angry confrontations. Olivia wanted a divorce; she was not prepared to tolerate more of this man. Their marriage had been a serious mistake to begin with and now, six years later, was a battleground. That night she sat out on the hotel balcony, smoking furiously, as she was under enormous strain. Peter sat beside her, silent and brooding.

"Peter, I can't go on like this. You know as well as I do that this marriage is just a complete sham. All we do is bloody well row. I'm not happy, and the kids aren't either. They want a proper life, not all this yelling and door-slamming. I want a divorce. Let's just be adults, cut our losses, and sort it all out sensibly. When we get back, I—"

"Oh you do, do you? Well, actually, I don't want a divorce. I think you just need to try a bit harder for the sake of your kids and mine. No wonder the last bloke you had slept around and you broke up. You're *self, self* and *more self*! If the slightest thing doesn't suit you it's tantrum time. You need to think hard about your behaviour. I've tried really hard, but you're a real pain in the butt. I don't want a fucking divorce, so forget it." He swallowed the remains of a glass of whisky and disappeared into the bedroom. Olivia sat biting her lip and holding back tears of anger and frustration. She stubbed out her cigarette and leaned back. She was determined to escape this prison. She had once more given her life—but not totally her heart—to a selfish, unfeeling, arrogant male, and she was again paying the price for that mistake. *When we get back*, she thought, *when we get back, I must do something to end this misery.* She closed her eyes and fell asleep.

Olivia's sister, Grace, seemed to be following Olivia's life pattern. She had married a man in the forces, and they had been posted to Germany. Her marriage was as rocky as Olivia's had been, and she frequently complained to Olivia of her discontent. When Grace's daughter was born in Germany, Olivia flew over to be with her sister, as she had nobody else from her family to help her. When Olivia went into the ward and greeted Grace, her sister's reaction hurt and surprised her. Grace didn't smile. She looked sullen and disinterested. "You didn't have to come over so soon," she said without smiling.

Olivia went to the cot, picked up her tiny niece, and carried her to a chair, where she cuddled her and talked to her. Her sister's chilly attitude continued throughout the visit, and to make matters even worse, Olivia managed to fall and injure the ligaments in her ankle. She arrived back in England hobbling on crutches.

Grace and her husband - who by now had two children -returned from Germany and were stationed in married quarters in the Midlands, the same town in which their mother and father resided. Their marriage continued to disintegrate, and Olivia drove up the many miles to pick up her sister and the children at least every three weeks and bring them back to East Anglia to stay in the big house with her family. This, thought Olivia, would at least give her sister a break from the strain of her domestic problems. The millennium was fast approaching, and everywhere there was great excitement as preparations were made for parties, bonfires, and fireworks.

Grace had asked Olivia to pick her up so that she could be away from her husband and with Olivia's family for the celebration, so

Olivia duly drove up and brought the three of them back, with the two children shouting and playing excitedly in the back of the car. By now Olivia owned her first beauty salon. She closed her office early, as most of the world seemed to be doing, to allow everyone to get home and prepare for the party of the century.

Olivia drove home and showered. She put on a lovely red-and-silver dress, matching shoes, and silver and ruby jewellery around her neck, on her wrists, on her fingers, and in her ears. She was just putting silver combs in her blonde hair when Grace came into her bedroom. She was holding a large glass of brandy and Coke.

"Here, get this down you. It'll help you relax after work and get into the party mood."

Olivia noticed that Grace was unusually cheerful and friendly; she put it down to the occasion. She picked up the glass and sipped at her drink.

"No, down it—drink it. Get ready to have a bit of fun. Come on!" Olivia obediently lifted the tumbler and swallowed the entire contents. She put on her fur coat, took her best handbag, and followed her sister down the road to the public house, which was full of noisy, happy people. As they walked, Olivia began to feel vaguely dizzy and unsteady. *Tiredness*, she thought. It had been a hectic week at work, and she had a house full of people to cook for; it must be the result of having far too much to do. She ordered another small brandy and Coke and sipped it. She felt worse. The room seemed to be spinning around, and sounds were distorted and disturbing. Olivia rose and went to the toilet; she stood in front of the mirror, trying to focus on her image, which seemed to be moving gently. She was still very unsteady and dizzy and beginning to feel vaguely worried. She knew she had only had two drinks and that she was more than capable of consuming five or six drinks and still be alert and able to walk normally. She opened the door into the lounge bar and almost fell onto the floor. Her stepfather lifted her up, and her husband soon joined him, each holding her firmly under one arm.

"Come on, lass, you've had a bit too much to drink. I think you need to sit down." Her stepfather guided her towards a chair. Olivia opened her mouth and tried to speak, but all that emerged was a nonsensical burbling, and saliva dribbled down her chin and onto her fur coat. Peter quickly steered her towards the door to the street.

"I think she ought to go home and sleep this off. She must have had a skinful before she got here; she's well out of it." He and Olivia's stepfather half dragged her outside and up the road to the house. They put her to bed. She remembered nothing for three days and then awoke feeling very unwell and very concerned. She was normally able to drink a fair amount without consequences like this. Why had this happened? She received a certain amount of humorous ribbing about the incident and some snide remarks from her husband about drinking on the quiet. She brushed them all off but remained worried, and the memories of what happened were still with her.

One evening in late March, Olivia was alone in her kitchen, preparing supper for her large household. That day she had been upstairs changing the sheets on her large double bed, when suddenly, from somewhere behind her, she'd heard a voice—one that she had never heard before—saying, "You won't be sleeping in your bed tonight."

Olivia had swung round quickly but there had been nobody there. It had been those voices again—that spirit that Olivia was able to hear and sense. She'd smiled and shrugged. Then she'd said, loudly and firmly, "Stop being silly. Of course I shall sleep in my bed." And she'd continued to make up the bed.

Everyone was out somewhere, so Olivia put the radio on and sang along with her favourite song of the moment. She was preparing Bolognese sauce from scratch, as she always did, and started by sweating down onions, garlic, and fresh tomatoes in olive oil and butter. She always added oregano and basil, freshly ground black pepper and a little salt, and then tomato puree and the ground steak, leaving them to simmer on a very low heat for a while. She was just adding the steak to the sauce when her eldest daughter came into the kitchen. Beth had left home and was living in her own flat with a partner. "I want a word with you." Beth was unsmiling and sullen.

"Do you, indeed," said Olivia. "Don't talk to me like that, please." "We need to clear the air. We have to talk about all the violence when I was young—all the punching, and kicking, and beatings—"

"What are you talking about!" Olivia was horrified and shocked. Was this some kind of dreadful joke?

"Oh yes, I remember it all right," Beth continued.

At that minute, Peter and Grace entered the kitchen together, almost as if they had been waiting somewhere in the wings. Grace stood in the doorway and screamed at her, "You abused your children, you bitch! You don't deserve to be a mother."

Suddenly they were talking, loudly, all at once, and Olivia's head began to spin. Was this real? Was she just dreaming? Almost blindly she grabbed her car keys and, still wearing her apron, ran out into the driveway. She unlocked the door of her car with shaking hands. Her heart was pounding furiously. She jumped into the car and drove, wildly and very fast, towards anywhere. She wanted to drive her car over a bridge and disappear from this horror. She had no idea where she was going but realised after an hour that she was driving to her mother's home. Tears rolled down her face and almost blinded her as she tore up the motorway in a daze.

Her mother sat quietly, listening to Olivia as she poured out their story between sobs. Minnie patted her hand and told her to try and calm herself down. She brought Olivia a large mug of hot, sweet tea and sat beside her, comforting her. Olivia was very tired but cried for hours before she was able to sink into a sleep which freed her from the burden of pain she carried.

The next day her mother went to church. "I'll be back soon, lass. Just sit and quieten down." Her mother left, the door closed with a click, and Olivia was alone. She paced up and down, smoked several cigarettes out in the garden, and then went upstairs to her mother's bedroom, where she knew her mother kept her quite considerable store of medication. She grabbed handfuls of blister packs of tablets and stuffed them into her handbag and pockets. Then she ran out and got into her car. She drove quickly towards the next town, stopped at a garage, and bought a large bottle of water. She continued driving, turning off the main road up a country lane that was deserted and quiet. She got out of the car, leaned against the door, and began to swallow handfuls of the pills, washing them down with large gulps of the water. Her world was devastated—her beloved daughter—her children—her babies. What was happening? She could not take this—she did not want to live. She put another handful of tablets into her mouth and was about to wash them all down when a voice—a calm, very clear voice—said somewhere in her head, "If you do this and die, who is going to fight for your children and safeguard them? Think. Stop, go back, and face it with courage. You *will* win."

Olivia stopped instantly. How could she do this and leave her children unprotected? Quickly she went to the side of the lane, pushed her fingers down her throat, and vomited, painfully and copiously, again and again. Tears were running down her face and chin. She gagged and gasped until she felt she had emptied her stomach of all the toxic load. She wiped her mouth and her eyes and drove swiftly back to her mother's home, where she ran upstairs and hastily returned the remainder of the medications to the bedside drawer in her mother's room. She went to the bathroom, washed her face and hands, and combed her hair. Shortly afterwards, her mother returned. Olivia was sitting in the armchair, trying to look as if nothing had occurred. She was surprised to realise that only two hours had elapsed since her mother had left the house.

How could I even think of doing this? she thought. *Causing my mother yet more pain and loss, with two suicides in her family— two of her children lost in such a terrible way!*

She smiled as her mother entered the room. "Cuppa, Mum?" She went into the kitchen as casually as she could, but her hands were shaking as she prepared their tea. She took a deep breath. She had to fight now, fight as hard as she could—and fight she would.

The following morning, Olivia showered and sat on the bed, plaiting her hair prior to drying it. She thought deeply and realised that her husband was trying to get rid of her and to gain custody of his daughter. Why he was pursuing this course did not matter exactly right then, but Olivia realised that he would have reported her missing almost immediately, in an effort to prove that she had abandoned her daughter. That guidance that she always seemed to receive in times of need was there—in her head and in her heart. Mobile phones had just bowed onto the social scene. Olivia used hers to quickly call the local police station and enquire whether she had been reported as missing. Not surprisingly, she had. She told the local police that she was not missing and had only briefly left her home to visit her mother. Her husband—who was a police officer—was very well aware of that fact. She was just leaving the Midlands to return to Norfolk.

Olivia sat on the bed, unplaiting and combing her hair. It had hit her like a thunderbolt just after she laid down the phone. He was plotting something; he was devious and cunning and unpleasant. She must at all costs return and fight to stop whatever he was planning and protect her children. As this thought came into her head, the phone rang. Olivia knew immediately that it was him. She picked up the phone and saw his number appear on the screen. She said nothing.

"So, you're coming back, are you?" It was a snarl.

"Yes, I am—right away—now." She was defiant.

"Well, you needn't bring that bloody old cow with you. I don't want her here. You bring her near me, and I'll slam the door in her bloody face"

He knew that Olivia's mother was formidable and would very soon have sorted out Grace—and he knew that Olivia would very soon face him up when she returned. Olivia told her mother that she would be returning alone. She was not going to subject her mother to any of this gathering blackness and verbal warfare. She could and would fight this battle alone. Her mother sobbed and begged to be allowed to accompany Olivia, but she held firm.

"No, Mum, it's OK; I'll sort it out. Don't worry. I'll sort the pair of them out." Inside her she knew what was developing and what had happened. Olivia kissed her mother and got into the car. She pulled away and left her mother still sobbing on the doorstep, watching her as she disappeared from sight. Olivia's heart pounded all through the journey. Thoughts and visions crowded her head. She had to concentrate desperately to avoid having an accident.

At last she was home. She jumped out of the car and ran to the front door. The door was unlocked, and the house seemed deserted. Olivia went into the kitchen, and there was Beth, her oldest daughter. Beth looked at her, confused and unhappy. Olivia held out her arms to Beth.

"You can touch me, Beth. I am your mother." Olivia said gently. Beth hesitated a second and then launched herself into her mother's arms. She held her closely and desperately. Olivia held her in return and kissed her long black hair.

"Come on love—let's have a cuppa." Olivia made two mugs of tea, and they went into one of the two lounges in the large house. They sat down opposite each other, and Olivia looked steadily at Beth. "OK, love, what's been going on? What's this all about?"

Beth looked confused. "But Mum, you did beat us, you know you did—"

"No, Beth, I never touched one of you, ever. You know that."

Again the look of bewilderment appeared in Beth's blue eyes. And then Olivia knew. In that second she knew with awful clarity just what had been happening. Peter and Grace—that little bitch—had been having an affair, and they had been brainwashing her children into believing that she had abused them. He, with his years of intense and professional training in police interrogation methods, had twisted and confused and trained her precious children to believe that they had been beaten and neglected. He knew too well of her dreadful childhood and her memories and terrors, and he had chosen to do this to her—but, worst of all, to them. She sat for a moment thinking over the horror of this realisation. Then the rest of it flowed over her, like hot lava. Peter and Grace had been lovers for some time, and they had planned this so that Olivia's first four children would be returned to their father, and he and Grace would keep his daughter. *The bastard*, she thought—*the bastard!* They had deliberately spiked her drink at the millennium celebration; Peter had access to drugs. This would guarantee that Olivia was safely out of the way so that he and Grace could have a flesh fest together. And as for her sister—Grace's marriage was finished, and Olivia realised that she had plotted this with Peter. She had plotted to get rid of Olivia's kids and move in with her lover and her own children to this beautiful house. Not for her a council house—oh no! She wanted this house, the home that Olivia had helped to buy and furnish and decorate by her hard work and skills.

Then Olivia remembered how many times she had driven up to the Midlands to pick up her sister and her children and bring them back, never realising that she was bringing the maggot to the rose, the viper to the nest. Her sister had said over and over again, "Why don't you have an affair, Livvy? After all, your marriage is a sham; it's over. Have some fun."

She'd constantly repeated this, and Olivia had told her, "No, I have no intention of having another man in my life until my marriage is properly and legally ended and I'm free to do it without feeling any guilt." *Of course!* she told herself now. *Of course—she was trying to push me into having an affair to give Peter grounds for divorcing me. It was all planned and plotted, so coldly and brutally and cunningly. My own sister doing this to me—after all the times in our lives that I protected her and took beatings for her, the times I got up at dawn to wash her sheets and nighties and turn the mattress to save her from beatings.* Olivia sobbed quietly as the hurt welled up and crushed her.

Then the anger rose, like a tidal wave, washing aside everything else in its path. *She tried to turn my own children against me, to have them taken from me, to make them think I had beaten them. She did this to part all of us, to hurt all of us. She tried to take my husband and my home. She tried to destroy me and everything I had and was. She knew what we both had suffered in those dark, terrible days of our childhood. Now I will face her, and I will take what is mine. I will take back my children and my home—but she may keep him. He is finished, and I will completely finish him.* She felt light and strength pouring into her soul. The pain was not gone, but it was generating power and the will to fight back. Olivia put out her hand to Beth, who took it and grasped it tightly. Then she began to cry and threw herself into her mother's arms. Olivia held her daughter and rocked her gently. She pulled her away and looked into her eyes. "Beth, how could you take my hand and hug me if you know I'm a monster who beat and mistreated you?"

"Oh, Mum!" Beth cuddled into her mother again. "What have I done? I know it never happened; I know." And then Beth explained to Olivia. She told her of the clandestine meetings in cafes, where she'd been subjected to hours of subtle, steady brainwashing and made to believe that, years before, when she could not remember, she had been systematically beaten, neglected, and mistreated by her mother. Her siblings had also been worked on and drip-fed a story of an abusive and terrible childhood. Olivia's youngest child, her son Matthew, who was only twelve at the time, had been forced to sit on the lid of the big chest freezer for over four hours, whilst the scientific and cruel verbal seduction slowly rearranged his memories and knowledge of his loved mother. It would take weeks before Matthew could be convinced that none of the allegations had really occurred. He was very badly affected and was left confused and depressed.

While Olivia and Beth connected and spoke, Grace was lurking upstairs, and Peter was creeping around in the second kitchen. Olivia was aware of them, and she felt the black, fetid, evil storm clouds massing inside the house. The door opened and there stood Peter, looking dark and angry and aggressive.

"Oh, so you're back, are you, the woman who abandons and beats her children?" And he launched into his fantasy accounts of what Olivia was supposed to have done.

Olivia was aware that her children had arrived at the house one by one and were gathered around, nervously watching and listening. All except Matthew were clearly uneasy and also clearly supportive of their mother. Olivia faced Peter with her head held high. "You know damned well that this is just a fabrication. You brainwashed my children. Where exactly is all this shit coming from?"

"Oh, the children told me—told us. They know exactly what happened; they gave all the details—"

Just then Olivia heard a clicking sound from Peter's pocket and realised that he had a recording device hidden there. "Oh—so you're recording all this, are you? Think you're at work with criminals or something?"

Peter pulled a small, thin Dictaphone from his jacket pocket. "Had to, didn't I? Can't trust you an inch—anywhere—with anything." Then he left the room abruptly.

Sally ran to her and held her very tightly, crying. This was the one they hadn't been able to turn. She had steadfastly refused to believe what they'd tried to force on her. Had Olivia succeeded in taking her own life, this girl would have maintained her mother's innocence. She refused to leave her mother; she was distressed and angry.

The atmosphere in the house was building to storm force. Tensions ran high. Nobody could settle, or sleep, or shake off the invisible mist. At two in the morning, Olivia went into the main kitchen and saw them standing there. The two of them were hand in hand. She would defeat them. Her palms were sweaty, and she was shaking, but her voice was steady, and quiet, and menacing. She looked them in the eyes. "You two think I'm really stupid, don't you? I know exactly what you're up to. Trying to convince my kids that I beat and abused them, so that they have to be given back to their father, and you can keep Cheryl. And you—" Olivia jabbed her finger at her sister—"You can move into my house with your kids and my husband. The pair of you have been shagging for months, and you tried to convince me to have an affair." Olivia laughed coldly. "You plotted and planned to take all I had, and my kids. Where was I supposed to live—on the streets? Not that either of you cares a damn. Well, my lady, you can just get out of my house, now! And don't imagine I shall be driving you back up there where you belong."

For a split second there was silence. Then Peter roared and ran to the kitchen counter, where he swept all the crockery and glasses onto the floor and smashed them further with his feet. He pulled cupboards and cabinets apart; grabbed a broom and smashed glass cupboard fronts; tore fittings down; smashed bottles of sauce against the walls; and emptied every packet, bottle and container onto the floor. Olivia had already sent Cheryl home with Beth for safety, as she'd known that what was to come would be too much for the already traumatised children. She closed her eyes and endured the noise of breakages, Peter's loud, violent swearing, and Grace's screams. Then she pushed them out, physically—out through the door and out of her home and her life. Then she held her other children close, and they stood, comforting each other, for a while. Then they began to clear up the devastation. There were two bin bags full of glass. They swept and washed and eventually made the kitchen safe.

The following morning, Olivia phoned the police and reported the incident. She showed the two officers who came the bags of shards. They knew who her husband was; they exchanged glances. They were sorry, but this was a domestic. Nothing could be done. No charges could be preferred. This was the man whose relationship had been launched on lies, had thrived on lies, and had just ended with terrible lies and scheming. There had been eleven years of falsehood, six years of marriage, but very little love or happiness.

At ten that morning, Peter returned. He wanted to borrow the car to take Grace back to the Midlands, to her home. Olivia told him firmly that he could get stuffed and that *she*—now Olivia's ex-sister—could walk or thumb a lift as far as she was concerned. Peter calmly informed her that after he had taken Grace home he was going to move back into the house and sleep in the spare room. Olivia did not relish this thought but was aware that the mortgage was in both their names and that legally she could not lock him out or refuse him entry. She had consulted a female solicitor and been advised as to what she should and should not do. She sat down and thought very hard and very clearly; then she called her office and asked them to stop paying her director's fees into the joint account she and Peter had. She drove into town, went into her bank, and opened a single account in her name, to which she transferred all the household direct debits. Then she informed the bankers that she and Peter were separated, and they automatically froze the joint account. She went for a coffee and a cream cake, and then she drove home and busied herself trying to cope with the damaged kitchen.

The phone rang. She picked it up. "Hello. Is that Mrs Rutter?"

"Yes."

"I'm John Priest from the bank's finance department, Mrs Rutter. I want to know who's going to pay these loans on the joint account."

"Loans. What loans? I know nothing about any loans."

"Two loans have been taken out on the account. One for £14,000 and another for £13,000. We need to know how they are going to be repaid."

Olivia was silent for a minute whilst she digested the news. "Well, first of all, I am no longer a party to that account, and secondly, where is the agreement that was signed for those loans? I know nothing about them. I didn't take them out, and I didn't sign anything. I suggest you ask the person who did sign the agreements."

"I'll be back to you after I've checked all this out, Mrs Rutter." And the phone clicked.

Ten minutes later the phone rang again. "Mrs Rutter, this is John Priest again. You are absolutely right; your name is not on either of the loan agreements. Your husband is the only person who signed those documents, so he alone is responsible for repayments. I am sorry to have troubled you. Thank you and good day."

Two days later Peter returned. Olivia did not mention the bank's call. She had busied herself moving all Peter's possessions into the spare bedroom and had dumped three large suitcases in the middle of the room as a hint. Four days passed while they lived their separate lives, avoiding each other pointedly in a cold, charged atmosphere. The next day he rushed downstairs and clutched dramatically at the doorframe of the kitchen. "God, I'm finished—fucking finished!" He was sobbing wildly. "The bank wants those loans paid off, and you've stopped your salary being paid into the account." He leaned against the door, breathing heavily.

"Of course I have," said Olivia. "I didn't take them out, and I haven't seen a bloody penny of the money. You borrowed the sodding cash—you pay it back." Olivia never did discover what the money had been used for. He refused to tell her, and she never worked it out.

Peter flopped down into a chair and put his head into his hands. "I'm finished! I'll have to go bankrupt." Olivia studiously ignored him and went about her routine. He had borrowed the money; he could repay it.

Peter disappeared for over a week. Olivia later found out that he and Grace had spent a week together in a hotel in the Midlands. Beth had found out and had informed Grace's husband before telling Olivia. Grace's husband said that, like Rhett Butler, he frankly didn't give a damn. Peter returned and began lurking around the house, engineering constant contact with Olivia and loudly goading her verbally. Olivia's son Matthew was witness to this. It didn't take him very long to realise that the brainwashing that he had endured had been a terrible lie and that his mother had never in his life abused him. At thirteen, he was a big, strong, muscular boy with a volatile temper. After a particularly prolonged and toxic tirade from his stepfather, he exploded and ran at him, shouting at him to shut up and leave his mother alone, and calling him a bloody liar. Olivia immediately knew that she had to stop this, because Peter, with his police background and training and his contacts in the force, would have made sure that Matthew was detained and suffered the full force of the law if he attacked his stepfather in the family home. Olivia grabbed Matthew's leather belt and, mustering every ounce of her strength, hauled him down the stairs. He fought and kicked and screamed, and Olivia was covered in bruises afterwards.

"No! That's what he wants you to do. Stop—come away," she told him. She dragged Matthew into the kitchen and stood with her back firmly against the door to prevent him escaping. Quietly and calmly she explained what would happen if he persisted in his behaviour. She told him she understood perfectly why he was doing this, but that if he were to be taken away as a result, she would be defenceless and alone. Matthew slowly calmed. He sat sulkily and unhappily in a chair, shaking and crying.

Olivia went upstairs after Matthew had quieted. She saw Peter standing in the corridor outside the bedroom. "I can see I'm not welcome here," he said defiantly.

Olivia faced him up. "If you had the balls to be any kind of man, you wouldn't have come back here in the first place, after what you and that slut did. Why don't you just get out and leave us all alone? We don't want or need you anymore." The solicitor had told her that there was nothing she could do to keep him out, but she wanted him out—right away. Every night he tried to antagonise her or the children, to cause friction. Olivia wanted him out. She glared at him and then turned and walked away.

During all this tension and trauma, Olivia hired a childminder to care for her youngest daughter. She still had a very responsible and taxing job and needed to ensure that Cheryl was being cared for properly. The following day, she felt some concern during the afternoon, and she felt that she should pick Cheryl up earlier than normal, as the atmosphere might be affecting her adversely. They drove home, and Cheryl ran ahead of her mother into the large living room. Then, almost as quickly, she ran out again, crying and looking frightened.

"What's the matter, pet?" Cheryl grabbed her mother's hand and pulled her into the living room. The place had been trashed. CDs were smashed, taken out of their sleeves, and thrown everywhere. Flowers and water from two large vases were scattered everywhere, the water staining the new, expensive rug, the vases smashed into a thousand pieces. Books had been torn and thrown around the room. Cushions had been cut with a knife; the stuffing was bleeding out and lying in various places. The suite had been slashed too, and one chair had had a bottle of red wine poured all over its once-pale-green satin seat. Curtains and their railings and hooks had been pulled down savagely and draped across the vandalised suite. The cupboards had been emptied. It was his mark, Olivia thought grimly. But it might mean that he had gone—and gone was what she wanted.

She put her arms around Cheryl. "It's all right, sweetheart. We haven't had burglars. It's just your daddy, who's got into a nasty temper because he's got to leave the house." She could not add, "Because he's been fucking your darling auntie, and trying to turn all your minds and hearts against me, your mother."

She went upstairs to the middle bedroom. All his stuff was gone—his clothes, his computers, everything. Olivia made a game of clearing the mess up so that Cheryl would not be too upset, and soon the house was back to rights.

Olivia called Peter on her mobile—they were still something of a novelty then. "This is the second time you've trashed my house," she said. "But you won't be doing it again, because you're never stepping inside this house again, ever."

"If I wanted to go in that house, I could walk in whenever I wanted, and you couldn't stop me—" Peter began.

"Oh really? I don't think so. I've taken photos of every damned thing you did, and I shall be going to a solicitor and then a judge. I don't somehow think you'll be showing your face here again—do you?" He went quiet. He realised what he had done at that point. He would fight to get Cheryl from Olivia and she would fight, fiercely, to prevent him. Olivia was relieved that Peter had moved out, but the nightmare was not yet at an end. The scheming and evil were to continue.

Olivia began to rapidly lose weight. It was not the deception, the lies, the adultery, and the scheming. Olivia was, after all, too used to men who lied, and slept around, who were devious and untrustworthy. It was the searing and wounding fact of her sister's treachery. This was the sister she had protected and defended—taken beatings for, comforted, kept warm and fed and clothed. She had physically and emotionally nurtured Grace as a child. She had cared for and done so much for her as an adult. Why had she turned on her, betrayed her, and plotted to defame and undermine her credibility as a mother? She had planned to throw Olivia out of her own home and take away her children. Grace had always been a selfish little thing, but this—Olivia huddled in her armchair, sobbing silently and brokenly. All trust had gone. Men were one thing, but her own sister—and after all they had endured together.

Peter and Grace had moved into a house only doors away from Olivia. It was torture to her. Had she encountered Grace in the street she would have ripped her apart limb from limb and stamped on her face afterwards. Peter turned up for his regular visit to Cheryl, as he had applied to the court to have Cheryl staying with him and Grace at their house; the court welfare officer had deemed it should be so. Olivia sat Cheryl down and gently told her that she had to go and stay with Daddy and Auntie Grace. It was as if she had torn the child's heart from her body. She wept brokenheartedly.

"I don't want to, Mummy. I don't want to go! Don't make me; let me stay here with you, please, Mummy."

Olivia hugged her fiercely. "I'm sorry, darling, you have to go. I can't stop it. Just see, you might like it." But tears were running down Olivia's face too.

Cheryl went. She told her mother that both Peter and Grace had sat her down for hours, trying to convince her that her mother did not love her. It was their same wicked tactic as before. Cheryl went only three times. After that she refused, and Olivia supported her decision. After that, contact ceased. Peter signed over all documentation, mortgages, and custody of Cheryl to Olivia. She signed over her rights to his police pension; she was so delighted to have got rid of them both. She still owned the huge, five-bedroomed, three-storey house, and she needed to sell it. She had stayed there for two years. She decided that the large place had to go. So it went on the market, and a stream of the usual sightseers and time-wasters materialised. One day the estate agent rang and said, "I've got a Mr Grant for a viewing today. He does actually seem to be a serious prospect."

"Hmm—thank the Lord for that. I'm fed up with all the ones who aren't really interested and take up my time." Olivia fervently hoped that this would be the buyer. He was due at six that evening, and she busied herself tidying and cleaning.

Mr Grant arrived with his two sons. They played with Olivia's two dogs, chasing up and down the staircases, shrieking and laughing. This seemed to cause Mr Grant to make up his mind immediately. "I want to make an offer." He made his offer, and Olivia accepted it.

"We can either go to the estate agent's or just sit here at the kitchen table and sort it all," she said—and so they sat at the kitchen table, and the deal was made.

Olivia moved out and bought herself a smaller house, which she didn't really like after her lovely, large, sprawling home. But there was only her, Cheryl, and Matthew now, so they did not need all that room.

Mr Grant became Michael. He worked in the oil business and often worked abroad for long periods of time. Every time he returned, he called Olivia and she went round; he would have bought in several bottles of wine for her. It was always red, and Olivia didn't drink red, so Michael always had to go out and get her some white. He would happily drain the bottles of red, and Olivia simply thought that he was on holiday, away from work, had worked long and hard, and was entitled to do as he wanted. She did not register his drinking then. They would sit talking into the early hours, but nothing happened. Then they went out to dinner, and slowly things moved on from there.

Two years after she sold the big house to Michael, Olivia moved back into it with her son and daughter. Two years after that, she and Michael married. Olivia noticed that Michael's drinking was heavier than what she would have called normal, but she was not one of life's drinkers, so she assumed that it was normal male consumption. She could not fault Michael as a husband; he was attentive, loving, and caring. There was no other woman in their relationship—just a vicious and tenacious rival called alcohol. Michael would get depressive moods, these would lead on to arguments, and these would be the excuse for him to disappear down to the pub to binge-drink. The binges would last at least a week. Each day he would surface, in a vile mood, and would soon be drinking again. And so each day would go like the previous one, until he had drunk himself into a stupor so often that he was forced to stop in order to eat, shower, and stumble back to some kind of normality. Olivia did love Michael, but she did not love his addiction or the problems it brought. When sober, he was the loveliest person imaginable. When drunk, he was quite horrible, and Olivia wondered why she had not picked up on his glaring flaw more quickly.

Then Michael was diagnosed with prostate cancer. Olivia searched heaven and earth to find some way of fighting the invader. She found that, from Germany, she could obtain irradiated seeds that could be implanted into the prostate, which would burn out the cancer. The treatment was arduous and trying. Olivia was there, always, beside Michael—encouraging and calming him, reassuring him, and fighting with him. He got through the course, with no damage to his genitals that would prevent him from having a perfectly good and satisfactory love life. The crowning glory was that he was clear of the killer. Olivia took him to Florida to recuperate in the sunshine. He made efforts to make love to her, but his libido had been psychologically affected, and he was only able to manage one night of lovemaking. After that he and Olivia were never again intimate. That she could have tolerated as the price of his cure, but only weeks after they returned home, he started to drink again. This Olivia would not endure. She had gone through months of stress and emotional hardship to help and support Michael. She had warned him so very often that if he ever drank again she would not stay to suffer the consequences.

Besides this, his treatment had been very costly. Olivia had paid a great deal of the cost privately, and the British National Health Service had borne the rest of the burden. Michael, having always worked abroad, had not paid a penny towards it, and this infuriated Olivia. After all that had been done to help Michael, he had gone straight back to his drug. Olivia was finished with him. She still, surprisingly, loved the man, but she could not and would not tolerate his addiction. Sober, he was loving, a perfect partner, but drunk, he was violent and frightening. He had dragged Olivia by her arms and tried to push her out of the front door; he had thrown cups, plates, and kettles at her. She had reached the end of her patience. She had fought to save his life, and now he was again abusing his health.

On her way to work the following day, Olivia parked her car and walked towards the office. She passed a solicitor's office and thought, *I have to do this—now—I can't put it off.* At the office, she wrote out a four-page statement and then rang the solicitors for an appointment.

She was there that same afternoon. A very aristocratic-looking man peered over his glasses at her and said, condescendingly, "I'll need all your details, of course."

"I've written them all down."

"And, of course, I'll have to have a full statement of the facts. Perhaps you could come back when—"

"I've already written you four full foolscap pages."

"Hmm, you seem to have done this before, Mrs Grant."

"This will be my third divorce." Olivia stood up. "The first one couldn't keep it in his trousers. The second one had an affair with my sister. This one's having an affair with alcohol. Yes, you could say I have some experience in this field." She handed him the statement. Eventually it cost her £6,000 to divorce Michael. He emerged from a three-week binge and found the divorce papers waiting to greet him. Olivia was living in the main bedroom of the house, and Michael was in the back bedroom. Her solicitor called and asked to see her, so Olivia dropped in on her way back from lunch.

"Ah, Mrs Grant, do sit down. I've had a letter from your husband's solicitor." The tall, gaunt man leaned forward and picked up the letter. He looked at it and then threw it back on the desk. "It seems that your husband wishes for an attempt at reconciliation to be made. What would you like me to reply?" He raised a well-polished eyebrow and then lifted his pen.

"Just this." Olivia grinned wickedly. "Tell him he'll need a new anorak."

The aristocratic eyebrow shot up, and a faint smile played on the solicitor's thin lips. *"Anorak*, Mrs Grant?"

"Yes, he'll be needing a new anorak—because it'll be a cold day in hell before I ever go back to him."

The solicitor pushed the paper away, looked up, and laughed. "I gather that this is a done deal then, Mrs Grant."

"Yes, I started this and I'll finish it. I told him that if he started drinking again, after all we've both been through, what it cost, and what I've put up with before, then it would be the end. Now he's on a three-week binge, and this really is the finish. He probably doesn't remember anything but the good times, but I don't, so no, there will be no reconciliation with Mr. Grant."

Olivia went ahead with the divorce. She sold the house. Michael had tried to block the sale by refusing to sign any paperwork, but Olivia told him that this would make no difference; the house was sold and he needed to move his belongings out. When she returned from work the following day, all Michael's paraphernalia had disappeared from the living room. A few days later they all had to move out as the buyers were moving in. Michael stood with Matthew in the garden, crying and asking Matthew to tell Olivia that he was so very sorry.

Olivia was sorry too; in fact, her heart was breaking, but she could not go back from this chosen path. She had endured too many broken promises, too many traumatic scenes, too much verbal and physical violence. She still loved Michael; she loved him a great deal. The normal, sober man was quite lovely. His high-flying job had taken him, and Olivia, all over the world. She had been to the Dubai Gold Souk many times, where Michael had decorated her fingers, wrists, and neck with expensive tokens, which Olivia called his "sorry gifts". These were attempts to atone for his weakness and addiction. Olivia had hoped that this would be her final and perfect relationship. Michael was ten years older than she was. He had a kind and caring nature, and she had really believed that he would be with her, to look after her, to the end of their marriage, when death alone would part them. He had been faithful to her in his way, but his addiction had seduced him, and trust had died. Olivia would mourn this loss—the loss of Michael's devotion, care, generosity, intelligence, and friendship—from then on. She loved him thereafter, but she could not stay. The search would go on.

During her marriage to Michael, something traumatic and significant occurred in Olivia's life. Her mother, Minnie, had worked for some years doing contract cleaning. She always attended to her hair, even when she was simply working, as she had meticulous standards. One day, lifting her arms to remove her curlers, she found she was unable to raise them properly. She had noticed that she was getting breathless easily and feeling less than well, but she tended to ignore things that didn't totally ground her, and so she carried on. But a visit to the doctor told her that she now suffered from COPD—chronic obstructive pulmonary disease—and angina. This was quite probably due to the strong chemicals used in the cleaning she did. She was only 58 years old. She struggled on, using inhalers and nebulisers, and on several occasions nearly died as a result of a serious attack. She had also been diagnosed with Paget's disease, a nonfatal but painful condition, and she was confined to a wheelchair. As well, she had had a hip operation which went wrong. When she was to take a demonstration of healing or mediumship, she would get out of the wheelchair and walk with a stick. Throughout the demonstration she would appear perfectly normal, but afterwards she would have to return to her wheelchair.

Olivia had heard of a new drug which could help her mother with the Paget's disease. Three weeks before the end, she had the drug prescribed for her mother. Ever afterwards she felt desperately guilty for doing this, as she felt that she had contributed to her mother's eventual death. Her mother told her repeatedly—after she went—that this was not so, but Olivia could not lose that guilt.

For six weeks Minnie was confined to her bed. It was Olivia's fiftieth birthday, but she didn't remind her mother, as she didn't want to worry her. When Olivia dropped in to see Minnie, she handed Olivia a beautiful watch. "Did you think I would forget?" she said softly.

Minnie told her husband, Adrian, that she was not going to make it to the usual Christmas dinner. She looked at him. "If this is what my life's going to be, then I don't want it, love." She knew she was not going to be there for Christmas. Olivia told her to hang on, she would be with Olivia for the big lunch, and Olivia would carry Minnie to her house for Christmas, if she had to, on her back.

Adrian and Michael, Olivia's then-husband, argued. Michael detested Christmas. Not everyone on the planet loved it. He would go through the motions and play the part but reluctantly. He wanted Olivia to go away for a break; he told her she was exhausted and that she looked it. At first she refused to leave her mother, but Michael won, and they flew to Dubai. Before she left, her mother told Olivia that she hadn't "been" for a full two weeks. Olivia had brought her round liquorice and a bevy of other aperients that she hoped might solve the problem. Whilst she was away, her daughters had attended Minnie and had tried her with just about everything they could think of. The doctor prescribed a powder called Movelat. When Olivia returned, her mother told her that she wasn't touching the prescribed powder ever again; it had achieved the desired result but caused Minnie much pain.

One day Adrian called Olivia and asked her if she was coming round to visit Minnie, something he had never done before. Olivia said she would pop round after work.

"Is everything OK, Dad?"

"Yes, fine."

Olivia arrived after work and was shocked to see her mother slumped in her wheelchair, asleep. When she awoke, her eyes were sunk into her head, and she looked terrible. Adrian explained that he had taken Minnie to a hospital appointment, then gone shopping, and she had suddenly gone into this decline.

"Why the hell didn't you tell me this before, Dad? I'd have been over sooner."

Olivia knelt beside her mother and stroked her arm. "Mum?"

Minnie opened her eyes and looked blankly at Olivia.

"Where's Michael? Where's your husband?"

Olivia realised that Minnie was confused. She knew that Michael was still in Dubai.

"Wake up, Mum. Wake up and talk to me." But Minnie was rambling. Olivia went into the kitchen and called for an ambulance. She didn't want Minnie to hear her.

Minnie wanted to go to the toilet; she was trying to get up. "I need a wee." Olivia went to help her stand up and walk to the downstairs wet room, but Minnie was like a rag doll, and her legs gave way.

Olivia's brother was there, and Olivia screamed at him, "Get the wheelchair! Get it—quickly!" Olivia assisted her mother to the toilet. Then she washed her and put a clean nighty on her. Because Minnie could no longer cope with doing her hair, she had had it cut short, and now she looked about 90, thought Olivia sadly.

The ambulance arrived and took Minnie to the local general hospital, where she was put into the high dependency ward. The family drove behind. It was now one in the morning. Soon Minnie was settled with oxygen and pain relief. She was comfortable but very confused. The doctor told Olivia to go home and rest, which she did; all of them did. At eight the following morning, after a sleepless night, Olivia arrived just as a line was being inserted into Minnie's neck. The consultant took her to the relatives' room and gently told her that her mother was doing extremely poorly. Olivia looked at him, wild-eyed. "Make her better—make her better!"

"I'm so sorry, but we can't. We can only make her comfortable, Mrs Grant."

"If it's money, then get the best specialists. Buy the drugs—money doesn't matter! Make her well, please."

The consultant laid a comforting hand on her shoulder. "I'm sorry, but money can't make any difference now. We're putting your mother on dialysis soon."

Minnie was moved to the high dependency special unit which was better equipped then the general ward, and linked up to a battery of tubes and machinery. She was almost comatose. Olivia went with her and sat beside her. Minnie began mumbling and was struggling to sit up. "Let me sit on the edge of the bed. I can't breathe." The doctor in the unit told Olivia that Minnie must remain in the bed. He administered a sedative to calm her struggles. She was, however, raised in the bed to help her breathing.

Adrian had arrived at the hospital and been taken to the relatives' room, where he was told that Minnie was seriously ill and would not survive the night. Olivia watched as she was attached to a heart monitor, unable to take her eyes away. The consultant spoke of dialysis again. Olivia said a firm no, but Adrian insisted that it be done. Olivia told him that a tube would have to be inserted through Minnie's groin, causing her agony, and she would have to endure this misery three times weekly. The doctor asked whether Minnie should be resuscitated if she started to go. Olivia immediately gave a strong no, but again Adrian wanted Minnie to be kept alive at any cost.

Olivia jabbed her finger in Adrian's face. "No—let her go peacefully." Eventually, feeling guilty, Olivia allowed the dialysis to proceed, and soon huge amounts of fluid were being removed from Minnie's ravaged body. The staff asked them to leave for a while, and Olivia went down to the canteen, where her children were gathered, waiting. They had phoned and informed all Olivia's siblings of the news, including the hated Grace and Peter.

Olivia was furious. She shouted at them in the canteen, in public, "Why the hell did you tell her—them?" She ran outside, lit up a cigarette, and puffed at it, tears of rage running down her face. She wanted her mother to quietly and peacefully slip away without her, yet at the same time she wanted so much to be with her mother at that last breath, when her spirit left her frail, sick body. They had been together at the beginning, at Olivia's birth, and they should be together at the end. She returned to the ward and sat by Minnie, stroking her head gently and talking to her.

Then the ward clerk told her that there was a telephone call for her. She took the phone. It was Grace, the last person Olivia wanted to hear right now. She cut Grace short. "You've never bothered with Mum for years, so why bother now?" And she put the phone down. Grace called again almost immediately. This time Olivia gave her no chance. "Sod off!" she snapped tersely, and again the receiver went down with a bang.

Soon the clerk came again and told Olivia that her brother-in-law was on the phone for her. Olivia frowned. "Brother-in-law? I haven't got a brother-in-law." It was Peter. He tried to plead for Grace, but Olivia would not be moved. Not after all the damage Grace had done to her, her children, her mother—everybody. She told him not to bother to come to the hospital or she would see that he never left in one piece. Again the phone went down. She told Adrian, who shook with rage. The nurse assured them that she would contact security so that they would not be allowed to get in, and this calmed the situation.

Adrian and Olivia's brother Paul left to go down and be with the children. Olivia sat by her mother, watching her laboured breathing and watching the heart monitor. Minnie was peacefully and blissfully floating in a mist of sedatives and analgesics. Suddenly she sat upright and flung her arms out to either side. "Enough! I'm full up," she said, and she fell back down onto her pillows.

When Adrian and Paul returned, she told her brother what had happened. "She wants to go; let her go. And back me up, please! Dad'll go crazy."

"Yes, let her go if she wants to go," said her brother. They persuaded Adrian. He was reluctant to allow Olivia to instruct the doctor, but he gave in. Olivia asked for everything but pain relief to be withdrawn. She also asked them to leave the heart monitor beeping gently, so that she could know when her mother was slipping away, but to turn off the alarm. Olivia sat stroking Minnie's hand, and they all whispered words of endearment to the departing woman. Olivia suddenly realised something that she should have been more aware of. Her mother was awaiting their permission to leave them and to pass out of the world of pain and frailty into the spirit world of peace. Olivia turned to Adrian and Paul and told them this.

Adrian's eyes were moist. He took Minnie's hand and leaned over to kiss her. "It's OK, Minnie. I'm going to be OK. Go if you want to, sweetheart. Just go. We'll be seeing each other again very soon." He kissed her again and stepped aside.

Olivia went close to her mother and held her thin hand. "You go, Mum, go home. I'll care for Adrian, I promise you. He'll always be looked after and loved."

Her brother broke down. He was unable to speak. They held their mother, one on each side. Then Minnie's eyes opened; she appeared to be looking intently at something or someone beyond the end of the bed. She nodded. "Yes, OK. Uh-huh," she said.

They looked at each other. They were all thinking that it was Wayne, Olivia's beautiful, lost brother, to whom Minnie was talking. Olivia held her mother closely. Minnie slipped back onto the pillows and closed her eyes again. The heart monitor slowed, and slowed, became barely detectable, and then Minnie was gone. She had gone into the world of spirit, and love, and peace. Olivia kissed her mother lingeringly; then she got up and quickly left. Out in the corridor, both she and Adrian broke down. He had lost a much-loved wife, companion, lover, and the mother of his children. Olivia had lost an adored and irreplaceable mother, a woman of strong character, who had left her mark on the world of spiritualism, on everyone who met her, and especially on her children. Minnie had asked Olivia to look after Adrian, and Olivia was determined that she would do this to the best of her ability until Adrian passed to be with Minnie again.

Michael returned from Dubai and cared for Olivia in her weak and distressed state. Christmas was a nonevent for them all that year, as Minnie had died on the nineteenth. Olivia took a three-week break from her business, and her staff rallied around to run it, excelling themselves to show their sympathy and liking for Olivia.

Olivia arranged the cremation. Minnie had told her not to let the funeral directors put her make-up on. She was as fastidious about her appearance in death as she had been in life. "I don't want them to make me look like a doll, and I won't go without make-up on," she had told her daughter firmly. So Olivia made up her mother's face herself, using all her skill and expertise and the finest cosmetics from her salon. She had her mother dressed in a smart purple dress and jacket and matched her eyeshadow to the colour. Her mother's face was so very cold as Olivia worked. She talked softly all the while to her mother as she gently applied the cosmetics. Then she stood back and looked at her beloved mother for the last time. She turned to leave and collapsed, totally overwhelmed by the trauma of her loss. As it was Christmas, the cremation had to be delayed, and it was January 6 when it took place. Thousands attended the goodbye to her famous mother. Olivia stood, hardly hearing or seeing anything as the service proceeded; then she left to look at the huge array of flowers. Minnie wanted her ashes to be interred with Wayne's, and so they were- in time.

Two to three weeks later, Olivia was drifting in a half-asleep state. It was nearly one in the morning. Suddenly the phone, which was in the bay window of the bedroom, rang shrilly. Olivia vaguely remembered how she and her mother had used to chat nightly. Olivia tumbled out of bed, went over to the phone, and picked it up. "Hello?"

"Hello, sweetheart, it's me." Olivia's heart leapt with a sharp stab. It was Minnie's voice.

"It can't be you, Mum. You're dead—"

Minnie interrupted her, saying very firmly, "It's me. Tell them all I'm all right. Just tell them that I'm absolutely fine and that I love them all very much."

"Oh, Mum." Olivia could hardly speak. Tears ran down her face. Minnie spoke again, strongly and authoritatively. "Just tell them, sweetheart."

Olivia turned and looked at the bed. She could see herself lying there—but this was very real. She looked down and saw her hand holding the phone receiver. "Mum, don't go. Please, don't go!" she begged Minnie.

"I must go. But tell them I'm here, and fine, and they mustn't worry. Goodbye, my sweetheart. I love you so much." Minnie's voice was fading.

Olivia put down the receiver and stood staring at the phone for several minutes. Then she went back to bed and lay thinking of her mother, her unforgettable, unique mother. Later in Olivia's life Minnie would return to her again, but this was the most significant and comforting of her contacts, and it helped Olivia at the worst time of her life.

Olivia moved into a new house. As life went on, she started to become lonely and feel the need for companionship. She went online and found a dating site, where she shopped around curiously. She found that she had not yet recovered from her sad parting with Michael, and so she stayed on the site but did not respond to the views, winks, and messages that flooded in. It was quite some time before her interest began to awaken. In 2013, on a beautiful, crisp, autumn day, she picked up her phone and looked at the dating site in earnest. Nobody on the site piqued her interest at first, but then one night she received a message from a rather good-looking Jamaican guy. He was tallish, handsome, and had those beautiful full lips of his race. He messaged her in a humorous, interesting way. Olivia knew that she was very physically drawn by this Caribbean stud and looked forward to his messages. Soon they were on WhatsApp, having left the site, and they texted nonstop. Olivia began to anticipate the *ping* of her phone when his messages came in. He was called Tyreese—Ty—but she knew little more than that about this mysterious, good-looking man. She found him very sexually attractive, even though they were just texting. When he first spoke to her on her phone, she found him totally compelling. He had a soft lilt, not quite American but not altogether Jamaican. He had been born in Jamaica but raised in the States from the time he was about 6, and this had coloured his accent. She loved the way he called her "hun" and "baby" and said "gonna". She looked forward to actually meeting him. He was only 42—a good twelve years younger than Olivia was, but she liked and preferred younger men. Apart from Michael, she had never really sought the company of older men, and she was not actually planning any long-term future with the men from the dating site. She just wanted a fling, sex, fun, a bit of relaxation. No more emotional roller coasters, untidy and irritating feelings, obligations and responsibilities. Just a man she could use for her own ends. No relationships, just fun—and sex.

One night she got a call. She looked at the incoming number and saw that it was Ty.

"Hi, baby." He sounded very serious and almost upset.

"Hello, Ty. What's up? You sound unhappy."

"Baby." A sob caught Ty's throat. "I'm sitting out here in my car with a bottle of vodka, hun—my dad." He paused, and again she heard his voice faltering. Something was upsetting him deeply. "My dad, baby. I've just heard that he's got cancer." Olivia had gathered that Ty's father was very dear to him. There seemed to be a large family and a close one.

"I just don't know what to do with myself, hun." His voice broke again.

"Well, come over here, Ty." Olivia felt compassion for the man. He sounded really broken. He arrived very soon afterwards and sat there, wiping tears from his face, sobbing, and drinking vodka and lemonade in fairly large quantities. Olivia registered immediate alarm after her years, and traumas with Michael, but she reasoned that this man was shocked by such news; maybe he could be allowed a few drinks in these circumstances. Ty sat crying and talking to Olivia about his father's condition. He had brought his laptop with him, curiously enough, and he opened it up and began to play his American soul music. It was hypnotic, and Olivia was lulled and seduced by it. Ty persuaded her to have half a glass of his vodka. She was no longer much of a drinker, and this made her yet more susceptible to his dark, sultry charms. Soon they were dancing, slowly, close together, and his cheek was next to hers. His body was large and warm, and Olivia found herself yearning to be very much closer.

Somehow, she did not remember how, they went up to her bedroom, and soon he was undressing her and laying her down on the bed. He used his tongue so very skilfully, and Olivia gasped as he ran it over her clitoris, slowly and gently, and into her vagina. He was a very experienced lover. He used every ounce of his knowledge and skill to send her into raptures. She moved, desperate for his body to go into hers. He pushed her up further onto the bed and knelt between her parted thighs. She felt what she thought was his fist at the entrance to her vagina. Then it was sliding into her, and she realised with shock that this was, in fact, Ty's penis.

"Oh my God!" Olivia gasped. She felt sure that she could never get this massive thing into her body. Ty was gentle, but Olivia was stretched to the limit she felt she could handle. He moved slowly, and Olivia's body responded eagerly. Soon she felt an orgasm building, and she pushed wildly into Ty's body. He responded by thrusting deeply. This took Olivia by surprise, and she felt pain, but she was too near a climax to register the discomfort, and they came together. Ty cried out and jerked wildly; then he slid down onto her breast and kissed her neck. They lay together for some time; then Ty kissed Olivia, slid away, and cuddled into her back. They both slept. In the morning Olivia made him coffee, and they chatted, and he left. They didn't meet again for nearly a month, and a pattern emerged. Ty would go off the radar, with no texts or calls for about two weeks, and then he would suddenly text and call again. Very soon he would be back with Olivia, cooking for her, playing his music, and making love to her. He would make her, amongst other things, Caribbean fried chicken with rice and peas, which she enjoyed. Olivia noticed that Ty tended to drink rather a lot, but she assumed that this was because he was relaxing with her. During this time he first told her that he was a single parent, raising his daughter alone. Then one evening he confessed that he was married but that the marriage had finished some while before and that he just lived with the wife, who was called Shirley. Ty said that he cleaned the house and picked his daughter up from school, as Shirley had a demanding and important job. He stressed that they had separate bedrooms and that everything between them had died some time ago. He also told her that the relationship was strained and that Shirley had a vindictive nature. Olivia imagined that this was why Ty drank so much when he was with her. It was a loosening of the control and unhappiness of his life. He made it clear that he wanted to move in with her, but because Olivia lived so near him and Shirley, he could not. The pattern grew. Olivia saw him on and off; the evenings and nights came and went. Then he started asking her to help him with money for his car. Olivia told him sharply that this was not the kind of relationship she had planned and made it quite clear to him that he had better not rely on her for financial assistance. The year had slipped into 2014. The visits continued, but it was a hotchpotch, and they fell out frequently. Ty told her that he did drug runs to get cash; he said that was why he had to disappear so often and be unavailable. Olivia was often extremely angry at Ty's failure to acknowledge texts, sometimes for days, or pick up phone calls, again for days. He expected his texts and calls to be answered immediately.

The lovemaking continued to be the one thing that held her in this union—that and Ty's talent for talking her round after the constant rows that ensued. Ty kept on pressuring her to allow him to move in with her. He insisted he could not stay with Shirley, as she made his life so unbearable. Olivia wondered at times why she allowed herself to stay in this drama. Ty's physical size was exciting and could be orgasmically blissful, but it was also something she had grown to dread, as it could also be the source of pain. She wished to hell sometimes that she had never met this man, and yet she realised that she would miss him, although why she would miss him she never quite understood.

The year 2014 rolled by. Their break-ups were frequent, often unpleasant, and often for long periods of time. Olivia ceased to think of it as a relationship. There was nothing concrete to build on. Ty was too unreliable, too selfish, and too unstable, both emotionally and financially. And she was very unsure of just how honest he really was. Olivia's working life was bringing her to the rewards of hard application. She was moving up towards expanding her business. She was elected to boards and committees connected with her chosen sector, and she was a firm and much-heard voice in those areas. She was busy, occupied with her job and her family.

Ty was mostly an annoyance, to be swept to the back of her consciousness but welcomed to her bed in the short periods when they reunited, welcomed warmly and lustily. Olivia could not resist Ty's body. She dreaded his size and the pain it meant, but the bliss it brought with it was something she could never refuse. The smell of his dark, velvet skin; the soft, gentle mouth; the combination of his fingers and tongue were his weapons, weapons which he used to defeat her attempts to push him out of her life. But there was always the dread, the seconds when she feared his hugeness, the intake of breath as he entered her and spread her so that she felt she would burst, the times when he became ferociously excited when near orgasm and thrust deeply, stabbing her cervix and causing her agony. But then would come the climax, when she screamed as she was taken to the edge of sheer bliss. For this she would have suffered anything. In those seconds she was his for life—she adored him and was his, body and soul.

Then would come the morning, and he would be leaving, and she would be angry, pleading and threatening, in despair. The door would close, and he would be gone. And there would be no texts, then brief texts, and then she would be firm and dismissive. She laid down ultimatums. He ignored her, made promises, pleaded, and found excuses. And so the carousel played on. Round and round it went, predictable, noisy, colourful, endless. The year slipped by, and still there was no real attachment. And still Olivia could not stop herself finding excuses for Ty's behaviour. She was beginning to realise that she could not trust him; he told her smooth half-truths and massively believable lies. He and his life were both dark, shadowy, and worrying. But always he could hold her where he wanted her with his body and his lovemaking. And always she wanted to believe him, and rationalise his behaviour, and make excuses for him. She believed she could tame him, make him her own thing. Christmas 2014 came. Olivia spent it with her family. She laid a place for Ty and texted him to invite him. He texted back thanks, saying that he might come, but he didn't. Christmas and New Year came and went, and nothing had changed, and still Olivia could not shake off the shadow of the handsome Jamaican from her mind and her heart.

In January 2015 Ty vaguely mentioned going on holiday to Egypt. The he went off Olivia's radar. Then he reappeared and was somehow back in her bed, and her body, and she was crying out with bliss and passion and twisting her hips with the rhythm of his dark, thrusting buttocks. And the fights resumed, and the endless texts, and disappearances, and they became Olivia's reality. She began to realise that she could not escape him. One night, after long, sultry, desperate lovemaking, Olivia was on the edge of a shuddering orgasm, and for a second Ty pulled back and looked into her eyes with his beautiful, deep-brown eyes. And she cried out, with all that was in her soul and her mind and her body, "I love you, Ty—I love you so very much!" And his body went deeply into hers, and Olivia screamed as she reached her paradise. She was committed now, bound to him.

In March 2015, Ty kept talking about going to Antigua in April, for his son's twenty-first birthday. Olivia was discovering that Ty had innumerable children, in England, the Caribbean, and the States. This one was, he said, his oldest child, his oldest son. Later Olivia found out that Ty had, in fact, got a son older than this, who had been born within weeks of the so-called oldest son. In April Ty flew to Antigua. Olivia assumed he had made the money for the fare from drug-running.

Ty kept nagging, insisting endlessly, that he wanted to move in with Olivia. It was an idea that she had entertained, but she felt very uncertain of the relationship. Every time she felt that some ground had been gained, Ty would go off the radar again, and they would argue about his failures to text, phone, or return. Eventually she weakened. Olivia had been thinking of moving anyway, as her newly opened branch was quite a way from her present home. She had to travel long distances every day, and the costs of fuel were horrendous. She decided to rent somewhere nearer her place of work and to rent out her present house.

The search for somewhere suitable began, but Ty did not make it easier with his constant disapproval of anything Olivia produced. Time and again she took him to houses she really liked and which had all the boxes ticked for her, but she could almost feel his lip curling as he stood, silently disapproving. *Why should he be so fussy?* thought Olivia. He *has no permanent home of his own; he appears to be constantly broke; his lifestyle is questionable.* Is *he even totally honest?* And yet she scampered around for him, looking for a home that met with his approval. The relationship had been anything but secure from the outset. Olivia kicked back at his casual and selfish attitude to anything that did not directly concern him or his needs and wants. Heated arguments were common, and he often stormed out angrily, after which she would not hear a word from him for weeks. Then there would be the resumption of his usual "Morning, baby"—and that only for days. Then he would put in the odd "You OK?" or even add "What you doing, baby?" Mostly it was his shorthand for wanting and needing help—usually financial—and that would kick off another disagreement. Olivia had made it quite clear that she was not to be considered as a cash cow, but always Ty asked, and always they fell out, and always he managed to talk her into helping him to a certain extent. But she would not be manipulated into financing his projected trips to Jamaica or Antigua or his dreams of newer and better cars. Now she wanted to move, and so did he. He wanted to move in with her, but his arrogant attitude and his refusal to like what Olivia preferred was causing her annoyance and stress.

Year 2015 rolled on, and still the relationship was a constant war. Olivia would not compromise on her ideas for what Ty's role should be—certainly not one of a man who turned up whenever he felt like appearing, to his routine, and in his time; someone who constantly pressured, and demanded, and wheedled, and managed to get all he wanted.

Olivia was sitting on the settee; she was smoking yet again, Ty's presence in her life had reawakened the habit she had managed to kill. She was thinking hard. *How have I managed to get myself so tangled up with this man? After all the experiences and traumas I've lived through, after all I've told myself about what I wanted and would only settle for, this is what I have. For God's sake—you're worth more than this, woman! What is it you really like about this man—if anything? Do you keep on having him back in your life just for his outsized dick? OK, he makes love with enormous skill, and you know that you really do yearn for that; in fact, you can't live without it, can you? Life is one nonstop argument. You can't rely on him, can't trust him to turn up, or text, or call. He's got that air of dangerous, quiet, menacing underworld about him—almost a threatening presence if things aren't going his way. You have to decide if you really love this guy—really want him in your life.* She sat motionless, smoking and thinking.

"The next time," she said out loud. "The next time that he starts any trouble, that's it, the finish." Olivia stubbed out her cigarette, turned out all the lights, locked up, and climbed the stairs to her large, luxurious bed. The bed that was the size of a small kingdom, made especially for her.

Not much later Olivia and Ty argued. Ty had been away; he had not texted her for days or picked up her calls, and then he drove up without any warning one evening. He was scruffy, and reeked of sweat. His eyes were bloodshot, and Olivia could smell vodka on his breath and body. She greeted him with a kiss, but all too soon he was talking of having to go to Jamaica to see his dying father. Olivia knew what this would lead up to. He would ask for money to go, but not directly. He would slowly and skilfully make her feel guilty that his father was so ill, and that he had no means to fly and see him or to send money for medical attention and drugs.

Olivia said a short, sharp "No!" She told him to do his drug runs and get another job to finance these needs. "Is money the only reason you want to move in with me, Ty? I shan't be keeping you. It's not what real men do. I've paid out more than my fair share for things for you already—"

A furious row followed. Olivia saw a nasty side to Ty, a side that wanted its own way in everything, at any cost, and did not welcome opposition. Ty stormed out with his possessions thrown into several suitcases and bin liners. Olivia attempted to speak to him as he strode to his car, but he pushed her away, jumped in the car, and drove off, raising gravel from the driveway in his acceleration.

Olivia imagined that he would be in touch when his rage had diminished, but there was a silence. She began to miss the brief "Good morning, baby" of the years before. She felt a slight twinge of yearning for his soft, deep voice when she heard certain music played. At night she sometimes put her hand out to the other, empty, side of the huge bed and wished for his large, hard body; his dark, sultry skin; his gentle, probing fingers; and his moist, skilful tongue. She tried to resist her urges, but she knew that he had captured her body and with it her heart. Some six weeks later, after a week of "Morning, baby", there was a phone call. She tried to reason, to point out, to complain, to reject, but he won her over—again. That evening, late, he pulled up, got out of the car carrying a bunch of red roses, and came back into Olivia's house and her life.

Several more stormy episodes followed. Always Ty left, quickly and angrily, and silence followed. Then brief texts would resume, and then, somehow, he always managed to reappear in Olivia's life to wheedle and whisper his way back into her bed and her heart. Olivia was now in the process of moving. She was tired of dancing around to Ty's wants and whims with regard to a house, and she had set her heart on a country cottage that was not too far from the town she worked in. At this point, her brother Paul needed a home, and her daughter Cheryl also was in desperate need of one, so Olivia decided that she would rent her present house to them both and find the cottage her heart yearned to live in. Ty had disappeared after another falling-out. It was difficult, if not impossible, to actually pinpoint the cause of the arguments that they had. Ty was a genius at making her the bad boy of each situation. He usually even managed to convince her that she should apologise, and often she reluctantly did. The making-up was incredible, and each time Ty rolled away from her, spent and docile, and Olivia lay in the afterglow of another orgasm, she had a spark of hope for this strange relationship.

Olivia moved into the cottage. It was the story-book place. It had roses around the door, a Victorian garden overlooked only by trees and farmland; it was remote, silent, and peaceful. Olivia loved it on sight.

After the move was over, and she was sitting drinking a cup of tea in the calm of the fading day, Ty called. "Hi, hun. What you up to?"

"I've finished moving. I'm in my cottage."

"Hell, baby, I forgot. I should have helped you."

"Yes, I would have appreciated the help. It was a lot to do almost alone."

"So where are you, exactly?"

"At the cottage I told you about. You know I wanted to be out in the country and nearer work."

There was a silence. "That cottage—but I didn't—it's a bit out of the way. I thought you would have asked me first." Olivia said nothing. "Well, give me the postcode. I'll be there as soon as I can make it." He drove up some hours later. He held her very tightly and kissed her. Then he went around the house looking at everything, pursing his lips and shrugging. He took his bags upstairs while Olivia went on with preparing a meal in the kitchen.

Ty came down. "OK, baby, I've put all my stuff in the drawers upstairs." He smiled, looked in the fridge, and found a beer, which he opened and drank. He sat down in the living room on the large red chair that was to become his over the months, turned on the television, and sprawled, beer in hand, laughing at the imported American comedy which Olivia hated.

It did not take Ty long to discover that the signal for both his mobile and laptop was almost nonexistent. This did not enthral him. Then Olivia asked him to go with her to visit her daughter. Immediately it was obvious that Ty did not want to go. His face told his feelings.

"Um, sorry, baby, I already promised to go and help my friend move. He's got a wife and kids and a lot to do. Must go and help him."

Olivia was angry. "Then why didn't you help him first and then come here afterwards? You knew he was moving." She knew he was going—and going for a while. She could feel it. He did not like her cottage, or the signal situation, or the quiet and peace that she loved. He hadn't wanted it from the start, and he was going to leave. Inside her head and her heart the red lights flashed, and the sirens screamed, "Let him go—go and not come back! This relationship is a travesty, ridiculous. Say 'Goodbye and don't bother to come back!' Get rid of him now—now." But she kissed him before he left and found herself agreeing to let him leave his clothes in the cottage. He drove away leaving Olivia feeling cheated, angry, and totally confused. That night, in her huge bed, she missed his body and that voice. What was this something that he had that always tempted her away from sense? It was nothing that she could really define. But she longed for him to disappear and never return—and she missed him achingly.

Months passed. Ty texted sometimes. Always she got the "Morning baby"; seldom did that not arrive.

Olivia was growing angrier and more impatient with the big Jamaican and his arrogant assumption that the world turned around him and his life. She texted him: "Please come and take your stuff from my cottage. There is nothing between us any longer, as you keep disappearing the minute you arrive and can't stay in touch even." There was no reply.

She sent the text again. This time he texted back: 'I can't, baby. I'm on my way to Jamaica."

Olivia replied, "I gave you plenty of notice. I'm putting them in bin bags and leaving them on the bench next to the front gate. Come and get them." She threw his clothes and trainers and other belongings into three large, black bin liners and dragged them down to the cottage gate, where she left them beside the bench. This was a remote place. Nobody was going to take them. She tried texting him again and again. No reply ever came. Then she texted, "The dustbin men come on the nineteenth; they'll take the bags if you don't pick them up. I'm not moving them."

Ty texted back. "Baby, I'm in Jamaica. I can't do anything. I'll see you when I come back."

The nineteenth came and went, and the bags were removed by the dustmen. They contained quite a few things that had never been worn; indeed, some of them were not even out of their wrappers and still had labels attached. When Ty returned he was as seductive and wheedling as ever, but when he realised that his new, unworn clothes and trainers had gone out in the bin, he was incandescent. He hadn't believed that Olivia meant what she had said. "For Christ's sake, baby! I told you I was in Jamaica, and you know my dad's very ill. You could have put them out in the shed if they were in your way. They were brand new—unworn—all that bloody money thrown away. I can't just jump when you want something done—"

"I gave you weeks to move them. You couldn't be bothered to even text me. You just disappeared, as you usually do. I can't be doing with this nonsense. You were the one who wanted to move in with me. I didn't force you to come here or anywhere else. You wanted to get away from her—then you just keep buggering off without a word. This isn't the sort of relationship I wanted Ty." Olivia lit up another cigarette. She was smoking heavily again. He was stress on wheels.

"Well, I have to go away and do my runs, earn money—I can't sit around here all day." Ty's eyes were growing darker; he had that angry look that Olivia had come to dislike a lot.

"Sit around all day? There's a lot to be done while I'm away at the office sweating my guts out. You want to be part of my life, live here, share things—well, you share the work. Stop just disappearing all the bloody time and not contacting me. If this doesn't suit you, then just bugger off!" Olivia slammed out of the room.

Ty soon opened his bottle of vodka and sat, glass in hand, with a thunderous look on his face. Then he got up, went to his car, and brought in several bags, which he unpacked in the kitchen. He started to prepare a meal of curried goat. Olivia did not particularly love the stuff, but the smell of the spices was tempting, and she was hungry. She went into the kitchen. Ty handed her a glass of brandy and Coke.

"Here, get this down you, baby. Lighten up, relax. Ty's here." He ran his fingers softly over her neck, brushing her hair aside. He kissed her neck gently and lingeringly and then moved down to her shoulders. Olivia tried to shrug him off but felt herself responding to his quiet, deep voice and the feel and smell of his skin.

Ty put the lid on the slow cooker. "That can cook nice and slow for a while. Come with me." He steered Olivia towards the living room, sat on the large red chair, pulled her down onto his lap, and began to kiss her deeply and fiercely. He removed her blouse and bra and sucked her nipples. Olivia took a deep breath. She was helpless. She could not resist his body, and she was desperate to feel him inside her. Ty laid her down on the chair and removed her skirt and panties. He stripped off his clothes and trainers and knelt in front of her. When his mouth went down onto her, Olivia cried out. She was so very ready for his huge body that she guided his massive penis in eagerly and pushed herself onto him. She could see his face clearly—that grin, those eyes closing with pleasure and desire. *God*, she thought, *he is so handsome. Just looking at him makes me wet.* "Please, baby, do it really hard! I want you badly. I'm almost there." She was frantic as orgasm gripped her belly. She dug her nails into his buttocks, pulling him into her even more deeply.

Their thrusts became a dance of lust, matched and liquid and shudderingly exciting. Then Ty began to breathe heavily and sweat, and he went into her deeply with his hugeness. Olivia screamed and trembled as she came with him, and he jerked and cried out, and then they lay still. He kissed her neck, her shoulders, her mouth.

A tear ran down Olivia's face. Ty wiped it away. "Crying, hun?" He smiled.

"I just needed that a lot; I've missed it." She smiled briefly and then came back to reality. "Hell, I'm naked. I need a shower."

Ty took her hand. "We'll take one together." They went upstairs, where Ty lathered and rinsed Olivia's body and then wrapped a large bath sheet around her. He put on his bath gown and dried Olivia. She climbed into lounging pyjamas and a robe, and they went down and sat, finishing their drinks, smoking, and just enjoying each other's company. *If only it could always be like this*, thought Olivia. *Like this. No rows, no sudden departures, silences, lies, and demands—no mystery and lack of trust. Just the two of us. Here together. Him cooking me Jamaican food—sometimes. Him helping me in the house and garden. Not him always driving off, the silences, the rows.* Deep inside her heart Olivia knew that this was never going to be. She knew that it was going to end in some kind of crisis. She knew she could not trust Ty. She knew, with a woman's intuition, that there was a woman or women somewhere out there. She didn't want to think about it—but she knew. And dark fear rose in her soul, because she realised that she was his, held captive, and that she had grown to love him. She could not, would not, share him with anyone. His stubborn refusal to tell her where he went, his selfish, uncaring lifestyle, and his ability to lie so slickly and convincingly all made Olivia's situation so much worse. She wanted to break away but could not. She needed and wanted him too much. She snuggled into his large, warm body and watched television. Soon they ate the curried goat, watched more television, and then went up to bed, where Ty held her closely and possessively. In the early hours of the morning, he rolled over onto her and slid into her body. She was almost asleep.

"No, Ty." She tried to push him away, but he covered her protesting mouth with his own mouth and kissed her as he moved faster. Olivia responded, reluctantly at first and then with passion, and they reached the golden land together. She slept in Ty's arms. He had her again—for now.

Over the next few months, Ty disappeared frequently. He was doing drug runs, he told Olivia. Then he would text her that he couldn't get to see her because the car needed a new tyre, or the windscreen had gone, or the exhaust needed repair. Olivia began to realise that she was being taken for a fool. His car was not that old, and it was a very upmarket model. After the tally rose to £450, Olivia refused to hand out any more cash to Ty. He seemed to frequently be at a place in Essex, and Olivia began to harbour a suspicion that there was some woman there that he went to stay with. There were certain places that he seemed to go often; he said that they were friends connected to his drug runs and drop-off places, but Olivia had her suspicions. She also knew, inside her, that Ty was visiting Shirley a lot and that he was sleeping with her, although he maintained stubbornly that he had not had sex with her for years. Olivia had managed to see a few texts on Ty's phone briefly and had seen several from Shirley, including one that said. "When are you coming here again?" She demanded to know what it meant, and Ty told her angrily that he wanted to see his daughter, that this was her home, and that he wasn't giving up his child for her.

She could never get a straight answer. Ty always managed to turn discussions into rows and to make Olivia feel unreasonable and demanding. He said that he was trying to change his ways for her and went away less often, but still he kept trying to get money for the many things that appeared to go wrong with his car, and still Olivia refused to pay out any more. He was always wanting to go to Jamaica—to his cousin's wedding, to his cousin's funeral ... "She was only 34, baby, shot in the head, a gangland killing, the wrong person." Sometimes it was his father's health or his mother's health—the list was endless. And when he went, he needed clothes, trainers, medications for his parents, who were poor and unable to afford them, as well as doctors' and hospital fees. Olivia supplied all these. She also paid the rent, the council tax, the water rates, the gas and electricity bills, the food bills—and Ty's vodka bills when he sneaked large bottles of it into her shopping trolley. He contributed nothing, except, she told herself grimly, a lot of his dirty washing—and a lot of his sperm. Olivia worked hard and now owned her own company. She did not need pressure and stress from Ty and his nonstop demands, crises, drinking, financial drainage, instability, insecurity—and his temper. *But here we are*, she thought, *hardly together, but tied together, because I cannot and will not break away. Maybe I can slowly train him to live in the way I want him to. Maybe I will win and get the person I want. He says he loves me, but if he did he would understand why he makes me so angry.* She tried to not love him—but she felt sudden desperation, emptiness, and loneliness. There was no life for her without Ty.

Ty had not liked the cottage on sight, and he used this dislike as an excuse to stay away from it often. He always had complaints: no Wi-Fi signal, no mobile signal, too quiet, too lonely, too far from the main road, too far from the town; it never ended. Olivia refused to give up the cottage that she loved, and so the year staggered on. The cycle repeated: the disappearances—sometimes for months—the rows, the short texts, the lack of texts, and then the reappearances, and the coming together. Always there was the reunion of their bodies. The hard, urgent, moist coupling and then the cries of relief and pleasure, and the intertwined, sweaty bodies, and his lips on her neck, and his whispered sweetnesses. Then would come the long time of separation, a time when Olivia felt Ty drifting almost imperceptibly away from her. She lay awake at nights, missing him, longing for him, yet telling herself that she was better off without this constant disruption to her life.

Her children did not like or trust him. Matthew had met him, acted frostily, and then told Olivia, out in the kitchen, "Mum, this one's just after money. I don't like him, and I don't trust him. There's something shifty and smooth about the guy. You just be careful. I hope to God you aren't thinking of marrying him."

"You have to be joking, Matt! If I ever did that, I'd have a prenup drawn up, and he wouldn't touch anything I've got, I can assure you, son. Don't worry. I don't totally trust him, believe me—"

"And yet you've been having him back again and again for years now, Mum. What is it this guy's got that keeps you dancing to his tune, for Christ's sake? He's bad, I can feel it. I wish you'd just kick him out."

Olivia thought, *I cannot tell you what it is about him that holds me, because even I don't totally know—and what I do know I won't be telling you!*

Christmas 2015 saw an empty chair yet again; Ty did not appear. Olivia's children made disparaging comments, and she was upset and angry. He had promised to come to her cottage to share their family Christmas. He often spoke of spending Christmas alone, and feeling sad for him, Olivia had wrapped gifts and arranged a good time for him. This was the second let-down. If he was so lonely, why did he not join them? At the end of a good family day, with her feet up on the settee and a brandy in her hand, she texted Ty. She was far from surprised when he did not reply for some time. Then, late in the evening, he texted back that it didn't really matter, as he never did Christmas anyway; he wasn't into that stuff. Olivia was deeply angry and not a little hurt. She texted back asking why he hadn't bothered to tell her this last year, and she wouldn't have gone to all the trouble she had gone to this year. She'd enjoyed her family Christmas, but was beginning to think that her relationship with Ty was something she should really forget. New Year came and went, and she did not hear a word. Not even "Happy New Year" on her phone. The next few months were sparse. They barely communicated. She heard that he had been to Jamaica a few times and vaguely wondered how he managed to afford all these trips. Drug-running maybe. He was always telling her of constant crises concerning his father's condition—mainly, Olivia suspected, to try and obtain funding from her. But she did not rise to this emotional blackmail. Then there was Ty's health. Always he had terrible headaches, or flu, or aches and pains; the list of things from which he suffered was endless and inventive. For a man in his mid forties, he was very unhealthy. Olivia worked very hard at developing her company, and it kept her occupied. Ty began to fade to the back of her mind, although she did sometimes think of him as she lay in her outsize bed. Then all his faults were as nothing, and she could only hear his soft, deep voice,; feel his large, warm body; see his dark, enticing skin; and feel the belly-wrenching orgasms he brought her to— *And that will be quite enough!* she thought. *It has achieved exactly nothing up to now; it will continue to be a total waste of time, effort, and emotion. So forget it, Olivia. Just forget it!* She threw every ounce of herself into the company, and it showed the results of her toil, enthusiasm, and skills.

Towards the end of autumn Olivia had still hardly heard a word from Ty, just an occasional "Good morning, baby" or "How are you, hun?" or the ubiquitous "What you doing, baby?". She sometimes replied, but he didn't answer after that. Then the texts became more frequent, and longer, and soon they were telling her that he missed her a lot and telling her that often. She texted back, telling him that she had tried to have some sort of relationship with him but that it hadn't worked because he kept disappearing and didn't appear to want to share her life. Also that he didn't seem to like anything she liked, or anything she did or said, so what was the point? Then, out of the blue, Ty called her. She hadn't heard from him for months and was quite surprised to see his number come up on her phone. There was an awkward pause.

"Hi, baby. So good to speak to you again. I've really missed you!"

"Well, yes, it's good to hear from you too, but you haven't exactly kept in touch, so I assumed we were over—*finito*. After all, we haven't really got on, have we, for some time."

"Hun, if you knew how I've missed you. I know I've been screwing up badly, I agree. I've missed you so much. I really will try to make an effort to make us work, I promise you. I really am going to make an effort this time. I know what I did wrong, and I've been thinking about it all and how I can show you how much I really love you. Just let me come back and show you—prove to you. I want to be your man. I want you to be my woman ..."

Olivia tuned out as Ty drifted into one of his endless monologues. She had been there before and heard it all before. When he finally paused for breath, she said, "You're going to have to change an awful lot, Ty, and your way of living, and reacting— everything—has got to change. If you want to come back with me, I'm not prepared to tolerate all that other shit I had to endure. It's risky for me to have you back living with me. I think you should just come and see me quite often, and I can get my head around it all. If you really are going to try, and if you really do want to come back here and stay and make a life with me, then I'll find out, in time."

"Hun, can I come round right now? I want you so much."

"No, Ty. I've had a very hard, busy day. Come over tomorrow evening. Bye." She cut off the call before he could argue.

The next day Ty texted her a lot. Mainly he told her how much he loved her, missed her, and wanted her. After work, Olivia showered and changed into a silk nighty with thin, floral straps, a matching silk gown, and velvet high-heeled slippers with a fur edging. She combed out her blonde hair and put on some expensive and tasteful jewellery, from the "sorry" collection from Michael. Just after eight, Ty rolled up. Immediately Olivia was slightly annoyed, as he was clutching a bottle of vodka, but she tried to forget it. He was just as she had hoped he would be—all animal. Dark, attractive, enticing animal, he exuded testosterone and desire. He swaggered in, grinning, and put his arms around her. "Oh, my baby, how I have missed you." He kissed her, and his kiss was hard, and lingering, and demanding.

Olivia felt her body react with a swiftness that annoyed her yet thrilled her. She wanted him—now—so very much. All she had planned to say was forgotten. Ty slowly slid her robe off. He kissed her shoulder, then her neck, then her ear, and then again her mouth. As he did so, he removed her silk nightie. It slid to the floor, and Ty kissed and nuzzled her breasts. Olivia had always had ample, attractive breasts, and Ty always had to suck her nipples and run his tongue over them and the blue-veined, swollen orbs, then take them into his mouth. His eyes were growing that flecked, orange-brown colour that signalled sexual urgency. He laid Olivia on the big red chair and then quickly stripped off his clothes. He went straight down onto her belly with his tongue and hands, slowly working to her clitoris. Olivia moaned loudly and arched her back. Ty looked up at her and grinned his shatteringly handsome grin. "You really want it, baby, don't you."

Olivia moaned again and reached for his penis.

"Oh no." He pushed her hand away. "Beg for it, baby. Beg for it."

He continued to send her crazy with fingers and mouth, and Olivia was desperate. "Please, Ty, oh please, just fuck me, really hard—I want you so much!"

"Am I your man, baby, and are you my queen?" He started to slide his magnificent penis into her very slowly.

"Yes, darling, oh yes. I am yours, all yours, and you are my man! Please—oh please—I want you so much!"

"This is all yours, baby, all yours when you're all mine." Then he thrust hard into Olivia's body, and she gasped and braced herself for the pain she was expecting, but the pleasure was overwhelming. She felt the rising storm and smashed herself against him as he drove into her harder and harder. Then she screamed out as she climaxed, and Ty gasped and rammed furiously and deeply into her. The momentary pain she felt was eclipsed by the flooding orgasm that brought her relief, joy, and a feeling that she could never let this man go. They lay together, joined, and their breathing slowly eased.

Then Ty kissed her, gently. "I love you, Livvy. You're my woman. I must stay with you." They kissed, rolled away, and Olivia went up to shower. Ty followed and showered with her. Then they came back down, and Olivia drank a couple of brandies with Ty. They had a light supper and sat watching television, Olivia leaning against Ty's huge shoulder on the big red chair. For that moment Olivia was truly happy. She felt very close to Ty. Her body purred with the afterglow of his lovemaking. If she could only freeze this moment in time, stay in this golden place, with these feelings. This was to be the pattern of the repair, the recipe for the following months, their coming together. There was always the joining of her body with his huge, dark body, the skill of his tongue, fingers, and his massive penis. He played her like some rare, delicate instrument and extracted exquisite and exciting melodies from her frantic body. Little by little Olivia began to fall in love with Ty. He would not totally change his lifetime habits for her, but he was trying, actively trying, to fall in with what she wanted him to be. He visited her often, on probation, attempting to establish the relationship she demanded. Slowly they became closer. Olivia was still annoyed by things Ty did, such as his failures to answer texts and calls, his haphazard lifestyle, and his disorganised routine. She still had fears about his having other women—she certainly suspected that he slept with Shirley—but was determined to tempt him away from them and towards her. She had begun to want him—fiercely at times. In October of 2016, they decided to take the step of living together. Olivia even gave in to Ty's demands to live in or near a town, to have a largish house with at least two bath and shower rooms and three bedrooms (so that one could be his man cave), and many other of his wants. She began to look for something that filled all these requirements, and the year slid into Christmas again. Olivia and Ty were now committed. Olivia was nervous. Had she made a sensible decision? Could Ty ever change? Did she really know enough about his life and him? *Oh hell!* she thought. *Is it my brain or my pussy controlling all this?* But she knew that she loved him, and that was what mattered to her. Once again she was giving her heart, her scarred, abused heart, and to a very uncertain future and a very unstable and unreliable man. *What the hell!* she told herself. *This may just be the one—my last and only love.*

Olivia had invited Ty to a family Christmas yet again. The children and grandchildren were all there, happy and excited. Olivia had wrapped and labelled Ty's gifts and laid them underneath the tree. He hadn't arrived by mid-morning, and the time for the Christmas meal approached. Olivia was upset and angry—yet again. Maybe he'd been delayed. She held the meal back by half an hour, but the grandchildren were getting hungry, and her children were annoyed that she was having to dance to Ty's whims. They began the meal. Ty's place was laid, with a red serviette and a large gold cracker. The meal went on for an hour, but still no Ty. The afternoon went by, the grandchildren played, and argued, and cried, and slept, and still there was not even a text. Olivia texted, and she called, but she knew she would get no reply. The silence continued for a few days afterwards, and then there was a tentative text. "You OK, baby?"

She texted back. "No, I am not. Call me *now!*" She was almost surprised when he did. She began a verbal barrage immediately. Did he know that this was the third time he had let her down so rudely? Did he know the trouble she had gone to? If he really hated Christmas, then why didn't he just say so and refuse to accept invitations and save everyone's time and money? Was it going to work out if he just continued being noncommunicative and letting her down again?

They sparred, hotly, for nearly an hour. Ty told her that he had been on the phone constantly to his family, as his father was again very ill, and they were all worried. It was the same old story, but it just might be true. She could not blame him for his father's illness, but she could blame him for his failure to contact her. Eventually Olivia went from a blaze to a simmer. She was still angry, but she wanted this relationship to have a chance yet again. She told him that she would have to accept his account but that she was still angry that he had not sent even one text. She was abrupt with him for some weeks, but she did not break away. And so 2016 limped into 2017, and the New Year came and went, and still Olivia had not got a real hold on Ty. But this man held her and her soul and her mind—she could not pull away.

OLIVIA AND TYRESE, 2017

In January 2017, Ty told Olivia that he was going to Jamaica for his birthday and his nephew's birthday. He managed to wheedle £100 out of Olivia for his trip, and after the date of his departure she heard little. *What else is new?* she thought.

On the day of his proposed return Olivia heard nothing, and then her mobile rang.

"Hi, baby. I'm back, but I'm in a mess. I need someone to come pick me up."

"I'll drive up right away," said Olivia.

He sounded irritable. "No, no don't bother. I've had a terrible time. I can't stop throwing up; I didn't eat at all in Jamaica these last coupla days. Maybe something I ate there—I don't know. Just feel terrible."

Olivia was mildly annoyed. Tyrese was always unwell. He gloried in ill health. Not a day passed when he didn't parade new symptoms.

"OK," she said. "Then you do need to be picked up, Ty. Just go and sit down, and I'll be there as quickly as I can."

"No, don't bother, hun. I'm trying to get hold of Amal."

Amal was a friend Ty had had for years; it seemed he lived just outside London. Although Ty often spoke of him and told Olivia he was visiting him and staying there, he also seemed to dislike him intensely. But Olivia had noticed that Ty extended this attitude to several other people; they seemed to have befriended him but he disliked them.

"What about our arrangement about moving, Ty?" Olivia asked him. "You were supposed to come back from Jamaica and come down here and help with the move to our new house. We are supposed to be living together; it's what you wanted, and I'm damned well not going to do it on my own. I can't. I've got a business to run. This is all for you—not for me."

Ty sounded sulky and angry. "Well, Amal's coming to pick me up. I'm too ill to do anything. Just let me go back with him and get better, baby; I'm really ill. You don't seem to care about how I feel and—"

Olivia cut him short. "Of course I care how you feel, but you did arrange to help with this move. OK. Go with Amal and get better, and I'll see you soon."

"OK, baby. Bye—I love you."

"Love you, too," said Olivia.

He ended the call.

He was gone for over three weeks. Olivia texted and called constantly, but Ty, as ever, was unavailable or did not return the texts. When she did get through to his phone or he called her, he told her that he was still very ill and could not return right then. There were still the inevitable daily texts of "Morning, baby" and, when they did speak, the loving and missing that were an inevitable part of any communication with the big Jamaican.

Finally he rolled up at the cottage without any warning. Olivia was packing things into a box; she was sweaty, dirty, and tired.

Unusually for her, she was not beautifully dressed and made up, as she'd had no idea Ty would be arriving. She was slightly annoyed but responded to his long, lingering kiss, realising that she had missed his body and his loving more than she wanted to. She went up and showered and changed into something she felt more normal and comfortable in. She applied make-up and perfume.

Ty stood in the doorway with one raised eyebrow and a grin on his handsome face. "Why bother, baby? I'm only gonna take them all off again."

He spoke softly and walked towards Olivia. He bent down and kissed her gently on her mouth and throat and started to unbutton her blouse. He slid it off and kissed her shoulders. Then he slowly removed her bra and brushed his lips over her breasts and nipples, which swelled as desire for his huge, beautiful body made Olivia oblivious to everything else. Ty carried her to the bed and quickly removed her skirt. Sliding the crotch of her small lacy knickers aside, he knelt and nuzzled into her, licking her clitoris with his skilled tongue. He stayed there for some time, using his fingers too, and soon Olivia was wet and desperate. He lifted her legs onto his shoulders and slid in slowly. Olivia gasped as she always did, because however aroused she was, Ty's hugeness was hard to take, and she tensed for the discomfort of his entry. He was gentle and slow, and Olivia responded passionately. Ty's desire increased, and as he neared his orgasm, he thrust into her very deeply. She cried out with pain and pleasure, mixed in one great second of bliss, as they came together. Then they lay still, and he pulled her into his arms, kissing her hair and telling her how much he loved her and how much he had missed her. Soon he fell asleep, snoring gently, and Olivia pulled away and crept to the shower. The sperm running down her legs was copious. *He has missed me*, she thought. *He has really needed me after all this time. He is true to me.* But it was a question, not a statement.

He stayed for only two days and made fierce love to her often. Then he took his bag to his car, said a brief goodbye, kissed her, and drove off. He was gone once again for some weeks, and again the morning texts arrived regularly, with "What you up to, hun?" and "You OK, baby?". But he rarely answered her texts or her calls.

Olivia had obtained the tenancy of the house that Ty had insisted she get. It satisfied all his continual demands. Everything was for him. She had arranged the move at the end of February, and her son Matthew, came to help. Ty arrived with several bottles of vodka, and the night before the move, he and Matthew sat drinking; they both got extremely and annoyingly drunk. Ty became argumentative, and Olivia had to pander to his whims to prevent him from becoming as obnoxious as she knew he could be. The next day the removal van arrived. Olivia had booked it but had had no idea that the removal men would be two hefty black guys from the Caribbean. Whilst she and her son struggled with the boxes, Ty lolled about, chatting with the men in patois and doing nothing particularly helpful. Olivia and her son grew more and more annoyed and resentful as Ty played the role of big rich guy with his pretty, blonde woman and showing off to these two other Caribbean brothers.

Eventually the move was finished. Olivia, her son, and Ty sat on unopened boxes, drinking coffee. Olivia's son looked at his watch. "Sorry, Mum, I've got to go. Got lots to do. I'm sure Ty will help you unpack all this." He shot Ty a meaningful glance.

"Sure." Ty waved his hand and glanced up from his phone, on which he had been furiously texting, as ever.

Olivia went out and kissed her son goodbye before he drove off. "Are you absolutely sure you're doing the right thing, Mum?" he asked her. Olivia realised that sons are always wary of males prowling around their mothers, and she tried to dismiss this remark as simply her son's natural biological reaction. Still he did not drive away. "Mum," he said seriously, "that bastard's just a bloody gold-digger. He's no good, Mum!" Olivia screwed up her face and tried to dismiss the subject. Her son shrugged and drove off. She stood, waving, as his disappeared around the corner of the road. Then she turned and went into the new house.

Olivia felt strange and ill at ease. She already missed her cottage and its beautiful, large garden. She had a distinct fear that she had made a mistake in asking Ty to share her life and her home. She knew little about him yet enough to know that he was rootless, unreliable, and, she feared, not totally honest. She went into the kitchen to make some coffee, and as she did so, Ty came down the stairs with a suitcase. "What's that for?" enquired Olivia.

"Baby,"—he put his hand on her shoulder—"I just need to go sort something out. I won't be long. Just a few days."

"What about all this unpacking?" Olivia waved her hand over the mountain of boxes. "You're here to help me with this, surely, Ty! I moved because you wanted this place. My cottage wasn't good enough for you, and now we're here you want to just bugger off again!"

Ty came up close to her and kissed her on the cheek, but Olivia turned her head away. "Just a few days baby. Got a little business I must sort out." Then he was gone. He got into his car and waved and smile as he drove away.

Olivia was furious. She dragged boxes all over the house, opened and emptied them, and packed things away. She was totally exhausted and angry and hurt. She went out into the garden and lit a cigarette. She had almost succeeded in kicking the habit, but Ty's hold on her life and his smoking had driven her to use them again. She stood there with her coat around her shoulders and thought deeply. *Have I made a dreadful mistake? I don't want to be here, really. I miss my cottage already, and this man is an unknown quantity. I cannot trust him.* She went back into the house and started to unpack more of her accumulated life. Darkness fell. She ate a little and then went up to bed—alone. She did not sleep well.

Ty was away for ten days. There were the usual daily "Morning, baby" texts and a few "Hi, baby" ones for two days, and then he called her. "Hi, baby. I really miss you. How's the house going? I wish I could have—"

Olivia cut across him. "I've done some deep, hard thinking, Ty. I think I've made a very big mistake leaving my cottage and taking all this on."

"But baby, we'll soon turn it into a real love palace—"

"No, Ty—it's not just the house. It's everything. It's us as well. I think I've made a big mistake deciding to live with you. No, don't interrupt. Listen to me, just for once, and don't hang up like you usually do. Since I first knew you we've argued over your constant disappearances and your refusal to answer texts or pick up phone calls. That's not the sort of relationship I want or need. I want someone reliable and permanent in my life, not an overemotional diva who flies off into a rage at nothing. I want peace and stability, not this—this never-ending row that just simmers and doesn't ever seem to end. It's all too bloody stressful. No, I won't put up with any more. I think you'd best come back and take your belongings, or I'll chuck them out like I did that last time at the cottage. Let's just say goodbye and write it off as a mistake."

"But baby, I can't live without you. Do you realise just how much I love you? I'll change. You'll see. I just had a few things to do."

"I don't think so, Ty." Olivia was firm. "It's been this way for nearly four years, and nothing has ever changed or got better. I don't want this anymore. I love you, but that doesn't change the reality of all this constant arguing and you disappearing and refusing to text or pick up calls." She put the phone down sharply and went out to light another cigarette.

Her mobile rang almost immediately. Ty was sobbing and pleading and promising to change. He insisted he loved her and couldn't live without her. She was his life. There was no one else but her.

Hmm, thought Olivia. *I wonder. You are away so much; you guard your phone like a dog with a bone; you are always out in your car, just sitting and texting and calling. And then there's Shirley. You said you were married, but you only ever went to see your daughter, because Shirley and you hated each other. Do I believe all this?*

Her mobile rang again. "Baby, don't do this to me! You just don't know how much I love you. It's killing me that you want us to end this relationship."

"What relationship?"

"Oh, honey, don't be silly. You know we're made for each other. Just give me one more chance. I can change." And it went on and on. Olivia would not relent, and Ty always ended with "OK, so it's over. Thank you for what you've done for me. I'm going home now."

Olivia often wondered where this home was but eventually realised it was part of Ty's arsenal of emotional blackmail weapons. He was going to go home—take his life.

The emotional onslaught continued for days, and the crying and the pleading, and Olivia began to weaken. She missed his lovemaking, cuddling into him in front of the television, even his not-too-well-cooked meals after which she had to wash and clear up, the early morning cup of tea, the smell of his dark skin, his handsome face, and sweet smile. Perhaps with this new house and his wants supplied he might change, might settle down. She waited for the next call; it soon came. He began to plead, and she stopped him. "Look, I love you, Ty—you know that—but you really have got to change. I'll give you that one more chance, but it's the very last one."

"Oh baby, my baby, you won't regret this! I love and miss you so much, my hunny. I'll be there soon." He arrived in just over an hour, and she wondered vaguely where he had travelled from. That night he made desperate and passionate love to her and held her closely as he slept. The lovemaking was pleasurable to Olivia, and she welcomed his warm, beautiful body into hers and climaxed joyfully. But in her deep mind there was still a faint, worrying whisper of doubt.

The next day Ty had the idea that they both needed a break together, away from all the stresses of life, but the togetherness was emphasised. Olivia thought of the Seychelles, Hawaii, India—anywhere exotic. Her bubble was burst when Ty insisted on again going to Jamaica. She argued against it, but he wheedled her with sulks and sex, and she gave in. Having got his own way, he began disappearing for days at a time again. He had so far contributed absolutely nothing towards the running of the house, and he continued to offer nothing towards all the planning and expense of the trip. Olivia had to do it all. She booked them into a hotel at Gatwick in readiness for a very early flight the next day. She drove them there and left her car with the employee of the secure parking firm.

At the hotel, Ty's mood suddenly changed. He had been drinking before they left, had brought a bottle of vodka with him, and began arguing furiously about everything and nothing. Olivia could take no more. She picked up her suitcase and made for the door. Ty rushed over and dragged her back roughly. She tried nearly seven times more to leave, but he blocked her each time. He screamed and shouted at her manically. Eventually she spent the night on the couch whilst Ty snored drunkenly on the double bed. In the morning, she woke to see him out on the veranda, drinking beer. She heard him muttering to himself and crept over to listen. "This is April 27th, and from now on I'm going to be a better person." He repeated this over and over again. Olivia found it bizarre and slightly worrying.

They travelled over by premier class at Ty's insistence. He liked the extra leg room; the luxury of real china plates and silver cutlery; the attractive hostesses in their red uniforms;

the endless free snacks; the champagne and the little bottles of spirits and mixers, which he drank from the start of the flight until they arrived in Jamaica. Ty was terrified of flying; he had flown many times from England to the Caribbean and the States, among other places, but his fear was unconquerable. He always managed to illegally obtain tranquillisers to mix with alcohol and help him to the state of nothingness that enabled him to face long hours of crossing the Atlantic. His heavy drinking continued throughout the entire holiday.

It was Olivia's first time in this exotic place, with its white beaches, palm trees, beautiful flowers, and calling birds with their jewelled feathers, tumbling through the waving fronds. They were booked into the most expensive hotel on the island because Tyrese would have nothing less. They had a luxury suite, with attendants on call and quiet, unobtrusive, ever-present security.

Olivia had to hire a large, expensive car so that Tyrese could impress his family and peers. This was her first introduction to a paradise that had its dark and seamy side. She was to meet Tyrese's family for the first time. He drove her to their house. They soon left the more luxurious areas behind and drove on dirt roads edged by shacks and run-down one-storey buildings. Thin, mangy dogs sniffed and ran in front of the car, and Olivia was surprised and amused to see a fat, snuffling pig wandering nonchalantly along the road and into a garden, Then they encountered a couple of goats strolling along aimlessly. She realised now why Tyrese was so desperate to share her style of living, but she felt that he was ashamed of his background and family, and she was not impressed or happy at this knowledge.

They parked outside the shabby house, and Ty went in, greeting his parents in patois. His father was not as tall as Tyrese. Indeed, Ty was the tallest of them all. His father, Sebastian, was not thickset like his son, but neither was he thin. He had short, greying hair and his dark skin could not conceal the greyness caused by the disease that was eating at his life. He stooped with the constant pain he suffered. Ty's mother, Mary, was a short, stocky woman of maybe 17 stone. Her long, grey hair was pinned up in a bun, and she was always smiling, always welcoming. She loved to cook for her family, friends, visitors, or anyone, and she spent a great deal of time in her kitchen. Olivia bought most of the food that was eaten during the visit. Her favourite dish was the beef soup Mary made with pumpkin. Olivia also bought her lobster and oxtail, which were beautifully cooked and delicious.

Olivia met the rest of Ty's siblings. The eldest brother was Michael, a smaller, not-quite-so-handsome version of Ty. His sister Carol Ann was a plump, happy, friendly woman, an ardent Christian who was always quoting long tracts of scripture and words of wisdom. Her husband, Denzil, was a skinny man with a calm nature. He had been sacked from his job at one of the leading hotels because he'd spent a whole weekend in the apartment of a female guest. Carol Ann had forgiven him because she was a Christian and taken him back to her bed. Denzil was friendly and considerate, and when everyone was babbling in patois, he translated for Olivia and tried to teach her a few words of this language so that she did not feel left out. Ty did not do this or attempt to help Olivia cope with the language or customs of his country. Two other sisters, Sanita and Yolanda, were in the States, and the youngest brother was called Sebastian after his father. He was skinny and almost as tall as Ty. He had long, tangled dreadlocks and always carried a bag of weed in his back pocket, which he smoked endlessly. He had little command of English, although he tried hard to chat with Olivia. Like his father, he had a great talent for carving lovely things out of wood and was a tactile, loving, calm person.

Carol Ann had a daughter, a lovely girl in her twenties, called Jolene. She had long, sleek black hair tied back in plaits. She was, like her mother, an ardent Christian who believed that everyone should have Jesus in their lives. She lived with her boyfriend and had a small daughter, but the boyfriend was violent; he drank and beat her. Ty's oldest brother, Michael, had gone round to the house, beat the boy to a pulp, and then held a gun to his head and told him, "Treat her right. Touch her again and I'll blow your *bloodclaat* head off."
Ty did not speak much to Michael or want to be anywhere his brother was. He told Olivia that his brother owed him money for stock he had bought for his brother's restaurant; Michael had flown back to Miami and left Ty in charge of the place. Ty said that his brother refused to pay the debt, and they had never made up this bitter quarrel.

Carol Ann and Olivia quickly formed a bond, and Carol Ann told Olivia that she'd felt immediately that Olivia was a good woman. Olivia realised that the family were impressed by her wealth, the way their Ty was living in such a style, and the fact that Olivia supplied food to them all. But thinking about it later, she realised that Carol Ann, as a committed Christian, loved her errant brother and desperately hoped that Olivia could be the one person who would be his salvation. Carol Ann knew all too well how crooked, dark, and dishonest her younger brother was.

From the start of the holiday, Ty drank unremittingly, and bitter arguments ruined Olivia's enjoyment of this paradise place. He would kick off at anything and everything, and Olivia began to wish for the moment that she could fly home to England. This dream break was turning into a horrific nightmare, and she began to have very serious doubts about this relationship— although each time Ty used his skilled tongue and fingers and whispered to her gently and enticingly, she was lost in the feel and musky smell of his dark skin and was helpless to break free. When they went to visit Ty's family, he changed very abruptly and noticeably. His manner was soft, loving, and respectful—so very different from the snarling, demanding, violent animal who dominated their hotel room.

Before this, Ty had shown Olivia pictures of a beautiful little girl with huge, innocent eyes that held hurt and despair in their dark depths. This, said Ty, was his niece, Leanne, a child with an insufficient mother and no clothes or toys or ornaments to call her own. Before they'd left for the holiday, he'd asked if Olivia could buy her a few things as a gift. Olivia had driven into town and shopped ferociously. She'd bought dresses, shoes, underwear, toiletries, toys, and sweets. She'd packed them all into a large suitcase, ready to take to the child. Olivia had fallen in love with the pretty, sad child instantly; she had somehow felt that this child was more than just Ty's niece. Looking at the photos, she'd realised that she was looking at Ty. She'd broached the subject as they sat snuggled into each other, holding hands, in the huge red armchair.

"Your niece is the image of you, Ty."

"Yes, baby, isn't she? Everyone says that." Then there was a taut silence, and she felt his discomfort. "Baby, I can't lie like this any longer. Leanne isn't my niece; she's mine—my daughter."

"Yes, I worked that out."

He squeezed her hand.

"How did this one happen, then?"

"I was working in Jamaica and rented a house. I had a housekeeper, because I was so busy. She was quite young, only 20. Well, you know how it is." He grinned nervously. "We slept together, and—"

"And you didn't use a condom, as ever," Olivia said sharply.

He shrugged. "No. I hate them. Anyway, they're always too small and they split, so I can't be bothered. She got pregnant after a few months, and by the time it was due I'd left. She contacted me on Facebook and put photos of Leanne on, so I saw her for the first time."

There was a further silence. Ty put his arm around her. "Everyone gets so moral and uptight at all the children I have. What's the problem, baby? Fucking's normal, and making babies is normal too. I have a lot of kids all over the place—I'm very proud of them."

Olivia faced him angrily. "When do you ever see all these children, Ty? How much do you contribute to their keep and upbringing? How often do they send you Father's Day cards?"

"I love my kids!" He was angry. "Blame the mothers who won't let me see them, not me!"

"Really," said Olivia. "They probably ban you after years of silence, no maintenance, all the other women and babies that just happened in between, and sheer disinterest."

He tried to kiss her, but she pushed him away. "It doesn't make any difference. She's still beautiful, and I'm still taking her the presents," she said. She pulled away from him and went to make coffee.

That night in bed he made long, passionate love to her. Afterwards, as they lay close together, he stroked her pale-blonde hair and kissed her face. "I wish I could give you a baby, hun," he said.

"Don't be so bloody stupid," she responded sharply. "It's the last thing on earth I'd actually want, even if I was young enough."

"I want to do that because I love you so much. It's my way of showing my love, baby."

"Really?" She rolled away from his embrace and sat on the edge of the bed. "You must have really loved an awful lot of women, then."

Ty leaned towards her and put his hand on her shoulder. "Get off." She shrugged his touch away, went downstairs, and poured herself a glass of wine. She seldom drank but needed the release to cope with her feelings at that moment.

They drove to see Leanne. The dirt road became potholed and the area shabbier and more rundown. The house was grim and sparsely furnished. Olivia was introduced to the mother of the little girl, a squat, ugly woman with huge breasts and buttocks, protruding eyes, a sullen mouth, and a lazy, annoying manner of speaking. She looked Olivia up and down with obvious dislike and stood with folded arms, not offering Olivia a chair to sit on or any refreshment. Ty took charge of the suitcase and brought it in as if he were Father Christmas and as if he had actually paid for the contents. That way his daughter and his family would see him as a caring father and a responsible person. Olivia sat back in the corner, ignored and seething. He opened the case and offered the child the contents, item by item, watching her reaction. The child did not respond to Ty or his attempts to kiss and cuddle her. In fact, she tried to get off his lap and escape this strange, loud, domineering man whom she did not know or like. She moved away from him, approached Olivia with her new dress in her hand, and smiled at her. Olivia's heart leapt with love for this little creature, and an invisible bond was forged in that second.

When they left the slummy house, Olivia turned on Ty angrily, berating him about his dishonesty and his failure to acknowledge her part in the selecting and buying of all these gifts. A furious row followed and yet another one when they returned to the hotel.

The following day started with more heated words and tension. Ty suggested they go to the pool, where he sat in the cool water drinking rum cocktails; it was still only ten in the morning. Olivia went off to the beach and sat on a recliner in the fierce, bright sunshine. Ty soon followed, sitting beside Olivia with a rum cocktail in his hand. On the beach, part of the hotel complex, there was a hut from which jerk chicken was being sold. Olivia went to get some for both of them and joined the long queue. At that point the hut ran out of plates to dispense the chicken on, so one of the staff went back to the hotel to get more. Two English tourists, a man and his wife, were in front of Olivia, and Olivia began to speak to them as they waited; they laughed and joked in a normal, friendly manner. The plates arrived and the chicken was doled out. With two plates in her hand, Olivia went back to where Ty lounged, drinking. She was aware that he had been watching her keenly as she stood in the queue and as she walked back. Olivia handed Ty his plate and put hers down on the table between the two sun loungers. Ty swung himself off his lounger and sat on the edge of it. There was a strange expression on his handsome black face.

"What's the matter with your face?" Olivia asked.

"Look into my eyes," Ty answered through gritted teeth. "What does it look like is wrong with me?"

"You look sad," replied Olivia.

"No, this isn't sadness; this is anger."

"Why?" she said. "Why are you angry?"

"I saw you talking to that couple in the queue. What were you talking to them for?" His nostrils flared. He leaned towards her. "You are *my* woman! You do not talk to any man, anywhere, while we're in Jamaica. Your eyes are on *me* at all times and nowhere else. Those two are probably swingers. I saw you bending down and whispering in his ear. What were you doing? Giving him your telephone number so you could meet him later?"

Olivia left her meal on the table, untouched. She leaned back in her lounger, put her sunglasses over her eyes, and pretended to be asleep. Ty's voice rose as he worked himself into a fury and ranted at Olivia. She was aware of glances from others around them on the beach and started to become tense. At that moment, Ty threw his plate violently up into the air. The chicken and rice flew everywhere—over the sand, the table, and the loungers. By now they were the centre of interest, and Olivia had to lie back and absorb the humiliation and stress. Ty ranted on as the afternoon passed. *Will he never stop?* she thought, still pretending to sleep. She eventually got up to leave, trying to ignore the glances and whispering of the onlookers. He followed her, and the tirade continued.

At last he stopped and said, "Why don't we just go to the pool and cool down." So Olivia obediently followed him to try and defuse his rage. They got into the blessedly cool water, and Ty continued drinking rum cocktails. Then he decided that he would socialise. Olivia was swimming around, trying to relax. Ty went to the end of the large pool, where three extremely well-built black women were sitting on the concrete stools in the water by the swim-up bar. There was music playing, and all three of them lifted up their bottoms and began twerking. Ty swam up close to them and leered at the three. One in particular had the build of a hippopotamus, and her buttocks quivered wildly. Ty grinned and said loudly, "Damn, baby!"
Olivia had had enough at this point. She swam to the steps and started to climb out of the pool. Ty chased after her. "Oh, come on, baby. It was just a joke."
Olivia told herself, *I must not react as he did. I must stay calm and try to placate him.* They stayed in the pool for another hour, and then people began to leave. The large pool was empty. Ty took her hands and swam her over to the edge of the pool. The lifeguard was on his lookout steps, and Ty called up to

him, "Hey, just disappear, will you? If you stay you might see something you don't want to."

The lifeguard seemed confused; he hesitated. "Go on!" Ty waved his hand at the man.

"OK, sir. Yes, OK." He hurried away. Ty leaned his back against the side of the pool and pulled Olivia onto him. He was very excited, and his erection was massive. He put his hand down and pulled the crotch of Olivia's costume to one side. She was suddenly desperate for his body, and he quickly went into her. She leaned backwards away from him so that she could control the depth of his thrusting and avoid the normal pain when he entered her. He looked at her with wild eyes; he had been drinking steadily all day. Then he lifted her legs around him, held her breasts tightly and thrust hard, moaning and panting. As Olivia was leaning away from Ty, he could see her, and she pulled her costume top down so that he could see and fondle her breasts. After ten minutes he closed his eyes, gasped, and Olivia came with him. He held her tightly for a while; then they swam to the steps and left the pool. Olivia thought that, spent, and satisfied, Ty would want to stay with her. But he changed into his shorts and T-shirt and headed for the bar without a backward glance.

She went back to their suite, hungry, tired, and unhappy. Ty remained down at the bar until late that night. Olivia ordered food from room service, as she hadn't eaten all day. Gratefully she finished her steak and salad and leaned back wearily. She had begun to feel very sunburnt when the sun went down. Her exposure to the fierce afternoon sun of Jamaica whilst Ty had been venting his angry jealousy had done damage to her fair skin. She was very uncomfortable and applied a good layer of aftersun to the affected areas. She decided to lie back in bed, relax, and watch television.

Ty came unsteadily into the room just after ten, and after urinating without bothering to close the door, he slumped into the other double bed in the large, luxurious room. Olivia was relieved. She didn't want him near her painful legs, and she particularly didn't want the clumsy, rough lovemaking which his drunkenness would have forced on her.

"Well, goodnight," she said. There was no reply. Ty lay on his back with his mouth open, snoring loudly. Olivia turned off the television and fell asleep. The huge moon turned the sea to silver and night crept on.

The following morning when Olivia awoke she was in great pain. Her legs were swollen, red, and blistered. When she tried to get out of bed and swung her legs over the edge, it felt as if hot metal bars were being driven into them; she was barely able to move. Just to drag herself to the bathroom took a full five minutes, and she slumped back on the bed exhausted. She could not bother to dress and carefully eased herself back into bed.

By now it was eleven in the morning, and Ty had crawled out of bed, showered, and dressed. Olivia explained her problem to him, but he just shrugged. "Well you stay in bed and sort yourself out and recover, baby, and I'll go see my family. I'll be back at about three." He kissed her and hurried off.

The day wore on, and Olivia felt very unwell. She tried to doze and endure the burning pain. To get to the toilet was a nightmare. She dragged herself step by painful step; it seemed like miles instead of yards. She had eaten nothing and could not be bothered to call room service. Ty had left her nothing to drink, and she was slowly becoming dehydrated. Three o'clock came and went and she tried to hang on, but she was beginning to feel very unwell. Towards evening she picked up the bedside phone and asked for the hotel's nurse to be sent up. The nurse lifted her eyebrows when she saw Olivia's legs. "You must go to the hospital, madam!"

"But my partner is out—he should be back soon."

"Madam, this is urgent. I will call the hospital and have you taken there." She disappeared and returned with a wheelchair. She helped Olivia into it patiently, as Olivia could barely put her feet on the floor now. The pain was horrific, like burning knives being forced into her bones. She was wheeled to the waiting ambulance. As they were leaving the hotel lobby to enter the ambulance, Ty came swaggering up. He turned to look at Olivia and the nurse and walked up to them. "I suppose I'm trouble for this as well," he said petulantly. The nurse wheeled Olivia up into the waiting ambulance, and Ty got in as well. On the way to the hospital he created more friction by saying that he supposed that he was going to be blamed for leaving Olivia alone all day. The argument raged until they drew up in front of the hospital building.

In the comfortable private room they took her to, they put her on intravenous rehydration and antibiotics. Olivia was told she had second-degree burns on her legs. The swelling and discoloration extended from her knees to her toes and was excruciatingly painful. Whilst the doctors and nurses were in the room attending Olivia, Ty was a model of concern, stroking her hands and head, looking worried, and offering her things she did not need or want. As soon as the door closed he became the sullen, selfish boor she recognised, complaining about being stuck there in the hospital. He went outside frequently to smoke, and she noticed him just finishing calls or texts on his phone when he returned to sulk and whine again.

Olivia was discharged after three hours. She and Ty took a taxi, which cost her £60, back to the hotel. All the way there he grumbled and muttered sullenly. At the hotel he did fetch a wheelchair and take Olivia up to the room and help her into bed. Then he left and went to the bar to drink. On his return, he showered and went to the other bed with scarcely a glance at Olivia. She realised that her reddish-purple, blistered legs repelled him and wondered where this great love he was supposed to have for her had gone. Each day was the same. He got up and disappeared until the evening, when he returned, showered, and continued his drinking—and what else Olivia neither knew nor cared at that moment. Only once did he ask if she had eaten, seeming unaware of, or indifferent to, her needs.

They were due to fly back to England on the Friday, but Olivia could not put her feet to the floor, and the pain was even worse, as was the swelling. She told Ty that they could not possibly return, and she phoned the hotel nurse once again. The nurse was about to call a taxi, but Ty told her not to bother. He lifted the phone and called the hire car company. When they had gone to pick up the car after their arrival, Olivia had noticed Ty holding the hand of the girl behind the desk and bending down to whisper to her. The girl had laughed. Now Ty spoke to this girl again. "Sorry, I can't bring the car back as planned. I'm gonna *have* to take Olivia to hospital again."

Olivia noted the emphasis on the *have*.

They reached the hospital for the second time. Olivia was wheeled in, and her credit card was promptly removed before they admitted her. Despite the antibiotic drip, she had had an allergic reaction and now had cellulitis in addition to the blisters and burning which had gone down to the bones. Olivia was in pain and depressed. Ty was seething. On her way out from the hotel, Olivia had been obliged to phone the travel rep and arrange another hotel for Ty, as the room they were in was booked out to another couple and there were no more vacancies. Eventually Olivia had Ty booked into a five-star hotel elsewhere, which she had to pay for on her credit card. Ty was becoming a very expensive and dependent luxury, and Olivia wondered whether he was worth it all. She wished that she could just stop loving him and being mesmerised by his cunning and his animal appeal. *Why?* she wondered. *Why can I not pull away from him? I give him chance after chance, but he gets blacker and more frightening hourly. I cannot truly trust this man.* As ever, he had been texting endlessly on his phone throughout their holiday, and she often wondered who he contacted on this closely guarded treasure. In the back of her mind she knew that he was not to be trusted, that he was not faithful, but she would not face this reality. She wanted him to change—to just not be what she feared he was. She tried to face her suspicions, but he could always wheedle, charm, bully, and seduce her into denial.

Ty did something uncharacteristic; he told the hospital staff that Olivia should not have to remain in a ward when she was paying so much money to them. They then put her in a very nice side room, with a modern hospital bed, good furniture, a new television, and an en-suite bathroom. For this Olivia was grateful. She was relieved to be away from Ty and his constantly changing moods, his possessiveness and anger, his brooding silences and unpredictability. *Anyway,* she thought, *he was never with me at the hotel. He just slept there, showered, and then disappeared to drink and do what he wanted to do.* Her illness had not stopped Ty from doing as he wanted; he was showing the true colours of his love and care again. At least she had some peace; she would see faces and hear voices here.

After half an hour Olivia was hooked up to another antibiotic drip, on which she remained for the next few days. She realised that she had arrived without toiletries, cosmetics, or clothing, and Ty hadn't bothered himself with her needs, despite trying to impress onlooking hospital staff with his apparent loving and caring behaviour. He had hurried off as soon as he could to return to his drinking and his own occupations. He did not come back until about two the next afternoon. He sat beside her, making silly jokes and annoying Olivia with his unconcern and the way he ogled the nurses who came into her room to check her needs. On the second day, he arrived with Carol Ann and her husband. Carol Ann looked at Olivia and said, "My dear, you don't look very comfortable".

"I'm not, Carol Ann. I haven't got anything to wash with or any make-up, and I've been in these clothes since I was admitted."

Carol Ann promptly turned to her younger brother and told him off very firmly for neglecting Olivia's needs. Then she said to him, "Come on, we're going shopping."

Ty already had Olivia's debit card. They all went off and returned later with a sundress, some toiletries, and fruit. Carol Ann told Olivia that she was coming back that evening. Mary, Ty's mother, was concerned and was making some of Olivia's favourite beef soup. Olivia was so touched by the thoughtfulness of Ty's family she almost cried. As they were leaving, Ty, in his usual showing-off mode, turned and said, "I'm feeling horny, babe. Can I come back and just slide it in and slip it out again, just a quickie up and down?"

Olivia was revolted and embarrassed. To say that in front of his own sister and her husband. Ty had no social etiquette whatsoever. "Just go, Ty," she said angrily. She felt trapped and helpless again. This man was a moron. She didn't feel good being his arm candy and his trophy white, blonde baby. Ty simply laughed and swaggered off.

That evening they all returned—the first time Ty had bothered to visit twice in one day. Carol Ann had brought a plastic container filled with the hot, deliciously tempting beef soup made by Mary. Although the hospital food was adequate, Olivia welcomed this gift, as it was so beautifully cooked; it was aromatic and satisfyingly full of lumps of tender beef. Ty told her that he had taken $200 out of the cashpoint on her card.

"What for?" asked Olivia.

"For the soup, baby. Mom needed the stuff to go in it.

"She needed $200 worth of stuff, Ty? That's about £150— expensive soup! Bloody expensive soup."

Ty grinned feebly and said nothing, his usual response to anything he wanted to avoid.

The next day Ty strolled in again. He only stayed twenty minutes and kept glancing at his watch and checking his phone. That was the pattern of the days, but Olivia was glad of the respite. Food was brought to her. She could lie back and watch the television and see old films that she enjoyed. She had her own pleasant bathroom to shower in. People spoke to her. She felt alive and wanted. She could rest. More importantly, she was away from the horrors of the holiday that was turning into her worst nightmare and revealing the man she had thought she loved as a dark, unpleasant, and frightening burden.

Two days later Olivia was discharged after paying a very large hospital bill. Her legs were enormously swollen still but she could walk. Ty collected her from the hospital. He still had the hire car, which she noted mentally was costing her every day, although they did need it. Ty took her to his hotel, and Olivia saw that even though it was expensive it was, frankly, grim. Ty was not happy in it, and Olivia had to agree with him that they needed a better place to stay for that price. Ty phoned around in a firm, businesslike manner. He was good at that, thought Olivia, good at getting what he required and good at using someone else's money to do it. But she had to admit that he did get them a really luxurious room in a top-class hotel. It was a paradise on earth. Ty had packed the suitcases and taken them there. The room was on the ground floor. It had windows opening onto a terrace, with a grassy area in front that led directly to the beach.

That night Ty decided that they must go to dinner, regardless of the fact that Olivia's legs were still massively swollen and she was in a great deal of pain. The hotel dress code was strict, and Olivia was obliged to dress accordingly. She had brought her usual beautiful clothes but was unable to put on her delicate high-heeled shoes. She could only manage to squeeze into a pair of sandals. The straps dug into her puffy feet and caused her agony. She put on a brave face and acted as if everything were fine, to avoid annoying Ty. They were shown to their table and Ty occupied himself with becoming extremely inebriated. As the evening wore on, Olivia was tired and in a lot of pain. It was nearly eleven. Ty had decided to socialise with the people at the next table, so he turned his chair around, leaned towards them, and began to chat, completely ignoring Olivia, who was a good six feet away from him. Ty turned to her and nodded. "Come here."

Olivia ignored him and bent down to pick up her handbag.

Ty swiftly pushed his chair back and sat very close to Olivia. He pushed his face into hers. He spoke very quietly but very menacingly. "If you get up and leave me here, this relationship is done."

Olivia looked him unflinchingly in the eye and said coolly, "Is it?" Then she picked up her handbag, got up, and left him sitting there alone. *How dare you!* she thought. *How dare you, after all I've been through! If you want to end this relationship, then damned well end it.* She tried to get back to their room, but the hotel was a maze of walkways, and she was soon lost. There were pathways everywhere, with jerk-chicken and coconut-water trolleys on them. If she could just find the entrance to the hotel, she could find the swimming pool, turn left, and there would be the corridor where their room was. She found the front doors, but they were locked. She walked past them and was soon lost in the eternally twisting paths. At this point she realised that she was being followed, and she turned to see Ty walking about six feet behind her. He saw her looking at him, dropped his gaze, and simply carried on as if they had no connection. Olivia thought that if she kept on walking she would have to find a way into the building somehow. She could get to the room and lie down. Her legs were an agony, and she felt unwell. She was sick of this man.

Then she heard him shouting, "Olivia! Olivia!" in a commanding and very unpleasant tone. She continued walking. People were looking at Ty as he continued to shout her name. The more she ignored his demanding shouts the louder they became. Then he was behind her, his mouth next to her ear. His voice was low and threatening. "Who've you made an appointment to go and fuck now? Which hotel room are you looking for? He's obviously expecting you, isn't he, so tell me which room it is, and I'll come with you."

"I'm trying to find our room." Olivia spoke softly to try and calm his rage. "I'm lost. I'm tired and in pain, and I just want to get back and lie down."

Suddenly he grabbed her upper left arm in a painful grip and threw her against the wall. "I know you've made an appointment with some man, and I'm fucking sick of all this. Who is it you're going to fuck this time, eh?" He was snarling and spitting like a wild animal about to attack its prey. Olivia tried to escape his grip, but the more she struggled the more he grabbed at her arm and the stronger his grip became. Soon her arm was a mass of fingermarks, and livid bruises were beginning to show. Eventually Olivia broke free and hurried to their room. He followed and the shouting and arguing went on.

"Ty will you just shut up! We have neighbours here. Everybody can hear this. They don't want to." The terrace doors were open, and their drama was on show to the world. Olivia had had enough. She just wanted to lie down and close her eyes and sleep. She needed to escape all this misery and violence. The beach was near and was warm, even at night, and there were recliners everywhere. She decided she would go down there and try to sleep. She walked out of the doors leading to the terrace and the beach. She had got halfway when he grabbed her from behind and tried to drag her back by her right arm.

"Get away!" She tried to push him off. "Get away and leave me alone." She continued towards the beach, but he tried yet again to stop her by grabbing her right arm. This time he squeezed it hard, very hard, and she knew that this was meant to hurt her. Then he grabbed her other arm and very deliberately twisted it. Olivia gasped and screamed with the pain. Ty dropped her arm, turned, and lurched away in the direction of the hotel. Olivia was thinking that she must rest. She was exhausted and in agony. She staggered down to the beach, to the welcoming recliners and the peace and the gentle swishing of the sea on the sand. *I must get away from this man*, she thought as she reached the recliner. *He is very drunk, and very dangerous, and very violent. I will sleep here, and in the morning I will check out, book myself another hotel, and get another flight home.* She sank back on the lounger. Her arms throbbed and she saw that huge, purplish-black bruises were appearing. She sobbed desperately. *Sleep*, she thought. *Just let me sleep and get my strength together to escape this hell.*

Then he was there beside her, kneeling down and rubbing her bruised arms very gently. Olivia knew that he knew exactly what he had done. He held her hand and said gently, so very gently and lovingly, "Come with me."

And she was his again in that second, and she got up, and he led her by the hand and she followed, not daring to protest, because she was in thrall to his dominance and under his dark spell—and, more immediately, she feared more of his violent anger. They reached the room, where Ty took off her clothes. He took them off tenderly and slowly, and she thought, *He will carry me to the bed, and then he will make love to me. I am too tired, but I want his beautiful, dark body in mine.* But when he had removed her panties and she was naked, he kissed her lingeringly on her mouth. He lifted her up, put her into the bed, and drew the cover over her. Then he undressed himself and climbed into the other bed. He was soon asleep.

Olivia lay awake for almost three hours, not daring to move for fear of what might happen if Ty awoke. She listened to the breeze sifting through the palm trees and the calling of exotic night birds, and she saw the great moon paint everything in the humid room with cold and unearthly light. Eventually, through sheer exhaustion, she drifted off to sleep.

When she woke, it was a bright, beautiful morning. Ty was out on the balcony. She looked at her phone; it was eight o'clock. He always went out there at about six in the morning with his phone and his laptop and sat messaging and texting feverishly, working his way through can after can of beer. Only when the beer that was always in the fridge in the room ran out would he take a shower, dress, and go out to the nearest bar in the hotel complex. There he would begin his day's drinking, moving from bar to bar until he had drunk himself into a black rage.

Olivia got out of bed. She was still in pain and tired. She had begun to smoke heavily on this holiday. She found her cigarettes and lighter, put on a sundress, and walked towards the terrace doors. She did not want to be near Ty. She wanted to be on her own on the beach, listening to the sea and resting in the shade. Ty turned. He put out his hand to her. "Just stay a minute, baby." Olivia hesitated but then turned and stood a little way from him. The first thing he said was "Baby, I'm so sorry about last night." Olivia stood there. Her arms from her shoulders to her wrists were covered in dark fingermarks.

"Please sit with me, hun." He smiled sheepishly.

Olivia sat down.

"I'm really sorry, baby; it shouldn't have happened. I love you so much, baby. You just don't realise how much I love and need you. I can't live without you. I got drunk and overreacted. I can't begin to tell you just how bad I feel, how sorry I am. I'll change, baby. You'll see. Just give me another chance; don't give up on me. What we have is so special, hun. I've never loved another woman like I love you. You're my only woman. I don't want anyone in the world beside you, baby. If I lost you, I couldn't live. I know you deserve much, much better than me, hun. Just give me a chance, baby. I'm gonna change, gonna be a better person. We could be so happy; we're so right for each other. You know you can't live without me either. I can see you really love me. I'm gonna kick the drinking. We'll be so happy, you'll see, my baby ..." On and on it went.

Olivia had heard it all before. She was weary with having to hear it all again and sat slowly drifting into a state of stupor.

Ty put his hand on her knee and gently stroked it. He ran his fingers upwards and spoke softly. "Who else can make love to you like I do, baby? You know you can't resist my body. I fuck you so well, hun—not many men have got all this—"

Olivia pushed his hand away and lit a cigarette.

Ty lit one too and then continued his pleading. Olivia steeled herself to listen to more of his prattle. Then he stopped, leaned forward, and kissed her very gently on her mouth, lingering there. Olivia felt her body react to his nearness, and her brain soon followed. She kissed him back, and he put his hand on her breast. She pushed his hand off and pulled away. "OK, Ty," she said reluctantly. "I'll give you just one more chance. I do love you, but this just can't happen again. Do you understand?"

"Oh, baby." Ty kissed her hand. "I promise you it'll never happen again. You'll see. Oh, I love you so much."

Olivia was amazed to see how much time had passed since Ty had begun his familiar monologue. Had they really been sitting there for almost five hours? She changed and they went to the pool for relaxation, where Ty immediately went to the swim-up bar and started on the rum cocktails. She just concentrated on keeping out of his way. That night another heated argument broke out and, fuelled by alcohol, Ty spat out accusations and insulted and abused Olivia. She had managed, during that afternoon, to contact her insurers and the travel company and arrange a flight back on the Tuesday. It was Friday; she had the weekend to endure. It turned out to be another nightmare. Ty's heavy drinking continued, and so did his loud abuse. Olivia was too embarrassed to go out at night to dinner so ordered room service. Apart from the stress of Ty's social incompetence, there was the very evident bruising on her arms. Everywhere she went she was painfully aware of eyes on her and on Ty, along with lowered voices and laughing. When they did go anywhere, Ty padded along behind her, shouting and goading her, oblivious to the entertainment and disgust he presented to the other guests and the humiliation he heaped on Olivia. Sometimes he would shout at them, too, and Olivia would tell him to stop as he was offending people. Ty would reply that he couldn't care less. He didn't know these people and would never meet them again, so they could just fuck off.

The hotel complex paths were always spotlessly clean, and there was always an army of sweepers with their brooms and barrows to be seen. As Ty berated and insulted her, these cleaners would look up sympathetically at Olivia. Ty would glare at them and shout, "What the fucking hell you looking at, nigger?"

When Olivia expressed her disgust at this, Ty just shrugged and told her it was normal for one black man to call another nigger, and it didn't have the same insulting meaning that it had if uttered by a white person. But Olivia knew that Ty had intended it to be insulting and demeaning, and it angered her. Ty was saying to his fellow men, "You are the menials, the cleaners here. I am the guest in this expensive place. If I shout at my expensive white woman, you must lower your eyes and go on sweeping—nigger!"

The days seemed like weeks to Olivia. Her legs were still agonisingly painful and swollen. All she wanted to do was lie down and rest. Ty's verbal onslaught was unending. He bullied her into going out with him and ignored her distress. Olivia had

179

now made up her mind. Ty was gone, finished, out of her life, just as soon as they got home. On the Sunday she told Ty to go out on his own and do exactly what he wanted. She was finished and wanted only to rest, to get back home, and to be rid of this selfish, ill-mannered drunken bully. She was in a foreign country where she knew no one but Ty and was dependent on him; she was stuck with him for now. But on her home territory she would soon deal with him.

Olivia had managed to get her flight home, with the willing assistance of her insurance company, but Ty was not happy. He insisted on their flying premier class yet again so that Olivia had to pay the difference out of her own pocket. As they drove to the airport, Ty said nervously, "I know you're gonna kick me out when we get back."

Olivia looked at him and said nothing. Had she told him that no, she wasn't going to do that, she would have been lying. She just looked at him, and Ty knew that he was going to be deleted from Olivia's life and all it had brought him.

On the nine-hour flight home, Olivia had to endure the babble again, the usual protestations of love and faithfulness. She heard that she was the only woman in his life. *Really?* she thought. He claimed that she was the only reason he was in England. If she didn't want him, then he would stay in Jamaica— although by then they were halfway across the Atlantic. Olivia closed her eyes and let the words skim over her head. Ty drank heavily. As Olivia fell into a sleep, Ty had reached the point in his monologue where his life was worthless if they parted—all the usual covert suicide threats, she noted as her eyes closed. The hostess was quite wonderful. She raised the footrest and put Olivia's handbag and a cushion on it to raise Olivia's feet and ease the swelling. Olivia was grateful to the pleasant, smiling girl for this care, as she was getting little from Ty.

They landed, and Olivia was able to clear customs on her feet, although she walked with difficulty. She was obliged to drive all the way back, as Ty was far too drunk. He was claustrophobic, refusing to allow her to use the Dartford tunnel, so she had to drive around the M25 and go miles further to get home. Her feet were swollen, her legs hurt, her head ached, and she just wanted Ty out of her car, her house, and her life. During all this, Ty was constantly on his phone. He said he was talking to Amal about a drug run he had to do, because he was skint. He told whoever he was talking to that he would be back in three hours. Olivia assumed it was Amal. She was beginning to have very real doubts about all the places, people, and events Ty presented to her. Why was he skint? she wondered. He hadn't spent a penny in Jamaica. Olivia had paid for everything, and Ty had even taken her debit card to pay for the food his mother had cooked for them. That was fine, but he had taken other money, too, while they were there. At home, he paid for nothing at the house she had rented just to please him. He explained that he needed to pay his car insurance and tax. Olivia was covering the credit payments for his smart new sports car, and Ty had promised, continually, to repay her for the quite large amounts of money she had already provided.

At last they arrived. Ty took the cases into the house. Olivia thankfully collapsed onto the settee. Ty came into the lounge and smiled at her. "Baby, do you fancy cooking me some tea?

I must go and do this drug run. Make me some spaghetti Bolognese, hun, OK?"

Ty knew there was no food in the house and that Olivia would have to drive into town to get the fresh ingredients and then stand on her swollen legs to cook it. She drove to the nearest supermarket and back, got out of the car slowly, and stood cooking while longing only to shower and sleep. Ty was gone; she neither knew nor cared where. He could eat the food when he got back. But he didn't return until the next day.

Olivia crawled up to bed and fell into a deep sleep. At four the next morning she woke with a sharp pain in her left shoulder. Thinking it to be muscular, she swung her arm around to relieve and loosen it and soon fell back to sleep. She was awake almost every hour. At eight she got up. The pain was much worse, and Olivia realised this was something much more sinister. Her daughter rang to talk about her holiday but was concerned for her mother when she heard. "Mum, ring an ambulance!"

Olivia didn't, but she rang 111, and they said they would send a rapid-response medic, followed by an ambulance. Olivia lay in bed, hardly able to breathe. Later she was to learn that she had a pulmonary embolism and any movement could have been fatal.

The ambulance was due when Ty came in. He stood at the bottom of the bed and glared at Olivia. "Well, I suppose I'm in trouble again, aren't I? Had to go to Cambridge, then that was wrong and had to take it somewhere else—"

Olivia was fighting for breath. "Ty, just shut up, and go away and leave me alone." Ty seemed to anticipate Olivia's leaping out of bed and giving him an argument; he seemed confused. At that moment the medic arrived with the ambulance.

Ty switched into normal, caring mode instantly. As the medic made her observations and examined Olivia, Ty spoke quietly and calmly, with great concern. "Are you all right, my darling? Are you in a lot of pain? I'll start getting a bag together, and I'll come with you."

The paramedics assisted Olivia down the stairs and asked Ty to bring her belongings to the hospital, as he had not at that point finished assembling them. They took her to the local main hospital. An appropriate scan was not available, and she had to sit for three hours, completely alone, in the A&E department. She had nothing with her, not even her mobile phone. Where was Ty? He should have been there within ten minutes. Eventually he arrived. "Where were you?" she asked him.

"Oh, baby, you know I don't like hospitals." He put his head on one side like a 5-year-old about to throw a tantrum.

Olivia ignored this. "Have you brought me any of my stuff?" she asked him.

He shrugged. "No. Just your phone." There was a silence. "Well," he said, "what's happening?" He looked bored and annoyed.

Olivia ignored him. She knew that no care or consideration would be forthcoming from this man.

Eventually she was wheeled up to a ward on the second floor. On the way, Ty turned. "Ring me," he said. "I'll see you later." He swiftly disappeared. Olivia resigned herself to her situation. The doctor in the ward questioned her about the circumstances of the burning to her legs, and Olivia explained, reliving in her mind the fact that she had been forced to stay in the punishing and damaging sun on the beach because Ty had been drunk and raging and she had feared his reaction if she moved. The doctor told her that he suspected that she had a pulmonary embolism. He sat down beside her. "We can't do a VQ scan now. You could stay in here and have the scan in the morning, or you can go home and we'll ring you tomorrow and tell you when to come in for it. Really," he said and paused, "it's better that you go home, because if anything happens, you know the score." He had found out Olivia's background and of her medical knowledge by then. "You know we can't do anything, and you'll be better off at home in your own bed."

Olivia nodded.

"OK, then; you go home, and we'll ring you tomorrow morning." Olivia phoned Ty. She told him that they were letting her out for the night. He went crazy; absolutely crazy.

"I've told my mate I'm going up there for the night to the American camp! He's my close mate, and he's had an accident and chopped his hand off, and they're flying him home tonight." His voice rose. "He's always been there for me, ever since I came to England—I can't not go! I might never see him ever again." It was clear that he was working himself up into another rage. Olivia's heart sank. Ty cut her off, and she sat, dreading his arrival. He strode into the ward and his face told all. He was clearly livid.

The nurse with Olivia looked concerned. "Are you going to be OK?" she asked.

"Look," Olivia said to Ty, "you want to go to the camp, just go to the bloody camp. Just drop me at home and give me my keys, so I can at least get into the house." She had nothing with her, as he had failed to bring a single thing with him save her phone.

Ty set off ahead of Olivia. She dragged and limped behind him, carrying the packets of injection paraphernalia the hospital had given her to treat her condition until she could return. He did not even offer to carry these. He just hurried on ahead of her, turning every now and then to see where she was and exhaling impatiently. They reached the main entrance. "Stay here," Ty snapped. "I'll fetch the car."

Olivia slowly and painfully climbed into the car, and Ty drove off, shouting and snarling at her.

"For God's sake, Ty, just shut up and take me home. I know where you're coming from now—"

"Oh yes," he cut her off. "Just so you can pack my bags, because I'm leaving you."

"Ty," said Olivia, "clearly there's no love there whatsoever. It makes no difference. I think we both know it's done. What's coming through is no love, no care—"

"Oh yes"—he cut in again. "We didn't have much of a holiday because you wouldn't have a bloody drink. People go on holiday to drink; they get pissed and they have fun. You're boring. You should go back to the nunnery you belong to." He lit a cigarette and dragged deeply on it.

Olivia took the insult without comment and sat there quietly. "It's all right, Ty," she said. "Don't worry about it. Like I said, I know where you're coming from. Just take me home. I'll make sure your stuff's ready for tomorrow when you come for it." She knew as she said this that the doctor had warned her not to stay on her own overnight; he had stressed this advice twice. The nurse had also told Ty as they'd left the ward, explaining the reasons and the dangers.

They reached the main dual carriageway, and Ty's rant increased in volume and intensity. Olivia felt desperately tired and very unwell. She wanted to be in her bed in her home and away from this man—this stranger she thought that she'd once known.

"All right, Ty, enough—enough! I can't take any more stress and hassle; I've been through enough. I'll have your stuff packed and ready in the morning. Just take me home."

Ty's voice became cold and menacing. "OK, so you're gonna pack my stuff up and kick me out, are you? Well, we're in this together for the long haul. If you're gonna finish with me, we're going together, baby. This is a fast car, and I'm gonna boot her up to 140, and then I'm gonna put it under a lorry. We'll both die together, and then we really will be together forever, won't we?" He pushed down on the accelerator, and the big, powerful car roared like a lion and leapt forward. Olivia thought, *I must not panic. If my heart beats too fast and my circulation increases, there is a danger of the embolism travelling and killing me.* Her knuckles were white as she clung to the door handle beside her. *I must not react. I must stay absolutely quiet. If I say a word, he will go even faster and do something terrible.* It seemed to Olivia to be an eternity as they screamed up the motorway at this terrifying speed, and then he slowed the car.

"I must go and see my friend," he told her.

"Go, Ty," she said. "Go, but just take me home first. I feel very unwell."

Ty swerved off the motorway and onto the slip road, and soon they were at the house. He turned the car around so that it was facing in the direction of escape for him. Olivia staggered to the door, clutching her bag of hypodermics and drugs, her mobile phone, and her keys. She stood there in her nightdress, dressing gown, and slippers. Thankfully, she unlocked the front door with shaking hands. She turned. Ty had gone, roaring away up the road. Olivia went shakily into the living room. Everything seemed to be moving, and there was a rushing in her ears. She put the bag of medications down on the coffee table, and all went black. She fell onto the carpeted floor as she lost consciousness. Later she came to, slowly, and still confused. She climbed onto the settee and stayed there all night, sitting up, fearful of sleeping in case she did not wake up again. But before that she set out determinedly, despite her condition and the risks she was taking, and went through the entire three floors of the house to find everything belonging to Ty and put it all in bin bags. She had told him it would be ready, and she kept her promises. If anything happened to her, she was determined that he would have no claim on her house or anything in it. She wanted him out.

The morning came at last, and Olivia stayed on the settee, getting up every now and again to get herself a drink of tea or coffee but resting to lessen her chances of the embolism shifting. Her children were frantic with worry for her and kept phoning, begging to be allowed to come and help her, but she insisted that they stay away and allow her to get rid of Ty first. Around ten he arrived. Olivia had put the bin bags of his belongings on the hall floor, locked the door, and left the key in the lock. The pounding began; she had expected it. Then the bell was rung repeatedly, and he started shouting angrily. Slowly Olivia shuffled to the door. She opened it. Ty stood there; he looked at his belongings in bags on the floor and then looked at Olivia. His face was a study in surprise. "Are you kicking me out, then?" He asked as if this was some sort of shock to him, as if nothing had happened.

"Yes, it's your stuff. I said I'd pack it. Now pick it up and go, and make sure you bring my car back in a fortnight." Olivia was quiet but firm. She went into the living room and sat down on the settee. Ty followed her. It took over two hours to get rid of him. Olivia knew exactly what would follow. He pleaded, cried, begged, professed his undying love, assured her he would change and be a better person—on and on it went before she could rid herself of his presence.

When he had finished his tirade, Olivia stood up, opened her dressing gown, and slipped the sleeves down, revealing the extensive bruising on her arms. She lifted her nighty to show him her swollen, blistered, discoloured legs. "Look at this—and I've got a pulmonary embolism. I could have died at any minute, and you could just go and leave me on my own like this! Get out!" Minutes later he left, and shortly after that the hospital called and asked Olivia to attend for a scan. She threw on some clothes and shuffled out to her car. It was then she realised that Ty was still sitting there, staring at her. She just wanted to get out, to escape him, to avoid more confrontation.

Olivia got to the hospital and, after the scan, learnt that she had, in fact, got multiple embolisms. One, albeit a very small one, was in her pulmonary artery. Her situation was not good. She then realised that she had left her mobile behind in her haste. She knew her children would be desperately worried. She drove home and thanked God when she saw that he had gone. Two of her daughters arrived rapidly, and the third, a district nurse, called to advise her on using an electric fan to help her inhale more oxygen. One daughter came laden with painkillers and creams for the burnt legs, and Olivia began her course of injections and tablets to thin her blood and prevent more thrombosing.

During all this, Ty did not give her any peace. He texted and called her mobile and landline ceaselessly. She did not pick up or reply. Just over three weeks passed. One night she was lying on the settee when her mobile rang. She did not look at the caller's identity; she was expecting a call from her son. She pressed the accept button, and the familiar Yankee-Jamaican twang hit her.

"Baby?" She paused. Her heart was pounding. For a second she was about to cancel the call and turn her phone off, but he continued. "My baby, I've missed you so much. I love you so much. I can't go on without you. Tell me you haven't missed me." Olivia took a deep breath. "No, actually, I really haven't, Ty. It's been bliss here on my own without you and all the shouting and screaming about everything and nothing—"

He broke in. "Hun, you know you do miss me—we had such a thing together, you and I. I really do love you more than any other woman in my whole life. Tell me, Olivia, tell me, you really do love me. Don't lie. In bed at night you long for my fingers and tongue, baby, for my big boy—you know you really can't do without it. Nobody can make love like I can, baby. OK, we row. Who doesn't? It's normal. You can be difficult too, hun. Please, Liv, please just take me back, give me a chance, let me show you this time. Let me show you just how I can change. This time I won't screw up. I promise, baby. You are my life, my world, my everything. Without you I can't do anything! If you kick me out and I never see you again, I won't want to live."

Here it comes again, thought Olivia. *The emotional blackmail, the suicide threat.* She spoke quietly. "OK, Ty, that's enough." There was a pause. "I can't stand any more of your vile and unpredictable temper, your disappearances, your refusal to answer texts or pick up calls, your selfishness, your total lack of consideration and care—a lot of things, but ..." Again there was a crackling tension. Ty was unusually silent. "But I do love you. I can't think why the hell I do, and you know it. I will give you this one—just one—last chance. If you screw up, then don't even bother to think about getting back again."

Ty was ecstatic. He arrived very shortly afterwards and was a model of attention. It took him only a short while to persuade Olivia to go up to bed with him, and he spent an hour showing her why she should stay with him and whispering adoring compliments in her ear as he slowly brought her to a shatteringly satisfying climax. As he held her close and nuzzled into her neck, Olivia said, "Ty."

"Yes, my darling." he murmured.

"Just promise me one thing, just this one thing—that you'll be faithful to me."

Ty kissed her neck and her hair. "My baby. How could I be unfaithful to a woman I love so much?" And then he was asleep, and Olivia lay close to his body, wondering what more lay in store for this relationship.

The following morning she found out. Ty announced that he must go to Jamaica for his cousin's wedding. *So this is why he was so desperate to get back*, thought Olivia. And her heart began to harden so very, very little but so very firmly.

TYRESE AND OLIVIA, JUNE 2017

Olivia sent Tyrese packing for a while. She was going to teach him that he hadn't just moved back in and taken over, so she told him to go away for a few weeks so that she could really think things over. He was shocked and not too happy, but he obediently packed and reluctantly drove away. He called daily and answered her texts promptly, which was a refreshing change for Olivia. She even began to miss him a little and, one night, told him that she wanted him back again. Ty was ecstatic and quickly moved back in. He was a much quieter man. Olivia even began to hope that he might have learnt a lesson from the events in Jamaica and from having been reinstated and then sent away again. When he first arrived back at the house, he was humble, clearly very pleased to see her again, willing to do as she wanted him to, and almost, Olivia found to her surprise, submissive. The first night in bed with him was unforgettable. He was cautious and almost afraid to upset her. He spent nearly an hour kissing, stroking, and talking to her before he began to run his tongue over her skin, slowly working down to her thighs. Olivia moaned softly. Ty gently parted the lips of her vulva, ran his tongue very skilfully over her clitoris, and worked down to her vagina and went into it with little darting strokes that made Olivia shudder and cry out. Ty stopped and went upwards. He began to flick his tongue across her nipples and suck them. She moaned again.

"Baby," he whispered, "do you want it in you?"

"Oh God, yes," gasped Olivia. Ty pushed her legs apart and slid in slowly and carefully. Olivia tensed, awaiting his usual move of pulling her legs up onto his shoulders, which gave him very deep thrust but caused her agonies because of his size. Ty let her remain lying flat and began to move very slowly, and Olivia was soon wanting him desperately.

"Oh God, Ty! Fuck me hard, just fuck me," she gasped, thrusting with his movements and on the verge of an orgasm. Oh how she had missed this, his beautiful body and his skilled lovemaking. Her climax hit her like a tsunami and she screamed out. Ty thrust into her forcefully again and again as he came with her, and he kissed her at the moment of their purest pleasure. They lay spent, sweating, and happy. He kissed her face all over lovingly and then rolled her over. They fell asleep with his arms firmly around her, tightly and possessively. Just before she fell asleep, Olivia whispered to him. "Please promise me that you'll be faithful to me. I won't ask anything else of you. Just be faithful."

Ty kissed her hair. "How could I not be faithful to you, baby? I love you so very much. You're the only woman in this world for me. I have nobody else. I don't need anyone else. I've missed you so much, baby. No sex like this for too long. I've dreamt of you." He kissed her again, and they both slept. In the early hours of the morning Olivia crept into the en-suite shower and cleaned the copious amount of Ty's sperm from herself. Then she put on her dressing gown and tiptoed downstairs and out into the garden, where she lit a cigarette. *I love him*, she thought.

I do love him, but is this all I really love—the fantastically skilled lovemaking, his size, the orgasms? What else is there? She finished the cigarette. She did not really want to have to think too deeply. For now, he was back with her. Would he stay? Would he be faithful? She went back quietly to the bedroom. Ty lay on his back; his mouth was wide open and he was snoring. Saliva trickled from one corner of his mouth. Olivia shut out this image, took off her robe, and climbed back into bed. Ty stirred and pulled her to his body tightly. They remained like this until the morning. Then Olivia awoke to Ty bringing her tea. He sat on the bed and stroking her cheek. She tried to keep these memories as life unrolled.

A week later Ty said, "We'll move this television up to the bedroom." He was pointing to the large smart television in the lounge.

"Why?" asked Olivia.

"I've got one just like this but bigger and better. It's at my friend's place down in Broomstead. I'll bring it back when I go there."

"We've already got them everywhere. We really don't need another one," said Olivia.

"Ah, but baby, this one is really something. Anyway, it's mine and it's free, so let's have it here, OK?"

Olivia shrugged. "If you insist, Ty, but this one's quite adequate." Daily life resumed. Ty brought her up a cup of tea at eight every morning and then went and sat downstairs, in his dressing gown, on his phone endlessly. Olivia left for the office just after nine and, when she returned, would find Ty still in his gown, sitting in the huge red chair, asleep or watching television. He would quite often make supper, leaving piles of dishes and pans for Olivia to clear up. She soon tired of the not-too-expertly-cooked curried goat and tasteless chicken concoctions, which were always accompanied by dry rice. She longed for something different, but she didn't want to rock the boat and risk giving Ty a reason to argue or become unpleasant. He did very little except loll in his dressing gown, watch television, and spend hours on his phone and laptop. He would ask her to go shopping with him for ingredients at the Caribbean food shop and then the supermarket, where he always added several large bottles of vodka to the shopping trolley, and Olivia, as always, paid for everything. Ty offered nothing towards the running of the house. Olivia paid the rent, council tax, water and sewage rates, the gas and electricity, the house insurances, and all the food, including Ty's increasing alcohol bills. Very occasionally he would say that he just had to do a drug run or go down to Norfolk to visit his daughter. Olivia thought darkly that this was an excuse to visit Shirley as well. Ty's daughter was 18 and quite capable of meeting her father anywhere.

Olivia was also suspicious of Ty's closely guarded phone and the time he spent on it; an enormous quantity of messages seemed to come in constantly. There were also calls that Ty immediately cut off—that was worrying. But Olivia tried to rationalise, ignore, and simply hope that her feelings of mistrust were unfounded. She was trying to make this work.

In June she bought a smart barbecue at Ty's insistence, and he set it up in the garden. That evening he cooked sausages and chicken legs and made a salad—even a dressing which Olivia actually liked. He washed his food down with a large amount of vodka and eventually fell asleep in the garden chair, snoring loudly and leaving Olivia to clear everything up. They had several barbecues after that, as the weather was very warm and pleasant. After the fourth one, Olivia was clearing up in the garden when she saw smoke coming up from underneath the closed lid of the barbecue. She lifted the lid, and smoke poured out. She then realised the cause; there was a large wad of paper in the barbecue. She was curious. She pulled a pile of it out. Because the lid had been shut, it had not been burnt entirely, and she saw that this was a pile of Ty's bank statements. She read down the entries and began to see an interesting pattern. Monies were being paid into Ty's account—quite a few of them and regularly. One name caught her eye, as it appeared more often than any of the others. Sophie. *Who is this Sophie?* she thought. Quickly she tore off the unburnt pages with the names on them and concealed them in the pocket of her apron. She took them upstairs quickly and copied the entries in a notebook; then she concealed the documents in her apron pocket again and took them back to the barbecue. Ty came out with a glass of vodka in his hand just afterwards and Olivia said quickly, "I saw smoke and found all this smouldering. You shut the lid, so they didn't burn properly."

Ty practically snatched them from the barbecue, then pushed them in again rapidly, and blew on them to ignite them. "I was just trying to burn my bank statements, baby."

"Why burn them, Ty?" she asked.

"Well, I have this money from my drug runs, hun, and I don't want any evidence, do I." He watched the paper reducing to black ash.

"Who is Sophie?" Olivia asked him quietly.

"Sophie?" For a second she saw panic in his eyes; then they flickered downwards and he turned away. "Oh, Sophie. You see, baby, they pay her the drug-run money, and she pays it to me in smaller amounts—sort of money laundering." He laughed nervously.

"But who is she?" Olivia asked him again.

"A godmother—one of my daughter's godmothers."

"Which daughter?" asked Olivia.

"Josie, of course, baby. My other daughters are all abroad."

Yes, thought Olivia, *all over the world, at least the ones you acknowledge. And all the other payments*, she thought, *all those other names. Are they godmothers too? And is that drug money too?*

She went into the kitchen and cleared up. That night she found it hard to respond to Ty's lovemaking; there was a tension between them. Afterwards he rolled away but then rolled back again abruptly and held her fiercely and possessively. He fell asleep like this, and soon Olivia was too hot and tried to escape. But he held her even closer and put his hands over her breasts so that she felt trapped and caged. Eventually she fell asleep and awoke to find Ty's imprisoning arms still loosely around her body. She pulled free slowly and gently and went to shower. Then she sat in the garden, as the sun had just come up in full splendour. She drank her tea, and smoked, and thought hard. All was not well. There were so many unexplained mysteries, and things explained that were still mysteries, and things she just couldn't quite grasp at, and clues but subtle ones. Ty could talk his way around everything and confuse and bemuse her; he could seduce her and wheedle her, make her feel stupid and demanding and suspicious. She knew all was not well—but she wanted this relationship to work, because this man had her heart and soul and mind and body. At that moment he came out into the garden, leaned down over her, and kissed her softly and lingeringly on her mouth.

"Morning baby," he said in that deep, treacle-sweet Jamaican drawl. And Olivia surrendered to the moment.

The new life illusion did not last, as Olivia had feared it might not. There were times when Ty disappeared briefly, telling her he had to do a drug run but would soon be back—and he would be. But the absences grew slowly longer each time. At first he would answer her texts and calls, but soon it was the familiar pattern of no replies and calls ignored or cut short. He started asking her for money for things he claimed he needed for the car. These repairs, logically, were not essential or even believable, because the expensive luxury car was almost new. He would turn up in an edgy temper and soon start drinking. Then the inevitable, endless fighting would begin to darken their lives yet again. One evening he told Olivia that he must go down to Norfolk to get his medications from his doctor's surgery the next day, and she realised that this was just an excuse to see Shirley. Ty's medications were almost a joke to Olivia. He was a man in his late forties who enjoyed the bad health of a 90-year old, a world-class hypochondriac who had everything fashionable and who went online to study the symptoms of whatever he decided he wanted to suffer from at that time. Everywhere Ty went, he carried his small suitcase on wheels that contained a small chemist's shop of what seemed to keep him running. There were sprays for his nose, tablets for his record number of supposed allergies, indigestion remedies, creams for his piles, numerous tablets for his headaches, skin creams, vitamin supplements, and dozens of other things without which this man seemed unable to function. He did, however, need several strong medications to cope with his extremely high blood pressure—which was not helped in any way by his drinking, heavy smoking, unreliable and labile temperament, and his lazy habit of driving just about everywhere in his car so that he was losing his toned, attractive body and starting to become overweight.

Olivia raised her eyebrows. "No, you don't need to go down there, Ty. Have you forgotten? I transferred you to my doctor's practice to save you having to drive all that way every time you need to see a doctor or just get your meds."

Ty narrowed his eyes and looked angry. Then he looked away and said quickly, "Oh, of course—I forgot." He went back to his vodka drinking and ignored Olivia completely.

That night in bed, Olivia was settling down to sleep when Ty rolled over onto her with force and without a word or any attempt at foreplay. He tried to push Olivia's legs apart, and she immediately pulled away and rolled over. Ty grabbed her from behind, and she shook him off angrily. "No. Ty—I don't want to be jumped on like that. I don't enjoy being raped."

"Baby,"—he was soft and wheedling—"baby, I really want you, and sometimes a man has to show that he is a man and the boss." He rolled into her and pushed his huge erection against her back.

"Does he really?" Olivia said curtly. "Well, I said no. Don't you understand that? *No!*—and this isn't Jamaica, and I'm not a submissive little possession, so get off and leave me alone."

"Oh, come on, baby. I want it so I'm gonna have it." And he tried to pull her over onto her back.

Olivia kicked out at him and said through clenched teeth. "I said *no!* No, Ty. No means just that, so go and masturbate, but don't treat me like something you own." And she rolled over onto her side of the bed and closed her eyes.

Ty flung himself over to his side and muttered angrily for a while, then gradually fell silent. Later he rolled back and began, very slowly, to wind himself around Olivia's body, clutching and clinging. Olivia ignore him and tried to sleep. He made no more efforts to initiate lovemaking, and slowly he relaxed and began to snore into her hair.

There were other instances of his trying to dominate and possess her, and she fought them all off. In bed he continued to hold her tightly, with a controlling and desperate embrace, and Olivia felt smothered, not just physically, but mentally and emotionally too.

The following morning Olivia awoke and lay waiting for Ty to bring her tea up, but time went on and he did not appear. She was annoyed. She was now late and had to shower very quickly. She dressed hurriedly and went down to look for Ty. He was nowhere to be seen, and when she went out of the gate at the side of the garden, she saw that his car was gone. *So,* she thought. *He's gone down to Norfolk—probably to see Shirley. The bastard. That's why he said he had to go and get his meds.* She went into the lounge, picked up her mobile, and texted him. 'Where the hell are you?' She waited for about ten minutes, smoked another cigarette in the garden, and texted him again. By the time she pulled out of the driveway in her car, there was still no reply.

She worked hard that day. There were important meetings to be attended and issues in her business that needed her complete attention. By lunchtime there was no reply to any of her texts, and her calls had been cut off abruptly. She arrived home as darkness was beginning to fall, having been kept late at her office. She was very tired and very angry at Ty. As she approached the house, she saw his car pulled up on the drive beside the house. She parked beside it and went into the house. Ty was in his dressing gown, lounging on the big red chair with a glass of vodka in his hand. As Olivia walked in and stood in the doorway, glaring at him, he looked up, smiling. "Hi there, baby." He put his hand out to her.

Olivia remained in the doorway, unsmiling. "OK, Ty, just exactly where have you been? You didn't bother to tell me you were going, and I was nearly late for a very important meeting. And you didn't bother to answer my texts, and you cut off my calls."

Ty's face changed rapidly. The smile faded, and the dark, frightening look Olivia knew too well was there. "For Christ's sake, baby. I had to go do a little job. Deliver something. Do I have to tell you every fucking move I make?"

"I have to account for my moves Ty. You call me even if I'm just out shopping or with my kids somewhere. You want to know who I'm with and what I'm doing and when I'll be back—it's getting stupid. But I do at least let you know where I'm going, if I can. I don't just disappear early in the morning and then refuse to answer texts and calls to let you know what's happening. If I did that, there'd be yet more yelling and rows. Where have you been, anyway?"

"I already told you." He was sullen; his mouth was drawn in tightly and his eyes were growing narrower and darker. He went over to the trolley, poured himself another vodka, and then took it out into the garden and lit a cigarette. He downed the vodka in one swallow. "I need to go places and do things. I have to earn money—be a man." He was almost talking to himself. "I can't do a bloody thing right, can I? I try to prove to you I'm a man and—"

"And what, Ty? And I pay for everything you do, and own, and wear, and eat, and a lot that you drink—a lot! And your expensive, state-of-the-art, brand-new phone—"

Ty spun round. He threw his glass and cigarette across the garden behind him and then hurled his phone into the room with great force. It bounced sickeningly off the wooden arm of the big chair and hit the table with a dull sound before skidding across the carpet and landing at Olivia's feet. "Fuck the bloody phone, and fuck you too!" Ty poured another vodka and stood there, shaking with fury.

Olivia picked up the phone. "I think you'd better leave right now, Ty. I warned you when I let you back the last time." She spoke very quietly but very determinedly. Ty sat down heavily on the red footstool and continued to drink sulkily. Olivia went upstairs and showered. She was very tired and just wanted to sleep— and to be rid of this man. Again she had let him into her heart and her life. Bad mistake. It would never work. She must get rid of him somehow. She had done so again and again—but still he talked his way back. She packed what she could find of his belongings into his suitcase and took it downstairs. She placed the suitcase firmly in front of him. "Come back for the rest of your stuff when I'm here. Leave your key."

Ty looked up, and the black anger was replaced, in a split second, by the pouting, pleading lips and soulful eyes of a hurt child. "Baby, don't just chuck me out because I had an accident with my phone. It can be mended—you've got insurance on it, hun."

Olivia ignored him and began to make herself a sandwich in the kitchen. He followed her in, and the familiar recital began— the pleading, the lying, the excuses. The love he had for her which she would be a fool to turn down. Then the tears and the sobs and the tantrums. The promises to change, to be a better person. Things were a little difficult right now, but she should not give up on him; she should stay with him. Olivia could almost say the words—she had heard it all before so very many times.

"Just take your stuff and go, Ty. Leave your key, and come back for the rest. Text me first." She didn't even look at him.

"Baby—" He spread his hands out pleadingly.

"Just go, Ty." Olivia carried her plate of supper into the lounge, sat on the settee, and began to eat, still ignoring him.

He took his suitcase—and the inevitable case of medications that were his life-support system—and went out wordlessly. Olivia heard the car door slam, the engine start up. and then the car pull away. She got up and secured the front door and all the other doors. She was so, so tired. She welcomed the prospect of a night's undisturbed sleep. Right now she cared very little whether Ty returned or not. She watched a little television, curled up on the settee, went up to bed, and was soon fast asleep.

The following morning Olivia woke and went down to get herself a cup of tea before showering and leaving for the office. She was a little surprised that she hadn't had a barrage of texts and whining phone calls from Ty; she almost missed the usual attack. She launched herself into the day's workload, and as she was breaking for a much-needed coffee about eleven, her phone pinged and there was a message from him. It simply said, "Hi". She ignored it. Minutes later came "You OK, hun?" Again she ignored it. Then there was silence until late in the afternoon. Olivia drove home and put her feet up on the settee, tired and actually missing Ty—at least she was missing the usual onslaught of messages and calls. At about seven a message came in. "I love you, baby." This was followed by "You are my life." and then "Please give me a chance to show you how much I love you."

"Nothing changes then." Olivia grinned to herself, but she was faintly annoyed and fed up with the never-ending cycle. She started to prepare herself some supper, and the doorbell rang. She opened the door warily, and there he stood, with a huge bunch of flowers and a sheepish grin on his face.

"What the hell do you want?" Olivia was not amused. "I told you to go and leave me in peace. This just isn't working—you can see that. All we do is fight and make up and fight all over again. You have an unstable and unpredictable temper, and I can't handle any more. There's nothing more to be said, Ty. Just go." And she slammed the door in his face. There was a barrage of texts, which she ignored, and then a nonstop attack of calls, which she also ignored. She went up to bed and was soon asleep, but her phone kept waking her, and she had to look to make sure it was not one of her children needing help. But it was Ty—sending one YouTube song recording after another. After the eighth one, she sat up and replayed them. The words seeped into her mind and soul, and part of her began to weaken. She sat, thinking, for some time. Then she texted him. "Shut up—let me sleep, and come back tomorrow. Goodnight."

He was back early the next day, contrite, cooperative, and quieter than usual—and as devastatingly handsome and animally attractive as ever.

Damn you! thought Olivia. *Why can you melt me and my resistance every time? I don't want you, but I need you.*

"I'm off to work," she told Ty. "Don't phone me or bother me or do anything else annoying—I've got a long, busy day ahead." And she slammed the door and drove off.

That night his lovemaking was exquisitely exciting, gentle, and satisfying. As he thrust his hugeness into her waiting womb in the last seconds of their mutual orgasm, she moaned, then began to cry, because she loved him very deeply and wanted their life to be always like this. Ty kissed her face and her tears and found a tissue to wipe her face.

"Why the tears, baby?"

"Because—never mind. You wouldn't understand anyway." She wiped the tears away from her face and got out to go to the toilet. When she got back in bed, Ty enclosed her in greedy, possessive arms and held her very close. He kissed her hair, and slowly his breathing became deeper, and he fell asleep. His grip was suffocating Olivia. She waited until he was fast asleep and beginning to snore; then she wriggled free, turned over, and fell asleep.

TY AND OLIVIA, JUNE AND JULY 2017

Since he had wheedled his way back to Olivia's bed, and house, and heart, Ty had talked endlessly and incessantly of the wedding in Jamaica and of the necessity for Olivia to be with him—on his arm as his woman. He wanted his family to see them as a unit, as belonging to one another and to Ty's family, too. There had been slight—very slight—talk of Olivia and Ty actually becoming engaged, but Olivia tried to play the subject down, as she was swinging from one extreme to the other with Ty. One week she would be determined to throw him out yet again; another week he would again be away, and she would be unable to believe what he told her—the places he said he was going and the things he was supposed to be doing. He did not answer texts or calls, and her brain built up pictures she did want to see. The next week he would return and slowly seduce her into calmness and trust, and her love would overwhelm her, and she would just want them to be together forever.

There were many long phone calls by Ty and Olivia to his family in Jamaica, and without remembering how or why, Olivia found herself deeply involved with Carol Anne. Not many weeks later, she had been talked into buying dresses for the female members of the family. For Ty's mother she had bought a dress, underwear, shoes, a handbag—so many things, and she scarcely recalled being asked or agreeing. The trip was going to be an expensive one, and Olivia told Ty that he would have to contribute to the cost.

"Baby, I'll have to go away and do a hell of a lot of drug runs," Ty told her. "I'll do a lot of stuff and get it together. You'll see." Olivia noticed that he was texting very frequently and often sat frowning at his phone. Olivia was less than eager to go on this second trip. She was still under the care of a consultant, as her embolisms had not gone, and she was on a daily drug regime. She told Ty that there was a possibility she would not be allowed to go. If this happened, then he could go alone— and she would *not* be paying for his expenses, so he would be on his own. Ty nagged her insistently, day after day, to call the consultant, make an appointment, and check it all out; he was clearly desperate that she went with him. He also dropped thinly veiled hints about their getting married. "Have you got your decree absolute, baby? You could take it with you, and we could get a special licence."

Olivia was puzzled. Ty had told her when they first met that he had married Shirley to enable him to leave the States and enter England. Then, after a fierce row some months before, he had denied that he was married to her; he'd said he was divorced. She wanted to believe him. She reasoned that if he were married and tried to marry her in Jamaica, he would bring down on himself a charge of bigamy—something he could certainly not afford to do.

Olivia had a short break in Cornwall with her eldest daughter. They stayed in a tiny cottage miles from anywhere and blissfully quiet, with only the cries of the birds and the gentle, breathy wind to disturb the green, granite space. They went to a small market town nearby to see what fascinating shops they could find, and discovered the perfect target. Hidden away in a cobbled passageway, it had large windows full of old, second-hand, loved and used jewellery and watches. Necklaces and rings and bangles and chains had been sold and pawned, to keep life flowing, to pay urgent bills, or to buy other gifts. The window was overflowing with these treasures, and Olivia was in heaven. She had her enormous collection already, but she could not resist any other baubles that beckoned to her. She and Beth went in. A small, frail, kind-looking man in a blue velvet waistcoat and matching bow tie greeted them with a small bow and a warm smile. Soon almost a third of the contents of the window were scattered over the counter, as Olivia tried on one beautiful thing after another.

Finally the friendly little man went out to the back of the shop and returned with a small box in his hand. "I observe that madam loves her rings and has a very excellent collection." He opened the leather box and held it out to Olivia. Nestling in the white silk lining was a breath-taking ring. Its band was studded with tiny diamonds and pearls, and the main gem was an oval shaped diamond surrounded, again, with exquisite pearls.

Olivia took a deep breath and tried it on the ring finger of her left hand, having removed the large diamond ring already there. It fitted perfectly—like Cinderella's glass slipper. Olivia smiled. "Gotta have this, Beth." Her daughter smilingly agreed. The deal was done for £600, and Olivia decided that, if a marriage were on the horizon, this would be her engagement ring. She packed it away and did not, as yet, say anything to Ty about it.

Eventually Olivia heard from her consultant, who told her that flying was not contraindicated. Indeed, she would be the safest person in the air, free from the threat of DVT, as she was taking blood-thinning drugs. So that route of escape was closed. Ty would get his way. Jamaica beckoned.

Olivia sat down with Ty, who had only drunk a small amount of vodka and was, for him, reasonably approachable. He was also happy because she had told him that she was medically fit to fly. She had shown him the ring and suggested that if—if—she decided to agree to marriage, then this was the ring that she had chosen. He, of course, immediately promised to repay the cost. He put the ring back in its leather box and slipped it into his jeans pocket.

Olivia stroked his arm. "Ty, hun, this trip mustn't be like the last one. I really can't see any future for us if there's a repeat of any of it. Let's try to make it a happy time—please."

Ty swung round and took her hand. "Baby, I promise on my parents' lives—my kids' lives—this will be such a wonderful trip! I'll be a different person. Give me a chance to show you. I can change, be different. This time we'll plan everything properly; it'll all run smoothly. I just need to spend time with you, baby. Just give me this chance, my baby ..."

Olivia sat listening; she almost knew what would come next, and depression edged into her mind. *We've been here so often, so many times before. I've heard all this before, but maybe—I have to give him just one chance—just one last chance.* She often wondered vaguely if it was her. Maybe she expected too much—but surely not?

"OK, Ty, we'll give it a go—but this is the very last chance. I won't take what happened on the last trip." She squeezed his hand and got up to make supper. Then she turned. "This trip is costing me a lot more than the last one, Ty, and I want your contribution." There was a silence.

Then he said, "OK, baby. But I'm gonna have to get a load of work—runs—to pay for it. How much will I need?"

"So far it's cost me £1,700."

"OK, hun, but don't get on my back if I have to be away a lot working. I'll have to get onto my guys right away." He disappeared into the garden and sat texting furiously.

The next few weeks were stormy. Ty disappeared, as she had expected he would, and communication disappeared with him. This led to heated exchanges and sarcastic texts from Olivia. He called her eventually and asked her to try and find out about a work colleague of Shirley's who, he said, was encouraging Shirley to "stir up shit" about him. And Ty suspected them of having an affair. *What?* thought Olivia. *He's living with me and kicking off about what she does. But they're divorced—I think.* She was angry and fed up. Then Ty called again and told her Shirley was threatening him. He sent her a text from his own phone—not a screen shot or a forwarded message—purported to be from Shirley, and it said, "Pay me back the two and a half thousand you borrowed before August, or I'll get you deported." Olivia asked to see a screenshot from Ty's phone, but he refused, saying that she might "misunderstand the other texts." He was away a long time with very little break. He told Olivia that he would get £200 for every year he would spend if he got caught running drugs. "So I have to do a lot of runs, baby." The simmering discontent lasted as the trip loomed on the warm, sultry July and August horizons. When Ty returned one afternoon, Olivia noticed immediately that the thick, solid-gold chain that he always wore around his neck was gone.

"Where's your chain?"

"I had to pawn it, baby—I need four hundred to get it back."

"Why did you pawn it?"

"I needed money for my kids. They all need things, and I just didn't have it." He spread out his hands and shrugged. "I need to get to Nantwich and get it back. I've only got another five months or I'll lose it."

Olivia was furious, but she transferred the money into his account. The trip to Jamaica was all paid for and booked, and it was just days until they were due to leave. He left the next day to get his chain. Olivia was more than sure that she had been conned and that he was up to something; the chain had never been pawned. Then there were endless days when texts were ignored and promised calls did not arrive. He needed money to get the car through the MOT test; then he called to say he needed it again, as he had given the money to one of his children. Tensions increased. Olivia was sure he was with Shirley—or someone else. She sent him pictures of the place she had booked, but he did not reply. This dragged on until two days before the trip was due, when he returned and behaved as if nothing had happened. A blazing row ensued. When this abated, he announced he needed to go into town for clothes for the trip, and yet again, almost without her being aware of what was happening, Olivia found herself paying out £600 to outfit Ty. He did hand her £600 in notes, but that was swallowed up by the cost of his chain redemption and the clothes.

Olivia wished with her whole being that she had not arranged and paid for this trip. She did not want to go, and she knew it was going to be a disaster. They had a blazing row the night before they left. Olivia caught him sitting in his car and having an animated conversation with someone. He swiftly cancelled the call and laughed it off, but she was furious and suspicious. Later she went into the garden, and the same scenario was repeated—but this time she heard him say, "I'll ring you later, baby." This caused angry words and an atmosphere which tainted the whole thing from the first.

The following day they set off for the hotel at Gatwick, where they were staying overnight for their early morning flight. Olivia handed her car over to the rep from the secure parking firm and went into the room to make herself a cup of tea and relax after the drive. She hadn't slept well the previous night. In the following hour, she showered and changed. She noticed that Ty had been drinking steadily. He insisted that she give him a pedicure and remove his ingrowing toenail, which troubled him continually. He also insisted that she take pictures of his feet before and after this operation. Olivia went on her knees and applied herself to this unsavoury task. She removed the large toenail, feeling nauseous as she did so, and then trimmed and cleaned the other nails. Again at Ty's insistence, she painted his nails with clear varnish, as he would be wearing sandals and felt his nails did not look good unvarnished. Somehow another violent row blew up, and Olivia had had enough. "This is exactly what happened last time, Ty. I'm not putting up with it again." She quickly repacked the few items she had removed from her case and walked out of the room. Ty dashed after her and dragged her back, none too gently. Olivia ignored him and dashed out a second time. She called the car security firm on her mobile; they brought the car to her within ten minutes. She was about to leave when she realised she had left her handbag in the room. "Bugger!" she muttered and dashed back.

Ty was sitting at the table by the window. Spread out in front of him were his complete arsenal of tablets and a bottle of vodka. "What the hell d'you think you're doing?" snapped Olivia.

"I'm not going to Jamaica, and I'm not going back to the house. If you get in that car and leave, I'm taking all of these."

Olivia scooped up all the medication and returned it to its containers. They argued, but it was muted. She fell into bed, exhausted, and turned away from him. They both slept heavily and awoke at dawn to board their flight.

At the checkout Ty downed 50 mg of diazepam, which he swilled down with half a bottle of vodka. This ensured an eventless and peaceful flight for Olivia, because Ty was semiconscious all the way. He woke just once to eat and to drink another half bottle of vodka; then he slid back to sleep again. Olivia, sitting in peaceful thought, realised that the diamond ring was in his luggage, and she was worried.

They landed, cleared customs, and picked up their hire car. The hotel was another plush five-star, breathtakingly expensive place. They met Ty's sister, Carol Ann, and Olivia gave her the dress that she had bought her for the wedding. Later, Olivia was to learn that Carol Ann went straight into town, sold the dress, and bought another one from the proceeds. Ty continued, as he drove them to the hotel, to try and pressure Olivia into moving from the hotel they were bound for to another one nearer the wedding venue. He argued that it would be nearer his home and his family, but Olivia knew that it meant that Ty wanted to drink heavily at the wedding and did not want to have to drive back a long distance. He had tried this on since before they left England, but Olivia had refused. She had already shelled out nearly five grand for this bunfight, and she wasn't being forced into any more expense.

Soon they were settled in their luxurious room, and Ty began to drink right away. He went out onto the balcony and began playing loud music on his laptop. He put on a local song with very explicit, bawdy words, which Olivia found offensive. She endured it until the singer started saying, "Show me the pussy." Then she had had enough. "For Christ's sake, Ty, turn the bloody thing off, or at least turn it down. It's disgusting! I don't want to hear any more." This, naturally, kicked off another argument, and Olivia eventually went to bed tired, angry, and depressed. Ty followed, after urinating loudly with the bathroom door open and then breaking wind even more loudly. He staggered to the bed, muttering, and climbed in clumsily. He reached for Olivia, but she was turned away and nearly asleep, listening to the strange sounds of the tropical night and feeling the warm breeze through the balcony shutters.

The next day dawned hot, sultry, and full of the bell-like calls of birds. There was a faint air of excitement. Today was the day of the wedding, the reason for this trip. The arguing began as soon as they got up and continued throughout their showering, coffee and cigarettes, and their dressing for the occasion. As was normal for this culture, Olivia was wearing a long dress. It was navy blue, and she wore her sapphire jewellery and cream shoes with it and carried a matching cream handbag.

She put her hair up, held in place by a gold comb studded with sapphires.

Ty was decked out in the clothes Olivia had bought him—every stitch he wore. She had to admit to herself that he looked devastatingly handsome and smart. He wore brown cord trousers, an expensive cream shirt with a grandad collar, a brown leather waistcoat, and brown leather boots. Olivia looked him up and down again. All that had cost her at least £600— and still he was rumbling, and picking, and arguing, and this before the day had even launched. Before Ty dressed, Olivia went to take his wedding clothes from the protective covers she had put on them. As she unzipped the long container, she felt something heavy in the bottom of it. Bending down she took out a mobile phone. It was an old one, small, with a flip-type cover. She stood up. "What's this then—a secret phone for your secret lovers?" She was joking, and she laughed as she said it. Ty's reaction was instant. "For God's sake! That's a present for my cousin—it's just an old one, for goodness' sake. Why do you always have to think the worst? Can't I give my family a damned present?" he roared and shouted at Olivia, who wished that she hadn't teased him. She hadn't expected quite such a reaction. They drove to the wedding in total silence. They were greeted warmly by the family, but Ty remained sullen. He continued to cause constant friction throughout what could have been a very pleasant day for Olivia. After about an hour, Ty turned to her and said sulkily, "Why don't you just bloody well leave? Obviously you don't like it here. Just go." He downed another glass of rum. Olivia stood up, picked up her handbag, and without a word or a glance at Ty, she walked away from the table, down the driveway, through the gate and out onto the dusty, potholed road. Very soon she was aware of running feet behind her, and she heard Ty calling. "Olivia, Olivia, stop, now! Come back here." Olivia paused and turned. Ty was coming towards her, closely followed by his aunt.

The aunt ran up to her and took her arm. "Darling, come back in. You can't be out in this road alone like this! This is a dangerous place for you. A woman dressed like this with all this jewellery, alone. No, child, you come right back. What you thinking, girl, running off like this?"

Olivia felt hot tears welling up, and soon they were spilling down her cheeks. Wordlessly she took the aunt's arm and walked back with her back through the gate, ignoring Ty. She sat down at the table. Ty sat down opposite her, and the aunt sat down beside her. "Now, child, what is going on here?"

The tears rolled down Olivia's face. "He told me to leave." There was a silence, and both the women looked at Ty.

"No, I did not tell you to leave." Ty looked so hurt, so convincing. "Ty, why are you lying?" He gazed at her steadily but did not reply. He just took another large gulp of rum. Olivia was hurt, and angry; she felt helpless and drained. "Go away! Just go away, and leave me alone."

Ty got up and walked away. Olivia was left alone at the table under the trees, below the shrill bird calls and the hot breeze that clattered the palm fronds. She felt abandoned. Nobody seemed to notice her. She didn't even have a drink to quench her thirst. She sat there for almost an hour, planning how she would get back to the hotel, pack her cases, get her air ticket changed, and dash to the airport and escape. Then Carol Ann came over. She put her arm around Olivia and persuaded her to come over and join the rest of the family. Olivia went with her and sat amongst them. Soon she was laughing with them, having real fun, and actually relaxing and enjoying herself.

Then Olivia looked up and saw Ty. He was dancing with a pretty black woman. His hips were rotating and undulating. His body was talking the rhythm, oozing raw sex, screaming virility and raunchy, black beauty. If he could do anything well, it was dancing—and singing. He danced towards Olivia, grinning and singing to the music, and moving very close to the girl who danced with him. He was almost next to Olivia.

"Aren't you going to introduce me, then?" she asked him, unsmiling.

"Oh, this is my cousin." Ty grinned, showing his white, even teeth and his attractive dimples.

"Let them get on with it—ignore him," Olivia heard someone behind her say. So she turned away and resumed her chatting with the other family members. Eventually the day faded into dusk. Little lights strung between the trees looked like stars floating above them. The bride and groom danced closely and lovingly, their eyes locked in love. Olivia watched them with a deep yearning in her soul.

Then Ty was demanding that they leave. He was incapable of driving, so his youngest brother drove them back to the hotel. There, Ty wanted to resume his drinking, and he swiftly disappeared. Olivia's feet were badly swollen, and she just wanted to get her shoes off and raise them. Thankfully, she sank onto the bed. She dozed. Ty came staggering in around two in the morning; he went into the bathroom and urinated long and loudly, not bothering to shut the door. Olivia stayed very still and breathed loudly and evenly, to give the impression she was asleep. Ty stood beside the bed, and she could feel his eyes on her; then he got into bed and was soon snoring loudly. Olivia slowly drifted into sleep. The next few days were a blur of uncomfortable and sometimes forgettable nothingness. On the Sunday they went over to Ty's parents' home, where the whole family were gathered for a meal. Olivia helped Mary and the other women to cook and serve the delicious stewed oxtail. They all chatted in patois for hours afterwards, and Olivia was left isolated and unable to understand or join in. Ty drank and was as sullen as ever. That night he again disappeared to the bar, and Olivia remained in the hotel room alone. Again Ty lurched in very late and, again Olivia feigned sleep to avoid any contact with him. Monday and Tuesday were monotonous repetitions, with all-day arguments, copious amounts of alcohol being poured down Ty's throat, Ty remaining at the bar until the early hours of the morning, and Olivia avoiding him at all costs by pretending to be asleep. On Wednesday they again went to his parents' home, where Mary expertly cooked another good meal of lobster and other sea delicacies.

Sebastian held court there. He had a strong, overwhelming presence. It was clear that his word ruled in that family. Olivia found out that Sebastian had many children who were not from Mary. He seemed to consider that this was normal and that Mary must simply accept the situation—even to the extent that Mary brought into her family and adopted two of the children that had been sired from other women during their marriage. Sebastian also seemed to think that he should be allowed to live his life as he chose, without comment or objection. He had great charm, but he also invoked a certain amount of disgust in Olivia. At the same time, she couldn't stop herself from liking him. *It was*, thought Olivia, *the same with his son Ty.* They both possessed this hypnotic charm, which could not be chased away by the anger, dislike, and fear that their actions also created. Sebastian had close links with the chief of police in that area, so Olivia was led to believe. In his former days he had done some pretty dreadful things and had got away with them because of this association with the law. He'd also used the friendship to punish anyone who got in his way or stood up to him. Despite all this, Olivia could not do anything but love this man. He was talented. He carved beautiful animals out of any scrap of wood that he could find. When in charm mode, he could chat for hours about many fascinating things, and he had a laugh and a smile to melt an Arctic glacier. Olivia enjoyed her day despite the gabble of patois and Ty's grim mood.

They returned to the hotel. Ty did not instantly go to the bar to resume his drinking but followed Olivia to their hotel room. He sat on the bed beside her and gently ran his fingers across her bare shoulders and neck. Olivia shrugged him off. He tried again, and she could feel herself, despite her anger, wanting this contact with Ty's body. Again she pushed him off. She expected an angry reaction, but Ty just kissed her shoulder and said very gently, "What's wrong, baby? Don't you want this big, sexy black guy? He wants your beautiful body, because he really does love you an awful lot." He continued kissing her shoulder, and his hand slid around and softly stroked her breast outside her flimsy sundress. Olivia tensed.

"You do want me, baby. You know you can't resist this body in yours." Olivia shrugged him away again, but he held her tightly and pushed her down on the bed. When she tried to protest, he kissed her hard, and she could not stop herself responding to his urgency. She kissed him back, and soon he had stripped her, throwing the garments across the room. He pulled his shorts, pants, and T-shirt off and moved her further onto the huge bed. He went down onto her, pushing her legs apart and running his tongue over her clitoris and into her vagina. Olivia tried not to show her desperate need for him, but she was writhing with desire and wet with her passionate lust for his hugeness and his skill. He slid into her slowly. He was massively erect. Olivia winced slightly as her body took his size; then she thrust back against him wantonly and furiously. He was more passionate and primitive than she had ever before known him to be, and soon she felt her orgasm looming; he was thrusting deeply and shuddering. As he came, with her, in one glorious second of satisfaction, he whispered into her hair, "Oh God, I love you, hun—I love you so much."

Olivia was glowing, and, for that minute in time, happy. "I love you too, Ty." And she really meant it. She did love him—deeply. If only his demons would go and leave them both with the happiness that could be theirs. They lay peacefully spent. He held her in his arms, gently but firmly, and they slid into a deep, refreshing oblivion. The moon walked across the island, sending beams of light through the shutters on the balcony, over the sleeping lovers, across the sand, and the palms, and the murmuring sea. For now this was paradise—just for now.

Thursday brought blue skies; screaming, warbling birds; a gentle, warm breeze; and the muted sounds of the busy complex drifting up from below. Olivia sat up and there, sitting on the bed, gazing at her with his dimpled, heart-wrenching smile, was Ty. She was surprised, as he was usually out on the balcony at this hour, on his phone or his laptop. He leaned over and kissed her. "You wanna cuppa tea, baby?" He smiled, drawling in his slanted, soft, Jamaican voice.

Olivia smiled back. "Yes, please—that would be just perfect." She lay back and, when the tea arrived, drank it with enjoyment. Ty was out on the balcony, making calls on his phone, but he frequently turned and smiled at Olivia. He came in and sat beside her. "Baby, I gotta go out and do something important. I promise I won't be long. You rest and take it easy." He leaned over and kissed her gently on her lips.

"Just have a restful day, baby. I'll try not to be long." He smiled again and swung jauntily out of the door.

Olivia wondered what he was up to but decided to enjoy this peace while it lasted. She could get to like the new improved Ty. She spent the day lounging, swimming, eating a steak with salad, smoking a little too much, and generally relaxing. As the day wore on, there was still no sign of Ty. Olivia felt a little stirring of unrest. She feared him rolling in very late and very drunk. *Please don't let it all kick off again.*

Then he returned, smiling, relaxed, and happy. "Baby, I'm so sorry I'm so late. I had to do something, and it took much longer than I thought it would. Look, I want you to really dress up tonight. We're going out to dinner, and I want you to really feel good."

"Why—where are we going?" Olivia was intrigued.

Ty winked and grinned. "You'll find out."

Olivia went to the shower room and had a long, satisfying wallow in scented gel. She couldn't decide what to wear, but Ty went to the wardrobe containing her large collection of dresses. He went through them until he came to the one which was his particular favourite—a beautiful, deep-sapphire-blue floaty dress which emphasised Olivia's pale skin and blonde hair. She was pleased at his choice, as she loved the dress.

"Here, hun. Wear this one for me, OK?"

Olivia put on the blue dress and blue shoes. She wore her diamond and sapphire jewellery and carried a matching blue bag.

"Be ready for seven, hun," Ty said as he went into the shower to get ready for the mystery outing. Olivia was ready at ten minutes to seven. She sat out on the balcony in the warm breeze, smoking. Then Ty joined her. He was looking very smart and very handsome.

Olivia was even more curious. "Where are we going?"

Ty smirked. "You'll see, baby. You'll see."

They went down to reception, where Ty steered Olivia out of the doors and to a waiting taxi. They got in, and the taxi driver simply drove away. Ty didn't direct him, so it was clear to Olivia that the driver knew exactly where to go; Ty had planned this. They stopped outside one of the most upmarket restaurants on the complex. A waiter came out with a silver tray, on which stood two fluted glasses of champagne. Olivia pulled a face. "Ty, I don't like champagne."

"Oh, go on, hun. Just take a sip."

Olivia wrinkled up her nose and took the smallest amount she could. She made a face and pushed the glass towards Ty. "Sorry, but I can't—I hate it." Ty took the glass and downed it. Then the maître d'hôtel appeared and bowed. "If you would like to follow me, sir." He walked on ahead, and Ty walked with him. Olivia tagged along behind, teetering slightly in her heels. They went along the side of the restaurant, down past the swimming pool, and then, to Olivia's surprise, down towards the beach. She was concerned that she would not be able to negotiate the sand in her heels. She walked on the boards that stretched from the grass over the sand, but soon these came to an end. Olivia stopped and looked at Ty. "I can't go any further. I'm wearing heels—it's the sand."

Ty put his hand out. "Come on, hun. You'll be OK." He held her hand and guided her as she lurched over the sand. And then she looked up and saw the table. It was under a canopy, and it was covered in candles, flickering in the dusk like stars. There were flowers everywhere. The table was laid out in perfect, crisp white linen and silver tableware. It was at the water's edge, and a trench had been dug to protect it from the sea. Olivia's breath was momentarily taken away by the sight. The waiter pulled out her chair, and she sat looking at the sight.

Even by Olivia's standards this was luxury. She looked across the table at Ty and smiled warmly. "Thanks, sweetheart—this is really lovely."

Ty smiled back. He laughed. "The night's not over yet, baby." Then began what Olivia was to find out was a seven-course meal. Ty picked at small amounts of each course. He never ate a full meal. He just pushed his food around and ate small portions of it. Most good food was wasted on him.

Then the waiter arrived and leaned down to Ty. "Could I have a word with you please, Mr Benton?" They went away a short distance, where they talked together.

Olivia was bemused. When Ty returned, she asked, "What exactly is going on?"

Ty grinned. "That's for me to know and for you to find out."

At that moment, Olivia knew—and she was not happy. *Oh God*, she thought. *He's going to propose to me! He has set this all up. He's going to propose.* The meal continued. The third course was brought in—the main course—and the waiter set it down in front of them both. Then Ty pushed back his chair, put his hand in his pocket, took out the pearl-and-diamond ring, put it onto his pinky finger, and walked around to Olivia. He went down on one knee on the sand, took Olivia's hand, and looked at her. Olivia's heart was racing.

"I've been wanting to do this for some time. You know that I love you—that I'm in love with you. You know that I want you in my life forever. All I want you to do is say yes. Will you marry me? If you do say yes, I will spend every waking minute trying to make you happy." Then he took the ring off his little finger and grasped Olivia's left hand. He slid the ring onto her finger. Her head was screaming no, but they were surrounded by people looking at them, watching, and waiting. The meal had been set up—so much planning and preparation. How could she burst his bubble, this man with the fragile psyche? There was nothing for it. She had to say yes. *But*, Olivia told herself, *this will be the longest engagement on God's earth.* She looked at the ring on her finger and then looked at Ty. The silence was tangible. Everyone was waiting.

"Yes, I will marry you, Ty," she said. She knew that she was lying. This argumentative, touchy, unpredictable, uncaring, selfish, hard-drinking, possessive, jealous man kneeling in front of her—was she going to tie herself to him for the rest of her life? Never. Both her head and her heart shouted no, but still she couldn't embarrass him by rejecting him in front of his peers. Ty stood up, and Olivia got up from her chair. He held her close, and they kissed. The onlookers shouted approval and clapped.

Then they sat down again and resumed their meal. Ty kept taking odd mouthfuls of each course and then rejecting the rest; Olivia had to keep nagging him to eat the expensive food presented. This began to grate on her, and it also began to spoil any enjoyment the evening might have held. Soon they were walking back over the sand, getting into the taxi, and returning to the hotel room. There Ty stripped Olivia roughly and pushed her down on the bed. He kissed her for a long time and told her that he loved her so very much. He kissed her breasts and nipples, whispering, "This is all mine now, all mine. Mrs Olivia Benton. My wife. My love."

He kissed her body all over and travelled slowly downwards to her belly. Then he used his tongue as he reached her clitoris, and soon Olivia was moaning and begging for his body to enter and thrill her body. He opened her legs wide and slowly slid inside her, gently, his eyes closed in bliss as she gasped. He moved inside her body slowly, leaning down to kiss her face, her mouth, and her breasts. Olivia could feel the hot excitement in her belly. She moved against Ty's body fiercely, crying out, "Oh, please, harder! Fuck me—just fuck me-e-e-e-e!" and she screamed as she climaxed. Ty rammed deeply into her as he reached his ecstasy with hers. They lay in each other's arms for some time.

Then Ty got up and went to the bathroom. He stepped out onto the balcony and lit a cigarette. Soon Olivia joined him. They sat without speaking for some time. Ty blew out a stream of smoke. "Baby, that was so good. I'm gonna make you so very happy."

Olivia did not reply. She was wondering what the hell she had done. She lit another cigarette and stared out over the moving, silvered waves. *Nothing will change*, she told herself. *Nothing will change, ever.* But still a part of her loved him, would not leave him—wanted him.

The following morning Olivia awoke to a sullen, quiet Ty. He had three extremes of mood, and these never varied. He would be sullen and quiet, dementedly overexcited, or extremely possessive and jealous. Today Olivia found him sullen. "Why are you so quiet?" she asked him.

He shrugged. "Nothing. Just enjoying the peace and quiet." So she left him to sit on the balcony in silence.

That evening, he wanted to go back to the Hilton for dinner, the place where he'd proposed. Olivia discovered that Carol Ann's daughter had arranged the entire previous night. Ty had just sat at his parents' home, directing and giving orders. He claimed he now wanted to go to the Hilton to thank the girl.

They arrived, still in silence, sat down, and waited for the waiter to bring menus. Olivia was not happy. "Ty, this is getting really uncomfortable. Why won't you speak to me?"

Ty did not say, "Because I can't be bothered." But he shrugged, grunted, and raised his hand, which was almost the same thing. Olivia could see where all this was going to end. She pushed her chair back and stood up. "I want to go back to the hotel—" she began, but just at that moment she saw Carol Ann's daughter, Jolene, approaching them. However, she continued walking out of the restaurant. Then she turned and saw Ty talking rapidly to Jolene; he was waving his arms around. She decided to go back. She knew Ty was probably telling a pack of lies about her, and she wanted to hear them.

As she approached, she heard Ty saying, "Oh, I don't know. I don't know." At that moment Olivia realised that Ty was very drunk.

Jolene looked at Olivia with concern on her face. "Are you all right?"

"No, not really, Jolene, I just want to go back to the hotel." It was about a fifteen-minute walk through the complexes to the hotel from the restaurant. Jolene couldn't get a taxi for Olivia, so she walked back with her. Ty trailed behind morosely. He was out of earshot. Jolene asked Olivia what was going on, so Olivia told her. It all spilled out—the drinking, the bruising, the jealous and possessive outbursts—everything.

"Thank you for everything you did to make last night so perfect," she said and smiled at Jolene. "But I don't think I can marry your uncle while he's like this."

"Yes, of course, I understand. I don't know what he's playing at." They walked further.

"Have you got your mobile phone?" asked Jolene. "If you have, don't let him see, but put my number in, and if you ever need me, just call or text me." Olivia managed to do this without Ty noticing anything. She felt that Jolene had seen all this before and knew what her uncle Ty was like. This did not encourage Olivia one little bit. When they arrived at the hotel, Jolene gave Olivia a hug and a kiss. "Keep in touch. Let me know you're all right."

"I will," said Olivia.

Ty came up to them then. "Bye," he said to Jolene without even turning; then he walked on ahead into the hotel. He ignored

Olivia, leaving her to get out of the lift alone and fumble for her key, as he had slammed the bedroom door on her. Inevitably another fight was brewing up.

Olivia sat, looking at Ty, mouthing, swearing, and shouting. "What do I do!" she said to herself. "Do I pity him? Get angry with him? Dump him?" Olivia eventually crawled into bed, totally exhausted and wondering just how much more she could handle of this nightmare. She was soon to find out.

The next day Ty asked Olivia to extend the holiday because he wanted to put right the arguing. He said that they had had no time to spend together to do things; they were always at his parents, he stated. In reality, he was always at the bar, on his phone, or being belligerent. He could still expect to get everything he wanted from Olivia—and he usually did.

They went to his parents' house and met his brother, Sebastian junior—or Titch—who had brought along his little daughter, Tia. Ty had brought along a large bottle of vodka, and this he shared, little and reluctantly, with his brother and a few ragtag friends. They were poor and dirty but cheerful and polite. Whilst the men drank, Olivia sat with Tia on her knee. The child babbled, smiled, and hugged and kissed Olivia, who hadn't seen her yet on this trip and had missed her a lot. Olivia told Ty that something should be done about his daughter Leanne. Her mother had agreed to Ty taking her back to England on the previous trip, but then he had decided it was all too much trouble, and absolutely nothing had been done since. Olivia noticed that the car she had paid to hire for Ty had somehow been lent to Ty's brother, who was zipping around everywhere in it. Few things surprised her anymore. Then Ty and his brother decided that it would be very nice for little Tia to spend a night at their hotel, as she had never seen anything like it before. They were all in the car, Olivia and Tia in the back and the men in the front. Ty turned round to Olivia and said, "It would be great for Tia to see a five-star hotel. Let's take her to spend the night with us."

"Yes, Ty, that would be very nice, but this hotel is for adults only. No kids are allowed. You know that."

"Oh, that'll be OK. We'll get her in."

"You can't take a child into an adults-only hotel. We'll get kicked out if she's found."

"Oh, we'll sneak her in; nobody'll find us."

Oh God, thought Olivia. *Here we go again.*

They arrived at the hotel. It was a half-moon-shaped building with rows of open balconies. Security guards were everywhere, watching comings and goings, watching suitcases going in and coming out, watching everything.

"How the hell can we get Tia in there?" asked Olivia. "She's a bit big for me to stick up my skirt and pretend to be pregnant." Ty turned round to Olivia. "Simple. We'll get her over that balcony."

"How on earth do we do that?" asked Olivia. They were sitting in a stationary car, and the security guards were too interested in them.

"You stay here, and I'll walk across and distract them," said Olivia. She strolled over to the front entrance with a lit cigarette and was about to speak to a hotel employee there when another couple took his attention. Olivia had to stand there, smoking. When she had finished the cigarette, she put it out and walked back to the car. This attracted further unwelcome attention from security.

"There's no way you're going to get her in there," she told the men.

Ty said impatiently, "Look, you go into the hotel, walk to the end of the corridor, and I'll take her into the bushes and lift her over the balcony." Olivia obediently went in and stood waiting. People passed by, and it was a long wait. Then Ty was lifting Tia up and over onto the balcony; he threw her into Olivia's arms. Olivia grabbed Tia's hand. "Run," she said to the bewildered child. They ran up the corridor and rounded the corner just as a housemaid was coming out of one of the rooms. Olivia pushed Tia into the nearby stairwell and put her finger to her lips. The child stared at her with wide, dark eyes. The housemaid disappeared into another room, and Olivia grabbed Tia and pushed her into their room. Just as she was doing this, the housemaid reappeared and looked up. Olivia realised that she had seen them and that she would report this. She waited anxiously inside the room.

Tia kept pulling at her arm and saying, "Can I have chips? Can I have chips?" Olivia calmed her and took her out onto the balcony so that if it all went pear-shaped and they were caught, Tia would at least have seen things she had never seen before. She stood there with the child, showing her the swimming pool and all the other trappings of luxury that were not part of the little girl's life. Then she took the child back into the room and closed the curtains. They sat on the bed together.

"Don't worry, love. Uncle Ty will be here soon," Olivia told Tia. They waited—and then Olivia saw the door opening, just a tiny fraction, just enough so that Olivia could hear Ty, talking to two security guards. He was letting her know that she must hide Tia.

"Don't be stupid. What you talkin' about? There's no child in here." It was Ty, trying to delay the inevitable. "Why are you picking on me? There's no child in this room." Then he pushed the door shut, and Olivia knew it was her cue to hide the girl. Olivia thought frantically and swiftly. The only thing she could think of doing was to push Tia into the wardrobe. She did this hastily and put her finger to her lips.

"Shush now; be very quiet. Stay in that wardrobe, and don't come out until Uncle Ty comes to take you out."

Then the door opened, and two security guards came in. Olivia raised her hands.

"Come in, come and have a look," she told them. The guard came into the room and began to search. Olivia went out onto the balcony to have a cigarette. She couldn't deal with all that was going on. She was so embarrassed. She knew they would find the child. The guard came out onto the balcony and looked around; then he went into the bathroom and the toilet and searched there, too. He stood momentarily next to the wardrobe and, as if by some instinct, turned to the door and opened it. Tia stood there, staring up at him with her big, brown eyes.

Then Ty shouted, "Olivia, can you come in here a minute?"

Olivia went in. She looked at Ty, at the security guard, and then at Tia. Then she sat the bewildered child next to her on the bed.

"Come and sit down here with me a minute, darling."

The security guard was saying to Ty, "You can't have children on the premises. We're not insured for children. It's for adults, over eighteens only. You'll have to get her parents to come and pick her up, or you'll have to cancel this reservation and move into the families' hotel next door." Ty lost all control yet again and started shouting abusively at the two guards. Olivia started packing up their belongings. She knew that Sebastian had disappeared with their hire car, and that Ty could not contact him.

"Ty, just come here and pack your stuff up." He ignored her and continued his rant. Olivia eventually packed for both of them. Ty berated the guards, accusing them of racism and picking on him. He said that the child was with him all the time and was perfectly safe, that it was just stupid health and safety. He went on and on. Olivia was stressed and fed up—what a holiday *this* one was turning out to be! She had got herself engaged to the man who was causing all this madness and trouble. She wished she could just get on a plane and fly back to England and sanity. She managed to pack everything and took the cases out into the corridor, where she was horrified to see people gathering to look at and listen to Ty's noisy performance. Olivia walked with her head high. The security guard was attempting to be helpful. He had radioed ahead and made a reservation for them in the next-door family hotel. A car was waiting outside to take them there.

As they came out of the room, the housemaid who had seen them came out of an adjacent room. When Ty saw her, he looked from her to Tia. Then he started on the housemaid. "You just couldn't keep your fucking mouth shut, could you, you bitch!" He screamed this furiously.

Olivia was terrified. She could see the look on the security guard's face, and she knew that he was on the verge of restraining Ty. She knew that if he did, a huge fight would break out. This must not happen, for the sake of little Tia. Olivia speeded up, dragging cases and holding Tia's tiny hand. *Just get the child away from all this*, Olivia told herself. Ty had the other two cases. They climbed into the waiting taxi and were at the family hotel in five minutes. They got the key and went up. The room was awful—dingy, dark, and old—nothing like the luxury hotel they had booked to stay in and which Ty's actions had got them thrown out of. Ty went down and complained to the manager. They had done this on purpose because of what had happened next door. It was disgusting; they wanted something better. The manager said that nothing could be done until the next morning.

Ty went back to the room; he had calmed down slightly. He climbed into the bed, with Tia cuddling into him, and Olivia took a photo of them both—Ty was actually smiling. Olivia bundled herself into the chair and tried to sleep. It was quite horrible. The following morning, after a sleepless night, Olivia took Tia to the dining rooms for breakfast. Ty did not go with them. He did not eat breakfast, and he needed to do his morning business of phone calls, texts, and emails. Olivia always wondered who these were all directed to. She had a lurking suspicion that they might be going to a few women.

Olivia and Tia went into the canteen. Everything was laid out buffet style. There were cereals, and fruit, yoghurt, bacon, sausages, tomatoes, mushrooms, eggs of all sorts, toast and bread, marmalade, jam, honey, and a cornucopia of other delights. Tia's little face lit up. Olivia took her to the counter. "Can I choose?" The little girl looked up at Olivia.

"You can have anything you like, darling." The child piled her plate with goodies so that Olivia had difficulty carrying the plate back to their table. They sat down, and Olivia watched the child as she started on the mound of food. The girl was cutting off tiny pieces, but she was not eating them; she was just sucking at them. Then Olivia realised that the poor child had such bad teeth that she was unable to eat properly! That explained her emaciated appearance. Health care in Jamaica was not free, and Tia's father, Ty's brother, was very poor. Olivia sat drinking her tea and feeling very sad for this child and her poverty-induced disability. When they were finished, Tia had left a great amount of the food she could not chew.

They were walking back, and Olivia decided to look for Ty, when she realised that he was behind them. He was following them. She turned. Ty had a face like thunder. Olivia looked at him. He just stood, staring at her wildly.

"What are you doing Ty, and why are you staring at me like that? And what time is Sebastian coming to get Tia?" She put a sunhat on Tia, as the sun was fierce and even the dark skinned of this planet needed protection. Then Ty took a packet of cigarettes out of Olivia's handbag, lit one up, and looked at her. He had calmed a little. He held out a small piece of paper to Olivia. It had the name Peter on it and a phone number. Ty spoke quietly. "Who is he? When did you get his number?"

Olivia looked at it and then at Ty. "This is the guy you hired to take us in the taxi to the proposal—remember?"

Ty looked unconvinced. "Why have you got his name and number on a bit of paper?"

"Quite simple. I thought he might come in handy, as he's someone you know, and he's trustworthy. So I asked him for his name and number and wrote it down on a slip of paper and just stuck it somewhere."

Ty looked at her; he seemed disbelieving.

Clearly, thought Olivia, he had been going through her bag.

"So he's a taxi driver. Where is he, then?"

Olivia took the piece of paper and took out her phone. She dialled the number. A man answered.

"Hello, is that Peter? I found your name and number in my bag and can't for the life of me remember who you are."

"I'm a taxi driver, ma'am. Did I take you somewhere?"

"To the Hilton on Thursday, perhaps—at seven in the evening?"

"Ah yes, ma'am; that was arranged by Mr Benton."

"Thanks so much! Sorry to have troubled you. I just totally forgot." She turned off her phone and looked at Ty. He was silent. He could not express anger, neither could Olivia, as Tia was there. They walked on in silence. Olivia went into a shop and bought Tia a bright, pretty swimming costume. Then she walked her to the children's swimming pool, which was supervised by a qualified nanny. She signed the book and left them her room number and mobile number. She waved Tia goodbye. The child was thrilled, laughing and splashing and clearly enjoying herself. Ty stood gazing at Olivia throughout all this, unusually calm and quiet. As she turned away, having safely left Tia at the pool, he came up to her.

"Sebastian's coming at twelve for Tia. Come with me." He held out his hand and took Olivia's hand firmly.

She looked at him quizzically. "Where?"

"Back to our room, baby. I wanna fuck you so much." Olivia followed him obediently. Back in the room, Ty threw her onto the bed. There was no undressing. He tore her pants off and pulled down his shorts and boxers. He went into her very hard and very quickly. His thrusts became vicious, and he was panting.

It was all over in about five minutes. Ty pulled out, smiled at her in an arrogant way, gave her a quick kiss, and then went to the bathroom.

Olivia felt revolted, abused and unloved. She felt as if Ty had just been restamping his mark on his possession; she was disgusted by the whole incident. She went to the bathroom after he had finished to clean herself up. Then she walked to the cafe, where she sat drinking coffee and feeling totally numb. She went to the pool, where she got Tia out, dried, dressed, and ready for her father's return. Ty went for the cases, as they had managed to get themselves booked back into their luxury hotel room. There was little communication between them for the rest of that day. Ty was quiet and remote; Olivia was still stunned and disturbed by everything. She was glad to be back in the room with all its comforts. Ty tried to make love to her that night, but she rolled away from him wordlessly, and he left her alone.

The next morning everything was quiet and almost civilised. They went to the beach to eat lunch, and Ty began drinking steadily. He was ogling the passing women, many of whom wore brief shorts and scanty T-shirts to suit the climate there. Olivia was not amused or pleased. "Do you have to stare at them like that?"

"Well, at least they dress properly."

"What exactly does that mean?"

"That they dress properly for the beach—not as if they're going to a dinner party."

"I choose not to wear tiny cut-off shorts and vests. That's my choice. I'm wearing a cotton skirt and top. What's wrong with that?"

"That's not proper beachwear. You stand out. You look stupid." A furious row resulted, which they continued back to the room. The balcony had huge armchairs, almost the size of beds, and Olivia flopped down gratefully into one of them and closed her eyes. She was aware of Ty coming onto the balcony and putting down a glass, and she heard him go back into the room and rustle around in his suitcase. Curiously she opened her eyes to see him taking a handful of beta blockers from their packet and putting them in the glass. She suddenly realised that the glass contained not vodka but liquid nicotine, a substance she and Ty used in their vapes.

"What the hell are you doing, Ty?"

"I need out. I can't take any more of this. I'm gonna swallow this, and—finish."

Then he went into the toilet and urinated. Whilst he was doing this, Olivia took the glass, threw the contents down the bathroom sink, and rinsed it out. She felt he had expected her to. The argument reignited an hour later, and Ty swore abusively and vehemently at Olivia.

She had had quite enough by this time and shouted back. "For Christ's sake, just shut up, Ty! I knew this was all a big mistake—I should never have trusted you. Just go away and leave me alone."

Ty glared at her. He went towards the door.

"Take your key." Olivia held the key out.

"No," he snapped and continued towards the door.

"Take the bloody thing, Ty. I can't just sit here all day and wait for you to come back." She knew that if he returned and had no key he would cause another scene.

"No!" He ignored her again and went out quickly, slamming the door behind him.

Olivia was furious. She had no intention of being trapped inside the room by his antics and temper. She changed into a swimming costume, overdress, and sandals and packed her large beach bag with sun lotion, water, cola, her sunglasses, a beach towel, and four pegs she had purchased to hold the towel down—and, of course, her phone. She locked the door and went down in the lift. At reception she handed over the spare key and told the clerk, "Mr Benton has forgotten his key. Please give this to him if he returns."

She had phoned him time after time, trying to let him know that she wanted to go out, and leaving messages, but he did not reply or pick up his mobile when she called. This was nothing new. He only picked up calls or answered texts when it suited him. Just before she left the room, she texted him and told him she was going to the beach; she was not going to be trapped in the room all evening waiting for him. She told him his key would be at the reception desk. He did not reply. She told the clerk that she had texted this information. Just as she turned to leave, she realised that he was standing behind her. His face was dark and very angry; Olivia had not seen him like this before. She assumed he was very drunk—yet again. She took the key off the desk and pushed it into his chest. "There's your key, then. I'm off to the beach."

Olivia swung round and made for the large glass doors of the hotel. In order to reach the beach, she had to go around the huge swimming pool and walk some distance. As she set off, she heard the doors opening and then Ty's voice split the air as he bellowed at her. "Where the fuck do you think you're going, then? Got a date, have you? Gonna meet him on the beach, are you?"

The place was swarming with people swimming and reclining on sun loungers. Everyone heard. Heads swung round, and Olivia was painfully aware of the keen interest in her situation— the stares, and sniggers, and whispers. She pulled her beach bag more firmly onto her shoulder, turned, and said quietly and firmly, "Just go away, Ty. Leave me alone. I want to go and sunbathe on the beach—in peace."

She continued walking, and he ran up behind her and snatched the bag from her shoulder. He sat down on the sun lounger with the bag between his legs. He continued his rant in a loud, aggressive voice. "Gonna meet your date here, eh? What's his name? Who is he? Do I know him? Gonna have a quick fuck somewhere, were you?" HIs eyes were wild, and Olivia felt real fear. People were again staring at them, and she just wished that the beach would swallow her up and remove her from this nightmare—this terrible repeat of the first one.

"I simply want to sit here and watch the sun go down over the sea, Ty. Just leave me alone."

"Oh no! You're going to fucking meet some guy to fuck with him, aren't you—you fucking slag!" The volume increased, and the stares and comments of the onlookers were driving Olivia to a state she had never before known. Suddenly, almost without her being aware of her actions, her arm came up, hard and fast, and she hit Ty across his face with strength she was unaware of possessing. His head snapped backwards, and he almost fell over. Olivia turned away and spread out her towel. Trying desperately to ignore the interest of the onlookers, she attempted to lie on the lounger and relax. The tirade continued unabated.

"Who is he, then? Do I know him? Go and meet him, then; I'll come with you. Should be fun. You're nothing but a fucking liar. Pretending to sunbathe. Think I don't fucking well know what you're up to—going to meet your bit on the side to fuck him. Don't you get enough fucking from me, then?" It went on until Olivia felt as if her head would burst. She held back the tears which were welling. Her dreams of a holiday of peace, sun, togetherness, and love were shattering around her. She closed her eyes again, and the toxic cloud of abuse continued to flow over her. She got up and walked to another lounger. Just as she was about to sit on it, Ty rushed up and grabbed her bag. He was carrying a large bright-orange bag to hold his precious, well-guarded mobile. He put one bag over each shoulder and hurried towards the sea. Laughing in a cold, manic way, he shouted at Olivia. "You're gonna meet some guy to fuck you, just watch me wade out to sea." And he began to walk into the brilliant blue water.

Olivia thought, *He thinks I'm going to run after him—I'm not that stupid.* Deep in her mind she knew that if she did so, he would grab her by her hair and push her under the water. She had no doubts at all. She was angry, because the bag contained things that didn't matter but also her sandals and, far more importantly, her mobile phone.

"Give me back my phone! How the hell can I keep in touch with home and work and my kids!" She stood watching as he waded in further and further. Now he was waist-deep, and she didn't care. She didn't care at all. Let him go on and on until he disappeared and drowned. She felt nothing. Ignoring the stares and comments, she turned quickly and walked back as fast as she could to the hotel. She went to the reception desk and told the clerk firmly, "You must be aware that there has been a very bad domestic between myself and Mr Benton. He has just decided to walk out into the sea with my bag and my door key and my mobile. Please, could you print me another key?" The clerk immediately did this. Olivia then walked over to security, where four strapping Jamaican guards were clearly very well aware of her situation. Olivia smiled at them.

"I know you know what's happening. Mr Benton has decided to wade out into the sea with his bag and mobile phone, and also my bag, which has a lot of my stuff in it, including my phone. If you do manage to recover my bag, please could you have my phone sent up to my room immediately?"

The tallest, a bearded, thickset man, smiled. "Yes, mam. Are you OK, mam?"

"Yes—so far." Olivia smiled back. "Thank you." She took the lift up to the room and went to shower. Her gown was hanging on the back of the bathroom door. Ty had thrown his gown onto the floor that morning, his usual untidy habit. The room maid had picked it up, thinking it was a large towel and put it in the laundry—Olivia found this out later when she went to retrieve it. Just as she slipped into her gown after a refreshing shower, she heard pounding on the door. Then the noise increased; he was kicking the door, shaking it with each blow. Olivia was terrified.

"Let me in this fucking room! Open it or I'll break it down!" She opened it, and Ty pushed her aside. He tore open cupboard doors and threw her clothes everywhere. He looked in every possible space—under the bed, out on the patio, even under the armchairs and in the toilet.

"Where is the fucking guy? Where is he! I know he's in here. I saw that security guard go running up the stairs to warn you. I know that guy's around here somewhere!" His eyes were wide and wild; Olivia was very afraid. Was this just his jealous raging suspicion, was it drink, or was it a lethal combination of both? Olivia knew she would be in the firing line, and she just huddled silently, trying not to attract his attention.

"So, I waded out in the sea, and you ran up here to find the guy you wanted to fuck, eh? You bitch, you fucking slut—I'll find the bastard, don't you worry! Look at you, all naked and waiting to be fucked. You shameless slag." He continued tearing open doors and looking in every possible place. Then he stopped in front of Olivia, breathing heavily, his face twisted with anger. He had noticed the absence of his bath gown.

"Oh, so now I see what happened. He put my gown over his uniform and ran for it, did he?" He looked around again, then strode over to the table where the telephone was, and picked it up. He dialled the front desk. He asked to speak to security. Olivia held her breath.

"Right, I want to make a complaint. One of your guards made a date with my wife to fuck her while I was away from the hotel, and I caught another one sneaking up to warn him I was coming back." There was silence. Then Ty said, "Whatever." He swung round onto Olivia and began to abuse her again, making sarcastic apologies for having disturbed her "date".

Olivia was totally bewildered. She had no idea what had spiralled Ty into this crazy outburst. She was at the end of her endurance.

There was a knock at the door, and a woman from management entered, holding a clipboard. She was flanked, very closely on each side by a hefty black security guard. They stood in the en suite, between the bedroom and the lounge, facing Ty firmly.

"I understand that you have made a complaint against my security staff, Mr Benton," the woman said, looking at Ty steadily.

"Yes, this guard arranged to meet my wife on the beach to fuck her. Her bag's full of condoms and KY jelly so that they could have a good time." The woman glanced at Olivia. Olivia tipped up her wicker beach bag, and the contents spilled onto the carpet. There were the pegs to hold her beach towel to the sunbed, a towel, a book, sunglasses, sun blocker—all the usual beach paraphernalia. Ty had taken her mobile phone. Olivia looked at the woman. It was clear that she thought that she was dealing with one very sane woman and one very disturbed man. Then Ty started another tirade, spitting his words out with hatred and blazing anger. He knew that their security guard had arranged this. He knew that he was walking around with his bath gown on so he would be seen easily. If they called the police, he wouldn't be there long, because he—Ty—Benton—knew the superintendent of police personally, and when the guy got out he would sort him out.

Ty subjected the two security men and the female manager to over thirty minutes of this. Then he said viciously and cuttingly, "The trouble with you lot is that you're still in slavery. You'll treat a white woman better than you'll treat me, because I'm black." The woman looked at Olivia, wide-eyed. "It's all right, I'm used to it," Olivia told her with a smile.

The racist rant continued. The woman tried to get Ty to write his complaint down, but he resisted. "Sir, I can't deal with a complaint unless you put it in writing for me."

"I don't need to do that. He's lost his job anyway, and I'll deal with him." The implication was clear. The guards looked at Ty silently; they knew he was threatening violence towards their colleague through his knowledge of the high-ranking police official.

After about fifteen minutes of this, Olivia had had enough. Ty was holding both his phone and her iPhone, one in each hand. "Give me back my phone, Ty." He continued ranting, ignoring her completely. She moved closer to him. "Ty, give that phone back. It's my only link with my family in England, and my business." Still he shouted, not even appearing to register Olivia's existence.

"Give it back to me ..." By now she was next to him. Then Ty raised his phone above his head as high as he could and threw it with enormous force down onto the floor, where it shattered. He picked up the pieces and stamped on them. The phone was demolished. Fortunately, whilst he was doing this, he had put Olivia's phone down on the bed. She walked over, took it, and went to sit on the settee. She was exhausted by all the drama. For the first time in this relationship she had felt actual deep fear. She looked up at the security manager.

"I think the best thing you can do is to leave. You're not going to get any sense out of him; it's a waste of your time."

The woman looked at Olivia, clearly concerned for her. "Are you sure you will be all right?"

"Yes, I'll be all right." Olivia ushered them all towards the door. Ty had gone out onto the veranda. "The phone's by my bed—and I don't want him back in this room. I would appreciate your swift arrival if I have to call you." She had already told them this. Ty had refused to move, and as he was a hotel guest, they were unable to force him to leave. Olivia had explained that he had family there, about the wedding, everything. But she was adamant. She did not want him in that room with her. He had told her that he was not leaving; if she didn't want him with her, she could move. She told him that he could sleep on the balcony then. It was massive and had huge recliners, more than adequate for comfortable sleeping. And it was warm.

Olivia went out onto the balcony for a cigarette while Ty was in the bathroom. She lit up a cigarette and inhaled deeply. She was annoyed with herself, as she had managed to kick this habit, but since meeting Ty she had resumed it in a big way. When she heard Ty coming out of the bathroom, she put out her cigarette and went back into the bedroom. Ty was standing in the doorway with a smirk on his face. It was a strange, disturbing look that made him look almost insane. Olivia looked at him. "I suggest that you go out onto the balcony and sleep," she told him.

"I'm not going to sleep." He spoke in a low, threatening voice. "You kick me out on the balcony like a dog—like you always do." Olivia gritted her teeth and willed herself not to rise to his aggression. Why start a war? When they got back, she was going to kick him out—and this would be final. This was the last, absolutely the last, straw that had broken her tough back. She faced him. "Ty, I don't know what the hell you think you're playing at. Your behaviour this evening was absolutely abysmal. I'm not putting up with any more of it. I've taken too much already. We're done." She walked into the room but then turned to him again. "You're not sleeping in this bed with me. You're sleeping on the balcony."

Ty was silent. Olivia went into the bathroom, ran water into the handbasin, and washed her hands and face. When she returned, Ty was not there. She went out onto the balcony and, to her horror, saw Ty sitting on the edge, overlooking a steep drop to the paving below. He was rocking to and fro— dangerously close to the edge. Olivia's heart leapt.

Oh my God, she thought. *Even if he doesn't mean to do anything real, he could fall accidentally, and if he does it'll kill him.* Despite everything, she did not want him to be harmed, certainly not to be killed in this manner. What should she do? If she just ignored him, he would think that she really didn't care a damn—and that wasn't true, because deep in her heart she still loved this wild, paradoxical, problematic man. If she went to him and tried to dissuade him, he might throw himself off the edge of the balcony just to prove something. He was desperately unpredictable and unreliable.

She walked towards him. "Ty." She spoke quietly but very firmly. "Just get down and come back in." And she walked back into their room. If the worst happened, she could say, truthfully, that she had asked him to get down. The hotel security staff would back up her claim that he was behaving irrationally and aggressively—if she had to face a coroner. By the time she got into the bedroom and turned round to see what was happening, Ty had simply walked back into the room again. Again Olivia ignored him. Then she saw him sit down with a glass of vodka in his hand, and she realised that he was also taking a handful of what she assumed to be beta blockers. Then he started to undo another strip of tablets. Olivia grabbed the strip and tried to take them from Ty's hand, but the strip was perforated, and as she pulled at them, they came away. Ty had managed to swallow about eight of them. *Oh God*, Olivia thought. *He'll go out and lie on the settee on the balcony, and he'll just die. I don't know what else he's taken.* And then she went back in time, back to her brother's suicide and her terrible guilt at not being with him to prevent it. She could not let this happen, although part of her longed to just walk away and let Ty get on with his own attention-seeking dramas.

She walked over to the house phone and picked it up. "Could I speak to the nurse, please?" There was a short delay, and then a click, and the hotel nurse was asking how she could help.

"Yes, I've got my estranged partner here, and he's just taken an overdose."

"Madam, please would you put the phone down, and I'll ring you back. It's security and medical policy."

"Of course." Olivia replaced the receiver, and soon the nurse called back. "He's still taking tablets," Olivia told her.

"I'll have to come up, madam." She was soon there.

"I've seen him take at least eight beta blockers," Olivia told the nurse, "and a whole strip of these other things." The wrappings were thrown all over the carpet around Ty.

"Mr Benton, how many tablets have you taken, and what are they? I've called an ambulance."

"I don't know how many fucking tablets I've taken, and I don't fucking care." Ty was slumped, sullen and aggressive. "And you can cancel the bloody ambulance. I'm not going anywhere."

"I'm afraid I have to, Mr Benton, it's hotel policy. I have no choice—"

Olivia interrupted the nurse. "If you're taking him to hospital, I'm not paying the bill, and I'm not claiming on my travel insurance policy, either. He's Jamaican—take him to the local hospital and he can sort the bill out himself."

The nurse walked to the phone, picked it up, and cancelled the ambulance. Then she went over to Ty and asked him, "What tablets did you actually take, Mr Benton?" Ty didn't answer. The nurse was trying to keep patient. She could see that Ty was unstable and was talking to him in a quiet, calm manner. She asked him once more to tell her what he had taken, or she would be forced to recall the ambulance and have him taken to the local hospital for a stomach wash. Olivia told the nurse that she had watched him take at least eight beta blockers as well as eight of the pills in the unknown strip.

At this Ty realised that unless he did something he would be forcibly removed and taken away to the hospital. He put his hand in his pocket and pulled it out again. His fist was closed. Olivia put her hand underneath his, and he dropped a small pile of tablets into her hand. These were the tablets that would do most damage, drop his blood pressure so low that his heart would stop. He had only pretended to swallow them! Olivia had simply assumed that he had taken beta blockers. The nurse watched this with some confusion. She asked Ty to pass her the strip from the pills that he had swallowed. He passed the tablets to the nurse, who looked at them.

The nurse looked up at Olivia with a raised eyebrow. The look on her face was not one of amusement, because of the annoying waste of her time and the time of an ambulance crew, but of mild resignation. "Mr Benton, what I suggest you do is drink lots of water to get these tablets through your system as quickly as possible." She smiled sympathetically at Olivia, and then she left.

Olivia looked at the strip from which Ty had actually swallowed pills. Her mouth twitched. They were strong laxatives. *Ah well*, she thought. *He's going to have the runs all day tomorrow. Serve him bloody right. I've had all the drama I can take, including the balcony scene.* She looked at Ty. "Just get out there on that balcony. I don't want you in the same room as me."

"OK, I'll sleep out there like a dog." He went out.

Olivia went to lock the door to the balcony, but then she reconsidered; Ty might just erupt and kick it open. What if he wanted to pee during the night? She pretended to lock it, closed the heavy curtains across the doors, and climbed, exhausted, into bed. She fell asleep immediately. At about four in the morning, she woke when she heard Ty coming into the room. He climbed into bed and rolled over to Olivia's side of the bed. "Get away from me—now." Ty obediently moved away and perched on the edge of the bed. Fortunately it was a very large bed. Olivia drifted back to sleep. She awoke at nine o'clock to blazing sun and a warm breeze lifting the curtains and touching her face. Ty was out on the balcony, smoking and drinking beer. Olivia made herself a coffee, very strong and very sweet, and sat on the settee in the room, drinking it thankfully. She looked up when Ty came in.

"I know what that security guard's name is now." He looked triumphant.

So he was still obsessing about it, was he? Olivia wanted to push him off the balcony. "I beg your pardon. What on earth are you talking about?"

"He sent a message. Says, "Stop snoring. I can hear you through the bedroom door'."

"Amir—that's that guard's name—Amir." Amir was a Tunisian friend whom Olivia had known for quite some years. She had known him, but certainly not in the biblical sense. He was a close friend who constantly WhatsApped her, chatting about anything and everything. There was certainly no sex involved. It was too good a friendship to ruin with that. Amir had a great sense of humour, and he knew Olivia was in Jamaica—it was the sort of thing he would send.

Ty moved over to the hotel phone on the table next to Olivia. He picked it up and dialled. "Is that security? Tell me, did you have a security guard on duty last night called Amir?" There was a pause. "Right. Thank you." He glared down at Olivia.

"Yes, there was an Amir on duty last night, and now I know what I'm gonna do."

Olivia knew that Ty was lying and that there had been no security guard with that name. "So, Ty, you've been reading my phone again, have you? You walk around with your phone surgically attached to you in case anybody dares to even glance at it, and I can't even go to sleep without you nosing into mine. Amir is just an old friend; I've known him for years. He lives in Tunisia, and the joke is that if he could hear me through the hotel door from there then I must snore very loudly. But it's a joke Ty, and you can't seem to understand jokes, unless they're at someone else's expense. But if you want to carry on like that, just get on with it. It makes no bloody difference to me anyway, Ty. At the end of the day, when we get to the airport, I'll make sure our seats are apart, and when we get back, we're done. Now go away and leave me alone."

"Oh yes, I'll go away, and you'll see; I'll get that Amir." His eyes were dark again. The angry, sulky look was there.

"If you want to get Amir, then you get him, but you'll have to go a bloody long way to find him." Ty went out onto the balcony.

Then there was a knock on the door. Olivia opened it. There was the woman manager, flanked by another two burly security guards. "Good morning madam. Are you all right? Can we speak with Mr Benton?"

"Yes, I'm fine, thanks." Olivia called to Ty, "There's someone here to see you."

Ty came into the room. He looked at the trio defiantly. "Yes. What?"

"Mr Benton, we've booked you on the eleven o'clock transport." It was then about nine forty. Olivia had packed Ty's belongings into his suitcases the night before, while the security guards were there to protect her. She had wanted him out then.

"If you want to get your things together, we'll escort you down there."

Ty sneered. "So you're gonna kick me out, and you're gonna leave *her* here ..." He indicated Olivia's presence with a toss of his head.

The manager spoke again. "I need you to leave here with us now, Mr Benton."

Ty moved around the room, picking up his various bits and pieces. One security guard was outside in the corridor with Ty's bags, and the other one held the door open. He had no choice but to go with them. Olivia heard him screaming at them as he went. "So you kick me out because I'm black—just like you—and you leave her because she's white, and she's the poor little woman ..." His voice faded as he disappeared down the corridor.

The manager had stayed. Olivia turned to her. "You've booked him on the eleven o'clock transport. Is my three o'clock booking still on?"

"Yes, madam, you're fine for three. I suggest you stay up here out of the way and try to relax." She smiled and left. Olivia sank down thankfully into the cushions of the balcony settee and lit a cigarette. She closed her eyes and gradually drifted into a half doze. The door was locked. Security would prevent Ty from returning. For now she had a temporary respite.

Then the texts started. "I know it's too late, but I will love you for the rest of my life." Then there was a text about changing his flight booking, and Olivia told him to just get on with it. She closed her eyes, leaned back, and blew out a stream of smoke. Her phone chirped. She looked at the screen. "I love you so much."

"Yes, Ty, you love me so much that you called security and told them I was going to meet some random security guard on the beach."

Then the message flashed back. "Baby, I'm so sorry. Please forgive Daddy."

Olivia was whirled back in time, back to the house up in the north, and the sperm donor, and the verbal abuse, and the beatings, and the sexual fumbling, and her poor, tiny siblings, and the whole black, painful misery of her early days. She shuddered. Then she turned to her phone. "You have to be joking."

Ty came right back. "You are my life."

"Ty, you have told me how you feel. I'm an idiot, evil, stupid, thick; you even told me it wouldn't take you long to hate me. Get on with it, then. I agree. I'm an idiot. You even told me you hoped I caught AIDS and died."

"I was angry when I said that."

"Good for you. Afraid it's unacceptable to me."

"I'm not leaving. I'm waiting here."

"As you wish." Then he asked her for cigarettes. She texted him and told him to go to the shop, get some, and charge them to her. He texted back that he refused to do that, as the cigarettes at the shop were nasty. Olivia only had two packets left, and she certainly wasn't going down to be anywhere near Ty. She called his brother Sebastian and asked him to tell Ty to go to the shop and get the cigarettes if he was so desperate. She told Ty this, and he said he would. He asked what Olivia was up to. He told her he felt sick to his stomach.

"Baby, dying to hold you."

"That won't happen again, ever."

"I know baby. When you coming down? Sebastian's borrowing a truck, and he's going to get us both some cigarettes, and he'll phone me from the gate."

"OK." There was a pause.

Then Ty texted, "Come back to me, baby." Olivia launched into a long text, telling him why there could be no love, how he had done so many dreadful things, mainly to her. About the accusations of sex with strangers. Lying to the security. Smashing his phone—everything. All she had wanted was his respect but she'd got nothing but disdain and abuse.

Ty replied, "OK, I get it." Half an hour later he asked her, "Please come down."

"No, I'm fine here. Just waiting for the bellboy to help me down to the transport."

"How long?" Olivia didn't answer.

"OK, I give up."

Still she didn't reply. She just leaned back into the cushions and smoked. Soon it was after two in the afternoon, and Olivia knew that she had to go down to reception, settle up an outstanding bill of some sort, and check out. She went down and did it. Ty was sitting in the lobby. The bellboy took Olivia's cases and loaded them into the transport, and she climbed in. The shuttle was almost empty, and Ty appeared and sat down beside her. Olivia ignored him. She looked out of the window all the way to the airport. On arrival, she got out, took her case and cabin bag, and went to stand in line to check in for the flight. Still she ignored Ty. She handed over her ticket and passport, and then the official came up to her.

"Madam, we have, unfortunately, overbooked. If you will volunteer to give up your seat, we'll put you up in a five-star hotel, and we'll give you a free return ticket to anywhere in the world." Olivia briefly considered this and then said, "No, sorry, I can't do this. I've got a business to run. I have to get back."

Then Ty was leaning over her shoulder. "Are you mental or something?" Olivia picked up her ticket and walked away. She hoped Ty would take up the offer, and she could get rid of him. She sped towards security, but he was behind her. She only had her handbag and her cabin bag with her, so she was able to elude Ty and lose him in duty free. She made for the coffee bar and stood in the queue, exhaling thankfully. But he appeared again behind her. She realised that he expected her to buy him a coffee, but she didn't. She just took hers and sat down at a table. He followed, sitting down opposite her.

"What the hell are you playing at, Ty? I don't want to see you or talk to you, and I don't want you with me, so go away."

Ty looked at her, then got up and walked away. Olivia finished her coffee, texted a few friends, and then got up to go to the departure gate. She had to pass Ty, who was sitting near the gate. He held up his hand. "Can I just have a word with you for a minute?"

Olivia walked over. "Yes, Ty, what is it?"

"Well, you know I volunteered to give up my seat—"

"Yes, Ty. Stay in luxury for another week and fly back premier class, because it's the last bit of high living you're going to get. You'll not get another thing out of me."

Ty told her that he knew it was all over, because of the previous night. Then he began the familiar, much-used rant of loving Olivia always—she knew it word for word. Ty sat there talking, but it just went into the air. Olivia didn't register a word. She looked at him and saw the familiar handsome face. He looked tired, and his eyes were pink—he had contracted conjunctivitis from his mother, she thought.

Ty approached the hostess on the boarding gate, wanting to know if he was on that flight. The hostess didn't know. Olivia knew that Ty would start insisting that he was contagious with his eye infection and thus unable to mix with the other passengers—anything to stop him flying back. Olivia boarded the plane and moved into premier class, where she settled into the large, comfortable seat. At least without him she got two seats to herself, and peace and quiet. It was done—finished. Olivia had rung her contracts manager at her business and asked him to remove the Audi sports car that Ty drove and hide it somewhere. The car was hers. She didn't want Ty returning and driving it away. She looked out of the window, impatiently waiting for the engines to rev up and change note, so she'd know that she was flying away from that bloody Jamaican and his stresses, moods, temper tantrums, illnesses, and financial demands. At last she could escape.

Just then a bottle of water landed in her lap. She looked up to see Ty standing there, smiling. "Well, it looks like we're flying back together, baby."

Olivia scowled. She threw the bottle of water onto his seat, turned away, and looked out of the window again. They hardly exchanged during the nine-hour flight. It was an awkward experience. Ty slept most of the way. He seemed to have been got hold of tranquillisers of some sort.

When they landed, he followed Olivia outside. "Are you gonna give me a lift? Or I'm stranded—got no way of getting home. I wouldn't leave a dog like this ..."

"That's all right. I won't leave you stranded—I'm not like you. I'll drop you off wherever you want me to." Olivia paid for a taxi back to the hotel and paid for the extra time the car had been in the secure parking. Ty loaded the cases into the boot. "Where do you want to go, then?"

Ty shrugged. "Suppose you'll have to take me to Hertfordshire." He gave Olivia the post code. She put it into the satnav and drove off. They hadn't gone far when Ty asked her to pull in, off the road. Olivia did so. Ty turned to her with tears running down his face. "Baby, please ..."

Olivia knew what was coming. She sat and listened, and she looked at Ty's face. He looked tired, desolate, unwell, and desperate. He was a human being with problems and needs. And Olivia's heart began to soften. She tried to resist—she tried to be hard—but she saw this man that she really loved, and she just wanted to curl up in his arms and feel his body on, and in, her body. Inside her she was crying for him. She said, softly. "Ty, stop. OK, just stop—I hear you. We'll go home." Ty put his hand over her hand and held it there. Then he lifted it to his lips and kissed it lingeringly. They drove home in silence. Ty fell asleep very quickly. Olivia was exhausted when they arrived. They brought the cases out of the car and into the house. They took food out of the freezer and defrosted it. Ty prepared it, and they sat eating. Ty glanced at Olivia from time to time with a look that unnerved her. It was undoubtedly a look of love and passion, but there was also a dark hint of uncontrolled anger—something just waiting to erupt, something that Ty was powerless to hold in check. He started drinking very soon, and then the manic talking began. Ty began laughing in a sinister way and talking to himself in an animated, frightening manner. Olivia was a tough woman, battle hardened and totally able to take care of herself, but Ty's behaviour disturbed her very much. She was well used to his vodka-fuelled rages, but now things were escalating to black madness. Ty was walking in and out of the garden, and the kitchen, and talking and laughing loudly to himself. When they went up to bed, he went into the en suite, where Olivia heard him again laughing inanely and talking. She went to the door and listened. Ty was saying, in a chanting voice, like a child reciting a nursery rhyme, "Wash your face before your arse; wash your face before your arse ..."

over and over again. He was laughing in a very strange manner in between each sentence.

Olivia was scared and disturbed by the bizarre performance. Ty got into bed and continued his chanting. By now Olivia was really frightened. She turned to him. "Either you go downstairs and sleep in the other bedroom or I will." Ty looked at her vaguely.

"No, no, I'll stop it now—I'll stop it now." Olivia barely slept an hour that night. Ty went downstairs, where Olivia heard him walking about, still mumbling to himself. He slept on the chair in the lounge, but Olivia was fearful that he would come upstairs again. She pushed a heavy chair against her bedroom door so that she would have some kind of warning of Ty's coming if the worst happened. The night passed. Olivia awoke, tired and dreading whatever was to come. She drove to her office and set to work; there was a lot to catch up with. She temporarily forgot Ty and his problem existence.

Then Olivia got a text at work to say that Ty had left for London. Olivia had returned the Audi to him, after stressing that the car was hers. Ty said he was going to London to see his eldest son, Jamari, who had flown over from Antigua. He had landed before Ty left for Jamaica, and they hadn't been able to meet up. He called Olivia to tell her that he was bringing Jamari back to the house and asked if that would be OK. Later he called her to say that he had turned up and found that Jamari had gone to the Notting Hill Carnival.

"I'm fucking furious, baby," he said, but he was laughing as if it were nothing. Olivia was very annoyed. Deep inside her she felt that this had just been an excuse to go and visit Shirley. Olivia no longer tried to pretend to herself that Ty and Shirley were just good friends—exes—or that Ty only visited to see his daughter. Indeed, Ty had frequently made it clear that his daughter had little respect or feeling for him, so Olivia realised with anger that Ty was off to see another member of his harem. Mentally she somehow knew that he had more than one other woman. It was a picture she tried to dispel from her thoughts, but little by little she had to face unpleasant realities. Ty told her that he needed to go and visit his friend in Nantwich, as he had nowhere to go for the night and he had to see him. Ty needed these breaks quite often. He seemed to run from one circle of friends to the other endlessly. Olivia let it go. Maybe a visit might calm him down a little. Then he sent her a WhatsApp photo of a gun and a magazine beside it; he said he was bringing it back with him.

"What the hell is that for?" texted Olivia.

"Tell you when I get there," Ty replied.

"You're not bringing that thing into my house. Not with my grandchildren around. Don't even think about it!"

Then followed many texts asking Olivia what she was doing; where was she going; was she going to see her son, Matthew; when would she be back …

Olivia texted back, "Good grief."

Ty replied, "Sorry, I shouldn't have asked. I guess we aren't talking, then."

"I guess not.'

"I'm talking to you, aren't I?" She felt he was on edge. Where was he?

Then, at ten-minute intervals, came "Baby?"

"Need to talk to you."

"I guess you win," Olivia messaged him. "Just go and see your son."

"Baby, I don't wanna do anything to upset you." Then silence. Then he asked if Olivia could sort out his recent speeding ticket that they had come home to. Olivia worked out that Ty had gone online and seen that he would have to go on an awareness course to avoid a fine and maybe lose points. The course cost £90 pounds. If Olivia sorted it for him, she would pay the cost. Olivia had just texted, "Yes." But when she looked at the cost, she simply closed the laptop and thought to herself, *Yes, this is what it's all about: money and sex—and God knows where else he's going for these things.*

On August 29, Ty texted that he was going to see his friend. Olivia texted back. "That's right. Run away again."

On August 30, Ty arrived with Jamari. He was a handsome younger version of his father, 23 years old, polite and helpful. Olivia and he got on well together. However, she was aware that the boy seemed confused. When they were introduced, he seemed puzzled at her name. Olivia just thought that it must be her. They had a pleasant time together that day and evening, and Jamari stayed overnight. Olivia went to work the next morning, and, when she was about to come home, she texted Ty to put the kettle on. He texted back that he had just left to take Jamari back to London. She heard little from him after that, but when she did have a brief word with him, he was tense and seemed under pressure. After that his texts were terse and gradually petered out. Then his phone was turned off.

On September 2, Ty kept texting her frantically all morning. He said he had an important meeting that he wanted her to help him with. She did not bother to reply until after one in the afternoon. She was going to have her nails done. Through texts that weren't answered, Ty worked himself up into a frenzy. They spoke as Olivia was leaving her nail artist and walking along the high street. As she stood, trying to hear over the traffic noise, a man walked by. He was shouting to his wife, who was ahead of him in the thoroughfare. Ty heard the man's voice, and instantly reacted. "Who the fuck is that? Who are you with—you're with a man! I can hear him."

Olivia switched her phone off abruptly. Later Ty texted her to say that there was something important; would she call him. Olivia called, but he hung up on her. Then Olivia texted him: "No point in telling me to call and hanging up on me yet again. Just come back, and I'll pack all your stuff." Olivia had taken Ty back reluctantly. She told herself that she did not need this. She didn't want him in her house. She had really had enough. When she returned home, she determinedly went around the house, picking up Ty's belongings and putting them in black dustbin liner bags. There were eight bags in all to show for his life. She went up to bed. At least she could sleep peacefully whilst Ty was away living his mysterious, sham life.

September 3, Ty texted and asked Olivia what she was doing. She told him she was working and was busy. Ty replied that it was a shame that he couldn't talk to the one he loved, and Olivia replied that yes, it was, wasn't it? And then there was nothing but silence. Olivia was relieved, yet puzzled. She was quite content not to have to tolerate his nonstop texts, which disturbed her demanding business life. On the other hand, she worried about what might have happened to him. She reasoned that he had spent the last four years disappearing, going off the radar, and not answering texts or calls. He would survive. Again Olivia was able to sleep soundly.

By the fourth of September, Ty was still away. He did not call or text. Olivia felt uneasy. She felt a gathering of storm clouds, an inevitability. She had a chilling, nagging sense of something about to unfold. She knew that this relationship was not going to work. But just as certainly, she knew that it would end disastrously. Meanwhile, she worked hard and tried to forget her personal burdens. The day ended, and Olivia drove home. Dark storm clouds were massing in the September skies. Thunder rumbled menacingly. Olivia shuddered slightly as she shut her front door. Ty did not contact her. She slept fitfully. In the early hours of the morning, the thunder growled across the dark sky again. Something was building. Olivia slept.

On the morning of September 5, Olivia drove to work. As she drove, Ty tried to ring her. She was negotiating heavy traffic and did not answer. He rang again, and again she could not take his call. She reached the office and picked up the large pile of mail from her desk. Then he rang again. "What's bloody going on? Aren't you picking up calls, now? Got another man there, have you?"
Olivia ignore this and said, "Good morning, Ty. What do you want? I was driving to the office. I don't take calls in traffic when I should be concentrating. Is this important? I'm busy. And I could remind you that you've ignored me for some days."
"Right. I've fucking well had enough of being treated like a fucking dog. I'm going back to the States and to normal people again."

"That's fine, Ty. If you want to go, then go; I'm not stopping you."

"I want my fucking passport. It's in the house."

"Oh, you can have that—and all your other stuff. It's packed up and ready for you to take. Come over just after lunchtime and get it all." Ty clicked off the line abruptly.

Olivia left the office, drove home, and put all the bin bags outside on the paved path in the garden. She put Ty's passport in a plastic bag and left it under a stone, next to the bags. She locked the front door and left the key in the lock, preventing Ty from using his house key. Then she went out of the patio doors and locked them behind her. She could get back in through these doors. Ty hadn't got a key for them. She left the gate to the garden unlocked. Then she got into the car and texted Ty. He actually answered her straight away.

"OK, Ty. I've put your passport in a plastic bag and left it under a big stone next to all the bin bags I packed for you. They're all in the back garden, and the gate is unlocked. Come and get them before five o'clock, please."

He rang after only a few seconds. "I can't make it until about Saturday. Don't leave them outside; it might rain. Baby, there's no need for all this. Just listen to me—please! I love you. You know that. I'll change—I ..." Ty's voice broke. Olivia had seen and heard the tears and sobs before. She wasn't going to listen. "OK Ty, I have to go. I'll put the stuff in the shed, with your passport." She switched the call off. Then she drove back to work. The day was stressful, but that was nothing new to Olivia. She ran a business, sat on committees, made policies, trained people, addressed important meetings—it was all part of her world. She drove home, pulled into the road, and then slowed, quickly. Ty had reversed his car into the driveway, right up to the back garden gate. Her phone told her that he had texted her. Olivia looked at the text. Ty told her that he had picked up his things and was soon going. He said he just wanted to see her again—just once, for the last time. Then he would go and leave her in peace.

Olivia drove away and around the surrounding back streets, hoping that Ty would be gone when she returned. It was nearly eight in the evening. Olivia was angry. It was her own home. Why could she not just park her car and walk into her own home? She would do that—just walk in and lock the door. When she reached the house, Ty's car was parked in front of the house, pointing down the hill. Olivia pulled her car up onto the driveway, picked up her handbag and briefcase, and went to get out of the car. And he was there, standing beside the door of her car. Olivia got out and shut the door.

"Ty, what are you doing?" Ty looked at her for just a moment, and that look was one that Olivia had not seen before. It was one of pain, despair, and total black fear. Ty was weeping. Olivia was not repelled, as she normally was. This was the wrenching, pleading crying of someone in genuine need. He was hysterical. Olivia did not want this to attract attention from her neighbours, as Ty's sobs were loud. She took his hand and led him gently into the garden, where she sat him down on a garden chair. She put a cigarette into his hand, lit it, and then lit herself one.

Then the pleading began. But it was different this time. This was a man in terrible need of help. Olivia felt part of her weaken. She still loved him, and she could not bear to see the real misery this man was in. He told her that he knew everything was his fault, that it was his drinking. He said that he was trying to get help with it, going to register with Alcoholics Anonymous. He grasped at Olivia's hand. "Baby, help me! Please don't throw me out. I really love you. I can't survive without you. I don't know what to do anymore." His eyes were full of genuine remorse and misery. "Take me back, baby, please! Let's start again."

Olivia looked at him. She spoke quietly but very firmly. "No, Ty, no more." Olivia was deeply concerned with Ty's seriously unstable mental state. He was so obviously ill and in need of help. As a decent, normal human being, she could not turn him out to drive away to nothing and nobody. He was not capable of it.

"OK, Ty, look. Tonight you can sleep on the big chair and stool downstairs, and tomorrow I'm going to ring the doctor's surgery and get a doctor to help you. You aren't well. But—when you've seen the doctor and got some sort of help—you're leaving." Olivia settled Ty in the chair, made him a milky drink, something he normally never touched, and went upstairs to bed. Again she put the heavy bedroom chair across the door in case Ty should venture up there. But he didn't.

September 6, in the morning, Olivia went down to make herself a cup of tea. Ty was still sitting in the chair, weeping softly. Olivia went to the phone and called the surgery. "My partner really needs a visit urgently. He's presenting with symptoms of a nervous breakdown."

"All right. The doctor will call him back and sort it from there," the receptionist told Olivia.

"The doctor's going to ring you. Stay there, and keep your phone by you." As if, thought Olivia, he had ever been separated from that phone.

"Yes, all right, all right, all right," Ty mumbled. He looked stressed and unhappy.

Olivia called him at twelve from work.

"Has the doctor rung you yet?"

"No, not yet."

"OK." Olivia called the doctor's surgery. She stressed that the doctor's call was urgently needed and had been promised. The reception told her to hold on for a moment, then came back to her to report that the doctor had called twice that morning, and the phone had been engaged each time.

Olivia called Ty. He picked up. "Look, Ty, the doctor's tried to get through to you twice, and you've been on that bloody phone twice. You need to stay off it! You need to talk to that doctor and get help. If you haven't spoke to the doctor by the time I get home, then you're out."

"Yes, OK. I will. Sorry."

Olivia continued her day's work, and later was driving home along the dual carriageway. She rang her daughter. She did not discuss Ty and the relationship. If her children had known the real truth about it, they would have reacted very swiftly and very angrily. Their conversation was quite long, and when Olivia looked at her call waiting, she saw that her housekeeper had called her five times. She did not particularly like the woman and was annoyed at this. "Cheeky mare. She can bloody well wait," Olivia said to her daughter.

Then she pulled off the dual carriageway and around the corner, and as she pulled up the hill towards her house, she saw a sight that froze her with horror. There were police everywhere. Policemen and police cars surrounded her house and were blocking the close so that nobody could leave or enter. She saw her housekeeper next to a policeman, and the woman pointed at Olivia. Olivia got out of her car with a sinking heart. Her legs were shaking. What had happened? Had Ty committed suicide? Great waves of fear, pain, and emotion flooded her. The memories of her brother's death overwhelmed her. She could hardly see. Was there a body in there? Everywhere there were faces—at windows, in doorways. Olivia was aware of the curious stares. She just wanted to escape it all. What had happened? Should she have left Ty like that? What had he done?

"Are you Olivia?" The policeman was speaking to her.

"Yes. What's going on? What's happened?"

"Just pull onto your driveway, and we'll have a chat." Two police cars pulled apart to let Olivia through, and she drove up beside the house and got out.

The policeman came over to her. "Do you own this house, or are you a tenant?"

"I'm a tenant; I rent this house—why?"

"We have to get your permission to search this house."

"Search it? Why?"

"A third party has reported that there might be a firearm in the house."

"A firearm?"

"Yes, a firearm—a gun."

Then, looking around her, Olivia realized that these were not ordinary police officers. They were armed—with holsters and rifles—and were wearing body armour. *Oh my God!'* she thought. *What has he done to himself—or someone else?* Her hands shook uncontrollably.

"There's no gun in my house, but feel free to search." The officer followed Olivia into the house, and a stream of armed policemen ran up and down the stairs, looking into rooms and cupboards. One turned to Olivia and asked, "Is there any room he's not allowed in, so that we can cut down the search area?"

"He lived here; he was allowed in any of the rooms." Olivia was in a nightmare—sleepwalking.

The officer who appeared to have been allocated the job of following Olivia, went out into the garden with her. Olivia sat, head in her hands, while faces peered down at her from bedroom windows and over fences.

"Oh my God. This so embarrassing!"

"Don't worry, my love. This is nothing, just tomorrow's fish-and-chip paper." He turned and waved animatedly at the chattering spectators. "Hello, hello!" He laughed.

"Oh, stop, for God's sake. You'll only make it worse!" Olivia was almost in tears.

"No, my love, it'll all be all right."

"But where's Ty—what's happened to him? Is he—?"

"He's outside, my love, in a police car. He's in handcuffs."

"Handcuffs? Why? What's wrong? What has he done?" Olivia got up. "I want to go and see him."

"Well, love, we'd much rather you didn't right now."

"Why? What has he done? For God's sake—someone tell me!"

"We're waiting for a police psychologist to come and assess him."

"Ah, so it's the doctor who's called and reported the firearm."

"We're not allowed to say, my love."

"He's obviously threatened to blow his head off then. I called the doctor this morning, because I really thought he was having a nervous breakdown."

The officer looked at her. "You know we can't confirm or deny that." Olivia had told them that she was an ex-police wife. She sat miserably, smoking, feeling like a fish in a public aquarium, as the curious neighbours continued to gawp inanely at her.

Then another armed officer came out of the house and into the garden. He spoke to Olivia's shadow. "We've found nothing here." Olivia saw a stream of heavily armed men leaving the house, causing more interest to the onlookers. Olivia's protector told her that the psychologist had finished her assessment of Ty. Olivia went into the lounge, where she stood and talked to a serious-looking, dark-haired woman.

"I've finished with him," the woman told her. "I can't find anything wrong with him."

Olivia was stunned. "Can't you?" Did this woman realise exactly what Olivia had witnessed and endured of Ty's bizarre and troubling antics? How could she not -as a trained psychologist- see just how disturbed Ty was?

"No. We've released him." Then she left. Olivia stood there in shock. What more could happen now? She walked out into the garden and dragged in several lungfuls of cigarette smoke, then she went back into the living room and, just as she passed the coffee table, Ty's phone rang. The phone that he wore next to his heart had been left behind when he was arrested. For a moment Olivia hesitated. Then the name Sophie came up on the screen with the call. It was quite an unusual name—the name that had been on those bank statements that Ty had tried to burn and destroy. Olivia picked up the phone.

"Hello, can I help you?"

There was a pause, and then a woman's voice, a slightly upper-class voice, sounding surprised, said, "Oh, I was looking for Ty."

"Ty can't come to the phone for the moment. Can I help you with something?"

There was a pause. Then the voice said, "Oh—can I ask who you are, please?"

"I'm Olivia, Ty's fiancée." There was a pregnant pause. Olivia's heart almost stopped beating. Was this woman real? Was this some sort of a sick joke—a ruse being played on her by Ty? No, it could not be. This woman was too, too real.

There was a pause again. To Olivia it seemed as if a thousand years were passing. Then the quiet, even, cultured voice said calmly, "Well, that's funny, because I've been with him for three years."

Olivia thought quickly. Suddenly everything was falling into place. "Here, take down my number, and ring me back later." Olivia hoped the woman could take the number down fast—could even find pen and paper. A few police were still drifting around in the house. As Olivia hastily reeled off her number, she looked up and saw the shadow of Ty standing at the door, laughing and joking with a policeman. The policeman was about to open the door and let Ty inside, when Olivia shouted, "Do not let that man over my doorstep! I do not want him in my house." Olivia quickly disconnected the call on Ty's mobile and replaced it on the coffee table.

The policeman shut the door and then came into the lounge. "What's going on here?"

Olivia looked at him. "I've just found out that he's got a girlfriend he's been seeing for three years. I don't want him in my house."

"Well," said the officer. "This is turning into a domestic, so I'll have to ask you a few questions. Has he any animals that he's ever been cruel to?"

"No, we don't have any animals. He doesn't—"

"Has he ever abused you, marked you?" Olivia still had bruising on the tops of her arms. She pulled up her sleeves and showed the policeman. He looked at it, pursed his lips, and wrote something down. Then he handed her a leaflet. "This will help you—you can get in touch with us if—"

Olivia pushed the leaflet away. "I don't want to know any of that. Just get him out of here and away from me. He's a done deal." The policeman went outside to answer his radio. He came back into the lounge. "He's saying he wants his stuff." During the day Ty had taken all his stuff, in its many bags, out of his car and put it all back in the shed. The officers had searched the bags, put everything back in them, and carefully knotted the tops back. Ty must have been outside the gate to the garden, trying to push it open, because the officer had his hand on the gate and was saying sternly, "Wait!" Soon the small, friendly guardian officer returned.

"We've packed all the bags into his car, but we've had to take his car keys, as he's been drinking. They're taking him to a hotel in the next town."

"I don't care where the hell you dump him—just get him out of here."

"Well, love, he'll have to come back in the morning and get his car and his stuff," he informed her. Then they were gone.

Olivia walked through into the lounge and stood in the doorway to the garden. She lit a cigarette. She felt numb, angry, and so terribly, terribly used. She had suffered all that verbal and physical abuse; been taken for so much money; given that man chance after chance; been wheedled back by his charm, and his body, and his sexual skills—and all this time he had been

270

running another woman. Olivia knew, had always known, that Ty did not just visit Shirley to see his daughter. Despite Ty's claims that he hated Shirley and that there was nothing at all between them, she knew there was something. Otherwise, why would he run back there so often? Olivia knew now that Ty was sleeping with Shirley, that her suspicions, which he denied so hotly, had been correct all along. But now—now this bombshell! He had been sleeping with another woman for some three years—when he'd been with Olivia, planning a future, proposing to her, talking about marrying her. What a bloody fool she had been!

She thought quickly. She couldn't trust him not to return. Drunk or not, he would try to get the car—despite the police. She quickly locked both the front door and patio door; then she pulled the curtains over. She sat, unable to really take in what was happening. It was later than she had thought. Had that woman got her hastily read-out number? Would she actually call? Why did she not call? Olivia lit another cigarette. Her head was almost bursting with the impact of what had happened that day—so many awful, traumatic, unreal things. Who was the quiet, well-spoken woman? A wife? A lover? She had been with him all this time—all the time Olivia and Ty had been going to Jamaica—and all the time before that. And Olivia had been suffering all Ty's moods, and drinking, and disappearances. But now Olivia knew; she knew that he had been with another woman. A woman who had shared his bed—maybe even his love—and his life. Olivia sat with her head in her hands. She was numb, yet burning with many emotions. What would she do now? If this woman did not contact her again, then she might never find out what had been happening.

Her mobile rang. She picked it up. "Hello?"

"Is that Olivia?"

"Yes?"

"Hello, this is Sophie ..."

And so the victims met.

SOPHIE, CHILDHOOD ONE.

She had known nothing but warmth and light and soft wools and silks since her earliest years. She had been fed on many things—even in the years of wartime when people were suffering shortages, there had been the connections and the backhanders. Her nanny in her crisp blue-and-white uniform ordered and arranged her days and nights. She was dressed in carefully laid out garments of the best materials: soft to the touch, warm or cool as the season demanded. Her friends were chosen for her. She, her sister, and their nanny would step into the big car, and the chauffeur, Barry, would drive them to other large houses set back in large gardens with long driveways, where butlers and maids opened doors, took coats, hats, and gloves, and ushered them subserviently to large rooms with log fires and Labradors sprawled before them with gently wagging tails. They would go up to nurseries with their friends and be entertained.

Sophie would always go straight to the bookshelves in the adults' rooms and carefully run her fingers across the leather covers and paperbacks and squint at the titles. Despite her round, metal-framed spectacles, she found the world a distant, out-of-focus place but had slowly grown accustomed to her myopic state. She would curl up with a chosen book until some adult, spotting her, would have her escorted upstairs to mix with her peers. There she would lie on the floor and read avidly, ignoring all requests to join in their games.

She rarely saw her parents. At nights her mother and stepfather would come up to the bedroom where she and her sister slept in two huge, walnut-framed beds. These were covered with large feather mattresses, duvets, and soft cotton sheets that smelt of lavender and were edged, as were the pillowcases, with lace. Lying there in her cotton nightdress, embroidered with flowers and also covered in lace and ribbons, she would await the arrival of her mother. Her stepfather was a shadowy, domineering presence whom Sophie would rather not have to acknowledge. Her mother would come in dressed for dinner. Sophie's favourite dress was the soft black velvet tight-fitting dress with the red velvet rose on the shoulder. With it her mother wore deep-blood-red rubies around her neck, in her ears, on her wrist, and on her finger. Her mother had black, shiny hair and pale skin. She had a snub nose and slanted eyes of deep brown. When her mother leant over her to kiss her goodnight, Sophie breathed in that wonderful odour of Chanel No. 5 that always evoked her mother's presence, and which Sophie remembered in the long periods of her life when she was parted from her.

Her stepfather planted a cold, begrudging kiss on her cheek, and Sophie always turned her face away, instinctively stiffening up. She knew that this was not the man she wanted to father her or to be in her life or that of her family. Her own father was discussed in secretive tones as if he were some kind of shameful secret. Later Sophie learnt that her father had been a war hero, killed when she was barely three. But this was a subject never to be raised, as her stepfather was jealous, and her father's name was anathema to him. Her father had been a professor of music, she learnt from his mother, her grandmother. Dreamy and creative but forgetful, he had once gone to the post office with her older sister in the pram. He'd completed his business, and promptly left the pram with her sister outside and walked home empty-handed, to her mother's horror. But he had loved music, and from a very early age Sophie had loved it too. At her grandmother's house she would sit on the floor of her father's studio, untouched since his death, and listen to Elgar and Beethoven and Chopin and Mozart on his gramophone, lost in a world of her own.

Sophie was a plain child, unremarkable with her slightly slanting eyes, turned-up nose, and straight hair, which was that beautiful shade of dark, coppery red known as Titian. From her earliest days she had been very short-sighted and was so used to her world that she could walk around in the dark even in strange houses, feeling the presence of furniture, walls, doors, and stairs as a palpable warning force. She wore steel-rimmed spectacles, which she often broke or lost; she was always being berated for this. She was remote; she spent hours reading or trying with one finger to pick out the melodies she had absorbed from her wind-up gramophone and its wax records. She sang loudly in strange places and elicited surprised looks. She often did not arrive for meals or arrived late. Then she would be lectured by her hated stepfather. He wore a blazer decorated with the regimental crest of the Royal Artillery in which he had been a captain in the First World War. He had a small, ridiculous moustache and smelt of tobacco and bay rum. He spoke sneeringly and sarcastically to Sophie and her sister and was domineering, controlling and abrupt with her gentle, yet cold and firmly businesslike, mother. Sophie feared and hated him with a deep burning resentment.

Her only sister was four years older than Sophie, an unemotional, hard child with a personality like that of their mother. She was brittle, judgemental, and unforgiving. Sophie wondered sometimes whether she—Sophie—had been left with this family by other beings, but then she would remember her dead father. Her sister, Rachael, was slim and had high cheekbones; so had Sophie, but they seemed inferior to her sister's. Rachael's eyes were deep green and large, and her eyebrows arched delicately above these eyes. Her lashes were long, while Sophie's were sparse and thin. Rachael's hair was a sheet of shining brunette curls. She was elegant and sociable and approved of by her mother and stepfather. She seemed to tolerate Sophie with ill-concealed malice and amusement.

The two sisters were cared for by a nanny and staff. They rose and ate and went out riding in their handmade tweed hacking jackets, jodhpurs, and leather riding boots. They visited with or without their parents, wearing appropriate and well-made garments. Sophie often thought that it would be quite pleasant to be able to choose her own clothes and shoes and her own daily routine. Their lives were organised and choreographed. The house was large, elegant, and warm, smelling of polish. Sophie had her books and music. They lived in a glass bubble which was not allowed to contain the common things of life, and Sophie was frequently amazed at what she saw whilst out in the car with Barry or her stepfather. Once she saw a child limping along, ragged, barefoot, and dirty. She urgently called out to Barry to stop the car. She pushed out of the car door before her nanny had time to grab her and ran to the small girl—who was very surprised when Sophie pulled off her patent leather shoes and insisted on putting them onto the girl's feet. Her nanny by then had reached her, and Sophie knew she would take the shoes back.

"Run!" she said urgently, pushing the bewildered girl forward. "Run quickly now!" The girl ran, and Sophie was carried back to the car by Barry whilst her nanny chided her severely. Her parents joined in when they returned.

Sophie was bemused that they did not understand that this poor child had no shoes, while she had many pairs, so why should she not give to someone who was in need of something she was not? She was not punished, but she overheard long conversations in low voices as she glided noiselessly through the large, whispering rooms of the comfortable house.

Sophie was taken up to London with her sister and nanny, where they spent hours buying uniforms and underwear. *School*, thought Sophie vaguely. Until now she and Rachael had been tutored at home, but now they were to be launched into a large school. Sophie dreaded the thought of hordes of noisy and unintelligent children and irritating teachers. Her friends had always been chosen for her and, if she did not like or approve of them, could be made to disappear from her little life stage.

Rachael and Sophie were driven to the school with their parents and nanny, dressed in their navy and saxe-blue outfits with new leather lace-up shoes and blue ribbons in their hair.

They drove up a long, winding driveway surrounded by sinister-looking tall trees and arrived at the front of a large building with white pillars beside a thick wooden door. The door was opened by a woman—or Sophie assumed by her voice that this was a woman—enveloped in dark, coarse robes and with an elaborate headpiece of white and black. There was a large rope of beads with a wooden cross on the end hanging down from her skirts, and her shoes were like those of a workman. She had a hard, mean face and a faint moustache that fascinated Sophie. She led them into a room with a desk and several uncomfortable chairs and beckoned them to sit, which they did, sitting stiffly and expectantly.

"You are Rachael," the heavily gowned one said menacingly to Sophie's sister.

"Yes," Rachael replied, looking uncomfortable.

"When you speak to me, you will address me and begin and finish your sentences with Reverend Mother," growled the person who Sophie now knew to be female.

"Yes, Reverend Mother." Rachael swallowed hard.

Reverend Mother showered Rachael with questions, most of which Rachael managed to answer to the woman's satisfaction. Sophie swung her little legs and kicked the chair. Reverend Mother frowned. "Please stop that, child." Sophie stopped but then began to fidget.

"You are quite right." The nun was addressing Sophie's parents. "She needs a great deal of discipline."

"Sister Mary Margaret will take them to their dormitories." Reverend Mother rang a bell on the wall, and soon a small nun with darting, shifty eyes like those of a rat came in and curtsied to her superior. She asked them all to follow her and led them out into the tiled hall, where there were paintings on the wall and an overpowering smell of lilies and polish.

Sophie noticed that Barry had placed two large trunks in the hall whilst they had been in that room. *Why?* she thought. *Why do we need all this just to go to school? We will arrive in the morning and go home in the evening.* Then they were led up several large, carved wooden staircases and taken into a room with rows of beds covered in uniform blue bedspreads and surrounded by curtains of the same colour. By each small bed in its small space was a wooden cupboard, on top of which was a large bowl with a jug in it and beside it a soap dish and an upturned glass. Barry and the convent's gardener and handyman brought up the trunks and deposited them beside two of these cubicles.

"Sister Mary Margaret will help you unpack," said Reverend Mother. "You may say goodbye to your parents now."

In that second Sophie realised with a knife-like pang of hurt that she and her sister had been abandoned to these austere and cold women. "No!" she shouted, flinging herself at her mother's legs. "No, I want to go home, Mummy."

Her mother unfolded Sophie's arms from her. "Stop this nonsense, Sophie," she said coldly, "and make sure you do exactly as you are told and work hard." And then they were gone, and Nanny and Barry were gone with them.

Sophie ran to the window to try and see them, but the window was too high, and she threw herself on the bed, weeping.

Sister Mary Margaret loomed over her. "Get up from your bed, and be quiet, and unpack this trunk immediately."

Sophie, still sobbing softly, unpacked her belongings. Her gym shorts and shirts had already been taken to the games room.

Her sister was unusually quiet and actually helped Sophie. Together they went down to the refectory to sit at a long, wooden table on a hard wooden bench with other pupils they did not know. They ate, in complete and utter silence, rough rye bread, hard, tasteless cheese, and an apple each. They drank cocoa with too much sugar in it. Afterwards they filed to the chapel, with its statues of Mary and Joseph and large angels and its smell of incense. The nuns were already there; Sophie sat listening to them chanting in Latin and almost fell asleep.

Tucked up in her hard, cold, and comfortless bed, she heard the duty nun who stayed awake all the night hours. She was reciting the night prayer Sophie would hear a thousand times more. "Matthew, Mark, Luke, and John, bless the bed that I lie on. Four corners to my bed, four angels round my head. One to sing, one to pray, and two to bear my soul away."

Sophie wept silently and piteously." Mummy! I want my mummy," she whispered and cried herself to sleep.

Sophie awoke during the night. Where was she? This was not her soft, large bed. The sheets were harsh, and there were only two thin blankets and a cotton cover that gave no warmth. She felt a wetness and put her hand down in the bed; her nightdress was wet and cold. Sophie was puzzled, then worried. What had happened? She lay shivering throughout the night, tired and frightened and longing for her mother and her nanny and her home.

As dawn streaked the sky with gold and pink, a bell rang loudly, and the nun ringing it threw open the door to the dormitory, "Get up, girls. Wash and dress and make your beds, and do so in silence."

Sophie slid down into her cold, comfortless bed. The nun walked up and down the space between the cubicles, flinging back curtains and checking the progress of the girls. She pulled Sophie's curtain aside. "Why are you not up as you should be, Sophie Harrison?" she barked, and pulling the bedcovers off, she dragged the shaking child from the bed. She looked at the bed and then at Sophie's wet nightgown. "What is this? Do you not have lavatories in your home, child? This is disgusting! You must be taught cleanliness, as dogs are taught."

She poured water from the china jug into the bowl and handed Sophie her sponge and soap. She pulled Sophie's nightgown off roughly. "Wash yourself, and be quick," the nun said harshly. Sophie dipped her sponge into the water. It was freezing. "It's so cold," she said to the nun.

"Wash yourself, and hurry up." The nun folded her arms and tapped her foot on the wooden floor.

Sophie washed awkwardly. At home she bathed daily and was wrapped in a warmed cotton bath gown. She had never been expected to wash like this—and in such cold water. Sophie finished washing and dried herself.

"Right, madam," the nun said harshly. "You need to learn to be clean." She grabbed Sophie's hair, pushed her forward onto the bed, and then forced her face into the wet area of the sheet. Roughly she rubbed the child's face in the urine stain until Sophie screamed for her sister. Rachael started to run to her sibling's aid, but the other boarders restrained her, whispering that she must not interfere. Rachael looked on in distress but was afraid to intervene. At last the cruelty ceased, and Sophie was allowed to stand up and dress. She sobbed until she was hiccupping. She wanted just to escape and find her mother.

They filed down to breakfast, and Sophie went to sit down next to her sister, but the nun who had done the terrible thing to her grabbed her by her small arm. "Oh no," she said. "You will come over here with me."

She pulled Sophie to the corner of the refectory and held up a written notice. She pushed it into Sophie's face. "Read it out loud," she commanded.

Sophie looked at the words and then pleadingly at the nun. Hesitating and swallowing hard, she stumbled over the words. "I am filthy and sinful. I wet my bed and must be punished." A tear ran hotly down Sophie's cheek. She looked over at her sister despairingly, but her sister was looking away and spreading her toast with margarine and marmalade. Sophie stood weeping while the nun affixed the notice to Sophie's chest. She was left to stand and watch the other girls eating toast, fruit, and porridge and drinking coffee and tea. She was so very thirsty, and hungry and tired, and her small heart was breaking. *Mummy,* she thought, *I want my mummy. I am unhappy here.*

Sophie was just 4 1/2 years old, beginning to learn oppression and rejection, and her sensitive soul was cowering. She wanted to escape to a place full of flowers and music and people who did not frighten and punish her. *One day*, the small girl told herself, *I will live in freedom, as I want to live, and I will try to learn not to be afraid of my oppressors.*

SOPHIE CHILDHOOD, TWO

Sophie was a very bright child, and she soon learnt that her oppressors admired her abilities and seemed to prize them. She was clumsy and dreamy, still late for almost everything, but she learnt soon to love the huge library with its glass-fronted cases filled with books of every kind. There were long tables in the room, smelling of wax polish, with rows of chairs. Sometimes Sophie would sit at the table with her short-sighted face close to the pages of her current book. At other times she would curl up on another chair by the white-painted radiator and immerse herself in words—words that described, and recounted, and explained, and educated.

She had music lessons with her favourite teacher, Miss Langridge, a tall woman with a long, hawk-like face and a beaked nose. Her skin was yellowish, and her eyes were like two large prunes sunk into their almost lidless sockets. The first time Sophie sat on the piano stool, which had an extra cushion on it to allow for Sophie's lack of height, she gazed in wonder at the ivory keys of the baby grand piano and willed her fingers to play the wonderful melodies which were dancing inside her head and her heart. Her first lesson was much more down to earth. She had to learn the names of the eight keys in each octave, but she mastered this very rapidly and was soon able to quickly recognise E from A minor and B flat from D sharp. She learnt her first scale in C major and could play it with both hands at the end of her hour-and-a-half session. Just as rapidly, she learnt to sight-read sheet music as if it were a story in one of her beloved books. The notes sang to her from the pages, and she would spend hours in the practice room, perfecting and speeding up her scales in both harmonic and melodic genres. She learnt to keep her hand in a curved shape and to move her fingers from their base joints smoothly and under control. Miss Langridge placed coins on the knuckles on the backs of Sophie's hands and Sophie had to play her scales without dislodging them. After a few months, Sophie had played her way through seven piano books, and Miss Langridge presented her with a new book of much harder pieces. Sophie looked at the front cover of the book. It told her that this was the official book of set pieces for Grade 1 of the examinations for the Associated Board of the Royal Schools of Music. Sophie's small heart leapt; she was to enter for her first piano exam. Closing her eyes, she felt a strong link with the father she had never known. She learnt and practiced and perfected those pieces over hours of patient and hard application. She could live without many things, but not without music. It was to comfort her in her darkest hours.

Sophie also observed and learnt that there was a sharp social divide between the nuns. The Irish nuns were the workers. They spent hours in the steamy, sweet-smelling laundry with their sleeves rolled up, washing and ironing and folding. They scrubbed, and polished, and dusted. They peeled vegetables, and cooked, and washed up, with their red arms plunged deep into huge, wooden sinks. They took the lower ranks in the back of the chapel and were, Sophie felt, rather looked down on and overworked. Only one of the Irish brigade—Sister Ancilla, a small, fierce woman with a hooked nose, bowed legs, and floppy breasts—was allowed the privilege of playing the harmonium in the chapel. She pedalled away gamely at the wooden slats that enabled the instrument to wheeze out the accompaniment as nuns and pupils sang heartily. One memorable day she grabbed at a stop to bring a more throaty sound from the tiny harmonium, and the stop came away from the panel. Sister Ancilla flew backwards off her perch and landed at the feet of the statue of St Joseph. The nuns continued singing without a break, as did those pupils who weren't covering their mouths and laughing. Sophie and two others hurried over to lift up the indignant nun and deposit her back on her seat. The harmonium picked up the melody in a strange, reedy, whining tone that produced more fits of mirth.

The upper echelon contained the English and Belgian nuns. They were very educated, aristocratic, and superior in all they did and said. In Sophie's time at the convent, the pupils had to curtsy to these nuns—the royalty of the order—every time they met, or passed them in the corridor, or when they entered the refectory. Even if the girls were eating a meal, they had to rise, curtsy, and bow their heads. And at prep in the evening, they were forced to rise, curtsy, bow, and then try to concentrate on their studies. These sisters looked down, very firmly, on their Irish companions, and Sophie learnt a lesson about human nature. She learnt about the intellectual arrogance and callous superiority of women who were supposed to be devoted to love, care, and God. She learnt of hypocrisy and cruelty and the misuse of intelligence. She appreciated the excellent education she was receiving from these highly qualified daughters of God, but she felt contempt for their social attitudes and behaviour.

Sophie did well at her studies and her examinations. She found a talent for playing games. On the hockey field, she played a full back and determinedly charged down the oncoming army of centres, centre halves, wingers, and inners intent on scoring; she repelled again and again their attacks. She was a defence in netball and played a reasonable game of tennis in the summer. At rounders, she hit hard and long and could bowl and catch as a fielder with great skill. When she and her classmates were made to go on cross-country runs, Sophie would lag behind, sit on the grass inside a sheltering bush, chew a couple of toffees, and then cut back the short way and join the pack sweating and lurching to the finish.

Socially Sophie was not quite so successful. She felt as if her fellow boarders sometimes behaved like aliens and fell out over things she later could not quite grasp. She was easily intimidated, which irritated her intensely and worried her. She stressed very readily over seemingly minor matters and was always too concerned by the opinions of others. She seemed to live her life for the approval of everyone except herself. She always had to please someone: her parents, her teachers, the nuns, her fellow pupils, God. God was the person she feared most. He was a remote, powerful, fearful and invisible presence that she could not escape. He apparently made very strict and sometimes incomprehensible rules that she was forced to learn and obey. In class she recited the Catholic catechism daily until it became a meaningless sound.

"Who made you?"

"God made me."

"Why did He make you?"

"To be in His likeness and image."

She could recite the seven deadly sins, and the definition of a venial sin and its more deadly big brother—a mortal sin.

She chanted her prayers in Latin in the incense-filled chapel heady with the odours of flowers picked in the convent gardens: lilies, and roses, and *muguet des bois*.

"Pater noster qui es in caelis, sanctificetur nomen tuum ..."

They sang hymns in two and three parts: *"Non nobis nomine, non nobis, sed nomine tuo da gloriam ..."*—"Not to my name but to thine be the glory given ...", and the chapel reverberated with their ardent voices.

Sophie was made a child of Mary; she wore a sky-blue cloak, and a veil, and a blue ribbon around her neck with a medal of the Virgin Mary on it. On the principal feast days of the mother of God, the children of Mary carried her statue, adorned with a wreath of fresh flowers, on a wooden platform with long poles at each corner. They bore it on their shoulders to the chapel after processing around the convent garden singing, "Protect us whilst telling thy praises we sing, In faithful hearts dwelling Christ Jesus our king. Ave, ave, ave, Maria—Ave, ave, ave, Maria." Smaller pupils walked in front, scattering rose petals at their feet. In class Sophie was taught that she must be as holy, pure, meek, and obedient as the virgin mother of God. Her role in life was to be a mother of endless children and a sweet, obedient, and demure wife who looked only at her husband and echoed his dominance with her submission. Men were creatures to be feared, avoided, and suspected until courtship and marriage loomed; then she must choose with due consideration and care and after much prayer. She absorbed this brainwashing with a mental sneer and instantly rejected it. But she continued to act the part she knew was required of her to keep her life with the nuns peaceful.

Ballroom dancing lessons were part of her training to be an upper-middle class female. She changed from her uniform into a pretty blue dress with organza skirts and flaring petticoats, stockings, and blue-and-silver dance sandals. She quickly picked up the dance routines and was adept and light on her feet. Being musical helped with the timing, and soon she was proficient at the waltz, the foxtrot, the quickstep, the tango, the samba, the rumba, and Scottish and country dancing.

Her life at home was far from happy or satisfying. Sophie began to dread the holidays, half-terms, and exeat weekends. She convinced the nuns that she had important scholastic work to complete and that going home would interfere with it significantly. Her hated stepfather was drinking heavily; when drunk he would throw violent temper tantrums like an outsized toddler. It was not a joke to Sophie. Her mother would be subjected to verbal and physical abuse, and Sophie was puzzled that her normally strong mother, who was a tough businesswoman, would be so submissive and placatory towards this unpleasant, cruel, and domineering tyrant. *Maybe*, thought Sophie, *this is how you have to be. Maybe you have to give in and tolerate all this hell, however angry you are inside.* She took refuge in her bedroom and read her books avidly, lying on her soft bedcover with her big brown teddy bear, Bruin, next to her.

Frequently her parents would go abroad, and then Sophie and Rachael would be left in the convent during the holidays. Sophie began to like this more and more, as she had no lessons and was left to fill the hours of the day in any way she wished excepting for meal times. She would talk to the gardener and help him with his tasks, and she learnt a deep love of plants and gardening. In the summer months she curled up in the garden and read whatever her hungry brain could absorb and digest. She also walked around the garden singing—music in any form filled her with a warm glow and lifted her to heights of joy. She did not look forward to the return of her parents. Solitude, flowers, music, and books were her delight. Her parents disturbed her small heaven.

On her tenth birthday, Sophie was told to go to the large drawing room to see her gift. She peered around the door curiously. There in the corner by the large window was a baby grand piano. Sophie drew in her breath. "Oh my!" she whispered and approached this wonderful thing. She ran her fingers over the dark, shining wood, then lifted the lid and touched the pale keys. She pulled out the stool with its red velvet cushion and adjusted it to her height. Then she sat before the instrument. She lifted her hands and brought them down on the new keys. She played one or two scales and arpeggios and then started on Beethoven's "Für Elise". The piano had a deliciously sharp and singing tone, and Sophie was lost in the joy of its melodious voice. She sat playing until she was called to lunch. After this she used loud piano playing to drown out the raised voices and the foul language of the unpleasant man with the moustache who seemed to want to own her mother.

School became Sophie's refuge, her world apart from the world, where all unwanted noises and people were blocked and forbidden. She loved the summer evenings, playing in the gardens with their rose beds which filled the air with a musky, sweet, soporific incense. She loved the huge ancient cedar tree, with its enormously long branches propped up with thick carved supports, under which they ran to shelter when the rain fell and under which they performed Shakespeare's *As You Like It*. Sophie played Touchstone, with his dry wit and striped jester's costume with bells on the hat.

Rachael, meanwhile, continued to be attractive—physically, at least. When her parents had visitors, her mother would introduce the two girls with "This is Rachael, and this is Sophie." Then she would add in a low, conspiratorial tone, "But Sophie is the *clever* one." From which Sophie deduced that her sister was, in fact, the pretty one, and her own plain appearance had to be excused by this revelation. She grew up aware of this; she absorbed the information until she finally knew that she was not attractive and therefore was undeserving. She would have to use other means to excel where her prettier peers and her sibling had the edge and a start on her. To comfort herself, Sophie developed the habit of chewing. She ate biscuits, sweets, potatoes, pork pies, bananas—anything that would give her a feeling of comfort and fill the void inside her where she felt her beauty should reside, but where, the world told her, she was deficient. As her teens approached, she ceased to grow upwards and began to spread in a very uncomfortable and worrying way. Excess fat seemed to accumulate on

Sophie's upper arms and her thighs if she as much as laid eyes on anything edible. She put herself on endless severe starvation regimes, which saw her losing ounces after weeks of a painfully empty stomach and sleepless nights in which she tossed miserably, yearning for anything to fill the aching void that dictated her feelings—and at times her life. She studied herself in the mirror, and depression gripped her. She was plain—horribly, boringly plain—and she could not shed her glasses, without which life would be like that of a goldfish in a very dirty bowl. And now her body was mocking her. She was a good athlete; she could run damned fast and stay the course of any match, but her fat cells apparently didn't know of her outside life and wanted her to remain this awful shape. They screamed at her daily to maintain their status. And when this misery hit home, Sophie wanted only to curl up on her bed with a pile of sandwiches or a bowl of ice cream and soothe her emptiness and depression.

As Sophie neared adolescence, she discovered that she had a talent for humour and biting sarcasm. She would compose sharp little poems about the nuns, teachers, and pupils who annoyed the rest of the school. At evening prep she would scribble these missiles with a grin on her face. They would be passed around from desk to desk amid hastily suppressed sniggers. Once Sister Mary Joan, an aristocratic, haughty nun, heard the murmur and strode down from the raised desk where she sat supervising the girls working. She snatched the piece of paper from the hand of Amaryllis Capelcure, who was desperately attempting to hide the incriminating document.

Sister Mary Joan held out her hand. "Give that to me," she hissed.

Amaryllis did so with a shaking hand. The nun looked at the poem and then looked at Amaryllis. "You do not have the wherewithal intellectually to have written this, Miss Capelcure. Kindly provide me with the name of the authoress."

Amaryllis looked around beseechingly. The other girls lowered their eyes and held their collective breath.

"I am waiting Miss Capelcure."

The silence seemed to scream into the warm summer evening. The haughty nun lifted her chin and glared down on Amaryllis. "Very well. The entire two classes will be punished. You will remain indoors at recreation times and learn two full scenes of Macbeth word perfectly over two weeks." She tore up the paper, walked over to the wastepaper basket, and held her hand up so that the pieces floated down into it like snow in slow motion. She paused for a second, and her eyes flickered onto Sophie like the eyes of a snake about to strike. Sophie knew that she must own up. Her fellow pupils would not tell on her, but she would not let them suffer for her. She stood up quickly, and her chair's feet scraped the floor loudly.

The nun looked at her coldly. "Yes, Sophie—you wish to say something?"

Sophie swallowed. "Yes, Sister Mary Joan, it was I who wrote that poem. It dropped on the floor, and Amaryllis just happened to pick it up. Please don't punish everybody for what I did; it wouldn't be fair. Just punish me, because I did it, nobody else did anything wrong—" She paused. She had been speaking louder and quicker and getting really warmed to her defence of her friends.

The nun drew herself up and loomed over Sophie. "You will indeed be punished, madam, and your friends will be spared, as you had the decency and morals to own up—and the spark in you to plead for justice. A small smile flickered on the nun's face. She turned away. "Stay here after prep, and we will see what you will do to make amends."

The bell rang to end prep, and her friends filed out, glancing at her with grateful and sympathetic smiles. Sophie remained at her desk.

The nun beckoned her over. "Sophie you have a great intelligence and intellect, but you have a leaning towards chaos and risk," she said, leaning back in her chair and tucking her hands into the long black sleeves of her habit. "Save your talents for better things, my child. At least you cared enough for your fellow pupils to confess and save them from injustice. You will learn two scenes from Macbeth—word perfect—within a fortnight, and you will miss two recreation periods." The nun rose and gathered up the knitting bag that she and most of her fellow sisters carried. "You are dismissed now. When you go to confession on Friday, do not forget to ask for absolution and penance for this episode."

Sophie assumed an appropriate expression of regret and guilt. She curtsied to the nun and then hurried off to her friends. They clustered around her and thanked her for her decency in taking the blame and the punishment. Sophie was warmed by their reaction. She had discovered her sense of fun and her ability to write hilarious and biting verse—but she had also discovered her love of justice, her deep loathing of wrongful accusations and consequences, and her yearning to help anyone who was oppressed. She was sliding into adolescence slowly and enquiringly.

Confirmation was a large event. The candidates had to remember long chunks of catechism and choose a middle name—a saint's name that would remain with them for life. Sophie's confirmation outfit was memorable. The dress was of white grosgrain, with a high collar and long sleeves and tiny seed pearls sewn all over it in floral patterns. With it Sophie wore a shoulder-length veil held onto her long Titian curls with a circlet of wax flowers and pearls. She wore white stockings, and on her feet were strapped shoes of white grosgrain to match her dress. She whirled around in front of the mirror, delighted with her appearance. She did not want to take her lovely clothes off to await the great day.

The sun rose strong and bright on that morning. Sophie rose early, bathed, brushed and combed her long, shiny curls, and donned her fairy-tale clothes. She had been dressed similarly for her first communion but had not felt so excited or so beautiful. The candidates for confirmation arrived at the church and processed inside quietly and reverently. They were to be confirmed by the cardinal archbishop of Westminster, Cardinal Griffin, and Sophie had to discipline herself not to openly stare at this exalted being.

After the ceremony, they filed out of the church. The cardinal stood in the lobby of the old church, resplendent in his purple robes. As each girl went past, she knelt and kissed the huge ring on the cardinal's finger, and he murmured a few words to her. Sophie knelt and kissed the ring which the cardinal held out to her. She stood up, and he asked her name. She told him, and he asked her, "What confirmation name did you take, child?"

"Theresa," Sophie replied.

"Ah, the great Saint Theresa of Avila?"

"No, Your Eminence, the little flower of Lisieux."

"Why did you choose her, my child?"

"Because she suffered a lot but had that toughness to get through."

The cardinal place his large hand underneath her chin, lifted her head up, and looked at her with a gentle smile. "Learn from that. Learn to suffer and to endure. Suffering is wasted on us if we give in too easily. Strength comes from discipline inside ourselves. Life can be overwhelming, my dear child. Be strong, whatever happens."

Then she was moved on, and they all walked back to the convent. There was a special breakfast following the ceremony, with hot, fresh buttered rolls, real coffee, fruit, and ham. The cardinal ate with them and joked and chatted. Sophie sat next to him and was able to talk with him. She found him fascinating and unusually attractive. *What a waste*, she thought, *of a sweet, intelligent, kind and interesting man who has to live a life of chastity and cut himself off from normal life.*

Thus, slowly but effectively, Sophie was taught self-discipline, the quality that would take her through many black times in her life. The convent and the nuns were her place of sanctuary from her desperate home life and the increasingly violent and heated arguments fuelled by alcohol and her stepfather's bullying. Rachael sneered at the chaos and seemed able to endure it. Sophie cowered under her bedclothes, hid in the garden or the airing cupboard, or sat at her piano, immersing herself in her beloved music to shut out the shouting and the misery. She was very frightened by loud voices and anger; she seemed unable to react with anything other than fear and a feeling of inferiority. Bullying angered her, and she longed to be able to hit back at it, but she was always paralysed with helpless terror and a feeling that she could not justify or defend herself. She felt she must always appease and accept blame.

Exams took up much of her life at the convent. She had reached Grade 5 in her music and had got as far as Grade 8 in her London Academy of Music and Dramatic Art studies. Recitation of poetry and prose were something Sophie really loved, and she also did exams in public speaking. When angry voices cut into her peace at night in the home she hated, she would whisper the words of loved poems to shut out the blackness inside her: "At the top of the house the apples are laid in rows, and the skylight lets the moonlight in, and those apples are deep-sea apples of green …" and the beauty of those words filled her head and her soul so she could fight the fear and discipline her timid spirit to endure.

Sophie was nearing a time she dreaded, the time when she would have to leave the sanctuary and security of the convent and be pushed out into an alien and hostile world. At the convent, the sixteen-year-olds were to be lectured by a priest from the Passionist Fathers of Mill Hill in London. The girls poured into the reception room at the front of the convent and sat obediently and expectantly on the chairs set out. Soon Mother Superior appeared, followed by a handsome, dark-haired priest of about thirty. He stood in front of them, and as was usual before just about anything in this Catholic world, he raised his hands and began to pray for enlightenment and for the Holy Spirit to descend and teach them all. Sophie glanced upwards but could see nothing descending. Increasingly she was irritated and offended by the religious blanket draped over every aspect of life in this place. They all sat down at the young priest's request, and he began to tell them what was expected of them as good Catholic young women. He spoke of their role as wives and mothers—no mention of careers or anything they might prefer to do, Sophie noted. He mentioned the obedience, respect, humility, and devotion expected of these little wives. As the young man droned on, Sophie had a mental picture of hordes of young Catholic women, dressed in sober, ankle-length black dresses, being herded onto a slave ship by a priest with a large whip in his hand.

Then the young priest hesitatingly reached the subject of sex. The room fell weirdly silent. The atmosphere was electric. They were informed that God intended that every sperm ejaculated should result in yet another devout (albeit impoverished) Catholic being. The prevention of conception was a terrible sin—the waste of sperm in withdrawal was the sin of onanism. He advised them that they must supply their husband's every sexual need without question; husbands were omnipotent, and they were inferior.

Sophie felt her nostrils flaring with anger. *What utter rubbish!* she thought. *Are we really supposed to act on this and screw our lives up?* The diatribe ended at last, and Mother Superior asked if anyone had any questions. Sophie raised her hand. There was an almost imperceptible communal intake of breath. The other girls knew Sophie and her way of thinking and reacting.

"Yes, Sophie. Stand up and ask Father Richard whatever it is you wish to know."

Sophie stood up. The handsome young priest smiled at her.

"Ah yes, Sophie. How may I help you, my dear?"

"Father Richard," Sophie began in an innocent, treacly voice. "You live in a seminary with many other priests, yes?"

"Yes, Sophie, I do."

"Of course, Father, you are not married, are you?" The gentle voice of Sophie led to the trap.

"No, of course not."

"You take a vow of chastity, do you not?"

"But of course, Sophie." He was looking slightly uncomfortable.

"So you cannot know what it is to be married, and what marriage entails, and all the daily ins and outs, and—" Sophie glanced at Mother Superior. The nun's face was set and angry. Father Richard looked as if he wished the Holy Spirit would strike Sophie dumb. Her fellow pupils were smirking and nudging each other.

"And you can hardly stand there and tell us what we should do, can you, because you have never, ever been in a situation involving sexual contact and are never ever likely to be. Furthermore,"—Sophie paused and her head went up defiantly—"you really think that all there is to life for a Catholic female is to be some sort of a slave to an overbearing, bossy, sexually demanding, Guinness-swilling lout and to scrub his floors, and cook his meals, and be pregnant for years, and drag up another race of brainwashed Catholics. If that's so, then the pope can accept my resignation right now." The silence trembled around them—all eyes and ears were on Sophie. "And

onanism isn't a sin. it's just a euphemism for masturbation."
Sophie smiled and sat down.

There was a very loud silence. Mother Superior worked her
jaws convulsively and clenched her fists. Father Richard looked
around for an escape, like a chicken in a room full of foxes.
Sophie's peers sniggered quietly, and some had to stuff their
fists into their mouths to prevent them from laughing openly.

Mother Superior broke the silence. "Well, girls, we must say
thank you to Father Richard for his enlightening talk, and you
must all go down to the refectory for tea." Her voice was shrill
and strained. She began frenziedly dragging girls from their
chairs and pushing them towards the door.

Father Richard stood with a sickly smile on his handsome
face, nodding at the giggling girls. As Sophie passed him, she
smiled alluringly, or what she hoped was alluringly. "Thank you
so much, Father Richard," she said softly, and the young man
blushed deeply. Sophie made for the door and, as she went
through it, muttered, "What a waste!"

A hand descended onto her shoulder and held her in a tight
and painful grasp. "You will go to my office immediately, Sophie,
and sit there and await me. Whilst you are waiting, you may
pray that God will forgive you," said Mother Superior through
clenched teeth.

"What about my tea?" Sophie asked innocently.

"You may consider the loss of your tea as a minor punishment
for your behaviour, madam." The nun pushed Sophie away
abruptly and turned her yellow-dentured smile on the terrified
Father Richard. "Come, Father. Come and have some tea
with me."

Sophie trudged up to the office and sat on a soft armchair in the corner of the large, gloomy room. She picked up a copy of the *Daily Telegraph* and began to do the crossword on the back. She had time to complete it, as Mother Superior did not return for almost an hour.

When the nun returned, she sat on her large wooden swivel chair facing Sophie and folded her arms. "Put that paper down and attend to me well, madam." Sophie met her gaze unflinchingly.

"You, Sophie, are heading for a life of damnation and sin. You will reject all we have taught you and pursue the life of the fleshly and the damned."

"A normal life, then." Sophie smiled annoyingly.

"If that is your normality, then yes."

"If *what* is my normality? Marrying someone you love? Getting to know them first? Choosing them for love, even if they don't follow your crackpot and stupid ideas? Experimenting with sex, as normal people do? Making love, and sensibly preventing the conception of unwanted children by using contraceptives? Having a relationship with someone who treats you as an equal—not a downtrodden baby machine for the pope? Then yes—that is what I hope to do when I go out into life. I can't see it as fleshly or damned, to be honest, and as for damned—well, God invented sex, so I doubt if he'd damn anyone for actually using his invention. It is supposed to be intensely pleasurable and enjoyable, so I'm told, not just endured for the purposes of creating unwanted children. Look at all the slum kids in Italy! Look at all the huge families in Ireland with kids they can't afford to feed and clothe! If there is a God who wants us to behave like that, then I don't believe in him and don't want to."

Sophie stopped and glared defiantly at the nun. Mother superior met Sophie's gaze coldly. "You were gifted with a high intelligence, Sophie, but you are a rebel, and your constant need to kick against convention and normality will take you to dark places and dark things. I can do nothing to change your nature and your future, save to pray for you daily. You will be leaving us soon, and your examination results will be good, I know. I regret your thinking, but I wish you all the very best in your life. I feel that you should apologise to father Richard and tell him that you did not mean anything you said."

"But I did mean it," Sophie said quietly but firmly, "and father Richard is a big boy. He should be able to take reality."

Mother Superior sighed. "It is as well that you are leaving, Sophie. Go and get your tea now, and think, child, think. We have tried to teach you things that will help you to survive life."

"Of course you have." Sophie stood up. "You've taught me tremendous self-discipline, and how to dance and speak and play the piano, and cook and sew, and how to have polite dinner parties, and sing—but not how to face a world I never ever knew and dread facing. But face it I must and will." She curtsied to the nun and left for the refectory and her tea.

The end of the summer term and the end of her time at the convent neared. In the gymnasium they had a session known as pirates and sailors. They dressed up and divided into teams of pirates and sailors, identified by the pirates wearing red bands and the sailors yellow ones. They swarmed over the apparatus, swinging, leaping, and climbing. The pirates attempted to catch the sailors by tapping them on a leg, arm, or back. The caught sailors had to go and sit on the benches along the side and cheer their team on. Any sailors who were still untouched when the final whistle was blown were lauded and presented with boxes of chocolates. Sophie was a pirate for her final game of her school life and happily pursued her fellow pupils and sent many of them to the bench. They then spent a day emptying their wooden desks, scrubbing them out and, when they were dry, polishing them with the beeswax polish that the nuns made. They scrubbed and polished all the other furniture in their classroom, and then they cleaned the windows. They cleared out and scrubbed their games room lockers and carefully packed away the hockey sticks that they would probably never ever use again.

The last ritual was the midnight feast. Families provided cakes and pork pies, sandwiches, fruit, crisps, pickled onions, and all manner of goodies. Lemonade was in huge supply, but the day pupils helped smuggle in several bottles of spirits. These were hidden upstairs, in the science laboratory where the feast was to take place. On the scheduled night, the senior girls who were leaving waited until lights out and then sneaked quietly up to the science room. They had all graduated to rooms of their own or shared with another pupil, so there was no night dormitory nun to evade. They crowded around the baskets of food, sharing them out and chattering happily. Glasses were filled with lemonade, and generous quantities of gin, rum, or whisky were added. Soon the volume increased, and the talk became more animated and risqué. The subject was, inevitably, sex and boys. Sophie, like those others who came from an all-girl family, had only seen male genitalia in cold, clinical pictures, which she found quite amazing. She asked those with brothers to give her a realistic description, and soon they were all laughing bawdily. As the night wore on, Sophie began to feel tired and unpleasantly woozy. Soon all the girls began to flag, and they trooped back to their rooms silently, with baskets full of rubbish. Sophie and her friend fell over each other and had to stifle their laughter. Once in her room, she fell into bed; she felt as if it were spinning round faster and faster. It was some time before she finally managed to fall asleep.

The morning came, soft, red streaked, and full of birdsong and the smell of the rosebuds. Sophie lifted her head and promptly dropped it back on the pillow. Her head felt as if someone had been hitting it with a 20-pound hammer, and she felt very sick. Every part of her ached as if she had flu. All she wanted to do was to crawl beneath her covers and die. *Oh my lord*, thought Sophie, *I have to get up.* Today was the finals of the end-of-year inter-house rounders matches. Her team, St Cuthberts, known affectionately as custards,(because 'custard' sounded like 'Cuthbert', and their house colours were yellow), were playing St Chads, or the bads. She dragged herself out of bed and went over to the open window, where she breathed in several lungfuls of fresh air. She crawled unsteadily to the bathroom and forced herself to stand underneath a freezing shower to wake up. She dried herself, dressed, and then made her way to the refectory, where several of her peers were hunched over cups of coffee, looking pale and miserable.

"Good morning, everyone!" Sophie tried to sound cheerful.

"Shut up!" said her friend Susan, propping up her head with her hands. An echoing chorus of shut ups followed from the rest of the table. Sophie sat down and poured herself a black coffee with two sugars. She didn't exactly want to eat, but she had to play a rounders match. She forced herself to have toast, fruit, and croissants and then went into the gardens to try and recover. Her friends joined her, sitting beside her on the bench, dozing in the sunshine. After an hour, Sophie sat up.

"Come on, you sleeping beauties," she said. "We've got a rounders match to win." Slowly they rose and straggled to the games room to don their shorts and shirts emblazoned with the Cuthberts yellow insignia. They drifted over to the huge meadow that stretched out behind the convent and on which hockey, lacrosse, and rounders were played. The entire pitch was surrounded by pupils, teachers, and nuns carrying banners for Cuthberts or Chads. After the toss, Cuthberts went in to field. Sophie was backstop; she had to catch missed balls and try to throw them quickly to the fielder at the first base to get the batsman out. Her head was spinning, and her mouth was dry. She threw her all into the match, but Chads batted well and achieved a high score, as Cuthberts began their bid to earn points. They all made superhuman efforts and fought their hangovers to nearly match Chads' total. In their second batting, Chads crept slowly well ahead of Cuthberts, and when Sophie and her team went in for their last batting, they had a huge gap to fill.

They fought grimly and slowly—so slowly—while the scores crept closer. Then they were closing and were tied, and the match had nearly run its course. Sophie stood before the bowler. She was the last one in; it all rested on her and her determination. If she could get just one more clear round of the pitch, her team would win. There was a tense silence amongst the spectators and the teams. The bowler hurled the ball at Sophie. Gathering all her strength, Sophie hit the ball with a sharp crack, and the ball flew up, over, and out into the grass at the edge of the pitch. Without a moment's hesitation, Sophie launched herself forward. She touched first base, dashed to second base, and started out for third base. Just one more and she would be home to victory. Her head hurt, her legs felt like lead, and she was nauseous, tired, and sweating profusely. In the distance she saw a fielder preparing to throw the ball to the girl who guarded the last base. Sophie pulled all her discipline and determination to the fore. *Run!* she told herself. *Run very fast! Give your all. You must not fail.* She accelerated, and the blood drummed in her ears. The ball was flying towards the fielder. Sophie gave of her last strength, hurling herself at the stop. The bat hit the stop a mere second before the ball fell into the fielder's hands. The referee raised her hand. It was a run— they had won! Sophie collapsed in a heap, and her teammates rushed to lift her up and slap her on the back. *What a way to go out*, thought Sophie. *Never give up. Fight all the way.*

Cars were leaving the gravelled driveway of the convent as parents collected their children. Taxis took others to the railway station. Sophie was awaiting the car that would take her home. Rachael had already left the school the previous year; she was at university. Sophie stood looking at the old ivy-covered buildings, the tall beech and oak trees, and the neat flower beds. She felt a deep pang of loss. She had wished the nuns goodbye and thanked them. She turned to leave for the last time. This had been her home and refuge for twelve long years. Now she must go forward into an alien world, and she was afraid. She stood for a few moments, taking in the scene and reliving flashes of her past few years. She was almost in tears. She turned away and walked to the waiting car. Sophie's childhood had ended.

SOPHIE'S ADOLESCENCE

Sophie's parents waited until she had returned from the convent for the last time and then announced that they were moving.

"Moving!" Sophie was aghast. "Moving where?"

"Down to Devon." Her mother was arranging lilies in a tall vase. The smell reminded Sophie of the school chapel, and she missed it greatly.

"Why didn't you tell me this before?" Sophie felt angry.

"Because your father and I felt you had your exams to take and didn't need any stresses or concerns."

"Well, it would have given me time to absorb the news—all the implications. I thought I would be seeing all my friends at the Catholic church and the youth club, and I haven't had time to say goodbye to them properly. And he's not my father." This last utterance was almost whispered. Sophie still did not possess the courage to speak out when she should.

"Don't mumble, Sophie." Her mother gathered up the cut leaves and stems of the lilies and wrapped them in newspaper. "Take these to the gardener to put on the compost heap, or do it yourself if he's not there." Sophie went out into the sun-drenched garden and looked for Harry. Not finding him, she put the package into the compost bin and went to sit on the garden seat under the willow trees. She felt nervous about moving; it might be fun, or it might be quite dreadful. There would be a whole bunch of strangers to get to know. Everything would be so different. Well, she must just face it; she couldn't change things. She went back into the cool, dark house and into the kitchen. She took a packet of biscuits and a glass of milk and sat on her bed, filling herself with comfort and soaking up Mozart as the evening deepened. There was cold beef and salad for supper. Sophie ate hers rapidly and then finished with a large bowl of stewed apples and cream. Her mother frowned as Sophie dolloped cream from the dish onto her apple.

"Cream is very fattening, Sophie, one thing you really do not need."

"Thank you, Mummy," Sophie retorted sarcastically. "But I am already too well aware of how unbeautiful I am to everyone, so why should I bother to remedy what biology has dictated and condemned me to?" And she spooned the fatty sweetness into her mouth. At bedtime she sat, supported by a nest of pillows, and wrote meticulously to each of her friends, explaining her situation. She enclosed the new address and finished her letters with "and I do hope you will be able to get down and see me. We're very near the sea, apparently, so the hols could be great." She absentmindedly chewed fruit gums as she listened to Elgar's "Enigma Variations" and read Nicholas Nickleby for the umpteenth time. She loved Charles Dickens and his wonderfully drawn characters, which sprang to life in the pages of his social commentaries and revelations of the hypocrisy, cruelty, and deprivation of the Victorian world. With music, books, and food, Sophie spun a cocoon around herself, an escape. Very soon she would have to start out in a new environment. For now the sun was sinking, and a slight breeze made the sultry summer night comfortable. Tomorrow was the future.

Sophie sat in the car, watching the last of her home being loaded into a huge pantechnicon. She clutched her shoulder bag, a flask of coffee, and a packet of water biscuits. She had wanted custard creams, but her mother had lectured her about their sugar content, so Sophie had had to settle for these, which tasted fine with a topping of mature cheddar and some farm butter but on their own were like the pages of her stepfather's *Daily Telegraph*—not that Sophie had ever consumed that national treasure, but she imagined it would be so.

They arrived as the sun was setting over the edge of the moors. The house was very beautiful, of old stone—and larger than Sophie had anticipated. Her room had a large window which opened onto a very lovely garden crammed with roses, perennials, and baskets and tubs full of bright annuals. Her mother cooked lamb chops, mashed potatoes, carrots, baked apples, and custard. Sophie ate hungrily and then went on a tour of the house. There was a large entrance hall and an imposing staircase. Off this hall were a large dining room, a panelled lounge which held Sophie's beloved piano, and a study for her stepfather, which looked out onto the garden through French windows. Along the corridor were cupboards and a door which led to steps down to a large cellar. At the end of this corridor was a huge kitchen, white-painted, well equipped, and light. The kitchen had a large porched door at the other end and beyond that a vegetable garden with currant bushes and fruit trees. The garden had apple, plum, and pear trees, along with other ornamental trees and shrubs; this delighted Sophie.

Sophie suddenly felt very tired and went upstairs with her heavy suitcase. The removal men had just finished placing the various items of furniture in their designated places and were beginning to unpack the large crates.

"Oh, leave those now," her stepfather said as he came out of the dining room. "I'll run you to the pub for tonight—you're booked in. Finish this lot tomorrow." He went out with the men, and the car engine roared as he drove the men to the local inn, the Dog and Pheasant, about a quarter of a mile away in the village.

Sophie went to investigate the bathroom and lay out her toiletries. She ran a bath and soaked in the perfumed water. Then she dried herself, put on her nightgown, and climbed into her bed. And what a comfortable bed it was, she thought. A new mattress had been purchased for her as a sort of compensation for the sudden removal. She read for a while and did not remember falling asleep. Her mother turned out her bedside lamp and closed the curtains. Sophie slept deeply and woke to a chorus of birdsong. She looked out of the window onto the garden and took in the scene. The removal men were just getting out of her stepfather's car and trudging over the gravel to begin unpacking crates.

Sophie dressed and went down to breakfast. This was her new life, and she was going out today to see, to speak, and to discover. After porridge, boiled eggs, toast, and marmalade with her parents, Sophie went up, cleaned her teeth, plaited her long red hair, and set out.

"Lunch will be at half past twelve, Sophie," her mother called to her as she opened the front door.

Sophie set out to find what life would offer her. She walked through the village, past shops with groceries, stationery, and loaves of golden bread and cakes with tempting chocolate and cream fillings. She saw a shop with all manner of buckets and bowls; it had wooden steps and garden benches outside. Sophie was interested; she walked into the shop. The wooden floor gave under her feet, and in the dim, cluttered vastness Sophie smelt wood, dust, metal, and oil. There were boxes and boxes of screws, tacks, and nails and all manner of gadgets made of metal, wood, and plastic, most of which she had never seen before. Against the walls were piled floor mops and brooms for kitchens and brooms for gardens—like witches' brooms—and rakes, and spades, and forks, and hoes, and a multitude of other gardening equipment. Sophie wandered around, gazing at everything in awe. She heard a door opening and saw a small, thin man shuffle in. He was suntanned and had sparse greying hair. He wore a leather waistcoat and a faded checked shirt which seemed to be missing many buttons. His corduroy trousers seemed not to have been washed for a very long time.

"Morning, miss. What can I get for you?"

"Oh, good morning. Actually I just came in to have a look and to get to know people."

"Oh, yes. New here, are you?"

"Yes, just arrived. We have the house at the top of Chequers Lane. How do you do—I'm Sophie Harrison." She put her hand out. The little man wiped his hand on his trousers and stuck it out awkwardly. Sophie shook his hand firmly.

"Well, you'll be looking the village over, eh?" He smiled gently. "I'm Tom Andrews. I have three sons, and you'll be seeing them around if you go to the youth club. The mobile cinema comes round every month, and they set it up in the village hall. My middle son, Terry, helps with that. I'll tell him to look out for you."

"Thanks very much; that's really kind." Sophie turned to go.

"If you're looking at all that's round here, you'll likely want to see the caves."

"Caves?" Sophie was interested.

"Yes. Walk through the main street and follow down the hill past the church—it's a very steep hill, mind you. About half a mile down on your left there's an opening in the hedge. Go through, and follow the path, and you'll come to the caves. Only go where there aren't notices warning you not to go further. Those bits are blocked off anyway. They're pretty and interesting. If you ever go after dark, always take a torch. I think you'll find them quite unique."

"Thanks—I'll certainly go there now." Sophie walked towards the door.

"Wait!" Sophie heard, and she turned. The little man was holding out a bottle of lemonade to her.

"Thanks! How much do I owe you?" She dug in her bag.

"Nothing, my dear, nothing. You'll need it today; it's hot, and climbing back up that hill is thirsty work."

Sophie smiled warmly. "You really are kind, Mr Andrews."

"Tom—not Mr Andrews, please—and enjoy yourself."

Sophie set off for the caves. She walked down the steep hill and past the attractive, ivy-covered church. There were fewer houses here, and soon she saw the hedge running alongside the road. There was the opening Tom had told her about. She turned in and followed the well-worn track.

The opening of the caves was a high, granite arch, and Sophie went inside feeling slightly overawed. Her footsteps on the damp floor echoed loudly. She could hear water dripping and see moss growing almost everywhere, apart from the path that everyone seemed to use. On the walls of the cathedral-like interior there were many colours which seemed to shine luminously. It was a magical place, cool, mysterious, and peaceful. It smelt damp and earthy but also somehow exciting and promising. Sophie went around the pathway for a while, until the place became a bit darker and gloomier and she felt slightly fearful. She turned back and was soon out in the hot sunshine again.

She walked back through the village, stopping to explore the church briefly, and was home again just in time for lunch. She told her parents of her morning's doings, ate her lunch, and then went to her room to finish unpacking her belongings and arranging her books and records. Her first day had been pleasant, and she looked forward to attending the youth club and the film at the village hall—and meeting Tom's sons.

A week later Sophie went to the youth club for the first time. It was held in the hall in the village centre. Sophie walked there and then stood outside, nervous and tentative. She knew nobody and felt suddenly very shy and uncertain. Several teenagers walked past her into the hall and turned to give her appraising stares. Sophie smiled but remained standing outside; she felt like going back home. Then two tall, blond, and rather good-looking young men came around the corner. They were both handsome, but Sophie felt an immediate attraction for the slightly taller one, who had amazing blue eyes, tanned skin, and a broad smile. They stopped, and the one who had struck Sophie's fancy spoke. "Hello, are you the young lady who's just moved into the house in Chequers Lane?"

"Yes, I am—I'm Sophie Harrison."

"Well, I'm Terry Andrews, and this is my brother Mark. Do you want to come in with us?"

"Great," said Sophie. "I don't know anyone, so you can introduce me."

They went in, and soon Terry had put her at her ease and she had met a few local teenagers. Some of the girls were a little frosty, and Sophie overheard them mimicking her accent. She flushed and looked distressed. Terry came up to her. "Ignore them stupid cows; they pick on anybody that's not as daft as them." He laughed. "Come on, let's dance. You do dance, don't you?"

"Yes. Love dancing." Sophie swung onto the floor with Terry holding her hand. Someone had put on the Deccalian record player, and Bill Haley and The Comets were belting out "Rock Around the Clock". Sophie bumped, ground, whirled, and rocked furiously and enthusiastically. Terry was a mean dancer, and Sophie was enjoying herself greatly.

They danced some more and then sat down. They drank Coke and chatted with a few of the girls she had met and who seemed friendly. "You going out with Terry?" a dark-haired girl asked. The others sniggered.

"No—I just met him tonight. He's danced with me, but that's all." Sophie swigged her Coke.

"You wanna watch him." Another girl with blonde plaits said with a grin, and the others exchanged glances.

"Why?" Asked Sophie. "Does he bite?" The girls erupted with laughter and elbowed each other.

"No," the blonde one said and grinned again. "That's about all he doesn't do."

Sophie shrugged. "He looks harmless," she said. The girls all got up to dance.

"Good luck," said the blonde girl, and she went to join the throng of rock and rollers.

It was nearing nine, and Sophie decided to walk home. She got up, picked up her jacket, and went to the door. Suddenly Terry was there beside her. "Leaving so soon?"

"I have to get back home, and I wanted to walk a bit first."

"Mind if I walk with you?"

Sophie hesitated. "No—no, of course not." They went out into the village street, and Sophie turned in the direction of her home. Terry took her arm.

"Why not come down and see the caves, eh?"

"I already saw them."

"But at night they're special. Come on—you'll love them." Again Sophie hesitated. Then she turned and walked with Terry. Through the village, down the hill, through the hedge, and onto the path leading to the caves Something inside her head told her that she should refuse and turn around and make for home, but she was faintly excited, and curious, and felt she was on the verge of something tangibly thrilling. They went in, and the caves were as Sophie had seen them, but now the walls had a glow. It was a magical greenish-pinky luminosity which seemed unearthly and provided a faint illumination.

They went further in, and the path became steeper and began to descend. As Sophie went downwards, her foot slipped, and

Terry grabbed her hand. Sophie felt a tiny shiver; it was not the fear of nearly falling but the reaction to the feel of his warm, firm hand in hers. She did not take her hand away, and they continued down the path until, to her amazement, the cave opened out into a large vaulted area, like a small room. Terry stopped. He squeezed her hand, then put his arm around her waist, and pulled her towards him. His body was very hard and warm, and Sophie felt a strange, overwhelming feeling. She knew that she wanted something, but she did not know what it was. Her body was hot and wanting, and the warmth was spreading down to her groin and further into that secret, dark, female part of her. Terry kissed her very deeply yet very gently on her mouth. She was not sure how to respond, but she opened her mouth and was fascinated by the sweetness of his lips. He was breathing deeply, and his eyes looked large, and greedy, and beautiful. He unbuttoned her blouse and began to pull it off her shoulders. Inside her head, Sophie knew she should have resisted, but she simply allowed him to continue. He unhooked her bra and gently removed it. Then he spread his jacket over the floor in a little niche of the cave wall, took her by the hand, and laid her down. He kissed and sucked her nipples, and Sophie felt them swelling. The sensation between her legs intensified, and she knew that she needed something—but what was it? Terry kissed her again. Then he smiled at her and began to remove her skirt. Sophie felt exposed and shy, but the fierce burning and longing in her body urged her on. Terry rolled her onto her back. He knelt between her legs, pulled off her knickers easily, slid them down and over her feet, and then spread her legs wide. He parted the lips of her vulva and rubbed, gently. Sophie was ecstatic—she trembled slightly.

Terry stopped, and she looked up to see what he was doing. He was rolling a condom onto what seemed to Sophie to be what she had imagined—but so much larger! *Oh my giddy aunt*, she thought, *that has to fit in me!* Terry kissed her again, hard, and then she felt the thing at the entrance to her vagina, and then he started to go into her, and the pain was sharp and intense. For a second Sophie wanted to pull away, to scream and run, but he kissed her again, and the hot desire in her overcame her fear, and she pulled him into her. The short pain as he thrust deeply was driven away by the wonderful sensation she felt as his thrusts grew more urgent and deep. She dug her fingernails into his buttocks and moaned as her need grew more urgent. At that moment Terry jerked violently, gasped, and slowed, panting. He lay on top of her for a little while and then pulled away. He smiled.

"You OK, then?" He eased the condom off and tied off the top. "Here, you'll need this." He handed her his hanky.

"Why?

"Because you'll be bleeding a bit, my lovely." Sophie looked down. He was right. She put the hanky inside her knickers to soak up the blood and started to put her clothes back on. They sat on the jacket on the cave floor and held hands.

Sophie knew there was something she had missed out on—something elusive and wonderful—but she knew soon she would find it. She put her head on Terry's shoulder and thought, *I am now a woman. A man has known my body and taken my virginity. He is now my love, and I am his love.* She had given her body, and with it her heart. They walked back together, up the hill, through the village, and to the big house, where Terry wished her goodnight and kissed her lingeringly before he left.

She gazed after him and then went in. Her mother asked if she had enjoyed the youth club.

"Yes, it was great. We danced a lot."

"Ah, that's why you're so flushed. Do you want some cocoa?" Sophie took her cocoa to bed, drank it, and then lay awake reliving every second of her deflowering. She fell asleep seeing Terry's blue eyes.

They met and he made love to her in those sultry, whispering, summer evenings. They did it out in the fields, in the long, sweet-smelling grass; sprawled over a hay bale, which prickled and scratched her bare back; under the willows beside the river, which whispered softly onto the stones of the bank; and one day in Terry's bed, when his family were away visiting his grandparents. Terry told her the grandparents did not like or approve of him. He and Sophie spent an entire afternoon exploring and pleasuring each other's bodies—but still something was eluding Sophie—some ultimate pleasurable something. Sophie had this beautiful boy in her life, and she floated, and life seemed to be so good.

Then one evening she went down to the post office to post a letter to Rachael, who was in Germany, staying with a family to learn the language. As she was walking home, she heard a murmuring laugh from across the street. Turning, she stopped. There, in a shop doorway, was Terry with the blonde girl from the youth club. They were kissing, and Terry's hands were down the back of the girl's jeans. Sophie was paralyzed momentarily. Then she ran, sobbing and panting, all the way up the main village street and home. She ran upstairs, threw herself onto her bed, and sobbed her heart out. He was a liar—a liar! He had loved her body, and she had imagined that he loved all of her—as she loved him. But he was a liar, and she had given her heart to him, and he had hurt her. After about half an hour, Sophie got up, went to the bathroom, washed her streaked face, combed her hair, took a deep breath, and went downstairs to her piano. She played furiously and with deep, torn, raw feeling. It grew dark, and she went to bed, where she cried some more.

She ignored Terry from then on. He tried to approach her in the street, but she turned away. He ran after her and grabbed her arm. "Hey, Sophie, what the hell have I done?"

She turned and looked at him, her head high. "My parents don't like you. They think you're common—not good enough for me. Please don't speak to me again—ever." She walked away quickly. *I'll have my heart back*, she thought, *and you're a liar.* She never went to the youth club again, or the caves, or the shop his father kept. The summer passed, and the evenings grew shorter and the weather colder. Her hated stepfather's drinking continued. Loud voices, and breaking glass, and slammed doors were all part of the evening's ritual. Sophie hated her stepfather, she hated Terry, she hated this new environment, and she hated life.

One day, wandering through the huge, grassy meadows outside the village, Sophie was fascinated to find a colourful group of hippies camped in the largest of the fields, under the trees and beside the river. They had wooden wagons, tents, horses tethered and grazing, open wood fires, and children wandering around happily. Their exotically decorated and fringed clothes intrigued and delighted her. She simply walked up to them and introduced herself. Within hours she had become one of their number and been accepted without question. The girls took her to a wagon and sorted out clothing for her, along with beads.

She went to the weekly market in Exeter, where she bought herself many long skirts, bohemian blouses, scarves, and velvet and satin waistcoats. She completed these outfits with necklaces and bracelets of beads and plaited leather, and tall, soft leather boots. She plaited ribbons into her hair and wore leather handmade bracelets and necklaces. She walked up to the commune daily, where she joined in everything. She brought food with her and prepared and cooked it with the other females. She gathered wood for the fires. She lay around the fires in the soft evenings and smoked very weak reefers. She did not appreciate the sensation of losing control of her feelings and thoughts as totally as many of the others there did.

Several of the young men there played guitars and sang, and Sophie got up and danced freely and joyfully. They would sit for hours around the red, crackling logs, whilst the sun slid down and the moon rose in icy, silvery beauty. They would talk about life, and their ambitions, and the madness and greed of the world, and how they wanted to reform its thinking and its corrupt institutions. And the firelight threw dark, sultry shadows onto the suntanned skin and long hair and muscular bodies of the men, and Sophie was pulled into the testosterone-fuelled interaction of eyes, and touch, and voices, and gestures, and compelling looks. She knew that she wanted them and that she felt good about her choices; she felt no shame, just deep satisfaction and joy. Everything was shared. Nobody declared ownership of material goods—or of bodies, or hearts and souls. Many of the girls had small children and slept with more than one man.

There was no moral fence. Sophie slept with four of the men there. They were all gentle, kind, loving, and passionate. By now she carried her own supply of condoms, and she insisted on their use, not least because they all had many partners and she wanted neither pregnancy nor a sexually transmitted disease. Here Sophie found a kind of peace. It was an escape from discipline of the harsh order she had been subjected to too often in her life. These gentle and genuinely loving people entranced and held her, and their mental freedom, their relaxed and generous lifestyle, became her credo.

Sophie's parents simply believed that she had adopted a new, trendy youth fashion. They were totally unaware of her new lifestyle, although they did remark that she seemed a lot happier—and they noticed that she had lost a great deal of weight and seemed uninterested in food. This was Sophie's quiet, silent, and visceral rebellion. Her spirit was struggling to free itself, and it had broken the first chains.

Sophie went to university and obtained a good science degree. She enjoyed this period of her life but avoided any associations with the men she encountered as she was, by nature, a serious person where study was concerned and wished to succeed. There were parties where pot was smoked and alcohol was consumed and Sophie attended a few of these with enjoyment but managed to dextorously avoid the expected after party bedding. There were males who attracted her but she turned her attention to her books. She loved the hours in the library, in the brooding and comforting silence, just Sophie and her books and the other silent students. It took her back to the beloved days in the convent library where her love of reading and knowledge had been nurtured. She felt confident, in her world, content and fulfilled. This was a part of her personality but other aspects of that personality could too easily intrude and she fought them. She worked very hard and, as ever, threw herself into achieving.

She was justifiably proud of her degree and had great plans to profit from it but, before she could use it to make some sort of life for herself, she met Rolf. She was in a hotel in Exeter with her friends, having a beer and a few laughs. She looked up and saw coming through the glass swing doors of the entrance another one of life's beautiful men. His hair was jet black and shining, with a natural wave at the front; his skin was olive and looked healthy and enticing. His eyes were sloe black, and his lashes were long, black, and sultry. When he smiled, he had sweet dimples and very white teeth. He wore a smart blazer, with a Royal Electrical and Mechanical Engineers badge on the top left pocket, and grey slacks with a knife-edge crease. He walked to the bar and ordered a beer. Then he lifted it, drank deeply, and turned to look at Sophie and her companions. He nodded his head and smiled before turning back to his pint and chatting to the barman. Sophie was entranced. She had fallen under his spell as soon as she'd set eyes on him. The animal chemistry had been put in motion. She volunteered eagerly to go up and get the next round of drinks. She stood next to the handsome stranger, going through the order with the barman. The stranger turned. "Hello," he said, smiling.

"Hello." Sophie smiled back shyly.

"Would you be offended if I joined your party?

"Of course not. Please do."

"I'll pay for the drinks." He turned to the barman. "Add another pint for me, and bring them over, Charlie." He handed over a note for the round and, after taking his change, followed Sophie to the table, where introductions were made. His name was Rolf Amery, and he was eight years older than Sophie. He had just come out of the army, having served as a regular soldier in the REME for seven years in England, Hong Kong and, very briefly, in British Guiana. They had been going home on a troop carrier from Hong Kong and had been diverted there when Dr Cheddii Jagan had caused trouble - or had needed help with trouble - Sophie couldn't quite remember. Rolf chatted with them about his army days, and Sophie was interested. She asked him what he was currently doing, and he told her he was in charge of a large workshop servicing heavy farming machinery, on a large estate belonging to a millionaire. This wealthy man also had two extremely unique racing cars, which Rolf had helped to build and maintain. Sophie enquired where the estate was and was amazed to find that it was only about two miles outside Chitterton, where she lived.

Rolf was surprised too and seemed pleased. "So we'll be seeing each other, then," he told her.

And they did see each other. Mainly they met in the local pub, the Chitterton Arms. The Chittertons were the local aristocratic family; they had a large residence outside the village, Chitterton Hall. Although Sophie had rejected Catholicism, she still attended mass out of sheer habit. As there was no Catholic church for miles, the public were allowed to attend masses said in the private chapel at the hall with the Chitterton family. Rolf started going with her eventually, although he had no real views on God or religion.

They met at the pub and chatted on and off for about three weeks before Rolf kissed her goodnight for the first time. Then he took her to a pub outside Exeter for a change of venue, and on the way home he drove off the main road and into a secluded wood. He was passionate and impatient, but Sophie was quickly aroused and longing for what she knew was imminent. When he entered her, she was a little shocked at how large he was and afraid she would not be able to take him into her body. She was also very concerned, as he had not put on a condom. She was certainly not taking any contraceptive pills; these were nonexistent at that stage of her life. She found that her body stretched to enclose his size, and she was in ecstasy as he thrust hard and deep into her. She started to wriggle her hips and match his thrusts with hers. The sensations inside her were building into something delicious and something that would not be denied her this time. Just as she knew that she was reaching the moment, Rolf pulled out and knelt with his handkerchief over his penis. He jerked his hand desperately back and forth and then groaned as sperm shot into the hanky. Sophie was shocked and disappointed. She lay there with a tear running down the side of her face.

Rolf cleaned himself up and zipped up his trousers. "What's wrong?" he said when he saw her tears. "Did I hurt you?"

"No. I just didn't quite—quite ..." Sophie didn't know what she hadn't quite managed to do, but she knew she had missed out badly. Inside she was still tingling and needy.

"You didn't come—is that it?"

"I think so."

"Ah—you've never actually ever come before, have you? And you nearly got there, and I stopped you. Sorry, Sophie. I could keep going to help you, but I might come inside you and make you pregnant, and we don't really want that, do we, sweetheart?"

"No, I suppose not." Sophie put her knickers and jeans back on. Rolf lit a cigarette. Sophie did not smoke. They sat in silence and then got up and walked to the car.

In the car, Rolf leaned over and kissed her. Sophie was quiet and unresponsive. Rolf sat back and lit another cigarette. "I suppose you want me to use condoms," he said. "I know I should, but they really spoil it all for me. Don't worry; I'll always get out in time. You'll learn to come quicker after a while, so you'll enjoy it too. Anyway, if you keep a note of when you have your period, we can do it just after your period for about ten days, and you'll be safe."

"You're assuming that I shan't have ovulated until halfway through my cycle?"

"I dunno—something like that. I did it with my last girlfriend, and I only pulled out after that ten days, and it worked fine. It was great."

I really needed to know that, Sophie thought. "It's a dangerous way to go on, Rolf," she told him. "Too easy to have an accident."

"OK, then. I'll use the bloody things."

"No, don't, Rolf—not if you don't want to. We'll use the rhythm method and just be very careful." Sophie was not happy really to do this, but she was afraid of upsetting and losing Rolf.

"Thank you, my darling." Rolf turned and kissed her. He switched on the engine, and the little Morgan roared throatily and bumped up the track to the main road. Eventually Sophie realised that she must introduce Rolf to her parents. She was very unhappy and nervous, as he had a strong South Devon accent, and her parents were very snobbish about such things.

She told them that she had met a young man and wanted them to meet him. Her stepfather immediately questioned her avidly about his age, what job he had, where he lived—on and on the inquisition went. He seemed satisfied on hearing of Rolf's army career and his job at the large park for the millionaire Silas Hay. "But have you met his parents yet?"

"No, I haven't met them."

"Where do they live, then?"

"In the gatehouse on the estate. They both work there." Her stepfather looked displeased, but he finished questioning her.

Rolf drove his Morgan into their drive at seven promptly a few evenings later. He was clean shaven, his hair was immaculate, and he was wearing his smart blazer with the REME badge and his regimental tie. He shook hands with her parents and sat down, whilst Sophie and her mother made drinks for all of them. As they heard Rolf speaking with such a strong local burr, Sophie's parents began to exchange subtle looks. Sophie's heart sank.

"And where does your father work?" her stepfather asked Rolf.

"Oh, he works on the estate," Rolf replied.

"In the office?"

"No, he helps with the cattle, and the chickens, and the gardening." There was a loud silence. Small talk followed, but the atmosphere was strained. Sophie was relieved when Rolf excused himself, saying he had a very early start the next day. As she walked with him to his car, he said, "They don't much like me, do they?"

Sophie was on the verge of tears. "I'm old enough to choose who I go out with, and they're a pair of damned snobs. He isn't even my father, and he's a bloody drunk, and he shouts at my mother, and I hate him!" She began to sob. Rolf put his arms around her and kissed her forehead.

"Tomorrow you must come and meet my parents. I'll pick you up at the end of the lane about six."

"OK." Sophie kissed him and walked slowly back into the house after watching him drive off. She entered and awaited the inevitable criticisms from her parents: *Didn't she even notice that thick accent? His father was just a farmhand. He went to the secondary modern school. He was only a sergeant in the army. Did he respect her? Had he touched her?* To this last question Sophie replied that he had only ever kissed her, and she didn't feel at all dishonest as it was not their business. She told them that she was going to meet his parents the next day. Then she went up to bed, unhappy and dreading the next evening.

At six Rolf drew up and opened the door of the Morgan for her. They drove in silence; Sophie was very nervous. She did not like his parents from the first second. His mother was a possessive, jealous, spiteful creature. Dwarf-like, with no teeth, she had little screwed-up eyes behind round, wire glasses and the dress sense of a scarecrow. His father had obviously been good-looking at some point, but now he had a hooked, threatening nose, sunken eyes, and sallow skin. Sophie was later to find out that he was a heavy drinker, gambler, and womaniser—and a vicious, calculating, and wicked liar. She was asked to sit at the table, and plates of cold meat and bread and butter were served, with salad and homemade pickles.

Rolf's mother peered at Sophie. "I hope it'll be good enough for her—her coming from such a posh family." She looked Sophie up and down and began to eat. She poured tea for everyone without asking Sophie how she liked her tea; then she started talking to her husband and son and totally ignoring Sophie. Sophie quickly realised that this was a mother who would not allow any other woman near her only son. She idolised and spoilt him and would even attempt to destroy anyone Rolf loved. After tea Sophie helped to take the dishes through and wash them up. Rolf's mother made half-hearted attempts at conversation, but it was very strained, and Sophie was glad to say goodnight and leave.

Both of them realised that they were disliked by the other's parents, and this did not much improve things between them. One week Rolf's parents were away in North Devon visiting an elderly aunt who was sick. Rolf asked Sophie to come up to the lodge and cook for him whilst they were away. He picked her up early in the mornings, and she cooked him a big breakfast; then he kissed her and drove up the big driveway to the workshops. At lunchtime she prepared him a light snack, and after that they went to his bedroom and made love until it was time for him to return to work. In the evening she cooked him a substantial meal and cleared and washed up, without any help from him. Then he would make love to her, kneeling in front of her outspread legs as she lay on the settee, and stroking her breasts and her belly.

One night they had a long, slow, arousing foreplay session, and Sophie was desperate for Rolf's body to be inside hers and bring her the orgasm she yearned for. He entered her, and soon they were both sweating and groaning. Sophie felt her moment of bliss approaching and pulled Rolf into her, digging her nails into his back and begging him to fuck her hard. As she felt the orgasm hit her body, she shivered and thrust hard against him; she was at the crest of the wave of liquid, tearing passion when she felt Rolf trying to pull away and heard him saying, "No, God no, Sophie—not now—we can't ..." And then he came with her, and she cried with the release and the satisfaction of her coming. Rolf pulled out of her quickly. "God, Sophie, this is about the worst day we could have done this!"

"Why?" And then she realised. They kept an eye on the dates. This was about fourteen days after her period, and she would be fertile. They both prayed that nothing would happen, but then Sophie's period was three weeks' overdue. She began vomiting, endlessly and painfully. They had to tell her parents, and it was not a happy event. There was much shouting and anger, and accusations flew viciously. Rolf's parents were not happy either, but there was nothing they could do about it. Abortion did not exist as an option; unmarried mothers were as guilty as murderers.

They had to marry, and they did so on a beautiful September day, at Lord Chitterton's Catholic chapel, with his kind permission. Sophie wore a very lovely wild silk, off-white gown and veil, with a diamanté and rosebud headdress. She carried an armful of tuber roses, carnations, and rosebuds. Rachael was her bridesmaid, dressed in a dusky-pink silk dress and carrying a ball of white rosebuds tied with white ribbon. The reception was held at Sophie's parents' home. Her stepfather refused to attend and went away for the entire week. Sophie's uncle had to step in and give her away. Sophie had to fight overwhelming nausea all the day long, and she had an infection in her urinary tract. It was on that day, of all days, that she realised that Rolf had a drink problem. She realised that she just hadn't registered how heavy his drinking was before. At the reception he slowly became unpleasantly and aggressively drunk, and Sophie realised then that she had made a huge, terrible mistake. His father came in a threadbare demob suit, which was too short in the arms and legs, and a hideous green-and-orange tie. HIs mother wore a slime green, hand-knitted dress that resembled a tea cosy with armholes. She also wore hideous, cheap costume jewellery in great profusion. She resembled a small, aggressive, ugly Christmas tree.

Eight months later, their first daughter entered the world, naturally and smoothly, without any gas and air or stitches being needed. The first stage of labour went on for three days, but husbands were not then allowed to attend or support, so Sophie lay in a dark room, terrified and in great pain. The birth relieved that agony. Her daughter had the thick, dark curls of her father; she had his looks.

Sophie did not find motherhood very wonderful, as she fought the interference of her in-laws and her husband's increasing drinking. With an inheritance from Sophie's grandmother, they bought a small thatched public house in the village. Sophie did not want it. It was not the sort of thing her alcoholic husband should really be running, but she was overruled, and they moved in. Her in-laws invited themselves and came to "help". This meant that her father-in-law worked behind the bar, helping himself to beer and cigarettes, on which there was a very small profit margin anyway. When the two of them left, her mother-in-law always had several bulging carrier bags with her, and Sophie would find meat and fish missing from her large freezer and tins and packets missing from her store.

One day Sophie noticed that two large cheques had been drawn on their joint bank account. Rolf had not put up a penny for the business but was very happy to draw from it. When she asked him what the cheques were for, she discovered that he had bought a second-hand car for his father—apparently the other one was finished—and he had paid a year's rent in advance for them to move, as his father had been sacked from the estate. He had been drunk on the job, stealing from the stores there, and selling the goods for profit. He had lost the lodge and was homeless, so Rolf had used her inheritance to pay his parents' way—without her permission. A furious row followed. Sophie pointed out to Rolf that this was her money, her inheritance, and it was to be used for them, but not for his parents—and most certainly not without her knowledge or permission. Rolf got very drunk and hit Sophie hard, bruising her face and arms. It was the start of a nightmare.

Sophie's parents had dismissed her from their lives. As far as they were concerned, Sophie had betrayed them socially and married that drunken, common, ill-spoken little runt; that mummy's spoilt brat. She was no longer of importance to them. They did not visit or phone. They had no interest in their granddaughter. Even Rachael became detached and cold. She hated Rolf. In later years she told Sophie that Rolf had made attempts to kiss and touch her, and she loathed his smell of alcohol and sweat. The small pub was not making any money. Rolf's parents had eroded the profits and their capital, and Rolf was drinking the rest. They were losing regulars at a serious rate. The stalwarts could no longer tolerate Rolf's drunken rudeness and his churlish treatment of Sophie.

They went bankrupt and had to sell the pretty little thatched place. Sophie was heartbroken. Rolf got a post as the manager of a fish and chip shop which had accommodation at the back. There were three downstairs rooms, a kitchen and two bedrooms. This did not last long. Rolf became very drunk one night; he was not at all happy in the job. He was appallingly rude to some customers and then threw a portion of chips across the shop at a customer. The owners sacked him immediately, and they were out on the street in days.

The only recourse they had was to live with Rolf's parents. They now had a three-bedroomed house—the year's rent having been paid for with Sophie's money. Rolf, Sophie, and their daughter were crammed into the tiny spare room. Rolf's mother interfered unrelentingly with everything. She took over their daughter and their lives. Sophie fought back, but if his mother was upset, Rolf would attack Sophie verbally and physically. He was drunk most of the time. He had one job after another. Money was thin, and Sophie had to sell her jewellery and clothes for them to survive. His parents charged them a pretty stiff rent and charged for their small amount of food on top of that. Sophie cried herself to sleep almost every night. She wrote to her parents weekly, but she received no reply. She begged her sister for help but was ignored. Eventually a letter arrived. With shaking hands, Sophie tore open the envelope. The writing was her stepfather's. Sophie was angry and hurt— she had expected her mother to write. She read the letter with a sinking heart and terrible pain.

Sophie,

Your mother and I have read your many letters with great annoyance and distress. You chose to associate with a no-good person of no family or background, with no education or career, and with common, ignorant parents of the servant class. We have spent a great amount on your education and upbringing and are certainly not prepared to waste any more, particularly if any of it will go to your drunken and indolent husband and his greedy parents. You must extract yourself from your predicament. We did make our disapproval clear at the very start, and you chose to ignore us. You have now learnt a very hard lesson. But it's one you brought on yourself. Do not write to your mother or to me for any money or any other kind of help again.

The letter was unsigned. Were it not for the address printed at the top of the page, it might have been anonymous. Sophie screwed it up and put it in the suitcase underneath her bed. She sank onto the bed and wept silently. She was alone—totally alone.

Rolf went from job to job, and they were so poor, so very poor and wretched. Sophie could scarcely buy decent clothes and shoes for her daughter. Her own clothes were threadbare; she had sold her good clothes with her jewellery. Rolf's parents kept him well dressed, but Sophie might just as well not have existed. Eventually Rolf struck up an acquaintance with a man who owned a large pottery in a tiny village on the river Dart. He needed someone to run repair workshops for a lorry and two

Land Rovers he had, which formed a small haulage. This man was an agent for small, locally built boats, which he delivered. Rolf took on the job and seemed to take on a new life from then on. His drinking lessened; more importantly, the man who employed him paid the deposit for them on a lovely little cottage in the village. It needed attention and repair, and they had virtually no furniture, but to Sophie it was heaven. She begged, borrowed, and went to sales, and slowly a home was thrown together. The large garden was derelict, and Sophie had to toil like a slave to even clear it, but slowly she turned it into a vegetable garden of some excellence. What they did not eat Sophie sold to the local shop and at the gate of the cottage.

Sophie suffered three miscarriages, followed by a stillbirth. She was deeply depressed. Rolf was pulling away from her mentally, emotionally, and physically. Lovemaking was pure routine, and he was disinterested. He still drank, and his violence returned and increased. He gave Sophie less and less money, and she was forced to hide under the stairs, with her hand over her daughter's mouth, to avoid the baker, butcher, and milkman as they knocked for their bills to be paid. Then local gossip let her know that Rolf's long absences were not just work. The haulage had developed, and he sometimes went away driving. The whispers told her that he spent hours with wealthy local women, usually older than he was. He was still a very attractive man and had a con man's ability to talk women into his shadow. Sophie realised that he was another beautiful liar.

They had a son by now. The birth had been very hard, as he was a huge baby—11 pounds and 4 ounces. Then Sophie inherited a fair sum of money from an aunt. She drew most of it out of her bank in cash and hid it carefully under the floorboards in the children's room. It was her last desperation money. The rest she used to buy the haulage for Rolf. He drove still and was transport manager. They employed two drivers, and Sophie did the office work. Rolf still had his mature lovers in the village, and Sophie tried to ignore the situation. Rolf's drinking and violence lurked unendingly in the shadows and tatters of their marriage.

One evening, one of their drivers, Dave, having set off for Scotland, was forced to return. He had had a breakdown and been obliged to leave his rig at a garage. He thumbed a lift to his home and went inside. In the bedroom he discovered Rolf, his boss, in bed with his wife. The affair had been going on for some time. A fight ensued. Dave went to live on his boat at Brixham, and Rolf moved in with Kate, leaving very suddenly. Sophie was shattered but almost relieved. She continued to run the haulage, but Rolf had been neglecting the business, and jobs had not been done properly. The rigs were in a state of disrepair. Money was being wasted and lost at a great rate. Soon creditors were demanding—first the cottage went and then the business. Sophie realised that she and her children would have to find a new home quickly. She thought of the money she had secreted under the bedroom floorboards; with that she could put down a deposit on a flat. She hurried up to the children's bedroom and prised up the old, splintery boards. Her heart stopped. There was nothing there—not even the box she had put the money in! She searched desperately. Nothing. Maybe rats had eaten it, but there were no shreds of paper or remains of chewed-up wood—just nothing. *Rolf*—she thought—*Rolf. He has stolen my money, and I have nothing.*

She faced him and accused him, but he just laughed at her and told her she was a fucking liar and an imbecile.

Rolf remained with Kate, and Sophie had to drag her children around a series of slums, fighting to exist again. Rolf gave her virtually nothing, and the pittance she begged the government for bought little. Rolf came to the cottage shortly before she left; he demanded a talk about the future. Rolf sat drinking steadily. They soon had little to talk about, and he moved towards Sophie on the settee.

"How about a quick fuck as a goodbye, eh?" Sophie recoiled and pulled away from him, but Rolf was a big, muscular man. He picked her up and turned her over so that she was kneeling face down on the settee. Sophie fought back and struggled to escape, but he was far too strong. He roughly tore off her clothes and her brief panties. Then he went into her from behind, very deeply and viciously. Sophie cried out as he hurt her but, to her horror, found herself aroused. Rolf fucked her, grunting and laughing, for a full twenty minutes, and Sophie pushed her hand into her mouth so that he should not hear her reach orgasm. When he came, he stayed inside her for a while. "Well, Sophie my girl, you'll have problems finding someone my size again." He laughed. "After me, everyone else will just be an anticlimax." He picked up his jacket and walked out. The door slammed. He was gone. Sophie was alone—and she didn't know it yet, but she was pregnant again.

The next few years were ones of poverty and despair for Sophie. She lived in substandard, slummy accommodation. She had no help, no family, and no money. She gave birth to another daughter. Rolf came to the hospital briefly to see the small girl. When he saw that she was blonde, although olive skinned, he told Sophie that the baby quite clearly wasn't his, and then he left. Sophie struggled to raise the children. Poverty dragged her down. She was thin and pale and depressed. She managed to get jobs but had problems with childcare and often lost good positions. The strain was making her ill, but she fought on. The years passed in a terrible sameness. She rarely saw her family. Rachael visited briefly but did not linger.

Rolf ran from his creditors, escaping to France with Kate, where he drove a lorry and continued to drink heavily. Kate had not told him that she suffered from epilepsy and took barbiturates to control the seizures. She gave birth to a small, sickly boy. Homesick, unhappy, and tired of Rolf's drinking, absences, and inability to handle money—disillusioned with him totally—she began to drink too. She mixed her medication with alcohol once too often. At just 33 years of age she was found dead with the now-6-month-old baby boy screaming in his carry cot. Rolf launched into a year-long drinking binge. The boy was taken into care. Rolf surfaced briefly, went to England, and met a nursing sister with property and rich friends. He did what he did so well. He lied his way into a marriage by weaving a sob story of a poor, sad man who had taken to drink only because his wife had suddenly and tragically died, leaving him with a baby to raise alone. And Sophie was a wicked, unfaithful bitch who had taken all his money and run away. The new wife lapped it up, of course. She wanted his body. Very soon she regretted marrying and believing this drunken con man—particularly a few years later, as she sat in a wheelchair, dying from terminal cancer, alone, while he lounged in the nearby pub chatting up a mature, wealthy blonde.

But that is how it is with the beautiful liars. There are the women of the moment, and there are the victims. Of the three, Sophie was the biggest victim. The other two were out of the misery he had created. She alone still had to cope with the aftermath. A journey of a million miles begins with the first step. Sophie walked onwards with her head into the wind—alone, frightened, and poor.

The years after this were terrible. Sophie never, ever wanted to relive them. She tried to get a job suitable to her education and qualification, but the problems she encountered with childcare and her children's behaviour saw her losing one post after another. Since the birth of her third child she had suffered from undiagnosed postnatal depression, and she struggled with this crippling disorder on top of her terrifying poverty. The stress bore down on her like an ambush, and she woke up one morning hardly knowing where or who she was. She was hospitalised and the children briefly sent to foster parents. She was discharged—far too soon—with bottles and packets of medication which shackled and imprisoned her mind and dulled her into a submissive, semicomatose state. She sleepwalked through each miserable day, while the house became a sordid, filthy prison and the children ran riot.

Oh God, she thought as she huddled on the settee, *I was so well raised and educated. How have I let my life become like this*? She fought to try and overcome the foggy misery in which she drifted daily, but she was losing, and she knew this. One morning, confused after not having eaten for days, dehydrated and ill, she accidentally overdosed on her medications. She was rushed into hospital. Her stomach was emptied, and she lay in a coma for days. Somebody from the social services came in and spoke to her. Sophie barely registered what the woman was saying. She seemed to understand that the children were being taken by their father to France for a while, to enable her to recover.

She was discharged after a week's rest in the hospital. She took the bus home to find the house empty. There were no voices and no movement. The mess was everywhere: toys, clothes, crisp packets, crumbs, combs, odd shoes. She stood weeping. After a while she determinedly attacked the house. She hoovered, scrubbed, tidied, and threw out bagfuls of rubbish. She remade beds and washed the bedding. She put the linen out on the line, ironed, mended, cleaned out the fridge, cleaned the filthy cooker, and rearranged all the children's toys in their rooms and downstairs. This left her very tired. She prepared a couple of boiled eggs with toast and a hot, sweet cup of tea. She sat down to eat, listening to some Elgar. How long had it been since she had played any music? She no longer had a piano—her means of release from the world's misery was gone from her life.

The following morning, having slept better than she had done for months, Sophie set off for the telephone box on the corner and made a long-distance call to France. The long *bweeee, bweeee* of the continental dial tone seemed to go on forever. Then there was a click, and she heard Rolf's voice.

"Hello, *bonjour.*"

"Rolf, it's Sophie. I'm out of hospital; I'm quite a lot better. How are the children? Can I speak to them? How soon can they come back home?"

"You can speak to them—but—well, I don't think, somehow, that they'll be back quite yet, do you?"

"Whatever do you mean! They were only there whilst I was ill. I'm well now—they can return." Her heart was thumping and she was shaking.

"Here—talk to them." Soon her eldest daughter was on the line. The children were all pleased to hear her voice and chatted eagerly. They seemed happy enough, but Sophie sensed that they wanted to return. She understood that they had not had a wonderful life with her. Poverty and her illness had not given them much of a childhood, but she wanted them back with her. Rolf was a selfish, insufficient father, and his girlfriend, Kate, was a party-loving, tarty, vain creature, although she had a warm heart and was a surprisingly good homemaker. But if Rolf behaved true to form, Sophie doubted that Kate could survive, and she did not want her children involved. She finished talking to the children, and Rolf came back on the line.

"They seem OK, Rolf, but I'm back now, and they should come home," Sophie said tentatively.

"They're settled quite well so far ..." Rolf hesitated. "The social services seemed to think they'd be better staying here with me and Kate."

"No, Rolf. No, their home is here with me. Let them come back."

"I'll contact the social services tomorrow Sophie—but I think they're better here. They can go over and see you, and you can come over and see them—"

"But they can't speak the language, Rolf! How will they cope with school? It's a strange country, and they—no, no, they must come back. I'm going to the social services myself tomorrow. They were only supposed to go there while I got better. I am better—they've changed my medication. I know I can cope now. You can't just take them away from me—" There was a click. He had put the phone down on her. Sophie ran home, crying. The next day she went into the offices of the child protection team and asked for her children to be returned. From then on her life became another nightmare, a daily struggle with authority and promises, promises that were broken and then later denied, a stream of different faces, people who seemed not to care or understand or accept the truth. Then she realised that Rolf was lying to them and they were believing him rather than her. She was helpless against this monstrous machine. She scraped and saved her tiny income and travelled over to see them. She was so happy to see them, and they were so happy to cuddle in to her. They looked ill fed and dressed. Kate was a good enough housekeeper but very young. Sophie sensed that all was not well between Kate and Rolf.

She returned home, despairing and feeling as if she wanted to howl to the moon for her babies. As soon as the council discovered that she was the only resident in the house, they demanded she give up the tenancy and move into a flat. Sophie argued that she needed the house for when her children returned. They informed her that in that eventuality she must reapply for suitable housing. She moved into a sordid upstairs flat in a seedy, derelict area. It was dark, smelt damp, and was very cold, even with the hissing, inefficient gas fire at full tilt.

Sophie got a job at an accountant's. She had lost her confidence and could not face the thought of holding down a job that she was really more qualified for. All day she toiled at her desk. She hardly knew anyone there, and she kept to herself. After the day's work Sophie took the bus home to her lonely, squalid box.

She hardly ate anything, as she had no appetite. But when she looked in the mirror one day, she saw something miraculous. Her face had thinned out, and her cheekbones were defined, almost attractive. She had changed. Her pallor did not even spoil the transformation. She hung onto this one tiny positive thing in her grim life.

The children came to stay with her. Her annual work holiday was a fortnight, and she had saved avidly for this occasion. She took the train and met them off the ferry. Tired and happy, they arrived at the tiny flat. She had put the two girls in her double bed in the one bedroom; she would sleep on a blow-up camping mattress on the bedroom floor. Her son slept on the battered settee. They had a good time and, when the time for their return came, were all quiet and sad. Sophie took them to the ferry. They said their tearful goodbyes, and Sophie stood waving and weeping as the ferry pulled out.

The next years were traumatic for all. Kate suddenly wrote to Sophie; the letter was clearly one of distress. Sophie's younger daughter was very unhappy, it said. The children were not happy; things were very bad. Kate had given birth to a boy who was sickly. Rolf was drinking very heavily. He spent most of his income on alcohol and had lost several jobs driving heavy lorries because of this. Money was in very short supply, and Kate was in despair. Sophie phoned Rolf. He insisted all was well and that the children were very happy. Sophie was in agonies of worry again. She went to the hated social services and tried desperately to get their help, but they were cold and unhelpful. They put every obstacle in her way that they could. At night she wept brokenly and tossed and turned hourly, waking tired and feeling more unwell with each miserable day. Slowly, slowly, the fight wore her down. She started to become unwell again. She had to start taking stronger medication again, and it affected her work performance. She was fighting for her children, her sanity, and her world. The children came to stay again, and Sophie knew all was very wrong with their father's environment. She waved them goodbye with a breaking heart and returned to the struggle.

Then she began, slowly, to make tiny inches of progress. The inhuman social workers began to notice her unending pressure, and they sent someone vaguely human to see her at the flat. They sat drinking tea in front of the chugging gas fire. This woman had actually got involved with the French system and agreed that something needed to be done. She was trying to get wheels in motion, but it would be a slow process.

"Please hurry." Sophie held out a letter from Kate. "She's at the end of her tether, and she has this baby who's unwell and never feeds or stops crying. It's all so urgent. Please do something—please!"

Two weeks passed. Then the news came to Sophie that Kate had been found dead. The baby had been put into care. Sophie's younger daughter had been placed in a convent boarding school. Her other two children were still with Rolf, who was drinking very heavily. Sophie phoned the woman who had promised her help. They would do what they could, but there was so much red tape, so many legal formalities. Sophie pleaded and wept.

That night she sat by her fire feeling very strange and unwell; she sat for a long time staring at the wall. Why was she here in this strange place? She could remember certain things—but so vaguely. She was very afraid. Her hands shook wildly as she held them out in front of her. She must get to France—yes, that was it. She fumbled wildly in her handbag. There was her passport, yes—and she had just enough in her savings to buy a ferry ticket over there and to pay the children's fares back. She must go to the school and get her youngest one out of that place. She turned off the gas fire, stuffed a few clothes in a duffel bag, dragged on her coat and scarf, and locked the front door behind her. Determinedly she went down the stone stairs and out into the cold night. She waited at the bus stop but realised that it was too late at night for buses. She began to walk. There would be a train—yes, there would be one to Liverpool Street. She picked up speed. The raw cold bit into her face, and she wrapped her scarf around her head. It took her over an hour to reach the railway station. It was silent and empty. Sophie looked at the board showing train times. It showed very little—just early morning times. Sophie searched desperately for someone to ask. She pounded on doors and shouted, pulling at he handles wildly. Then something inside her burst.

She kicked furiously at the door which said Information. Screaming and crying, she kicked it again and again. Then there was a man asking her something, and someone else, and she was trying so hard to make them realise that she had to get to France because her children needed her now. The man tried to pull her away from the door, and Sophie hit out at him. And then there were police everywhere, and they were holding her arms roughly and dragging her out of the station, and she was imploring them, and weeping, and trying to get back to the trains—the trains—the boat—her children!

"Let me go—no! I must get to them! Don't you see? They need me—please!" They took her to the police station, where a kindly elderly doctor spoke to her. They gave her a cup of tea and then they took her out to an ambulance. *They will take me home, and I can go to France tomorrow*, Sophie reassured herself. But they didn't take her home. They sectioned her, and she spent several weeks in a dreadful, lost, underwater world. She was filled with drugs and watched constantly. Finally one day she went home, and the realisation hit her like a blow to the face. She had not been able to save her children. From then on, they were to remain in France, and settle in schools, and marry. Sophie felt that they never forgave her; Rolf lied about the reality to them and made sure that the blame he should have taken was poured onto Sophie. Her son Sean, now 9, was very unhappy, and he did blame his father. He hid his passport, scraped together money for the crossing, and slipped out of the house. He ran to the terminal and boarded the ferry. He had forged a letter of parental permission and safely docked four hours later. He thumbed lifts all the way, and then he knocked on Sophie's door. When she opened it, he fell into her arms, laughing and crying. Rolf made indignant noises of accusation and tried to involve the authorities in France. The English social services told her to forget about it and gave her some help to get benefits. Sophie had a reason to get better, and so she did.

As her son matured, he began to develop his father's liking for alcohol. Sophie was angry and distressed. She tried many times to obtain help for him, but he would refuse to attend meetings and therapy and then a placement in a very good and sought-after clinic. Slowly his life ran down into the mud of alcoholism. He was always shabby and unshaven. Sophie struggled to pay her way and keep him too. Frequently he went away saying that he had a job in some town somewhere, but he would soon be back with stories of being let down or the job not being what he'd been told it was. But Sophie knew that he had lost it because of his unreliability and the erratic performance caused by his addiction. One morning he brought his various backpacks, stuffed with his belongings, into the little living room and set them down. He pulled on his jacket.

"I'm off, Mum."

"Off—where?"

"I'm going over to France to try and get a decent job. I speak French fluently, and I've got friends over there. We can go grape-picking; there's work on the docks and the markets. I'll be just fine."

"But what about—" Sophie stopped. She had meant to ask him how he was going to survive with his addiction. She realised that she could do nothing to stop him. He was very young, but he was old enough to sort his own life out by learning the hard way. She went to her handbag and took out a bundle of notes. It was her entire month's housekeeping money, but she had things in her freezer and her cupboards—and she ate little these days.

"Here, take this. It will help for a while."

"Thanks, Mum. Are you sure? It's a lot—"

"Of course I'm sure. I wish you wouldn't go. I wish you'd stay here with me and try to beat your drinking—"

He was frowning at her. "I'm fine. Stop worrying so much. I'm not like that arsehole of a father of mine." He picked up his bags and heaved them onto his broad shoulders. "Must go now, Mum. Take good care of yourself. I'll try to stay in touch." He leaned down and kissed her warmly. Sophie pushed his bags out of the way and flung her arms around him, crushing him to her body. She cried as she held him. Then he gently pulled free and picked his bags up again.

"Bye." He stood for a moment looking at her, and then he was gone. Sophie heard his feet on the stone staircase outside the flats and then the silence. He was gone, her only son—gone to face life, vulnerable, addicted, and young. She sat weeping silently for some while. So many partings. So many goodbyes, and silences, and so much emptiness. *Goodbye, my darling. My heart goes with you.* And Sophie faced the next phase of that dark journey—alone.

Sophie did not know quite how she found herself involved with Michel Navarre. She took an evening job at a wine bar to try and save money to go to France to see the children. She worked upstairs in a small, pleasant, relaxed bar. She soon took to the tasks involved and was at ease with the customers. Some of the single men chatted her up, but Sophie took all this talk, with its inevitable sexual innuendo, as just a part of the job and brushed it off. She had begun to dress rather more smartly, buying her clothes at second-hand shops and from market stalls. Her now-slimmer figure, combined with her beautiful long, red hair and more attractive clothes, made Sophie look very much sexier and even prettier. She used quite a lot of make-up, defining her eyes sharply and rouging her high cheekbones. The results pleased Sophie, and her confidence began to return.

One night, as Sophie was restocking the shelves, he came in. He was hardly attractive. There was no instant internal *wow*, no chemistry, nothing. He was very tall and gangly. He had pale-brown, very tightly curled hair and a rather cruel, beaky nose. There was nothing in him that moved Sophie in any way—except his eyes. They were a beautiful shade of deep, jewel-like green, with bluish and yellow flecks. It was impossible not to stare at them. Sophie learnt that he was called Michel Navarre. He was from a French family but had been brought up in England. He was a machinist at a local engineering firm, and he lived alone in a bedsitter. He came in every night from then on. They talked, and Sophie saw that this was a very lonely person she had met—as lonely as she was. She went to the pictures with him, to a restaurant, for an evening riverboat trip on her day off from the wine bar, and for walks on the river path. She found that she was not lonely anymore, but she did not really feel too much for Michel.

One night they went back to his bedsitter. She registered that he had rather cheap, tasteless furniture and fittings, but she did not take in his meanness of spirit, his tight, obsessive control of money for its own ends, his abnormal and neurotic personality. She met his parents. HIs mother had been a beauty in her youth. She seemed welcoming and pleasant enough, but there was something vague about her that Sophie could not quite grasp. His father was a man who held very firm views on everything, and he held them noisily, jabbing his finger like a dagger at the person he was inflicting them on. He was biased, bigoted, and boring. Like most people of this ilk, he was also, inevitably, a total know-all. On having discovered that Sophie suffered from severe migraine, he said in his whiney drawl, "Well, there you are, then." When Sophie enquired as to what this meant, he looked at her witheringly.

"Parents, bad blood, weak stock. Bad diet." Sophie made the mistake of laughing loudly at this ignorant garbage. Michel hastily swept her out of the house with his father muttering to nobody in particular that Sophie was "an overeducated, stupid, stuck up, silly, modern woman—and mark my words, you'll regret meeting her!" Sophie was glad to reach the bus stop and get on the bus to escape. Michel did not have a car. He could not even actually drive. Again these facts seemed to have washed over Sophie. She was not really all that desperately happy with his company, but she was so lonely that even this brought her some kind of relief from her solitary existence.

Sophie did not know quite how she drifted into marriage with Michel, but one September they married in the registry office of the local city and drove with Michel's brother down to his parents' home on the coast for the reception. The meal was, quite evidently, cheap and budgeted to within a farthing. The wine was little short of disgusting. Sophie's mother had condescended to attend with Rachael, and Sophie watched her mother's expression as the torturous meal progressed. Sophie felt herself becoming more and more humiliated and angry; then the speeches began. As there was no father of the bride, Michel's father had decided that he would conduct matters. He leapt up and delivered a boring, nonsensical rant. Everyone fidgeted and looked uncomfortable. Sophie's mother whispered to Rachael and kept glancing at the door. At last the ordeal was over. The tables were cleared away and music was put on. Drinks were poured. People danced. It became reasonably bearable. Michel danced, stiffly and badly, with Sophie and talked interminably, irritating and boring his tired, disappointed, disillusioned bride. That night they slept at her in-laws' home in a hard, noisy bed. They had slept together before, and Michel had performed pretty well. He was equipped with a good-sized penis. It had been quite a good experience for Sophie then, but tonight she was tired and unhappy, and the damned bed made such a bloody awful racket, squeaking and creaking each time Michel thrust into her. She did not reach orgasm. Michel did. He rolled off his condom, tied it off, went to the toilet, kissed her goodnight, and then fell asleep with his back to her.

In the following three years of her grey, loveless marriage to this thin, dull, selfish, neurotic creature, Sophie enrolled on and completed a nursing qualification. She enjoyed it greatly, although she had to get to her duties by bus and on foot. But this helped her to achieve a slimmed-down body. She was about to launch into a job as a nurse, but life had already dug her another pit into which she was about to fall with a dull thud.

Life was grim again for Sophie. She discovered she had married a man with meanness imprinted throughout his being like the name in a stick of rock candy. He once bought some second-hand timber, and Sophie had to spend two days of her weekend prising out the nails. Then she had to hammer the nails to straighten them out to be reused. She was forbidden to light the fire until ice formed on the inside of window panes. Michel refused to take a driving test or purchase a car. He went everywhere on his bicycle. The fact that Sophie was unable to even ride a bike was of no interest to him. She had to drag her shopping home up the steep hill to save the bus fares. They had taken a mortgage on a house that they had bought in a foreclosure sale. It was a miserable terraced house with two bedrooms, one of which they had to walk through to access the damp, gloomy bathroom, with its sloping roof and ancient bath, toilet, and basin. Its tiled ceiling was black with mould. Michel decided the redecorations. The results were rooms decorated in colours that Sophie was to describe later to her friends as dark mushroom, frog green, mud brown, and vomit. He and his mean habits and spirit crushed Sophie. She was by now on the contraceptive pill, as the last thing she wanted to add to this miserable situation was another baby. One day, after eating a Chinese lunch with her friends from the hospital at which she had just completed her nursing studies, Sophie felt violently sick. By midnight she was vomiting profusely and passing copious amounts of watery, stinking faeces. To her shame, Sophie totally forgot that this would affect the action of her birth control pills. When she missed her period and the early morning coffee she usually enjoyed made her feel nauseous, she sat down with her head in her hands. She thought, *I'm going to get an abortion. I don't need his approval or permission. I can hide the pregnancy and go and have it done when I'm supposed to be at the hospital on duty. He'll never know.* But his keen eyes and brain had registered her lack of periods, her large, swollen breasts, and her morning sickness. She broke down under his interrogation. He was delighted. This was the crowning moment of his marriage and his life. Sophie was trapped.

Michel burbled on unendingly about the son she was about to present him with. He attended the antenatal check-ups and classes and subjected Sophie to a daily ritual in which she was made to lie on the bed whilst he examined her swollen belly, feeling the unborn baby kicking and moving. This usually excited Michel, and the inevitable outcome was his needing sexual gratification, which involved Sophie lying sideways across the bed whilst Michel entered her from behind. He panted and gasped, and stroked her huge belly as he came, making little whining noises. Towards the end, when she was huge and unwieldy, he insisted on her lying on the bed on her side and sucking his penis until he reached a climax and pulled out, jerking and moaning, and finished the process with his hand and a tissue. Sophie loathed this. She had by now realised that she had no love for this cold, mean person. Having to take his unwanted flesh into her mouth nauseated her, and she had to resort to pretending to be asleep or groaning with invented back pain to avoid contact with Michel.

The birth was induced. It began early on Easter Sunday. The sun was shining fiercely through the windows of the delivery room, and the trees outside were a riot of cherry blossom. Sophie was growing very tired. She was nearly thirty-nine; Michel was thirty. She was given an epidural to help her endure the pain that was wearing her strength down. Michel strode up and down the delivery room, irritating the nursing staff with his unending commentary on what his son would look like, be called, wear, and do when he grew up—it went on and on. The evening wore on. Michel was sent out. It was a forceps delivery. Sophie was pulled to the end of the bed with her legs in supports. She could not feel the contractions, but the midwife told her when to bear down. And then, suddenly, she was there—her daughter. The child had pale, unmarked, smooth skin, with not a wrinkle, or mark, or any redness. She had a fuzz of pale, golden hair. And then she opened her eyes, and Sophie saw for the first time those unforgettable eyes. They were the colour of cornflowers and the summer sky and the Caribbean sea. Her eyes actually shone with their fantastic and mesmerising blueness. She was truly beautiful. The nursing staff commented on this, as did the gynaecologist who had delivered the tiny girl. She had weighed in at 8 pounds and 3 ounces; she was not plump and beefy as Sophie's other children had been, but she was long and so beautifully shaped—all of her. When she had been weighed, measured, had her umbilical cord clamped, and been wrapped in a pink blanket, the baby was handed to Sophie, who held her close and kissed her little mist of blonde hair. How had she produced this so perfect and incredibly beautiful child? She drank in every part of the tiny girl's sweet face: the turned-up nose, the rosebud mouth, the incredible eyes, and the miniature golden curls. She was flooded with hot, protective, fierce love. Michel was allowed in. He came to the bedside. He was smiling broadly, but suddenly his expression changed. "Why is my son wrapped in a pink blanket?" He was clearly angry.

"Because your son is a daughter—and a very beautiful one, with fantastic blue eyes." Sophie pulled the blanket back so that Michel could see the little girl.

He looked at her, unsmiling. "Yes, she is very pretty—but damn it—I didn't want a bloody girl! I wanted a son." He stamped his foot like a toddler, hard, on the floor of the delivery room. Couldn't you even get that right? My father's right—it's your bad blood. You planned this, didn't you?" He was breathing hard, and his face was very red.

"Don't be so silly." Sophie laughed. "It's you who decided the sex of our child. You produce two types of sperm, and the one with the X chromosome got there first. But this is your child, your daughter. Surely—"

Michel erupted, swearing and shouting at Sophie. The staff hovering outside, hearing raised voices, intervened swiftly to protect Sophie and her baby.

Michel slammed out of the hospital—and their lives. When Sophie recovered, she took her daughter home. She called her Ella, after her grandmother and because she liked the name, and because the little thing looked like an Ella. Sophie went to a solicitor. The marital home was put on the market, and Sophie moved to Cambridge, where she got a good job at a university college and a brand new single-parent, two-bedded, terraced house, which she furnished with some of the money she got from the house sale. She had to fight Michel in the county court for maintenance of his child, but she won. He visited the child briefly, but Ella did not like him and rejected his attempted kisses. Michel was living with a woman he had moved in with shortly after he'd stormed out of the hospital. It became very clear to Sophie that he had known this woman before they'd parted. The woman had two sons. Michel idolised these two and eventually put all his energies and time into their upbringing. His lovely little daughter was of no importance. He did not send her a card at Christmas or on her birthday, but it was obvious he knew when her birthday was, because he remembered to stop her maintenance the day after her eighteenth birthday.

Sophie discovered a lot about herself in that time. She found that she was attracted to the young students and the younger dons at the college. She was unashamed of her predilection for younger men. She sampled those who came into her office, sat on the desk, chatted, flirted, and invited her to coffee or dinner. She took them to her bed with delight and animal passion; now she could reach orgasm with ease and shivering wetness. She learnt every trick to please the hard, young bodies that thrust and grunted and jerked above her. She could massage, suck, stroke, and kiss sensuously and teasingly. She gloried in the pleasure she extracted from these beautiful young bodies. She did not think of herself as abnormal in any way. A man who indulged his fancy for younger—much younger—women was called a man. She was just a woman who preferred firm, sweet, young bodies that filled the air with testosterone. Sophie took her contraceptive pill religiously. She loved to have seed splashed on her belly and breasts, and on her face and in her mouth—and inside her—but she wanted no accidents. She just wanted the hedonistic thrill.

Sophie had no interaction with her parents. She very rarely visited them, and when her hated stepfather died of a heart attack during one of his noisy rages, she felt nothing, nor did she attend his funeral. Her mother developed dementia, and Rachael had her put into a home. It was a grim place, dark and cheerless, and it stunk of stale urine. Sophie wasn't able to visit a lot, as she had a struggle to keep herself and Ella, but she went when she could manage the time and the journey. Her mother didn't recognise her, or she told her that she should be back at school or the nuns would be phoning to find out where she was. "Mummy, I left school years ago." Sophie would say gently.

She wished she loved her mother more. She wished also that her mother had shown her even the slightest affection and the merest hint of love. Her mother died of a massive stroke just before her ninetieth birthday. She had asked that no flowers be wasted at her funeral. On the day of the cremation, her coffin was covered by a solitary, pathetic bunch of flowers from her daughters. Sophie cried afterwards on her own. She cried for what could and should have been. She cried for the mother she'd missed and yearned for so often in her childhood, the mother who had been so far away physically, mentally, and emotionally. She closed her eyes and saw the beautiful, dark-haired, dark-eyed woman in the black velvet dress. Then she closed her mind and her heart on another chapter and journeyed on.

Ella was beginning to be a problem. She had since the age of 18 months been very stubborn, wilful, and aggressive. When Sophie worked, Ella went in the nursery provided by the college for its employees. There she earned the nickname of Miss Bossy Boots, because she bullied and domineered the other children. Sophie dreaded picking her up, as she was constantly being taken aside for details of the day's incidents involving her child's worrying behaviour. Sophie spent as much time as she could with Ella to compensate for the partings. She sat playing with her, read to her, established routines to calm her, let her help with cooking and housework, and took her for long romps in the park and on the swings. She tried to keep a stable discipline, but sometimes her day's work left her exhausted. She was now in her early forties, and motherhood and the task of raising a difficult young tearaway were eroding her patience. Life was lonely. Sophie did not form liaisons with her young bed partners. Emotionally she was wary. She had had enough hurt for now. She often gave in to Ella's tantrums when she should have stood her ground. The small, intelligent, single-minded girl began to control and dominate her mother's life.

When Ella had chickenpox, Sophie had to take time off to nurse her. She was quite surprised when she was called into the office manager's lair when she returned. "Sit down, Sophie. We need to talk. You've taken rather a long time off."

"My daughter was ill. She had chickenpox. You know this. I phoned you, and I posted you a certificate from the doctor. When I was interviewed for the position, I made it very clear that my child's welfare must be a priority."

"Well, yes, but your work has piled up, and nobody else here can do it. You'll have to work overtime to catch up."

"I can't do that. It's totally unreasonable. Ella is young. The nursery stays open for late workers, but Ella already has a long day, and she's tired enough with my normal hours. You're discriminating against me because I have a child to raise alone." The office manager sat back in his chair and made his well-manicured hands into a steeple. "Hmmm. This work must be done. You will have to do it in your lunch hour. You could have a sandwich and a drink at your desk. This will have to do this time. Other absences must be made up in a more satisfactory way." He waved her away brusquely.

Sophie made up the work. She worked throughout her lunch period and sneaked work home with her and completed it at night when Ella finally fell asleep. She was very tired and even more impatient with Ella. Her daughter was incredibly physically attractive and intelligent, but she was a terrible handful—a problem in the making. The nursery staff continued to complain to Sophie about Ella's many outbursts and her domineering, aggressive behaviour. Slowly the situation ground Sophie down. She was called to the nursery continually to apologise to other parents because of Ella's aggression towards their offspring. She had been forced to take Ella home more than once. Her absences and the effect on her work at the college brought her into conflict with the steely office manager yet again. She sat before him, tired, despairing, and at the end of her tether.

"This is just not good enough, Mrs Navarre. You are constantly absent because of your child. Most people have some kind of a family to assist with child problems—"

"My child is a 'problem'?" Sophie raised her chin and glared at the sallow, unpleasant man.

"Well, it does seem to cause more problems than one would expect it to—"

"It?" Sophie's voice was very quiet and cold. She was dangerous when quiet. "My child is a girl, not an *it*. You will stop referring to her as if she were an object. I have no family. Many people have no family. Has that now been made a national crime?"

"Your work is suffering as a result of the problems your child causes. We really have to consider your position here. I have set up a meeting with the domestic bursar later today so that we can all discuss this. I think, Mrs Navarre, you should realise that—"

Sophie rose from the chair and leant forward towards the cold, robotic man. "And I think you should realise that I am not going to suffer this discrimination and persecution a second longer. You can take your stupid, boring, badly paid job, and stick it up your anal orifice. And while you're at it, learn to be human." Sophie picked up her belongings and cleared her desk. She escaped and went to pick Ella up from the nursery, where she gave them notice. The matron smiled sympathetically. "You've got a big problem there, my dear. Best, really, to give up trying to hold down a job like this for a while. Pity you have no family to—"

Sophie shot the woman a look which silenced her. Sophie thanked her and promised she would pay what she owed when she knew whether or not she would receive any salary. The woman patted her arm. "Don't worry, Sophie. If things are tight, we won't chase you. You've got enough to cope with."

Sophie pushed Ella home in her pushchair. She made her some tea and played with her; then she bathed her and got her ready for bed. She held the little girl close. *How are we going to manage, my little one?* she thought. She tucked Ella up in bed, and soon she had settled. Sophie sat up, thinking and sipping wine. She fell asleep in the armchair through sheer exhaustion. When the first silver and red streaks of dawn lit up the house, Sophie made herself a coffee. Later she asked her neighbour to take Ella for a while to play with her two children. She ran up to the phone boxes at the railway station and dialled her friend, an old school chum, who owned a farm in Suffolk.

The number rang endlessly, but then she heard Helen's voice. She poured out her tale, crying as the conversation progressed.

Helen was immediately in friend mode. "Look, Soph, I have this massive house. There's just me and Harry and the two kids—and loads of Labs, of course. Why don't you move in with us for a bit while you look for somewhere to live? I won't charge you a penny. You can just help with things. You'll need what cash you've got to rent a place."

Sophie's tears were now those of relief and gratitude. She ran back and picked up Ella. Soon they were both packing up their few possessions.

The next day, Harry came in the large Land Rover towing a horse box, and his brother, George, was driving a 7 1/2-ton truck to put all Sophie and Ella's worldly goods into. They all worked hard. Even little Ella helped, although she was manic at times and tired Sophie out. As evening drew on, they were all done. Sophie had left the key with her neighbour and paid her to clean the little house. She went around saying goodbye to the other lone parents in the complex. She felt a little sad, and nervous about her future and Ella's as they pulled out. They stopped shortly at a petrol station and café, where they all had burgers and chips, and Ella had a drink full of harmful chemicals and sugar. Then they were off to Suffolk and the next phase.

Late that evening, they pulled into the yard of the huge farm. The Labradors ran out, barking and welcoming. Sophie loved Labradors above any other breed of dog on the planet, and she jumped out to pet them. Ella also ran up to them and was soon embracing the big, loving animals delightedly. Helen came out with her two boys and kissed Sophie warmly. They had kept in touch for years by letter and the occasional phone call, and

Sophie had been a guest at Helen and Harry's wedding. Helen linked Sophie's arm and took her into the large, inviting kitchen with its red-and-black Aga, shining copper pans hanging from the heavy beams, long oak table and chairs, and the inviting smell of cooking. The men were going to unpack and store Sophie's furniture in one of the barns the next day, and now they came in to mugs of tea and kisses from Helen and the children. They all sat around the table and ate large bowls of beef stew and homemade bread. The children ran off to play for a while, after which they were bathed and tucked up to sleep. Ella was exhausted. She was in a small bed next to Sophie's large one in a room overlooking the rolling fields of the Suffolk countryside. Sophie sat with Helen, Harry, and George, drinking wine and chatting avidly. They were making up the lost years of life, and soon Sophie was yawning and drooping. She kissed them goodnight and gratefully sank into the deep, comfortable bed.

The next morning the place was alive and stirring with the first shaft of light. The farmyard noises awoke Sophie and Ella, and they were soon down in the kitchen eating a large cooked breakfast and drinking tea. Then Sophie went outside to help Harry and George to put all her belongings in the barn. This took up most of the day. Then the men went off to attend to the farm tasks. Sophie helped Helen prepare supper, and soon they were all eating roast lamb and fresh vegetables and chattering happily. Sophie again slept very well, as Ella did, and was up and raring the next day. She helped Helen in the house. Such a big house required a great deal of work, but Sophie enjoyed it. She, Helen, and the three children walked the Labradors along the fields and paths and down by the sea; they went to see the horses, cattle, and tractors.

After supper, Sophie and Helen often sat and talked deeply. Sophie told Helen of her life's journey to date and of her grim experiences with men. "I really have had enough of men and all that love stuff," Sophie told Helen. "We want them to be handsome, and fit, and good in bed, and rich, and kind, and caring, and good mannered, and well educated, and well brought up—but I can't seem to get more than one of those requirements!"

Helen laughed. "Sounds as if you interview them after you've read their application letters! Most of us just get a few of the nice qualities. It's not always film-star looks and porno star movie stuff in bed. Harry suits me. He is kind and caring, and a really good provider and father." She sipped her wine.

"I want to suddenly see my life's love." Sophie was staring into the distance. "See him and suddenly know, in a flash, that he is the one I always dreamt of. Know that my heart is his in that one second—and know that whatever happens I'll never leave him."

"So that means that all that other stuff doesn't matter? You're stricken, he gets you to bed, and you tolerate all the rest."

"I suppose I do mean that, yes." Sophie giggled. "Don't really seem to know what I want, do I?" They sat in silence. Then Sophie spoke softly. "One day I will meet my love, and it will be love at first glance, and I will love him, and follow him, and tolerate his weaknesses, and be there for him whatever he does and needs. He will put out his hand, and I will follow." Sophie sipped her wine and curled down into the armchair. "One day, soon, there will be that time of my life."

Helen smiled at her. The silence was comforting.

Sophie had received her salary and holiday pay from the college. She and Helen searched the papers and estate agents' windows for properties to let, without immediate success. Rents were too high, or the properties were too secluded and far from schools, or they were too near dangerous main roads. They kept at it daily. Sophie and Ella were settling down well and were very happy on the farm. Sophie realised that she must move before they both grew to love the place and the company too much. One evening at supper Harry told them that he knew someone in a nearby market town who was looking for a tenant for his two-bedroomed cottage; he had asked Harry if he could recommend anyone. Sophie was interested. Harry suggested that Helen could take her there the next day to view the place and meet the prospective landlord. Sophie was excited and pleased but also a little sad at the prospect of leaving her friends.

The next day they drove to the little market town. It was seven miles inland from the sea and on the river, with a quay where cruisers full of holiday-makers moored in the summer holiday season. The cottage was old and pretty, with a largish garden, The back of it formed the bottom of a cul de sac, and in this cul de sac there was an infants' school, just yards away from the back gate of the cottage. The cottage had two small bedrooms and a reasonably modern bathroom. Downstairs there was a narrow, galley-style kitchen which led into a dining room. Off this was a tiny utility room with a sloping roof, and off this was the living room with an open fire. Sophie felt at home the minute she stepped into the place. It seemed to embrace her. She had a déjà vu feeling of coming home. She asked the rent and was relieved to find that it was less than she had feared.

The man arranged to meet her at the end of the week with the contract to sign, and she would then give him a month's rent in advance. Then the key would be hers, and the tenancy. Sophie was happy. They drove back to the farm, and Sophie told Ella, who had stayed with George and his wife that day, that they had a new home and would be moving in next week.

"Have I got my own bedroom, Mummy?"

"Yes, darling—a small one, but it's all yours." Ella whirled round, whooping and singing. That night Helen, Harry, and Sophie cracked open a bottle of champagne and toasted the future. Sophie went to bed with her head full of plans and worries. At the end of the week she signed the letting contract, paid the month's deposit, and got the gas, electricity, and water supplies sorted. Harry and George loaded up the horsebox and the truck with her life's belongings and drove her to the cottage. Before she left, Sophie cuddled Helen as they kissed goodbye. Helen had given her bags of fresh vegetables, fresh meat from the farm, eggs, homemade cakes and scones, and several bottles of wine. Sophie thanked her warmly and tearfully and waved from the window of the Land Rover as they bumped down the driveway to the main road.

At the cottage, the two men unpacked and moved in all Sophie's furniture. They laid what carpeting she owned and some that Helen had given her. They also put up curtain rails and hooked the curtains and nets up, and soon the cottage looked alive, friendly, and warm. Ella had been running about excitedly, exploring and helping Sophie and arranging her toys and trinkets in her new bedroom. As dusk fell Sophie said, "Come on baby, let's eat. I'm starving."

"I'm starving too," said Ella. They went into the little kitchen, where Sophie unpacked the things that Helen had given her from the fridge. There was a large steak and kidney pie, which looked absolutely delicious. Sophie peeled potatoes and Ella chopped them, with a plastic knife, into tiny pieces to boil and make mash. Sophie prepared cabbage and leeks to go with all this feast, along with more gravy. Soon the little kitchen was filled with mouth-watering odours. They sat in the dining room and ate their feast. Afterwards they were totally stuffed with good things. Ella helped Sophie wash up the dishes, and then they sat on the settee with mugs of tea and watched Sophie's ancient television.

Soon Ella fell asleep, and Sophie carried her upstairs. She gently undressed her, put on her nighty, and tucked her into her bed. She kissed the golden curls and the snub nose, drew the curtains, and then went to her own room. She put on her nighty and was about to turn off the light when she remembered the card Helen had given her. She had been too busy to open it earlier. She went downstairs, found it, and opened it. On the front was a picture of a beautiful black Labrador. Sophie smiled and opened the card. "Be happy in your new home, both of you. We are always a phone call away if you need us. Hold on to your dreams. Soon it will be the time of your life. XX, H and H." Sophie kissed the card and put it on the mantelpiece. Then she went up to bed and lay sleepily worrying about her future. She could no longer work because of the problems she had with Ella's behaviour; she had to rely on government benefits and the small maintenance that Michel paid her for Ella. She knew she could grow her own vegetables in the large garden. Somehow they would survive. The large moon brightened the bedroom and spoke to Sophie of life to come. She slept. Ella slept. The moon slid silently across the night sky.

SOPHIE AND BEN, ONE

At this time in Sophie's life her hair was thick, wavy, Titian, and tied in a plait down her back and spilling down her face. She was high cheek-boned, had almond-shaped hazel eyes, and was now almost exotically attractive and quite slender—and this was when she was already forty-two. Ella was still a little girl. They were lonely and poor, but she struggled on proudly and determinedly. The winter nights were long and cold.

When Ella was at school, Sophie dressed up in her heavy coat, scarf, gloves, and fur boots and took her shopping trolley up onto the common. There were thick woods along the edge, and she spent hours picking up loose wood to burn on the open fireplace to keep them warm at night. At lunchtime she huddled up by the empty fireplace, still in her coat and boots, and drank a cup of coffee and ate a piece of bread. Then she went back to the common and worked in the raw wind and grey light until it faded into colder lateness. Returning to the cottage, she built a small fire with just four pieces of coal and piled wood on it so Ella came home to at least one warm room. When Ella asked her why she wasn't eating, she told her casually that she had eaten her share at lunchtime.

Night-times were empty and bleak, and Sophie huddled in her cold bed, listening to the wind keening and banging the windows and the snowflakes hitting the window panes like bits of metal. The loneliness of her existence ate at her soul, but she struggled to survive. There would be a day when life would be better. Something would happen to change her misery; she dreamed dreams to keep herself sane.

It was a warm June evening when her son, Sean, came to the cottage with a friend. Her son had not been able to survive long over in France and had come back in haste. Sophie suspected he had got himself into some kind of trouble there. He had found Sophie and Ella and was living on a boat on the river with a friend. When he came to visit, he was always wanting to borrow things—money, usually—but he would happily take the small amounts of food she had without regard to Ella's and Sophie's needs.

The friend stood behind her son shyly. She noticed vaguely that he had dark-blond hair tied back in a plait, was very brown from the sun, and was very tall, with a massive, attractive, muscular body. He wore many hippy leather and bead bracelets and necklaces and a gold ring in his ear. "Hello," she said. When he turned his eyes to hers, she saw they were bright, bright blue and full of warmth, humour, and a strange deep appeal. She felt a shock deep inside of her being. They stayed for a cup of tea, and Sophie learnt that his name was Ben. They left as darkness fell. Sophie remembered his blue eyes all through the next day; she seemed to be distracted and clumsy. She bathed Ella, put her to bed, and then went to sit out in the garden in the fading warmth.

The gate creaked, and she looked up to see Ben standing there hesitantly. "Well, hello," she said. "What can I do for you?"

He held out a wrapped package. "I brought this for you and Ella," he said quietly.

She looked at the proffered gift. "What is it?" she asked.

"Fresh fish," he replied.

"Well," she said, "I haven't had anything like that for one hell of a time." Sophie smiled. "Thank you," she said, and she took the package. "Well, come on in and have a cup of tea."

"Actually, I brought a few beers," Ben said. He grinned at her, and she saw white teeth and a dimpled smile. A tiny shiver ran through her, but she told herself, *This is just a boy, probably only twenty-five—if that.* But her body spoke to her, and tiny feelings awoke and disturbed her.

They sat sipping the beer, and Sophie put the CD player on. She felt pleasantly relaxed and fuzzy; she hadn't drunk alcohol since she'd left Helen and the farm. Poverty had seen to that. Ben chatted away, and she listened, observing him quietly. Ella was tucked up in bed, fast asleep. When he turned his blue, blue eyes on her and held her with his deep gaze, she was frightened but unable to move or act. She felt like a rabbit standing before an oncoming car's lights.

"Well, I have to go to bed," Sophie said. "Ella has to go to school tomorrow."

Ben stood up, looking at her for a minute or two, and then he said very, very softly, "Will you let me come with you?"

"Come with me where?" she asked, puzzled.

"To your bed," he said and took her hand.

"But—" she said, "but you're so—"

"Young?" he said, grinning.

She dropped her eyes and blushed. "Well, yes," she murmured. "Come," he said. "Come with me." She followed as if hypnotised. She was terrified and nervous, but her body screamed for contact with this virile young man. He led her upstairs and took her to her bedroom.

"The bathroom's round the corner," she said with a grin. "After all that beer, you'll need it."

When he returned, he began very gently to undress her. Soon she stood naked and trembling. He laid her on the bed and then said suddenly, "Wait." He went to the bathroom, and she heard running water. When he returned he had stripped, and she saw his tanned, strong body in the dim light. He was very big; his shoulders were wide and rippling with muscle. She felt suddenly awkward and inexperienced before this young, beautiful man, as if she were a virgin again. Ben climbed in beside her, leaned over, and kissed her very gently on her mouth. Then he kissed her neck and her shoulders and her breasts and flicked her nipples with his tongue. He gently ran his tongue down, down until he was brushing her clitoris. She moaned softly and arched her back slightly.

"Is that good?" he whispered.

"Oh yes, yes," she breathed jerkily. He guided her fingers gently to his penis, and she gasped at its massive size. She seemed to always be blessed - or cursed - with well endowed men.

"Am I frightening you?" he said. She saw him grinning in the half dark. Suddenly she tried to sit up. "Hey, hey—what's wrong," he whispered.

"You've only known young girls," Sophie told him. "I've had babies, and I've got scars, and I've been stretched, and—" she stopped, feeling stupid, inadequate, and embarrassed.

"I'll let you know if that's a problem. I've actually had women as well as little girls, you know." She saw his white teeth and his grin. He eased her gently back onto the bed and went down onto her with his tongue and fingers until she was breathing hard and burnt with a yearning for his body. "Do you want me, sweetheart?" he murmured as he began to push into her gently. She cried out to him to go in, and in, and in, and she was astonished and excited at his size and hardness. She felt like some bride on her wedding night.

Her body was screaming for his thrusting and his hard, sweaty maleness. The smell of him stimulated her beyond anything, and she arched her back and twisted against him. Her nipples hardened as she neared her climax. She began to moan softly and then louder. As she reached the point of beauty and release, she screamed, and he put his hand gently over her mouth.

"Come on, my lovely," Ben whispered. "Let go, let go—give it all to me." Sophie climaxed again and again, and he kissed her mouth as he came, with her fifth orgasm, and gasped as he fell across her.

Ben kissed her hair and neck and murmured endearments as her breathing returned to normal. Tears rolled down her cheeks, and he wiped them away with her hair. "It's been too long since you lived normally, my sweetling," he whispered. He pulled out gently, and his seed spilled down the insides of her thighs. He drew a deep breath. "I forgot to cover it, didn't I?" he said. "I hope you're on the pill."

"I've been sterilised," Sophie said very quietly. "Otherwise I would have insisted on protection. But you're quite safe to come inside me; you won't make me pregnant."

"Well, that's good," he said. "I won't be making you pregnant the first time I sleep with you. But, for the first time in my life, I'd actually love to." And he grinned his dimpled, sweet grin down at her. Then they slept, arms around bodies and legs entwined. When the first flush of dawn came, Ben bent down to kiss Sophie's mouth and slipped silently away. Sophie pushed the long curls from her sweaty face and smiled. Young he might be, but she wanted him and she didn't care what was right or wrong or normal. She wanted him so very, very much. She stretched like a great, lithe predatory cat and slept.

SOPHIE AND BEN, TWO.

Ben returned the following day. Sophie was sleeping in the sun and Ella was playing in the garden in a little plastic pool. He stood shyly inside the gateway. Ella asked him, "Who are you?" and Sophie woke.

"Well, come in; I was just going to make myself a drink," she said to him. She felt Ben's eyes on her and was shy and ill at ease. He followed her into the house and leaned against the frame of the kitchen doorway watching her making tea. "Sugar and milk?" Sophie asked.

"Two sugars and just a splash, please." Ben watched her all this time, and she glanced at him and saw how very young he was and how very smooth, muscular, and beautiful his body was through his thin cotton shirt.

Back in the garden, Ben played with Ella, and she laughed happily. She was at ease with this young man, and he seemed to delight in her company.

"She's a lot fairer than you," Ben said, "and boy, her eyes are so blue—rather like mine are, I think." He grinned, and tiny dimples came up by his mouth. Sophie drank her tea feeling tense. Each time Ben came near her or almost touched her, it was like electricity. She expected sparks to fly, blue and crackling, through the air between them.

He wasn't in a hurry to leave. "May I?" he asked, looking through her CD collection. He chose ZZ Top. He stood watching her again, singing softly along with the lyrics, and she felt her cheeks flushing gently as her body began to react to the innuendo.

Sophie called Ella in and cooked her some supper. Then she took her upstairs to pack her little bag. When Ben saw it, he asked, "Is she going somewhere?"

"She stays overnight with my friend's kids," Sophie told him. "It's good company for her, and it gives me a break." As she prepared Ella for her outing, she was aware of Ben looking in the fridge and the kitchen cupboards. She was vaguely annoyed but curious.

After her friend had picked Ella up, Sophie went into the house and began to tidy up Ella's toys. "When are you going to eat?" Ben asked her gently.

"I'm not very hungry," she said quickly, avoiding his eyes.

"I think you are," he said quietly, "but you can't afford to eat."

She flushed but held her head up proudly. "Don't be so stupid," she said in what she hoped was a casual and confident voice.

He walked over and took her hand. "Please," he said. "Please let me help you."

"Why?" she said quietly but angrily. "Because you owe me for the one-night stand? I'm not a prostitute!"

Ben held onto her hand, and his grip increased. "Please," he said, "don't be offended. I couldn't imagine treating you like a hooker, and I'm so sorry." He wouldn't let loose her hand. "I want you very, very much. I haven't been able to stop thinking about you. I can't eat or keep still—I really need you." He paused to looked at her, and the deep-blue eyes held her, held her. "But I know what a struggle you're having to keep both of you. Please don't be offended. I've got a biggish haulage business, and I don't go without much. I can't bear to see you struggling so. You don't eat properly."

Sophie raised her head defiantly. "Ella has everything she wants," she said proudly.

"And you have virtually nothing," Ben said quietly. He still held her hand tightly. Her hand was so tiny in his massive one. Slowly he led her towards the stairs.

She pulled her hand away, shook her head, and backed away from him. "You're only in your twenties," she said.

"Twenty-four, actually," he said and grinned.

"Well, I'm ..." She paused.

"Eighteen years older than me?" Ben finished for her.

Sophie shrugged her shoulders and wrapped her arms around herself. "What happened was—fantastic." She couldn't look at him. "But people will think I'm a cougar and preying on you, and I'm not, and I'm completely confused and—just go away. Go away and find someone your own age, and be happy, and have lots of babies." Suddenly she was weeping uncontrollably and Ben was holding her very, very tightly and rocking her.

His body was hard and warm, and she realised again how huge and muscular he was. He smelt sweaty, and dangerous, and enticing. He took her hand and led her once more towards the stairs. "Come up with me?" he whispered.

"I have to lock the door," Sophie said quickly.

"I locked it already." His grin was her undoing.

She followed and stood unresisting while Ben slowly undressed her and himself. He kissed her delicately on her face, neck, and breasts. Suddenly he grabbed Sophie by her long hair, pulled her head back, and kissed her very hard on her mouth.

He pushed her roughly onto the bed before she could cry out. He forced her knees up to her shoulders and thrust into her with force. She winced but he did not ease the force he was using; she felt desire rising in hot waves in her belly. He held himself up so that she could see his face. His blue eyes became brighter with lust as he pushed into her with an urgent desire that frightened her. "I can't hold out any longer, my sweetling. Are you going to come?" he said gently. He slowed a little and then leaned down and sucked her nipple. It swelled and hardened, and he knew she was nearing her climax. She arched and wriggled, but he pushed her back down. She could not fight his superior strength. He pushed her hands above her head and held her down by her wrists. She rolled her eyes ecstatically as orgasm ripped through her. She screamed and whimpered again and again. Ben rammed into her as he came, and they lay still at last, sweaty and spent.

He ran his fingers very gently through the little curls by her ears, picked up her hand, kissed her fingers, and ran his tongue over them. "Was that too rough for you?" Ben asked her softly. "No," she answered shyly. "I actually enjoyed it—it really made me very, very turned on."

Ben stroked her face. "Rough sex can be fantastic," he said "It was a bit naughty of me to push it on you like that without your knowing it was coming, and I'm truly sorry, but I know you really did enjoy every bit of it, sweetheart. That was really nothing; it gets a lot rougher, but you have to want it, ask for it, and agree to it. Otherwise you have every right to ask me to stop. If I ever hurt you too much, even after you've asked me for it, then you must tell me right away, OK? I think I did hurt you a bit—did I? Honestly."

"OK," Sophie said. "Yes, it did hurt a bit at times, but that was what actually excited me a lot. You're just a lot—well, a lot bigger than anything—anyone—I've been used to before." She blushed again.

Ben grinned, and then he leaned over and kissed her gently on her mouth." Yes, I'm a big guy, Sophie, and I have to keep remembering it. Usually I'm careful and quite gentle, but it's one of my bonuses." He grinned again, looking into Sophie's eyes. She blushed, and Ben laughed and leaned down and kissed her mouth again. "I think I'm in danger of falling in love with you, my sweet Sophie."

Sophie grinned at him. "You hardly know me. This is only the second time you've made love to me, and we've only known each other for hours. Do you always fall in love so easily?" she asked him. "And what did you mean last night about wanting to make someone pregnant the first time you slept with her?"

Ben shrugged. "I'm usually more concerned about *not* getting girls pregnant, but for the very first time ever, I just wanted to—well, I just wanted to give you a baby. It's not my style, but you have this effect on me. I know it sounds irresponsible; I'm actually very strict about that sort of thing, but you're so different. I would love to have children of my own very much, but I've never found the person I'd want to be their mother. I've always had girls running after me quite happy for me to bang them up, but no way. I'm not sure just what's happened to me. Call me crazy, Sophie my lovely, but from the minute I laid eyes on you, my life changed."

Sophie looked at him keenly for a minute. "You really don't know me at all yet, Ben. You've slept with me twice; you're a lot younger than me—how much can you possibly know about me? And still you want to give me your child the first time you fuck me?"

Ben kissed her hand. "I wasn't just fucking you, Sophie my lovely; I was truly making love to you, and I still am. I know enough to see that you're unique, loveable, intelligent, and interesting. I've never made love to anyone so sensuous, responsive, and raunchy in my entire career. And one who blushes so easily." He smiled at her teasingly.

Sophie's eyes were closing. She slid so gently into sleep and he, too, slept, with his hand cupping her breast. The sun had gone down and she stirred, stretching like a jungle cat and yawning. She turned onto her side and felt the stirrings of his manhood against her back. He stroked her belly and thighs, and she was amazed at the quickness of the tingling desire she felt.

He went into her from behind quite hard and she winced. "Oops," he said contritely. "I must be a bit gentler with you." He moved slowly and carefully inside her, and she pushed her buttocks back against his body. She gasped and cried out as she climaxed again and again.

He lay with her all through the night and made love and lust to her once more. When she awoke he was gone from the bed. She heard him moving around downstairs. She inhaled the sweet odours of his young body—sweat, and testosterone, and his seed which had soaked her sheets. He came up with two mugs of tea and a plate of buttered toast. Sophie noticed with great amusement that he was naked, and his breath-taking beauty made her tremble.

Ben sat on the bed drinking his tea, and now and then he would stroke Sophie's hair, lift little curls from her face, and look at her with narrowed eyes. She drank her tea and looked back at him with eyes of wonder. Why should this young, young, lovely man desire her?

Later he left, and she listened to the drone of the diesel engine in his four-by-four in the distance. He returned laden with shopping, and Sophie instantly became tense and angry again. "You don't have to keep me—I'm not your responsibility!" she said tersely.

"Yes, you are." Ben's blue eyes became bluer and wider. "You're mine now. I own every part of you, and I intend to protect and care for you and for Ella."

"Own me?" she shouted. "I'm not a bloody car! You may have fucked me, but you don't own any part of me and certainly not my soul. Just get out and find another baby your own age."

Ben stopped as if she had slapped him. His eyes narrowed in a way that disturbed Sophie. He went to the door, turned to look at her again, then shrugged and left. Sophie stood, sobbing and confused. She crouched down on the kitchen floor, rocking back and forth in pain.

SOPHIE AND BEN, THREE

Sophie went through the next few days in a daze. What was happening to her? How could she have let this happen? She hated him. She wanted him. Her body ached for him. She could not eat even the small amounts of food she normally allowed herself. She found herself tensing every time she heard a diesel engine or the gate opening. Sleep eluded her, and then she dreamt of him, in the distance but out of her reach.

Ella was at Sophie's friends house. Sophie sat down to watch television in a frantic attempt to forget him and her feelings. She dozed, and was awakened by a knocking at the back door. She glanced at the clock; it was nearly midnight. She opened the door to find Ben there, leaning with one hand against the doorframe. She smelt alcohol very strongly, and his face was dark and unpleasant.

Feeling uneasy, she tried to close the door, but he held it open with just his fingers. He laughed. "You aren't strong enough to keep me out, are you?" He swaggered in and smirked down at her. He was very, very big and very, very strong. She felt very small, very weak, and very vulnerable.

"Please leave my house," Sophie said in a small, shaking voice, backing away from him.

Ben laughed again, and his darker blue eyes terrified her. "So I'm a baby, am I? Let's see what this baby can do." He pushed Sophie hard up against the wall. When she struggled, he held her easily with one muscular arm. He unzipped his jeans, pushed up her skirt and, to her horror, ripped her pants off. She still tried to escape, but he just laughed and laughed as he pushed into her with tremendous force. "So I'm a baby, am I?" he snarled at her. "You'll find out just how big a baby I am. There aren't too many babies as big as this." She was pinned and pushed against the wall; her back was hurting her terribly and he was hurting all of her.

She screamed at him to stop. "Please, please, you're hurting me! I can't take any more of this."

He stopped for a moment and grinned down at her. "Really— but I'm just a baby. How could I possibly hurt you?" He thrust back into her harder and harder while she sobbed with fright and pain. Suddenly Ben groaned and climaxed, laughing as he did so. He pulled out of her roughly, hit her across her face, and pushed her away. Sophie slid to the floor. She was trembling, and her teeth were chattering. Ben went out, slamming the door. She lay crying weakly and shaking until she fell asleep.

Hours later Sophie crawled upstairs. In the bathroom, as she attempted to clean herself up, she discovered that his seed, running down her legs, was mixed with blood. She was sore and badly bruised. She lay sobbing, unable to sleep. Should she call the police and charge Ben with rape? She wanted to, but something inside her felt strangely and abnormally protective towards him. She slept out of sheer exhaustion and suffered confused and disturbed dreams.

The following morning after Sophie's friend took Ella to school, Sophie dragged herself downstairs, where she collapsed into a chair with strong coffee, then sobbed until she slept. She woke just before the school closed for the day and went to collect Ella. Absently she fed and bathed Ella, read to her, and tucked her up in bed. "Why is your face a funny colour, Mummy?" asked Ella.

"Is it?" she answered and said nothing more. She mentally thanked God for the fact that Ella had not been there overnight. She washed up and cleaned the kitchen; then she curled up in her armchair again. As darkness fell, there was a gentle knock at the back door. She froze, unable to speak or move. She waited, her heart pounding. The knock came again. She got up and walked to the door. It was locked, and she called out. "Go away. Don't come here again. I'll call the police."

Ben spoke very gently. "Please, my love, let me in. I must speak to you."

Sophie shook at the sound of his voice; it was partly fear and partly an emotion she couldn't recognise. "I'm not your love— you don't rape someone you love. Go away from me."

"Please, sweetheart, just let me in and listen to me, and I'll go away forever." Suddenly she couldn't bear the thought of never seeing him again, although she was very, very afraid of him. Slowly and nervously she unlocked the door.

She couldn't look at Ben as he stood in the doorway, hesitant. He lacked the cocky, arrogant assurance he had always shown. In his hand was a huge bunch of red roses. "I don't know what to say ..." He stopped and put his hand out gingerly towards her. She flinched away, and he withdrew his hand and stood quietly. She looked up and saw his face. She could tell that he had been crying, and her heart was torn for him.

"Why?" she whispered. "Why? You hurt me very badly, I—"

"I know," Ben broke in. "I know; I found blood on myself and I knew what I'd done to you. I was so, so—frightened to lose you, and angry and confused. I just wanted to own you completely. I can't bear the thought of anyone else even touching you. I just want to be the only one who makes love to you. When you called me a baby, you really angered me, and I had to show you what a big, big boy I really am. I'm not usually like this. I feel so differently about you than any other girl I've ever had. I've never behaved in this awful way with any other girl ever before. I don't know what's happened to me—I just can't bear the thought of losing you, but I've only just met you, and I'm acting as if I own you, and you're not really mine, are you?" He looked down awkwardly. "And this big, big boy did that to such a little, helpless girl." He touched the bruises on her cheek. Sophie winced and bit her lip. "And I scared you and hurt you. You're right. I am just a child, really." Ben put his hand out to Sophie again, and she took it slowly and timidly. He took a step forward, and she still backed away.

"I don't want to be fucked; I want to be loved," she told him.

The look on Ben's face was one Sophie would never, ever forget—even after she'd lost him forever. "Oh my lovely, precious lady," he said gently and took her in his arms. He touched the bruises on her face and kissed them. They stood together for a long, long time; he rocked her tenderly and kissed her hair. He led her to the chair and took her on his lap. She fell deeply asleep, and he held her there until the sky turned pale gold and red with dawn.

Later she woke in her bed. Ben had carried her upstairs as she slept and put her in the bed and covered her with her duvet. Sophie looked about her and saw the roses in a vase on her dressing table. She smiled a little, stretched her jungle-cat stretch, and yawned. And then she saw Ben standing by the window, watching her with great tenderness in his eyes.

"Are you OK?" Ben asked softly.

"I think so," Sophie said. Then turned to look at her alarm clock. "Oh good Lord! Ella should be at school." She started to climb out.

But Ben pushed her back, saying, "I got Ella up, gave her breakfast, and took her to school. She seemed to like the arrangement. Stay there. I'm going to get you a cup of tea," he said, smiling his dimpled smile. He came back with tea, two boiled eggs, and a pile of toast.

She protested feebly. "I can't eat all that. I never eat in the morning."

"Or any other time," he rebuked her, raising his eyebrows. He sat on the bed beside her, broke the top of the egg, and spooned it into her mouth. She grinned and ate it obediently. He made her finish both eggs, taking small spoonfuls himself. Then he fed her toast and tea. Afterwards she lay back, feeling deliciously sleepy, and he slid into bed beside her.

When Ben put his arms about her, Sophie instantly stiffened and moved away from his body.

"I know, I know," he said quietly. "I won't touch you until you tell me to. I just want to cuddle you to sleep."

She reached out and pulled his arms around her loosely. "I'm sorry," Sophie said.

"Sorry for what?" He was puzzled.

"For being so rude, and ungrateful, and proud—and calling you a baby."

"Why? I am."

"Oh no, you're not; you're not a baby. You're a very, *very* big boy." Ben chuckled into her hair. "I told you not to worry." He touched her cheek carefully. "You're blushing" he said.

As Sophie slid into a deep sleep, she was aware of Ben kissing her neck softly. When she woke, Ben had made her a cup of coffee and was sitting on the end of the bed drinking a mugful himself.

"Are you really all right?" He seemed worried. "Do you need to see a doctor or something?"

"What about?" Sophie queried. "I don't need emergency contraception. I told you I was sterilised. My tubes were tied off. I can't conceive. I still produce eggs and have periods but the sperm can't get up there to fertilise them.

"OK." Ben seemed slightly amused. "But you were bleeding ..." He frowned. "Did I damage you or something? I was very rough. I'm so, so sorry."

Sophie looked at him for a while. "I'm very sore and things there hurt a lot," she told him. "I may have some tears inside, or you may have opened a scar. I'm not going to a doctor because the police would be called in, and I don't want that."

A silence hung between them. Ben looked down and said very quietly, "Will you ever let me touch you again?"

Sophie's heart screamed out to him that she wanted him there and then, but her body was afraid of more pain, and her bruises made contact difficult.

"Maybe. Soon. Give me time. Please."

Ben picked Ella up from school. He had been to the supermarket beforehand, and soon a delicious smell drifted up to Sophie. Ben had told Ella that Mummy was unwell and was having a day in bed. He brought three plates of cottage pie with carrots, cauliflower, and broccoli up for them all. Ella sat on the floor and ate with them, loving her picnic-style evening meal. Ben sat on the bed beside Sophie, glancing at her anxiously from time to time. When she slowed and could not eat the large amounts of food, he took her fork and fed her. Later he bathed Ella and tucked her up in bed. He read her a story, using a variety of funny voices, which amused her.

After Ella was asleep, Ben brought Sophie up a cup of chocolate and sat next to her, watching her drink it. She settled down, still very tired after her ordeal, and he slid in beside her, fully dressed. He held her loosely and gently, and she soon fell into another deep and healing sleep. Later she stirred and felt his lips on her cheek. She was soon deeply asleep again and stayed that way until the first streaks of morning appeared.

Ben stayed with Sophie for over a fortnight. He cared for her and for Ella with love and good humour. Sophie's bruises faded and the rawness inside her healed. Ella went to stay with her friend again, and they were alone. Ben had done the washing up, and he came into the living room with a cup of tea for Sophie. Their hands brushed, and she felt a shock pass through her entire body.

Ben's blue eyes were on her, and they were questioning. "Will you let me try? Please?" he begged. Sophie nodded nervously, and Ben led her up to the bedroom. She shook with fear and desire as he laid her down so very, very gently. He used his tongue and fingers to arouse and pleasure her. He was about to enter her, but she pushed him away fearfully. He continued to caress her with his fingers until she arched her back and moaned. Sophie cried as she climaxed, and Ben kissed her tears away. She slid down onto his belly and ran her tongue down the line of blonde hair from his navel to his penis. She ran her tongue inside his thighs and over his testicles and slowly, slowly took him into her mouth. She sucked the huge hardness of his manhood until he gasped and his seed spurted into her mouth and throat. She swallowed it, smiling at him shyly. "Thank you so, so much," he whispered, smiling back. Then he held her very tightly in his arms. "I love you so very much," he said into her ear. He lay her down to sleep and put his arms around her very tightly and protectively.

As Sophie held him to her breasts, an overwhelming desire to mother and protect him flooded her—but she also wanted his body and his entire self. The feelings seemed strange, wrong and confusing, almost incestuous.

Ben kissed her ear. "I love you so very much," he murmured as he slid into sleep.

Ben moved into the cottage with Sophie and Ella, and life changed considerably for all of them. There were always large amounts of food in the new, large fridge-freezer that Ben had bought her. Soon she had an automatic washing machine, a tumble dryer, a new vacuum cleaner, new beds for her and Ella, carpeting that thrilled her with its depth and lushness, and—the crowning gift—a British Racing green Mini with white stripes. She took Ella for drives and was able to develop a social life for them both.

Ben took her to shop for clothes. Before, Sophie had managed on what she'd bought from jumble sales and she had worn the same shabby coat and shoes for years. Ben brought her flowers and chocolates and beautiful little undies that thrilled her. She could afford to wear make-up again and expensive perfume, which Ben loved to buy her. Her morale lifted and her confidence returned; life was good at the little cottage.

Ben sometimes went away driving for several days but phoned her almost hourly. Their partings were hard for her. When Ben returned, she greeted him with joy, and their lovemaking was passionate and beautiful. Soon Sophie was in his strong, hard embrace, and he would bring her to one orgasm after another. "Oh God, how I love you, Sophie," he murmured as he slid his hugeness into her waiting warmth and wetness. Then he fucked her very, very slowly, whispering adoring words into her ear. He sucked her nipples and ran his tongue over her shoulders and neck. Sophie lay quietly, moving her body gently with his rhythm until she felt orgasm building up yet again, and her movements became jerky and intense. "Are you coming again, my little one?" Ben asked her.

"Yes, oh yes," Sophie gasped, and Ben pushed into her harder. Soon she was moaning and crying out for him to go faster and even deeper. She orgasmed time after time until Ben asked her if he could let go, and they both climaxed together, and Sophie wept with happiness and relief.

Life drifted into a disordered but peaceful existence for the three of them. Ella adored her Ben, and he loved and spoilt her with equal adoration. Ben helped Sophie with all the household tasks whenever he was home from driving; he also helped her in her garden with her beloved plants and vegetables. Often he would cook delicious meals for them all and help Sophie to wash up afterwards.

"Please, God," Sophie prayed. "Please never let this end." This was her man. He had her heart. She was his—whatever he did she was capable of forgiving. For these moments in time Sophie was content, fulfilled, and loved.

Sophie's son, Sean, was not happy at what had happened. He deeply resented his mother's relationship with his friend. It had taken away his company and - more importantly to Sean - someone who paid for the drinks, and the gas bottles that provided the heating and cooking on the boat, and the food. He didn't hide his anger and was very verbally abusive to Sophie. If he came to the cottage he always managed to leave with something he had stolen. A bottle of wine. Chops from the freezer. Eggs. Milk. If he had asked for them they would have given them to him - willingly. Tension always simmered between him and Ben and Sophie feared that it would erupt into violence. One night, fuelled by vodka and jealousy, Sean became very mouthy towards Ben.

"Why can't you find a woman your own age. Why do you need someone old enough to be your fucking mother?" Ben answered good humouredly.

"She'd have had to be a very young mother."

"Can't you keep someone your own age then. Do you need a mummy to hold your hand."

"Sophie is a woman - my woman. I happen to love her and I don't care about her age - neither does she actually. I can understand that you might be jealous....." Sean lurched towards

Ben. His teeth were gritted, his hands clenched. "Well I fucking well care that you're fucking my mum….." Sean took a swing at Ben. Ben held Sean's wrist and prevented him from landing a blow. The contest of strength continued with both men's faces showing the strain. Finally Sean dropped his hand and sat down in an armchair. He took a swig of his drink and slumped sulkily, muttering darkly. Ben looked at Sophie who was standing with her hand in her mouth biting her knuckles. He turned towards her and was about to put his arm around her when Sean gave a huge bellow and came at Ben like a maddened bull. The fight that followed was one of Sophie's worst memories. Both men were very big and well built and strong. Ben had the advantage of fitness and muscle - and he was less drunk - and soon he was winning the struggle. After Sean had taken a hard blow to his face which split open his cheek and caused blood to spray everywhere, he pulled away and dropped his arms. Ben wiped blood from his mouth, then held his hand out to Sean.

"Come on man, this isn't the way. Your mum's happy - doesn't that mean anything to you? This is upsetting her a lot…" Sean ignored the proffered hand and turned to go. He picked up the bottle of vodka from the table, turned and made for the back door. Sophie went after him desperately. "Sean…" He went on walking and opened the door. Sophie grabbed his arm.

"There's no need for this Sean. Ben is part of my life now. There's room for you both." Sean turned to her. He looked at her intently. Blood ran down his face.

"Is there?" He said softly. Sophie lifted her hand to wipe the blood from his face but he gently pushed it away. He leaned forward and kissed her cheek, then he walked into the darkness and away from them all.

In later years Sean came looking for Ben because he needed work. Ben - willingly - gave him work as a driver but Sean managed to screw up deliveries. He arrived drunk and drugged and damaged the goods. He stole diesel which he sold for drugs. He failed to turn up for work because he was sleeping off binges. Ben and Sophie tried hard to help him. They invited him to the cottage to eat but he never arrived. He would turn up to see Ella occasionally but he drifted away slowly and inevitably. Sophie transferred money to him often and she always overpaid his wages. But he was going - going away from her and she felt the loss of her only son deeply.

SOPHIE AND BEN, FOUR

When Sophie began to help Ben with the business, she was expected to work as hard as he or any of the other drivers did. But she was only qualified to drive the small A-Series truck—known to all as the "A Serious" because of its mechanical and bodywork problems. In order to steer it she had to wedge her elbow in the steering wheel and fight it. She developed muscles and gained a reputation amongst the drivers as a feisty, strong-willed fighter who would never give up, even when she hadn't got the physical ability to continue.

She cleaned the trucks inside and out; she cleaned the yard; she did the professional checks on each rig that was about to leave; she made sure each truck was fuelled up and the oil was checked; she checked tachographs. As well, she tackled all the paperwork in the office, chased debtors, paid bills, banked cash, and tackled transport managers from other firms when she got return loads for the trucks.

Sophie soon knew what was worth picking up from where and which firms would subcontract work worth having and would pay up in time. She learnt to be polite when it paid and when to swear hotly at people—mostly men—who were rude to her. The first time he heard her arguing and swearing at another transport manager, Ben lounged in the doorway, grinning. "Way to go, honey," he told her as she slammed the phone down after winning the bout.

She made endless cups of tea for drivers and did the weekly wages after checking all the POD slips.

After sitting night after night with Ben for some months whilst he took her through all the legal, technical, and professional aspects of haulage management, she drove off for a fortnight's tuition and her CPC: her Certificate of Professional Competence in Road Haulage Management and Administration.

"What a mouthful," she said with a giggle. Ben's certificate, framed, hung in the office, and she couldn't wait for hers to join it. He had paid out £500 for her tuition and exam fees, and she was very conscious of the investment he had made. He preferred to call it her birthday present.

Leaving every morning and returning every evening to study, as well as still tackling her normal yard and office duties, was tiring for her. Sophie found, for the first time in their relationship, that she could not totally respond to his lovemaking. He seemed to be patient with her and appeared to understand the pressures— but he did seem to go out rather frequently with his friends and often didn't return until very, very late when she was asleep. He did try to wake her, but she would not roll over into his arms as she normally did so eagerly.

The day of her exam arrived, and she was irritable and nervous. He put his arms around her. "You'll walk it sweetie." He kissed her twice for goodbye and once for luck and waved her off. He phoned her mobile at lunch break.

"How's it going, little one?"

"I think I might have scraped through. See you in a couple of hours. Love you."

"Love you too. Drive carefully."

When the notification of her having passed with a mark of 100 per cent arrived, she put the letter in her pocket, smiling to herself. Ben was out driving locally today and she had some work to do at the office, but she would be back home to tell him the news.

Darkness fell. Ella was asleep in bed. She rang the yard, but the office phone rang and rang and clicked onto answer phone time and time again. She tried his mobile, but although it rang, it suddenly went dead as if it had been switched off. She felt vaguely uneasy. She could ring his friends, but she knew this was not wise. He resented being chased by her and especially in front of his friends. *What friends!* she thought. *They're mostly wasters and druggies and heavy drinkers.*

She could do nothing to prevent him going to those people. Sometimes he came home very late and his blue eyes were almost grey or bloodshot and narrowed and angry. On these nights he was often difficult to deal with. She stayed up to make him a drink. He returned at three in the morning.

"What are you doing up?" he slurred at her.

"I just thought you might like a coffee." She smiled at him.

"Checking up on me, eh?" He swayed. "Well, make the bloody stuff, then." He drank it and fell asleep in the chair. She crept up to bed, slipped under the duvet, and was soon asleep. She was awakened by a hand pulling her roughly out of bed. She fell onto the floor, half asleep and confused. He was looking at her with hard, frightening eyes.

"Let's have this off, shall we?" He sneered and pulled her T-shirt off. "We'll get those off too." He pointed to her pants. Afraid of his temper she stepped out of them. "Right, now—what fun can I have? I've had to go without while you took your fucking CPC." Trying desperately to distract him, she said with a smile. "I've passed with 100 per cent."

"Oh you have, have you? Aren't you the clever one? You just had to get a higher mark than me, didn't you? Just had to show me that I'm just a little boy and you're the grown-up."

She was shocked and sad. "I just thought you might be pleased that I worked so hard—" she began.

He twisted her arm roughly behind her back. "I'll be pleased when I can fuck you again. I'm the man here, the boss. You might think you run the haulage, but I'll teach you who's in charge." He let her arm go. She turned her head slightly and saw him taking off his belt. She tried to crawl away, but he pinned her down by her neck on the bed. She was shaking with terror. When he hit her with the belt, she pushed her face into the duvet, trying not to scream in case Ella heard. He hit her four times more, threw the belt down, and forced her onto the floor on her hands and knees. He went into her from behind, very hard and very deep.

He fucked her mercilessly, grabbing hold of her long plaited hair and pulling her head backwards while he thrust ferociously. He climaxed loudly, grunting and panting.

After he pulled out, Sophie was too frightened to move. She was shaking and sobbing quietly. He staggered to the toilet. She got up and crawled into bed, where she lay silently praying he would go to sleep immediately.

He got into bed. She tried to sleep, thinking he had drifted off. She was unable to lie on her back or her side, as the belt marks on her buttocks were agonising. She turned onto her stomach, almost asleep from sheer exhaustion, when he suddenly rolled over onto her.

"Good idea," he mumbled. "Stay right there." To her horror, he was pushing into her from behind, but he was sodomising her, and she was in absolute agony. She pushed her face into the pillow to stop herself screaming out loud.

She thought the pain would never end; he seemed to go on forever. Then he groaned, pushed into her harder, and her ordeal was over. He rolled off and fell asleep. Sophie sobbed. She was in agony. What was happening with the man she loved? He was abusing all manner of drugs and alcohol, and they turned him into some kind of wild beast.

She crept out of bed and curled up on the settee downstairs with a blanket. She hardly slept. Dawn came in with a red-streaked sky, and she got up to see to Ella. She had a bath to try and soothe her badly bruised buttocks, but the other pain was still unbearable.

She cooked Ella's breakfast and took her to school. When she returned, Ben was still fast asleep. She went through the house finding his belongings and put them into a suitcase. She put it outside the back door. She wrote him a note, which she left beside the bed under his mobile phone.

"Please will you leave my home. I forgave you before, and it was never, ever to happen again. This is beyond terrible. I could have reported you to the police for a lot of dreadful things. I never want to see you again. Ever. Just take all your stuff with you. Post the key through the letterbox after you lock up. I will never stop loving you. Ella will want to know why you've gone. What do I tell her?" She signed her name and put the letters

CPC after it, as she was entitled to do now. She looked at the short note for a while. It was nonsensical. She should have said, "Get out and leave my key"—and no more. She stared at it for a full minute, and then put one solitary kiss at the bottom. She did not alter a word.

She went back upstairs and gazed at him. He was naked, and his huge body was uncovered by any bedding. He looked angelic with his blond hair down his face. She looked at him, maybe for the last time, and remembered the wonderful pleasure and orgasms that body had given her. He could be so incredibly sensitive and loving. Now she could no longer trust him. He seemed to prefer his alcohol and drugs to her and Ella. She drove up to the yard. The welts on her buttocks made every movement agony. She went into the office and dealt with the mail. She checked the diary and movements list, phoned drivers who had left to check their locations, sorted delivery notes, and tidied up cups. She was so, so tired. She climbed up into Big Blue's Iveco; she was sure he had taken out another rig that day. She rolled into the bunk on her belly. She sobbed until she fell into an exhausted sleep.

Blue came into the yard about eleven. He saw her car and noticed that she had been in the office. He went to his rig and jumped in. He was puzzled to find her in his bunk. *She must be really worn out to have slept here,* he thought. He put a gentle hand on her.

Sophie's reaction amazed him. She jumped up, her face white and the terror in her eyes pitiful. She cowered in the bunk with her arms over her head. "No—please, no!" she whispered in a shaking voice.

Blue put his huge arms around her. "Sweetie," he said. "Darlin'. What's he done to you?" Blue was no fool; he knew what the spoilt blond idiot was capable of. He had hoped, as all the drivers had hoped, that this feisty little female could change Ben or that he would have the intelligence to change for her and that lovely little kid of hers.

She put her hand on the back of her jeans. Blue undid her belt and pulled her jeans down. He was a father figure, unthreatening. He saw the huge bruises blackening her buttocks. "Where's the blood coming from, sweetheart?" he said.

She was shaking. "He, he—"

Blue narrowed his eyes. "Oh, no—he didn't!" He shook his head and looked at her. She nodded. "You stay here, my precious lamb," Blue told her.

She fell back to sleep with relief. Some hours later she was awakened by raised voices in the yard. Rolling over awkwardly, wincing, she looked out of the window. Ben's car was by the office. Blue and another hefty driver, Fossie, were talking to him. He glared at them and shouldered his way past. Blue grabbed him and held him in a vice-like grip while Fossie hit him—hard—twice. He buckled, gasped, and fell. In an instant she had opened the cab door, fallen out, picked herself up, and raced towards them. With strength born of her desperate and primal need to protect him, she threw herself at Fossie and hit him in the stomach.

"Leave him alone!" she screamed. "Leave him alone!" She pushed herself between Fossie and Ben's body. She tore at Blue's arms. He could have brushed her off like a mosquito, but he dropped his arms, afraid of hurting her.

The two drivers backed off. She knelt beside Ben and laid her head on his huge chest. She sobbed. "Are you all right?" He opened his eyes and saw her. She stroked his face, where bruises were appearing. Blood was coming from his mouth and nose.

As he lay there, Fossie suddenly kicked him in the ribs. She threw herself at Fossie again and dug her nails into his arms. "No!" she shouted. "No! Leave him alone."

Fossie shrugged and turned to go. "Why do you waste yourself on that spoilt, cruel bastard?" he muttered.

Blue put out his hand to her. "You've got my number if you need it, my lamb. Are you sure you're all right?"

She nodded. Ben lay there breathing slowly and deeply. Then he put his arms out to her, and she went into them. He held her very, very tightly. "Please, please don't make me leave you both," he pleaded.

Sophie did not reply. She got up and put her hand out to him. He took it and got up slowly, wincing as he felt his face and ribs. He took the scarf he wore round his neck and wiped the blood from his mouth. He bent over. "Christ, it hurts," he said.

She stared at him. "Yes, oh yes—I know all about hurting," she said quietly as she walked towards the office. She continued with the pile of paperwork on the desk. He came into the office and stood silently, watching her sorting and filing. She called several drivers to tell them about their return loads, touted for more return freight, and chased subcontractors for payment. She ignored Ben and went to make a cup of tea.

"Don't I get one too?" he asked.

399

She pointed to the kettle and mugs. "I think you're just about capable of making yourself a cup of tea," she said shortly. "After all, you'll be living on your own now, won't you?"

"No, please. Please, my sweetheart. I didn't mean to hurt you."

She folded her arms. "Well, what did you mean to do when you did this to me?" She took her belt off and pulled down her jeans and pants. "Look," she said. "Take a good look. You've really left a sign of your love, haven't you?"

Ben looked shocked and confused. "What's all that dried blood?" he asked.

She pulled up her pants and jeans but left the leather belt off, holding it loosely in her hand. "Don't you remember?" She walked towards him and looked into his deep-blue eyes.

He dropped his eyes.

"Look at me," she demanded.

He looked.

"You hit me with your belt after you pulled me out of bed and stripped me." She looked intently into his eyes all the time she was speaking. "Then you made me kneel on the floor and fucked me from behind so hard that it made me really hurt." She took a deep breath and continued to stare at him. "Then, when I was falling asleep on my tummy because I was hurting too much to lie on my back, you rolled over onto me—and you didn't really fuck me, did you?" He raised his shoulders and spread his hands helplessly.

"What did I do?"

"You don't remember?" Suddenly she swung her belt round and hit him forcefully and angrily across the chest. She would have preferred to hit his face, but she was too short to reach it. She hit him again and again. When he tried to defend himself with his hands, she hit his hands hard. She stopped and began to shake uncontrollably. "You sodomised me—butt-fucked me. You hurt me very badly."

He stared at her in horror and then put his hands over his face. "Oh Christ, no! Tell me I didn't do that to you! Oh God, no."

"I waited up for you to tell you I'd passed my CPC with 100 per cent, and you accused me of trying to make you look young and inferior. I thought you'd be pleased, but you were only concerned with the fact that I hadn't wanted to make love when I was tired from studying and running the haulage. No, actually that's not true. You were only concerned with the fact that you wanted to fuck me—not make love to me—so you decided to beat and sodomise me to make up for the nights you'd missed. And you wanted to teach me a lesson for beating your CPC mark and thinking I ran the haulage." She picked up her car keys. "I think I've summed up what happened." Sophie turned and walked out to her car.

He came after her quickly. "Please don't walk out on me. Please, at least talk to me."

"I just did," she said without slowing her pace. "I hope you took your stuff, because I don't want you in my home again. And I hope you left the key, because if you didn't I'll have the locks changed."

He stared at her. "How will you keep yourself and Ella?"

She stopped and turned to face him. "I have a job as your transport manager. The car goes with the job, and I want £250 a week. I'm a qualified TM now, just like you are. I can't drive the big rigs yet, but give me time. Try to sack me, and the boys will walk out on you."

He knew she was right. The drivers, to a man, preferred her as a manager. She was efficient and hard-working. She treated the men with fairness and cared about their lives and families. They also felt very protective towards her. The skilful way she moved and parked the 42-tonners in the yard earned their admiration.

"I can't take all this in right now—but yes, the job's yours. I know what's good for my business." He stood looking at her still. "I don't want to leave you. Please talk to me. Oh God, this can't be happening."

She got into the car. "You'll be on your boat if I need you for the business?"

"Yes," he said in a defeated voice. He raised his hands. "What are you going to tell Ella?" he begged.

She ignored him and drove away.

Ben had a large cruiser on the river on a private mooring. It was well fitted out, with three bedrooms to choose from and a new, modern kitchen. He could look after himself quite splendidly there, she thought. If he wanted a life of alcohol and drugs and dark friends, he could have them—but not her and certainly not Ella.

After Ella had gone to bed, she eased herself painfully onto the settee and watched a little television. She opened a bottle of wine Ben had bought her and downed a few glasses.

The next day she would go to the local police and charge him with rape on two occasions. She drank another glass of wine. She relaxed. *Yes*, she thought, *I'll do just that. And he'll go to prison.*

The night wore on, and she found another bottle in the fridge. She opened it and started to drink again. Her determination to teach him a lesson began to waver. She could not get out of her mind his beautiful, muscular body; his heart- achingly attractive smile; his huge, huge blue eyes with their tiny laughter lines; the sweet endearments he whispered as she climaxed. She thought of the shattering orgasms he coaxed from her body without even going into her. The sweetness of his love for Ella and the way he tried so hard to father her. His endearing, childish, silly, humorous ways. His generosity—*This is ridiculous!* she told herself. *He can't be trusted; he has a bad alcohol and substance problem. He has raped, sodomised, and beaten me; he can be verbally and physically violent, and yet …*

And yet her whole body ached for him. Her soul yearned for him. She wanted to hold and protect him and defend him. If anyone hurt or threatened him, her maternal instincts kicked in with terrifying force. *No*, she told herself. *No. He must stay away from me and from Ella. He must think hard about this relationship. He wanted it and he started it.*

She put the wine back in the fridge and went up to bed. She lay awake thinking of him. Was he eating? Was he out with his toxic friends, wasting his life and his money? Was he missing her? Because she was missing him. She wanted to feel his body, so hard and muscular and warm against hers; she wanted to snuggle into his huge, hard back. She wanted him to wake her with his wonderfully gentle and experienced fingers and tongue.

Shit! she thought. *There's more to a relationship than fucking! Even if he has such a wonderful big body. There are other men in this world. And if you're that desperate, just buy yourself a vibrator.* But she felt as if part of her had gone.

She drove into the yard the next morning to see the drivers in a huddle, talking. When she drew up, they all stared at her and smiled. She went on into the office. Blue came up and cuddled her, saying, "My little princess." He kissed her. "Are you OK?"

"Fine, Blue, fine" she said breezily.

"Where's the blond fuckwit?" asked Randy.

"I couldn't tell you," she said casually. "Probably on his boat." The drivers exchanged glances. "Come on! Chop," she chivvied them. "There's driving to be done."

She turned to Jago. "What have you forgotten to check?."

"Nothing," Jago said in surprise.

"Well, take a good look behind your cab. Your suzies are loose. Next time you tell me when your air lines are faulty. Check, man, check."

Jago grinned. "Yes, boss," he said and blew her a kiss.

She handed out collection and delivery slips, and she checked each massive blue-and-white rig that pulled out, waving the boys on their various ways. She went back into the office and made herself a cup of strong coffee. She powered into the work that was piled up on her desk. Then she took a set of keys from the key safe, locked the office door, and walked out into the yard, pulling on her leather jacket.

Ben's car pulled up just after half past twelve. He walked in and stood watching Sophie. She swung round in her chair.

"Well, how good of you to turn up at all. You should have been in Stowmarket at half past nine."

He was sullen. "So we lost a job?"

"No. I don't lose runs. I took it myself."

"*You* took it?" He looked bewildered.

"Sure. I took the seventeen and half-tonner and drag. Loaded it myself. Dropped off by eleven, and here I am back, and there's your little blue baby safe and sound." She pointed at the new rig standing gleaming in its blue and white livery.

"You took my draw bar out on your own?"

"Well, it can't drive itself can it? Handles nicely, doesn't it?" He stared at her open-mouthed and then burst out laughing. "You just got in it and drove it?" He shook his head and laughed again. "You are something else completely!"

"Blue'll be back after four," she told him, "and you can take the Iveco up to Scotland. I've got three return load pickups for you already. Then Blue can take the drag over to Beeston tomorrow.

"OK," he said slowly. "I suppose I won't see you until about Thursday, then."

"Probably not." She went on typing and ignored him. "I'll be out when you come back," she said without looking up. "I've got a date." She still did not look up.

"Oh." He stopped, bewildered. "Well, I might see you around, eh?" Still she did not look at him. "Maybe," she said. "And don't show up late for work again, please." She waited for the reaction, but he just went out and began to examine his new rig.

"Oh God, how I miss him," said her heart and her body. She had to fight a strong urge to run after him, drag him into the cab, strip off his thin cotton shirt, and—*Oh no! I'm not even going there*, she thought. *I won't give in. He must change and prove it.*

The week went on, and Sophie was run off her feet with an intense workload. Moving the Arctics around the yard, she couldn't slot the fifth-wheel into the trailer of the biggest rig and suddenly lost her temper. She screamed and swore angrily at the trailer. She tried again without success and brought her fist down on the side of the cab till her knuckles were bruised and bleeding. She curled up into a ball on the ground, sobbing.

Jago rolled into the yard in his Iveco rig. Seeing her on the ground, he pulled up sharply and jumped out. He knelt down beside her and put his arm around her. "What's up, petal?" He saw her knuckles. "He hasn't touched you again?" he said darkly.

She shook her head. "No, J. It's my own fault. I lost my cool and hit the side of the cab." She sniffed and grinned at him.

"Why?" said J., looking amused. "What's the problem"?

She thrust her thumb back towards the trailer. "Can't slot it in; don't seem to be able to do it."

"Leave it to me, sweetie." Jago jumped up into the cab, and soon the big lorry was parked neatly in line. She went into the office, made them both coffee, and then went into the side room to photocopy and tidy. While she was there, several drivers came in. They made themselves coffee and sat chatting. She heard Jago say, "Little boss is edgy today—smacked her hand up on the cab on purpose; couldn't slot the fifth-wheel in and got in a state."

"Perhaps she's premenstrual," volunteered Fossie. "My old lady's hell when she's like it. Keep out of her way then."

"Has he been around?" said Blue.

"Nope. He's still up North. Not back until about Friday. I reckon she deliberately got him one hell of a backload schedule to keep him out of her way."

"Maybe, but her problem's that he isn't here to slot *his* fifth-wheel in." Several of the drivers laughed bawdily. "Got the jackpot hasn't he just? Spoilt rich kid and he's hung like a stallion and he gets a woman like that. He only has to move his finger and she jumps. He says 'jump' and she says 'how high?' Compared with some of the brainless little bitches he's had in the past, she's a gem. All that lot just wanted his cars and his money."

"And his dick." More bawdy laughter.

"God, she works hard, and puts up with all his shit, and defends him if anyone says or does anything to him or about him—and all she gets is a leather belt across the arse because she beat his CPC mark."

"That's not all, so I heard."

Blue growled. "Shut up. Don't go there. She's kicked him out, and she's feeling pretty upset. She just happens to love the little fool, and if he's the guy she can't do without, then so be it."

"If she's missing a good seeing-to, I'll be first in line."

"Shut up," said Blue angrily. "You so much as stand too close to her and you're dead."

"Yes," agreed Jago. "She's a protected species here, and don't you forget it. I'd love to ask her out, but she's his for life; like a little tiger if you attack him."

Bernie had been listening quietly. "Or a cougar maybe—"

"A what?"

"A cougar: a beautiful, stealthy, prowling big cat that has fierce loyalties and protects its young fiercely—the females do anyway."

"What are you talking about?"

"Nothing. But who's stalking who? This is confusing."

"You on mushrooms or summat?"

"Never mind," said Bernie. "Where's the girl, anyway?"

"Here," she announced, emerging from the store room with a bunch of papers under her arm. There was silence. Some of the drivers looked uncomfortable.

"Haven't you homes to go to?" she chided. She tidied her desk and then picked up her jacket, bag, and keys. "Lock up for me please, Blue." She walked to the door. Then she stopped and turned. "If there's ever a vacancy in my bed, none of you had better apply for the job—I don't think you've got the skill levels or the equipment." She grinned as she walked to the car, swinging her hips.

"I wouldn't mind an interview," said Jago.

Blue laughed and shook his head. "That's my princess," he said.

SOPHIE AND BEN, FIVE

Sophie missed Ben a great deal in the next two weeks, but she was absolutely determined that she would not give in to her feelings or his wheedling. She went to the yard daily and worked very hard. She saw him as she saw the other drivers. They discussed work and the running of the haulage, as it was, of course, his business. Whenever he was alone with her, he would try to talk to her about them rather than work. "Hi, are you busy?"

"Yes, actually. Was there something urgent? I'm busy right now."

"Well, I wondered if you might like to come out for a drink."

"No, thanks. I have to pick Ella up, and then I've got a lot to do at home."

Ben sighed. "OK. I miss Ella a lot."

"Yes, she misses you too. It's been hard for her."

"What did you tell her?"

"Just that you're very busy and you can't come and see us."

"Oh." He looked down. "Couldn't I just come to visit her, and perhaps when she's gone to bed we could talk?"

"What about?"

"Well about—about us and things."

"What things?"

"Well, you know about—things."

"Will that change anything?"

"Please, just let me come round and talk to you."

"If I ever allow you in my house again, it will be as someone I've just met and am getting to know in a formal way. Do you understand?"

"Sure. I'll do anything you ask, Could I come round tonight?"

"No, it's not convenient. Friday will be better. It will be my rules, you understand?"

"Sure. I will behave, I promise."

"You'd better or you'll never get another chance."

When Friday came, Sophie put Ella to bed and waited anxiously for Ben to arrive. She had showered, washed her long plait, and put on some of the perfume he had brought her back from a trip. She felt nervous and excited. She must not, she thought, just give in and be persuaded by his blue eyes and smile to follow him upstairs as she had done before. She must keep her cool and try to make him realise that their relationship could not survive unless he grew up and left behind his harmful and toxic friends. Sex alone could not be a basis of their union. If she couldn't get through to him, this love she had for him would be wasted, and their relationship would be shattered. Could she cope? She must.

As the sun went down, there was a gentle tapping on the back door. Ben stood there looking sheepish and uncomfortable. "I brought a couple of bottles of wine. I thought you might like a drink; it's very good wine." He held the bottles out to her and remained in the doorway.

"Well, come on in." Sophie saw that he had washed and braided his long blond hair and was wearing carefully ironed jeans and a white shirt. She smiled to herself.

They went into the little sitting room. Ben remained standing, unsure of himself. He looked so very young and almost frightened.

"Why don't you open the wine? You know where the glasses are?"

"Yes, sure." He came back with two full glasses of red wine and handed her one.

Sophie sipped it. "This is really good." She smiled.

Ben looked down at the floor.

She didn't know what to say, how to begin; but he was too shy and wasn't going to start any sort of dialogue. "You said you wanted to talk about things."

"Yes—I wanted to say ..." Ben looked at the carpet.

Her heart went out to him; he was so young, so very young, and so ill at ease. She wanted to take him in her arms and cradle him against the world. But she wasn't his mother; she was his lover. She was so confused. "Yes?" She wasn't going to make it easy for him.

"Well, I just miss you and Ella a lot. It's very lonely on the boat. I know I did a dreadful thing to you. I can't begin to say how very, very sorry I am. I can't believe I did what I did. I don't even remember doing it. It really upsets me that I hurt you so badly." He looked down awkwardly. There was an uncomfortable silence.

"Yes," Sophie said quietly. "Being hit across the buttocks with a heavy biker's belt just for telling you that I had worked my guts out to justify the money you spent on my CPC by getting a full 100 per cent in my exam. Yes, that hurt more than you'll ever know—not just physically but mentally and emotionally. I thought you would be proud of me. But no, you had to hit me really hard, and with that big studded belt too. It was agony, just sheer agony. I can't do a thing to defend myself against you. You know that. You can hold me down with one hand, and talking to you only makes you worse. Have you any idea what it feels like to be so helplessly unable to do anything against someone so big and so strong? It's terrifying. You're so huge and so able to defend yourself; you haven't a clue what it's like for me. Or perhaps you have, and you take mean advantage?" Sophie drank a large amount of her wine. "Then you pushed me down onto all fours and fucked me so, so hard. It wasn't love or passion, just a nasty desire to completely dominate me. That hurt a lot too."

Ben looked distressed, and his blue eyes were pleading with her. "Oh please, please forgive me. I was drunk and spaced out on drugs. I couldn't do that to you if I was in my right mind. Do you know just how much I love you?" He shrugged helplessly.

Sophie sipped her wine. "Then," she continued softly. "As if you hadn't hurt and degraded me enough, you hurt me more—very, very badly."

Ben looked down at the floor, and tears rolled down his face. "How could I have done it to you? You're so tiny and so helpless, and I adore you. If anyone else hurt you, I'd kill them."

"But you did do it," Sophie said. "And before that you pushed me hard up against the wall and raped me viciously and laughed at me whilst you did it. Then you just pushed me onto the floor and walked out. So you were angry and offended that I called you a baby, but did that justify such a terrible attack? Did you realise just how frightening that was for me? Just me alone against you—with no way of stopping you. Suppose Ella had been in the cottage when I screamed at you to stop because I couldn't stand the pain anymore? What would it have done to her if she had witnessed what you were doing to me? She loves you very deeply, and it would have terrified her to see you attacking me like that."

Ben wiped the tears from his face with his hand. Sophie saw that his hand was shaking; she wanted, quite desperately, to stroke his hand and soothe him. "You were out of your mind on drink and drugs. That's your explanation, but if you want any part in my life or in Ella's life, you're going to have to kick those habits. I forgave you the first time, but the second attack was too much, and I can't offer you more forgiveness. You'll have to earn that. I've still got the marks of your belt across my buttocks to remind me just what you did to me."

Ben looked down and tears ran down his face once more. Sophie sipped her wine and fought an overwhelming urge to rush to him, hold him in her arms, and comfort him.

"I can't tell you just how awful I feel when you tell me the things I did. If I'd known what I was doing, I could never, never have hurt you like that. To have hit you with my belt—you're so little and so defenceless against me, I know. Oh God." Ben drank half a glass of wine and wiped the tears from his face with the back of his hand.

"You came to me after you raped me, and you'd been crying then," Sophie told him. I was sorry for you, and I forgave you. I really thought you'd shocked yourself into leaving drink and drugs alone and putting Ella and me first in your life. You say you love us both, but your actions don't mirror your words, do they?"

Silence fell between them; she sipped at her wine again. "What are we going to do about it?" She paused and drank the remains

413

of her wine. She went into the kitchen and brought the bottle back with her. She refilled both their glasses.

"If you will continue to visit—just visit—to make Ella feel better, and we behave like two people just getting to know each other, and that may take a long time; then I will give you one very last chance to prove that you do love me and Ella as you say you do. If you ever try to hit me, or sexually abuse me, or use your size and superior strength to frighten or threaten me again, then it's over—completely over. Do you agree to that?"

Ben looked up at her with relief in his blue eyes and nodded.

Sophie raised her glass. "Well, here's to that last chance. You'll never get another." They drank; then Sophie turned to him. "I'm going to bed now—alone—and you can go to the boat and think this all over. I'm free on Sunday, and you're not driving until Monday, so you can come round for lunch and to see Ella. Is that OK with you?"

"Yes, oh yes, that's—that's fine." Ben said. He stood looking awkward and uncomfortable and made a move to kiss her. She turned her head away, moved back, and held out her hand. "Goodnight, Ben," she said firmly.

He looked dejected, but she followed him to the door, closed it, and locked it firmly behind him. She stood for a while thinking, before she went up to bed. She lay sleepless and yearning for his sweet fingers and mouth, his whispers of love, and his hard, strong young body thrusting into her eager one. "Goodnight Ben, my darling" she whispered and fell asleep.

On Sunday Sophie cooked roast beef with all the trimmings, which she knew Ben loved. He arrived mid-morning, arms filled with flowers, wine, and sweets for Ella. Ella was ecstatically happy to see him. She sat in his lap, playing with his plait and kissing him. He was delighted to see her too, and they played together with her board games, laughing happily while Sophie prepared lunch.

They ate the large meal, and Ben helped her wash up and tidy the kitchen. The afternoon was given to playing with Ella and taking her out to the play park by the quay. After her tea, Ben bathed Ella, read to her, and settled her in bed. He came downstairs and opened the first of the bottles of wine, bringing two large glasses in for them. He sat opposite Sophie.

"Well," Sophie began, "I'm going to ask you to tell me what it is about me that you first liked—even loved—and tell me what it is about me that makes you want to stay here with me. If you want to stay, that is." She looked at him expectantly.

Ben took a sip of wine. "The first thing that I loved was your voice. Your classy accent, your intelligence. That and your beautiful hair and your hazel eyes—I think, anyway. It was just something that happened; I can't explain it. I looked at you and wanted to take you to bed at that second. You were so different from all the girls I had known and slept with. They were empty-headed and childish, and I somehow felt I would be ..." He paused—"I would be safe in your arms; you would protect me and understand me. And yet I also saw you as very sexy and passionate and deeply loving." He gazed at her intently and continued. "I loved your shyness and embarrassment because you thought that your having had babies was something that would bother me. And then the look of amazement on your face when you realised that I'm a pretty big guy and it didn't matter at all. Then—although you can be very shy and blush sometimes, and I find that sweet and touching—how raunchy and abandoned you are in bed with me, and how much you really, absolutely love fucking. You give everything to me; you know what I want and love, and you do your utmost to give me pleasure. From the first time I went into you, you and I seemed to know each other's bodies as if we had been together for a lifetime."

"That's just a category of my sexual abilities." Sophie half grinned. "I'm talking about me as a person."

Ben appeared not to hear her. He was looking into space and into a dream. He stopped and drank his wine. "I love the way you twist your hips and arch your back and moan and scream when you reach orgasm. I love the way your eyes get wide and bright, the way you dig your nails into me; I'm gobsmacked by the number of orgasms you're capable of reaching. I really love the way you make me hold back until I'm gasping to come, then kiss me hard and come with me. I adore the way you sometimes cry when you come; the way you hold me against your breasts as if I were a small child; the way you giggle when we try to sleep and I immediately get another hard-on."

Sophie grinned.

There was more. "I adore your little temper fits when you try to square up to me—and you barely reach my chest!" Ben shook his head and laughed. "I love your beautiful, full breasts, and I love it when I run my tongue over your nipples and they go hard and you close your eyes and look dreamy."

"This is getting a bit too sexual," Sophie told him. "You must like more about me than just my performance in bed."

Ben grinned, and Sophie felt her insides melting with yearning for him.

"Of course," he said. "I love the way you cook and how much you love your garden. Hearing you singing in the bath. You have a beautiful voice. The classical music you play and how much you know about it; and the fact that you know and love heavy metal too. The feisty way you tackle running my haulage, and the way you cope with the drivers when they're being bloody-minded; although they tease and taunt you, you keep your dignity." He grinned. "Usually you do, anyway. I love and admire you for your bravery; you face up to anything and, usually, tough it out, although you're really so timid and nervous. I love the way you've worked to build up my business; the work you put in to turn the rigs out spotless, legal, and mechanically perfect. We're getting a name for it, and although you had to fight the drivers to get things done, you fought and won, and you now have the total loyalty, respect, and love of all the boys. And I know it was for me you did it. And I love and admire you for it." Sophie smiled. "I love working in the haulage; you know that. It's hard work, but it's my world now."

Ben went into the kitchen to get crisps and nuts for them to nibble. He sat by her and continued. "I really admire and appreciate the way you push yourself to do things beyond your physical capabilities. I love your gutsy bravery; the way you ran to defend me when Blue and Fossie gave me a well-earned going over You could have got hurt badly getting between us like that; and then the way you suddenly switched and put me firmly in my place. The way you forgave me for the dreadful thing I did to you when you called me a baby. I was dreadful, so dreadful. I used my size to intimidate you and to hurt you when you couldn't possibly defend yourself, but you forgave me. You could have gone to the police. I raped you and bruised you all

417

over, but you forgave me and gave me a chance to redeem myself. And I screwed up again." He stopped and looked on the verge of tears.

"I love you for your ability to survive terrible poverty and to go without even food to make sure Ella has what she needs in life. For your fierce pride when I offered to help you because, unlike the empty-headed stick insects I've always attracted, you really don't want me for my money or what I own. You really care for me as a person, and you go all out to help me in every way you possibly can. When I buy you presents, even small ones, you act like a little girl at Christmas and as if you think you aren't worthy of such things."

"But you buy me such a lot of skimpy underwear," Sophie broke in.

Ben grinned wickedly. "Because I like taking it off you."

Sophie blushed.

"I love your intelligence, your quick wit, your sense of humour, your serious intellectual side, your creative nature, the beautiful poetry you read to me, and the lovely way you use language to express your feelings.

"I really love you that you gave birth to Ella, because I adore her and she's more than just beautiful. I just wish—" He stopped.

"Go on," Sophie said quietly.

"Well—I can't not say it," Ben continued hesitantly, "I just wish that I could give you another lovely baby that looks like us." He stopped and looked at Sophie from under his eyelashes.

"Ben," said Sophie quietly. "I told you the first time we made love that I've been sterilised." She shrugged. "I'm sorry, but that's how it is. It is a method of contraception, for goodness' sake. There is a possibility that my tubes can be untied and then conception could take place naturally, but it's all so—so—" Sophie shrugged." Anyway, having your baby would be a huge decision right now. It's one I'd only think over when we had sorted our future out, which is what we're trying to do right now. I understand how you feel, but you can't bring children into an uncertain relationship—especially one as unusual as ours."

"What's so unusual about it?" Ben looked at her.

"The fact that I'm eighteen years older than you," said Sophie rather sadly. "If I were ten or even twelve years older it wouldn't be so bad, but I'm 43 now, and you may grow weary of me in a few years' time. In about seven or eight years' time I'll be going through the menopause, and it will affect my skin and looks and everything about me. Trying to bring up another child of only 7 when I'm 50 would be hard."

"But I'm here," Ben said.

"Yes," said Sophie quietly, "but so far your track record isn't too good, is it? Could I trust you to support me through a pregnancy and birth, and then help me with the responsibility and hard work involved in bringing up a child? Anyway," she continued, "this isn't what we were talking about is it? It's a subject for another day. OK, Ben?"

"OK," Ben agreed. "Now why do I want to stay with you?" He sat down next to her and drained his wine glass. "I want to stay with you because you've made everything in my life better and more meaningful. Because you're what I think about from the time I wake until the time I sleep. You've built up my business by sheer hard work, loyalty, and dedication. You're always there to comfort, defend and shelter me. I can run to your arms and the world goes away and I feel safe. I want to give you all the things you've been deprived of for so long, all the most basic things in life. I want to protect you and Ella, and one day, when I've managed to prove to you that I really do love you and that I can change, I want to ask you to marry me."

Sophie's eyes opened very wide. "Marry you?" After that she was speechless.

"Yes," Ben replied. "I know it's all too soon, and a lot of time will have to pass before you trust me again, and I understand, but that's what I want. Not just to stay with you but to make you my wife, my lifelong love and companion. I'll stop talking about that now; it's not the right time, but one day I want to put a large, expensive gold ring on your tiny finger and really make you all mine. I guess you could say I do want to stay with you."

Now," he said as he looked at her. "It's your turn."

Sophie refilled the wine glasses. "The first second I saw your blue eyes," she began, "I was swept away. Like you, I can't really say what happened to me. I was yours from the moment you held out your hand to me and said, 'Come to bed with me.' I knew you were a lot younger than me, and it worried me at first, but after the first fantastic night when I experienced lovemaking such as I had never, ever known before, I didn't care. It just seemed so normal, so inevitable, so destined. And there are so many things I love and like about you, Ben.

"I love your blond plait and your sweet curls that stick to your face in the rain or when you sweat. Your astoundingly blue eyes that can mesmerise me and bring me to orgasm when you gaze at me with the adoration you do when you love me. I love your huge, strong body when you hold me tight; your strong arms which make me feel so safe and protected. I adore your musky, male body odour; it can turn me on sexually even if I just smell it on your clothes when you're not here.

"I love the way you whisper beautiful things to me when you climax and after we make love when we're falling into sleep. I love your gentle, skilled fingers and tongue and the way you use them to bring me to one orgasm after the other. Your experienced gentle loving; your raunchy, rough loving when you hold me down and pull my plait back and kiss me hard and long. When you hold my hands down above my head I know I'm unable to move unless you allow me to; and then you fuck me really hard, and really deeply, and I want to move, and you won't let me and I have to fight you, and it gives me out-of-this-world orgasms—"

Ben interrupted laughingly. "Now who's rambling on pornographically!"

Sophie raised her hand. "Let me just finish this bit, Ben. I know it seems strange that I do actually like really rough lovemaking after what's happened, but it's what I ask for and allow—not what you dish out when you're drunk and stoned and I don't want it. That's assault. When I say yes, go ahead, then it's terrific. There's so much about our sex life that's wonderful, and I've learnt a lot from you although you're so much younger than me.

Ben nodded. "OK, sweetheart. I understand, and I'll take that really seriously—I mean that." Sophie touched his hand gently and then continued. "I love the sweet, gentle way you made me feel better about my body when I thought that having big babies made me somehow undesirable. The way you changed my embarrassment into bliss."

Ben interrupted her, grinning broadly. "That was due in no small way to my rather large equipment, don't you think?"

"OK, Ben," she said without dropping her eyes. "Yes, you are a very, very big and well-endowed guy, but it would be useless if you weren't also experienced and sensitive when you use what nature gave you." Ben grinned and moved closer to Sophie.

"Anyway, to continue, and to stop just talking about our sexual relationship, although it is hugely important to both of us," Sophie said. "I love your sharp, intelligent, well-informed mind. Although you haven't told me yet, I suspect you went to a private school?" She raised an eyebrow. Ben nodded.

"I love the way you can beat me at chess; I love the fact that you are very well read and willing to explore the poetry I love. I was fascinated to find that you know and love classical music as well as heavy metal and rock; I love your fast, skilful driving; I love working on the lorries with you, sheeting and roping in all weathers, travelling miles; I love long journeys with you and the fantastic love we make at night snug in our bunk. I love it when Ella comes with us, and you entertain her by telling her the names of cars and lorries and her whoops of joy when she recognises one and gets the make right.

"I adore you for the sweet, loving way you have with Ella; how proud you are of her and her beauty; how you both have curly blonde hair and striking blue eyes; how you're teaching her to ride a bike, and swim and fish from your boat, and drive a tractor; the hours you spend feeding, and bathing her, playing with her, telling her all about the lorries, explaining the countryside to her, and taking her to school. The way you discipline her when she's naughty and defiant; you're so quiet and firm, and she really listens to you. The way you read to her after you've bathed her, and you put on your funny voices and she giggles and so do you—just like a little boy. The skilled way you braid and tie up her hair with your huge fingers—" Sophie stopped, and a tear ran down her face.

"I love all those lovely little gifts you bring me; flowers or just one flower, handmade chocolates, exquisite little lacy panties and bras—and you get the sizes right! How you put up with my PMT with terrific tolerance and patience—and I know it's not easy for men to really understand."

The tear ran down into her mouth. She wiped it away. "I want to stay with you because you've brought something into my life I've never had before. You're my lover and, at the same time, almost my child, but I never want to be away from you ever. As soon as you're out of my sight I miss you. I love you deeply and very sincerely, but I won't let you stay with me and Ella if you continue to drink heavily and especially if you take the vile stuff that makes you violent and aggressive. I can't imagine life without you. I feel as if we've been together forever. I don't want us to split up, but you have to make your decision, my love."

The tears were running down Sophie's face and into her mouth. They looked at each other at that second, and Ben put his hand out to Sophie.

"Oh no, no," she said. "No, Ben, it would be too easy to just take your hand and follow you upstairs, but we've got to make this relationship work, and just giving in to your wheedling and charm won't help me to do it. You don't get even a kiss until you've faced up to a few home truths and reality."

When Ben looked at her, his blue eyes were very bright and very large. Sophie realised that he was very sexually charged. She felt sorry for him and yet slightly afraid.

"You know, my little Sophie, that I could just pick you up, carry you to bed, strip you, hold you down, and fuck you very, very hard. And you couldn't do a damned thing to stop me, could you?" he said with a faint grin.

"But you're not going to, are you?" Sophie said briskly. "Or you'll never get to even kiss me ever again."

"How about opening that other bottle of red wine?" Ben suggested.

"Why not?" replied Sophie. "It's very good. What is it?"

"Italian Chianti—a very expensive one," Ben told her. He went into the kitchen, opened the wine, and brought the bottle into the tiny living room. He filled their glasses.

"Now," said Sophie. "I want you to tell me the things you don't like about me: my faults and the things that worry or annoy you, OK?"

"Right," said Ben. "Let me think. First it has to be your PMT every month, when you turn into somebody else. You bite my head off, terrify the drivers, drop things, forget things, scratch my cabs—"

"Only once," protested Sophie. "And that was the first time I'd ever reversed an Arctic."

"Yep." Ben grinned. "That was really entertaining, that was. I can't think of too many things I don't like about you, Sophie. You fuss a bit about me changing my clothes, and I've never showered or washed my hair as often as I have since I moved in with you. But it's cool, and it makes sense; I'm on you and in you a lot, so I should be fussy about hygiene.

"If I look at friends' babies when we run into them in town or anywhere, you get very quiet and a bit off and snappy. And if I even bring up the subject, I can feel you getting cold and pulling away from me. I know what's upsetting you, I think, but you won't often just talk about it to me—you just close up.

"Then there's the subject of my friends. I know you really dislike many of them, and I can understand, because they haven't exactly helped our relationship, and they pull me back into a very dark place. But I've known most of them since we were kids, and some of them have actually been good friends at times. You just refuse to mix with them, and you shut them out of our lives, and it hurts and annoys me, Sophie. Some of them think you're a stuck-up bitch, and I have to defend you to them."

"Really?" said Sophie, tossing her head. "Can't you see that these wonderful friends of yours have been the cause of our break-ups, and I've suffered the results of your alcohol and substance abuse, which they encourage? If you want to spend the rest of your life turning into a monster who can't remember his actions the morning after, then continue like that. If that's what you choose, then you'll be saying goodbye to Ella and to me and to what we had. You can't really expect me to like them or encourage them into your life and mine." Sophie took a big sip of her red wine. She was clearly upset.

"I can't just cut my friends out of my life," Ben said. "For you and for Ella, I'm prepared to have just the odd drink but no binges and no hard drugs. Even you smoke a little weed now and then, and it just makes me last longer in bed, so I'll keep that vice." He grinned.

Sophie grinned back.

"When am I allowed back?" Ben asked anxiously.

"I'll tell you later," Sophie said. "Have you finished telling me all my faults and annoying habits?"

"Not quite," said Ben. "There's the question of your driving." He tried to hide a grin and look severe.

"Oh, that," said Sophie resignedly.

"Where shall I start? You could get out and push the Mini round corners faster than you drive around them; you brake as soon as you see a fly in the road; you're not aggressive enough; you stop when you could go straight onto roundabouts; you hold the car on the clutch when you should have your handbrake on; you have your handbrake on when you should be holding the car on the clutch; you can't reverse or park properly; if I tell you, you get all female and bitchy and yet—and yet—the amazing thing is that you can move big Arctics and drags around the yard and position and park them perfectly. I just don't understand. I'm going to take you out for a long driving lesson at least once a week. Deal?"

Sophie glared at him and then sighed. "OK, deal," she said. "Anything else?"

"Ah, yes, just one small thing," Ben said. "I wish you'd cut your nails more often. I just love it when you dig them into me and run them down my back and arms when you're flying and climaxing, but I'm fed up with having the piss taken out of me by all the drivers when I have great grooves gouged out of me almost daily. Just file them down so they're blunter, please, my love."

"Sorry—I'll remember." Sophie said. Her blushing amused Ben greatly.

"Now," said Ben, "it's your turn."

Sophie looked at him with her head on one side and took a deep breath. "This will seem a strange thing to start with—strange to you, anyway, Ben. When you first slept with me you didn't use a condom, and you didn't ask me if I had any or if I was on the pill, or had a coil, or anything. You commented on it afterwards, though, so you were aware, weren't you? Apart

426

from the fact that I could have become pregnant, there was the risk of STDs, AIDS, and hepatitis. Are you always so careless and irresponsible? Because if you are, there may be a lot of little Bens around this area, and I don't want their mothers pushing in on our relationship."

"Wow," Ben said. "First of all, before I have to defend myself, what precautions did *you* take to protect yourself against infections? OK, you're sterilised, so there was no danger of being impregnated by me the very first time we made love, but you should have insisted on me using a condom too, to protect me as well as you. Neither of us did too well there, but I just had that gut instinct that you had enough intelligence and maturity to be using an effective form of birth control, and I felt you were super clean."

"Yes," said Sophie. "I felt that too about you. Normally I wouldn't have had sex with any guy without a rubber, but with you ..." She shrugged. "It's just that ..."

"I understand," said Ben. "You think I've been riding bareback all over the place and casually filling up local bellies with what you call little Bens. It ain't gonna happen, Sophie. I'm very, very careful, sweetheart. There's a lot of scheming little bitches around here who would love me to impregnate them, but I'm not going to oblige. If I was to believe all the gossip over the years, I've apparently fathered half the kids in this town. Actually, I know I haven't. I just honestly felt safe with you. It was the very first time I didn't use a condom. I don't have to with you anyway, and bareback is fantastic."

"Just as long as you only ever sleep with me and don't mix me in with the local bikes," Sophie said darkly.

"Oh no," Ben said seriously. "No Sophie. You're the only one for me, sweetheart. I'm not short of offers, but I've let it be known that I'm off that particular market. I don't find the young girls who chase me very interesting any more. Most of them drink far too much, and they're total crap in bed, anyway."

"Why?" Sophie looked up sharply. "Have you been sampling them? How do you know?"

"Whoa there, Sophie" said Ben. "I haven't touched any female in this area since I first slid into your beautiful body, and I don't want to. I'm just going out of my mind not being able to even kiss you, let alone—"

"Yes, Ben?"

"Oh, Sophie, all I think and dream of is you and your sweet, warm, body."

"Keep dreaming, Ben. You'll have to earn even a fingertip on my clitoris." Sophie grinned to herself. She had seen Ben's huge erection straining his tight jeans. "You can put that away," she told him sternly.

"Soph, darling, please," Ben begged her. "I've been trying to hold out for weeks now, and I'm going slowly mad. I've got into fights at the yard because I'm so bloody frustrated."

"You'll just have to use a bit of self-control," said Sophie haughtily. "I have to, Ben; it's not easy for me either."

Ben snorted. "Soph, you're a liar."

"A liar!" repeated Sophie, raising her eyebrows. "Why am I a liar?"

"Because I saw your nipples getting hard through that thin T-shirt and through your bra—and they're still erect," Ben said. He was laughing at her.

Sophie blushed hotly. "We're going to get this sorted on my terms," she insisted. "And there's no going to bed or even kissing until we agree on things, Ben, so just go back to the boat and look at porno movies if it's too much for you."

Ben grinned. "I could always just carry you upstairs and give your hard nipples a bit of relief," he proposed.

"I thought we agreed that you're not going to use your superior size and strength to overpower me," Sophie said angrily.

Ben shrugged. "Can I come back tomorrow, please, sweetheart? This really is a bit too much for me, I'm afraid. Mind you, there's a whole bunch of girls up at the pub who'd pay me to fuck them. Maybe I'll go up there." He was laughing, but his back was turned to Sophie.

"Go there then if you can't control yourself for a bit longer," she mumbled, upset.

"Of course I won't, Soph, and I won't pick you up with one hand and carry you up to your bed and have my wicked way. I'm just going back to the boat. I'll come round tomorrow after school hours so I can see Ella, if that's OK with you."

"Yes, that's fine," said Sophie.

Ben hovered in the doorway, clearly anticipating a kiss. Sophie gave him a swift peck on the cheek. "Off you go," she said. She pushed him out and locked the door.

Oh Ben, my Ben, I miss your body so much, she thought as she rubbed shower gel across her swollen nipples. In bed she kicked and tossed the covers off; she couldn't settle. Her body was aching for him, and she wondered just how long she could endure this separation.

She fell asleep from sheer exhaustion and woke tired and still missing Ben.

The next day, Sophie worked hard at the yard and returned to pick Ella up from school. "Is Ben coming again today?" enquired Ella.

"Yes, sweetie," Sophie told her. Ella skipped ahead of Sophie down the road to the cottage. "Ben's coming, Ben's coming," she sang excitedly. Sophie smiled. *Those two really love each other*, she thought, *and I love him too*.

When Ben arrived shortly afterwards, he handed Ella a large parcel. "Can I open it now?" Ella said happily.

"Of course you can, my poppet," Ben told her. Ella peeled away the layers of wrapping paper and came to a large box. Impatiently she tore away the lid. Inside was a perfect replica baby, with soft hair and beautiful lace clothes, complete with nappies, a feeding bottle, and a lovely, lacy woollen shawl.

"Look, Mummy, look, look!" Ella thrust the doll at Sophie. "I've got my own baby!" She knelt down and undressed the doll, exclaiming at the lovely clothes it was dressed in. "Show me how to put the nappy on it, Mummy, please," asked Ella, pulling Sophie down on the floor beside her. Sophie showed Ella slowly how to fold and pin the small nappy; then she dressed the doll and picked it up in her arms, holding it close to her heart. Suddenly huge tears rolled down her cheeks, and she handed the doll back to Ella. "I think she needs her bottle, darling," she said quickly.

Ben looked down at Sophie anxiously. "Hey, Soph, my love, what's wrong?" Sophie shook her head. "Nothing, nothing. I'm just tired, that's all, Ben." Ben put his arm around Sophie and pulled her into him.

"I know what it is, sweetheart. I know. I just wish you'd talk to me about it instead of putting up a wall and shutting me out."

"Not now, please, Ben. Let's pay some attention to Ella." The wall was up again. Sophie shrugged off Ben's arms and started to prepare their supper.

Ben helped Sophie to cook, lay the table, and serve the meal. Then he helped with the washing up, bathed Ella, read her a story, and tucked her up for the night.

Sophie brought in two glasses and poured wine for herself and for Ben. "Let's continue from yesterday, shall we?" she asked. "I got sort of sidelined in the middle of telling you your faults." She smiled.

"We got past the lecture on birth control, I think." Ben grinned. Sophie smiled. "Just that you spoil Ella rotten. I know and appreciate that you also discipline her very well; she rarely disobeys you now. She's got just about everything she's asked you for, and she can twist you round her little finger, Ben. She has to learn that she can't have it all."

"She's stunningly lovely," Ben said, "and she'll be even more beautiful as she gets older. She'll always get what she wants from men if she's canny and intelligent. I'm just teaching her to use her fantastic looks to get what she wants in life."

"Is that really a good thing to teach her, Ben? She needs to learn to earn things, to wait for them; this instant gratification based on her looks can't be good for her, really. I know how much you love her, but please don't spoil her too much. Already she's started to tell me, if I don't give in to her every whim, that you will give this and that to her and let her do what I forbid. She's playing one of us against the other, sweetheart. Just be careful."

Soon it was time for Ben to go back to his boat. Reluctantly he left Sophie after giving her a tiny kiss on her cheek, which was all she would allow. Just for a nanosecond he felt like kissing her deeply on her mouth, pushing his tongue under hers, and stroking her sweet face—but he had to wait until she allowed him to. He would wait, because she was a prize worth waiting for.

That day, when Sophie had picked up Ella from school, Ella had said, "Mummy, I want Ben to be my daddy. I really love him. Can I call him Daddy—please, Mummy, please?" Sophie was a little taken aback but not too surprised. "I miss Ben, Mummy. When will he be not busy? I want him back."

"Soon," Sophie murmured. "Soon."

They arrived at the cottage to find Ben waiting outside; he had a huge bunch of flowers clutched awkwardly in his large hands. Sophie smiled. "Thanks Ben." She took them into the sunlit kitchen, filled a chipped blue vase with water, and arranged the bright, pretty blooms. Ella flung herself around Ben's legs and kissed his knees. He laughingly scooped her up and kissed her nose. Sophie told her to go up and change out of her school uniform, and she dashed away.

When they were alone later, with Ella tucked up in bed, Sophie said, "Ben, Ella asked me today if she could call you Daddy. I know what you feel for each other, but—" She held up both her hands helplessly.

Ben's blue eyes lit up, and he smiled warmly. "Did she really? That's—that's wonderful, mind-blowing, and a terrific compliment. If she does, then people will really believe that I actually made her. Lots of people believe that already, because we look so like each other. Somebody thought she was my secret love child! I said that she was. Would you let her call me Daddy, Soph, please?"

"Yes, of course, Ben. You've earned it. You've really been a wonderful substitute father to her. I'm very happy for Ella to really have a daddy that she loves respects and trusts. However," Sophie said and she frowned. "Remember that, because if she ever sees you doing to me what you have done, you'll lose her respect and trust instantly. You've got a choice to make. You can have Ella as a daughter; me running your haulage efficiently and properly; a home here; and someone who loves you more than you could ever understand—someone who'll always be ready to comfort and defend you through everything life can throw, who'll always be ready to make love, and who'll do anything to pleasure and satisfy you."

Ben took her hand. "I choose you and Ella and that over everything and everybody else," he said soberly. "Sophie, I've got something to give you to seal this promise." He put a small box into her hand. Sophie opened it slowly. Nestled in the white satin and expensive leather was an exquisitely beautiful ring; there were deep-red stones and white ones, obviously diamonds.

Sophie gasped. "Ben, it's fantastic."

"It's rubies and diamonds in platinum," Ben told her. "I remember you saying how much you loved rubies. I had to guess at your finger size, but I think it's OK. Here, hold out your left hand." Ben slipped the lovely ring onto Sophie's finger. "Now you're engaged to me, Sophie. You really are all mine, and I'm all yours, and I want one day to add a wedding ring to this."

Sophie gazed at the ring speechlessly. Then she put her arms around Ben's neck and kissed him very slowly for a long time.

"Whoa, Soph," he pleaded. "I'm getting a massive erection, and you've forbidden me to go there."

Sophie grinned up at him. "Oh, did I forget to tell you? The ban just ended."

"Oh, Sophie, my little darling," Ben murmured. "Come here and let me love you a lot."

Ben carried her upstairs, kissing her all the way. He slowly and gently lowered Sophie onto the bed. "Have you got those knickers on that I bought you last week?" he asked, grinning. Sophie grinned back. "Yep."

He ran his hands down to her belly, slowly eased her jeans off, and then removed her T-shirt and bra. He quickly stripped off all his clothes and then very slowly removed her tiny, beribboned, lacy panties. "Oh my God, Sophie, I've missed you so very much. I want you so badly. I think it'll take me all night to show you how much I love and want you."

He kissed her gently and then harder and harder. "Sorry, darling," he groaned. "I've just got to go into you. I'm nearly coming now. Is that OK?" Sophie took his huge penis in her hand and fed it into the warmth and wetness of her yearning body.

"Fuck me hard, Ben; fuck me very, very hard. I want you and need you like hell."

Ben went into her passionately, and she reached orgasm within seconds. Ben lasted another minute and then groaned. "Oh, Sophie, my darling! Oh God, Sophie, how I love you. I'm coming, my lovely. Take it all in your belly. Take it all." He pushed into her furiously, and she climaxed again and again. Ben kissed her passionately, tears running down his face as he poured all his frustrated love and lust into Sophie's body. "Oh, my sweet darling, how I've missed you." He wept into her hair and kissed her neck and her shoulders and breasts.

"Ben, my Ben," Sophie whispered, stroking his body and nuzzling into his neck.

They held each other tightly and dozed. But very soon Ben was aroused again, and he slid down to Sophie's belly and ran his tongue over her navel, and down, down until he reached her sweet, wet warmth. He ran his tongue across her clitoris gently and then pushed into her. She moaned and pushed his head away.

"No, Ben darling, no gentle stuff, please, I want to be fucked really hard."

"Really, really hard, Sophie?"

"Yes, hard and rough, Ben."

"Until you call me the safe word—*Benjamin*?"

"No, just don't listen this time; make me fight back."

"OK, my honey, but it will be hard, and it will be very rough. Think you can take it?"

Sophie looked into his deep, blue eyes and begged: "Give it to me, Ben—I need it!"

Ben took off his thick leather necklets. He tied several around Sophie's wrists and then pushed one into her mouth. "You'll need to bite on this," he told her. Sophie felt shivers running over her, shivers of excitement and fear and deep need and passion. "Get on your knees." Ben pushed her forward. He lifted her pinioned arms up over her head and behind her neck so that she was unable to do anything at all to defend or help herself.

"Head down and bum up," he commanded. Sophie raised her buttocks obediently. "Spread," said Ben tersely. She spread her legs, and Ben went into her from behind, very hard and very forcefully. He grabbed her shoulders and thrust his full huge maleness into her. Sophie held her breath; she was in some pain, but great waves of pleasure rolled through her body. She arched her back, although with some difficulty because of Ben's great weight. Ben slapped her hard across the buttocks. "Keep still!" he snapped, pushing down on her shoulders

Ben pulled out suddenly and ordered Sophie to turn and face him. "Open your mouth," he demanded. Sophie obeyed him. He took the leather gag out and thrust into her. He moved very quickly, and Sophie felt rising panic. Her arms, tied behind her neck, were hurting badly, and Ben held her head back by her plait so that he was almost wedged down her throat. To protect herself she could bite, but he would punish her for that and probably push harder. She put her tongue across the back of her throat to give herself some protection. Despite her position, she was very, very sexually aroused; the pain and danger added to her passion.

Sophie watched Ben's eyes and listened to his gasps. She felt him tensing and his groans became deeper.

Ben pulled her head up by her plait and slid out of her. "Good girl," he said and kissed her hard on her mouth. Then he pushed the leather gag back into her mouth. "On your back," he ordered. Sophie lay back; the pain in her arms was agonising. Ben pulled them up and tied them to the bed head. Then he went down onto her with his tongue; he brought her near to orgasm time and time again, each time stopping at the crucial moment and leaving Sophie wriggling and begging. He pinned her down to stop her movements and laughed at her as she begged him to let her reach orgasm. Sophie fought him, throwing her body upwards and turning her head away from him as he tried to kiss her mouth. She twisted and attempted to kick out, but Ben held her down with his heavy body. He pushed two of his huge fingers into her and moved them in and out; she tried to writhe about again until he prevented her once again. "I told you not to move," he growled at her. "See how this feels." He inserted four fingers and pushed really hard. Sophie winced. Ben pushed another finger in and twisted his hand around. Sophie cried out and bit hard on her gag, but she was still excited; she wanted rougher, raw handling.

Ben stopped, withdrew his fingers, and pushed Sophie's knees up to her shoulders. He inserted his penis as far as he was able and rammed into Sophie, grunting and gasping with each tremendous thrust. Sophie bit into the gag and whimpered; this was really painful. She cried out "No, no, no!" and fought him ferociously, throwing herself sideways forcibly, but this just made Ben push into her harder. He stayed in her for some time but then withdrew without climaxing. "Roll over," he instructed tersely. "Kneel." He untied her wrists and then retied them behind her back so that she was completely helpless. He commanded her to spread her legs apart once again.

"Are you sure you want me to go on?" he asked her. "This is really going to hurt. You've got your word to stop me if it's too much; I promise I'll stop."

Sophie murmured, "Keep going."

"You know you're going to get my belt again. You can call a stop now if you can't take it," Ben said. "Do you want me to go on?"

Sophie nodded, and Ben pushed another leather strip into her mouth for her to bite on.

Sophie was trembling with excitement and terror; Ben took his biker's belt from his jeans and stroked her buttocks gently with it. He leaned down, kissed her buttocks, and ran his tongue over them. He continued to do this for some minutes. Suddenly he grunted and brought his belt down hard across her buttocks. She jerked and screamed, biting hard on her gag. She fought to escape, but Ben held her down with one huge hand. "Did that hurt, my little sweetheart?" he murmured, kissing the weal he had raised.

Sophie felt his huge penis rubbing against her from behind. She realised, with a pang of delicious fear, what was about to happen, but she said nothing. She was still incredibly aroused. Ben slid his penis into her slowly and put his fingers into her vagina, moving them hard and rubbing her clitoris with his thumb. Sophie was very aroused, and Ben began to thrust into her anus really hard. Sophie was near her orgasm; although Ben was hurting her, she was stimulated and excited. Her orgasm hit her, and she moaned and wriggled. Ben pulled out of her and hit her buttocks viciously with his belt again. "Don't move, Sophie!" He pushed into her hard again, and Sophie cried out with pain and pleasure as she climaxed again and again. Ben pulled out of her, rolled her over onto her back, and sprayed his seed over her face and her breasts. He lay across her, panting and sweating.

"Benjamin," Sophie said softly.

"Yes, Soph," he said.

"Please untie my hands; they're hurting a lot."

Ben rolled her over and released her hands. She spat her gags out and stretched out on the bed. Ben rolled onto her and held her very tightly. "This has nothing to do with what I did to you before," he told her, stroking her hair.

"I know, Ben," she said. "I asked you for it, and I wanted and needed it. It's very different."

He kissed her on her mouth and she pushed him off gently. "I'm covered in your sperm," she told him.

"So what?" He grinned. Come on, let's have a shower. Then I could murder a beer."

Sophie smiled gently. She stretched out on the bed and yawned. She was learning that she loved certain dark things, the things of the night, and the half-light, and the painfully languorous. And they and Ben were one, and he was the sun in her universe. They slept together, skin on skin and soul in soul.

The starlight poured over them.

SOPHIE AND BEN, SIX

The first day Ben took them both in his truck was sunny and bright. Sophie loved the huge blue-and-white rig, with its throaty 310-horsepower diesel purr; its amazing display of gear shifts—she learnt what a splitter was—its air clutch; its array of flashing lights and bleeping alarms; and the *whoosh* of the air brakes. Along with his usual array of leather and beaded bracelets and necklets, Ben was wearing one gold earring and a thick neck chain with a gold locket that held pictures of Sophie and Ella.

Sophie was able to study his tattoos of stars, moons, crosses, and dragons. She loved his Celtic bands and noted with an inner grin that there were no female names in the array. When she asked him about it later, he joked that there wouldn't be enough room on his skin for them all. She adored his arrogant self-confidence. As the day wore on, she became more and more entranced with the great truck and the road life she was seeing. He was wearing only his jeans in the heat, and she was continuously aware of his bronzed skin and the strong male odour of his young body.

As evening drew on, they stopped at a truckers' café, where Ben and Ella ate huge platefuls of shepherd's pie and a mountain of vegetables. Sophie had a mug of strong tea and a sandwich. She was unable to eat large amounts after spending so many years going without to feed Ella, and Ben's presences and absences had also taken away her appetite.

They slept in the cab when darkness fell. Ella had a top bunk with safety bars, and they had a huge double bunk behind the seats. After they left Ella with friends, they drank, smoked weed, and then made love for hours. Ben took her from behind, hard and excitingly, and they went down on each other. When he was tired from driving, she pushed him back onto the bunk and rolled onto him, kissing his mouth and hands and the thick, blond hair on his body. He could look up at her and stroke her breasts while she moved slowly, slowly, stopping time and time again just as he was reaching his peak. She held him back until he begged her for release, and she let him go, and he cried out her name, and called her his precious one and his darling. Later Ben went down on her and sent her into raptures with his tongue and fingers. He covered her mouth with his to silence her cries when she climaxed. Sophie slept deeply and peacefully. Just before dawn, she woke and went down and took him into her mouth. She ran her tongue over him skilfully and adoringly until he groaned, and she took his seed into her mouth. Then she spat some onto her hands and rubbed it over her nipples whilst he watched her with his blue, blue eyes and grinned the grin that made her senses spin and her heart miss a beat.

They got home tired, dirty, and stinking of diesel. There were always sleeping bags to be washed and paperwork to be done. She noticed as time went by that she was doing more and more of this while he would disappear and come home late. His blue eyes would be duller, almost grey, and he would seem disinterested in her. She tried not to think too much about why. She told herself that maybe he needed to get away from her and be with his men friends, but in her heart she knew that he was in a bad place. He could not break free of addiction, and she wept inwardly as she saw the end of their happiness looming.

Ben adored Ella, and she worshipped him. He had taken her with him to deliver fertiliser at a farm one sunny, frosty early morning, and the farmer's wife had brought them in to sit by the Aga while she cooked them a huge fried breakfast. She turned and looked at Ella. "What a beautiful child," she said, "and how like her daddy with those blue eyes and golden hair." Ben had smiled proudly.

"Yes, she is like me, isn't she," he said and winked at Ella, who grinned back adoringly.

When Ella became ill and was very feverish, Sophie woke to find Ben sitting by her bed, watching her anxiously. Sophie sat with Ben, holding his hand and resting her head on his shoulder until he fell asleep as dawn swept up the darkness.

Ben bought Ella a pink tricycle with balance wheels, and she tore around on it, chortling with delight. The day came when he took off the balance wheels and took her to the top of the little hill behind the cottage. "Stay there," he said solemnly, and she stayed there whilst he walked to the bottom of the hill. He turned and opened his arms. "Come on!" he shouted, and she hesitated, wobbled, and then flew down to his waiting arms. He lifted her up into the air, and she screamed with joy and love for him. When he looked at her it was as if he were looking on a precious gem. They had a bond that was palpable.

The lovely blue-eyed, blonde child with her handsome blue-eyed, blonde adoptive father were inseparable and, physically, strangely similar. Sophie was often deeply moved by their mutual delight in each other's company and being.

Ben, yet again, stroked her cheek and whispered, "All we need now is a little boy to go with her, eh?"

She stiffened. "I can't have any more babies; I thought you understood."

"I think you can have it reversed; they can untie your tubes again or something," he said, shrugging. "Then you can conceive again naturally. I saw it on tele a few weeks ago—"

"Maybe, but had you thought that I might not want to go through another pregnancy and birth at my age? We've been through this already, Ben. I've had problems with very big babies before. You know all this, Ben—and look at the size of you! I can't face the prospect of a 10- or 11-pound baby. It really frightens me."

Ben was silent, and a chill ran over Sophie's heart. This was what she had secretly feared and dreaded, why she had told him to find someone younger.

"You'll want babies," she had told him as they lay in the afterglow of lovemaking. Ben had traced patterns on her belly with his fingers and remarked casually that any children they had would be quite beautiful. "I can't have them, you know that," she'd said and asked him quietly and sadly if it really mattered so very much. Ben had said that no, it didn't matter to him, but Sophie knew that it did matter, and she had tried to push it from her mind.

Sophie thought very hard about this; she agonised over the problems she would face and then felt very guilty about Ben's deep desire to have a child with her. One day she went to her doctor and discussed the problem with him; he arranged for her to see an obstetrician/gynaecologist, and Sophie kept the appointment without telling Ben. She was told that she could, indeed, have a procedure that might enable her to conceive Ben's child. She decided to tell him when they went to a celebration they had been invited to by friends who had just had their first child, a baby boy.

Ella went to their friends', and Sophie dressed herself up and put on make-up and perfume. Ben wore his best jeans and white shirt and red neckerchief. He washed and braided his blond hair in leather strips. The gathering was large; there were tents pitched and horse-drawn caravans and very old motorised homes. It was noisy, colourful, and fascinating. The noise was overwhelming. There was music everywhere, with people playing guitars and singing, shouting, laughing, and talking loudly. The smell of wood smoke came from many open fires and the familiar smells of marijuana, unwashed bodies, dogs, cooking—a wonderful potpourri of brightness and noise. Sophie was pulled back to her hippie days and felt nostalgic and excited. Many of the young, attractive girls were in various stages of pregnancy or breast-feeding small babies, and young children ran around everywhere, shouting excitedly.

The people there were all hippy, traveller, biker types, and Sophie knew a few of them vaguely. She was slightly nervous of the presence of some of Ben's druggy friends. Ben was drinking quite heavily, and Sophie watched him carefully. He was talking to the young parents of the new baby boy. The mother was a dainty, thin, very pretty girl, with curly blonde hair and pale skin. The father was a tall, slight, handsome lad with jet-black hair in a long plait. Like the others at the celebration, they had multiple tattoos and piercings and wore leather and bead bracelets and necklets.

Ben called Sophie over. He held the newborn child in his arms and showed it to Sophie.

"Look," Ben said. "Look at this beautiful little boy. His mother could conceive him and give birth to him, which is more than you can, isn't it Sophie?" Sophie felt as if he had slapped her across the face. She felt tears welling in her eyes. "Look," Ben continued. "Look at all these other proper females." He emphasised the word *proper.* "Look, Sophie, can you see that some of them have got big, big bellies because their guys have fucked them and the seed they put in is growing into babies? There's a lot of other females with nice flat bellies, but if I fucked them and filled them with my seed, their bellies would soon swell. I've put one hell of a lot of my seed in you, Sophie, but no, no babies. No babies for Ben." He took the baby back to its parents, while Sophie stood shaking and fighting not to cry. She was aware of people looking at her and talking softly to each other. The child's parents looked sad and sympathetic, and she could see empathy and pity in their eyes.

Ben went off to join a group of friends, and soon several girls were quite blatantly flirting with him. He paid a great deal of attention to a strikingly dark, thin girl with long hair and large sloe-black eyes. Sophie was distressed to see Ben put his arm around her. The girl laughed up at him, ran her fingers over his chest, and went on tiptoe to play with his long plait. He was drinking more heavily and kept his arm around the girl.

Sophie had planned to tell Ben her news about the operation and was determined not to let his behaviour deter her, despite her deep hurt at his comments. She walked over to Ben and the dark girl. The girl looked at Sophie arrogantly and raised her eyebrows. "What do you want?" she demanded rudely.

"I just want to speak to Ben," Sophie said very quietly.

"Why?" the girl said with a laugh. "Do you have some sort of priority over the rest of us?"

Sophie looked at her calmly. "Yes," she said softly. "Yes. He's my—" She stopped.

"Your son, perhaps?" The dark girl roared with laughter. She took Ben's hand. "Come on, sweetie; there's treats to be had over there." The girl pointed to the small wooden Romany caravan, where a group of Ben's dark friends were, doubtless, fixing on substances.

Sophie stood her ground. "Ben, I need to talk to you—alone—privately, please."

Ben looked at her drunkenly, swaying.

The dark girl pulled at Ben's hand. "Come on, Benjy. Your mum can put herself to bed." They both laughed, and Sophie felt hurt, like a hot knife, tearing at her heart.

"Please, Ben" she said very softly. "Please, it's important." She took his arm, and he turned to face her.

"What's this very important thing, then?" he said irritably.

Sophie took a deep breath. "I've seen the doctor and a specialist, and I can have an operation—"

At that moment the dark girl dragged Ben away. "Come on, Benjy. They're all waiting for you." Ben turned away from Sophie and followed.

Sophie stood shaking; huge tears ran down her face and into her mouth. She felt arms around her. She turned to see the parents of the newborn boy. The concern and pity in their eyes made her weep even more.

"Don't let it get to you, darling," the girl said. "That Bella has been after Ben since they were at school together. She's a jealous, bitchy troublemaker. Ben won't give her what she wants—he does really love you a lot; everyone knows it."

Sophie looked at her. "But why is he going back to those awful people and their drugs yet again? He promised me and Ella that he would stay away. He's been so different up until today—" She sobbed and shook.

The young, tall man put his arms around her and cuddled her tightly. "I heard what he said to you, Sophie. Some of us know that he wants your baby, and the problem you've got, and we're really gutted for you. That was so cruel and out of order. He can be a really sweet, kind guy."

The girl put her hand on Sophie's shoulder. "Stick with it, Sophie. Be strong. He really needs you more than he realises." The baby cried then, and the girl lifted him, in his shawl, to her breast and sat down on the ground to feed him. Seeing the tiny creature nuzzling into his mother and suckling made Sophie sob again.

The man put his arms around her more tightly and stroked her hair gently. "Dear Sophie, you've done so much for Ben, and he just won't grow up. Don't throw yourself away forever—there's a lot of men just waiting for Ben to go."

Sophie looked up and saw Ben in the distance, staring at her in the man's arms. Their eyes met, and Ben gazed at her for some time. Sophie pulled away from the dark, sweet, comforting lad and ran to where her Mini was parked. She had brought her Mini and Ben his Land Rover, as they had given several people lifts to the gathering. She quickly unlocked her car, got in, and drove back to the cottage. She took a bottle of wine out of the fridge and poured herself a large glass. She put some music on the stereo and sat listening to it, trying to cope with her anger and disappointment at Ben's return to alcohol and drugs. She emptied the bottle of wine and went upstairs to bed. She stripped off her clothes, as the night was warm and humid. She curled up in the bed in which she and Ben had made such torrid and beautiful love. She cried herself to sleep but awoke after a short time. She took the letter from the hospital from the bedside table. She read and reread it, opened one of her drawers, and pushed it in.

In the early hours, when the birds were starting to sing and the light was coming up over the trees and the river, Ben came in very softly. Sophie woke but did not stir; she kept her eyes shut tightly and breathed deeply so that Ben would think she was asleep. He got into bed, leaned over her, and kissed her mouth. Sophie could smell alcohol and marijuana. She rolled away from Ben and buried her face in the pillow. Ben began to stroke her back and her buttocks and kiss them gently. Sophie wanted to scream at him to go away, to go and fuck the black-eyed bitch, but try as she might to resist and shut Ben out, she felt herself responding to him. He pulled her over towards him and began to run his tongue over her nipples. Sophie tried to roll back away from him, but Ben was far too strong for her. He wasn't rough, but he held her very firmly down so that he could roll over onto her.

"You know you want me, my lovely," he said gently. "I know I've been a sod to you, and I let Bella hang round me, and it upset you. I wouldn't give her what she's always wanting, and I told her off for what she said to you."

"Did you?" said Sophie. "But you didn't defend me when she said it, did you? You just laughed and followed her. I wanted to talk to you, and you couldn't stay and listen to me—she was more important and so were the drugs." Ben kissed her hard on her mouth, and she felt his erection growing yet harder and bigger. Sophie wished she was not reacting with such desire and that she could just be cold and refuse Ben his assumed rights. She wanted to talk to him, not make love to him; she was still very hurt and very angry. She turned her head away and tried to push Ben off.

He grinned down at her. "Getting rough with me, eh, little one?" He held her down even more firmly with one hand.

Sophie got very angry and hit out at Ben, but he held her wrist and she was unable to move an inch.

"I love you when you're angry," he said, still grinning. He kissed her very hard on her mouth, and she could smell again the alcohol and marijuana. Ben lay on top of her without moving and brought his face down to hers. She could see the deep, deep blue of his beautiful eyes.

"Sophie, my lovely, my little one, my sweetheart, you know how much you want me. You're angry, but you're not going to push me away." He opened the fingers on her left hand. "Look at this ring," he said. "It cost several thousand pounds, and it says that Sophie Navarre belongs completely to Ben Benedict, and he wants to fuck her beautiful body right now. So little Sophie must stop fighting him off and open her legs." He grinned cheekily at her, which made Sophie furious.

"You don't own me!" She said through gritted teeth." I own me, and I'll decide when I want you to fuck me. Right now I want to talk to you, not be fucked, so please get off me, Ben—I mean it!" Her hazel eyes were hard.

"Soph darling, please, no. I have to have you right now. Can't we talk later? Just let me make love to you, little one—please, please."

"Get off me, Ben." Sophie tried to escape from his huge body, but he held her down. In desperation she scratched at Ben's face, and blood began to pour out of his cheek. His eyes became dark with anger. Forcing Sophie's legs apart, he went into her hard, hurting her.

"No!" Sophie screamed. "Leave me alone, Ben! Get off me!"

"Oh no, Sophie." Ben breathed hard as he continued thrusting deeply into her. "Oh no, you're mine, and if I want you I'm going to have you. You don't want me to have any of those other girls, so keep me happy and let me fuck you one hell of a lot, and you won't have to worry, will you, my little one?"

Sophie sobbed with anger and frustration.

"Are you coming yet?" Ben asked her. "No? Well tough, Soph, tough—because I am." He groaned and thrust deep into Sophie as he climaxed.

Sophie was left desperate and frustrated. She was very angry with Ben but also highly sexually charged and in need of an orgasm.

Ben laughed at her. "You should have been a good little one and played Ben's game. Then you wouldn't be uptight and still needing a good fuck, would you, my little tiger." Ben went into the bathroom and bathed his scratched face.

Sophie wept with fury at her inability to prevent Ben from imposing himself on her sexually when he was in the aftermath of a drink and drugs orgy. He had made her promises and solemn vows, and all had been well and truly happy for them all for some time. But now, suddenly, Ben was sliding backwards into the seamy, murky darkness of his former addictions. Sophie was angry, but she was also frightened.

She heard Ben going downstairs, and soon he came back up with two cups of coffee. He gave Sophie one and sat down beside her on the bed.

"So what did you want to talk to me about that was more important than us making love?" He grinned at her. "It must be bloody important," said Ben.

Sophie decided in that instant that she would not tell him about the operation and the possibility that he would have what his heart yearned for—her belly filled with his child. She would not do so because she could no longer trust Ben to support and care for her through a pregnancy, a likely difficult birth, and the care and support she would need afterwards. She also doubted that Ben would help her raise a child when he was in his addiction moods.

"It was important," Sophie said, lowering her eyes. "But I've sorted it now."

Much later, when days were dark, his drinking was heavy, and his moods were becoming almost too much to cope with, Sophie felt that she could not continue in the relationship. As she was preparing herself to face the fact that it was hopeless and she was losing him, she began to feel very tired and vaguely nauseous. She realised, with a stab of fear, that her breasts were larger and tender and that she could no longer drink or stand the smell of coffee. She was frightened and puzzled. She lay with her hands on her belly, thinking of the not-unheard-of possibility of conception after sterilisation.

She knew she was pregnant but tried to deny it to herself. She visited her doctor, and he confirmed it. He wanted her to visit a specialist as a precaution because of her age and the sterilisation. She did not keep the appointment. She was terrified. How could she stay with Ben now that he had broken his pledge to her and to Ella? But how could she leave? And how could she face this unwanted and abnormal pregnancy while living in fear of Ben's unstable, drug-fuelled temperament and his increasing violence towards her?

She did not tell Ben. She was becoming increasingly afraid of his changing and unpredictable moods. His frequently rough and selfish lovemaking left her unsatisfied, awake and crying quietly long after he had rolled away and fallen asleep.

She wept because she loved him and he was pulling away from her; he was lost in a world of drugs and alcohol. She wept for the beautiful lovemaking that he no longer gave to her. Her sexual longing for him was unfulfilled. She yearned for the sweet, long, gentle foreplay they had once shared for hours, the fierce but loving passion of the final thrusting and orgasm. She missed the sweet and sincere love he had whispered to her as he held her tightly while they lay spent and happy. He still remained a tender and caring father substitute to Ella, however; his darkness seemed to be aimed at Sophie.

Now she almost dreaded Ben's advances: his roughness and impatience; his lack of foreplay, which made his thrusting painful to her and often left her bruised, physically and mentally.

Just once in a while he would emerge from his substance-fuelled stupor, and her beautiful Ben would be back with her for several days. Then he would constantly kiss and hug her, call her "little one," and bring her flowers, trinkets, chocolates, and skimpy underwear. They would be back in the world she knew and longed for, and their lovemaking would be something she tried to remember and carry with her through the darker days. On one of these nights their lovemaking had been sweet and intense, and she had climaxed with a passion she had never felt before. Ben had pushed into her very deeply, and she'd been almost unable to breathe as they reached orgasm together. Later, in the dark, lost days, she liked to think that this was the night that Ben's seed had somehow breached her tied-off tube and created a tiny life inside her. She knew it was likely to end in tragedy and pain, but deep inside of her a faint hope flickered that nature might have beaten the science that had closed off her ability to conceive the baby Ben longed for and that it had implanted in her womb and was growing normally.

Ben did not seem to notice how tired she had become, but when he did notice he snapped at her for her inability to do all he demanded of her. She ate little, and often what she did eat was vomited back forcibly. When he did see her vomiting, he was cruel and dismissive and accused Sophie of attention-seeking. Sophie became nervous and tense; she tried to hide it from him when she felt nauseous. When he made love to her he seemed unaware of her growing breasts. She was so sick and eating so little that her belly did not swell as rapidly as it had done in her other pregnancies.

Ben's moods had become darker. Sophie was so tired that her normal patience with and understanding of his drinking and temper had all but gone. He was always somewhere else when there was work to be done, work he had always shared with her before. Some of the work was physically almost beyond her capabilities, and her pregnancy was beginning to exhaust her. She would not give in—she was a stubbornly determined character. This was Ben's haulage business, and she could not let it fall apart—she would never stop helping him.

Some of the drivers had noticed. They saw Ben's flash moods and his apparently cruel pleasure at Sophie's growing fear of them. They saw her devotion and love. They also saw her increasing tiredness and her continual vomiting. Once she had fainted at the yard but begged the drivers to say nothing to Ben. They worried about her and tried to help her, but she was proud and would force herself beyond her emotional and physical limits. A few of the drivers had faint suspicions that poor Sophie, struggling with overwhelming problems and trauma caused by Ben's addictions and violence, might be pregnant. Over the months her breasts were enlarging, but she seemed to be getting much thinner, and her belly was barely swollen. So they imagined it might be some kind of female problem but were still fairly sure that they were right. Thus they shadowed her and treated her like china, but they did it discreetly so that she was unaware of being protected.

Only Blue, a man with extraordinary knowledge of reality, relationships, and women, could see the subtle changes. These changes told Blue that Sophie was carrying new life in her body; she was carrying the child of a young guy who seemed unable to break his dark habits for this tough, loving, and beautiful woman whose love and devotion Blue would have died to own. But Blue could see that the immature fool really did love her deeply. *What has to happen to teach him that losing her would mean the end of his world?* wondered Blue. He watched Sophie dragging the hose over to start cleaning the trucks. She always ensured that their blue-and-white rigs were head-turningly clean, smart, and mechanically and legally perfect.

Sophie was unaware of Blue's presence when she stopped suddenly, dropping the hose and pressing her fist into her belly, her face screwed up in pain.

He was immediately by her side. "Are you OK, my love?"

She turned and smiled at him. He adored her suntanned, freckled face; her tilted, almond-shaped hazel eyes; her long, wavy copper-red hair that was plaited with ribbons, beads, and tiny bells. She was small, almost delicate, but her hard work, day in and day out, had made her tough and muscular. Blue was always amazed at what her stubborn self-discipline enabled her to do.

Why can't Ben see what a prize he has there, thought Blue. He wondered how Sophie would handle this—even her tough little spirit couldn't keep her going through a pregnancy at her age if she pushed herself like this. How could that stupid young idiot not have the sense to protect her against it? Did he even know he had put a child in her belly? Blue had noticed Sophie's, often-severe vomiting and knew she frequently brought back even the liquids she drank. He worried about her risk of dehydration. The day she fainted whilst cleaning one of the cabs, he was very tempted to speak to Ben. But Blue knew, too, how afraid Sophie was becoming, and he did not want to be the cause of Ben's temper being vented on her—especially now that she was pregnant. He was puzzled that Sophie was afraid to tell Ben, but he reasoned that Sophie was confused and frightened and struggling with Ben's addictions and moods. Blue prayed that Sophie had medical support and supervision. If not, then disaster could be looming for the increasingly frail and tired Sophie.

Blue knew that Ben had pulled himself together after the split-up with Sophie and that life had been wonderful for them both for a while. But he also knew that Ben had drifted back to the companions and substances that changed him into the violent, uncaring, and selfish bastard and that Sophie was suffering stress, unhappiness, and perhaps more violence. Blue knew too well that she had no defence against Ben's massive size and strength. Ben could pick her up with just one hand. She was brave and loyal, but all the drivers had seen the bruising on her arms and sometimes her face and her body; they pitied her helplessness. But they all knew that Sophie would continue to loyally and stubbornly defend Ben, work for his benefit, and bear his physical and emotional abuse, because she loved him very, very deeply and could not leave him or turn away from the path she had chosen.

"Let me help you, my darling," Blue said, picking up the hose. Sophie turned to him and smiled, and his heart melted with pity at the exhaustion in her eyes and the tiny lines of weariness around them. "No, no. You go on home, Blue," she said. "Your missus will want you back for a long, sexy weekend!"

Blue grinned and kissed her hair. "I'll stay if you need a hand. You look a bit tired." He hesitated. "Got a bit of tummy pain, eh?" Sophie looked up quickly and smiled. "Sure, just been eating too much."

More like too little, thought Blue. Sophie was becoming thinner, and Blue knew the growing child inside her was wearing down her strength and her health dangerously.

Blue got into his car, still worried about her. Something was wrong and he sensed it. Sophie had been in pain; something she would always hide and cope with. Her pain must be pretty severe if she had winced like that. Blue had also noticed that she was very pale and seemed to find difficulty in simply walking; he'd also seen her hands shaking slightly. Should he stay and keep a fatherly eye on her? He was aware of her pregnancy, but not all of the other drivers had yet realised it. If she were on her own and became unwell, they would not realise her situation when they arrived at the yard. He waved to her reluctantly and pulled out.

When he was out of sight, Sophie took a deep breath and picked up the hose. She was left alone to clean all seven lorries. She felt so weak; even her stubborn spirit seemed to have failed her. She could scarcely climb up into the cabs, and as she jumped down from one, she felt another sudden stab of pain in her belly. It was agonising and made her shake. She caught her breath and doubled up. She remained like this for several minutes, sweating and retching. Then she forced herself to straighten up and continue.

There was a mountain of paperwork to face. Ben might return. Sophie knew he had been away with his sinister friends, since he'd driven back and left his rig parked in the yard with delivery notes thrown everywhere and full of the debris of a week's driving. He would expect it to be cleared and cleaned and readied for another pull-out. What they had once done together was now her sole, backbreaking, never-ending burden. She never had time, and her body was so very tired.

Ben had come back recently from a long trip, slightly drunk and aroused by the sight of her wearing only a brief vest over her jeans as she reversed the trailer into its parking space. Watching this tiny female wrestling the big trucks skilfully always excited him strangely. He'd got into the cab and forced her back into the bunk. She did not dislike rough lovemaking if she consented to it; it was a part of their normally loving union. But he had hurt her arms, holding her down very, very hard with his hands. He had not bothered with his usual long, sweet, erotic foreplay but gone into her hard.

She had worried, as Ben did not know of her pregnancy and she had experienced cramping pains recently. She'd been concerned that Ben's increasingly violent sexual handling would damage her unborn child. She'd been afraid to tell him, and the stress of this made life very hard for her. She had winced.

"What's the problem now?" He had been angry. "Scars, or what?"

"I'm sorry, Ben. I can't help them."

"Why have you got scars like fucking zippers?"

"Because I had very big babies, and I couldn't manage to get them out without being cut or splitting."

"So you couldn't even do that properly."

Sophie had not been able to reply and tears had rolled down her cheeks.

"Oh, for fuck's sake, stop crying. I'm supposed to be the baby, and you're supposed to be the older one. Why do you cry so much?" Ben had emphasised the word *older*, and she felt something die inside her.

She wanted to say, "Because you're often so rough and selfish when you make love, and you hurt me, and because I'm pregnant with your child, and I've been having cramping pains, and I'm worried sick that your huge size and hard thrusting may harm our baby. And I've very probably got an ectopic pregnancy, and I'm terrified of what may happen, and I'm too frightened to tell you." But she was so afraid of his unreliable temper, and so she held all the fear, stress, loneliness, and pain inside.

She had tried really hard to respond to Ben's body and his need but, unusually for her, had not felt anything at all. She'd been frightened. He'd climaxed quickly, pushing into her hard and painfully, and rolled off her and lit a cigarette. She'd lain there in the bunk, quiet and weeping. *Please*, she had prayed, *please let him stop this drinking and drug abuse. He's so different when he's away from it all. I love him so much, but I can't defend and protect him or run this haulage on my own much longer.*

Sophie was just going into the office to begin tackling the mountain of paperwork there when Ben's Land Rover pulled into the yard and he got out. She saw that he was in a black mood and drunk as well—she could always tell. Normally she was wary and patient, but she felt suddenly exhausted and resentful.

Ben looked at her with arrogant, angry eyes. "Haven't you done the paperwork yet?" he demanded sullenly.

"No, not yet." She tried to sound casual, as if she was oblivious to his threatening presence.

"Why?"

"I had to clean the trucks."

"Really. Is that a criticism of me? Should I have been here and done them? Have I been somewhere I shouldn't be? Don't I work hard enough, with all the fucking driving I fucking do!"

Suddenly something inside of Sophie snapped. She wanted to slap his face, drag him by his long hair, and force him to see how tired and unwell she was. At that minute, the pain ripped through her like a knife, and she shouted at him: "Yes, you do work very hard, but so do I—boy!" In that second she realised she had made a terrible mistake. The word hit Ben like a whip across the face, and he turned towards her with a look she had learnt to dread. It was the same sneering, black angry look that she'd seen when he had raped her, and other times when life had been difficult and his moods had dominated their life.

"What did you call me?" His voice was terrifyingly soft. He swaggered towards her, and she was suddenly hardly able to see with the terrible pain which was tearing her inside. Her face was deathly white. "No, Ben," she pleaded. "Please, no." Backing away from him, she doubled up in agony, trying to protect her belly with her shaking hands.

"I'm sorry; I'm not well. Please, please help me, please Ben. It hurts so much—oh, help me!" she begged him, sobbing with pain and holding out her hand imploringly. He pushed her away roughly. "I'm so sorry. I didn't mean to say that. Please, Ben, oh please—help me!" She whimpered with pain, and her eyes were slowly closing as the room began to spin around her. She felt warmth and wetness running down her thighs, and the pain became unendurable. *Oh, my baby,* she thought, *my baby. I'm losing my baby—Ben's baby. Oh, please help me; someone please help me. I can't take any more.*

Ben's smile was nasty. "Big mistake, my lady. You know what you're going to get. Will you ever learn that I'm no baby, and no boy, and you're not the boss?" Suddenly he hit her hard across her face, sending her backwards. Sophie's body hit the wall with force, and she slid down onto her hands and knees, blood pouring from her nose and mouth.

Shaking with pain, she managed to get up and stand, dazed and terrified. "Please, Ben, please; help me. I can't—I can't—" She was swaying, and the warmth, and wetness, and pain were overwhelming her.

Ben grabbed her wrists in a crushing grip and dragged her towards the desk. She did not resist; she could not. She was slowly losing consciousness. She slid down from his hands, sweating, retching, and shaking. He stopped, confused. And then he saw the blood running down her legs and soaking her jeans.

"Oh my God!" he said, holding her tightly in his strong arms and easing her limp body to the floor. "Oh my God. Sweetheart, Sophie, what's wrong?" He held her closely and desperately, watching in horror as the blood cascaded onto the floor in a crimson torrent.

"I tried to tell you," Sophie whispered. "I tried ..." She slumped into Ben's arms, struggling for breath. "I'm so sorry," she gasped. Ben hardly heard her. Her eyes closed, and she was gone from him.

He knelt down, stroking her face, trying desperately to revive her. "Oh, my love, my love, what have I done "? In a second he was sober. He gently covered her with his jacket and ran to call the emergency services. Soon the yard was filled with paramedics, an ambulance, and returning drivers who stood speechless, concerned and desperate for her.

Jago cleaned up the blood from the floor and sat in the office with tears running down his face. "What's the matter with her?" he begged of Blue.

"She's losing her baby," Blue said quietly, "but there's something not quite right—it shouldn't be like this. Not this serious."

"Baby? What baby?" Jago asked. "I didn't know—I didn't realise—is that why she fainted the other day?"

The other drivers sat around helplessly. "God, how much blood can a person lose?" asked Fossie. "Did you see how white she was? I suspected the poor little thing was pregnant, but she's been getting thinner, not swelling up like they normally do."

"He didn't hit her before it happened, did he?" asked Jago.

"Dunno," said Blue quickly. He had guessed why Sophie had blood coming from her nose and mouth and had told the paramedics that she had hit the desk when she collapsed. Despite his anger at Ben's violence towards Sophie, he felt Ben had enough to cope with right then. "But she wasn't right when I left about an hour ago. I shouldn't have left the kid; she was doubled up in pain then but pretending to be fine. I should have known better; I knew she had a baby in her weeks ago. Why, oh why, did I let this happen to her? Poor little thing."

"How has she managed all this time? All that work, and he did nothing to help her. The bastard just terrified and bullied her.

Surely he knew she was carrying his kid? Lousy, cruel bastard!" exclaimed Fossie angrily.

"He didn't know about the baby," said Blue. "I've just had to tell him."

Blue had been worried and had returned just as the ambulance rushed into the yard. He had found Ben and Sophie together in the office and had comforted the weeping, shaking Ben, trying to reassure him as the paramedics worked swiftly and rushed Sophie into the ambulance. He realised then that Ben hadn't even known that Sophie was pregnant. He told him, and Ben looked shaken and distraught.

"Pregnant? But how—how, Blue? She's sterilised. Believe me, Blue, even if she had been able to have kids, I wouldn't have deliberately made her pregnant. I wanted us to have our baby, but she didn't want any more babies. Oh God," Ben said, "it's all my fault; I got angry with her. I didn't realise what was going on. She asked me to help her, and she was shaking and crying, in awful pain. I didn't help her; I didn't listen to her. She was white and could hardly stand, and she was pleading for help—she was begging me, Blue—and I did nothing. I just ignored her. I pushed her away. Oh my God—I hit her, Blue! I hit her across her face; I dragged her by her wrists; her tiny little wrists." Tears ran down Ben's face. "Then there was all this blood everywhere. Oh, what have I done to her? My poor, darling little Sophie. Christ, Blue, I've been such a fucking bastard. I love her so much. Will she die?" he begged of Blue.

"She was already in trouble hours ago," said Blue. "She's been losing the baby for some time. What you did to her certainly didn't help her any. If you'd listened to her, she might have got to a hospital before all this happened. This isn't just an ordinary miscarriage, Ben. If she was sterilised, the baby's probably grown in her tube or something, and it's ruptured out. That's why she's bleeding so much. There's something seriously wrong, but they'll get her there," Blue said gently. "Look, there's the police car arriving to go ahead and clear the way. Just go with her, and we'll all pray for her."

Dimly Sophie heard the paramedic's voice. "Stay with us, darling. Stay with us, Sophie."
Loud sirens screamed, and blue lights flashed, and then she slipped into the blackness again. Voices buzzed confusingly; the sirens and lights were like something she must hold onto, but she kept drifting away into a peaceful, warm place. Was that Ben's voice? Still the nightmarish noises and lights came and then, nothing. Thankfully she let go of the pain and the fear as she began to let go of life. Her last conscious thought was of Ella.

Ben sat by her bed in the intensive care unit. Sophie was very, very white, despite her tanned skin. There were endless lines and drips into and out of her body. Machines bleeped and ticked, and a heart monitor told of Sophie's fight to survive. To Ben she looked very small and fragile, and he was desperately guilty—and lost. He felt wretched as he looked at the dark bruising on Sophie's mouth and cheek. How could he have hit this woman he adored and depended on for his very existence? She had begged him for help, and he had denied her what she had always given him in his many needs.
She had been rushed into the operating theatre, and Ben waited helplessly and afraid until the surgeon had come out and put his hand on his arm. He said, "I'm so sorry. I managed to save

your partner, but the babies could never have survived. It was an ectopic pregnancy. She was carrying twins—a boy and a girl. One grew inside her fallopian tube and the other out in her body cavity; it's sad and tragic. She lost a lot of blood—almost half her total body volume—and she suffered a great deal of pain and severe shock.

"Didn't you realise she was pregnant? She was about twelve or thirteen weeks into the pregnancy. You almost lost her, as well. Because she'd been sterilised, she should have been seen earlier by a specialist because of the implications and risks. At her age this isn't a good situation. She's underweight and anaemic, and she was severely dehydrated on admission. The babies took a huge toll of her reserves. She's 46 years old, and pregnant women of that age need a lot of extra care. Had this been a normal pregnancy, she should have been resting and eating adequately. Has she been working at all?"

Ben hung his head and felt ashamed as he thought of how much work Sophie had been doing. He should have been doing it, but he had chosen instead to drink, take drugs, and abuse and ignore her.

"She was running my haulage." he said quietly.

"She shouldn't have been doing a lot of physical work without proper rest, and she doesn't seem to have been eating much. Also, she hasn't had proper antenatal care from her surgery or the hospital. For a 46-year-old woman who *isn't* pregnant, running a haulage is a heavy job—but for one carrying twin babies, it's, well, amazing that she could carry on," the surgeon informed him. "Her health would be affected anyway, without this trauma. She must have been very tough to survive. She really should have had proper rest and care.

"I didn't know she was pregnant," Ben admitted. "She didn't say anything to me at all. If I'd known, I could have done more to protect her." *Would I have?* he asked himself. *Would I have protected and cared for her properly, or would I have gone on drinking and getting high and nasty and making her poor little life hell? Why did it take her nearly losing her life to wake me up to how much I love and depend on her?*

"She's very ill; she's not out of the woods yet. That's why she's staying in the intensive care unit for now. You'll need to look after her when she eventually goes home," the surgeon told him. "The psychological kickback will be as bad as the physical trauma."

"But—" Ben was lost. "But she's been sterilised. How—?" The surgeon explained to him that, very rarely, these things occurred, and it wasn't anyone's fault—just a sad, unpredictable mistake. The sutures tying off Sophie's fallopian tube had loosened, and Ben's sperm had managed to get up through the gap. The eggs, being very much larger, couldn't get down to her womb to implant and grow normally. "But suppose it happens again?" Ben asked, still confused. "Couldn't she have the ties taken off, so we can try again normally, and maybe the baby will grow inside her properly?"

"Well now, I've made sure the remaining fallopian tube is completely cut off and stitched, so it's irreversible now. I'm sorry, there are no more chances, and to be professional and honest, your partner's really too old to be having another child." Ben sat thinking about how he had threatened Sophie, had hit her across the face and dragged her by her wrists. How terrified she must have been! How much terrible pain and fear had he made her suffer? *It's my fault. I drink too much. I went back on the stuff, too, after I promised her I would kick it. We were so happy. I love her so much, and Ella too. If she had died—if I'd lost her—my life would be over.* He reached over and stroked Sophie's hair. *My poor, sweet, lovely lady. I did this to you. You're brave, and unselfish, and tough, and you love me so much, so very much. You told me to go, you told me to find someone younger and have babies. But I don't want anyone else's babies—just yours, because I love you so very much. But I wouldn't deliberately have given you a baby you didn't want, even though I really did want your child and mine.*

Why? he asked himself. *Why, my darling little Sophie, didn't you tell me? Did you hope that some miracle would happen and we could have our own baby? Or were you so afraid of my drug-fuelled moods? So terrified of my temper, my unpredictability. My sweet Sophie. I know you'd follow me to the ends of the earth. Please, my beloved, please pull through for me and for Ella. Fight, little Sophie, fight as you've always fought to help and love me. And forgive me, my darling little Sophie; please forgive me for being too damned selfish to see what I was destroying. I may lose not just your love and respect, I may lose you completely. I love you so very much that I would give my own life right now so that you could live. You've suffered all alone for months, and I deserted you. You were always there for me, and when you couldn't go on because you were in such dreadful pain and almost bleeding to death, you begged me for help, and I just pushed you away. You dragged your poor, tired little body on until you collapsed. You should never have had to suffer so much all on your own, with nobody to talk to. You must have been so frightened; you were so ill, so lonely, and so in need of someone just to care for you. I should have done that, my little sweetheart. I failed you—and you never failed me. My selfish negligence has nearly cost you your life.* Ben wept silently.

Darkness fell. Still Ben sat beside her. In the early hours of the morning, Sophie slowly regained consciousness. She looked at him and the pain in her hazel eyes seared his soul. He could barely hear her when she whispered, "Ben, my Ben—are you there, my darling? Sorry, I'm so sorry. Have I lost your baby? I'm so sorry." She tried to raise her hand to touch him, but it fell uselessly and weakly onto the bed. Her eyes closed, and she slipped into sleep again. He kissed her eyes and her mouth and her hands and resumed his sad vigil.

Ben would not leave her bedside; the hospital staff tried to persuade him to eat and to go home to sleep, but Ben stayed stubbornly by Sophie. He dozed in the chair, waking at the slightest sound when staff came to check Sophie and adjust the life support equipment. Once all the alarms went off, and staff came rushing in. A doctor was called, and Ben was asked to leave, but he refused. For over an hour there was serious concern for Sophie's condition, but she rallied, and Ben sat by her again, refusing to sleep and watching her every breath. Their friends cared for Ella, and between them the drivers kept the haulage ticking over.

Sophie regained consciousness from time to time, whispering Ben's name always. She would look at him and cry. She'd ask for forgiveness for losing his baby; she did not know then that she had lost twins. Ben stroked her hair and told her that she had done nothing wrong and that he loved her. The episodes were always brief, and she soon slipped back into her comatose condition. It was a full five days before she was awake and responding to normality.

Slowly she recovered. Food did not interest her. She did not glance at the ward television or read. Only Ella's visits caused any reaction. Ben visited her often and sat chatting aimlessly about the haulage and anything he felt she might want to hear. He held her hand and kissed her face, but she looked at him as if she did not know him. He felt deserted and abandoned. Guilt drove him to seek drink, but he drank only one beer and then left. He looked after Ella, tended the house, and ran the haulage. He never ceased thinking of his beloved Sophie.

He could not get out of his head the picture of her gasping, retching, and crying in agony as she collapsed. He remembered her weak and desperate plea for him to help her. She must have been in terrible pain, and he had simply ignored her. He recalled the torrent of bright-red blood soaking her jeans, the tense urgency of the paramedics, and the screaming of the sirens as the ambulance raced along with a police car in front clearing the roads. He would never forget watching her face losing colour as she and their dying babies slipped away from him.

The time came when Sophie was discharged, and Ben took her home. She seemed confused and wandered around looking at things as if she were in a strange place. She ate little and spoke even less. Weeks passed. She slept in Ella's room.

At nights, as Ben lay sleepless, he heard Sophie sobbing softly. He yearned for her warmth and the sweet smell of her skin, for the lovemaking they had had before he'd been stupid enough to shatter their lives yet again. He longed to stroke her warm, loving little body, to feel her tensing as she arched her back and pushed into him and screamed with the intensity of her passion. He longed to pour his love into her as he climaxed, to wipe the tears she often cried at orgasm, and to kiss her face all over and tell her what she was to him, before they both slept entwined and sated. But he could not speak about anything to her. He was terrified and lost.

One afternoon he could not find her, and he panicked. One of the drivers phoned him. "Boss, I think you should come up here right away. Sophie drove up here, and—and she won't listen to any of us. She's not right, not well. We want to help her, but she doesn't seem to know any of us. Please hurry up." Ben drove to the yard very quickly, where he found Sophie furiously washing the trucks in the yard. The drivers stood around helplessly, concerned for her. Twenty-stone Blue was puzzled and desperately worried about her. He needed to take his truck out on the road, but Sophie wouldn't let him touch it. The big man would not try to stop her. He just wanted someone to help her before she broke down completely.

Ben leapt out, ran to the lorry, put his hand up to Sophie wordlessly, and lifted her down. Still holding her hand, he led her to the pickup truck and helped her in. She did not speak but followed as if in a dream. Back at the cottage, he made her a cup of coffee and sat beside her. Her hands began to tremble and the coffee began to spill. He lunged forward to save it, and their hands touched briefly.

She dropped the cup and raised her arms to him. "Help me— help me, please. Oh Ben, my Ben," she pleaded. He held her tightly, and rocked her. She started to cry, softly at first and then with wrenching, painful gasps which shook her whole body. "Ben, my Ben, I love you, but I'm no good for you. How can you ever look at me again?"

"Why, Sophie darling? Why? "Ben asked, stroking her tear-stained face, "You're beautiful. I adore you."

"All those scars," she sobbed. "All those scars. I can't even conceive and carry babies properly. I'm old—old and useless and ugly. How can you ever touch me again? I lost your babies, and now there's no chance of my ever conceiving your child—our child. I should have had my tubes untied when you asked me, but I was so frightened—so frightened of another pregnancy and birth, and of having a huge baby, and afraid that you would go back to drink and drugs and leave me alone when I needed you. I did have an appointment to have them done. I was going to have the operation, but you were with that dark girl and you wouldn't listen and—and—"

"Sophie, my love," he whispered as he kissed her hair and stroked the tiny curls back from her ears. "Shush, my little one. You've done nothing wrong at all. It was entirely my fault. I let you down very badly; I should have been there for you. I found that letter when I was looking for your things when you were in hospital; it was in your bedside drawer. Poor Sophie, you went to all that trouble, and you were prepared to have surgery to give me the baby I wanted. But I opted for drugs and flirting with that poisonous Bella when you wanted to tell me. It's all my fault, and I've lost the chance of giving you our baby because of my lousy selfishness and stupidity."

After a while Sophie's shaking and sobbing ceased, and she looked up at him. She took his hand and kissed it. Then she led him upstairs. She undressed and stood naked, looking at him intently with her slanted hazel eyes. Her beautiful, Titian curls tumbled over her shoulders.

"This is me," Sophie said quietly and put her hands over the scar on her belly. Ben knelt before her and kissed her belly, the scars, and her hands.

"You are so utterly beautiful," he whispered, "and I love your body, every part of it."

She stroked his hair and then gently lifted him up. She slowly unbuttoned his shirt and slid it off his body.

Ben hesitated and then quickly undressed. He kissed Sophie hard and passionately. Ben lifted her in his arms and carried her to the bed. He was almost afraid to touch her, but Sophie guided his hands to her, and she was warm and moist with wanting him. Slowly, with fingers and tongue, he pleasured her, and she stroked him sensuously and teasingly. Ben was desperate to make love to Sophie after weeks and weeks of not even being able to touch her. When he slid into her, she groaned with desire and wanting; she arched her back as she felt his massive erection. He pulled back from her and gazed into her eyes. "I love you so very much," he told her.

Sophie's eyes had become large and bright, and her cheeks were flushed; she dug her nails into his buttocks. "Oh my sweet, darling Ben, I want you very, very much. I love you so very much too!" She pulled him into her. "Oh, love me, my precious Ben. Fuck me, please fuck me, fill me with you!" she pleaded. They had not made love like this ever before. They had never had this depth of feeling, desire, and pure love. She stopped him before she climaxed and rolled over on top of him. Grabbing his wrists, she pushed his hands above his head. He grinned at her because he could so easily have just pushed them up again, but he submitted. She fucked him slowly, twisting her hips sensuously and pushing down hard so that he went deep into her. She held him from his orgasm time and time again; then her breathing quickened, and she leaned forward and kissed him hard on his mouth. He felt her nipples rise and expand, and she kissed him harder as she reached her orgasm, sobbing and gasping that she loved him, at the same second as he let go and flooded her with his love and his seed.

"Your body is so, so beautiful," whispered Ben as he held her close and nuzzled into her breasts. "It's given life to children, and fed them, and I love every sweet inch of you; all your scars are precious to me. You suffered so much for me, and I adore you. I'll never, never treat you badly, ever again. My sweet little Sophie, I've said and done unforgivable things to you because I've been selfish and stupid and a total bastard. I'll never leave you; I couldn't live without you. Watching you struggle to live was the turning point for me.

"Can you ever forgive me for what I've done to you, my darling little Sophie? I broke a solemn promise to you and Ella. I treated you ill and neglected you; I used my size and strength to terrify and domineer you; I used you sexually without any thought for you or your needs; I didn't even see the changes in your body because I was so into myself and my addictions. And you, poor little Sophie, you clung on loyally and lovingly and tried so very hard to bear the verbal and physical abuse I inflicted on you. You must have suffered so much, my darling. The drivers told me you fainted and begged them not to tell me, and you were sick every single day, and you even brought up liquids. Blue said you had been unwell for some time and that you were trying to clean the lorries and tackle the paperwork when you could hardly walk.

"I'm so ashamed of myself, Sophie. I saw nothing because I was selfish, and I've always been spoilt and self-interested. Everyone else watched you struggling. But I treated you with contempt, without love or care or humanity, and you took it and fought on. You're brave and beautiful, and I adore you. You pleaded with me for help when you couldn't stand the pain you were suffering—you put your little hand out to me, the one person who should have helped and protected you. You begged me to help you, and I hit you, and I hate myself. You've stood by me always, and I pushed you away when you were seriously ill and needed help so very much. Please, please forgive me, Sophie."

Sophie wrapped her arms around Ben. "Hush, my darling, hush. We've both suffered, but you're back now. Please stay with me. Please don't go back to your drugs and drink. I couldn't bear to lose you again." Ben kissed her hair. Sophie had slipped into sleep.

They slept entwined and exhausted. Sophie awoke in the early hours. The full moon was painting the room with silver. Ben was awake and looking at her. She held his hand and looked up at him. "Oh my darling, precious Ben, I'm so, so sorry I couldn't give you the baby you wanted," she whispered. "I would have done anything to be able to do this for you, but my body can't do what it should." She began to cry softly. "I'm just too old for you. You need someone younger." Her sobs increased. "I lost both your babies, and I know how very much you wanted a boy. I'm so, so—"

He held her tightly and stroked her hair. "No, my little one. *We* lost *our* babies. It was your loss as well, not just mine. We made those babies together, but we didn't know we were doing it or that it could even happen. You did nothing wrong, nothing. But if only you'd told me. I was a bastard. You were working harder than me. I wasn't doing a thing to help you, and you're so little, and not as strong as you seem to be, and you were doing things that I should have done, things way beyond your physical abilities. How did you manage to keep going, my poor little one? Why didn't I notice anything? Blue knew. How?"

"Blue's older than you, and he's been around life longer than you. He's got seven kids. How could you know what to look for?"

"I did see things, but I was so busy getting drunk and stoned that I didn't take them in. I remember how sick you were all the time and how I thought your breasts were getting a lot bigger while the rest of you was getting smaller. I remember thinking that you hadn't seemed to have a period for a while, but I just thought it was something about women I didn't know—like I don't seem to know how to look after someone I absolutely love and adore, who's my whole existence, and who would do anything for me." He held her closer. They lay in silence.

She pressed into him. "I think you should leave," she said quietly.

"Leave?" It was as if he had been slapped hard across the face. "Why?" he said. "Why would I do that?"

"I think you should go and find someone younger than me, who can give you the children you long for. You're a wonderful father to Ella. Any children you have will be lucky—if you can grow up and stop drinking so much, and the rest."

"Ella," he said. "Ella. What would I do without her? And what would she do without me?" He suddenly pressed his mouth hard down onto hers and kissed her passionately. Pulling away, he said, "And what would I do without you? I wouldn't exist without you. I love you; I really do love you more than anything in this world. I nearly lost you, and I know now what a stupid fucking bastard I've been. If you'd died I don't know how I would have gone on living. Please don't make me leave you. I'm here because I always wanted to be here—from the first second I laid eyes on you and knew I wanted you and your body as my own, and learnt to love you as a person. From the first time we made love, I've been part of you and you've been part of me. I've tried to go with younger girls—" He stopped.

"Yes, I know," she said.

"You know?"

"This is a small town, and the drivers all knew. Two of them warned me."

"But you said nothing?"

"Why? You're a free spirit. I almost wanted you to find someone younger."

"And you would have just let me go, just like that?"

"How could I hold you?

"And you wouldn't have missed me just a little?"

She turned to him, placed her finger on his lips, and ran it across his face so, so gently. Then she twisted a tiny lock of his curly hair around her finger. She leaned towards him and kissed his lips. She looked straight into his blue eyes. "My world would have ended. I would have lost one of the dearest things I've ever had. I would have had to see you around all the time and see your babies arriving, knowing that your new young love could conceive and carry them normally; and imagine you holding her close in the way you used to hold me. I'd imagine the wonderful lovemaking you used to share with me being shared with someone else; imagine your beautiful body pleasuring someone else; imagine your fingers and tongue giving her the fantastic orgasms they gave me; imagine someone else with the man I adored. I would miss holding you close to me and shutting out the world and comforting you when you couldn't cope." Her breath caught, and she started to cry. "Yes," she said softly, "I would have missed you just a little."

Sophie stopped and put her hands over her face. The tears slipped through her fingers. "I would have let you go, because I love you so much that I would want you to have what made you happy, even if it broke my heart."

Ben held her tightly and gently stroked the tears away from her face. He kissed and stroked her hair.

"Don't make me go, please. I tried to go with those other girls, but nothing happened, nothing at all. I felt nothing for them, not even sexually. All I could think of was you, Sophie, you and Ella. You're my world now, my love and my life. One of the girls was just about the sexiest, prettiest girl around here, but she did nothing to me at all. I love you too much to throw everything away on a quick fuck with someone just because she's younger than you. I didn't even want to sleep with her; all I could see was your hazel eyes." Ben chuckled. "It was the first time I'd ever been unable to get a hard on. Nothing happened. You're the only girl my body responds to now. I only want you, and I want you more than anything in this world. Making love to you is the most wonderful thing in my life."

He rolled over, took her hands, and linked his fingers with hers. He pushed her hands above her head. He kissed Sophie ardently on the mouth and then ran his tongue over her body, stopping when she arched her back. "No," he said, "no—you must wait until I let you."

Ben made love to her with his mouth and his fingers for nearly an hour, constantly pausing whilst she moaned softly and begged for his body to go into hers. But he just grinned at her and looked at her hazel eyes with his blue ones, saying, "You want me so much, don't you?" Sophie's almond eyes narrowed and her face flushed. Ben continued, "You want this so much, my little love," and he put her hand on his hugely erect penis. She begged him to go into her, but he still held back. "You want all of this inside you, my little sweetheart, don't you? You will always want and need me. Who else could fuck you and love you like I do?" He grinned his beautiful grin, staring into her eyes. "Tell me, Sophie, tell me that you want me." She begged again for him to push into her and fill her.

"Yes, I want you, Ben," she gasped.

"And tell me you love me, Sophie, my sweet little one."

"I love you! Yes, I love you, Ben. I will always love you; whatever happens, I can never stop loving you."

He increased the pressure of his fingers, and she began to buck and twist. When her orgasm came, it made her scream and tear at him with her nails like a great cat. He went into her hard, and they came together, panting and sweating. He told her that she was his life, and his love, and his world. He did not pull out of or away from her, and they fell asleep conjoined in body and spirit.

Later, as dawn flushed over the horizon, Ben woke to find Sophie crying soundlessly and desperately. "Sweetheart, what's wrong?" He wrapped his arms tightly around her and kissed her wet face.

"Oh Ben, my babies—our babies—they're gone! They're dead, and I'll never have another chance to have your baby." Sophie wept silently.

"But we still have Ella," he reminded her. "I adore her because she's part of you, and she looks like me, and people think I actually made her—which makes me feel really proud, because she's so beautiful. And I still have you, my precious little Sophie." She wept in his strong arms, and Ben shed tears too for the tiny lost babies they had both wanted, those babies made, unknowingly, in the heat of brutal, imposed sex—or from passion and love.

Then he rolled onto and into her and, once more, made sweet, slow, adoring, passionate love to her as the sun climbed into the blue, blue sky.

SOPHIE AND BEN, SEVEN

The drivers were at the cottage, smoking and drinking coffee, sorting out POD slips, and discussing the following week's work.

"Did you hear about Big Bubba, who works for Hill Haulage?" Blue asked.

"No," Sophie said. "What's he been up to now?"

"Rollover on the 25/11," said Blue. "Couldn't get him out. Dead at 28, and his missus expecting a baby in two weeks' time."

The drivers made noises of sympathy. They decided to consult with other haulage companies locally and start a fund for her.

"Nasty intersection, that," said Jody. "Built one motorway and didn't work out how to join it to the existing M11. Hellish twists and turns, and the camber's a pig."

"What was he pulling?" asked Rusty.

"Blue CHEP pallets," answered Blue. "On the flatbed."

"Loaded too high?" said Rusty.

"His trailer had a low centre of gravity," said Blue. "It's just that fucking road. They ought to do something about it." The others agreed.

Ben sat listening as he checked paperwork. He was at the yard and the office nearly all the time now. He did his share of the work again and watched Sophie, tenderly, for any slight sign of tiredness. He allowed her to do as she wished but was always as near to her as he could possibly be.

When Ella was with their friends and he took Sophie with him on journeys, he would lie beside her in the bunk, gazing at her as if she were some new and wonderful treasure he had just found. He no longer so often indulged his liking for the slightly rough sex that they certainly both enjoyed but he had sometimes forced on her. He spent hours pleasuring her very gently, and even in the most passionate moments he was caring and controlled.

He often stroked her belly with careful fingers and kissed the scar which reminded him how nearly he had lost the mother/ lover figure who was the centre of his universe. He lay with his head on her breasts while she stroked his hair.

Slowly he had pulled himself away from the companions and situations which had led him into the dark side of life. He sometimes drank a couple of beers but then left quickly and came home to her and to Ella.

"I'm not afraid of going," Ben said.

Sophie looked at him. "Going where?" she asked.

"Of dying on some motorway when my time comes," he answered.

She felt stunned. "Don't say that, please! Nothing's going to happen to you."

"I know," he said. "Nothing's going to happen, but if it does, I'm not afraid to die."

She made cups of coffee for them all whilst the drivers chatted and laughed noisily.

Ella came in from playing. She saw him and ran up and flung her arms around him.

"Hello, baby girl." He grinned and then suddenly he frowned. "Have you taken your pills today?"

"Pills?" said Ella. "What pills?"

"Your ugly pills—if you get any prettier, I'll have the too-pretty police calling here to arrest me for having a too-pretty daughter." Ella flushed with pleasure and laughed. "Don't be daft. They don't do things like that."

"Ah, but they do. I've already been in prison because Mummy's too pretty."

Ella strode up to him and began trying to arm-wrestle him. He allowed her to nearly bend his muscular arm down to the table, groaning and pretending she was hurting his arm. At the last second he grabbed her and slung her over his shoulder, where she chortled with pure happiness.

"Time for your bath," Sophie called to Ella. Ella did the rounds of the drivers, kissing them goodnight.

When Ella went to Ben for her goodnight kiss, he hugged her closely. "I love you so very much," Ella told him.

"And I love you very, very much too, my poppet," he told her.

About to close the door, Ella turned to him. "I'll never have a boyfriend if he isn't like you," she said adoringly.

He blew her a kiss and grinned. "I won't let you have a boyfriend like me. Nobody will be good enough."

Sophie lay awake, thinking of what Ben had said. Losing Ben like that was something she had never contemplated. She was always hearing of drivers who had lost their lives in ghastly smashes, and she tried to shut it out of her consciousness. No, not him. She rolled over and hugged him tightly.

He took her hand sleepily. "What is it, honey?" She rolled him over and began to kiss him frantically. "Hey, hey," he said, laughing. "Am I being ravished for my fantastic body?"

"Love me; please love me," she begged running her fingers down his belly.

"A pleasure, my sweet lady." He rolled over onto her and kissed her gently. "Would you like to choose from the menu?" She saw him grinning. "I do a good bondage and other sadomasochistic side dishes. What can I offer you?"

"Just love me. Please, love me as if you'll never see me again," she pleaded.

"Hey, little one, what's going on?"

"If anything should happen to you—"

"It won't. Please don't stress so much." He kissed her again and slowly slid down to pleasure her with his tongue and hands. He loved her so sweetly.

Little did she know that the days of his beautiful loving were almost finished.

SOPHIE AND BEN, EIGHT

They told her, told her of an accident, and a tangled, twisted mass of metal, and his crushed, dead body. She screamed at them that it was not true—it could not be true! No, he was coming back. He couldn't die, not him!

At the funeral parlour she gazed uncomprehendingly at his dead body. She didn't want them to touch him. She plaited his beautiful, blond hair, talking to him softly as she did so. She took the diamond-and-ruby ring off her finger and put it onto the heavy gold chain around his neck with his gold cross and the locket containing pictures of her and Ella. She ran her fingers lovingly over his cold, cold face. She leaned down, kissed his cold mouth, and whispered words of love that he would never hear. She sat beside his body talking to him, until someone gently led her away.

The funeral was like a strange dream. So many people. So many haulage firms, so many friends. So many flowers dying in the sun. She looked across the crowded churchyard and saw Sean looking very sad and very thin. Their eyes met. Sophie went over to him and opened her arms. Sean held her closely and rocked her gently.

"I know how much you loved him - how much you loved each other. I'm sorry mum - I really am sorry. Sorry he's gone and sorry that I was so awful to you both." Sophie did not answer. She took his hand and took him back to her car and they drove to the wake. It was a long, traumatic afternoon and Sophie was cornered by so many well meaning people who made her long for solitude and space to curl up and rock with pain for her searing loss. When she looked around for Sean he had gone. He had slipped away and she felt his loss as well

At last she sat in her armchair at the cottage. Alone with a glass of wine. Ella was with friends as Sophie was incapable of consoling her at that moment. Her world had ceased to function. From that moment she never forgot Ben and their time on earth together.

He was her boy, her lover. So young and beautiful, and she had adored him, and feared him, and fought him. Now she was alone again. The nights grew colder, and faint lines appeared around her eyes—time was creeping up and winning. He was no longer there to keep her youthful with his love and lust.

"How can I live again?" she screamed into the night. "How can I ever live without him? I loved him so very much, and I will never see, or hear, or feel him again." Part of her body had gone; part of her soul had gone too.

She drove up to see Ben's grave every day for months. Then she could do it no longer. He was gone, and she lay in her cold, lonely bed. The world had changed, and time ground on. She thought of him often and cried at nights for the loss of his strong, warm, musky body and his sweet whispered endearments. Sometimes she almost wished that she had been able to bear his children, their two dead and lost babies, but it was a selfish, unrealistic thought. They were gone forever, her beautiful boy and their babies.

She was sucked back into the muddy river of life again, and loneliness and poverty. And the days of her beautiful, golden boy were gone.

She could not, would not, ever forget the days and nights of his loving and lusting and she knew that nothing and nobody would ever bring that bliss back.

And when life was cold and unbearable she closed her eyes and saw, heard, and felt him again, and tried to hold on to him as time and life attempted to pull him away, away and beyond the horizon of her memories.

SOPHIE AND BEN, NINE

The days after his death were some of the worst in Sophie's life. For months she would put two coffee cups out without thinking. When the lorries roared out of the quay car park at two in the morning, she would be awake, her heart rolling with them and the life they had brought her. Ben was everywhere. She reached for his hard, beautiful body in her near-sleep moments. He sat in the chair by the log fire; he was out in the garden under the willow tree in the gathering darkness, his white teeth flashing as he grinned at her; he was with her and in her, in her movement and her being. Wine dulled the keen edge of the pain, and she stumbled through the days expecting him to come back when the weekend was over or after a long journey.

Later she stood out in the warm June night thinking of him and feeling a strange and inappropriate sense of great peace. She remembered that it was on exactly this night, some years ago, that he had first held out his hand to her and taken her to bed. And now she would never see his blue, blue eyes ever again, or hear his hearty laugh, or see his beautiful smile that turned her heart over, or feel his gentle experienced fingers and tongue exciting and enthralling her arching body, or hear his sweet whispered words of adoration as he neared his climax, or feel his hard body pouring his love and his seed into her.

Blue had brought Ben's things back from the cab. He sat with his huge arm cradling Sophie as she unpacked them and sat looking at them numbly. The leather jacket, stained and shaped to him and smelling of him; she held it to her face and rocked whilst the hot tears coursed down her face and onto the sleeve, making more stains. The leather ties that held back his plait. A photo of the three of them that had always been on the dashboard of his cab. The hand-knitted patchwork blanket that she and Ella had made to keep him warm in his bunk, and which also held his precious odour. His pipe and tobacco. She laid them on the mantelpiece, where they remained year after year, the tobacco drying to a powder, until Ella took them to hold as a memory. A half-eaten sandwich—and one of his leather boots. *Why just one?* thought Sophie vaguely. She and Blue sat close together as she kissed and hugged the coat and the blanket, and hot tears ran unchecked. *Oh, my Ben, my boy, my love, my child, my passion, my torment, my pain, my life. I am alone now. Where are you, my darling? Can you see and feel me and Ella and hear me calling for you in the terrible and lonely nights? Or are you gone into a silent blackness, with nothing, for the great and grinding life of the planets and time?* Sophie put these items away in her wardrobe, save for his blanket, and that she slept with. She held it fiercely, breathing in the musky smell of him and breathing her sobs into its warmth as if she could resurrect him with her pain and yearning. The pain was unrelenting—it flooded her body and her mind. She could not eat or sleep. She stood and stared out into the garden, with the gathering darkness blotting out any tiny shards of comfort and hope. She saw the gate where he had appeared that evening with his fish—that second in time when their lives had collided and he'd become her everything. He was her love and her being, her reason to face life and embrace existence. Her days slid by in an automatic blur, and oblivion came with the wine and tears as she rocked in her chair in the impending dark, with the ripping, burning claws of pain tearing her without cease.

When they told Sophie of Ben's death, Ella was at school. After school, she came running in, golden curls flying. She ran to Sophie and hugged her. Sophie hugged her very hard in return, and Ella cried out, "Mummy, why are you squeezing me so hard"? Sophie tried to cope for the next few hours, but then Ella said, "Where's Ben, Mummy? He's very late." There was a pause that seemed to last for hours.

Sophie stuttered, "Ella, Ben—he's not—not coming back."

Ella was lying on the floor with her books. "Did he have to go somewhere a long way away?" she asked, not looking up.

"No, my darling." Now the tears were running hotly down Sophie's face. She swallowed hard. "He—he's never coming back, baby—"

Ella turned her face up and frowned. "Why, Mummy—why not? Have you been arguing? I thought you never did that. Why not?" She searched Sophie's face.

"Mummy, why are you crying?"

"Oh, my darling." Sophie's chest was tight and painful. "He can't come back—he's dead, my baby. His lorry rolled and killed him. I ..." She stood shaking and put her arms out to Ella.

Ella got up quickly, her face becoming dark and angry. She pushed Sophie's arms away, picked up her books, and flung them across the room. "No!" she screamed at Sophie, her face twisted with pain and fury. "No—no, my Ben isn't dead! He is coming back. No—don't say that!" Again Sophie attempted to put her arms around Ella, but Ella abruptly repulsed her. She turned and ran upstairs, sobbing. Sophie ran up after her, but Ella was lying face down on her bed, shaking with sobs. When Sophie laid her hand gently on Ella's shoulder, Ella shrugged it off fiercely.

"Go away!" she shouted hoarsely. "Leave me alone!" Sophie tried for several hours to comfort Ella, but the anger and terrible grief were consuming the poor child. Eventually Ella fell into a restless sleep, occasionally sobbing even in her slumbering.

Sophie went downstairs and poured a glass of wine. The phone rang; friends were calling to speak words of comfort. She sobbed to them that Ella was distraught and rejecting her, and soon they were at the cottage, enfolding her with love and silent sympathy. They called her doctor, and a handful of medication and more wine aided her escape into deep sleep. Her friends stayed on watch through that grim night, watching for any signs of Ella's awakening and needing them. The moon-bright sky flushed with a red-streaked dawn, and Sophie and Ella stirred to the beginnings of a new and unwanted life.

Life without Ben.

SOPHIE AND BEN, TEN

Day followed dreary day. Sophie scarcely ate or functioned. Ella remained sullen, unapproachable, beyond comfort. Ben's brother had taken the haulage whilst Sophie dreamed through the nightmarish days. He had slick solicitors who had made it clear that she and Ben had been unmarried and their relationship and partnership were immaterial. She did not fight back. She was unable to function, unable to reason. A small lump sum was paid to her, and she existed on it with a minute government handout which did not last many months.

Sophie took Ella over to France to her eldest daughter for a short while, trying to bring some pleasure and respite to Ella and herself. Her other children were much older than Ella and hardly knew her, but they tried to comfort her. She and Ben had spent time there when her third daughter was married. They had had a magic week there together, lying in the big bed in the stone house, listening to the gentle rain whispering on the slates and smelling the dust from the courtyard, just drowning in each other's bodies. Ben had lain beside her, stroking her face and hair and gently kissing her mouth. "My sweetling," he'd whispered, "you are all in all to me. I can't imagine any life without you."

"Then we must both live forever," Sophie had answered, quietly running her finger over his lips.

She found Ben there still—everywhere—in the long evenings. He was in the orchard; in the courtyard; in the tangled, flower-filled gardens; and in the fields stretching to the edge of the blue Normandy skies. The pain consumed her and dulled her perception of everything. She longed to be courageous enough to end this agony and join her beautiful boy, but she had Ella to care for and comfort. She did not belong only to herself; she must step out on the road life had hewed for her. She bowed her head into the storm and the darkness of her fate and took the first painful step—alone.

ELLA

Ella found herself unable to cope with Ben's death. The handsome, big, hot-tempered, generous, loving man had entered her life and changed everything with his warmth and vibrancy. He had been the father she had always wanted. He had taught her to ride her first tiny bike, taught her to swim and fish off his boat, let her drive lorries and tractors and his four-wheel-drive Jeep when her mother didn't know. He'd let her stay up late and watch films on the television; let her live on junk food; let her use her mother's make-up. He'd danced with her to heavy-metal music. He had even once let her take a puff of his spliff. She'd adored him and been proud to be his blue-eyed baby girl, hating any other female who spoke to him or stood too close. He'd been her giant—strong, kind, and understanding, with a dangerous, dark, undefinable something that Ella did not then understand. His death was the finish of her universe. She cried until it was not possible to cry any more. The pain twisted her body and mind ceaselessly. She tried to, but could not, comprehend the reality of never seeing him again. She tried to cope with what remained of her small life, but everything seemed pointless and exhausting.

At the funeral, when she began to sob, someone put a hand on her small shoulder, but she shrugged it off fiercely and swallowed back the tears. She had worn her bright-red dress for the occasion, because Ben had bought it for her, and he'd loved it. At the wake afterwards, they'd played his heavy-metal discs and had slowly got very drunk and high on pot. Ella wandered out to the lorries and climbed up into one, where she sat talking to Ben. She knew that the only way she would ever see him again was to die and join him. She wished she knew how to.

Blue found her there. He gently lifted her down and cuddled her closely. "It's hard, my baby, very hard. You'll find him again someday."

The wake went on all night. Sophie was stoned and drunk. Ella went up to her and kissed her; then she went back to the lorry, climbed up into the big bunk at the back, and soon fell asleep. In her dreams she was riding the motorways with Ben, and then he turned off and drove into the clouds, laughing and singing. Ella sang too. Then she was singing on her own, and Ben was gone, and she was curled up in the bunk, alone. From now on her life would be like that—she'd be alone. Ella knew it was that way for her mother too.

Ella was a highly intelligent and gifted child. She did very well at school but was in constant trouble for bullying other children. Sophie was worried about her. She would be invited to her small friends' homes for tea and to play, but there would always be some incident, and the invitations would not be repeated. Sophie took her to the local happy-clappy Christian fellowship, where the children were divided into age groups and taken out for instruction and activities. It was not long before Sophie was summoned to face the all-knowing mouthpieces of the setup—the "elders" as they termed themselves. They told her, with serious faces, that Ella was "problematic"; she was "causing concern" and "perhaps needed discipline". Sophie left and did not return.

She alone knew how hard she tried to control Ella's manic and worrying behaviour. She lacked respect for everything and everyone, particularly Sophie. She did as she pleased and ignored rules and restrictions. She invited friends and gave them every scrap of food Sophie had in her home. That was little enough, on Sophie's tiny income. She demanded the best of everything, wanted every new craze that appeared. She was angry that her friends' parents had new cars. Sophie had a small, very cheap wreck that embarrassed Ella, who demanded that Sophie never arrive outside the school in this humiliating evidence of their extreme poverty.

For some years Sophie bought Ella clothes from a second-hand shop and turned her out well for very little. One day Ella came home from school in a fury. Her school friends had called her a gypsy because they had found out that even Ella's school uniform was second-hand. She ranted vitriolically at Sophie and told her she would not attend school if she did not have new clothing. Furthermore, she didn't want any of that rubbish from the second-hand shop any more. Sophie was in agonies. She simply didn't have the means to buy Ella all the things she wanted. When Ben was alive, they had become used to having every single thing they wanted and needed. Ben had bought Ella the best of everything. Now she was suffering from the sting of poverty as well as the pain of losing her adored Ben. Sophie had a few bits of her jewellery still, and she sold some of them and hoarded the proceeds to buy Ella clothes. After that, there was nothing else to be done. She must go out to work. She started looking the next day.

To return to teaching Sophie would need to complete an eighteen-month refresher course. Unfortunately, the government had forgotten that she would also need to exist, paying for bus fares, childcare, and maybe car fuel during this time, but they offered nothing to cover this problem. Sophie tried the benefits office, where she was informed that if she began to train for anything she would have her existing benefits removed immediately. Sophie tried explaining that she was not training—she was already trained—but was being forced to complete a course to allow her to teach again. The department was unmoved. Sophie gave up. She took a deep breath and joined a social care agency.

This was Margaret Thatcher's plan of care in the community. Something which should have been provided by the government had been farmed out to the private, profit-obsessed area. The agencies did not care in any way, either for the clients who used the service or for the overworked, undertrained, and often underskilled carers. Sophie worked illegal and killing hours. The office staff who had begun as former trained nurses at least knew what was happening. But they slowly disappeared and were replaced by what Sophie could only refer to euphemistically as illiterate teenagers. These self-important little madams hadn't an hour's experience of the art of caring or, indeed, any idea at all of what was involved. They couldn't have organised a piss-up in a brewery, Sophie told many of her annoyed colleagues, as they arrived at bookings at the same time as three other carers, or were blamed by the office for not turning up at a client's when they had not been asked to.

The work was hard. Sometimes it was rewarding; more often it was frustrating and frankly awful. Clients ranged from sweet, grateful, good-humoured, generous, understanding, and welcoming to bad-mannered, rude, selfish, ill-tempered, antisocial, and cruel. Sophie drove mile after dreary mile in sun, snow, fog, thunderstorms, and driving rain. Her car broke down with sickening regularity. She often worked back-to-back night duties and then went straight on at seven in the morning to a back-breaking list of clients which ran into lunch visits. She raced home to take a shower and change her uniform, look through her mail, and try to catch up with the housework. She ate sandwiches whilst she drove. It was not a healthy life. Sophie went down hard with a serious throat infection which spread to her lungs. She took her antibiotics and after only a day's rest was back in harness, struggling to keep going.

And Ella. All of this time Ella was running wild. Sophie hardly had a second to control or monitor her daughter's life. She tried very hard. Ella had matured into a rebellious, disobedient, violent teenager. She had a ferocious temper and had on more than one occasion attacked Sophie, hitting her, dragging her around the floor by her hair, kicking her, spitting in her face, and calling her the vilest possible names, totally ignoring her mother's position. One day Sophie discovered that Ella was not attending school. She drove around looking for her, and following a tip she had been given, she found her in the house of a woman addicted to heroin, whose children had been removed and put into care. This woman loathed her parents and had taken Ella with her whilst she stood outside her parents' home shouting filthy abuse at them for having been instrumental in having the unfortunate children rescued. Ella seemed to think that this person was somehow to be admired. Sophie forcibly removed Ella from the house.

Sophie was realising that she had a major problem. Over the years of Ella's adolescence, life was a nightmare of manic behaviour, violence, abuse, bad companions, theft, disrespect, and much more. There were times when they travelled to France to the family for breaks, but Ella's exploits caused constant friction there, too. Sophie's life was agonising. She still mourned and missed her Ben. The pain was always with her. She needed to work horrific hours to pay the increasing bills. Ella was in real trouble. Her behaviour was that of a manic-depressive, with a great deal of mania. She had many boyfriends who did not last. The calm, dependable ones were dubbed "boring". The wild ones were interesting but did not stay around long enough.

Eventually Ella hooked up with a selfish, moody, spoilt, unpredictable, abusive man. Sophie disliked him immediately. Ella seemed to recognise exactly what this man was but persisted in the relationship. She had wandered from one job to another, never settling or being able to keep a post. She had got herself a place at college and could have qualified for a decent job or career, as she was far from unintelligent. She should really have been at university. But Ella spent her college hours with a bunch of time-wasting dropouts and drifted into the world of drugs. She was a beautiful girl, with her Madonna-like wavy, blonde hair; luminous, stunning blue eyes; and face that drew instant attention. She had an intelligent and enquiring mind and great abilities and potential. But she was working in a factory, throwing her life away on a useless and pointless relationship.

Ella became pregnant. She acted happy, but Sophie knew that she was frightened and far from happy. Sophie was with her and the father in the hospital when Ella gave birth to Freddie in the early hours of one spring morning. Ella was 21. Freddie was a truly lovely child. Sophie loved him from the second she saw him entering the world. Ella was a good little mother and breastfed him tenderly. She soon tired of the selfish, childish antics of Freddie's father, and she moved back with Sophie. Here she stayed for just over a year, bonding with her sweet boy. Life was calm for the first time in Ella's life. Sophie began to hope for normality and a happy relationship with the daughter she loved. Sophie worked and kept them both. Freddie's father intruded from time to time but was of little help.

Ella moved into her own little house away from Sophie, and soon a rather pleasant young man moved in with her. But he was "boring" and did not last. There was a stream of others. Sophie lost count. She also lost contact with the reality of her daughter's life, as she was still working so hard. She often helped Ella out financially. The girl had no father, and Sophie tried to compensate for this. But she did not realise at first that her darling, blue-eyed girl was drifting dangerously into a life of drug dependency. Again and again in the following years Sophie took Freddie to save him from the drug-fuelled, violent arguments and unbearable atmosphere created by his mother's unsuitable boyfriend of the moment. They became very close, Sophie and Freddie. Ella depended very heavily on her mother's help, but she was aggressive and ungrateful.

She continually blamed her mother for her problems and told awful lies about Sophie to her friends, who were unaware of just how much Sophie actually did to help her errant daughter.

Ella was by now living with a young, arrogant know-all, a mouthy, unpleasant lad. Sophie already knew him, and of him. He was a cruel exploiter of emotions, a parasite, a waste of space. He was turning Ella into a wreck. He taunted her for her drug abuse yet deliberately encouraged it. He told her one minute that he loved her and the next that he could not care a fuck about her or her life. He bullied Freddie mercilessly, and Sophie soon discovered that he mentally and physically abused the helpless child, bruising his body and his mind. This man walked out on Ella one day. He simply packed his possessions and left after calling her a "stupid, dirty, hopeless junkie" amongst other insults and vile abuse he mouthed at the sick, dependent girl. She clung to him, sobbing and pleading, but he shrugged her off and laughed at her distress. That night, very drunk, she drove to his home and pounded on the door, begging him to just open it and talk to her. He ignored her while she kept on knocking and pleading. He called the police, and Ella was taken home; her car was taken to the police station until she sobered up. From then on, Sophie could chart Ella's spiral into despair and serious depression, her loss of a grasp on reality. Sophie tried again and again to get into Ella's house and talk to her, but Ella shut her out completely. Her mother was the enemy, the person to blame for everything that had ever happened to Ella. Sophie continued to put cash into her daughter's bank account and leave food on her doorstep, but she was unwanted. She cried often and broken-heartedly. She yearned to hold her daughter close, to soothe her and comfort her, but Ella was not hers to help. Ella had rejected her mother and was wandering, lost and ill, in her own world.

Sophie had a live-in post as a housekeeper in a large house that was hard to run but very lovely. Her client was a retired consultant and pleasant enough to work for. Sophie frequently had to drive over frantically to Ella's home and pick Freddie up, when Ella was out of her head on some substance or another. Sophie had given Freddie a small mobile phone, which he hid from his mother and used to call his beloved grandmother when he was frightened and could no longer handle what was going on. Sophie had contacted the social services, Ella's doctor, and the school—who had also reported Freddie as being at risk—but little help was offered. Sophie was even accused of interfering. She explained that she was trying to help her daughter, who had serious problems and, as a result, her grandson, who was at serious risk of harm and neglect.

One day on her day off Sophie drove to Ella's house to take Freddie out for some relief from his mother's stressful presence and to give Ella a break. Ella was wandering about in her nightie, clearly under the influence of drugs. She was talking to, and smiling at, some person or persons she seemed to be seeing. Sophie told Ella calmly that she was taking Freddie out to give Ella a chance to sleep. Ella seemed not to hear, but at the last minute she grabbed at Freddie, who cried out and ran to his grandmother. Sophie took Freddie's hand, and they ran out to the car. Sophie took Freddie to the swimming pool and then to a restaurant, where they had a lunch of roast beef with all the trimmings. Freddie ate as if he were starving.

There followed months of problems, with the school frequently reporting Freddie's absences, his inappropriate clothing, his need of a wash or a haircut, his mother's unacceptable responses, and her failures to attend meetings that were set up. Freddie called Sophie often on his little mobile. Sophie's heart was breaking as she saw her daughter's life crumbling and with it her grandson's tiny world. She didn't want them to have to be parted, but no help was forthcoming, and the small boy was suffering in every possible way.

One evening Freddie called her in desperation. Ella had hit him, and he was bruised and terrified. Sophie called the social worker who was monitoring the case. This woman went to the house with a policewoman and removed Freddie. He was driven to Sophie's place of work in the big house. Her client had died recently, and she had been retained to look after the house, keep it clean and presentable, and show around prospective buyers. Sophie and Freddie lived there in happiness and peace. Freddie spent hours in the swimming pool, supervised by Sophie or the gardener, Thomas. He helped Thomas, worked with Sophie in her greenhouse, and assisted her in the kitchen, where he carefully made scones and rock cakes and waited for them to be lifted out of the large Aga for Thomas, Sophie, and him to consume. He was truly relaxed and happy, which pleased Sophie, but her heart was torn in half for her daughter. She was addicted and fighting mental illness, and now her son had been removed from her.

Sophie left Freddie with his father and the father's very lovely girlfriend one weekend, and she went to try and see Ella. Ella would not answer the door at first, but when she eventually did, she was horrifically abusive. She screamed at Sophie, who tried, gently and calmly, to reason with her. When Ella lunged at Sophie, she was forced to retreat and drive away. Sophie continued to seek help for her daughter and eventually was promised that help.

By now Sophie was very tired. She was 70 years old. She had worked very, very hard year after year. She made a decision to move away to France and live with her eldest daughter. She would travel back often and see Freddie and Ella. Had she thought the whole thing through when she was not so stressed and exhausted, she would have realised that it was not a good decision. But at that moment Sophie was despairing and tired. All would be well, she told herself; she just needed to get away and rest. She did not register that she was deserting her daughter and her vulnerable grandson. Freddie's father did not like Sophie at all. He did not care that she had done so much to help his son. Life was all about him. That he had failed his son by not fathering him and taking his share of care did not matter to him. He was not to blame.

Sophie gave notice to her landlords. The house she was looking after was soon to be sold. She left it for the last time and began to pack her life into cartons and boxes. She sat with a glass of wine in her hand, remembering Ben's beautiful face, hearing his laughter, feeling the touch of his hands on her waiting body. Where had all that youth, that happiness, and love gone?

Ella phoned her. She needed to be somewhere quickly. She sounded strange and drugged. She wanted Sophie to drive her there. Sophie said that of course she would. She was very worried about Ella. Another of her grandsons was helping her to pack, and she asked him if he would go with her. Understanding the situation, he agreed. When they arrived at the house, Ella was standing in the porchway, ready to leave. She seemed annoyed that Sophie's grandson was sitting in the front seat but climbed into the back of the car. Not long after they set off, Ella started waving a wad of papers about and accusing Sophie of breaking into her house and stealing from her. Then she accused her of failing to inform her about some family matter, saying that her birth certificate was not right and that Sophie had lied to her for years.

Sophie and her grandson tried to calm Ella. Sophie was nervous, as Ella was moving nearer her; she knew that Ella was quite capable of attacking her without warning. Sophie spoke to Ella very softly. "OK, baby, shall I take you to the police station, and we can ask them to sort out these problems for you? I can take you there—we're almost there now."

Ella shook her head furiously. "No, I'm not going there! Drop me off, now—now! Give me some money. I need food."

"Come home with me, darling. I'll cook you a nice meal—"

As they approached the police station, Ella was trying to open the car door; she was next to the road. Sophie feared she would jump into the path of an oncoming car, so she quickly pulled over to the kerb. Ella grabbed at Sophie's shoulder. "Give me that money!"

Quickly Sophie dug in her bag and took out her purse. She found £20 and gave it to Ella. Ella snatched it, jumped out of the car, and ran swiftly up the road. She was soon out of sight. Sophie was very concerned. She suspected that Ella would go drinking and, when she was drunk, trouble would ensue. She turned the car into the driveway of the police station and went in to the reception. There she spoke to a policewoman she knew who was sympathetic, explaining her fears. She was assured that help would be available if it was needed and that an eye would be kept on any disturbances in the local pubs.

Sophie did not want her daughter arrested—she wanted her to be helped. She drove home with her grandson. He stayed at the house for some time, being concerned for Sophie's safety. He knew all too well what his aunt's temper was like and how violent she could be, especially towards her mother. After half past ten he decided he could safely leave. He kissed Sophie goodbye and left. "Call me if you need any help," he said. He walked down the pathway to the gate, turned, and waved. Sophie waved back.

Sophie decided to go next door to her neighbours, who had been her friends for over thirty years and who knew Ella's history. She sat and told them what had happened and what she was afraid might now occur. They said they would listen out for sounds of trouble; she was to phone them if she needed help.

Sophie went back to her cottage and sat, biting her lip and worrying. She was so tired that she soon fell asleep. Suddenly she was awakened by a loud crash and the sound of breaking glass. She leapt up and went into the kitchen. A large plant in its heavy container had been thrown through the kitchen window. Broken glass and earth were in the sink, over the draining board, and on the floor. Ella was there with her hand through the gap, trying to open the window and climb through.

"Be careful of the glass—you'll cut yourself!" Sophie cried anxiously. Ella ignored her and clambered in, onto the draining board, and then jumped down onto the floor. She was clearly inebriated. Her eyes were pink and she was swaying. "There's the fucking cunt that took away my kid." She jabbed her finger into Sophie's face. "The bitch who ruined my fucking life. She did all this shit to me. She deserves a good kicking." Ella grabbed Sophie by her hair and pulled her onto the floor. She dragged her along, then let go of Sophie's hair, and began to kick out at her. Sophie covered her face with her hands and curled into a protective ball.

"Stop Ella—stop!" she shouted loudly so that her neighbours would hear. They had a key to her home and could let themselves in. Ella continued to kick out at her mother and to shout obscenities and accusations. The kicks were landing on Sophie's back, arms, and legs. She was terrified and praying for rescue when she heard the back door opening. Then she heard both of her neighbours; they were telling Ella to stop. She looked up and saw the husband restraining Ella.

The wife knelt down next to Sophie. "Are you all right?" She looked very concerned. Sophie pulled herself up. She felt badly bruised and her nose was bleeding. She sat on the armchair with her head between her knees and a wad of kitchen roll across her face. Ella had been calmed but was still ranting manically. The wife went to make tea for them all. They sat with their mugs whilst the neighbours tried to talk to Ella, but she was in a world of her own. Eventually the wife had to return next door to check on her evening meal. As she left, she told Sophie that she had called the police before leaving her house; they would soon be arriving. This whipped Ella into another frenzy. She shook off the husband's restraining hands and pushed him away. She grabbed Sophie's handbag and went through it desperately; she took out Sophie's purse.

"This should do nicely." With that she ran out of the door and out of the house. The husband ran after her, but she was gone. Shortly after this the police arrived. They were kind and helpful. Sophie begged them not to further distress her child.

"She needs proper professional help. Let her sleep this off, and get her assessed tomorrow morning." They assured her that this was exactly what would happen; then they left to search for her. Not long afterwards they picked her up walking towards her home—which was seven miles away—on the main road. She was talking to herself. They took back Sophie's purse, then drove Ella to the station. There they gave her food and tea, bedded her down, and kept a close watch on her all through the night hours. The next day a police doctor and two psychiatrists declared her in need of sectioning, and she was driven to a local secure unit.

Sophie drove to see her daily. Ella was aggressive and agitated. A staff member stood near as Sophie gave Ella tobacco and papers, chocolate, toiletries—all the necessities she knew her child would ask for. Day after day she went. Every day she was shut out, insulted, and abused by Ella. On Christmas Day, Sophie drove through thick fog to bring Ella presents and cards. Ella sat and opened them, looked at them vacantly, and then got up and left. Sophie drove home, hardly able to see for the fog and her hot tears.

Sophie was due to leave England at the end of December, so the day before that she drove to say goodbye to Ella. Ella was unresponsive and unemotional. Sophie went to kiss Ella goodbye and was pushed away. She turned to look at her daughter one last time before she left. She had left cash with a friend who lived nearby, who had promised to use it to get tobacco and papers for Ella, and anything else she needed. This she did faithfully.

Sophie's heart was breaking. She had given up her rented home and everything. She had no job or home any longer. Leaving Ella and Freddie had been agonising, and she realised that she might have done a very unwise thing. On the last day of December, Sophie left her small home. She stood, looking at the empty, echoing rooms. She could hear the small blue-eyed girl as she laughed and played. She could see Ben, tall, muscular, handsome, grinning and reaching out to hug her. Sophie blinked back the tears. Then she handed the house keys to her landlord and walked to the waiting car. She knew one thing—she would be back soon.

Sophie tried to settle in France. There were things she loved but things she did not much like, and she soon began to feel bitterly homesick. Sarah, her eldest daughter, could be very difficult to exist with. She had a temperament which upset her children, and her life with her recently deceased husband had been a very stormy and sometimes unpleasant one. Sophie wished for her own home and her own habits. Sarah would not allow Sophie to drive her car, so Sophie was imprisoned in this tiny, spread out, isolated village. She phoned daily to check on Ella's progress. She learnt that a few weeks later Ella was to be discharged back to her own home. Sophie was concerned about how Ella would cope on her own but was assured that somebody trained would visit her daily until she was considered fit to manage.

Ella did not want to remain in the large, isolated house the council had provided for her and Freddie. In the year or two before all this happened, Ella had left her lovely little original home to move in with another of her destructive men. This one had abused her emotionally and physically and had introduced her to hard drugs. Ella and Freddie had moved back into Sophie's home for a while. She'd been actually beginning to settle down just a little when she'd got herself tangled up with another of life's rejects. Sophie was away often at her private, live-in posts, and upon returning one day had found that Ella had moved her current loser into the cottage without asking Sophie's permission. Sophie had not been happy and was even less happy when, on returning from a couple of weeks' working, she discovered both jewellery and cash missing from her hiding place underneath her wardrobe. Words had followed, and soon Ella had got herself moved into a large, remote house. It had a lovely large garden, but on one side the neighbours were neurotic and spiteful. Ella had been unable to handle anything about it all, and after her discharge from the clinic, she had got herself quickly transferred to a small flat on the main road nearby.

This did not last long. She found the flat claustrophobic, the neighbours loud, and the traffic noises disturbing. She had mentioned this to friends of Sophie's—who had known both her and Ella for years—and they had offered her a home with them in their beautiful three-bedroomed house in a tiny, exclusive village near the river. *At least*, thought Sophie gratefully, *Ella will be looked after, and by people who really love her.*

In August of the following year, Sophie took the ferry and the coach back to her old home town. She had booked into a very nice boarding house and had hired a car for her stay. She drove out to see Ella, who was genuinely and warmly pleased

509

to see her and greeted her by throwing her arms around her. Sophie was so relieved. Ella seemed a lot better and happier. The friends invited Sophie to stay with them and Ella, and so Sophie drove back, packed her belongings, and then moved into the twin-bedded room Ella slept in.

The friends were mother and son—an only, idolised son. Taking after his half-Italian mother, he was olive skinned with curly black hair and sloe-black eyes. Enrico was arrogant, overconfident, self-indulgent, and vain; yet, in the same breath, he was caring, warm, tolerant, loyal, and devoted. He was 45 years old and still lived with his mother, who doted on his every move and utterance. His father had died a few years before, and Enrico cared for his mother. When Sophie had first moved into her little cottage, Enrico and his parents had lived a short way up the road from her. Enrico had delivered her morning papers on his bicycle. As he'd grown up—and as Ella did—Enrico had fallen in love with Ella and wanted to marry her. Ella had not shared his feelings. She'd seen him as just a friend, most certainly not as a lover or material for marriage. He was twelve years her senior, for a start. And he was a spoilt mother's boy. He had a fast sports car, he was a disc jockey in the local pubs and clubs—he had everything he wanted and more. But Ella wanted something else, and that something else was not Enrico.

Now she was content to live in his home with his mother and him, as she needed a home and help. Sophie's visit was a good one. She felt that Ella was making progress and was being cared for well. She returned to France with a flickering of hope in her heart. She continued to be less than happy there and tried to plan a return, but it was very difficult, if not impossible, so Sophie tried to bear the burden she had brought on herself. The following January saw her in Provence, a live-in private-care job in a beautiful house that was built down a steep hillside in the Luberon. There were olive groves and lavender on its huge, sprawling grounds. They were in the foothills of the Alps, and the mistral blew cuttingly and viciously. On the second day of her four weeks there, it snowed, heavily and silently, blotting out the distant Alpilles and coating everything in flashing white. It was peaceful. Her client was a famous artist, an intelligent, kind, sociable guy. Sophie drove on narrow, twisting roads to the nearby village for bread and the *Telegraph* daily. She also shopped for fresh, expensive, excellent meat, with which she cooked memorable meals. There was a plentiful supply of fresh peppers, onions, courgettes, garlic, and aubergines, which Sophie oven roasted daily with the sweet, nutty fresh olive oil that was produced from the garden's trees and stored in huge earthenware jugs in the kitchen. The wines that accompanied the meals were of the very best, and Sophie enjoyed her stay to the fullest possible degree.

Despite the underfloor heating, the stone floors were always cold. There was a huge log fire in the living room, and Sophie heaped the logs up high, but she was always cold. She was chilled by the screaming, angry Mistral that clawed at the shutters and fought to enter the house.

Sophie returned to Normandy. She boarded the TGV train at Avignon and hurtled through the snowbound French countryside, which slowly turned whiter as they sped north.

When she got back to Normandy, she learnt that Sean was unwell. His alcoholism was now a serious problem. His life was a total mess. He lived in a tiny flat, which he had allowed to become slummy. Sophie tried to visit him often, when she had any time over from working away and chasing Ella's problems, but often he would not open the front door, or if she phoned he did not answer. His health had been uncertain for some time, but now, she learnt, he had serious problems with his spine. His legs were also implicated, and he had had several falls from which he had been unable to get up. His good friend had raised him the first time, but the second time an ambulance call-out had been necessary. The friend had contacted Sophie, as he'd been worried about the neglect of his health that her son was guilty of due to his drinking.

Ella seemed to be settling down and trying to create some sort of a life for herself. She only saw Freddie once a week, which was hurtful to her, but that was better than never seeing him at all. She sent loving messages to Sophie on Facebook and Messenger, and these encouraged Sophie to believe that her daughter would pull through and be able to resume her life with Freddie.

Sophie determined that she would get back to England again and set up a home for the three of them so that she could help Ella. She took the ferry to Portsmouth, and the coach up to Victoria and from thence to Suffolk. She stayed with Enrico and his mother once more; then she took Ella back with her for a break. The night before they were due to leave, Sophie noticed that Ella was behaving strangely; she feared that her daughter was again using hard drugs. She had imagined that this phase was well over but did not realise that the prescription drugs that Ella took had inflamed her yearning for the stronger substances. The next day they travelled to Portsmouth. Ella was black under the eyes and half asleep. She was irritable and rude to Sophie, and the crossing was a nightmare. Sophie, as always, had booked a cabin. Ella wandered off and came back from time to time, staggering and smelling of alcohol. Sophie was angry and told Ella so. At Ouistreham, Ella lurched off the gangplank. She dropped her case and then fell while trying to retrieve it. Sophie was mortified and despairing. Sarah picked them up in her car. On the way back, Ella tried to light a cigarette. Her sister told her not to smoke, as it affected her chest. Ella then tried to open the car window and nearly opened the door as they sped along the motorway. At the house, Ella behaved badly and was soon sent off to bed, as she was nearly unconscious anyway. Sarah said that they would give things a day or two and, if this went on, would send Ella home. Sophie prayed desperately that Ella would redeem herself—in fact she did and was very helpful in every way. She tended to sleep a lot and did not appear to want too much company, but things went better than Sophie had feared they would.

Sophie had a few bad moments with Ella. She discovered that Ella was snooping into her mobile phone and sending Sophie's messages to her own phone. She was also doing this with Sophie's laptop and sending copies of her emails to someone. Sophie took up Ella's phone and deleted the copied messages; then she locked her own phone and changed the password on her laptop. Ella said nothing about the matter, but Sophie was not happy. The visit came to an end, and Ella was put onto the ferry. Her journey home was uneventful, and Sophie breathed a sigh of relief.

Not many weeks later, Sophie heard that Ella had fallen out with Enrico and his mother and had moved out to live with some man she had known for a while. He was a very quiet, retiring type who lived very simply. He was thrifty with money, almost mean but sensible. He adored Ella, but he really knew very little about her. Very soon Sophie heard that Ella had been sectioned again. She had appeared to be making progress and had even had a date to start a college course, but just as suddenly she had begun talking loudly to nonexistent people in empty rooms, laughing wildly and frightening Freddie, displaying rages and manic outbursts, and even attacking the man, who was trying to help her. He sounded decidedly shaky and not a little tired of it all. Ella, he told Sophie, had been going to pubs and meeting some unpleasant character who supplied hard drugs. She was always out of her head on her return and took days to recover. He had now found out the extent of Ella's problems, having been told by Ella that Sophie was the cause of everything, was cruel, evil, and underhanded. He was now realising that all this was untrue and that Ella's problem was hard drugs and her constant use of them. The drug abuse had triggered severe manic-depressive psychosis. Sophie thought, *She was manic from the first. This is nothing new or recent.*

Sophie planned a trip to England again. As she booked her passage, she received the disturbing news that Sean had been rushed to hospital. He had collapsed yet again. His friend had been unable to raise him from the floor, and he had seemed unable to respond. He had been scanned and a tumour found in his spinal cord, in the area of his neck. He was going to be transferred as soon as possible to Addenbrookes Hospital near

Cambridge, which specialised in such neurological surgery. Sophie now had two firm reasons to speed to her home country. On arrival she hired a car. She took Ella with her to Cambridge, where she booked them both into a Travelodge. The following day they drove to the hospital, where her son was being prepared for his surgery; it would be a long business. The surgeon spoke to Sophie and explained that the tumour had been biopsied already—it was benign. But that did not make anything better, as the invading thing was still intertwined with the vertebrae and might even have penetrated the actual spinal cord.

Sophie and Ella kissed Sean as he was wheeled away. Then they sat for eleven long hours in the cafe, outside whilst Ella smoked (Sophie even had a few drags), and outside the ward—waiting, waiting. Then her son was back in his bed, and the surgeon was telling them that it had been successful to a certain extent but that he had been unable to remove all of the tumour, as it was embedded in sensitive nerve tissue. He could not say whether Sean would walk again; only time would tell. When he regained consciousness, they sat with him, handed him drinks and talking with him. When he fell asleep, they drove back to the Lodge. There was a restaurant next door, where they had a good supper, and then they went to bed, totally exhausted. This was their routine for almost three weeks. Then Sean was transferred back to Norwich, and they went back to Ella's friend's home. They visited the Norwich hospital for a week, and then Sophie's son was sent home with little notice. She and Ella drove there and knocked on the shabby front door, with its broken glass and peeling paint. There was no reply. They tried again and again; then they sat in the car calling his phone. Still nothing. Sophie knew that Sean would start drinking again very soon. He would not admit anybody. They were being dismissed. They had served their purpose.

Sophie was deeply worried for Ella. She was in an almost vegetative state. She had no interest in anything but just sat motionless. She seemed to want to do nothing except sleep, smoke, and stare into space. She decided she would take her to France again. The boyfriend was visibly relieved. He kissed Ella goodbye as he saw them both onto the coach, but Ella did not speak or respond. She slept all the way over on the crossing and was withdrawn and uncommunicative on arrival. She spent most of her day curled up in her bed. Her bedroom was downstairs; it opened onto the main living room, and she would lie there with the door open, seeming to want to hear people talking and moving about. Ella was ill—very ill.

Sophie and her eldest daughter had been trying to monitor Ella's medications. She was supposed to be taking large daily doses of strong antidepressants and tranquillising medications, but there seemed to be very few in Ella's belongings, and they were unable to establish whether or not she was actually taking the prescribed doses. They did try to question her about it, but Ella was lethargic and uncommunicative. She was living in a world of her own. Sophie felt powerless at being unable to help her beloved child as she struggled through the darkness of her illness.

Sophie's other daughter, Kate, who was also living in France, with her second husband and her four sons, had been in contact with her. She was not happy that her birthday was imminent and that her mother had not arranged to visit her on this day. Sophie had explained that Ella was very unwell and that she needed to keep an eye on her.Kate was openly jealous and annoyed, and Sophie was put in a very difficult situation. Eventually they agreed that Sophie, Sarah and Clara - her daughter- would travel up to Kate's home and stay for a birthday meal. They would stay overnight, and then Sophie would remain there for a week. Her daughter and her granddaughter would drive back the next day.

Sophie asked Ella if she would like to go with them, but Ella refused, weakly and quietly. Sophie was not happy at leaving Ella alone. There were many animals in the house and outside that needed attention—horses, chickens, goats, and sheep—so Ella could help with this whilst they were away. Sophie left a few things she knew Ella liked to eat in the fridge. She asked her again whether she would go with them, but Ella again refused. Sophie kissed Ella goodbye, and as she held her tightly, she felt a wave of fear and a feeling that she should not go. For a few minutes she fought with the idea of calling her other daughter and opting out of the arrangement, but she was concerned that she would upset Kate. In that split second, Sophie decided to go. She turned and took one last look at Ella standing in the doorway with her hand raised, her golden-reddish, wavy hair spilling over her shoulders, her once deep-blue eyes now faded to almost grey, watching the car pulling out of the driveway. Sophie turned her head and strained to see her daughter once again. Then the car pulled away into the Normandy countryside and towards the motorway.

The birthday party was pleasant, with everyone chatting, good food, and a cake. Sophie joined in, but part of her mind was with Ella. She went upstairs and called the house on her mobile phone. It rang and rang endlessly. Nobody answered. Sophie rang several times that evening and the next day, but still there was silence, no pickup. She slept fitfully and was distracted and worried all the next day throughout lunch and the early afternoon. Her eldest daughter and her granddaughter were leaving to return, and Sophie was remaining. She felt as if she wanted to run after the car and beg them to take her. Deep inside her there were hot waves of worry and dread rising and suffocating her. When Sarah drove away, Sophie went into the house and tried to settle. For some hours she wandered about restlessly. She was helping her other daughter to prepare supper when the phone rang. Kate picked it up. There were low, terse voices. Sophie felt that something bad had occurred. When her daughter returned, she stood looking at her mother with a look of terrible desolation. She went towards Sophie, slowly, with her arms out. "Mum, I'm so, so sorry. It's Ella ... she's taken her own life—it was an overdose. They found her—oh, Mum—" She held her mother closely and began to cry.

Sophie felt as if her heart would stop beating, as if she couldn't breathe. She pulled herself free. "I—I can't breathe—" she whispered and sank down onto the settee. Time had stopped. She had heard something awful. But it was not true. She had known all along, of course—but what had she just been told? Was it about Ella? No, not her Ella, her baby girl.

"Oh, my baby, my baby!" Sophie rocked to and fro. She could not cry. She must get to Ella. That was it. She must get there, and they would see that Ella was just asleep. Not dead. Asleep. Just very tired. Someone handed Sophie a glass of brandy, and she downed it rapidly, welcoming the warm hit to her stomach and the calming sensation. The evening passed. Sophie did not register time or events. Now it was night-time, and she must sleep. Tomorrow they would go back, and Sophie would see Ella and wake her. She climbed into bed and lay there motionless. She stared into the darkness. Was Ella in the dark—alone—frightened? Where was she?

Sophie put out her hand. "Ella, my baby girl, are you there? I'm here, my baby. Don't be afraid of anything. I'm here." Sophie slowly fell into a sleep full of strange and disturbing dreams. She awoke early to a dull, cloudy day. For a split second her life was normal, and then the realisation hit her like a knife thrust into her chest. Ella was dead. Her Ella had taken her life. Her beloved, wild, disturbed, unhappy child had chosen this way to end her pain. Sophie's whole body ached with grief. Nothing about her seemed real or meaningful. Sophie felt guilty. She had left Ella when she knew she should have stayed. Oh God, I should have stayed there—I should have followed my heart. I should have seen that she was desperate, that there was no way out of her misery that she could see. And Freddie. Poor darling little Freddie. Who will tell this child that the mother he adored, whose illness caused him to be taken away from her, had taken her life? That he will never hear her laughter again, never see her beauty—those exquisite and uniquely blue eyes and that red, full, smiling mouth—ever again. He'll never help her to bake cakes ever again or help her dig, plant, and cut back and mow in the garden she loved. He'll never feel again the touch of her soft, loving hand or the whispering glance of her kiss on his face. Will he understand? Can he accept and cope? Sophie wanted to hide Freddie in her arms and shield him from the searing pain. She wanted to rock him gently, to take his hurt, to shut out the world and the horror of reality, and life, and death. Sophie trod her path one painful, terrible step at a time. She must face the storm; she must go through all that must be gone through; she must survive; she must not go down. Freddie would need her for a long time. Sophie closed her eyes, took a deep breath, and stepped into the future.

The next week was a whirl of visiting the undertaker, buying flowers, and contacting people. It was full of noise and stress and distraction. In the evenings Sophie sat in her bedroom, playing the last songs that Ella had played on the big computer downstairs and that she had posted to Facebook. The tears came hot and wrenching. Sophie curled up on her bed, rocking with pain and grief. She wanted to see Ella but was discouraged from doing so by the undertakers. The cremation was to be in Caen. Ella's father had been located and contacted. Kate had spoken to him on the phone, and she had been abrupt and angry. She had called him many names after this and held him in even more contempt than before—if this were possible. She had asked him whether he intended to foot the funeral bill or even contribute towards it. He told her to send a photocopy by email so that he could "consider" it. Afterwards there was a resounding silence. He never offered a penny towards the considerable bill, and neither did he attend his only child's last rites and cremation. A basket of flowers was sent; these contained a message from Ella's "father" and from the obese, porcine, alcoholic, domineering harpy for whom he had abandoned his daughter and her mother. Other family members sent flowers. Sophie had two velvety deep-red roses placed on the coffin from Freddie.

They set off on the first day of December in the dark, cloudy cold. Ella's coffin was placed in a plain white van. *Just like a commercial delivery van*, thought Sophie. *No proper hearse.* The family followed this to the crematorium and filed inside. Sophie had not had time to compile any kind of service. She selected readings and poems, which she and members of the family read out. Ella's music was played. Then the coffin was taken to a side room to be sealed. In France, two armed gendarmes had to be present to ensure that the correct body was sealed inside the casket. Sophie was distressed at the guns they wore, and seeing her state, they removed them. Sophie stood looking down at her child's face. Ella had a curious, knowing, smile. Her face had been made up, and she looked truly unearthly in her beauty. Her reddish-blonde hair, thick and shining, was spread out in waves on the silken pillow, and little ribbons and flowers had been plaited into her curls. She wore a hippy blouse and a long hippy skirt that Sophie had bought her only a few days prior to her passing.

How fitting she looks, thought Sophie, *to go to Ben.* Sophie leaned down and kissed her daughter's closed eyes. They were so cold. She kissed her cheeks and forehead, and she stroked her hair. "My darling," Sophie whispered. "My darling baby girl." She stroked Ella's cheek gently. "Sleep peacefully, my love. I promise you I'll look after Freddie. I'll protect him to my last breath. It won't be too long before we meet again, baby girl. Oh, my darling—my darling!"

Tears ran down Sophie's face and fell onto Ella's cheek. Sophie brushed them tenderly from her child's face. "I loved you from the moment you were born. I tried so hard to help you, but ..."

Sophie paused, and again she kissed her child's cold cheek. "Goodbye, my sweet Ella. Go to Ben—he'll look after you."

Sophie stepped back. The younger of the gendarmes looked at her sympathetically. The coffin was sealed. It was wheeled towards the doors leading to the ovens. Suddenly Sophie could not bear the thought of her child's body being consumed by fire. That body she had carried inside her body for nine months. That beloved child she had struggled to raise, had starved for, and been cold for, had walked the streets searching for when she rebelled and ran wild. Sophie ran to the coffin and flung herself at it. Strong arms pulled her away and held her. Choking sobs tore her throat to shreds. She wept until she could hardly breathe. The doors opened, the remains of her beautiful daughter were taken inside, and the doors closed, silently.

There was silence—just silence, and eternity, and the aching grief that would never go. The winter wind was crying at the window.

Ella was gone.

Afterwards they all went to a restaurant by the sea. Sophie had fish and some vegetables, which she picked at. She joined in the conversation but felt as if she were in a parallel universe. After a pudding, which she didn't recall, and coffee, they all trooped down to the beach with the funeral flowers. The grandchildren undid the blooms from the frames and scattered them on the incoming waves of the sea. The petals and leaves were taken out by the receding waves, like Ella's spirit setting out on the sea of eternity and another existence. Sophie's 32-year-old grandson, Matthieu, stripped off his trainer trousers and, in his underpants and sweatshirt, walked out as far as he was able into the flat slate-grey channel to throw flowers into the water. They floated into the distance under the dull winter light. Evening swooped down quickly, and they all walked to the waiting cars. Sophie was tired, terminally tired. When she got into bed, she fell asleep and spent a restless, disturbed night. The morning was grey again, with heavy, cheerless rain. Sophie booked her ferry crossing and her coach journey online. She could pick Ella's ashes up on the fourth; then she would take them home to the East Anglian countryside and to the tiny churchyard where Ben was buried. There she would lay Ella to rest next to the father whose untimely death she had never been able to cope with. There would be a memorial service in the church first, for all Ella's friends to attend.

Sophie began to feel very unwell. She had a throat and a chest infection, and when she coughed, she had a very bad pain on one side. Her head was burning, her eyes were weepy and hot; she wanted to just sleep.Sarah drove her to Ouistreham and left her there, clutching her cases and bags—and Ella's ashes in a Chinese-style container inside a plastic carrier bag. Sophie was visibly ill. She was sweating and shaking; she could hardly climb up the gangway to board the ferry. Sophie had been obliged to ask the shipping company if it was permissible to take human ashes on their ferry. They had told her, kindly and understandingly, that it was. As she boarded and went to enter the doorway, a stewardess stepped forward and gently took her arm. "Mrs Navarre?"

Sophie nodded.

"Please come with me, Mrs Navarre." The woman led her to the luxury-class cabin deck and unlocked the door to a beautiful first-class cabin.

"But I had booked—" Sophie began.

"This is with the compliments of the ferry company and the captain, Madame. You use our line a great deal, and we are aware of your terrible grief and loss. Please feel free to ring for the steward if you want anything at all." She smiled and left.

Sophie looked around. Then she laid the bag containing Ella's ashes on the dressing table. She felt weak, hot, and shaky. Her side hurt whenever she breathed. She lay on the bed and was soon asleep.

She was awakened by the steward knocking; he came in and looked down at her. "Are you all right, Madame?" He was holding a tray with teacups, teapot, hot-water jug, and a tray of thinly cut sandwiches. Sophie sat up. Her side hurt badly. She smiled, and the steward put the tray on the table next to the bed. He bowed and then left. Sophie poured a cup of tea and gratefully drank it. She took a bite of the ham sandwich. It was delicious, but she could not eat. She drank several cups of tea and then sank down onto the bed and slept again.

The tannoy woke her about half an hour before they arrived in Portsmouth. Sophie put on her warm coat, scarf, and boots. She picked up her luggage and Ella's ashes, which she cradled in her arms, and left the cabin. Most of the crew had disappeared, and the cleaners were the only people in evidence. Sophie began the descent of the gangway. The tide was high, and it was a long trek. The port seemed deserted, too, at this late hour. Halfway down, Sophie found herself struggling. She could not breathe properly, and her legs were failing her. She reached the bottom and stepped out onto the quay. Her legs collapsed completely, and she fell, clutching Ella's ashes to her heart. She heard, faintly, voices, and footsteps. She was aware that drizzle was falling on her, wetting her hair and face.

"You OK, my love?" came a masculine voice.

There were other voices. "Put a blanket over her. Here, take my coat. Put that jumper under her head."

"Think she's had a stroke?"

"Is she on her own?

"Is anyone meeting her?

"What's in that bag? She won't let go of it."

Then she heard the wail of an ambulance, and the paramedics were down beside her. She told them that she was unwell and thought she had pleurisy. She just needed sleep, she told them. They wanted to take her to the hospital, but she refused. She insisted she would get a taxi to the Travelodge she was booked into. "I must take my girl home," Sophie told the paramedic. He looked at the bundle in her arms quizzically.

"My daughter," said Sophie. "I have to take her home to sleep." The man looked at her with great pity in his eyes.

"Are you quite sure you'll be OK? You're not very well. You need antibiotics and care."

"We'll be fine." Sophie put out her hand to him. "Please, help me stand. I'll call a taxi." The paramedic lifted her gently to her feet. "I'll do that," he said. The taxi arrived quickly, and the paramedics and the taxi driver helped Sophie into the cab with her luggage and her precious load in her arms. The driver helped her up to her room when they arrived. He told her to take care, and then he left. Sophie made herself a coffee, but she was in a great deal of pain. Then friends of Ella's contacted her on her mobile, asking her how and where she was and how she was going to get home from the port. Sophie told them she was travelling by coach, changing at Victoria in London. Immediately they told her that she was not to do that; they would arrive the following morning by car and drive her back. Sophie cried with relief. She was at the end of her physical resources and afraid she might not be able to drag her body any further. Holding Ella's remains close to her, she fell asleep.

The friends arrived mid-morning, and soon they were on their way. Enrico and his mother had phoned and told her she must go to them straight away, so they were driving there. Sophie dozed fitfully in the heat of the car. They stopped to refuel and for coffee. Night fell too soon; then they were back in the familiar fields, marshes, and broads of Suffolk. They pulled into the driveway and helped Sophie with her luggage. The girls sat, drinking tea and chatting with Enrico and his mother. Sophie kissed them and thanked them, and soon she was in bed. Ella's ashes were on a table downstairs with a candle burning next to them. She was nearly home.

The next few days were filled with visits to the doctor, antibiotics, rest, and talk. They talked nightly for hours, with vodka and roll-up cigarettes. Enrico helped her arrange the memorial service and printed out the service programmes with really lovely photos of Ella on the covers. There were calls from people, Ella's old friends, wanting to say things and do things. Sophie tried to accommodate their wants. She was fighting her illness hard, and now she felt that everyone wanted to be in on this memorial—everyone was claiming her daughter's soul.

Claiming they "knew" her, as if Sophie did not. Sophie tried to go with the flow.

The day was sunny. A lot of people went to the beautiful little church. There were Ella's songs, played on a CD recorder by the boyfriend she had last lived with. Poems and tributes were read by close friends of Ella's. A long and deeply felt tribute, written by Sophie, was read by the young clergyman. Then they lit candles, and there was a silence, and "Fields of Gold" was played. Many people sobbed. Sophie was next to Freddie and his father with his girlfriend. Poor little Freddie cried but seemed totally confused. At the end, when "Over the Rainbow" was being sung, Freddie and Ella's boyfriend took the container with Ella's ashes and went out to where Ben's grave was. Enrico had dug a hole and lined it with plastic to keep it dry. The container was placed there, and friends threw in single flowers. The young priest said the last prayers, and the earth covered her baby girl's ashes.

"Rest in peace, my darling. Go with your Ben. Be happy—be free—" Sophie whispered. She stood in the winter sunshine, numb and insensate.Sean stood next to her on his crutches, still suffering after his operation and illnesses. They went to the cars and back to the wake. Sophie stayed until she was unable to register any more feelings. She had drunk a lot of alcohol. Her friend came to pick her up. She wasn't going to ask Enrico to come that distance for her—he would be drowning his own sorrows. They went back to her friend's house and sat talking. Then Sophie fell fast asleep. A journey of a million miles begins with the first step. Tomorrow Sophie would take that first step.

Five days later, Enrico took Sophie up to her first live-in client's home. He was working nearby, so could come and pick her up at the end of the booking. Sophie was going to have to work very hard. She had been left with a huge funeral bill to foot— nobody had offered her a penny towards it. She had no home and no possessions, just her stubborn spirit and the need to go on. She wanted to make a home for herself and for Freddie. She had promised Ella that she would protect and raise him, and she would.

The post was not a happy one. The elderly widow was a selfish, domineering bully. The house was overheated, but the attic room where Sophie slept was unheated and dreary. The adjoining bathroom was unheated too, and Sophie froze daily as she showered. At the end of the miserable ten days, Enrico picked her up, and she drove back with him. He had told her that his uncle was coming to stay with them and they could not offer her a home just then. Sophie understood—just as she understood why so many other people had no room or time for her in the months that followed. She asked a friend for help and moved in with her. From then on, her life slipped into a nomadic, gypsy style. She had no home, no real base. She slept on settees, on floors, on broken beds, in cold houses, and anywhere else she could beg a place to stay.

At 72, Sophie found this lifestyle hard, physically and emotionally. She wanted and needed a permanent home where she could pull her resources together and try to establish a home for Freddie. His father was trying to prevent them seeing each other. He had parental control, and this power fed his control freakery and twisted personality. Being able to keep them apart delighted him. He didn't care a damn that Sophie was all

Freddie had left of his much-missed mother—or that Freddie was all that Sophie had left of her daughter.

Sophie went back to France for Christmas 2013. She did not enjoy it; she felt unwelcome. She went back a week later to the home of another friend, who put her up in a comfortable room and made her welcome. He was a hippy, slaphappy character. The Wi-Fi often went off, as did the television, the bills being unpaid. Sophie often paid these and other bills. She did not mind too much. She put money on the gas card, as the friend was often away getting stoned and drunk. She cleaned the house and washed and ironed. Mostly she was away working. She got a well-paying post in Lincolnshire. The elderly clients were bearable. But their niece, who ran their affairs, turned up unannounced, using dominance, threats, and bullying—both verbal and physical—to make Sophie's life there a stressful nightmare. This woman also drank heavily, which did not improve her personality defects.

Sophie had to have a cataract operation on her eye. The hippy friend picked her up, and she took some time away from work to recover. She began to think of Enrico and his mother. Sophie had driven over to see Enrico's mother on occasions when she had a hire car. His mother had become rather ill. She had fought cancer twice, but she was a very heavy drinker, and it was now obvious that her liver was involved. On Sophie's last visit she had been told that the mother had been diagnosed with liver and bone cancer. It was a death sentence. Sophie had meant to visit her often but had no transport. She texted Enrico and explained. She asked how things were and whether she could do anything to help. He texted back that he had been nursing his mother at home for some months, that it was hard, that his mother was near death, and that he would be glad to see Sophie. She was not working for a couple of weeks, so she took a taxi over there.

Enrico's mother was in a hospital bed in the downstairs lounge of the house. Sophie's trained eyes saw that she was very near her end. Sophie had brought her toilet things, a nighty, and a change of clothes. She suggested that she should take the night watch, to allow Enrico to get some much-needed rest. He was clearly relieved. Sophie sat with the dying woman. She moistened her mouth, helped her take sips of water, bathed her hands and face, and adjusted her pillows and covers. She helped her to get up and onto her commode and then helped her back into bed and settled her. As dawn broke, Sophie went into the kitchen and made herself a strong coffee. Her patient was sleeping peacefully. Sophie took a cup of tea up to Enrico. He sat up and took it gratefully. He drank it and then asked about his mother. Sophie told him, gently, that she was very near the end. Enrico put his arms around Sophie and sobbed. She held him and rocked him. This was an idolised child who had worshipped the ground his mother walked on. He'd been spoilt and indulged. This would be for him a trauma to extinguish all others. Sophie held him until his sobs stopped. During the day, carers came to assist. Sophie took charge and directed the care she wished to be given. The carers were good, realising that she knew what she was talking about, and cooperative. There was only one who was slightly arrogant and, Sophie felt, overfamiliar with Enrico and his mother. The day went by. Sophie took the second night watch. During the night, she called Enrico. She had to tell him that a syringe driver should now be put in to ease his mother's pain—and shorten her life. Enrico knew the implications. He sobbed but consented. Sophie called the on-duty community nurses, and they soon came, followed by a doctor, who agreed with Sophie. The driver was put in. Enrico sat drinking Bacardi and smoking. He eventually went to bed, and Sophie stayed on watch next to his dying mother. The next day she went up early with a cup of tea for Enrico, who got up and prepared them breakfast. Sophie waited for the carers and instructed them to wash Enrico's mother carefully and with little disturbance. She was now drifting far away. Enrico went in to speak to her, but she did not respond. A friend of the family came around eleven that morning and sat by the bed while Sophie went up to wash and change her clothes. When she came down, Enrico was going out to the garden to smoke. Sophie went to check his mother. She realised immediately that the end was imminent and sent the friend out to get Enrico. He rushed in and was with his mother as she took her last breath. He drank a great deal and cried a great deal afterwards. Sophie quietly comforted him. She understood all too well.

The funeral involved a lot of people. Enrico's cousins were noisy, common, and lovely. Two of the women—with their big, black, handsome partners, oozing sex—and their beautiful mixed-race children, were really friendly and warm towards Sophie. A lot of alcohol was consumed. The wake involved this, and weed, and music. People danced. One of the big black guys, called Errol, danced with Sophie. He held her very tightly, and she could feel his hard, fit body; it disturbed her. Then he was kissing her. She pulled away and looked around anxiously. The cousin whose man he was bore down on them. She grabbed his arm. "You can leave that out, nigger." She turned to Sophie. "Not your fault, darling. He does it all the time. Wonder why I keep having the bastard back." The situation was defused.

The wake continued until everyone was too drunk, stoned, and tired to continue. They all slept, Sophie on the settee. She had to leave the next morning to go back to Lincolnshire, to the hated place of work and the bullying niece. On the train she thought of the funeral—and of the beautiful black guy who had danced with her and kissed her. Deep inside her something flickered gently.

When she had been at her place of work for three days, she received a phone call from Enrico. She was pleased to hear from him and listened to him as he poured out his sorrow. Then he said, "I'd love it if you moved in with me. You need a home, and I need some help to recover from Mum's death. I could drive up and pick you up from there. When do you finish?"

"On Friday. Ten in the morning. Only another week. I'd be really happy to be with you. It's been so hard without a proper home."

"You can have Freddie round whenever he can come. You know that." Sophie's heart sang. It was another step on the journey towards her dream of having Freddie with her in their own home, another step towards fulfilling her promise to her Ella.

The next week they drove home, very fast, in Enrico's black Mercedes sports car. On arrival, Sophie was delighted to sit down with a hot cup of coffee. Then Enrico cooked her an Italian meal. He was a very good cook—as long as he was cooking what he wanted to cook and it didn't involve too many extra vegetables. That night, as they sat drinking and smoking,

Enrico told her he had booked a villa in Fuerteventura in the Canaries. Would she like to go? Sophie was delighted. She quite desperately needed a real holiday. They sorted out the bookings and the finance immediately. Sophie confessed to Enrico that she had never flown in a jet plane. Older prop aircraft, yes, but she was a jet virgin. He assured her that he would talk her through it. The day came. Enrico weighed the luggage, checked all the documentation, loaded his Merc, and they were off, tazzing up the motorway to Gatwick.

They left the Merc in the secure park, took the shuttle bus to the terminal, stood in huge queues in the sweltering building, checked in their luggage and, at last, were sitting with coffee and burgers waiting for the call to the boarding gate. Sophie was calm. Enrico was close to her as they boarded. She had a window seat. "Just in case you get hot and want to open it," Enrico had told her laughingly. He settled her in and chatted with her to calm her. They taxied to the runway, and Enrico explained to her how the engines would rev up and they would gather speed; then there would be a big *whoomph*, and up they would go. Sophie sat entranced. She was too busy watching the cars on the motorway below becoming toys before her eyes to be afraid. The flight was uneventful. The clouds beneath them were like fields of snow, and the island of Tenerife had its own crown of cloud. They descended and were quickly at the small air terminal near Puerto del Rosario, the capital of the island. They landed so gently that Sophie was unaware of their having touched down at all.

They rescued their cases from the luggage belt and went to the car rental desk. After a few problems which were not their fault, Enrico managed to charm the female desk clerk into upgrading them to a lovely, brand-new four-wheel-drive Citroën. They soon found their villa, as the island was small. It was nearly nine at night and very warm. On the way there, Enrico called into a McDonalds and got burgers and some lemonade to go with his Bacardi. When they arrived, they unpacked and went to sit with their feet in the pool. Enrico threw back his Bacardi, while Sophie drank rather too much vodka and ate too little of the burger. She leaned her head on his shoulder. He had begun to call her Mamma a few weeks before this. He was an Italian boy from a Mafia family—he needed a mamma—so Sophie had taken on the role. But Sophie had noticed in the days before the holiday that she had become Sophie again.

She felt pleasantly drunk. She walked around the warm garden. There were not many plants, because it was too hot and dry there, but some exotic shrubs were scenting the late air. Sophie felt strange—*nice* strange; *new beginnings* strange. Something was going to happen. She could feel it. She gazed up at the jewel-like stars cascading above the island. Once, in a far-off time, she had loved deeply. She felt that her lost lover was, somehow, returning. *Too much to drink, Sophie*, she told herself. She kissed Enrico goodnight, got herself a bottle of water, and went to her bedroom. She opened the shutters, as the heat was something she was unused to. Very soon she was deep in sleep.

ENRICO, ONE

Sophie didn't sleep for many hours. When the sun was still struggling over the edge of the horizon, she went out to the side of the pool in her kaftan with a cup of coffee. There was a slight breeze and a huge stillness. She lit a cigarette, watched the sun lighting up the surrounding white villas, and felt the first strong rays of its warmth.

When it was nearly eight, she went into the kitchen and made Enrico a mug of tea. She took it to his bedroom, paused, and knocked on the door.

"Mmm?" he said faintly.

She went in and put the mug beside the bed. "Nice cuppa for you, Godfather. Did you sleep well?"

"Pretty good, thanks," he said stretching and rolling over. He was naked except for a tiny pair of black silk boxers, and his deeply tanned olive skin was covered in thick, black curling hair. He lay on his stomach with his arms above his head. When he rolled over, it was as if she were seeing him for the first time. She sat on the edge of his bed and chatted to him while he drank his tea. She felt vaguely uncomfortable. The nearness of his naked body, the sweet, musky, masculine smell of his skin shocked her; she had never noticed it before. Yet she had done this at other times without being so deeply affected.

Suddenly she was swept back years to another bed in another bedroom and a beautiful young, blond-haired man with his ponytail, tattoos, his leather and beaded necklets and bracelets. She caught her breath as she smelt the same raunchy male smell.

He was here, here again. Without thinking, she put out her hand and touched him very gently. She stroked his skin, his hair, his beautiful body. Then she was pulled back into reality. She realised she had touched not her dead blond lover but her dark olive-skinned Italian friend.

He regarded her with amusement. "Oops," he said.

"Oh, I'm so sorry!" She was confused and embarrassed. "I thought you were someone else."

He raised one black eyebrow and looked at her from under his coal-black lashes. "Well, that's the most original excuse I've heard yet," he said with a laugh.

Sophie turned away and, to her surprise, found herself crying large, hot tears.

"Hey, hey," he said perturbed by her grief. "Whatever's wrong"?

She slumped down on his bed. "I know this will sound ridiculous, but just for a minute I thought you were my partner who died— you know, he was killed in his lorry; he was Ella's substitute father."

"Yes, I know—it was terrible. What made you think that?" He was puzzled.

She felt increasingly confused and embarrassed. "It was—"

"Was what?" he asked.

"I don't know how to say it, but it was the smell."

"Smell?" he said. "What smell?"

She dropped her eyes; she couldn't look at his huge, dark, searching ones. Suddenly they threatened her in a way she could not understand. She almost whispered. "It was the smell of your skin."

"So," he said, "are you trying to tell me I need a shower or sumfin'?"

She felt flustered. Normally she would have laughed, but she was lost and sad and bewildered. "No," she said very slowly. "It was the smell of sweat and—and maleness. It somehow brought back my past in a huge way, and I saw him there, and I wanted to touch him again." She wiped tears from her cheek and mouth.

"Why are you suddenly thinking of him, after all this time?" he asked her.

"I told you, it was the body smell. It made me feel ..." The tears flowed again.

"Come here." He put his arms around her and hugged her. She was comforted at first, but suddenly she felt as if it were the other whose arms were around her. She wanted to run, run and escape, because too much past was surfacing; the feelings, desires, and love she had left behind were transferring onto this dear, dear friend, and she was totally lost and frightened.

Sophie slept in the chair beside the pool, and Enrico woke her with a warning to oil her fair, freckled skin more often, as the Canarian sun was powerful. He had no such problem with his almost-black Italian skin. But he cared for her and everything about her with a sweetness that made her feel like weeping at times.

He brought her a beer. "Do you want to talk about it?" he asked, sipping his beer and lighting a roll-up.

"I don't really know what to talk about," she said, gazing up at the tiny, high clouds.

"When was he killed?"

"On June 22, 1988. At twenty minutes past three in the afternoon," she said. Her eyes were sad and thoughtful. "He was only 30 years old. Just 30 years and 11 days old."

He frowned. "That would make him 56 now," he said. "So you must have been a lot older than he was."

"Yes, he was younger than me, but we didn't think about that; it made no difference to us."

"Why did you want someone so much younger?"

"I didn't want—he chose me."

"But surely it felt wrong."

"Wrong? Of course not. He was 24, not 16. He was an adult with a mind of his own. I did tell him that he should find someone his own age, but he wanted me."

He looked at her keenly over his sun shades. "Have you always been attracted to younger men?"

"Ella's father was twelve years younger than me. That was a total disaster. And there were the American students in France—they were 18 and 19, and I was about 29. And the guy I met in a motel. I was about 25 and he was 19, I think.

"Phew!" He grinned at her. "And since Ben's death, anyone?"

She paused. "Yep, actually. I was 55 and he was 30; and there was the one with the BMW, but he was 51 and I was 60." She lit a cigarette. "None of them mattered, really. I never had the feeling for any of them that I had for him. One or two were just beautiful, and they fucked spectacularly, but ..." She shrugged.

"Don't you like older men or men your own age?"

"My first husband was eight years older than me. I hated him then and I hate him now. And I'm just not attracted to men my own age. Many men prefer females younger than they are don't they -?"

"But you shouldn't chase boys like that. Don't you like sex with men your own age?"

"I don't chase them. That's not fair. And they are hardly boys, as you put it. They seem attracted to me, or seemed to be—in the past tense now. And no, I just told you that I don't really warm to the thought of sex with men in my age group."

"But be honest. You do seem to be attracted to younger men. I've watched you."

"Watched me what? I like Brad Pitt, and so do millions of older women. Does that make them weird or perverted?"

"Yes, but I've seen the look on your face sometimes when a good-looking young man is around! And you'd be lying if you said you don't fancy me." He grinned wickedly and ran his tongue over his white teeth.

"Fuck off," she said, smiling.

He drank his beer and lit another roll-up. "Don't they have a name for women like you? Something like panther or cheetah or—"

She interrupted him. "*Cougar.* What you don't seem to understand," she said, "is ..."

"Is what?"

She finished her beer and leaned back in her chair, stretching like a large, lithe cat in the sun. "I don't want to talk anymore," she said. Closing her eyes, she went to sleep.

He stared at her for a moment.

The sun climbed higher.

ENRICO TWO

It was like this on that day.

The clouds were thin and fine, and the sun was a huge burning presence. The dust sifted finely over everything. The white villas stood in rows. The water in the pools reflected the heat and the blue of the sky above; the sea was like lapis lazuli. He walked out of the French doors, swaggering gently, aware of his maleness, his dark-olive skin, his jet-black hair, his deep-brown eyes with their unsettlingly piercing and all-seeing stare. He suddenly dipped and flicked his long, black lashes, swinging those eyes onto her. He was oblivious to his own attractiveness and to the unsettling effect he had on women, especially older women.

She recalled that woman at the airport who had started to chat to him about her twin daughters and breastfeeding them. She had suddenly said she was too hot and taken off her jacket, revealing a flimsy top that barely hid her breasts. Her husband had been glowering, and when Sophie had asked him about it, he had shrugged and said, "But I didn't do anything, did I?" and grinned. But the tension and the imperceptible aura of maleness was there, always there. It was disturbing her more and more deeply, despite her happiness.

This was her friend, the one she shared her problems and secrets with. He had supported her through terrible and ugly times, and she had carried him through his tragedies. Night after night she had cradled him as he drank and wept, and they'd laughed uncontrollably as they bandied jokes and repartee and talked away the night. She had chopped, and peeled, and washed as he cooked his delectable, irresistible Italian food. She'd protected and cared for him and his needs and wants, and he'd protected her and pandered to her tiny whimsical outbursts, correcting her irrationalities and ignorance. They'd teased one another, swapped confidences, and shared everything. Their friendship had been forged in the fires of shared tragedy and heartbreak, and in a remarkably short time they had become conjoined spiritually. An unbreakable and unusual love existed between them, which seemed to have always been there. It had an inevitability, a naturalness, which made it easy for her to sense his needs and thoughts.

Then he had brought her to this place, away from all the misery they had both suffered and were still struggling through. And it was like this on that day.

She turned her eyes on him, and something went through her like a hot and frightening wave. She knew in that second that everything was different. The handsome Enrico she had shared some of her life and her pain with was not the person who had adopted her as his mother when his own mother had died. In that second of terrifying revelation, she realised the impact of his lethal sexual attraction.

It had always created a rather fascinating tension between them, because his dark, sultry Italian presence was impossible to ignore. They'd talked about sex and lovemaking in sweet but sometimes overtly bawdy tones, and he'd amused and delighted her with his pornographically detailed descriptions of his many girlfriends.

She felt herself tumbling helplessly into—what? This beautiful dark, gentle friend was her universe, but now she realised that he was more, and her whole being wanted him as something more, and there was no going back. She caught her breath, and the slight sound she made attracted his attention. He swivelled his eyes towards her. Deep, deep brown eyes; piercing and riveting, they were eyes that seemed to look into her soul. Those eyes could expand with the stare of an animal stalking its prey, and they suddenly made her young and needy again. And that—*that*—was the end for her. She wanted to fight the feelings but could not.

"You're getting too hot, Sophie," he said. "You need a drink; I keep telling you to drink enough in this heat." He was gentle, chiding her. He stopped. "What's wrong?" he said softly. "You look strange."

She couldn't speak. The world had changed.

And it was like this on that day.

ENRICO THREE

It was evening, and the sun had slid down; it was still very warm, and they sat on the terrace. She had changed into her kaftan; it was too warm to be encumbered by her bra, so she'd left it off. He had noticed it and observed, "In cougar mode tonight, eh?"

"Why do you call me a cougar?" She was hurt and surprised.

He looked at her with narrowed eyes, those deep, dark eyes that were beginning to disturb her. "Because you always seem to end up with boys a lot younger than you, don't you?" he said quietly, lighting up a cigarette.

"They were men, not boys, really." She almost spoke to herself. "Anyway, why use that word? It's been invented as a term of contempt for women who seem to attract and be attracted by younger men. What's so terrible about that? If an older man has an affair with or marries a much younger woman, he doesn't get treated with the same attitude. They don't call him by some brand name—"

"Dirty old man, perhaps?" He broke in.

"Anyway, why should chronological age define the quality of a relationship?" she asked tersely. "Why do people have to invent spiteful tags for people who find love in ways they can't share or understand? Why must they be gays, or dykes, or cougars?"

"I dunno." He shrugged and took a swig of drink. "I'm just a normal straight guy."

"Your normality is yours, but other peoples' normalities are theirs," she pointed out. "Suppose you met someone much younger than you and fell for her very deeply. Not just sexually, but say this person was your very best friend as well, and you could tell her anything, and you shared everything and helped each other through life and felt desolate without her. Why should anyone label you with a contemptuous, cruel label?"

"Mmm." He shrugged. "I suppose you could be right, but older women preying on young boys just to get sexual kicks seems to me not very nice."

"I didn't prey on him for sexual kicks." She was remembering his blue eyes; his stubby, childish, gentle fingers; and his sweet probing tongue. She breathed deeply. "He wanted our relationship. I told him to go. I did actually love him a lot, you know. I felt really protective and maternal towards him ..." She paused.

"But you still wanted him to fuck the hell out of you?" He looked at her from under his dark lashes.

"Yes, I did. He was big and experienced and fantastic when he made love." She paused. "And I wanted to fuck the hell out of him, too." She smiled at the memories. "But I loved him very, very much. It's not all about fucking."

She felt his eyes on her; and she knew he was grinning. "Well, it's still like fucking your own mum," he remarked.

"He was 24 when we met, and I was nearly 42," she said, annoyed that she sounded defensive. "That's only eighteen years' difference, and it's not so bad when you're younger, is it really?

Someday," she said, "someday I'll tell you about it. What really happened. That's if I can bear to go back there. It really hurt. I suffered, and I think it may have damaged Ella ..." She couldn't continue, and he understood when she mentioned Ella.

He put his hand over hers. They had both lost someone they loved when Ella went.

They sat in silence for a while; then he went into the villa and brought her out a glass of wine. She thanked him and took a sip. "What's so very wrong, anyway, with falling in love with someone older or younger than you are?" she asked him. "If it's real love, the age difference doesn't matter a fish's tit." The silence fell again. He lit another cigarette.

"The thing is," she said, "that the word *cougar* is associated with women, usually around 40 or so, who deliberately set out to trap younger men by dyeing and painting, lifting and tucking everything to make themselves appear younger. And it's purely for sex." She sipped her wine again and drew on her cigarette. She knew his dark eyes were on her. "Sometimes a woman just happens to fall for a man who is younger, and it's not just the sexual magnetism of the guy; it's the personality and the close friendship they build. And she genuinely and deeply loves the guy.

"After all, you know the guy's not going to fuck you, for Christ's sake, because he's—what—45 and you're over 70? So you have this close, very close friendship, and you can say anything to each other, and you're both unshockable, and you'd do anything for each other. You make love verbally, because that's the only way it's going to happen. You can talk about anything to each other, and he understands just where you're coming from, because he loves you enough to realise that you would never overstep the invisible boundaries; he also has enough compassion to realise that it's hell for you but you'll stick it out because you love him so much. But it's hard on the one who's older and who loves, because every day's a fight to cope with hellishly strong urges."

He gazed at her quizzically. "You seem to know a lot about it." He grinned again. "Are you writing a book on it or something?"

"No," she responded quickly. "I just imagine that's how it might be."

He was silent for some while. He poured himself another Bacardi. "Funny thing that, isn't it?" he said. "Because I just happen to be 45, and you just happen to be over 70—a bit."

She shrugged. "It was just a sort of example."

"Was it really?" There was an edge to his voice that she had never, ever heard before.

"Well, we're close friends and—"

"And what?"

"I don't know." She was uneasy. He flicked his dark eyes sideways at her and set his mouth in a hard line. He had on what she laughingly called his "Mafia Face." But she didn't feel much like laughing, because there was a steely glitter to his gaze.

His voice became very soft, very worryingly soft. "You're always honest with me. That's why we get on so well, isn't it?"

Where was this going? She answered carefully. "Of course, yes. I trust you with my life."

"And I trust you with mine," he said. "But I am just starting to feel that there's a lot I don't know about you, and I'm starting to feel a bit uneasy."

"Why?" Her throat was dry. "You know almost everything about me, surely."

He downed half a glass of Bacardi and turned to face her. "I want very honest answers," he said, "and I mean honest."

"OK," she said slowly. What was coming? He held her with those eyes—she was powerless to avoid them. When she was caught in their deep, deep gaze, she could deny him nothing. They widened and bored into hers.

"If I were to invite you to come to bed with me tonight, would you say yes without hesitation?"

For a second she was stunned. She dropped her eyes, unable to look into his. "That's not fair," she muttered quickly.

"Why?" he said." Why isn't it fair? I want an honest answer, that's all."

"What I want to do and what I would actually do aren't the same thing, are they?" She was struggling. "Anyway, you would never, ever make that invitation, so it's totally irrelevant."

"Be honest with me," he insisted. He held her arm, and the force in his grip frightened her. He was the gentlest of men although he was so well built and strong.

She put her head down. She couldn't look at him. She swallowed and said in a whisper, "Yes, I would, and you bloody well know it."

"Why?" he said.

She was puzzled—why? She took a deep breath. "Because I find you sexually irresistible, and good-looking, and your eyes are so dark and beautiful that they take my breath away, and when you look at me intensely, and they grow wider and darker, I feel, I feel—lost. And the smell of your skin makes me dig my nails into my hands to stop myself practically—"

She stopped, lit a cigarette, and drew on it, deeply. "And I—I love everything about you. Does that answer your question?" She wanted to cry. She was totally confused. But she went on. "And there's something else you really have to understand."

"What's that?"

"I've always kept the sexual urges and performance of a 35-year-old. I've always been raunchy and very highly sexed; but I have to have feelings, too—I don't just fuck. I'd rather just masturbate. Most people would think it a blessing and a gift, but I don't think you would—I don't know ..." She stared deliberately into his eyes. "But I'm damned if I'm going to feel ashamed of it. I'm proud of it."

He stared at her emotionlessly, and she felt terrified.

She found it almost impossible to continue, but she knew she must explain what she felt, or he would never understand her. "I would also give my life for you. Please don't be angry, because I can't help my feelings. I love you as if you were my child, and I love and value you as my dearest and closest friend, but I really can't help what I feel. I can control what I do, but the feelings are impossible to ignore. I fight them all the time. I didn't plan for this to happen. I couldn't bear this to part us. I love and value you so very much. Even if you did say, 'Come to bed with me'— and, for Christ's sake, you won't—I wouldn't give in. Although I might say yes because I love and respect you too much—so very much—it would be a fight to say no. You shouldn't have asked me. It's not fair, is it? Can you really understand what I am and how I have to fight my needs and desires—" She couldn't carry on. She was so confused. He stared at her, and his beautiful, brown eyes seemed still so cruel.

Sophie didn't know what else to say. She was tired, and she closed her eyes to doze in the powerful sun.

Enrico dived into the pool and swam strongly; then he suddenly splashed her. She shrieked and jumped up. Enrico climbed out of the pool, threw his arms around Sophie, and hugged her tightly.

"Damn you, I'm soaked!" she said, but she was laughing.

They went into the cool villa, where Sophie changed out of her wet clothes while Enrico showered and dressed. They sat on the terrace sipping beer. Enrico looked at her for some time. "I'll always love you," he said, and then he turned away and lit a cigarette.

Sophie was falling asleep; she heard him and her heart echoed his words.

The evening drew on. Enrico prepared chicken and steaks on the barbecue in the garden of the villa. Sophie fixed up a salad with an oil, garlic, and balsamic vinegar dressing. They sat eating on the terrace, under the orange-yellow moon. Sophie sipped wine but Enrico was making inroads into a bottle of Bacardi. Sophie had noticed that he was drinking more, and earlier, as time went on. He could be quite difficult and disagreeable when he was drunk, but tonight he seemed just to relax and mellow. They finished the meal and carried the plates into the kitchen, where they worked together to wash, wipe, and put away the crockery and cutlery. Sophie made herself a cup of coffee, but Enrico continued to drink Bacardi. They went back to the terrace and sat smoking, Sophie with her coffee, and Enrico with his rum. They chatted about the holiday and about where they would go the following day.

Sophie stretched and yawned. "Gosh, I really am tired. Must be all that sun. I'm turning in. I want to be up early and get going." She rose. Enrico squeezed her hand and wished her goodnight, and she went to her room. She changed into a thin, cool nightdress and went into the bathroom to wash. She was there for some time, and when she came out, she saw Enrico standing at the end of the corridor, outside his bedroom, looking at her. She smiled and went into her room. Minutes later, her door opened, and Enrico came in. He stood for a few seconds, looking at her keenly with his large, dark eyes. Then he took her hand and pulled her onto the bed, where he sat beside her. He held her hand very tightly; then he leaned forward and kissed her naked shoulder.

"You are really very attractive. Sexy in a different sort of way—I don't know—those high cheekbones, maybe. Your slanted eyes. Or maybe it's your voice—just something." Again he leaned towards her, and Sophie felt fleeting attraction—but then panic.

I am deeply attracted to this man's body, and I do love him a lot, but I don't want a spoilt, temperamental, mother-fixated toddler, her brain said decisively She wanted him as a friend but certainly as nothing else. She was desperately attracted to him physically, but now that he had actually touched her, she was almost repelled. *What do I do?* she thought frantically. *I know I really love him—and I want him—but he is too complex, too much work. If I knew he would take me tonight, and many nights after, and remain my friend, then I would say yes and sink back and allow him to give me what I crave. But it would be a trap. He would demand too much emotionally. He is too possessive.* In a second, Sophie had decided.

"No, Enrico. No, please. Just let me think about this. Give me time. You said this would never happen and now—well, now you seem to have completely changed your mind."

"I thought this was what you wanted." He pulled away from her.

"Let me think about it, please. This is so sudden—I didn't expect you to—"

Enrico stood up and left the room. She heard him unlock the door and go out onto the terrace. After a few minutes, she followed him out there. She sat down, lit a cigarette, and then put her hand on his arm. He shrugged it off.

"I think we'll drive up to the observatory tomorrow," he said. "There's a cafe and gift shop up there. The road winds a lot; it's very narrow and steep. You'll be terrified." He had switched off. She did not exist for him as a prospective lover now. He had been calling her Sophie since they'd boarded the plane. Now he turned to her and said, "Best go to bed, Mamma. We have an early start."

She was his mamma again. She still loved him deeply—but not as his mamma. In those few seconds all had changed irrevocably. And now Sophie would have to live with the decision she had made. She hoped she would not live to regret it.

ENRICO, FOUR

Sophie and Enrico had a close partnership, and she helped him improve the house that was now his inheritance. He wanted to rent it out so that they could go back to their island in the sun for the rest of their lives. But despite her feelings for him, and although it was a tempting prospect, Sophie knew that she would never go. She would never leave Freddie. She had not yet told Enrico this, but she would at the right time. Her love for him was powerful, but her love for her motherless grandson transcended all her other emotions and loyalties.

Sophie cleaned, tidied the garden, and made it beautiful with tubs and hanging baskets. She dug out weed beds and hoisted rubbish into barrows. She put the house in order, turned out and threw out, washed and ironed, and exhausted herself, trying to show her endless and unconditional love for him. Despite what had happened on that holiday, he still treated her as a closely loved person. But he had started to call her Mamma again, and Sophie was completely confused. She did not know whether she was supposed to be his mother or his lover—although that possibility had ended on their holiday. He still kissed her on the mouth, held her hand whilst they were driving in the car, and touched her shoulder and face gently when he walked past her. Maybe he was confused too.

She went off on a job, working till she was exhausted to help him pay bills—helping them. She missed him achingly when she was away. They texted for hours, and he told her that he loved her so much and missed her, too. He picked her up in the car, and she sunk into the seat beside him, tired but so glad to be with him again. They held hands as he drove fast and furiously in his Mercedes Benz sports car. They joked as they always did, and she warmed inwardly at his precious nearness. One day when she had returned from a particularly exhausting work schedule, they spent a wonderful day together, but she noticed the next day that he seemed uncomfortable and preoccupied. He took a shower in the evening, which was quite unusual. As the evening wore on, she felt uneasy. He was texting quite a lot, and he didn't seem able to meet her gaze as he usually did with his beautiful smile.

At eight o'clock he told her, "I'm going out tonight."

"OK," she said, thinking he was going to visit his friends. She had noticed that he hadn't been drinking, as he would normally have been doing.

He looked uncomfortable. "I won't be back tonight," he said. "I'm going to see Karen."

Sophie remembered her as one of the carers who had looked after Enrico's mother. Sophie hadn't liked her, as she'd sensed competitiveness and too much interest in Enrico. Once when Sophie had gone to take a cup of tea up to Enrico, Karen had pushed in, taken it from her, and said, "I'll do it; I usually do."

Sophie was stunned. She felt numb—and strangely jealous. Why hadn't he given her more time to absorb and deal with this? *I must not overreact*, she thought. *He is 45 years old and has sexual needs, and he doesn't want me. And this woman,*

553

who has no part in his life, and who doesn't know him as I do, and who hasn't been through what Enrico and I have been through together, will have him totally.

Enrico tried to reassure Sophie that it was only a liaison for his sexual needs; but she was hurt, and he knew it. He held her close and told her he would always come back to her. He pulled out of the drive in his sports car just after ten that night. She waved him goodbye. After the sound of the engine died away in the distance, she wept. She opened a bottle of wine and drank it, too fast. Suppose he fell for this woman and no longer wanted her? Suppose he brought her into their shared home? How could she cope?

She drank steadily, opening another bottle of wine and becoming more and more distraught at the thought of losing Enrico's friendship and love. She had already lost her beautiful young lover and her daughter. What more would life take from her? Three o'clock in the morning came, and she was rapidly sliding into deep, deep despair. She was very drunk, and she staggered upstairs and fell into bed, still fully dressed.

Struggling up from the mists of deep, deep sleep, she felt Enrico kiss her cheek. He crept out of the room, and she saw that he had left her a mug of tea. She sat up. *Oh God,* she thought, *I feel terrible!* Her mouth was disgusting and furry, and her head ached with a dull persistence.

She crawled out of bed, still fully dressed, sweaty, and wretched. She went downstairs to the patio, where she drank her mug of tea and lit a cigarette. She sat in the lounging chair and shivered slightly in the early morning sunshine. She heard him coming down but dreaded having to see him

He came out to the patio with his tea and stood looking at her silently. After a minute he sat down opposite her. He lit a cigarette. "Well, that was a stupid thing to do, wasn't it?" he said quietly.

She could not look at him. She longed to run to his arms and hold him close and smell his sweet, musky smell. But she feared that she had now alienated and angered him, and she did not know how to cope.

"I came in, found all the lights still on, the front door unlocked, an empty glass, a full ashtray, and two and a half empty wine bottles. It wasn't exactly a good thing to find, was it?"

Sophie nodded and looked at the ground; she could not meet his gaze.

"I told you I'll always come back to you. I told you I love you, and I'll never, never leave you. Can't you believe that this is nothing? I went for shag, a fuck, nothing more. I love you very much; she'll never replace you."

Sophie looked up at him, and tears rolled hotly down her cheeks. "You could at least have given me time to take this in and deal with it. You just sprung it on me. The shock was pretty awful, and I couldn't cope. We had just come home and everything was so, so ..."

She could not go on. Didn't Enrico really understand just how he had hurt her? How impossible her situation was? What it was like to know that the man who had seemed to be your close friend, and who said he loved you so specially, had walked away to another woman? She was angry, jealous, hurt, and insecure. He did not want her, and he expected her to silently endure the situation with indifference and good humour and wish him happiness.

"For you it's an all-win situation; you have all of me you want to have. I have nothing of what I really want. So you will never leave me. Why should you? You have me captive and doing everything you want me to do, but you don't really consider my plight and my frustration and misery. I wish to God I could leave you and start again, but I know my life would be empty without you. I have thrown my lot in with you. I thought we had a future, and life *was* sunny and bearable for this short happy time. Now I can feel you pulling away from me slowly and almost imperceptibly, but it is happening. You pretend to me that this is just a sexual liaison, a need that you are fulfilling coldly. You are just using her. If you are, then I am seeing you as selfish, hard, and uncaring, and I am terrified because you are using me too, only for different reasons.

"I cannot believe that you do not tell her you care for her. I see you texting her for long periods, and you glance at me if I watch you, and you look guilty. You leave me to see her, but you have already left me during that day. You cease to notice me and what I do and say. You are already with her, and you have no use for me then.

"You tell me that you love me more than you love her, but in a different way, and that I have more of you than she does. I cannot trust you, because I have never been able to trust any man I have had a relationship with. Even my darling, much-missed Ben, if he could have lived, would inevitably have found someone younger—or would he? It was better that I lost him to death than to another, younger, woman. And now this has happened again, and already I have lost even the friendship and closeness we shared."

Sophie went up to her bedroom. Lying on the bed feeling headachy and exhausted, she suddenly made a decision. There were dating agencies all over the Internet. She would find a man—or men—to dally with, to use and leave. Maybe one would fall for her, or she for him. *Never mind that*, thought Sophie. *It's just a game.* She picked up her mobile and began to search the Internet.

By the evening it was all under way; her life was moving to a new phase.

Sophie registered with an agency for older people, but this did not seem to stop a lot of much-younger men from continually popping up and inspecting her profile. She examined them all carefully but could see nobody who gave her that "wow" feeling. For her profile she was supposed to write a piece on what she was looking for in her ideal man. She trotted out all the expected adjectives: kind, caring, reliable, honest, educated. After a pause, she added "solvent." Then she felt a bit dishonest, because she owned nothing. It did not take her too long to realise that most of these men weren't remotely interested in anything they claimed on their profile blurbs. They might as well have written simply, "I want your money or your pussy, preferably both." It was an online street corner, with cruising men hidden behind false names and invented personalities. She browsed the men presented hour after boring hour. One of them looked nice, but he seemed to want anything female. Not very promising. Amongst the photos was that of a really handsome black guy. He looked big, and there was a kindness in his dark eyes that fascinated and called to Sophie. She felt instant attraction. He described himself as kind and caring and said that "age is just a number." He was, he wrote, 45, which was younger even than Enrico. *No,* thought Sophie. *He is too young for me, and he is very good-looking. He will have his pick of attractive women, and wealthy ones too, no doubt.* She decided, with sadness, that she was out of her league, and she tried not to look at his profile again. She looked at the men in and near her age group, but she found herself left cold and disinterested. She simply was not attracted to older men. Why should she be? There were no rules carved in stone. Age was, indeed, just a number. Sophie thought young, her body was still young, and her sexual urges and performance had not altered with the years. She stopped looking at the site and the notifications which popped up regularly on her phone. She had other problems to address.

Enrico was in deep debt, although he pretended to a life of easy wealth. He had inherited his mother's home, but he had also inherited a stack of bills. Most of these dated back for several years. His mother had been claiming benefits to which she was not entitled, and the government department concerned was chasing Enrico for repayment. The house was in a very poor state of repair, despite all the work Enrico and Sophie had put in to spruce it up. His business had closed down, because he had been issuing certificates of training for things he was not licensed to do so. Sophie had paid more than her share from her earnings, but now Enrico was stressing about his car insurance and tax, unpaid phone and electricity bills, and unending other liabilities.

Sophie was giving him every penny she earned, but it was like a leaking dam. Then one morning Sophie received a letter from her bank telling her that she was being compensated for PPI she had paid on loans she had taken out in the past. The sum was interesting, £22,000. Sophie was in raptures, but she decided to keep the information to herself. She decided that she would move to her own home as soon as she could. Enrico was frenziedly trying to sell the house to pay his debts and move to the Canary Islands. Sophie packed the letter away in a drawer in her bedroom and went off to work for ten days. When she returned, she was glad of the rest. She stayed in bed for a lie-in the next morning and decided to surf the Internet for furniture and curtaining. She also wanted to look for properties to let in the town where she had once lived, the town where she had raised Ella and lived and loved with Ben. She decided to check her bank statement on her phone, and when she did so, her heart began to race. Large amounts of money had been paid out to various companies and people. The electricity company that Enrico owed so much to, British Telecom; the local council—that would be his overdue council tax for over three years; his insurance company; the DVLA for car tax, and on it went. Sophie was hot and angry. She got up and ran down the stairs, where she found Enrico smoking and drinking coffee.

"Morning." He smiled. "Want a coffee?"

"No," Sophie snapped. "I want an explanation as to why my bank account has been used to pay your debts."

"What? You're joking."

"No, I'm bloody well not! I recognise the amounts and the people you owed them to. How the fuck did you know I had this money—and how did you get my bank card details?"

"You had all that money and you weren't going to tell me. I found the letter in your drawer."

"You snooped through my private mail?" Sophie was incandescent with rage.

"It's my fucking house. I'll do what I like in it."

"I pay all the bills in this place! Nothing's yours. But you've stolen money from me, and you've read my private mail. You must have copied my card details, which means you've taken my card out of my purse at some time. You're a cheap, common little thief and con man. From now on I'm paying for my food and my share of the house expenses, remembering I'm away from here working a lot, but nothing else. I might have helped you if you'd asked. But you stole from me, so it's all finished now. I was never going to the Canaries with you. Freddie comes first in my life. I shall take all my mail and personal possessions with me when I work, and I shall get a new bank card immediately, so you won't be stealing any more from me." Enrico, switching to little-boy mode, tried his sultry, begging look.

"I shall sell the house soon; then I'll pay you back every penny, Mamma. I promise. I'm sorry, but I was desperate. You kept that money from me, all to yourself."

"Of course I did. It's my money! You have a damned cheek reading my mail and going through my bedroom drawers—not to mention taking my debit card and copying the bank details. If you'd had the simple decency to ask me for money to pay all your bills, then I might have helped you. I'm bloody angry and disgusted, and I don't trust you any more."

"But Mamma, I ran up these bills because I couldn't work when my mother was dying—"

"Oh no, you didn't!" Sophie cut in sharply. "These bills of yours go back over three years. Long before I was here. And I've more than paid my way since I moved in here. You and your mother seemed able to live the very good life, so you weren't making any effort to pay your debts then, were you?" She went upstairs, angry and bitterly disappointed. This man was just another thief, liar, and self-interested bastard. She surfed on her phone. She went onto the dating site just for some kind of distraction. She was pleasantly surprised to see a message waiting for her. She went to the messages, and there it was— and her heart leapt. It was from the big handsome black guy. He was called Ty—Tyrone. He was Jamaican. He chatted with her online, and she discovered that he only lived about nine miles away from her. She went downstairs to get a glass of wine and found Enrico swilling back Bacardi with a sour, angry look on his face.

"Stay down here and talk to me," he demanded.

"I don't want to," said Sophie. "I don't find you very good company when you drink too much."

"You're on that bloody phone or your laptop all the time!" Enrico's smart television told him who in the house was using the Internet.

"I'll use what I like! I pay for the Wi-Fi, and the phone, and the electricity, and the heating oil—"

"Fuck you!" Enrico threw back the remains of his Bacardi.

Sophie messaged the handsome Ty again before she went to sleep. She was awakened at three in the morning by Enrico playing loud rap music; it shook the bedroom floors. She put her television on and put in her headphones; then she drifted off to sleep again.

561

The messaging between Sophie and Ty continued for a couple of weeks. After returning from being away at work, she sat on her bed and messaged him on her phone. She texted with her tongue in her cheek. "My friends tell me that all Jamaicans have pretty big equipment—is that true? LOL."

Ty texted back. "Why don't you come and find out—just as a friend, if you like. We could meet then."

Sophie was ecstatic, and she was also terrified. This guy was very young and very handsome. But she really did like the look of him and his body. Her feline instincts roused from their long slumber. Yes, she would use his body, get all the pleasure she could extract, wallow in his beauty and youth, and take her pleasure. He texted her that they would have to meet in a hotel, as he had his teenage daughter at home and didn't want her walking in on them. Sophie understood. Then Ty texted that he was actually broke, so she would have to pay for the hotel room. Sophie was fleetingly angry, but then she thought, *It's just a night of steamy sex with a really good-looking guy. I'll pay for my pleasure. Why should I care?* She texted back to leave it to her. Then she booked a local room online and texted Ty the date and room number. He texted back that it had to be the Wednesday, no other day. She wondered why. Work? It didn't matter. She changed the booking immediately with no problem.

That night Enrico was visiting his fuck buddy. He left at six in the evening. Before he left, he tried to kiss Sophie goodbye, but she turned her face away and ignored him. As soon as his car left the drive, Sophie ran upstairs, showered, changed into sexy undies, put on a lot of make-up and expensive perfume, and donned her leather jacket. She left the house lights on so that any nosey neighbours would think she had been home all night. She got into the four-by-four SUV that Enrico had given her. It had been his mother's car but had sat for over a year in the drive, untouched and neglected. It had seemed a wonderful gift, but it had started off needing a new battery. Then there was an MOT check, which threw up new tyres, a lot of welding, brake pads, and light problems. Sophie cheerfully shelled out almost a thousand pounds to get the vehicle on the road. She loved it nevertheless.

She drove it this night through the December murk to the hotel. She booked in and opened a bottle of wine from the three she had brought with her. She was terribly nervous. *Relax, this is just a night of fun and sex. You like young men, and this one is young and handsome, and he could be good in bed. Just lie back and enjoy it. Just use him. He probably uses women all the time.*

Then he texted. "Which number room are you in, baby?"

"Ten," Sophie replied.

A pause. Then he texted again. "I'm so worried about my big stomach."

Sophie read it and laughed. She texted back. "Mine's enormous. Stop worrying."

Seconds later someone started to open the door.

SOPHIE AND TY, ONE

2014 to 2016

The door opened and I saw you, and the beauty of you slayed me at that second—your black skin, and your deep brown eyes, and your sensuous mouth. I drowned in your maleness and youth and sensuality. You held a plastic carrier bag in your hands that contained a bottle of vodka. I had brought wine. I did not see the significance of your dependency. I could not have known. I saw only a man I knew I could adore and pleasure and sacrifice for. That night I experienced pain and pleasure, the price of loving your body, but I could not know the extent of your abnormal and destructive personality. Who could tell? The childish hands. I wanted to protect and help and love you. Like a goat, I was the sacrifice. My role was that of cougar. This was not the script.

I took your hugeness and you took my heart and soul. This was not the script.

He was big and handsome, with dark eyes, the slightly snubbed nose of his race, and a full, sensual, beautiful mouth that stunned Sophie at first sight. He stood in the doorway, smiling, and said just one word. "Hi." He had a slight American drawl. Sophie was even more attracted. The voice was deep, dark, and honeyed. He grinned, and dimples showed by his mouth. The mouth was full and the lips spoke to her of softness and sensuality. He swaggered in and put his carrier bag down to the side.

"Hi, baby, I'm Ty—Tyrese. I brought my vodka with me. You drinking anything?"

"I brought some wine." Sophie felt shy. "Hi to you, too. I'm Sophie."

"Nice name. Let's drink to our meeting." He found two glasses near the kettle and the tea and coffee equipment. He poured Sophie some wine and then himself some vodka, which he topped up with lemonade.

"Here's to having some fun, and some really good sex." He raised his glass, and they both drank. He walked over to the side of the bed, holding Sophie's hand, and sat her down on the edge. Then he sat on the chair next to the bed, facing her. He was very close to her; their legs were touching. Sophie took a long gulp of wine, and Ty sipped his vodka. Then he took her glass and put it, with his, on the table next to the bed. He leaned forward. Sophie closed her eyes instinctively. Then she felt that mouth on hers—warm, soft, and pressing hers gently and caressingly. He put his tongue into her mouth and kissed her harder. Sophie responded, opening her mouth wider and pressing back. Then he took her hand and pulled it down between his legs. He had pulled down the front of his trainer trousers, and Sophie encountered what she thought was his leg. But then he put her hand around something really huge, and warm, and hard. Sophie's eyes opened wide. She pulled her mouth away from Ty's and looked down. She saw the largest penis she had ever imagined in her entire life. It was not just long but so very thick. Sophie had never seen a black penis before either, and she was fascinated by the black glans. She stared at it.

"Wow, that is so big—"

Ty grinned. "Yep. A lot of women have said that to me."

"I don't think I'll get that in me." Sophie was worried.

Ty laughed. "Of course you will, hun. You said you've had four babies, yes?"

"Yes. But that thing will be like pushing one of those babies back!"

Ty laughed, wrinkling his nose. "Funny, baby, funny. You just relax. Just enjoy what I've got." He leaned forward again and kissed her hard. He pushed her gently back onto the bed and continued kissing her. He slowly and carefully undressed her, throwing the garments across the room. He kissed her nipples and ran his tongue over them, then used his tongue on her skin as he worked his way down to her waiting clitoris. Sophie groaned and moved her hips as he flicked his tongue over her. Ty moved onto the bed, and she felt the hugeness of his penis at the entrance to her vagina. She thought, *I'll never be able to take this into me.*

Ty said gently, "Relax, baby, relax. Just let me in. Relax." Then he was sliding in, and Sophie's eyes opened wide. She tried to let her muscles expand to take the great thing. Then Ty kissed her again, and the smell and heat of his skin, and the softness of those lips made her desire swell, and he went into her fully. She gasped, but her body followed his, and she was in heaven. She was so stimulated. She felt every tiny movement.

Soon she was nearing her orgasm, and she moved quickly and desperately.

"Oh God—fuck me! Fuck me, please—harder—fuck me!" As she climaxed, gasping and shuddering, Ty pulled out. After a moment, Sophie asked him, "Aren't you going to come too?"

He grinned down at her. "I can keep going all night, baby." He kissed her again, lingeringly, and then went to get himself another vodka. He poured Sophie some wine. She sat up and he sat on the bed beside her. Sophie leaned against his shoulder and sipped the wine. He kissed her hair.

Just then Ty's mobile rang. "Damn." He picked it up. "OK. Call me if you have to. Bye." It was short and abrupt. He smiled at her. "Just my daughter, baby." He did not elaborate on the situation. Then he was beside her again and pulling her down towards him. He went into her again, and she felt herself on edge as he slid into her body. Already Sophie was quite sore from that first encounter, but she was very attracted to him physically, and she realised that she felt considerably more for him already. This time he pushed her knees up to her shoulders, and this enabled him to go into her deeply. Sophie cried out. He was hitting her cervix, and it was like being stabbed with a blunt knife. Sophie pulled away, but she was pinned down with his greater weight.

"Please—oh please, stop. That really hurts. I'm sorry, but I can't handle it like that."

Ty pulled away and lowered her legs. He grinned at her. Then he lay back on the bed with his head on the pillow and pulled her onto him. "Here, baby, you come ride me." Sophie slid down, carefully, onto the beautiful black thing that she both wanted and feared. In this position she could control the depth, and she thrust her hips and slid up and down on him. He looked into her eyes and groaned with sincere pleasure. Sophie's actions grew harder. Ty put his hands on her buttocks and pulled her into him. Sophie felt another orgasm building, and she went harder and harder until she cried out and the waves of pure heaven gripped her belly.

Ty suddenly said, "Oh God, oh my God!" and began to thrust harder and harder until he caught his breath and then lay back, smiling and sweating. Sophie sank down onto his huge chest and kissed his neck and mouth. She put her hand up and played with the thick gold chain around his dark neck. He stroked her hair and kissed it.

"You OK, baby?"

"Oh hell, yes. That was great."

"Think you can handle the big guy?"

"I may get used to it—but it's scary." She giggled, and Ty grinned again and kissed her.

They lay quietly together for a while, and Ty's breathing made her think that he was almost asleep. Then he sat up. "Want another drink, baby?"

"Yes, please." They sat on the bed and drank. Then they smoked, leaning out of the window, as smoking was, naturally, banned. Ty pointed out his silver BMW sports car in the park nearby. Sophie looked. It was impressive. She felt that she ought to ask Ty what he did for a living and about his life set-up. But maybe this would just be a one-night stand, and they would part and never meet again. They drank silently. Then Ty kissed her again. She kissed his face and worked down to his chest and belly. Then she lifted up the massive penis and ran her tongue over it. Ty moaned softly and shivered. Sophie took the thing in her mouth and slowly sucked and licked it. She could hardly fit it in her mouth; she was terrified that it might choke her. Ty held her hair and moved her head down further, and then he began to push into her mouth, hard. Sophie just managed to stay with the action. She pulled away and went down on his testicles, sucking and licking them whilst she took his penis in her hand and rubbed it. Ty was loving this. Sophie kept it up for another twenty minutes, until Ty began to groan, stiffen, and beg her to take it in her mouth again. Sophie did, and she sucked as hard as she could, trying to prevent the thing from choking her. When she knew he was coming, she pulled her mouth away and held his penis whilst he spurted sperm into her hand. She was amazed at just how much he produced. He smiled and kissed her.

Sophie went to the bathroom and washed her hands. When she went back, Ty was lying there, holding his arms out to her. She rolled into his shoulder and lay there while he kissed her hair. He said, "Thank you," very quietly. She kissed him, and then she rolled away, tired. Ty snuggled into her back and held her tight, kissing her neck. Soon they were sliding into sleep. Sophie felt safe, and warm, and needed in those large, strong arms.

Suddenly Ty's mobile rang again. He leapt up to answer it. "OK. I'll be there in about fifteen minutes." He turned to Sophie and sighed. "Sorry, baby. I have to go pick up my daughter. She's a teenager. Been out somewhere. Can't get home." He shrugged and grinned. "I'll come back first thing tomorrow morning, baby. It was really good. We must meet again. You sleep. I'll see you soon." Then he was gone.

Sophie lay dozing. She was sore, but she had just had sex as she had never had it before—except for Ben. Ben had loved her, and she had loved Ben, and it had been lovemaking, not just sex. But this Jamaican guy was—what? She knew nothing about him—nothing—but she had fallen for him. For what? His size? What was that, really? He was gentle, good in bed, and his smile slayed her. Then there was the voice, and the smell and colour of his skin. She fell asleep still thinking about it all.

Sophie awoke early. Ty was coming back. She showered, dressed, and put on her make-up, ready for him. Then she made herself a strong coffee and tidied up the room. There was a small smear of blood on the sheets from when Ty had first entered her. She was not surprised. She sat drinking her coffee, smoked a cigarette out of the window, and waited.

Ty did not come, and neither did he call. She texted him but got no reply. She called, but her call was cut off. She called three more times, and each call rang until it went to voicemail. Sophie was faintly annoyed. Why could he not simply text her a reason for not coming back as he had promised? She packed up her belongings and took them to the car. She drove home quickly. She knew Enrico was never back from his fuck buddy until at least ten thirty. She parked on the driveway and ran in with her bag. She took it upstairs and unpacked it. Then she went down to the kitchen, made a coffee, poured it down the sink, and then stood the cup on the draining board. She turned all the lights off, opened the curtains, let the cat in and fed it, put the mail on the dining room table, and then texted Enrico that she was popping out for some shopping. The car engine would be hot, so she needed to go out so that it would seem normal. She had, in any case, things to get from the supermarket. She drove to town and parked in the Morrisons car park. Then she texted Ty again. She sat waiting, but there was no reply. She tried calling, but again, either the call was cut off or it rang until it went to voicemail. She thought, *He just used me. He probably has a whole harem of women. That wasn't his daughter. It was just an excuse to get away.* Sophie went for her shopping, and then she drove back home and got on with life. She tried to forget Ty.

Two weeks later, when she was at work, Sophie received a call from Ty. He wanted to meet her again. He seemed slightly annoyed that she was far away at work. She explained that she would be back after Christmas; she had to stay and work. Nobody else would, due to the vile niece. It meant extra wages, so Sophie was staying. She wouldn't celebrate Christmas with Enrico, as he did not want to acknowledge Christmas. He was not a social creature but rather a lone drinker. He preferred to get nastily inebriated on his own. Then he would call people very late at night to insult and bore them.

Ty was anxious for another meeting. Sophie told him she would arrange one when she returned. He continued to text her daily with "Morning, baby." Then she would get the occasional "Hey, baby" or "What you doing, hun?" But there was little real conversation. Nor did he reply to her texts, and if they started any kind of a conversation, he would just disappear in the middle. Sophie found him very irritating—but she was fascinated by him and unable to forget his dark, handsome face, and that smile, and that voice …

Christmas was grim at her workplace. The inebriated, domineering niece ensured that nobody enjoyed the season of goodwill. Sophie could not wait to return to Suffolk. The station was freezing. The train was packed, but Sophie had booked in advance so was assured of her seat all the way to Norwich, where Enrico picked her up in the Merc. He seemed pleased to see her. This might be, she thought, because he had run out of Bacardi and expected her to stock him up. She texted Ty and was surprised when he replied immediately. They arranged a date. Sophie told Enrico that she was going out on a girl's night with her friends, as she had been away for Christmas. He seemed quite happy with this. He was beginning to be possessive and controlling, seeming to think that Sophie should obtain his permission and approval for everything she did.

Sophie booked a hotel, showered, dressed, made herself up, and set off in the SUV with a bottle of vodka and some lemonade. Ty was late, but he was pleased to see her again. This time he was less gentle, however, and seemed not to want to indulge in foreplay. After he had taken her on her back, and allowed her to suck his penis and testicles, Ty pushed her over onto her knees facing the pillows. He held her tightly by her hips and then went into her from behind, quite hard. It really hurt Sophie, and she cried out. This just seemed to inflame Ty, and he went in very deeply and hard. He was hitting Sophie's cervix viciously, and she pleaded with him to ease off. But Ty was nearing his climax, and he just went harder and deeper. He grunted and gasped as he came, and despite the pain, Sophie found herself coming with him. He lay across her back for a few minutes and then pulled away.

"Oh my God," Ty said. "Not again."

Sophie turned around. "What is it?"

"Look. Blood everywhere."

Sophie looked. There was blood all over the sheets. She went into the shower room and cleaned herself up.

"Don't worry, baby. This happens to me all the time." He was laughing, but Sophie was sore and upset. They drank, smoked out of the window, and then lay holding hands. Sophie wanted to ask him so very many important things, but the words didn't come. She knew she was falling under this man's spell, and she felt she was on dangerous ground. But she just could not ask him all the things she should ask. They fell asleep. He slept with his arms tightly around her. His mobile rang often during the evening and late at night. He just turned the calls off. Sophie wondered if he turned her calls off like that without even looking at who was calling.

Ty left early the next morning after receiving a call that he took in the bathroom. He sounded angry. He kissed Sophie briefly and left. She got up and soaked the sheets in the bath to wash out as much of the blood as she could. Then she drove home. Enrico was sitting with his coffee in the living room.

"Have a good night out, then?"

"Yes, terrific."

"All the girls there?"

"Yes, all of them."

"Funny thing, that. I went to town to get some Bacardi last night, and I ran into Sally and Brenda. They didn't know anything about this party. Haven't seen you for weeks. So, where were you, then?" His face was not pleasant.

"I went out somewhere, with someone—and because you make such a lot of fuss about everything I do and refuse to let me live my own life, I decided not to tell you. It's none of your business, anyway."

"You're just a bloody liar! Who were you with, some man?"

"What if I was? You go to your fuck buddy, don't you? My sex life is my business."

"Not while you're in my house, it's not! You tell me what you do, and where you go, and who you go with." He was red-faced and breathless.

Too many cigarettes and too much Bacardi and anger, thought Sophie. So she told him. He would probably follow her anyway.

"You've slept with a fucking nigger? Are you crazy? You'll catch something nasty. And he'll be after money. They all are. What does he do for a living? Where does he live? Bet he's got wives and kids everywhere—here and back in Jamaica. You're a bloody idiot. You'll regret this!"

"I know that he's Jamaican, was born there and raised in New Jersey—" Sophie began. Enrico snorted. He stamped out of the room and upstairs, and Sophie heard the shower running. She'd known that Enrico would react like this. He was possessive, domineering, and controlling. He could go to hell! She was going to get somewhere to move to as soon as she could. Enrico would be going to Spain as soon as he could sell the house. He had planned to go to Fuerteventura but had cousins in Spain and had changed his plans.She wanted out, her own space, a home for Freddie and perhaps somewhere for Ty to visit her. She just had to tolerate Enrico's drinking and his unpleasant personality a bit longer. Now that his true character had emerged, she wondered how she could have felt anything for him.

Ty texted Sophie daily. He seemed quite genuinely concerned about the bleeding and asked Sophie whether she had visited a doctor. Sophie had, and she'd discovered that it was a childbirth scar that had torn under the pressure from Ty's oversized member. The doctor had given her oestrogen pessaries to insert every day for a fortnight and then twice a week continuously, to keep the tissues supple and able to give. Ty's concern went on for a few days longer. After that Sophie received brief good mornings, and then Ty texted her only from time to time. Then there was silence. Sophie just got on with her search for a home and kept working hard. Then, one day she was lying on the bed and thought of Ty, so she picked up her phone to text him. She was surprised to find that he had texted her three times over two weeks. She texted back. "Hi. Only just saw your texts. How are you?"

An hour later he replied that he was on holiday in Egypt. He sent a photo of him posing in front of a troupe of camels and looking very laid back and happy. Sophie noticed that the person taking the shot was a woman; her shadow was thrown across the sand in front of Ty.

A week later Ty texted her again. What was she doing?

Sophie told him that she was looking for somewhere to move to. What was he doing?

"Packing," he replied, "to come home and fuck you again."

She replied that she didn't want just fucking; she wanted lovemaking. Ty said he could do that with no problem. After he returned, he texted quite often, complaining that she was only six miles away from him but was unable to see him. He claimed he wanted her badly. Sophie had explained about Enrico to Ty and had emphasised that she had to live in his house. Ty didn't mention Sophie coming to see him, but Sophie had formed the impression that Ty was a single parent, raising his daughter alone, and that he didn't want his sleeping partners around the house.

By this time, Enrico had sold his VW camper, a prized possession. He had imagined it to be worth a considerable amount of money, but like the house, it had been badly neglected and needed attention. He had to settle for less money. Sophie imagined that Enrico would use this money to repay the people he had borrowed from over the last few months. He owed her the most. But when she asked for her money, Enrico simply told her she would get it all back when he sold the house. She later discovered that he hadn't paid back his other friends, either. They were married couples who had lent him small amounts they'd put away, believing his promise to repay them when his camper was sold. Instead Enrico announced that he was flying to Spain "on business." Sophie knew full well that this was a blatant lie. He had no money and was in no position to look for any kind of property. In any case, he could have browsed online for what he wanted. No, this was just a holiday, a break paid for by other people for the selfish, hedonistic, spoilt guinea brat.

Sophie did not care a damn. She was getting rid of him for just over a week, and she'd be able to bring Ty into the house. Enrico left at six o'clock two nights later, zooming off to Gatwick for a night flight. Sophie waited until he texted her that he had handed his car over to the secure parking and was on the shuttle bus to the terminal. Then she called Ty, and he drove over. He backed his silver sports car into the hedge so that it was hidden from the road. The immediate neighbours were abroad. Ty came in with his bottle of vodka. He had brought food, and he cooked her jerk chicken and rice and peas. They ate, loaded the dishwasher, and then sat watching a video and drinking and smoking. Sophie went up and showered, and soon Ty followed her up. He was very gentle with her, taking his body weight on his forearms and going into her very carefully. He did not go in too deeply. Sophie loved being able to look into his eyes as he climaxed with her, very passionately but with great restraint. Afterwards they slept close together.

In the morning, Sophie took up coffee. She offered to cook breakfast, but Ty said he never, ever ate that meal. He showered and then told her he had to go. Sophie was disappointed. She had expected him to make the most of this opportunity to be with her. It was the same the whole week. Some days he didn't turn up or even call. Sophie was less than happy. She wanted to tackle Ty about it, but somehow she was unable to. One evening, as they sat in front of the television, he turned to her. "Baby, I need to tell you—"

Sophie's heart sank. He looked unhappy. "What is it, Ty? Are you leaving me?"

"No, hun. It's just that … I'm married."

"Married? But—"

"To my daughter's godmother, baby. I owe her £500 for doing it—it was to help me stay in this country."

"Oh—I understand." Sophie was relieved. It was an immigration thing. "You don't live with her, then?"

"No, hun, but …" Again Ty hesitated. "But I actually live with my daughter's mum. She's my ex. Nothing at all between us, of course, but I need a home, she works long hours, and I do the housework and look after my daughter when I can. It's just a convenience. Don't worry—we were finished ages ago."

Sophie was relieved but at the same time rather concerned about the continuous baggage that Ty was dragging into their relationship. Sophie knew that she couldn't leave this man. His body sent her to heaven. He was young and killingly handsome. She wanted to just use him for what he could give her, but her nature was such that she was unable to sustain this as a sexual playground. She felt a great deal for Ty. Deep inside her head the warning bells were ringing loudly. Ty was secretive, casual, unreliable, and maybe not too honest. He had told her quite openly that he was broke, but Sophie didn't know whether this was just a temporary thing that would be remedied soon.

Sophie had been changed by Ella's tragic death. Nothing in her was the same as it had been—except maybe her ability to love men who were harmful to her, dangerous, unpredictable, and unstable. She was vulnerable and fragile, easy prey for the unscrupulous. Half of her knew this, but the rest of her was just drifting. She was shutting out reality as she shut out the daily pain of the loss of her beautiful girl. And she was yearning to find Ben again, aching to find the physical bliss she had gloried in before her life had been plunged into blackness and loss all those years ago.

Except for Ty's disappearances and silences, the week was quite wonderful for Sophie. She did not miss Enrico for one second. It came to an end all too soon, and she had to kiss Ty goodbye and stand watching his big silver car turn out of the driveway and disappear up the road. She went back into the house and tidied up. She cleaned the kitchen, bathroom, living room, and most particularly the bedroom, stripping the sheets off and piling everything into the washing machine. She expunged every trace of Ty, every clue that Enrico might pick up on.

Ty texted her briefly every morning. Sophie came to welcome the "Morning, baby," and "Morning, hun" that greeted her daily. Sometimes she heard little other than that that for days. Eventually she came to recognise Ty's pattern of communication. He would ask her what she was up to; if she was OK, he would build up a link to carefully and cleverly lead to her wanting to see him, his half-promising to meet her, and then his letting her know, "I need gas money, hun." She would always pay some small amount into his bank. He did not always turn up. Sophie let that go. Then one day he said that he needed to go to London to get some money together to pay the instalment on his car. Sophie had not known that he did not own it completely, but it was an expensive car, so that did not seem unusual. She asked how much he needed for the instalment. He told her three hundred and twenty pounds. Sophie found herself transferring the amount from her bank account into his. She already had his bank details, as she had been giving him small amounts for fuel. She texted him that she had done this and got his much used "OMG, baby." She felt good about this. But she also felt concerned that she was giving him so much money, money that she already knew she would never get back again. One day Ty had met Sophie at the lay-by where she would drive to, leave her SUV, and then go in his car. Usually they went to the nearby McDonald's, where Sophie bought two coffees to drink in the car. They opened the car doors, smoked, and talked. When Sophie told Ty that she was looking for her own home, he hinted that he would move in with her, as he was far from happy with his present set-up. Sophie's heart leapt at the prospect of sharing her life with this handsome, virile man—despite all the misgivings she had about him and his too-complicated life. They drove back to the lay-by and sat there, Ty holding her hand. He looked at her directly. His deep-brown eyes held her. "Baby, I need to ask you something."

Sophie felt alarmed. Ty looked serious. "OK—yes, what is it Ty?"

He hesitated. "Do you love me, baby?"

Sophie was suddenly shy, unsure. "I—I think I loved you from the moment I met you, Ty. But I couldn't say anything because—well—you're so young and good-looking. You're too young to love me, baby. And I am a lot older than you are—you do realise this, Ty. I'm thirty years older than you. It's a hell of a lot! But yes, I do love you. I love you a lot, Ty Benton."

Ty kissed her on her mouth with that soft, sweet mouth of his. "And I love you too, baby. Age really doesn't matter a damn. You're like a 40-year-old in bed, and you don't seem like your age in any way. It honestly doesn't matter to me at all, baby. Would you do anything to help me, hun?"

"Well, yes, if I could, baby."

"Baby, I need your help."

"Help? Are you in some sort of trouble?"

"No, baby, not trouble, but I need to go see my son for his twenty-first birthday."

Sophie was slowly learning that Ty had been a prolific breeder; he had many children. Each time she saw or heard from Ty there seemed to be yet another one. She knew that he had a daughter by the ex he lived with, a son in London, and another young daughter by an Italian woman in Florida. That, Sophie thought, was three. But it seemed she was to learn about another one. She now discovered that Ty had not just a son but also his sister living in Antigua with Ty's ex-wife. When Sophie worked out the ages of the various children, she realised that his first son had been born, out of wedlock, only weeks before his first legitimate son in Antigua. And the daughter he lived with now had been born within months of his legitimate daughter in Antigua. Sophie thought, *This is a real mess. This man seems to have no sense of responsibility for his children.* But she heard that Ty was proud of and loved all his children. She suspected that there might be more that she hadn't been told about.

"OK, baby. What, exactly, do you want from me?"

"Baby, I desperately need the money to pay my plane ticket and to get Jamari a present. I'll have to get Samantha something too, as I don't see them that often."

"OK, Ty. How much are we talking about?"

"I hate to ask, hun—"

"How much, Ty?"

"About a thousand, baby."

Sophie pursed her lips and frowned. "I can't do that right away, Ty. I have to earn it first." *Perhaps just this once*, she thought. *Just this special occasion, but no more! I can't establish a very bad habit.*

"OK, hun. But as soon as you can, OK?"

Sophie promised that she would do her best. She kissed Ty goodbye and drove back to Enrico.

The following day, she took the three trains she had to take to get to Lincolnshire to the job she so hated. At first Enrico had driven her there and picked her up again, but that had stopped as things soured between them, and Ty's arrival on the scene had caused an even bigger rift. Sophie endured a long fortnight at work. Ty texted her erratically, usually to nag her about the money he needed. He kept dangling the carrot of moving in with her when she found her own home. Then he texted her asking if she wanted him to pick her up from work and drive her home. Sophie was delighted and accepted the offer. But it had conditions attached. Sophie would, naturally, pay for the petrol. That would be quite costly, as the sports saloon had a thirsty 4-litre engine. On top of this, Ty wanted her to pay for his accommodation the night before she left.

When Enrico had taken her to work, he had always got up at six in the morning, driven her to work, and then driven the four hours' journey straight back again. When he'd picked her up, he'd got up at six again, driven up there, and picked her up just after ten thirty. They'd stopped for a strong coffee and a break, and they'd got home by about three in the afternoon. When Sophie asked Ty, over the phone, why he could not do that, he became sullen and difficult. Sophie told him that even a Travelodge in that area was expensive. Ty said he could not drive all that distance in one day. If she didn't want him to go there, that was fine. He had offered, but she was being unreasonable and selfish. Sophie gave in. Ty booked himself a room for £68, which was not too bad—but Sophie had looked online and seen reasonable rooms for a lot less. She nevertheless transferred the money for the room and the petrol. On the morning of Sophie's departure, Ty's car purred into the driveway. Ty got out and swaggered up to Sophie, who was waiting with her luggage in the doorway. The other staff looked on, and one of them mouthed a "Wow" at the tall, handsome man as he kissed Sophie and put her cases in the boot of the impressive silver saloon. They drove back to the hotel to pick up Ty's case. Sophie wondered why he hadn't brought it to the house with him, and then she found out. Ty wanted her, and he took her on the rumpled bed, greedily and passionately. Sophie wanted him, too. She had missed him desperately. They lay spent, hand in hand. Out in the car, they had a cigarette. They stopped off for a coffee a little later and then sped off towards Suffolk. They stopped in a lay-by as the afternoon progressed, so that Ty could doze. Then he woke, kissed her, and felt her breasts through her blouse. They kissed passionately, and Ty became very aroused. He turned off the main road and drove through back roads until he found a remote wooded track; he drove up it and parked. He kissed her again deeply, his excitement growing. He pushed back the seat she was in as far as it would go and knelt in the footwell. He pulled her skirt up and her pants down and threw them on the floor. Then he went down on her and sucked and licked her clitoris until she was desperate for him.

"Fuck me, Ty—fuck me, please!" He was in her quickly, which was painful, but she wanted him so very badly. Soon he was thrusting frenziedly. He had opened her blouse, pulled away her bra, and was sucking her nipples as he rammed into her. Sophie whimpered and gasped as her climax built, and Ty breathed heavily as he, too, neared his orgasm. They reached the peak of their pleasure together.

Ty continued to thrust slowly as he filled her with his seed; then he lay on her breasts, his breathing slowing. He kissed her nose and grinned as he pulled himself up. "Thanks, baby. That was really good. You OK?" Sophie just smiled. She cleaned herself up, and they both leaned back and had a smoke.

They returned to the motorway and stopped for a coffee. Soon they were back in Suffolk, and Ty dropped Sophie a little way from Enrico's house. He would not go any nearer. Sophie thanked him and kissed him. She got out of the car and dragged her cases to the house. Ty texted her soon afterwards. Had she got that money for his trip? He had to book his flight. Sophie transferred just over fifteen hundred pounds to Ty's account. He texted, "Thanks, baby. I love you." Then she heard no more for almost a week.

This became the pattern of her life with Ty. Sophie was sleepwalking through life. She was tired, deeply tired. She needed a home for herself and Freddie. Her job was stressful and demanding, and her health was suffering. She knew that she should stop bankrolling this man. She knew that she was being used, that he did not really love her, that he had another life with someone else—maybe with several others—and that the way he earned what he did earn was not totally legal. He was not honest or dependable. But still she dreamt of him living with her. Then she would be his woman, his queen. Sophie had to push reality away in order to survive, and she struggled on.

Ty flew to Antigua. He kept in touch with Sophie, mainly because he needed still more money. A birthday party for his son, a car hire—it was endless. Sophie gave it to him. She had gone online and found cottages to rent in Antigua for very reasonable prices, but Ty had sneered and called them roach motels. "They're not safe, baby. There's a lot of crime. You don't know about these things."

He also wanted clothes. She had, unwisely, let him know that she had an account with a mail-order firm. He wheedled, and she let him order a couple of pairs of trainers. But then he needed T-shirts, and shorts—and so it went on. Soon she had added a rather large amount to her account. It was just another expense she had taken on for him.

Then Sophie found her cottage. It was a tiny, sweet place. It had only one door, the front door; a living room; a quite large kitchen; a winding, weirdly dangerous staircase leading to a large bedroom that would be Sophie's; a tiny bathroom; and a really tiny bedroom with a walk-in cupboard almost as big as the actual room. *This will be Freddie's room*, thought Sophie. The cottage had a small garden, which delighted Sophie. It was situated in a better part of the town, in a tiny lane running between two roads. It was what Sophie could afford. Furthermore, she knew the tenant who was leaving and had been recommended to the private landlady by this tenant. She thus had no agent's fees to pay, just the usual one month's rent in advance. She was over the moon.

Sophie had absolutely nothing except the few bits she and Enrico had brought back by van from her daughter's home in France. She had a new table-and-chairs set, a dishwasher, and a patio set, which she left with Enrico, as she could not, at that point, fit them all in the cottage. A friend had a van, and he and Sophie's grandson James helped her move her few bits, a washing machine and tumble dryer, her microwave, the second-hand fridge she had bought, and her personal effects. Soon Sophie acquired a second-hand settee, which opened up into a double bed. When she'd first moved, she'd only had a blow-up camping double bed, on which she and Ty made love when he came round. He never stayed long. When he'd first arrived and looked at Sophie's little home, he'd had a look on his face that upset Sophie. She realised instantly that he had expected her to be in something that equalled Enrico's home and the area he lived in. Clearly this cottage was not good enough for Ty. How could he expect something better, she wondered, when he was so broke and always pleading for money? Sophie was hurt.

Ty finally came round and agreed to spend a night with Sophie. She simply could not understand why he'd been unable to before this. She had thought that once she had her own little private nest he would be with her often and would stay overnight. Ty would not provide a reason. He had a very clever and exasperating way of avoiding questions he did not want to answer. Ty was hungry this night, so Sophie ordered in Chinese takeaway. Ty picked at the food and simply threw away most of it. Sophie would have saved and reheated it, to save money. Then Ty started to drink vodka as if it were going out of fashion, throwing it back mixed with lemonade. Sophie was dismayed. Ty was clumsy and rough when he eventually made love to her. He insisted on her lying across the sofa bed whilst he went into her doggy style; she cried out when he rammed into her. He did not ease up but pulled her head backwards, holding onto her hair. Sophie was frightened but also highly stimulated. Ty was hurting her, but she was reaching a climax. She reached a tremendous orgasm, and Ty came with her, grunting and thrusting deeply into her body. He laid his head on her back whilst his breathing slowed, and then he pulled away. Sophie turned around and saw Ty looking at the sheet.

"You're bleeding again, baby."

"Oh God—I thought I'd got over that!" Sophie was distressed.

"You really came then, hun. Big time. But it's still a bit too much for you, baby."

"You need to be a bit gentler, Ty. You go in so hard, baby."

"Sorry, baby." He kissed her and held her briefly. Sophie stripped the sheet off and put it straight into the washing machine. She went up to the toilet and cleaned herself up. The bleeding had stopped, but she was very sore. She went down with a clean sheet and sorted the bed out. Ty pulled her to him. He was still drinking hard. Sophie drank a fair amount of the good red wine she had bought.

"Do you like my little cottage?" she asked him.

Ty shrugged. "It's a bit small, hun, more like an apartment."

"Well, it's big enough for me." Sophie was defensive. Ty quickly changed the subject by switching on the new television that Sophie had rented. It was a large smart model. Ty flicked through the channels until he found a gangster film with non-stop gunfire and bloodshed, which he settled on. Sophie put on her robe and went to the kitchen to make a coffee. She had had enough wine for one night.

A little later, Sophie snuggled into him. "Ty."

"Yes, baby."

"You're supposed to be moving in with me, hun. You promised—"

"Yes, I will, baby. Next time I pick you up from work."

Sophie was tired. She settled into bed and was soon dozing. Ty sat watching the television. Soon Sophie was asleep. She woke later to silence and Ty cuddled into her back. She slept again but was awakened several times by his loud snoring. She just smiled and rolled him over, and he stopped for a while. The next morning he woke her with a kiss and parted her thighs. She was on edge.

"Please be careful, Ty. I'm terribly sore, baby." He kissed her again.

"I will, hun. Relax." And he was gentle, and he did not go in far. He moved slowly and watched her face as she screwed up her eyes and moaned with pleasure. She opened her eyes and looked into his brown, beautiful eyes. He smiled at her and then he closed his eyes, and they climaxed together. Even then he was very careful not to go into her too hard. After he was finished pumping sperm into her waiting womb, he kissed her face and slid out of her. He held her tightly and lovingly. Sophie held onto those moments, and the feelings she had, and Ty's sweetness. She knew that she loved him enough to endure anything. This was her man, her world. She could not leave him, although she knew she should do so. Ty got up and made them both coffee. He put the sofa bed back and helped Sophie tidy up. They sat for a while, Sophie leaning on Ty's shoulder and drinking in the sweet smell of his ebony skin. Then he was up and leaving her. They kissed. She went out and watched the car pulling away. Then she busied herself with living.

As he would be leaving England and would not be able to take much furniture, Enrico had given Sophie a king-sized bed for her room and a single bed for Freddie's room. Her friend with the van brought them to the cottage that week and helped Sophie assemble them. Sophie went online and got herself a television cabinet, a very large pine wardrobe, a computer desk, two bedside cabinets, a chest of drawers, and a nest of tables. Her grandson James helped her to assemble them all, which was quite a task. She also acquired other pieces from sale adverts and friends. She rented a smart new electric cooker and bought a second-hand chest freezer. She then bought new bedding for both beds. After all, Ty had promised to move in with her after her next work assignment. She cleaned and tidied her little cottage. The working fortnight was long and hard. Sophie longed for Ty. She paid for his petrol and for a hotel. The morning of her escape arrived. Ty picked her up and they drove back, Ty holding her hand in the car. For the first time after a very long and heartbreaking blackness, Sophie felt real happiness. They arrived at the cottage, and Ty went in with Sophie's case and his own small suitcase. Sophie kissed him. "Oh, baby, you're moving in with me! I'm so damned happy. At last! I'm going to try and look after you so well. You'll see, hun!" Ty stood in the doorway of the cottage, smoking.

Sophie went into the kitchen to make them both a coffee. When she returned, she saw Ty leaving, holding his case. "Baby? Where are you going?"

"Just gotta sort some stuff out, hun. I'll be back in about two hours."

"OK, baby." She kissed him. Ty turned and waved.

The evening drew on. Darkness fell. There was no text from Ty. She texted him. No reply. She called him. Again and again the call went to voicemail. Then the calls were cut off abruptly. Sophie sat on the settee in the dark, hot tears rolling down her face. She understood a lot of things then. Ty had rejected her. He had lied to her. He had never intended to live with her. He was using her. He did not love her. But she also understood that, despite her rising anger and her terrible pain, she was tied to him. She could not escape his cruel beauty, his sexuality, and his youth—and there was something else that she could not explain to herself. She was weak and unable to pull away— to tell him to go to hell, to leave, and not to be enticed back again. He had spun his web with stealth and cunning. Sophie was in the middle of this web, paralysed as she watched her own destruction, powerless to fight back. But right now, she was angry. Terribly angry. She had been cut to the soul by his cold, uncaring lies and deceit. The night crept by. Sophie drank a few glasses of wine, and then she crept up to bed. She lay shivering and crying until the ghost-grey dawn pulled her into the stark reality of her life, her life with Ty.

Sophie cried out inside her head: *Oh, Ella, my darling, baby Ella. I miss you so much! Your blue eyes, your beautiful long, wavy hair. The sound of your voice. Your laughter. Your energy. You have taken away my life with you. But I must go on, for your lovely boy.* Ty had broken her heart, and she was in terrible pain. Grief was ripping her soul apart. As always, the depth of her sadness dragged up searingly hurtful repressed feelings. She sobbed until she could hardly breathe. Then she struggled into wakefulness and rose, exhausted, to face another day.

Ty never stayed. He always had to go somewhere else and do something else. There was always so much going on in his life. He was constantly stressed out, and this stress was spilling over into Sophie's life and beginning to wear her down. There was no happiness in Ty. She tried humour, but he seemed not to understand it. He seemed to understand very little of what she said to him—except when money was needed. He kept insisting that he couldn't handle long texts—he couldn't be bothered to read them. He said he preferred phone calls and talking to Sophie. But Sophie called him often, giving up when he never picked up. When she tried to contact him on WhatsApp, she could see that he was online for hours, but he ignored her texts, so she gave up that, too. When she tackled him about it, Ty told her that he had been talking to his family in Jamaica and it had been important. He often became angry that she dared to question his failure to contact her. He had a busy life. He did the same with his own family, he told her, ignoring texts for weeks because he couldn't be bothered.

However, if Sophie was busy and did not reply to his texts or at least acknowledge them, or if she did not pick up his calls, then it was a very different matter. He became very annoyed. As time went on, he began getting angry. He accused her of sleeping with other men when she was unable to answer his texts because she was busy working, or sleeping, or her phone was on charge. Her phone was beginning to slow down and run out of charge more quickly, and Sophie could not afford another one—for the same reason that she could not afford anything else. Ty was taking everything he could wheedle out of her with promises, and stories, and lies, and half-truths. And Sophie loved him so stupidly, and so deeply, and so hopelessly. The hurt still tearing at her from the deaths of her most loved ones was blinding her to reality, and her torn, fragile soul was being abused and ripped apart.

2015 limped on, and nothing really changed in the relationship. Ty had sold his iPhone for extra cash when in Antigua, despite the large amounts that Sophie had given him, and he was making very obvious noises about his need of a decent new phone. Sophie bought him a cheap good one. She simply could not afford the things that Ty seemed to take for granted as his right to own. He seemed pleased with the phone, but very soon he began to complain about aspects of it that had apparently gone wrong. Then it seemed it had died on him. Sophie scraped together the money for another, slightly better, phone. Later, that one disappeared too. She was never told why. Sometime afterwards, she learned that the first one had not gone wrong at all. Ty had given it to his daughter. The second one had also been a gift to a family member when Ty was on one of his many trips to Jamaica.

Ty's visits to Sophie were infrequent and quickly over. He came for sex and for money. He told her in texts that he loved her and could not live without her, but his words and his actions did not match. Sophie was servile. She dreaded losing Ty, so she gave in, apologised to him, and endured neglect, insults, and lies. Then one day, tired, stressed, and infuriated by his constant failure to appear or contact her for days on end, Sophie snapped. She texted him, saying that he was just using her for sex and for money, and that she had reached the end of her tether. Ty became angry, whingy, and self-righteous. Sophie gave in, and everything resumed as before. This happened several times, and the day came when Sophie really had had too much. Her job was exhausting her, physically and mentally. The financial burden of Ty's needs was dragging her down. She desperately needed a break, a holiday, new clothes—a lot of things. Ty was ignoring her. He had not so much as texted her for over a week.

Unable to sleep and miserable, Sophie texted Ty. "OK, baby. I think that you want to say goodbye but you don't know how to do it. I may be wrong, but my gut tells me that you don't want or need me any more. I've served my purpose. You said you loved me and wanted to live with me, but your actions tell me something else. You said you were scared of being hurt, but you let me love you very deeply. I've stood by you and cared for you and helped you, but I feel you pulling away. Tell me I'm wrong or tell me the truth and say goodbye."

Immediately Ty replied. "You are so wrong, hun." It was a phrase Sophie was to see over and over. Then her phone rang, and it was Ty. He was pleading, desperate, passionate. "Baby, I really do love you so much. I couldn't have got this far without you. Don't walk out on me now. Just stay with me. Work with me. Things are gonna be so different soon. You'll see, hun. I have things I must do. Soon we will be together. I know you haven't been treated right, my hunny, and I'm so very sorry for that. Believe me, I love you very much. I can't live without you—" And so it went on. He was almost in tears.

Sophie relented. Her soft, caring heart melted. She wanted him to want her in the way she loved and missed him. Hearing his voice and his words made it all so different. She had been unfair, impatient, selfish. She was pressuring and stressing this man, the man she loved so very much. They exchanged loving words. Sophie fell asleep. She was tightly enmeshed, captive and helpless.

Ty continued to bleed funds from Sophie. He told her continually, "I have no money for gas, baby, or I'd come and see you." And Sophie gave him ten pounds here and fifteen pounds there, although often he didn't turn up. Once he was supposed to travel up to Lincolnshire and pick her up from work. She had paid for a motel for him along with a large sum for fuel. On the night before and then the morning of the departure, Sophie heard nothing. She called Ty, and eventually he picked up.

"Where are you, Ty? I'm ready to leave."

"Leave where, baby?"

"Work, baby. You're picking me up—aren't you?"

"Oh, hun, it's so rough and windy. I can't drive in this." There had been a storm the previous day and the wind was still strong.

"Then why the hell didn't you let me know yesterday, Ty! I can't get a cheap ticket now—" Sophie hung up. She was furious and very hurt. Usually she bought her ticket online in advance, for a much reduced fare. Now it would cost a huge amount. She called a taxi to take her to the station; she was not at all happy when she had to pay out nearly £85 for her train fare. The most she had previously paid was £30, and often she only paid £15 or £20. On top of this, Ty had the fuel money of £60, and she had paid out £50 for his overnight accommodation. All was totally wasted—nearly £200 down the drain! She never again asked Ty to pick her up from work.

Sophie wanted Ty to go to France with her to visit her family. She explained that he could drive directly onto the ferry at Portsmouth, off at the other end, and then onto the motorway. This did not please Ty. He wanted to fly there and hire a big upmarket car. Sophie went online and found a firm that flew to the area she needed. The fare would be reasonable, but the car hire was extortionate. Meanwhile, Ty told her that he would need a visa, as he was not an EU citizen. Sophie gave him £80 to get it. Eventually she realised that Ty simply didn't want to go. In any case, she could not afford Ty's way of getting there. By ferry would have been affordable and easier. The idea just faded away. Sophie had lost the money for the visa. She knew that. She also realised that Ty had used the situation as an excuse to take yet more money from her. Slowly Sophie was losing heart, but she stubbornly hung on to her love for this charming, handsome crook. She knew that she was being duped and used in every kind of way. She felt herself being whirled into a dark place and unable to fight her way back. But she told herself, *I love this man.* And somehow this seemed to justify everything that he did and said.

In May 2015, Ty was harassing her for money to go to Jamaica. He said that his father had gone back there to die, having been in the States with Ty's brother before that. He was due to have surgery, and Ty wanted to be there in case his father didn't make it. That made sense to Sophie, and she tried desperately to raise the cash for Ty to go. He was still pressuring her for funds for his car, which seemed to constantly need work. Sophie was already paying his car instalment monthly, which was over £300. Thank God, she thought, that it was not winter time, so she didn't have to shell out a lot for prepayment on gas and electricity meters. She had to juggle her bills to help Ty, and her income wasn't regular. She was well paid, but sometimes, after working nearly three weeks, she would be laid off for the next three weeks. Her client's niece would engage her for a period, Sophie would pay for her rail ticket and arrive, only to be told a week later that the niece wanted to introduce another member to the team. Would Sophie mind going home for four days and returning afterwards? These new recruits never stayed, or if they did, they never lasted long. Sophie was the only employee who stuck out the misery of the place, and she was constantly inconvenienced and robbed of her income by this unreliable employment.

Somehow Sophie managed to scrape together the fare money for Ty. He was grateful, and she received the usual texts telling her how much he loved her, thanking her profusely, and calling her his angel. But still he failed to show when he promised. He texted her one evening just before he was due to leave for Gatwick and his flight. He wanted to bring some of his ironing over and do it at the cottage. He hinted that he might stay overnight with Sophie. She showered, put on perfume and make-up, and donned her decent jeans and shirt. She changed the bed sheets and tidied up the bathroom. The evening wore on, but no Ty. She texted him—no reply. She called him, but her calls went to voicemail. At nine she gave up, undressed, and went to bed. She heard no more for two days. She realised that it was a long flight and that Ty's phone would be on flight mode. She also knew that he would not always be in a good area to send and receive messages. She had managed to find another £200, which she'd transferred into his bank account. Then her phone pinged, and there was a text from Ty.

"Hey, my baby. I'm missing you."

"I'm missing you too, my darling. Did you get your money? And how is your father?"

"Thank you, baby. He had the surgery yesterday and is doing OK for now. Love you."

"Please send him my best wishes. Love and miss you terribly. Hope it's good to be back in Jamaica, despite the stress of your father's health. I love you so much."

"I will, and I miss you."

A few days later Ty texted Sophie that he loved and missed her a lot. She enquired about his father, and Ty told her that he was doing well. Then he asked her if she was still going to pay his car instalment. Sophie had wondered why Ty would wake her at 01.30 just to tell her he loved her; she thought there had to be a motive—and she was right. Later he texted that he loved and missed her. He thanked her for the money she had sent but reminded her again not to forget his car payment.

A week later he had returned, and he texted her. "Hey, baby."

"Hi darling. You OK?"

"Not really, hun."

"Why, hunny?"

"Each time I used my card in Jamaica the bank charged me, and that's why all my money has gone."

"Charged you how much? I put £450 in your bank over two days and then £310 for your car. That can't have all gone, surely, hun." Ty didn't reply.

Days passed, and Sophie went back to work. Then she found out Ty was stuck in London because the turbo on his car had gone wrong. That cost Sophie £145. She returned home after another trying, unhappy stint at her job. A few nights later, she was lying on the settee watching television when Ty texted. He led the conversation into sex chat, and then he said, "I want to ask you something."

"OK. Fire away."

"You want you and me to be swingers?"

"Swingers?"

"Yes. Just light swinging."

"I don't understand, baby."

"Invite other couples or single females to join us." Sophie's heart sank. Ty had hinted at this sort of thing before. He had also blatantly suggested that he bring one of his friends with him so that he could watch Sophie being fucked by the friend. Sophie had resisted, furiously. She had told him that she didn't want to do such a thing. How could he ask her to do it if he really did love her as he claimed to do? Slowly, Ty had pressured Sophie.

He'd made her feel prissy and overly moral, even abnormal. He'd dropped very unpleasant hints that he could easily find another woman who would do this for him, which put Sophie into a panic.

"Oh, that," she said now. "But another guy touching me, someone I don't know or like. And having to watch you fuck another woman—no, Ty! We've got different ideas about loving someone, hunny. To me you're mine, and I can't easily handle the idea of you thinking about shafting another woman in front of me. I don't think you really understand."

"OK."

"Just OK? Please tell me I'm wrong to doubt if you really do love me, when you want to fuck a stranger and expect me not to be very hurt."

"Baby, it's something I have to try, and I don't want to do it without you." Then he promised to call her soon and went completely offline.

That had been at eleven in the morning. By eight in the evening Sophie had had enough. She texted Ty. "Thanks for the call," she said. He did not reply. At a quarter past ten she lay in bed and texted. "Remember what you said to me a while ago? 'I can't do this any more. I want to end it all.' That's when you were very depressed and down. Well, that's how I feel right now. I couldn't have done any more for you. I never lied to you or let you down, ever. But you've done it to me again and again. You even asked me if I was seeing someone else—but do you know something? I don't know if I really trust you. I've been honest, loyal, caring, understanding, and everything you asked of me, but you continue to ignore and neglect me, lie to me, and let me down. Let's stop it right here, Ty. I know you don't love me. I'm just a convenience, and hurting me is not a problem to you. You've never been honest with me, ever and, whatever you say, you have used me, cruelly and deliberately. I'm walking away now, because I can't take any more. I know very well that you neither love me nor want me. I'm worth a lot more than this neglect and emotional abuse. You'll soon find another fool on that dating site, if you haven't already. Take care. You had someone who really loved and cared for you, but you lost her. Bye, my babe." Sophie sent the text. No reply. An hour later she wrote, "The biggest tragedy is that I love you—I really love you, and it's a cross I have to bear alone. Take care. You mean the world to me, but I know that you don't and can't feel for me what I feel for you. Goodbye, my beautiful guy. I hope you find what you want and need." Sophie pressed the Send button. The phone pinged. There was no reply. Nothing. Sophie slept.

The following day Sophie heard nothing. No text came through. She called his phone but her calls were quickly cut off. She resigned herself to the fact that he was finished with her and that she must just face the misery she would surely feel.

At four in the afternoon, she heard her phone ping. There was a text from Ty. "I am here stuck in London, and that's all you can think about??" After that there was silence. Again she called him and was rejected. She was resigned to what was happening, almost relieved. A day passed, and then he texted her again. He had no money for petrol. Sophie had little, but she transferred her last £40 to his account. She didn't even receive a thank you. She tried to forget the handsome Jamaican, tried to be angry at the way he had treated her. Life had to go on.

Sophie had to go to a physiotherapist for neck and shoulder injuries she had sustained when her SUV was hit. Enrico had offered to take her, as she had no vehicle. Their route took them past the house where Shirley lived, and as they approached it, someone with a large truck was attempting to turn round in the road in a series of three-point turns. Enrico had to stop directly in front of the house, and just then Ty came out to go to his car. He stopped, looked up, and saw Sophie sitting in the car. He also saw Enrico beside her. She saw him take his mobile out of his pocket and tap away at it. Then her phone pinged, and she looked at it. "Baby, I am so, so, so sorry. I really love you and I can't go on without you. Please forgive me."

"I love you too. OK. I'm on my way to physiotherapy for my accident injuries."

They drove off. Enrico came into the cottage for tea after the appointment. He was a minor nuisance too. Deeply in debt, he owed Sophie a lot of money; he was always asking her for money to help him put credit on his phone, to pay for his electricity, and to buy tobacco and Bacardi. He didn't ask for the large sums that Ty did, but he was another drain on Sophie's resources. She wished he would sell the house and repay her and solve her problems.

Ty turned up the next morning very early, without texting first. Sophie was half asleep still. Ty climbed into bed with her and cuddled her tightly. He kissed her warmly and more lovingly than he had done for some time. His lovemaking was just that—lovemaking. It was gentle, caring, and considerate. Sophie climaxed joyfully and repeated this ten minutes later when she and Ty came together. Sophie wept with happiness.

Ty wiped her tears away and kissed her face. They lay in silence. Ty held her hand tightly. "I mustn't lose you again, my baby. I do love you. Very much. Just try and understand that I have things to do, and I am away a lot."

"I do understand, hunny, but you must understand that one small text is all it takes to let me know that you're OK, and it stops me worrying."

"Okay, baby. I know. I'm not good at that. I do try." Ty stayed, and Sophie cooked him scrambled eggs, with two thick slices of ham, buttered toast, and a coffee. He sat in bed, eating and smiling at her. Her heart was full to bursting with love for him. They kissed goodbye at the door, and Ty stopped to wave and blow a kiss.

Sophie didn't hear a word from him for over a week, but she held herself back patiently and waited—and waited. He got in touch then. He needed money urgently to go to Jamaica again. Sophie would have to find yet another £1,000. She returned to her hated job and worked—blinkered, tired, resentful, stressed, lonely, and missing Ty. He texted to pressure her for the money, peppering the texts with declarations of love and half-hearted interest in her welfare. Sophie had to find the money. She worried, as usual. Her SUV was becoming a problem. She had nowhere to park it and had to leave it in a nearby road where she was unable to see it. The soft top at the back was getting tatty around the zips that fastened it, and one day, after she had had to leave it there for over a week, Sophie was told by a resident of the road that a group of teenagers had tried to force the back open. They had been driven off, and the resident had kindly kept an eye on the vehicle for her. She thanked him warmly, but she was dismayed. She went online to discover that replacement top covers would set her back over £700, and then she would have to pay for the fitting of them; it would end up costing her over £1,000 in all. Then the rear tyres needed replacing, and the brakes were dodgy. She would have to sell it. Sophie had approached the insurance company about the damage the teenagers had done to the weakened cover, but they were not happy that the car was no longer in Enrico's private driveway; they wanted to almost treble the premium she paid. That was the finish. She advertised the car. She was sad to lose it, but she could not afford the expense or the worry. She knew that she would have to use what she got for it to help Ty get to Jamaica. She found a buyer and told Ty. He followed her as she drove the SUV to a rendezvous with the prospective buyer. He had come with his father, and being a mechanic and a dealer, he was pleased with the vehicle's mechanical state. They agreed on £900. Sophie handed over the log book and the keys, and the man counted the cash into her hand. Ty behaved very strangely. He came over and looked at every note as it was counted; then he snatched the money and counted it again and again. The two buyers exchanged glances. Ty went back to his car, which was parked a distance from them, to get his cigarettes. Whilst he was walking away, one of the men asked her, "Is he always like that, darling?"

"I don't really know. I don't think so." Sophie was embarrassed. "A bit naughty, acting as if we'd cheat you because we're black and you're a white woman." They shook hands, and then Sophie watched as the powerful SUV roared away. She felt sad. She got into Ty's car. He had pocketed the money, assuming that it was all for him. Sophie did not argue. He turned and kissed her.

"Thank you so much, baby. I can go over after Christmas now."
Sophie had managed to get together £300 already. They drove
off. She hoped that Ty would come into the cottage and stay a
while, but he kissed her goodbye, thanked her again, and drove
off as soon as she had shut the car door. She saw very little of
him after that and heard very little too. He came over for a very
quick sex session one morning but left hurriedly. It left Sophie
numb, miserable, and frustrated. They talked about Christmas.
Ty said he didn't "do Christmas." Sophie didn't either, because
Ella had been laid to rest, with Ben, just before Christmas, and
she preferred to be alone. Sophie asked Ty where he would
be for Christmas.

"Alone," he replied.

"Well, come over and see me. I'll be on my own too, so pop in."

"Yes, I probably will. Thanks." But Christmas came and went,
and Sophie sat alone watching boring television and missing
Ella. Freddie was with his father. Sophie texted "Happy
Christmas" to Ty and got a reply but nothing after that. New
Year came. Sophie texted Ty again and wished him a happy
one. He replied briefly. Then she heard nothing. The year 2015
was over, and 2016 loomed on the horizon, and Sophie did not
know yet how dreadful it would be.

TY AND SOPHIE, 2016

Sean had a terrible addiction to drink. He resisted all kinds of intervention and, throughout his life, had been offered the best and most revolutionary care available. But he didn't want anyone's help. He just wanted to live in his own twilight world of escape and nothingness. Sophie was deeply concerned for him. Since his operation and subsequent health problems just before Ella's sad death, he had become more reclusive. He would not answer phone calls or open the door of his flat to visitors. Only one staunch friend was able to constantly keep an eye on him, to bully and persuade him to eat and to keep himself and his flat reasonably clean. The new year saw him failing in health again. Sophie was afraid for him.

Her job was becoming more stressful and depressing. She was beginning to hate the long journeys to and from Lincolnshire. Ty had taken her a few times, but he was unreliable. He had let her down so often that she could not even think of asking him again.

Ty's relentless begging for money continued. Sophie scraped, and worried, and cut corners. She turned the heating off and sat wrapped in a blanket, cold and unhappy. In January, Ty relieved her of several hundred pounds; he had to go to Jamaica. Again the excuse was his father. This time he really was dying, and Ty had to be there. Early in February Ty flew over there and lost touch with Sophie. He'd texted her before he'd left from Birmingham, but only to make sure that she was going to transfer him the money for his car insurance in the middle of the month.

Sophie texted him: "Bring me back some sun!"

"I will. I'll text you when I get there." Ty did text her whilst he was there but only to complain that he thought he had the flu. He was unwell and felt awful. Then he told her that he had run out of money. Could she just send him maybe a couple of hundred? Sophie, with great difficulty, shaved her costs more, and by living frugally and miserably again, managed to send Ty the £200. He sent her his usual protestations of true love, promised to drive straight from the airport to see her, and then went off the radar. Sophie texted frantically, and eventually Ty informed her that he had landed, was very tired, and needed a hotel to sleep in before he could think of driving back. Sophie had nothing to give him. She told him that, and he texted back that he would just have to pull off the motorway and sleep, as he was not fit to drive. He did not turn up, and he did not text or call.

Sophie sent Ty a Valentine's Day greeting text. Ty responded that St. Valentine had been a batty boy, a gay, and he didn't celebrate people like that. A few days later Ty texted Sophie asking her to send him some photos of her pussy. He missed her and was desperate. Sophie hated this. She tried to reason that they were a couple in a relationship and that Ty had sexual needs. He had a high sex drive, and they were, for reasons unknown, separated a great deal. This was not a bad thing; she was just helping him to survive. She could not give him her body in reality, so she was giving it this way. She sent him the pictures. Immediately he texted back.

"Why is the bed wet?"

"It's not wet, baby. It's just the pattern on the bedding."

Then Ty went offline for days.

Ty had told her often recently that he was going to apply for his British citizenship papers. He came to see her, bringing his laptop, and he went over and over the different test papers, trying to memorise the answers. He turned up more often than he normally did, but it was all about the citizenship, not about Sophie. She went back to Lincolnshire for another horrible, long engagement with the client she quite liked and his niece whom she hated intensely. The atmosphere there was unbearable. Staff were leaving weekly after heated arguments, and Sophie had twice the work to do. The niece was drunk a lot more often, becoming argumentative, interfering, and unbearable. Sophie was nearing breaking point. She worried constantly about what crisis Ty would land on her next, and she was anxious about her financial situation. She was due to leave the job in March and travel home. Ty texted and asked whether she wanted him to pick her up. It quite surprised her. Part of her wondered what he really wanted. Naturally the trip involved fuel money for the car and a hotel for Ty to stay in overnight. Sophie shelled out, as she so longed to see him. He rolled into the driveway just after ten that morning and came inside to pick up Sophie's luggage. The housekeeper looked at Ty longingly and began to flirt with him verbally. Ty played along, obviously enjoying the attention. Sophie hastily went out to the car, and Ty followed. He took her back to the hotel, quite obviously wanting sex. In the room, he sat her on the bed and kissed her lips gently and lingeringly.

Sophie was surprised and pleased. She hadn't seen this Ty for some while. He slowly undressed Sophie, took off his clothes, and then laid her back on the large bed. He used his fingers very gently to stimulate her, and Sophie rapidly became very wet and very excited. He kissed her nipples and her shoulders and then slowly slid his large penis into her. Sophie caught her breath, always expecting to be hurt, but she was ready for him, very ready, and soon he was in her body and moving slowly and sweetly. Sophie was in bliss. Ty looked down at her and said, "Baby, I love you so very much." Then he closed his eyes, his movements became hard thrusts, and Sophie felt him reaching his climax. She let go of herself and thrust back, hard and wanting. They reached the peak together, and Sophie cried as Ty's final jerking thrusts stilled and he lay beside her, holding her hand.

"Why you crying, hun?" Ty wiped a tear from her face with his finger.

"It's just that this was so good today—and I want it to be like that always—and I hate being away from you so much! You keep saying that soon everything will be different, that soon we will be together. You tell me to just work with you, to bear with you. I don't know what I'm working or bearing with, Ty! I don't know anything much about you or your life, really, except what you choose to tell me." Sophie stopped. It had all come out in a rush. She could sense Ty's growing annoyance. She knew she had spoilt the moment, but she couldn't take much more of the uncertainty.

Ty rolled off the bed. He started to pack his bag. "Come on, then," he said abruptly. "I must get on. I have to get home." *Wherever that is*, thought Sophie. *Not with me.*

They drove off and the long journey was continued almost in silence. Sophie fell asleep from sheer exhaustion and was disturbed only by the constant messages *pinging* into Ty's phone. They stopped for coffee and a toilet visit and Ty sat quietly chatting to her in a pleasant, relaxed manner. He rarely did this and Sophie treasured every second. Ty had travelled extensively and could tell a good traveller's tale and it all fascinated Sophie. Then they pulled quickly back onto the motorway and Ty drove very fast, holding Sophie's small hand in his broad, strong hand. Too soon they arrived at Sophie's cottage. Ty carried her luggage inside. It was evening, and Freddie was with his father. Shortly after Sophie had moved into her little cottage it was Freddie's 16th birthday and he could legally make his own life decisions. He began spending time with Sophie whenever he could and, in June, he left school and moved in for the holidays and stayed, He took over the small bedroom and installed the computer he had built, gradually adding to it until it became very state of the art and powerful. Freddie had autism - that gift that some people consider a disability - but he had an unmeasurably high I.Q. and the logic of a 30 year old. Sophie and Freddie loved each other deeply. They communicated almost silently. Sophie's life was rich and fulfilled in this relationship and she was keeping her promise to darling Ella. Freddie spent the occasional day and night with his father and they went out to the cinema and ate out. This was one of these dad days and nights for Freddie.

"Are you staying?" Sophie could only hope.

Ty shrugged. "No. Can't do that, baby. Too much stuff to do. Sorry." Swiftly he kissed her and went out of the door. Sophie stood watching him, nearly in tears. It had been such a lovely day with him until now. Ty turned as he reached the gate; he waved and smiled. Sophie raised her hand. He would never be hers. Why didn't she just finish the whole saga, get away from this destructive relationship? She was frightened, because she felt that she was unable to live without Ty in her life—even if he was only on the very margins of that life. She was so very tired, too tired to think about the reality facing her. She went upstairs, unpacked, showered, and went to bed early.

The next morning Sophie received an email from the hated niece. She was accusing Sophie of being responsible for a fall that her client had had during one night. He had a baby alarm that enabled Sophie to hear him calling. During the night in question, the client had called her twice for aid with going to the toilet. The third time, Sophie had heard a noise, gone into the client's bedroom, and found him on the floor. He'd been slightly shaken and had managed to cut his knuckles on the side of the bed somehow. He'd been very apologetic and blamed himself, calling himself stupid, and told Sophie not to worry.

Now Sophie rang other staff, who told her that he had maintained this to everyone. He had told the niece that he had caused the incident, but she seemed determined to blame Sophie. Sophie sat down, picked up her phone, and emailed the niece.

"I was not responsible for the incident involving the fall your uncle had and the injury to his hand. He has told you, as he told me and other staff members, that it was entirely his own fault. I am totally sick of being spoken to and treated like a moron, accused of untrue things, and expected to cover for the times other live-in carers walk out—which is all of the time. You cannot keep any staff, let alone good staff. I have had enough of you and the situation, and I shall not be returning." She pressed the Send button.

There was no reply for some hours, and then she received a reply. "You have misunderstood me. I want you back, as you are a very valuable member of my team. I have transferred a month's wages into your account just now, as a thank you for all your services, without which I could not manage. I shall not need you for a few weeks yet but will inform you when I do."

Sophie checked her bank account. The money was there, all of it. She called a staff member who had been a close friend.

"OK, what's she up to?"

"She's found these two carers—or so they call themselves. She's starting them off this week, at least the first one. Probably hopes they'll stay, and then she'll dump you. She's paying them a lot less, but you get what you pay for."

"Right. Keep me posted."

"Sure will. Bye."

A week later the friend called to say that the two carers had been disastrous—inexperienced, unqualified, ignorant, and everything to be expected from those not timeserved or trained. They had both, in any case, fallen out very swiftly with the niece and loud altercations followed. The first one had not even stayed the full week. After a heated row she had packed and left. The second victim arrived the next day - and stayed for one day only before she, too, slammed out. Sophie emailed the niece to thank her for the money; it was due to her anyway as holiday pay. She would not be returning. Then she blocked the niece on email, messaging, cell phone, and landline. What a relief! She had no worries about other employment. A friend - Gloria - with whom she had worked before needed a partner, and the client was very near. No driving was needed. Sophie would have a few weeks' break. She slept soundly that night.

The next day Sophie received a phone call and learned that Sean had been rushed into hospital. He was in a coma. Sophie imagined it was connected to the operation for his spinal tumour. Her grandson, James, drove her there. They entered the ward, and the charge nurse took them aside. Sean had been admitted feeling very unwell and had collapsed on arrival; he was now comatose. His liver had ceased to function because of his alcoholism, and his condition was serious. They went into the side ward where he lay. He looked yellow and was breathing noisily. Sophie stood stroking his face and talking to him. He roused briefly and then slid back to sleep. After about three hours, Sophie and Sean's son, James, left.

Sophie sat in her little cottage shaking and crying. She realised that she hadn't heard a word from Ty since she had told him that her job had finished. She texted him that her son was very ill, but no reply came through. After a while she gave up checking for his response.

The next day Sean had roused, and he was responding to treatment. When Sophie and James visited him, the consultant seemed surprised that Sean had rallied so quickly and was improving with treatment. "We can only make good the situation and treat the symptoms to alleviate Sean's discomfort. He may, and this is a remote possibility, may just improve enough for us to consider a liver transplant. However, his condition is serious at present, so don't hope for too much."

Sophie had started her new job, which she liked, although she was wary of the client; she could sense problems ahead.

Every day she took the bus and visited Sean. He was cheerful, resigned, and brave. He knew that he was in that condition through his own actions. He admitted that he had turned away all the help that had been offered to him. Sophie was torn. She realised that he was addicted and that addiction is a terrible thing to try and fight, so she was deeply sympathetic. But the other half of her was angry that Sean had wasted his considerable intelligence and abilities and done nothing in his life except drink. His actions had resulted in him serving several prison sentences. He was penniless, unemployable and, until the last few years, homeless. Sophie had tried to have him living with her, but it just hadn't worked. He'd stolen, lied, and destroyed things and people. He'd caused friction and bad feelings. His was a sad life—and Sophie could do nothing to change or help the situation. She knew that this was going to be a dreadful journey for her, for Sean, and for his son. She worked hard and tried to face with courage what was to come. She wished that Ty would not be near her at this time, and in a sense he wasn't. He had gone off the radar—disappeared—and she was too occupied with Sean and dashing to the hospital to worry about it. Looking at her phone one day, she realised that she hadn't had even a good morning for over two weeks. Then Ty suddenly texted that he loved her. She was happy to hear from him again, and they texted about one thing and another. Not once did Ty even ask her about Sean. She was unhappy and even a little angry at his selfishness. If he or his father were ill, then she was expected to know and to comment.

Then one night she had a text from him. "Goodnight to the woman I love, to my future wife."

Sophie was puzzled and a little pleased. The following day she texted him, after he had sent her the usual good morning. "Were you drunk last night? You asked me to marry you—LOL."

"Will you?"

"You're already married, aren't you? And we hardly ever see each other, do we baby!"

"Is that a no, then?"

"Baby, I'd marry you tomorrow, but I thought you were already married. You know it's not just sex that I love you for. I just love all of you, and about you, and I want you in my life. I understand that you don't want a clinging vine, and you need your space and your men friends. Yes, I'd marry you tomorrow. Love you."

"You are and always will be in my life and my heart."

"So, when do I become Mrs. Benton!"

"ASAP."

"But honey, aren't you married to your daughter's godmother? Don't tease me, hun!"

"I'm getting my divorce as soon as I do my Life in the UK test."

"I can give you the money you need very soon. When I get paid. Will be in touch then, Mr. Benton."

"LOL. OK, Mrs. Benton."

Later that evening she texted him. "Hi, Mr Benton, baby. Have just put £450 in your account. Love you."

"OK, baby, thank you so much. I can pay the rest I owe on my car tomorrow. You are my angel. I love you."

Sophie continued her visits to Sean. He was beginning to respond positively to the treatment, and there was a faint glimmering of hope that he could have a transplant. One morning Ty texted her that he was coming to see her. Sophie hadn't seen him for quite a while, and she had missed him a lot. She was excited. "When are you coming?"

"I'm bringing someone with me, hun."

"Who?"

"A friend. I want to watch him fuck you." Sophie's heart sank. She was shattered. "I don't want that! I told you. I don't care if it is something you want—it's unacceptable, horrible. How can you say you love me and then ask me to do something like this?"

"I'm sure you'll love it, baby. Do you really love me? Are you loyal? If I like it, then you must like it too. If it pleases me, then you should want it too."

"I don't want it—any of it."

There was a pause. Then he texted again. "I can't stop thinking about it. Him sliding his big dick in your pussy, and you moaning. I'm gonna sign us up on a swingers site as a couple."

"Don't bother. I won't do it. Stop pressuring me like this."

"Well, baby, if you don't want to do it, I suppose I can find someone else who will." Always the veiled threat, the suggestion that Ty could easily find another woman who would satisfy those black wants. He was a very handsome man. He could soon find anyone. Sophie sat and cried. She felt pressured and unhappy. Why did Ty keep demanding these things? Sophie was broadminded, but this disgusted and frightened her.

There was a silence of some hours and then, "Baby, if you want to keep me, just answer me and keep me happy. Even if you have to pretend. I'm away from you a lot, and I need sex. It helps me not to miss you."

"I'm still not happy, Ty. If you love me, you don't need this sort of thing."

"Just humour me, baby. Keep me happy."

Sophie heard nothing more until the following day.

The pressure to sleep with a friend, to join a swingers group, to do anything unconventional and stimulating for Ty continued, as did his demands for money. His car needed spares, taxing, tyres—it was unending. He was always desperate for more money. He only initiated loving chat to lead towards asking Sophie for more cash. He was manipulative and relentless, able to sweet-talk Sophie every time. He was full of promises and explanations. If nothing else worked, he became angry or implied that he could leave Sophie. She felt helpless. At the same time, she was worried, worried every hour of every day, about Sean. He had managed to reach a point at the end of June where he could be sent home to his flat. Friends, Sophie, and his son all visited to help. Sean was fragile and weak. Sophie wondered if he really would make it. She prayed nightly that he would recover and live out his life in sobriety and some kind of happiness. Ty hardly ever mentioned him. He seemed to resent the time Sophie spent travelling and visiting Sean if it interfered with what he wanted.

Sean did not manage well. His condition had them all concerned, and he was readmitted to hospital in July that year. Sophie took the bus there daily or went in the car with Sean's son James. They were able to take him, in his wheelchair, down to the hospital grounds to sit in the sun, where they would smoke and chat. Gradually the once-handsome boy was becoming an old, shrivelled man, with grey skin, sunken eyes and mouth, and the bony hands of the terminally ill. One day the doctor took Sophie and James aside. He told them that treatment was no longer working, that nothing more could be done except to make Sean comfortable. The two of them sat and wept. Then they went in together and told Sean, as gently as they could, that he was dying. In the sunbeams from the window, a butterfly danced, beautiful and unreal. Sophie felt detached. This was not happening. She was just looking at herself, watching herself telling her only son that he was soon to die.

Things were done then. A will form was brought. Sophie filled it in, and Sean signed it with his shaking, claw-like hand. Soon they moved Sean into a side room, the little room of death. He asked that they did not hook him up to any devices save a syringe driver, at the very end. He was content to go as soon as his life ended naturally. Sophie, her grandson, his beautiful little girlfriend, and Sean's stepson Charlie and his lady, all sat in the room with Sean. He was too weak to be taken down in a wheelchair now. He was sleepy and drifting, getting weaker hour by hour. Sophie barely slept. She still went to work and then rushed to the hospital the minute she was free.

One day when she was on the bus going to see Sean, Ty texted. She hadn't noticed any messages, but when she did she saw a row of them saying "Hello?"

"Hi, baby. I'm at the hospital."

"I've been worried about you. I've texted you about ten times without an answer."

"Sorry, hun. I was on the bus, travelling here. I've only received one message."

"And couldn't reply? You aren't thinking about me at all."

"Baby, I'm thinking about my son and a lot of other things that are worrying me. You know that I'm always thinking about you. Sometimes *you* ignore *me* for days. I've only just seen the WhatsApp message anyway. My daughters were phoning me."

"I know you are worried about your son, hun."

"I never fail to answer without a good reason."

"I wasn't arguing. Just worried about you."

I really do miss you. It's not fair that you go back to Shirley and leave me alone so much."

"What am I supposed to do?"

"I don't know, because you never really explain anything to me. I thought you hated her, but you live with her and your daughter in a two-bedroomed house."

"Are you serious? Is that why you've not been texting? We don't share a bed, so please stop."

"We're taking Sean out in his wheelchair now. I can't keep texting you. He's more important."

"I love you. Please don't forget to do that thing for me."

"Were you worried about that or me?"

"You, hun. Call me."

"I can't; I'm in the ward. I'll transfer the money when I can."

Sophie turned her phone off. Ty had only wanted to know where his money was. *Sod him!*

He called her later when she was at home, still wanting his cash. He said little about her son, just said he needed to go to London. Sophie knew that this meant he wanted more money for fuel. She texted. "The day after tomorrow is my son's birthday—the last one he'll ever have. He's 53."

"OMG, baby. I am so sorry for you right now."

"He's facing death with great courage and dignity—doesn't want tears and moping. I'm just numb. I can't believe I'm losing another child."

"You make me want to cry. I'm sitting here with tears in my eyes right now."

Sophie looked at his words. They seemed unreal, meaningless. "I'll need you when it's all over," she told him.

"I know, my love. I'll be there for you."

She finished the conversation quickly. She was very tired, and her son was very near death.

The following day Sophie went up to the hospital again. Sean was weak but cheerful. He ate some sushi that his son, James, had brought in and clearly enjoyed it. The next day would be his fifty-third birthday. The family sat around him, trying hard to joke with him. Death was creeping into the little room. Sophie could smell it and feel it. Death had taken her daughter, sneakily and cruelly. Now it stood in the corner, waiting and watching. Sean was getting weaker, his swollen abdomen causing him pain. Sophie went to the nursing station to get palliative care, which was immediately dispensed. He was facing his death with courage and dignity.

They all came on the day of Sean's birthday, laden with gifts, cards, and more sushi—but Sean had slipped into a comatose state. He lay against the pillows, grey and breathing noisily. He stirred when James sat by him and held his hand. All day they kept vigil, talking and laughing nervously. Late at night they left. Sophie was exhausted and fighting to stay in touch with reality. She fell into bed and slept deeply. At three the next morning her grandson phoned. Sean had slipped away, peacefully and painlessly, just after two. His close friend, who had cared for him through thick and thin, had been with him. A Catholic priest had also been there. That afforded Sophie some comfort. Sean had been baptised as a Catholic. He had fallen away from his faith in later years but had asked for a priest to be with him when he passed. Sophie wanted to believe that somewhere there was a place of peace and happiness, where Ella and Sean could find some kind of joy and eternal rest. She had her beliefs, but they had been shredded by her losses.

Now Sophie was sleepwalking, unable to really register that she had lost her only son. She sat on the bed, staring at the light as it grew brighter. She had lost Ben and then her precious Ella—and now her only son was gone. Losing a child was unthinkable. Losing a second child barely four years later was a nightmare nobody would want to enter. And she was there, in that desolate, black place—totally alone. She felt helpless and totally useless as a mother. She had failed her children. They should have lived, coped with their demons, and recovered— they should never have had those problems to begin with. Why could she not have saved them? Why had she not been there to save Ella? Why had she not been able to prevent Sean from growing into a hopelessly addicted wretch?

Sophie dressed with shaking hands. James, his girlfriend Lola, and other family members were waiting in the car. At the hospital they went up to the little room and stood looking at Sean. Sophie stroked his face and his hair. He looked very peaceful. He was almost smiling, as if he had seen something, something that had changed everything in that last second as he left his earthly body and made his final journey to—what? Who? Where? The merciful, loving God who would grant him the peace he could never find on earth? They sat around, drinking tea and talking. Sophie was drifting into her own world. Sophie texted Ty. "My son just passed away, baby. Please stay in touch with me. I miss you."

"Oh, baby, I'm so sorry."

"Baby, my heart is breaking. Sean was so brave. He died peacefully and painlessly. My only son—my darling boy. I miss you so much."

The *you* was intended for Sean—not for Ty. But he replied, "I miss you too, baby. I wish I was there. Poor hun."

"I wish you were here too, baby. I'm so tired."

"I'm sure you must be, hun."

Later that day, around noon, Sophie texted, "I'm going to try and sleep now. Please keep in touch baby. I love you."

"OK, baby. I love you, too." That evening he texted her to ask how she was, and Sophie told him she was in a bad, sad place. Ty immediately told her that he was too, as his father was ill, and he could not even afford a ticket to see him. Sophie could see how selfish and uncaring Ty was being. She realised it, but part of her was detached, wandering in a strange land. She was seeing but not comprehending, unable to react appropriately, unable to defend herself. She was like a fawn, standing vulnerable in the open jungle, aware of her position but helpless and prey to the dark, smooth hunter who stalked her. From then on, Ty constantly pleaded with and threatened Sophie over money. Even at a time like this he would not leave her alone. He had to have money to go to Jamaica, he insisted. His father was dying, and his sister was begging him for money for drugs to relieve his pain. It was unremitting. Ty texted her that he wanted to be with her in her time of need. But there was a slight condition attached, one that Sophie was already used to. He hadn't the cash to get there. Sophie dug up £50 for him. Still that was not enough. Sophie did not always reply to Ty. He complained, edgily and selfishly.

"Be patient. I'm very stressed out trying to sort my son's funeral. My family are coming over."

"I'll call you, hun."

Sophie waited, but Ty did not call. She texted him. No reply. Late at night, she texted, "Thanks for upsetting me and messing me around."

An hour later Ty replied. "Baby, are you serious?"

"But you didn't call or answer my call or my texts. I'm so fragile right now and so easily upset that it only takes something like this to reduce me to tears. Please try to understand. I have just lost my son, the second child I've lost. I'm sad and down, and I can't handle your tricks and silliness and selfishness. I have to sleep. I have to work tomorrow."

"I'm sorry, baby." But Sophie had turned her phone off.

In the next few days, Ty told her to "keep on top of it" and "don't make too much of it."

Sophie replied, "I'm coping bloody well. I'm a lot stronger than you seem to think, but having to lose two children in four years is a hell of a knock to take!"

"I know, baby."

"Do you?"

And then Ty was pleading and bullying for money again. He announced he was coming to see Sophie, but he just needed the cash for fuel for his thirsty car. And Sophie squeezed her slender purse yet again for him, but Ty did not arrive, or text, or call.

She texted him. "I can't handle any more of this contemptuous treatment. You just take me for granted. When I need you most you let me down. I have never once let you down! You said you wanted the cash to come and see me—you wanted to be with me because of my son's death. I fall for it every time, don't I? If you want me, you know where I am."

Ty sent her texts that were full of sympathy on the surface but were really just a way of keeping her attention so that he could pressure her for money.

The funeral was to be in ten days' time. Sophie's daughters, Sarah and Kate, and two of her grandchildren, Mattieu and Marco, came over from France. They supported each other in their mutual misery and grief. Ty kept pushing into her life. Why she did not simply turn her phone off, block Ty, ignore him? She had no idea. She blindly followed his demanding lead, almost obeying him in her terror of losing him. Now she was so fragile and so easy to use. He texted unendingly. He put in a few words of sympathy but followed them with whining about his worries over money, his father's health, and his family. Whatever issues anyone had to bear, Ty had more. His problems were worse than anyone else's. Sophie had lost her second child, but still Ty tried to make her feel guilty for his mess of a life. Sophie asked him to come to the funeral to support her. He told her had nothing to wear. She asked him a second time, when they were talking on the phone.

"I can't go, baby. I don't know anyone. Anyway, I hate funerals."

"But I need you, Ty. I need your support."

Ty's voice became edgy. "Would you come to my dad's funeral? I bet you wouldn't. You don't just go to anyone's funeral—"

"If you asked me to, Ty, if it would help you and if I was supporting you, yes. Of course I would." Sophie was deeply upset. She had run herself ragged to help him. She had always been there for him. She'd never broken a promise—and most of those promises had concerned money. Now she really needed him.

Where was his love, and his care? He had told her she was his woman and his angel. Sophie was too hurt and too numb with the trauma of her loss to register any of the real impact of all this.

The service took place at a beautiful little country crematorium. "Fields of Gold" was played, as it had been at Ella's farewell. Everyone wept brokenly. Sophie's French grandsons, James, and Sean's old friend who was James's godfather, together helped carry his coffin into the chapel. They said their goodbyes, and the coffin slid out of sight. Another young life was gone, another child gone before her. Sophie felt nothing any more. She was acting out her life, playing a part. She was losing touch with reality.

They went to hotel at the edge of the river and sat reminiscing and drinking. Sophie drank many gin and tonics and tried to appear normal. She and her close family all went back to her little cottage, they ordered Indian takeaway, and everyone sat, eating and talking. Sophie fell asleep. She was slightly drunk and desperately tired.

The family stayed a few days longer. They went down to the coast, and the cousins all went crabbing on the river for relaxation. Sophie sat in a deckchair and dozed. Despite the heat of the August sun, she felt cold. She had left her mobile in the car, not wanting to bother with it. When they returned to the car to drive home, she found a mass of texts from Ty. The last one said, "I know you are with your family, but you can drop me a text every now and then."

Sophie stared at the screen. "Like you do all the time, Ty!" she cried angrily. And she turned the phone off again.

That evening they were all sitting in the garden eating supper. Sophie's phone pinged endlessly. Eventually she looked at the texts. They were all from Ty again.

"I need to talk to you badly."

"Very important."

"I know you read my message."

No, I didn't, Sophie thought. She texted back. "Baby, I'm eating supper. I'll call you directly after. I have my family round me, Ty."

"I really need to tell you something. I've found a flight to Jamaica and I've managed to raise most of the money."

Sophie knew what he wanted. "How much more do you need?"

"The ticket is £647 with Virgin Atlantic. I've managed to come up with £390."

"Sorry. I have to work first. I can find it at the beginning of September."

"Do you have anything at all to help me pay for it by tomorrow?"

"Sorry. I told you. Can't you wait until September, or find another deal?"

"Just looking" texted Ty. "There's a flight September 9 for £679. I can pay for it next week. Next week—I need it by next week—"

"I just told you, baby" Sophie texted irritably." Next week. Please leave me be now. I want to spend time with my family." There was peace for a few hours, and then Ty was texting again, demanding that Sophie let him have some clothes from her club. Sophie decided to say no—she owed a horrendous amount already, mainly for stuff Ty had got himself. He'd got two expensive watches, amongst other things. She told him she had closed the club; she didn't run it any more. She told him that she wished she could just fly off to the sun, rest, and take a break from life.

Ty just said, "I know, baby." But he didn't know. He didn't want to know anything that didn't involve him on centre stage, with the spotlights on him and his silly, unimportant life. Sophie registered this, but some part of her brain could not process it.

In the next few weeks, Ty texted, as ever, only when he felt like it or when he wanted something. Sophie was never allowed to voice her grief. If she even said that she was feeling a bit down, Ty would come straight back with, "I'm feeling really down too." This meant he needed more money.

Sophie texted, "Managed to get through another day. Just don't want to be here any more." Ty didn't reply. In the next few weeks he begged non-stop for money. It was usually for small amounts, £15 or £30. He said he was hungry, but Sophie realised that this was the amount he needed to buy vodka; it was about £15 a bottle. So he was still drinking—broke but drinking. Sophie was feeling unwell. She was tired, achy, and weak. Ty pressed her for the money to go to Jamaica. Sophie told him she was very low. She asked him if he could just take her for a drive somewhere, anywhere, to get out of the house. She needed to get away for a few hours. Ty ignored her and continued to insist that he had to buy his ticket. Sophie did not exist for him. She could not remember when she had last seen him. When she had a day off, he told her he was coming to see her. She waited in for him. By four o'clock she was desolate. He did not reply to her texts or pick up her calls. Then he did text, with no apology for letting her down yet again. He was flying the coming Friday. He needed cash to take. He had nothing. Sophie sat down, desperately doing complicated sums, trying to avoid paying bills, shaving down her gas, electricity, and food money. Eventually she managed to scrape up £250. She texted Ty. He told her he loved her and would soon be there.

"I'm desperate for you, baby. Wanna make love to you. Need you so much." Sophie waited. She waited for three days. Ty made excuse after excuse or just ignored her.

The evening came. Sophie texted, "Night. I'm going to bed early. There's nothing to wait up for."

Ty didn't reply.

Sophie texted, "Bye. Have a good trip. Think of me sometimes. I'll never forget you." Then she fell asleep.

The following day Ty texted. "I texted you this morning but no reply."

Much later Sophie replied, "My electricity meter ran out, and I had to walk into town to get credit. My phone was charging overnight and was dead until I could recharge it, which was nearly one in the afternoon. When do I ever just ignore you without a reason, Ty? You know I've been hoping to see you for days, and I'm fragile because it's only three weeks since I lost my son. You don't text me for days, and I have to just tolerate it, Ty. Didn't you think that there might just be a very good reason? I could have been ill—but did you think to check instead of shutting me out and ignoring me? I'm ignored for days all the time, and I'm supposed to not get hurt and upset, but I fail to reply just once in a very long time and you treat me coldly and hurtfully. I don't need this right now."

"But I told you. I texted you this morning and got no reply, baby. I'll come see you tomorrow." But then he started pressuring Sophie again, telling her he wanted to see his friends fucking her. He told her that it turned him on, so she should like it too. Sophie resisted weakly. She had no fight left. She was deeply distressed. Ty wheedled with her that all she had to do was to agree with him, to text back that she loved it and tell him what she wanted his friends to do to her. He spoke very softly, telling Sophie that he could easily find someone who would want to do this to please him. Sophie panicked. She could not lose Ty, not lose the man she adored. This was so very wrong, so cruel. But Sophie gave in, miserably. She verbally agreed to humour him, but she was hating all of it.

A few days later he told her he was coming over, and he actually turned up. He swaggered in, oozing charm, and testosterone, and good looks. He kissed her lingeringly and then led her up to the bedroom. He undressed her and spent more time than usual kissing her, gently stimulating her with his fingers, and telling her how much he loved her and had missed her. As usual, Sophie put her hand down to slow his entry; she had never overcome her fear of his size. He smiled and was very gentle and very slow. He moved with her body's moving, and soon Sophie was desperately pleading. As she came, he drove into her and pleasured her until she screamed and clawed at his back. He did not reach an orgasm then. He pulled her to the edge of the bed and pushed her to face downwards. He seemed to hesitate for a while, and then he went into her, slowly, and continued slowly and carefully. Soon Sophie was aroused again. She pushed back against him. Ty's thrusts became harder and deeper and then so deep that it hurt Sophie, making her cry out. But he held her down and slammed against her as he neared his climax. Sophie was in agony, but she so wanted him. They reached heaven together. Ty lay against Sophie's back, breathing heavily. Then he pulled her up onto the bed and cuddled into her, holding her hand. She lay against his shoulder. Tears ran down her face.

"Hey, what's this? Did I hurt you, baby?"

"No, hun. I just missed you so much. Life isn't good for me right now. You've been a bit shitty to me, and I just can't handle it."

Ty kissed her tears. "Come on. I have a lot to do. I'm away a lot. I have to get to see my father in Jamaica. I have problems too."

But not like mine, Sophie thought. They lay together and were soon asleep. Sophie loved these too-few precious times when she and Ty were close, lying together, with Ty breathing deeply as he slept, his arms tightly around her. They never lasted, though. Ty's phone would always intrude into these rare times of relaxation. Then Ty would wake and turn over, push Sophie away, and pick up his phone. Often he just switched off whatever was waking him or turned off calls. He would look at the screen and frown, and then Sophie would know that the moment was gone. He would swing out of the bed and start to dress. He always had to go somewhere or to something or someone. This time was no different.

"Gotta go, baby."

Sophie sat in bed, hunched up with her arms around her knees. "Can't you stay, Ty—just a little longer, baby? I haven't had you here to myself for so long. I don't see you much any more." She was sad and wistful.

Ty looked annoyed, as he usually did. "I have a lot to do, baby. I have to try and get to Jamaica. My father's dying, for God's sake. I'm very stressed. Think of me, instead of yourself."

And when did you ever really think of me, thought Sophie. *After all I've suffered recently. Where were you? What comfort or help did you show to me? What love and care?*

Sophie went to get out of bed, but Ty stopped her. You stay here, baby. You look tired." He bent down and kissed her quickly on the cheek. "See ya." He waved and smiled and was soon gone down the stairs. Sophie heard him moving about downstairs but thought nothing of it. Often he would look in the fridge and take a bottle of water. Then the door closed, and soon the car fired up and she heard the four-litre engine echoing down the hill as Ty sped away.

That night Ty began pressuring Sophie about doing threesomes with him. She sat crying whilst she texted the answers she imagined he needed. She was wretchedly unhappy but so desperately afraid to lose him. Her life was unbearable, and she felt that if she lost Ty the very foundations of her sanity would crumble from beneath her.

Then he called her. "Baby, I've signed us up for a swingers' club. I've signed up onsite and put some photos on."

"Photos? What photos?" Sophie's heart tripped.

"Oh, those ones I took of us the other day when we were together." And then Sophie understood it all. Ty had hesitated before he'd entered her because he'd been adjusting his mobile to take shots of them making love. *Really?* she thought. It was just having sex—love was nowhere in the frame. And when Ty had hung back before leaving, he had doubtless looked at her passport, in her handbag, and got her date of birth. No wonder he hadn't wanted her to come downstairs with him.

"You didn't ask me, Ty! I don't want to be on anything like that. I didn't give my permission. Take me off the bloody thing. You've no right to do this. How can you sleep with some other strange female you've only just met—"

"Ah, come on, baby. Don't be such a fucking prude. It's just a bit of light-hearted sex. I've always wanted to do it. Just try it out. You're a long time dead, for God's sake. If you don't wanna do it, then I'll just have to find a more willing woman who really cares about me and likes what I like."

Sophie wanted to scream. "I do care about you, one hell of a lot, and you know it. And I like what you like, Ty, but this is totally different. Asking me to sleep with some strange man that I might not even like, and having to watch you fuck a strange woman—no! I can't do it."

"Come on, baby. Try it. You'll love it—" Sophie cut the call off. Her hands were shaking. Then Ty sent her the pictures; they arrived on her phone immediately. And there was a video of Ty taking her from behind, across the bed. Sophie wept. That was supposed to have been their time together, with Ty making love to her—but this was a cold, pornographic insult. Sophie closed her phone and sat motionless. She wanted to do something or say something to make Ty understand how she felt. But she was unable to—her brain was incapable of dealing with what had happened and what was happening. She was too weak to defend herself. Her self-image had been dragged down into the mud of subservience and apathy. Her vulnerable psyche had been torn by the winds of terror—terror at the prospect of never seeing Ty again. She tried to forget what he had said. She had so much to deal with. Just forgetting seemed the way to react for the moment.

Sophie did not hear from Ty or see him for quite a while. She texted him that she missed him. He replied that he was a bit down. Sophie responded, "You only live up the road from me, but you never come over to just talk to me. I get pretty down too, baby. I miss my kids terribly, and I'm trapped here with no car, unable to escape. I'm missing you and wondering why you never come to see me."

"How do you know where I am, hun?"

"I don't, because I never know where you are, or who you're with, or what you're doing—and you say you don't trust *me*, baby. You've stopped wanting me, so you must have someone else. You're handsome and you like sex too much to be without a woman." Ty had taken to accusing Sophie of being unfaithful to him if she didn't answer texts quickly enough for him or if she said something that he didn't like because it was too true.

"Huh?" came back from Ty.

"Well, you've often accused me of cheating and I'm not—and you disappear for weeks and you're a good-looking guy, so I find it hard to believe you don't have the odd fuck. Lately you haven't wanted me, so I can't help thinking you're with someone else. You have a home here with me, but you always go somewhere else. You never tell me where you are or where you're going. I see you less and less. I really love and care for you, but I sense you pulling away from me, and it really hurts me."

"I am not pulling away at all."

"So why do I see you so rarely? I simply don't understand why you can't come over to see me, and you are too stubborn and secretive to tell me why you always go back to Shirley. After two years, I see you less than ever and get nothing but promises that things will change. Maybe the whole situation is so hopeless that nothing can ever change. I've stuck by you and helped you and never broken a promise. I deserve some kind of happiness, but I never even see you."

"I hate all this texting shit. Why are you moaning so much?"

"I've hardly seen you in the last few months. I'm finding life very tough since my son died. You just get into your car and escape."

"OK, Sophie. I know." Then he disappeared from her phone and her life for some time. There were the usual "Good morning, baby" texts but little else. He would want to come and see her, but it was always when Freddie was there. Ty was visibly annoyed that the boy took precedence over him. Sophie went to great pains to arrange days and nights off, often losing pay to do so, but after she had arranged these dates, Ty would let her down again and again. He still chased her continually for money. On his recent trip to Jamaica he had forgotten to turn off his roaming data and had run up a bill. He needed cash for the car and cash for his car insurance. He was on a drug run, and the guy hadn't turned up to give him his cash, so he needed money for a hotel, or for fuel to get back. There was an endless and subtly destructive flow from Sophie's slender funds.

Ty came to see her a few weeks later and was soon in bed with her. He was very gentle with her, very considerate, and did not even insist on his favourite rear-entry position, which caused Sophie pain. They lay together afterwards, and Ty stroked her face. "I want to set up a meet with this couple—" he began.
But Sophie pushed his arms away and sat up abruptly. "No, Ty, no! Not that foursomes stuff. I told you I don't want any of it. Why did you have to spoil a really lovely time by saying this?" Now Sophie realised why Ty had been so loving—not because he wanted Sophie to feel loved but because he wanted to persuade her to do what he wanted and what he knew she most certainly did not want. They argued forcefully, and Ty slammed

out. Sophie did not even get a "Good morning" for days. Then Ty called her, saying his parents desperately needed money for painkillers for his father. Without hesitation Sophie transferred £110 to Ty's account.

The pressure continued from Ty. Sophie had to reply to his texts and tell him she wanted him to bring his man friend to fuck her and that she loved the video of them. She refused absolutely to do this at first but Ty's threats and continuous demanding forced Sophie to, very reluctantly, text what he wanted her to. She sat weeping after she sent the texts off. She felt soiled and angry.

Then he texted. "Are you bi?"

"Bloody hell, no. Why do you ask that?"

"I think you are, LOL."

"Why do you think I am? I'm totally heterosexual."

"I don't mind if you are. In fact, I wish you were."

"Baby, I only like fucking men. I'm understanding of gays, but am not gay or bi."

"Shame. LOL."

And then Ty dropped the sky on Sophie's head. First he called and asked her to take a night off work, as he would be able to spend a night with her. Sophie was overjoyed. It was what she had prayed for. She got cover for her work and was looking forward to her night of love with Ty. On the afternoon of the date, Ty called her. "Baby, I won't be alone. We're meeting a couple—nice people."

"What, Ty?"

"A couple from the swingers' website. For a foursome."

"But I told you I didn't want—this was supposed to be my night with you, Ty!"

"Don't be a fucking bore, baby. You'll love it. I'll be there—you'll be OK. I'll bring stuff to eat and drink. Just chill out. See you soon." Sophie sat there shaking. She wanted to run away, to get as far as possible from Ty and all this nightmarish pressure. Almost as if in a dream, she changed into a long dress and applied make-up. She had already showered in readiness for Ty and the night that he had promised with his lies—to trap her into this.

Ty arrived with his laptop, an armful of bottles, and various nibbles, crisps, and cheeses. He arranged the food on the sideboard and put the bottles out on the kitchen work surface. He had already drunk a fair amount before he arrived, and now he poured himself a large rum and tried to persuade Sophie to drink some. She hated rum and pushed the glass away. She poured herself some wine. She felt she would need it.

Ty opened his laptop and went to Skype to talk to his brother in Jamaica. Then he put his music on very loudly—too loudly. Sophie asked him to please turn it down. She had good neighbours and had no intention of upsetting them with all that noise. Ty was defiant: It was early evening; Sophie had rights. He was totally unconcerned with anyone other than himself. He was also rather drunk and was becoming unpleasantly argumentative and aggressive. Sophie considered running out and finding somewhere to stay overnight. Freddie was with his father so she had only herself to consider. Then the couple arrived. He was small, skinny, plain, bespectacled, ginger, and boring, yet quite pleasant and considerate. She was a huge woman. Sophie was overweight, but this creature made her feel almost normal. The woman wore a large garment that looked like loose covers on a settee. She panted whenever she moved and smelt strongly of sweat. They sat, drinking and nibbling. Sophie was almost frozen with fright and unhappiness.

Ty took Sophie's glass. "Go upstairs with Liz, baby. You two can start."

Start what? thought Sophie. They went up the stairs, Liz panting and sweating profusely. Sophie did not like her or the situation. Liz lay on the bed and motioned Sophie to join her. Sophie lay down, and Liz unbuttoned Sophie's blouse and began to pull up her bra and stroke her breasts. Sophie was repelled. She pushed Liz away. Liz took Sophie's hand and tried to make her do the same to her, but Sophie pulled her hand away and shut her eyes.

Liz had a hoarse, grating, common voice. "You aren't much good at this, are you? Done it before?"

"No, and I have no intention of doing it now—or ever." Just then the men came in. Ty was quickly at the side of the bed, pulling Liz over and pushing her face down on the bed. Then he had undressed and was in her. Sophie was distressed and hurt. She could not bear this a minute longer. The man, Harry, got undressed and got into bed with her. He tried to kiss her, but Sophie turned her head away sharply. Then he tried to remove Sophie's pants. She put her hand down and held his wrist in a vice like grip.

"Let me alone! I don't want to do this. I hate it. I want to go back downstairs." Harry obediently released her, and Sophie ran downstairs and sat with her glass of wine, hunched up and crying. Harry came down and sat beside Sophie. He poured himself a glass of wine and put his arm around her.

"Come on, lovely. Don't be so upset. You didn't want to do this—did he force you?"

Sophie shook her head. Then she said, "Well, yes and no. I told him I didn't want to—I find it horrible! I can't bear it if I have to watch. He hardly ever sees me ... and then this—" Harry squeezed her shoulders affectionately.

"Then stand up to him, darling. I only do it to humour her. She's at it all the time. It's the only way we can keep this thing together. You see, I really do love her, and I have to go through it all to hold on to her. I know what it's like for you, but you just stand firm. If he has to bully you into doing this sort of thing, then is he really worth it?" Sophie drank her wine and thought about it. Harry cuddled her quietly.

Then they heard Liz saying, "I'm going down now anyway." There was a lot of loud banging from Sophie's bedroom. Sophie could also hear Ty talking loudly to himself. She went upstairs nervously and looked around the door.

Ty had pulled out all three of her bedroom drawers and thrown the contents all over her bed. As she went in, he turned. His eyes were bloodshot and dark with anger. "What's this then, Sophie?" Ty pointed to the articles on the bed.

"What's what, Ty?"

"This—a box of Durex! This lube, this KY jelly! How many fucking men have you had up here! And you tell me you love me and miss me, and I'm the only man in your life." He threw the bottle of lube across the room and it landed on Sophie's dressing table, scattering all her creams and cosmetics.

"Ty, I bought those Durex the first time I ever went with you, and you said you wouldn't use them. I bought the lube after I found out how big you are. I really needed it to make things less painful for me. Then you told me you hated the lube and asked me to buy K-Y Jelly, so I bought it. I have no other men. The only other man who has been in this house and in my bed is the one here tonight. The one you forced me to have here against my will."

Ty glared at her. "So, you've been fucking him on the settee down here, have you?"

"No, I have not. I didn't want to do anything with a stranger, or with anyone but you, so I went downstairs. We just talked and had a drink."

"Huh! Really."

"Yes, really. Go down and ask Harry."

Ty went downstairs, leaving Sophie's room in a complete mess. As she started to pick things up and put them away, Sophie could hear Harry telling Ty that nothing had occurred between them, that he respected Sophie for her stand, and that Ty should listen to her or he would lose her. Sophie went down as Liz and Harry were preparing to leave. Sophie wished them goodnight, and they went down the path. Sophie turned to Ty. "Are you staying, Ty? You did say you were coming for the night—"

"You think I'm gonna fuck you, when you've got another man's sperm in you?" He pushed Sophie out of the way, picked up his bottles of rum and vodka, and went quickly to the door.

Sophie grabbed his arm. "Ty, you can't drive, you're too drunk. Stay here and sleep it off—" She stepped backwards as Ty hit out at her. He left, staggering and muttering. Sophie heard voices and then the engine of Ty's car being over-revved and driven away.

Liz and Harry came back up the path. "We were worried, love. He was in a very nasty temper! And he shouldn't be driving. We tried to stop him, but he just swore at us. Is he always like this? He's not likely to come back and harm you, is he?"

Sophie shook her head. No, Ty was not likely to come back tonight—or any night. He might never return. She thanked the two of them, wished them goodnight, and went back in to clean up the house. She couldn't bear to see the bed where Ty had spent so long with Liz, so she stripped all the bedding and remade the bed. She showered and put on a clean nightie. Then she crawled into bed, stunned and miserable.

Why had she allowed this to happen? Ty was not nice in any sense of the word. He was a con man and a liar, who used sex casually and meaninglessly as a weapon to back up his toxic charm. She should just kick him out of her life. But the apathy engulfed her like a fog. She could not mobilise the strength to do what her intelligence told her she should. Maybe one day—someday—things would change, and Ty would come and see her more often. He had once told her that he was able to steal from the drug dealers he ran for. He could easily just lift £50,000, run to Jamaica, open up a little shop or restaurant, or run a taxi service, and then all would be sunshine. And why wouldn't Sophie go with him? Sophie had told him that he would be running a stupid risk doing that. Those sort of people would find out and hunt him down. Anyway, she was never going to leave Freddie. Ty's eyes had narrowed at this. He was very jealous of Freddie. Sophie was continually trying to set up meeting times for her and Ty that didn't interfere with Freddie. She went to endless trouble to do this, but then Ty rarely turned up. Sophie lay thinking. She loved this man—but why? She felt protective towards him. She felt as if she must keep the world and his worries away from him. When she took him into her arms, she was holding her two dead children. Sophie was confused; she sometimes felt as if she were teetering on the verge of insanity. She lay awake until nearly dawn. She got her "Good morning, baby" late the next day. She ignored it, as she ignored the others that arrived for days afterwards.

In late October, after having only sent "Good morning," and "What you up to, hun?" and "You OK, hun?" for some time, Ty texted her again. "Morning baby."
"Hi."
"What you up to?"
"Just going to work."
"OK, my baby. I need you this evening. What time you done?"
"I have to work this evening as well. I can get cover if you really want me to. But don't mess me about, Ty, please."
"Let me sort something, baby."
"OK, hun." *Maybe this is it*, Sophie thought. *Maybe he is going to spend an entire evening with me—maybe even a night!* Her heart sang.
Later her phone announced a text from him. "Baby, would you like to go to a party tonight?"
"Party? Not one of those sex things with a bunch of strangers, Ty."
"Baby, stop being so afraid, please. You will be with me, OK?"
"Yes, Ty, but I haven't forgotten that other miserable time when you got horribly drunk, disappeared with that woman, pulled stuff out of my bedroom drawers, threw it everywhere, accused me of having men at the house, made a scene, and went away without touching me. On top of that, you drove when you were

very drunk. I don't want any stranger touching me. I hate the whole idea."

"OMG."

"Why OMG, Ty? I'm just being totally honest. I was very hurt and very upset."

"It won't happen again, OK?"

"I don't want to go, Ty—I've already told you."

"We'll need to stay in a hotel overnight—"

"I don't want to go, and I'm not giving you cash to go and have an orgy with a bunch of strangers. You want me to go and spend a night with you at that sort of thing, but you can't spend a night here with me."

"Well, I can't go then, and don't you start that fucking shit with me, OK. Why do you think I fucking asked you?"

"Ty, stop being so aggressive. I have the right to say no to anything I don't want, and I don't want this."

"I'm sorry, hun, but it's just that you don't think sometimes before you say shit."

Sophie closed her phone. When she checked it later, Ty had sent her this: "Call me when you can. I hate texting."

Sophie texted, "I love you."

"I really do love you too, Soph."

In the following weeks Sophie's body began to react to the events of that year. She had crippling migraines and was desperately tired. Ty continued to text; he wanted money to go to Jamaica again. He kept her dangling on the long, firmly attached string from him to her. He would say just enough to keep her hoping, promising things and letting her down. She sent him various sums of money. His demands continued. Sophie scraped together the money he needed.

Sophie sat wrapped in a blanket again, cuddling her hot water bottle. She only turned on the central heating when Freddie was home from college. Freddie went to his father's home for Christmas, and Sophie spent Christmas alone.

Ty had promised to call and see her, but Sophie knew that he would not come. She had told him that she had all of Christmas and New Year off from work and would be alone. It was the perfect opportunity for him to call. He had become slightly more loving in the last couple of weeks and seemed to want to keep her happy. *It's money*, Sophie told herself. *Money and Jamaica. Next year must bring something different. Something positive*, she thought. Sophie hunched into her blanket. The cold easterly wind rattled the dead leaves in the garden. It was dark by three. The streets were bleak and cheerless, as bleak as Sophie's heart.

On Christmas Eve she learned that Enrico had taken advantage of her preoccupation with the illness and death of Sean to quickly sell his house. He got a lower price than he wanted, but it enabled him to sneak away to Spain, leaving behind a pile of debts—including nearly £20,000 he owed to Sophie and had promised her faithfully to repay. He had also taken her expensive dishwasher, her dining room table and chairs, and her costly patio set. Whilst Sean had been dying and Sophie coping with his death, that spoilt mummy's boy whom Sophie had helped so much had run off and taken all Sophie had. Sophie listened to the wind. She almost wished she could dry up and be blown away by it, scattered where she could find the laughing girl with the blue, blue eyes and her handsome dark-haired brother. The year was dying—and with it Sophie's spirit.

SOPHIE AND TYRESE, 2017

It was Just after midnight on New Year's Day. Sophie texted Ty.
"Happy New Year, my darling. Love you."

At 7.30 the next morning he texted back. "Happy New Year to you, my love."

At just after 10 he texted. "Baby?"

"Yes, hun?" Sophie replied.

"Are you ignoring me?" Ty messaged her.

"No, why? I replied immediately," Sophie answered.

He asked her what she was doing, and she told him she had slept in because she'd stayed up to watch the New Year in. She told him she needed her usual strong coffee in order to become human.

Ty texted that he needed some pussy.

"Well, mine's hot and ready, like my coffee," Sophie answered.

Ty told her that if he left right then he could be with her by 12.30, and she said that was fine. It would give her time to wake up and have a bath.

Then he spoilt it by saying that he was going to bring a friend. "I want to watch him fuck you," he messaged her.

"NO, Ty—no! I don't want any of that. I keep telling you. Stop pressuring me." Sophie was upset.

"Come on, hun. You know it turns me on. I want you to like the stuff I like. If you loved me you would."

Sophie felt angry and afraid. She hated Ty's constant pressure on her to join him in foursomes and his non-stop insistence that he was bringing a male friend and wanted to watch Sophie performing with this friend. He made it clear that he wanted her to text a response that would excite him sexually, and he implied subtly that his interest in her would disappear if she did not meet his demands. She loved him deeply, irrationally, and she forced herself to please him even when she wanted to cry out that it was unfair and she felt bullied. Ty didn't arrive that day, but she was used to that.

"Love you," she texted. "Night."

"Love you," he replied much later, when she was already asleep.

The next day she received the usual "Morning, baby" and his explanation of his failure to arrive. He'd had no gas and hadn't wanted to ask her for money.

Sophie was annoyed. "So you just left me worrying for a whole day—and now I can't see you for over a week again, because I have to work. I had the whole of Christmas and New Year off and was on my own so I could have time with you. Why the hell can't you just ask me or tell me, baby?"

That was at 11.45. He did not text her until 13.12.

"What time you done work?"

"Soon," Sophie replied. "Two."

"OK," Ty replied.

An hour later he texted, "Love you."

Sophie was annoyed still. She knew in her heart that Ty had gone to see Shirley. She had tackled him about this before, and he had told her that he had been running to Shirley for over ten years and didn't know anywhere else to go. Sophie asked him why he had to run to Shirley—what was he always running from? And why couldn't he come to her? She had a home, and he had promised over and over again to move in with her. He had told her that Shirley was just the mother of his daughter, and that he simply lived there, and did the housework, and picked Josie up from school, and kept an eye on her whilst her mother worked. He was most insistent that they did not sleep together. From time to time it was clear to Sophie that Ty and Shirley had had a row; Ty would disappear to his friends in the Midlands or somewhere in Hertfordshire. But still he always returned to Shirley, despite his insistence that he hated her and only stayed there under protest.

Sophie had all but given up asking Ty why he would not move in with her. He always mumbled that he might soon or changed the subject very skilfully. He still had no job that Sophie could notice. She knew he did drug runs and got paid for that, but he couldn't live on that income, she realised. She had never really asked him how he survived, but he was always broke and always pleading and pressuring her for money. After just over two years of this, Sophie was struggling to keep pace with his demands. Just as she thought she could scrape together enough for yet another flight to Jamaica, he would want cash for car repairs, fuel for his car, a hotel so he could escape Shirley, or clothes. It was endless. If she tried to explain to him how it was affecting her health and how bad her own financial situation was, he just made sympathetic noises and ignored her.

Since the end of the previous year Sophie had been seeing Ty less and less. He promised, as he always did, to visit her and stay a while, but when Sophie asked him why he could not stay even one night with her, he always claimed to have so very much to do. He had to be away somewhere; there was always an explanation. Rien ça change, thought Sophie. *He will never talk to me about anything serious, unless it involves him and his needs and wants. I have to be sympathetic about his father, but what sympathy did he extend to me when my son died? A few words in a few texts, words which seemed to be copied from a standard letter to an annoying girlfriend just to keep her quiet. I tolerate all this*, she thought, *and I know I am being conned and cheated on, and I know he lies, but a part of me refuses to accept it. I want him so much; I adore his big, loping, arrogant body and his handsome face. I melt when I hear his soft Yankee drawl with the undertones of Jamaican. I long for, yet fear, his terrifying size and the pleasure and pain it causes me. But he frightens me when he gets angry and abusive and when he drops subtle hints that he could leave me. And yet—and yet,* she thought, *when I threaten to leave and tell him I can't take any more and why, he wheedles and seduces me back. Again and again I succumb to his demands for money and his rough sexual handling.* She longed for him to make love to her as he had done at first, but now he made no pretence of foreplay. He had not even kissed her as often or as genuinely before or during intercourse for a long time. She wished she had the mental and emotional strength to leave him and forget him, but when she steeled herself to do it, she would relent within hours and sit crying brokenly at the thought of never seeing or hearing from him again.

Sophie's life was tedious, and there was no respite. She worked, walked home, and then worked some more. She no longer had a car, and could not escape the monotony of her life. Ty's financial demands ensured that she was unable to plan the cheapest holiday; even essentials like new shoes were becoming a luxury. She felt beaten down and hopeless.

Ty was pleading yet again for money, claiming he had to go to the States. When Sophie asked why, he told her his parents had gone to stay with his sister and her husband, and he was flying to his brother in Miami so they could drive up there together. Sophie did not know where "up there" was exactly but had learned not to press things with Ty. He was desperate to get the money, dropping continuous hints that he would have to sell his car. He also kept sending her texts telling her how much he loved her. This was the usual foreplay to the act of extracting large amounts of cash from her, Sophie knew. She was annoyed. If he loved her so much, why couldn't he spend at least one night with her at the cottage? The hints continued: Ty had to get together £700 or his car had to go. He also needed clothes and trainers.

"Can you get them for me from your club, baby? I'll pay you back soon, I promise." he texted.

Sophie scraped. She turned off the central heating yet again while Freddie was away at college. The shoes she desperately needed were put on hold. She paid her rent and her council tax a week late and worried daily about being in arrears. Ty phoned her one afternoon as she sat wrapped up in a blanket in the freezing cottage.

"Hi, my baby. I need to come choose some stuff from your catalogue. God, I'm horny for you. Haven't had sex with you for so long. I must come fuck you. You about tonight, hun?"y

"No, darling. I have to work. And Freddie's here at night—you know that."

"OK, hun." He sounded annoyed. "I'll try and get to see you soon."

There was a pause. Sophie knew he wanted money. She waited.

"Baby, have you got a little cash on you?"

"How much, Ty? I've already had to scrape up enough for your trip to save you having to sell your car."

"Whatever you can manage, hun. I'm just so hungry, baby. Don't give it if it leaves you short—"

Sophie immediately said, "Baby, why can't you come here with me? I can feed you and you'll be warm and it'll be easier—"

Ty cut across her. "If I'm being a nuisance, I won't ask again." She knew that tone. It meant "I don't want to move in with you; I don't want to discuss it; I just want money—now."

"OK, darling" she said resignedly. "I can dig up about £30 in all now. That should buy you some food. Will that do?"

"Yep, I suppose so. You couldn't dig up a bit more? I need money for gas too, baby."

"OK, darling. I'll transfer it now."

Sophie started to ask how Ty's father was, but Ty said he had to go, he had so much to do, and rang off. Sophie transferred the cash on her mobile and texted Ty that it was in his account. Immediately he texted back. "Thank you, my darling. I love you so very much." Then he disappeared.

Sophie texted him, "Night, and sweet dreams. I love you," as she did almost every night. He rarely replied and this night was no exception.

The next morning she had her usual "Morning, baby" from Ty. She was not working the day shift, so she had two strong cups of coffee and had a soak in the bath. She got back into bed in her bath gown and was dozing when she heard a noise from downstairs. Then she heard footsteps on the stairs. Ty sat on the top step and put his head around the open door.

"Hi, my baby. Surprise!" Sophie was really happy but also a little nervous. Usually Ty gave her texted notice before his infrequent visits. That gave her the time she needed to prepare herself mentally for what was becoming an ordeal. Sophie did enjoy his lovemaking sometimes. She longed for him, yet she dreaded him at the same time. Ty was becoming impatient and uncaring. He rarely spent time on foreplay and sometimes just used his fingers for insufficient time to stimulate Sophie at all. When they had first met he'd been very considerate and had spent some time on oral foreplay. When this disappeared and Sophie complained to Ty about it, he told her pointedly, "I don't do oral sex. No tongue stuff down there. Don't you know, we Caribbean guys never do that, baby." and Sophie was hurt and angry because she knew full well that Ty was very experienced and capable - and also a liar. But he loved Sophie using her tongue and mouth on his massive penis and would lie back, groaning ecstatically and grabbing handfuls of her hair and telling her he loved her.

Ty swaggered over, bent towards Sophie, and kissed her forehead briefly. He picked up the television controls from her bedside table and tuned the television to his favourite American programme. Sophie winced inwardly. Why must he always have the damned thing on all the damned time—especially when they were together like this, about to make love, and she hadn't seen Ty for ages! He undressed, keeping his vest on as he always did. This was to cover his stomach, as he was touchy about its size. Sophie always told him that she preferred him naked. She was naked and had bulges she would rather he didn't see, but she stripped because he wanted her to. Ty got into bed and began to finger Sophie's clitoris quite roughly. He didn't kiss her; this always crushed her. The kissing had gradually got less and was forced and unconvincing. It was just one of the things that was driving Sophie down into depression slowly and relentlessly.

Then Ty's mobile rang. He rolled away from Sophie, picked it up, and began chatting away animatedly. Sophie shrank into her inmost self. She wanted this man; she loved this man; she missed him so very much and saw him so little—and all he could do was to chat on the phone when he should be gently preparing her for his entrance. She took the opportunity while Ty's back was turned to lean over and get the bottle of lube out of her bedside drawer and apply it to her pubes and inside her vagina. Ty hated the stuff and preferred to just use saliva, which was useless when he was trying to insert such a huge thing, thought Sophie. Ty finished his conversation and put the phone down on the bedside table next to him. He climbed back on the bed and pushed Sophie's legs open. This was the moment she dreaded. She took a deep breath and closed her eyes.

"Come on, baby, just relax." Ty began to slide into her. Sophie automatically put her hand down to try to slow and control his entry.

He smacked her hand out of the way. "No! Stop that—leave it! I'll do it my way. It's mine, not yours." He looked angry for a second, but then he gave her that grin, that dimpled grin with his even teeth so white against his black skin.

She winced as he went into her and caught her breath, as she did every time. She longed for this but also feared it. She was afraid that he would be so passionate that he would become rough; that was agonisingly painful if she wasn't very ready for him. He began slowly, and she started to calm down and even enjoy his body. Then he did what she dreaded; he lifted her legs up, put her feet onto his shoulders, and drove down into her, hitting her cervix with force. She cried out, but he did not ease his thrusting.

"No," she pleaded. He continued pushing hard into her and she winced. Then Ty stopped moving. He looked down at her and grinned and shook his head; then he pulled her legs down. She lay, relieved, waiting for him to continue. In this position she actually enjoyed him, but he didn't much like it, as he couldn't get deep enough. He moved slowly, and Sophie could feel herself responding to him. She smelt the musky warmth of his skin and felt his great, hard body straining against hers. She moaned softly as her desire grew, and she felt her orgasm gathering like a storm. She loved him so very much; she had missed him and his body so very much. She moved with his moving, and her moans turned to a scream as she came, digging her fingernails into his huge shoulders.

"Hey, baby, that was good, eh?" He stopped and withdrew. "You know what I want now."

Sophie knew. She knelt on the bed facing the pillows and leaned forward, using them as a support. She was tense as he spread her legs from behind, raised her buttocks, and entered her.

"OK, baby, relax. I won't hurt you." He always said that, but there were times when he did hurt her—a lot. This time it was not bad. He was at an angle when he wasn't driving against her cervix, and as he began to thrust into her body again, Sophie felt another orgasm rising. She pushed backwards against him and cried out with pleasure as the intensity mounted and she reached her peak again and yet again. Now Ty was really ramming home, and she felt pain, but Sophie was too far out on her cloud of sheer animal lust to register it. Ty began to gasp as he neared his orgasm. They moved hard into each other's bodies as he cried out and thrust forcefully once or twice. He stayed inside her for a few moments while his breathing slowed; then he pulled out and rolled her over. Usually he kissed her and held her for a while, but on his last few visits he had simply moved away and picked up the pack of baby wipes that she kept on his side of her bed and cleaned himself up. He did this now, turning to smile at her.

"You OK, baby?" He got into bed beside her, and she cuddled into him. He held her hand but did not kiss her as he had used to. He was watching the television and ignoring Sophie. Then his mobile rang, and he picked it up and chatted briefly. "OK, I said I had something to do. I'll be about an hour." He looked annoyed, Sophie thought.

That's Shirley—I know it is! He's come to see me because he's on his way to her. She frowned and sighed.

Ty looked sideways at her. "What?" he demanded sharply.

"Nothing," said Sophie. "But I just thought you might have stayed with me for a while. I haven't seen you in ages, and I miss you. I just wanted—" She stopped.

"Just wanted what?" Ty was looking displeased.

"Just wanted to be in your arms and hold you, hun. You won't stay with me for a night, and I hardly see you now. You run away so soon—I feel unwanted."

Ty squeezed her hand. "Don't be so silly, baby. You know I want you very much. Always will."

Sophie pulled up her courage from the deepest recesses of her being. "*Do* you want me, Ty? You hardly ever come here, do you? Remember when I first moved here, you came to visit a lot more often. You were going to move in with me, baby—"

"I didn't say that." He had that pouty expression and his eyes looked large and angry.

Sophie normally backed down when Ty showed annoyance or anger, but now she squared up to him. She spoke quietly. "Yes you did, Ty. From the minute I told you I was leaving Enrico and moving here, you said that it was great, and you couldn't wait to move in with me. But I know that from the second you walked in that door and saw how small and humble this place was you decided it wasn't good enough for you. You seem to want everything to be really expensive, and you're so fussy over everything you eat, and have, and—" Sophie stopped and then continued, "I and my little home aren't good enough for you, Ty. You were going to move in with me and set up home, and we had some sort of a future."

Ty raised his hand but Sophie took hold of it and pulled it down. "No, don't interrupt me, Ty. Don't say I'm talking shit, like you usually do. We talked about all this two years ago when I had just moved in, and you came and actually stayed overnight— don't you remember? We slept on the bed settee because my beds hadn't been delivered. I made you breakfast in the morning, and you had that very thick bacon that you like, and scrambled eggs, and toast, and really good coffee—"

Ty looked at her. "Yes, I remember the breakfast, and the other breakfasts you made me, but I don't recall us talking about other stuff, baby. What stuff was it?"

"Surely you can't have forgotten, Ty. It meant a lot to me—and still does, because none of it ever happened after all your promises. I asked you to tell me exactly what was going on and why you wouldn't keep your promise to me to move in and live with me. You had brought me back from Lincolnshire, Ty, remember? You were supposed to stay with me, and that was to be the beginning of us as a couple. We got back here, and you said you would be gone for a couple of hours because you needed to sort some stuff, and I thought you were going back to Shirley to pick up your stuff and tell her. What a stupid fool I was, wasn't I?" Sophie pulled her hand away from Ty's grip and sat up. The tears were running down her face.

"You didn't come back, did you, Ty? You didn't even answer my texts. I was shattered, but I loved you so much I couldn't do the sensible thing and end it once and for all. The next week you dropped in to see me, and then I did ask you why you treated me like that, and you went on about how we didn't know each other well, and maybe we wouldn't get on together—"

"And?" Ty sounded tense.

"And I told you we were never likely to get to know anything about each other if you saw so little of me and I was just your bit on the side who only existed for sex and money."

"Yep." Ty was now grinning. "Yep, I remember that, baby. I pulled you onto the settee and took your clothes off and gave you a really good fucking for the second time that day. Come on, hun. I've got stuff to sort out; when it's sorted I will move in with you, baby, I promise." He kissed her cheek and then got up to go to the bathroom to urinate and wash.

Sophie sat slumped and defeated. He would always joke or talk his way out of any confrontation—either that or run. She dressed and went down the winding stairs of the tiny cottage. She made coffee for them both. When Ty came down, they stood in the doorway of the house, smoking and drinking the hot, aromatic Colombian brew.

Ty turned. "You've got a new telly, baby. Wow, that really is something." He walked over to it and examined it. "That must have cost a fortune."

"It didn't. I rent mine; it was an upgrade." Sophie took the cups into the kitchen and then returned to sit on the settee. "Come and sit with me and talk."

"Talk—about what?" He started to put his trainers on.

"A lot of things. I hardly ever see you, and you rarely call me or answer when I call you—and you say you hate long texts and refuse to read or write them."

"Yup, baby, I hate those damned long texts, can't be arsed to read them. Prefer calls. Why don't you call me more often?"

"Because I do call you, and you hardly ever pick up, and when you do pick up you tell me you've got company or you're with Shirley or something and put your phone down on me."

"Oh, for Christ's sake, Sophie, are we gonna have another moaning session? Just as well I didn't bloody well move in with you, if that's all life would have been!"

"But don't you see, Ty? It's because you aren't with me, because you broke your promise to me to move in, and because I see less and less of you that we row like this! Anyway, I'm not rowing. I'm just trying to get you to listen to me. How can I have a relationship with a man who hardly ever turns up, who never keeps a promise, who just shows up long enough to fuck me and run, and who only rarely texts or phones when he wants money—" Sophie stopped, and the tears ran down her face. She couldn't win like this, but her temper was rising and she had to tell him.

"You're away a lot, and you keep wanting me to text sexy stuff and send you pics, and to text you pretending to want all this foursome stuff and your men friends—and you know I detest it!"

Ty put his arm around her. "Baby, you know I have to be away a lot, and I miss you, and I get horny, and it helps me to survive. I have to go without for ages sometimes."

Sophie glared at him. "Ty, I've told you this before—you're a very good-looking young guy, and I find it very hard to believe that you exist without any sex at all when we're apart. You've accused me of sleeping with other men just because I haven't answered my phone quickly enough for you. I don't hear from you or see you for ages sometimes. For God's sake, you pick up your bloody phone and talk to Shirley when you're in bed with me!"

Ty's jaw set. "I've told you a million times I do not sleep with that bloody woman! She's my ex and the mother of my daughter, and I go to see my daughter—is that wrong? Am I not allowed to see them then? Do I have to give them up for you?"

"For God's sake, Ty—you've never given up one damned thing for me." She turned her back on him.

Ty folded his arms and leaned against the sideboard. "Tell you what. If you're so damned unhappy, I'll just leave and never bother you ever again. How about that, Sophie?"

She turned to see him picking up his shades and cigarettes and going out of the door. For a moment Sophie hesitated. "No, Ty—no, don't leave me! Please, just listen to me, talk to me." She grabbed at his arm, but he shook her off and went swiftly down the path and out of the gate. She stood sobbing. The big sports car roared throatily and was gone. Ty was gone. Sophie sat sobbing. She got on with her chores and then went to work until late in the evening. Afterwards, she fell into bed feeling worn out and desperate. Her head ached. She fell into a restless sleep.

In the early hours of the morning she was awakened by her phone pinging as a message came in. She picked it up to find a message from Ty. "I'm sorry, baby. Please don't leave me. You know I love you and you're my life."

Sophie sat up and texted back. "I'm sorry too, hun, but I did mean what I said. I don't want us to split up. I really love you too, baby, and you really are my world."

She turned over and fell asleep. Ty had spun his web around her yet again. She was his, unable to exist with him or without him. She was unhappy in his presence and out of his shadow. However far away he was, he held her in the palm of his dark hand.

The year drifted on. Sophie was finding it very hard to cope with her newest loss. Ty did not really help her. When she told him how desperate she felt, he would say things like "I'm here for you, baby" or "I know how you feel." But these were hollow, meaningless phrases. He didn't know, and he certainly wasn't there for Sophie—ever. In a fit of deep depression after being let down yet again by Ty, Sophie told him that she could take no more. She poured out her feelings. Ty ignored her.

That same night Ty texted, desperate and upset, telling her that he had been kicked out of the place where he lived. He told Sophie that he had no proper home, only a room in a house occupied by "a bunch of guys who all drink too much." He said he couldn't escape the drinking, and it was a problem to him, as he was trying to stop. He told her he had no television in his small room, and again he pressured her to get him one like the smart television she had in her living room. She repeated that it was not hers; it was rented. She owned the smaller smart television in her bedroom, and he could have that. But it was not good enough—as so many other things were not. After the kicking-out incident, Ty's phone broke down. He was very angry about it. Sophie told him that it was an expensive phone and the manufacturers should repair it. Ty did not reply. He was becoming increasingly edgy and stressed. Sophie scraped up yet more cash, For His car's MOT, its windscreen, and its tyres. The usual list of needs. Again she wrote a long, heartfelt text to Ty, pouring out her disappointment and shattered hopes. She said it would be better for her to say goodbye before she was hurt beyond healing.

Ty texted back. "OMG, OK. Thanks for all that. I guess I'm on my own now. I won't bother you again."

"I really love you, and I don't want to leave you. You're not on your own—I can't leave you or desert you. Just understand that I don't want to leave you, but you don't seem to see just how much you've hurt me."

"It's OK—you've left me. I understand and I don't hate you for it. I'm just gonna go home now." Sophie was weary of this phrase. Ty was always "going home". Maybe he meant he was flying back to Jamaica or the States - or was it a suicide threat.? Often when he was depressed or desperate he would say he was "going home". Sophie could never quite understand this.

"Please, Ty, no—please don't go." Sophie was desolate.

"Thank you for all you've done for me. I will always love you."

"No, Ty, no—don't go! You are the love of my life, my world. I just can't cope with all the separations, the never seeing you, the not knowing; I can't take it! Darling, don't just leave me." He did not reply. Sophie sobbed herself hoarse and slept badly. She woke at two in the morning and checked her phone—nothing. At seven her phone pinged. Ty had sent "Morning, baby." Then he sent her a link to Charlie Wilson's song "You Are." Sophie listened and cried. They continued exchanging loving texts—but Ty did not see her, and he still wanted cash far too often.

At the end of June he texted, "I need to get out of here today. I'm going mad." Sophie imagined that he was talking about the house he appeared to lodge in. She thought he had been thrown out but had heard no more about the incident so supposed that all was forgiven and he was back there. She was sorry for him. But she had offered him a home, and he would not take her up on her offer. She could do no more.

"I need to get to Nantwich today, baby."

"You need fuel money?"

"Yes, hun." Ty spoke of getting rid of his car, of being unable to pay for it. He texted her a few days later and informed her that he'd used the money she had given him on groceries. "I was so hungry, baby." He pressured her about his car.

Sophie hadn't the means to do anything to help him and told him so. He was stressed about it, and his texts showed it. Sophie noticed that he was slowly becoming more and more unhappy; he was short-tempered and preoccupied. On the rare occasions that she saw him he smelt of vodka, and he was smoking far too much. He had always been troubled, but now he seemed to be wrestling with something bigger, something out of control. He arrived a couple of times and made love to her—at least Sophie told herself that it was lovemaking. Ty was always in a great hurry, and he seemed to want to get it all out of the way as quickly as he could. He seemed to not notice Sophie as a person. He would smile at her vacantly and get the whole process over without much feeling in evidence. They continued to text, but Ty was drifting away, slowly but evidently, and Sophie's heart was breaking. She did not know how to help him, and that hurt her. She loved him very deeply, despite the way he treated her. She wanted him to be happy, free of worry, content. But she knew so very little of the reality of his life—and of him.

Near the end of July, Ty texted her. "Morning, my love."
"Hi, my baby."
"What you up to? Seems so long since we talked." And that caught Sophie's throat—the sadness and yearning in Ty's words.
"Yes, baby, I miss you a lot."

"I miss you too, my baby."

"Can't you just come here for a while, Ty—just a few hours together?"

"I really do want you so much, my baby. I'm just going through some shit at the moment, hun. But like I asked you before, please don't give up on me, OK?"

Sophie was trying not to give up. Always Ty promised he was going to change. Things would be different after he came back from Jamaica, from the States, after next month—but they never changed. Ty's life was a mess, a mess that Sophie had been sucked into when she fell deeply in love with him. She longed to escape it, but she could not desert him, and she didn't want to live without him.

As July went on, Ty frequently told her he loved her, and he sounded sad and genuinely sorry. He told her that he had to get to Jamaica, as his father was going downhill quickly, and he asked if she could help him with the fare. Sophie worried, and plotted, and juggled the rows of figures, as she always had, in order to help Ty. He promised to come and see her but didn't turn up. Sophie tried not to be angry with him. She told him that he could at least phone or text if he wasn't going to turn up. She had explained so many times before that she had to swap work shifts and sometimes lose income in order to see him. She told him that he had let her down so often that she was past caring whether or not she made time for him. The last bit was not true, but Sophie had to try and make him see what he was doing to her, and to them.

The next day, Sophie had a day off, and Freddie was with his father. Sophie was in the kitchen, making a cup of tea and some toast, when she felt a kiss on her neck. Ty put his arms around her and hugged her tightly. They stood there for a little while, and then Ty turned her around and kissed her. Sophie took her tea and toast into the living room, sat down, and started eating her toast. She fed Ty with tiny pieces, which he ate, grinning. Then he took her upstairs, took her clothes off quickly, and was inside her before she had time to even think. He was rough and impatient, and he smelt of vodka. Sophie responded, but when she asked him to kiss her, he turned away, and Sophie felt rejected and sad. Ty looked down at her, kissed her very hard on her mouth, and then drove into her body with great force. Sophie wanted to respond, but she felt that Ty was not really with her. This was animal lust, pure need, an obligation he was fulfilling. Ty pulled out and rolled Sophie off the bed. He pushed her face down, and was soon inside her from behind. He was rough, grunting as he thrust into her with all his weight. He was hurting Sophie; she cried out and willed it all to be over. Then Ty's phone began ringing. He swore, turned away, and picked it up. He held Sophie down with one hand and leaned his elbow on her back whilst he spoke into his phone.

"What? Just be patient, will you! I told you I'll be there soon." He slammed the phone down, climaxed noisily, pulled out of Sophie, and hastily cleaned himself with the baby wipes.

Sophie struggled up. Ty looked at her as if he had only just become aware of her. "Sorry, baby, I have to go."

Sophie said nothing. She was crushed and lost.

Ty dressed; then he leaned down and kissed her briefly. "Bye, hun. Thanks—don't forget the money for my trip, will you."

Still Sophie did not speak. She could not. She so loved this man; she so wanted to help him. He had just treated her like a one-bit hooker—a nobody. She felt her world slipping into hopelessness.

Ty leaned down and kissed Sophie's hair. He smiled, that devastating smile that sucked Sophie into the trap that was destroying her. "Have to go. See ya soon, baby. Don't forget my money for Jamaica."

"No, I won't." It was almost a whisper. Then he was gone, and she heard the gate close and the car start up and drive away. She sat for an hour, staring vacantly at the wall. She was feeling unwell, strange. Part of her was giving up. She had been through so much and mostly alone. Ty had done nothing to support her emotionally. She must cut all ties with him. He was not good for her or to her. But she could not live without him—this she knew. She showered; it was as if she were washing Ty's presence from her body. She watched the television blankly, hardly comprehending what she saw and heard. Then she slept.

Over the next few days Sophie scraped together yet more money for Ty's trip to Jamaica. He was stressed and texted her frequently, asking her not to forget her promises. Sophie had never broken a promise to Ty. She found what he asked for this time too, and soon the time for his departure was imminent. Sophie had hoped that he would call and say goodbye. He had half-promised. But he did not arrive. Her birthday was at the end of July, but Ty forgot it. He pressured her, by text, for yet more cash and then asked her for some propranolol pills. He wanted them for his trip. She got them on prescription, while Ty had to pay for all his medication. She frequently gave him half of her supply. She earned the bulk of the cash for him at the end of that week and suggested he come down to pick it up and see her at the same time, maybe even spend the night with her.

He texted, "I can't stay the night, hun. So-o-o busy getting stuff together."

"Stuff is more important than I am. I learnt that a long time ago, Ty."

"What you talking about?"

"Just that you always seem too busy with other things to spend any time with me."

"Oh baby, please stop saying that."

Sophie picked up her phone and transferred the large sum of money. It would keep her poor for several weeks. She texted Ty. "It's in your account, baby."

"Oh my baby, thank you so much. I love you." Then she heard little from him. On August 12 Ty texted, "Hi, baby. I'm in Jamaica. I'll keep in touch. Love you."

"Love you too, baby."

August 13

"Hey, baby. I'm missing you so much—love you.

"Me too. Hope your dad is OK. Love you. X"

"He's not too bad, baby. What you up to today?"

"Not a lot, hun. What's Jamaica like?"

"It's OK, hun. Wish you were here."

"Is it very hot there?"

Yes, hun. Is my car insurance sorted out?"

"Yes, darling. Don't worry. Wish I saw more of you."

"When I get back, hun."

August 15

"Morning, baby."

"Afternoon, darling."

"How are you today, baby?"

Tired, hun—just leaving work."

"Did you sort my insurance out, baby?"

"Yes, baby. I paid it into your bank."

"When, hun?"

"Two days ago."

"OK, hun. I'll have a look."

"I also paid in £50 for you."

"Thank you very much, hun. I need it so much. Talk soon. Love you."

August 18

"Hey, baby. I'm gonna have to stay a few more days, hun."

"OK, baby."

August 20

"Hey, baby. How are you?"

"Tired, as usual."

"I'm stuck here till Wednesday, hun. I am gonna have to buy a whole new ticket to get home, because I missed my flight home. I do love and miss you so much."

"I don't know what I can do, baby. Your ticket will cost thousands."

"I've contacted Virgin, and I can get a ticket for £740 with my Virgin miles."

"I haven't got that kind of money, baby. Not until the end of September."

"Baby, anything will help."

"Where will you get the rest?"

"Not sure, but I'm gonna have to."

"Why didn't you get your existing ticket changed?"

"I did try."

"And?"

"They wouldn't."

August 21

"Can you put some in for me, hun?"

August 22

"I haven't got much, baby. I've managed to put in £150 for you. It's all I've got. I'm broke now."

"Morning, baby. I miss you so much, and I love you so much."

August 23

"Hun, I only need £200 to get on the plane."

"Hun."

"Yes, baby. Give me a minute."

"Did you get my text?"

"Baby, I don't have £200 until Sunday—I can scrape up £100 now."

"OK, I'll just have to try and get the other £100."

Later that day

"Did you get the £100 I put in your account, baby?"

"Yes, my love. I'm on the flight for 6 this evening—I love you."

"Love you, too. Hope I'll see you again. Have a good flight."

August 25
"Morning, baby."
"Hi, darling."

That evening
"Night, my love. Sleep well. Miss you."
"Tired, hun—jet lag. Love you."
"Sleep, my hun. Love you, too."
"Love you more.

August 30
"I'm just driving up to pick up Jamari, baby. I'll bring him to meet you."

Later that day
"Can you help me with some cash, hun?"
"I haven't got much, but I'll try. I managed £85. Did you get the money?"

23.15 that night
"Love you, baby."

August 31
"Morning, baby."
"Hi, hun. Working hard. Am free tomorrow."
"OK, my baby. Love you."
In the next few days, Sophie paid more money into Ty's bank account. Ty said he would give it to Jamari.

September 4

"Hey, baby."

"Hi, Ty darling."

"What you up to?"

"The usual, baby. Working and sleeping!"

September 5

"Morning, baby."

"Hi, hun."

"What you up to today?"

"I thought we were supposed to be seeing Jamari before he flies back."

"Baby. Ty—Hello?"

September 6

Ty texted Sophie at 08.25. "Morning, baby. XX" Two kisses from Ty was unusual.

Sophie was fast asleep. She had had a very bad night and not slept well.

At 11.42 Ty texted, "OK. I get the message."

Sophie woke at midday. She had a bad head and was very tired still. She read Ty's texts. "What message?" she responded. "I only just woke up. I had a very bad night."

"OK."

"OK? That's all you can say to me, baby?"

"Well, you don't want to talk to me."

"Ty, I tried to talk to you yesterday, but you first let the phone ring and then didn't pick up. The next two times the phone went straight to engaged or cut off. I told you about it, but you didn't answer me. You don't make any effort to stay in touch, apart from saying good morning. That's nice, but you won't answer my texts or pick up my calls, and if I text, you complain my texts are too long. You're ignoring me now. You keep coming online—sometimes you're online for ages, but you don't bother to look at my texts. It's been like this for nearly three years." That was at 13.13.

Then Ty rang Sophie. "Baby, I'm really bad. I don't know what's happening to me. I feel so ill. I need antidepressants or something. I keep drinking—" Ty's voice broke. He was crying. She was shocked at the weak desperation in his voice. She felt terrible for having been so harsh to him in her text.

"I just can't stop drinking, my love. Everything is falling apart. Help me, please, Sophie—help me! I need to get Jamari some clothes to take back. I promised him, hun, but I've got no money."

Sophie's heart was filled with instant pity and love. "Sweetheart, I can spare you £150—Is that OK?"

"Oh, my baby. Thank you so much. I love you."

"Ty, you sound dreadful. Can you come down to me and stay here, baby?"

"No, hun, I wish I could. I've been drinking; I can't drive."

"Sweetheart, if you need me I'm here. Please get some medical help. I wish I could do more."

"Thank you for all you do for me, my love. I am waiting for a doctor to call now. I will get help—I wish you were here ..." His voice trailed off into quiet weeping.

"Call me if you need me, baby. I have to sort out money now. I'll transfer it as soon as I possibly can. I love you."

"I love you, Sophie." He ended the call.

At 16.28 Sophie texted Ty. "It's in your account, baby. I love you, and I'm here for you always."

"Thank you, my love."

Towards the evening Sophie felt concerned. Ty had been unwell and had sounded at the end of his tether. Something was happening to him, something she knew nothing about, and he was breaking down. She had felt it all these weeks and months—his ability to cope going, his edginess increasing, and his attention completely gone. She had better call him, just to check. He might need to talk, to hear her voice. Sophie hesitated; she walked past her phone; then she picked it up and pressed the phone symbol next to Ty's name. It rang and was picked up. There was a short silence. Sophie was nervous. "Hello," she said.

Then she heard, not Ty, but a woman's voice—a cool, authoritative voice. "Can I help you?"

Sophie reeled. This must be a policewoman or a doctor—Ty had tried to take his life! Oh, God. What had happened to him?

Then the woman spoke—and Sophie was stunned at what she said. She stood numb, shocked. Her head swam for a second. *Fiancée?* How could Ty have a fiancée without her knowing about it? She had always had fears about being pushed out of sight, about Ty's secretive life—but engaged? Going to marry someone? He had only just come back from Jamaica—she had paid a lot of money to help him go on that trip! She had gone without a lot; she'd cut corners and sacrificed.

Oh my God, thought Sophie. *I have been helping him to survive—to eat! I thought he was alone and destitute—and he has a fiancée.*

This was the evening of September 6. And the blackness that had chased Sophie for the last five long years filled up her soul and almost drowned her.

THE EVENING OF SEPTEMBER 6

Sophie stood staring at her phone for a while. She felt nothing. It was the same black nothingness she had been thrown into after the deaths of Ben, Ella, and Sean. She looked at her phone and went onto WhatsApp. On Ty's site she typed, "I suspected this all along. I knew you were cheating and using me. Goodbye." She pressed Send. Then she sat down and looked at the screen. He would not answer. She looked at the clock—it was nearly time for her to go to work. She steeled herself to behave normally and went through the motions. She locked the door of the cottage and climbed the hill to her place of work. She had hardly begun her duties when her phone rang. It was Ty. He immediately launched into a furious tirade, with no hello or greeting of any kind.

""Why did you do this to me?"

"Do what to you? What are you talking about Ty? All I did—"

"All you fucking did was to lose me everything!"

"I did nothing! I called your phone because I was so worried about you. You sounded so—"

He cut across her, his voice a snarl. "Why did you bloody talk to her? Why?"

"I thought she was a policewoman or a doctor. I thought something dreadful had happened to you when you didn't answer—you usually keep your phone very close. How was I to know?" Then Sophie cut off the call with, "I can't stay here talking. I have to work." She was shaking. She dug her nails into her palms to force herself to concentrate on her job. Ten minutes later, she was in the kitchen when Ty rang her again. He started talking immediately. There was anger and menace in his voice, like the low growl of a tiger at bay.

"Do you know where I fucking am? Do you? The police dumped me out on the motorway, dumped me, with nothing but a few bags of stuff. I haven't got a fucking penny, or my car—nothing. It's all your fucking fault—"

"No, Ty, it's not my fault at all. You've been cheating and lying to me for three years. You have another woman, a fiancée—*fiancée*—you're going to marry her? For Christ's sake, Ty! I've been scraping and saving, going without, worrying myself sick, thinking I was helping you to just survive, helping you to get to Jamaica to see your dying father. I know you've been going to see Shirley—you seem to be surgically attached to her. But a fiancée?"

"Shut the fuck up, you stupid bitch. I'm stuck here with no car, and no money, and no home—nothing—because you couldn't stop yourself from calling her and telling her—"

"What are you drivelling on about, Ty? I called *your* phone. How could I call someone I don't even know on your phone? You're even more stupid than I thought you were. You haven't said one word about what you've been doing to me—and to this other woman. She says you two are engaged, but you conveniently forgot to tell her about me, and me about her. When were you intending to tell me? Were you going to invite me to the wedding and introduce me to the bride: "And this is Sophie, the woman I've been fucking, and bleeding dry of money, and lying to, and letting down, and conning, and using for the last three years—I'm sure you two will get along just fine."? Tears were running down Sophie's cheeks. She wiped them away defiantly with the tea towel she was holding. There was a short pause. "Shirley put you up to this, didn't she! I know it was her—" Sophie snapped back, "What the hell are you on about, Ty? I don't know Shirley or her phone number, and she doesn't know me or my number. She has absolutely nothing to do with any of this—but yes, she actually does, doesn't she? She's the other victim. I've no doubt you've been living off her as well as me. I suppose I've been keeping this fiancée—I must have been; you've had enough cash out of me. Did I pay for her ring? Were you going to con me for the money for your wedding?" The tears ran down into Sophie's mouth. They were tears of heartbreak but of pure anger as well. "When were you going to tell me about her—and her about me? No wonder you've been so stressed and drinking so much. Just calling in to keep me happy—to take more money."

"What about me? I'm stuck here on this fucking road without my car. Because of you I've lost all I had! I've got to try and … you stupid bitch! You should have put the bloody phone down … said nothing."

"Said nothing? Are you crazy? She tells me she's your goddamn fiancée, and you expect me to say 'Sorry to bother you. I'm his chiropodist, and he missed his appointment?' What the hell would you say if it was the other way round, Ty? Quite a lot, I imagine. You've got one hell of a bloody cheek to talk to me like this! You've been cheating, lying, sleeping around, and getting yourself engaged to another woman, and all you can do is to blame me for calling your bloody phone to see if you were OK when I was worried about you. I don't really care where you are! Anyway, why did she answer your phone? You always keep it next to your heart—attached with superglue. Got careless, did you? And you're blaming *me* for all this? Fuck you, Ty."

When Ty spoke he was whining like a 5-year-old whose conker had fallen off its string. "But what can I do? They just dumped me here. They handcuffed me and put me in a police car, and they just dumped me. I've got no money—"

"Yes you have, Ty. You conned me out of £150 a few hours ago. It was supposed to be for Jamari, but I'll lay bets that he hasn't got it, not a penny of it. Use that and get a bed for the night. What were you doing being arrested, anyway? What the hell is going on, Ty?

"I'm stuck on this fucking road! I want my car—"

"Oh, for God's sake, thumb a goddam lift, or call a taxi and go get your sodding car. Is it your car? Or hers? Or mine even? I paid for so bloody much. And what about the word *sorry*, Ty? Are you sorry? Do you even damned well care about what you've done to me and to this other woman? I doubt it; all you care about is yourself and your car. Well, I hope you have to walk to wherever you're going, and I hope it pours with rain, and I hope this bloody fiancée of yours kills you, slowly and painfully. You've hurt me so badly. You knew my son had just died and that I'd lost Ella—you bastard! You took every penny of my earnings. I should have been able to stop work and rest—" She stood, unable to move.

"What about me and what you've done to my life?" Ty bleated.

"Just fuck off, Ty—fuck off. I hope she kicks you out of wherever you live and makes your life hell."

"I'll make fucking sure you pay for this, you fucking bitch! You'll find out that I'm not just some unimportant nigger—you'll pay for it, believe me."

"Why not, Ty? I've paid for every damned thing so far. And stop playing the racist card. I'm not a racist—you are. And you're engaged to this woman. She's your fiancé; nothing at all to do with me, Ty, so call her, and she can sort it all out."

Sophie cut the call off and switched off her phone. She got on with her work, putting the situation out of her mind. She would deal with it all later. She would have to phone this woman when she got home. What had she said her name was, Olivia? Yes, that was it. She would phone her as soon as she got back, and then she would find out exactly what and who Ty really was.

SOPHIE AND OLIVIA MEET.

Olivia paced up and down. She had gone around the house very thoroughly, making sure that the police hadn't disturbed or moved any of her possessions. She was restless, angry, and confused. She had already kicked Ty out before all this drama had blown up. Now she had a further, very big, reason to wave goodbye. She wanted to know exactly what had been going on. She had asked the woman called Sophie to call her in half an hour. Maybe the woman wouldn't call. Maybe Ty had run to her, and they had both done a runner together. But he hadn't got his car—her car. Then again, just maybe this Sophie had a car and had driven to pick Ty up. Olivia's mind was running at breakneck speed. In the silence of the room, her phone pinged. She jumped. She had been expecting a call from one of them, but the sound startled her. She saw there was a text from Ty, a lengthy one for his standards. Olivia read it.

"Thanks. You kicked me out like a dog. Didn't even listen to what I had to say. If you'd just allowed me to come in, I could have explained everything, but hey, that's OK."

Olivia thought that Ty clearly didn't realise just what had actually happened. She texted back.

"Well, it doesn't have anything to do with armed police tramping all over my house because you were going to blow your head off—yet again—but it might just have a lot to do with the conversation I had with your girlfriend!!!!!!!! DO NOT contact me again."

She sent the message. No reply arrived. There was another loud silence. Clearly Ty was caught on the back foot and thinking, desperately, how to explain each of them to the other. Time was passing. Olivia had no way of contacting this Sophie. Maybe she hadn't got that telephone number, or maybe she had taken it down wrong. Maybe the woman had just called Ty and warned him. Maybe she was more than just the other woman—maybe she was his wife. Olivia gave up. She paced nervously, and she smoked. Time seemed to crawl by so very slowly. Nothing was happening, and she could do nothing. Ty had spent time away so often—clearly he had been with this Sophie. Olivia knew that Ty had spent time with Shirley. She had driven past Shirley's home and seen his car outside often enough. What a bloody fool she had been. Paying for his trips to Jamaica. Buying him a new car. Putting up with his temperament and drinking. Financing a lifestyle he could never afford but which he demanded. Doing all this because she'd loved him. She was so frustrated because she could not get to the people she wanted to talk to—her stress levels built and built.

Then her phone rang. It was just after half past nine in the evening. The incoming call was from a strange number. She picked it up and took a deep breath. "Hello?"

"Is that Olivia?"

"Yes."

"Hello, it's Sophie."

Sophie was quite obviously very nervous. She launched into a long apologetic explanation of how she'd had to work until nine thirty. Then she told Olivia that Ty had called her at work, had been very aggressive and nasty, and had blamed Sophie for the whole crisis. Olivia just wanted to know where Sophie fitted in this whole triangle. Originally Olivia had thought that it was just her and Shirley, but now it seemed there was a third one. What sort of relationship was it? Obviously it was a sexual one—but what else? Sophie was making it clear that she and Ty did not live together. Ty just called in for very short periods of time, obviously on his way to visit Shirley. Olivia discovered that Sophie lived in a small market town en route from her to Shirley. Olivia heard how Ty had texted Sophie the same sickly sweet propaganda, had told her he loved her and couldn't live without her, that she was his angel, and on and on. It seemed that Ty had been calling her less and less often of late. Had been cooler towards Sophie. Olivia heard how Sophie had been bankrolling Ty, non-stop, how he had been calling her from Jamaica on his latest trip and demanding more money to get another flight, as his had been delayed.

Olivia stopped Sophie at this point. "You do realise that I paid for this trip to Jamaica—and the last one? I went with him. We flew premier class and stayed at the most expensive hotel on the island. He proposed to me on this trip. Set up a romantic dinner on the beach, with all the trimmings, and then went down on one knee and asked me to marry him. To be perfectly honest, I didn't want to, not after the way he's behaved on both trips and after. But I said yes and accepted the ring—I paid for the bloody thing! But it was going to be the longest engagement in history, believe you me. I kept him for nine months—he was living with me. Didn't you know that?"

Sophie was quiet and she sounded very beaten down. "No, he told me he was living with a bunch of blokes in this house, that he had nothing but a tiny room, that he barely had enough money for food—I was always giving him my last tenner because it hurt me to think of him being hungry and alone. I kept telling him to move in with me so he could be warm and share our food, but he kept refusing. No wonder, if he was living with you, and getting his holidays paid for. He told me his father was dying each time; he just had to get there. So he took everything I had—and it was all a lie, and he was living with you—"

"He lived in total luxury with me here. I left my lovely country cottage and moved in here because he kept demanding that I did. It's been like that since I met him four years ago—"

"Four years ago? I met him only three years ago! You must have been together then—"

"We kept breaking up—arguing—on and off. Maybe it was then, when we were split up."

"But you got back together again, and you lived together, and he went on conning me and lying to me—all that money that I really couldn't afford. And I thought I loved him—I think I always knew he didn't really love me. I never really trusted him. But this is a terrible shock—he's taken me for a goddamned patsy. The bastard!"

Olivia felt that she, too, had been taken for a patsy, but an even bigger one. He had cost her a fortune to keep. She had financed his upmarket car. Certainly his disappearances had grown less frequent of late, and he had given her about £800 towards their recent trip, of which £200 had been spent on the beach dinner and proposal. The other £600 had just gone back to him, because she had spent it on the pricey outfit he'd worn at the wedding. However, that £800 had, Olivia learnt, been given to him by Sophie when Ty had pleaded for cash to go and see his father, who seemed to have been dying for a rather long time. The man was terminally ill, but Ty had used his condition quite shamelessly as emotional blackmail on Sophie—on Olivia, too, but at least she had met the family and knew the score. Sophie had actually paid for Olivia's proposal set-up! Olivia was furious, not just at Ty's deception and lies but because he had conned this woman by using his father as the reason. He had texted her still whilst they were in Jamaica and begged for more still! Olivia was outraged. Ty had had the best that was on offer. Why had he needed to take this woman's meagre earnings? Sophie had explained her circumstances to Olivia—the losses of her two children, the way she was bringing up her grandson, and the fact that she was still working at her age. That was another thing Olivia couldn't quite cope with. Sophie was in her seventies. She didn't sound it when she was talking, and Olivia would not have known if she hadn't told her. Olivia's anger grew. She told Sophie that the earlier trip to Jamaica had been to attend a family wedding. Sophie had not known this. She had scraped together a fair amount of money towards the trip, believing, as ever, that it was the final time for Ty to see his father. Then Olivia told Sophie that this was not the paradise she might be picturing, that Ty had already been kicked out, and what had actually had happened on that fateful day and evening. She explained that things had been very bad for some time and that the two trips to Jamaica had been total nightmares.

Sophie told of the two phone calls she had had that evening, and how Ty had accused her of causing the situation, blaming her irrationally.

Olivia suggested that they meet. She wanted to see the woman Ty had been running to and talk to her face to face.

Sophie said she could try to get up there, but she didn't have a car.

Olivia realised that this was not the woman she had imagined. She agreed to drive down to see Sophie. Sophie gave her the address and the post code. They were talking on Sophie's land line when her mobile rang. Sophie knew it was Ty.

"Stay on this line, Olivia. He's calling my mobile. I'll get as close as I can to the landline." She picked up the mobile but said nothing.

He was breathing quite heavily. "Oh, so it's you."

"Yes, Ty, it's me."

He was clearly very drunk, almost unintelligible. He mumbled to himself for a short while, and Sophie could only pick out "white trash" and "bloody women ask for it."

"You've got them all there, haven't you."

"No, Ty. There's only me here."

"Well, they're listening, all of them, I know—Olivia and Shirley. You're all fucking in on it, I know. And you—you're bloody evil,

681

an evil, fucking bitch. You've been working away at this in the background. You set it all up." Ty rambled on for almost forty minutes. They couldn't actually hear a lot of what he said, but they did hear, "Shirley, I had more than twenty years of total bloody misery with you. Olivia, well, I still love you, always did and always will. You're a miserable, controlling cow, but I still love you, and I'm gonna get you back. I want you. And you, Sophie. Well, you—what can I say? It is what it is. You just tried to buy me. I got damned sick of having to get the men you gave me money to buy for you, just so you could fuck them."

Sophie took a deep breath. She spoke very quietly. "That is, as you well know, a total lie. Just a way to try and explain why you took so much money from me and lied to me so badly. It's not a very good story really, is it, Ty?"

"Ah well, Sophie, you forget I've kept all my WhatsApp texts." He laughed triumphantly.

> Sophie's voice was even, almost a whisper. "And you forget, my dear, that I have all mine, too. Every single one. Shall we compare them?" She could almost hear Ty gritting his teeth.

"I know about all those other men you had; your neighbours told me about them. Dozens of men—always there. They told me—"

"And exactly how did they tell you, Ty? They don't know you, or anything about you, or your phone number, or your address. But I'll happily go round now and get them to tell you what a goddamned liar you are." Ty mumbled something incomprehensible.

"Then there's your kids. You're such a fucking bitch that it's no wonder they wanted to leave you—die and leave you to get away from you. No wonder you keep that fucking grandson of yours away from his father. It's just guilt, isn't it, guilt over her death!"

Sophie dug her nails into the palms of her hands. She had turned to ice inside. "Do not even mention my children. They are something that scum like you is not worthy of talking about." Her voice was even, calm, dignified. She did not rise to the provocation.

Olivia, listening on the end of the land line, was pushing her knuckles into her mouth to prevent herself from screaming out at him, "You evil bastard!" She wanted to leap at him and remove his eyeballs. In that second, Olivia saw Ty for what he truly was. She had seen glimmers of it over time, but she had tried not to see reality. Now the light shone, unwaveringly, on this vile person. She could not have taken this as Sophie was taking it. Her opinion of this woman rose with this incident. Olivia would have flared up and hit out verbally and physically. Sophie remained icy. She could cut Ty to pieces with a few quiet words. The overpowering tone of Ty's voice throughout this monologue was one of total contempt towards them all— but mainly Sophie. After that it was just banal drivel.

Ty had been brought up in a family in which his father had several children out of wedlock. His brother's wife packed Durex in her husband's suitcase when he left Florida for Jamaica on business trips. Ty expected women to react in the same way, to accept unacceptable things as normal, to shut up and give way. It showed in his final outburst: "You've all got AIDS! You're all going to die!" And then he laughed, and the call ended.

Sophie and Olivia talked some more. They discussed the way Ty had tried to convince Olivia that she had spoken to Shirley and not to Sophie. He had tried the same lies on her as he'd tried on Sophie. Olivia told Sophie how furious she had been when Ty had made those awful comments about Sophie's dead children. They laughed at his comments about Olivia, about her being "miserable and controlling." They spoke about his nasty reference to Shirley. After all, the woman appeared to have tolerated him and his lies, infidelity, and disrespect for a very long time. And she had his child. Then they spoke, very briefly, of the children he had—those they knew, or knew of, or had been told of. Ty was a man who cared little about any other human besides himself. They spoke of his temper, and of how he might very well try to get even with one or both of them. Olivia was very fearful, because he loved her, and that was quite frightening. He wanted her, and if he wanted something, he would pursue it, never giving up and using every ploy in his arsenal.

"If I were to have another man, he'd find out, and God help me, Sophie."

"Well, I know he used to accuse me of having other men if I didn't answer his texts and calls immediately, but I didn't realise he was that bad. He'll want to pay me out, because he blames me for this little episode, but he isn't interested in me love-wise. He hates me. I've lost my interest, because he can't squeeze any more money out of me. He'll just forget me because he'll be so busy trying to get back to you. I think I'm safe in that way—I hope so, anyway. I feel savaged enough as it is—ripped apart. God knows how you feel!"

Both of them were thinking the same thing. Neither of them blamed the other. She was not the other woman; she had not known; she had done no hurt. They even felt a certain sympathy for Shirley. She appeared to have taken the burden for a long time. Maybe she even loved him. There was so much they didn't know about everything. But Olivia realized that it was just the beginning of another chapter, maybe a worse one. Ty did not easily surrender what he wanted, and he wanted her. She was a fighter. Sophie, however, was weaker—easy prey for Ty's kind.

Both sat for a while after the call ended, deep in thought. Midnight slid over the moonlit horizon. Both were inextricably linked now, linked by the sisterhood of hurt, and of life.

TYRESE AND SOPHIE, BETRAYAL

I leaned my head against the pillow, the one he used to sleep on after he was spent, mouth open and teeth opalescent against his black skin. I leaned against his shoulder, absorbing his warmth and smell. The voile curtains stirred in the silent breeze; he said he liked those lacy, whispering curtains when I first hung them. I lay there trying to remember the feel of his body, his strong arms smelling of cologne and sweat. The deep tones of his voice, that soft Yankee lilt with the faintest trace of Jamaica and the dangerous, slummy sun he came from. The fingers so dark and stumpy, almost childlike, so that I wanted to hold and stroke and protect them—and all of him—and keep the splintering away from us in our transience.

It was an illusion, a fabrication, and I knew it. I had known it even as his raw and savage passion had driven his hugeness into my wanting and waiting womb and I'd cried out with joy and pain. There had been too much mystery and covertness. He had guarded the mobile phone with the savagery of a tiger with its prey; at times he had swung round from my body to search its screen. I'd known it all even then.

I want you again and for all time, but I hate you, and I hurt. It's as if I have dropped into scalding oil and cannot escape, and every movement I make towards normality hurts more. There are those little smooth, sneaky times when I feel calmness and relief; I am rid of your stressful lack of concern for me, and my life, and my feelings. I can breathe again; no longer do I have to evade your technological, snarling control. "Where were you? I texted you. I know your family are there, but you haven't texted me for hours." And I had been with my family, laying my son, my only most precious and adored son, to rest in a pure and terrifying heat that would reduce to pitiful ashes the child that my body bore.

You were beautiful but deadly, scarred and sinister, and you were my all. I knew you lied, that none of it hung together sanely, that what you said then was dismissed later. The answers were too smooth and too carefully constructed. But I was sleepwalking, sliding into the ebony depths of your ego-fuelled, insane game.

The curtains whisper in the warmth of the fading day. I built this little home for us, for *us*, you said. I would live in here with you and we would be happy. But I slowly realised that none of my safe haven was good enough for your greedy wants and needs; you craved only the very best, and you had to command that and be the owner of it all. My simple and poor surroundings, my meagre possessions, soon elicited your contempt.

I so wanted you to just be with me. I so want you now, here in my bed, lying quietly in my arms. I want all the drama and pain not to have happened. I want my soul to be able to fly, not to drag in this exquisite torment of loving you one second and hating you with a burning savagery the next. I cry with anguish and fury; I writhe with a wish to hurt, and hurt, and hurt, as you have hurt me. Then I raise my face to the fading daylight, and the hot tears stream unchecked, and I cannot move. I want you, I want you—but you are evil. You have hurt so many people, and to you it is a game. This is a game you love to play. To you this is life, and triumph, and amusement—and you have to win. I was not the prize. I was incidental. And when the prey turns and catches you out, your revenge is terrible and pitiless.

Like a tiger, you drag me across thorns and stones and I am torn and bleeding. You drag me and abandon me and turn to raise your lips in a snarl. Then you look to the other object of your chase, but she will be spared for now. And then she will be a victim for the second time, and she will need her gazelle-like intuition and her ability to swerve to outsmart you.

I am leaning on the pillow and weeping for you, and the darkness is falling.

TYRESE AND OLIVIA, BETRAYAL

I am standing here in this home I made for us. For you and all your wants and demands I left my country nest, my retreat from stress and the world and the pressures of my business, and I came here at your insistence. The light is fading. The breeze is coming gently through the French windows. I walk to the chair where you used to sit, the large red chair with the big footstool, the one where we used to curl up together with your soft, dark skin against my skin. One day you sat on the footstool in one of your too-frequent fits of depression and weeping. I knelt to comfort you, and you dragged me to you and pulled me onto you and made fierce and possessive love to me so that I cried out as a primal orgasm seized me and swept me to the heaven you could create with your great, animal body. And you cried out with me as you climaxed, greedily clutching at my breasts.

I am coldly angry at your betrayal and your lying. Whilst I granted your every whim and endured your violent tempers and terrifying outbursts, your absences, your silences, your repeated lies, your dark possessiveness and jealousy, your arrogance and vanity, your dishonesty and deviousness, and your often rough and pitiless lovemaking, you were giving your body to her. You were in another woman's bed and in her body. You were talking to her and kissing her and making promises to her. I endured all you threw at me because I loved you and adored you. I asked only that you stay faithful to me.

I light a cigarette and stand out in the garden. I shiver because it is chilly and because my body is reacting to the shock of this betrayal. We were at the point of parting. After Jamaica I packed your bags time and time again and told you to go and leave me to a life of peace, without your sulking and tears and pleading. Your endless drinking was destroying our life, and every day brought new grinding tensions and words and silences. But I took you back over and over, and you would have worn down my defences yet again and slid your way into my affections and heart and bed and body. You would have spent a long time slowly and skilfully pleasuring my body until I begged for you to enter me and then begin another of my nightmares of pleasure and pain.

I am crying silently; tears pour down my face and run onto my breasts. I feel such fierce love for you—my man—a worthless traitor who has enslaved me so cunningly and inescapably.

Like some dark, beautiful, deadly jungle creature you have pursued me, sometimes holding me lovingly and then snarling menacingly without warning. I want you to suffer as I am suffering, to know hopeless and painful love that cannot have what it cannot live without.

I must leave you, but I am your possession. You will not let me go. I feel pity for the other woman but no hatred or jealousy or resentment. She thought she was the one you ran to and adored and that her body was the only one your body pleasured. Her shock and grief was palpable—and your reaction shocked me when I discovered the truth. I knew she was telling me no lies and that she loved you as I did. Your rejection of her in a second without a shred of feeling, your filthy lies designed to degrade her, your derisive laughter—did you think that sort of cruelty would win me back?

You savaged her, like a great jungle beast, and I am left as your prey and feast. I must win the chase and outrun you, because I know that you desire me as a prize, as your prey, without any feeling for my wounds. This is a game I must win. I stand at the edge of the jungle whilst you rest and recover your cunning and guile. You want me for your needs, not for mine. I will outrun you. I will help your other victim because she is so weak and so wounded. You have betrayed and savaged her, so I must fight for us both.

But my body cries out for you. My heart beats with your heartbeat. To be held in your arms during the rare moments of your gentleness was my all, my life. Why can this not be some terrible dream? I will turn, and you will be standing there, smiling with that beautiful and inescapable invitation for my forgiveness and love. You will step forward and hold me very firmly and passionately ... but this has all gone into the darkening world of betrayal and lies, and I am crying again. The wind blows my hair into my eyes, and I am blinded— blinded and lost.

The other has been dragged mercilessly, and hurt, and rejected. I stand here, wounded too, but stronger. I know you will not let me be until I defeat you.

I stand in the garden, crying.

OLIVIA AND SOPHIE, AN END AND A BEGINNING

In the next couple of days, texts flew between them. Olivia told Sophie about the first trip to Jamaica, and she sent pictures of her badly bruised arms. Then Sunday arrived, and Olivia set off to meet Sophie. It was very difficult to find her tiny cottage; the satnav seemed to have developed amnesia. Olivia drove around the one-way system of the little town for some time before she gave up and called Sophie. Sophie directed her, and Olivia soon pulled up in front of the row of tiny cottages. Olivia felt very strange. Sophie had told her that this was where Ty had parked on his visits. She sat for a while, thinking of Ty arriving here, getting out of his car, and going into the other woman's home. He probably came straight from her house, her bed, her body. She took a deep breath, got out of her car, and went to the door of the small dwelling.

Sophie was waiting, heart in her mouth, for Olivia's arrival. The knock at the door came, and Sophie opened it. The woman who stood there made Sophie realise why Ty had lived with her and wanted to marry her. She was a delicate, very pretty blonde with large, firm breasts. She wore a tight-fitting black-and-white dress, very high black-and-white shoes, and jewellery that was very real. Her fingers were covered in gold rings, mainly diamond rings, and they looked genuine. Her nails were the type that were stuck on, and they were black and white too, with tiny jewels set into most of them. Her make-up was pristine. She was the epitome of a smart, elegant, rich woman. Sophie felt a total mess. She was in her shabby trousers, a loose hippy top, and her old slippers. She wore no make-up, as she normally didn't, and she felt extremely dowdy and inferior. Then she saw that the woman, Olivia, was holding out a box of cream cakes, almost like a peace offering, a way of saying, "All is well. I mean you no harm."

Olivia looked back at a woman who was into her seventies. Untidy and not well dressed, she looked like an unstylish hippy. Olivia had expected to see someone prettier—why else would Ty have been unfaithful to her? But this woman was quite plain and unremarkable. She had high cheekbones, a snub nose, untidy hair, and was overweight. Her nails were worn down and unpolished. Olivia noted that some of her fingers were twisted badly with arthritis. On the phone she had sounded much younger than she actually was. Olivia could have accepted a woman younger than Ty; she had felt her fourteen years ahead of Ty to be quite bad enough. But when she had heard that this other woman was in her seventies, she'd been very shocked. Whatever did this woman have that Olivia could not give in large measure already? Finding out that she had virtually nothing and was very plain, not well dressed, and overweight, Olivia could almost have despised her. But she realised in that instant that Ty had used this poor woman, mercilessly and coldly. He'd lied to her and stolen from her, just to back up the lifestyle he pretended to—and already had on demand from Olivia.

Sophie smiled at her. "Come in."

Olivia stepped into the tiny living room. She held out the box. "I brought you some cream cakes."

Sophie took the box. "Wow, lovely—thanks. I shouldn't eat them, but what the hell! I've given up worrying." Sophie looked at Olivia. *She's even lovelier than I imagined she would be. No wonder Ty wants her back*, thought Sophie She felt sad, inferior, and defeated. She realised with terrible clarity that she had been used for nothing more than money—and occasional sex. She was no competition for this classy blonde. She hadn't had a ghost of a chance from the start. Ty had singled her out as prey—to be fleeced of her earnings, and to be used, coldly, for sex—not for lovemaking. There had been no love of any sort.

Sophie asked Olivia to sit down on the old settee. It was covered in brightly coloured throws. One was a union jack and the other two were the stars and stripes of the USA. Olivia thought to herself, *This must be for Ty.* She looked around when Sophie disappeared into the kitchen to make her a coffee. Above the filled-in fireplace was an amateur painting of President Obama—rather a good one, Olivia thought, but another thing put there for Ty. Later Olivia learned that this had been up on the wall since Sophie had moved in; her grandson, Freddie, had painted it. He had autism, and thus was not—or so the school had informed them all—someone with great creative ability. One day the class had been asked to paint a picture of their personal hero. Freddie had produced this masterpiece out of his head, and it hung there not for Ty's benefit but because it was a triumph for Freddie. Sophie was very proud of the work.

As Olivia sat on the throw, she thought, *He sat here—Ty sat here—next to her, in this room, on this throw. She has brought all these Americanisms to make him feel at home in this place. He is a Jamaican, brought up in the States, and she has done all this for him.* She was sitting in the place where he had committed adultery—yes, it was adultery to her. He had proposed to her and called her his wife. Should she really be here? Was this right? Yes, she would stay here, and she would talk with Sophie. She had done no wrong—she had been as cheated on and mistreated as Olivia had. She'd heard the way Ty had spoken to Sophie on her mobile that night. There had been no love there. He'd been vile and hurtful, had made it so clear that she was nothing to him. Olivia was sorry for her, not angry with her. She was angry at Ty for his cruelty to her. Olivia want to talk to Sophie and find out what had been going on.

Sophie came in with coffee and the cream cakes that Olivia had brought. The two women sat side by side on the stars-and-stripes throw, drank coffee, ate the cakes, and talked. They talked of Ty, of how they'd first met him, of the things he had said and done, of the intertwining of their lives. They discussed the texts, the excuses, the enormous amounts of money he had wheedled out of Sophie, and the lies he had spun to elicit her sympathy. Sophie told Olivia of the miseries she had suffered when Ty had demanded that she pretend to want his threesomes and of the horrible night when he'd almost forced her into a foursome. She described how she had resisted and how he had been so very drunk and had thrown everything out of her drawers. His temper, his accusations—there was so much to tell, to get out of her system. She showed Olivia the exercise book full of carefully written figures copied from her bank account. It showed that Ty had taken the astonishing amount of £42,000 from her earnings in less than three years. "Why did I let it happen, Olivia? I knew what he was doing! I knew I couldn't trust him. I knew he didn't really love me—I just wanted to believe him. I closed my eyes to reality. He has a sneaky, velvet way of creeping into your heart and mind. After all the men I've had in my life—total arseholes, to a man—you'd think I would know better, and at my age!"

"Don't blame yourself, Sophie. I've had more arseholes than you have, and I'm a pretty shrewd businesswoman. I should really know better, but you're so very right. That man can talk a woman into anything—just anything. I didn't trust him, and I closed my eyes to it too. That little voice at the back of my head kept on telling me, and I told it to shut up. He is just a very, very cunning and dangerous con artist. He plays a woman like an instrument. I was on the point of kicking him out for the last time when all this blew up. It wasn't all love and roses—no way, Sophie. It seems as if I had the best of it all I know—"

"Well, at least he lived with you; he spent days and nights with you. He wouldn't stay with me more than a couple of hours. At first he picked me up from work; then we would make love at his hotel before we drove back, and sometimes he would spend a night with me, but it wasn't often. It was very clear to me from the first second he cast eyes on this little cottage that it wasn't good enough for him, Olivia. He had that expensive car and expensive tastes, and he was always demanding money. I was such an idiot. He said he'd move in with me, but he had no intention whatsoever of doing that. Once he even brought me back here and said he had to go and pick something up; he would be back in two hours. He never came back. He never

697

answered my texts. And I just let him keep doing it—hurting me, stealing from me, lying to me—"

"Sophie, you were a victim in a way other women aren't." Olivia put her hand on Sophie's arm. "You were fragile and vulnerable, such easy prey for that unfeeling bastard. You had just lost your children so tragically, and he knew that."

"Yes, I know. I was just sleepwalking through life. He really used me—" Sophie was near to tears. Olivia's description of her world, her home, the life she and Ty had lived together, and the obvious love Ty had for her was like a hot knife in Sophie's heart. Everything she'd thought she had shared with the man was fake. She felt so exposed and unclean. He must have laughed at her as he looked at his bank statement and saw each deposit he had earned from his lies, the pleas of hardship, the tales of his dying father, and the stories of hunger, cold, and homelessness.

Then Olivia told Sophie her tales. She described the cost of keeping Ty in luxury in every aspect of life—the expensive car, the trips abroad flying premier class, the most expensive and luxurious hotels on the island, his clothes, and the clothes Olivia had bought for his family for the wedding. She spoke of the food, copious amounts of alcohol, specialist barber's fees, and the costly hair products. She mentioned the trips to Jamaica, the horrors of Ty's drinking, violent screaming rages, racism, suicide attempts, disappearances, and lying. She told of the terrible suffering she'd had to endure when her legs were seriously sunburnt, of Ty's appalling performance when they'd returned to England, and of how he had driven off and left Olivia on her own—maybe, even, to die alone.

Sophie was shocked that Olivia had still taken him back, after all that—just as she had done. Neither one of them had been able to resist his pull, his mesmerising personality, his silent, deadly, sweet web-spinning. They talked for nearly four hours, and dusk was falling when it became clear to them that Ty was still in love with Olivia but that he probably hadn't meant to fall in love with her—just to love her whilst he was fleecing her. And they agreed that he would not let her go lightly. He always wanted his own way. His attempts to marry Olivia so quickly in Jamaica had been his way of ensuring a hold on her. He wanted control and access to her wealth, body, and soul.

Olivia warned Sophie that Ty was more deadly and evil tempered than she realised. Sophie had really had very little contact with him.

Sophie decided that she, at least, would be safe, as Ty now hated her. He had decided to blame the entire situation on her. He had insisted for a while to Olivia that Sophie was actually Shirley and that Sophie did not exist. Not being man enough to admit the truth, he'd continued trying to convince Olivia that it was true.

Olivia needed none of his fabrications. She had sat beside Sophie and seen all of his WhatsApp texts on her mobile. The woman was open and honest. Not arrogant or belligerent, as she could have been. She was just shocked, and saddened and, like Olivia, angry at what this man had done to both of them. She was angry for Sophie. There was a warmth, a closeness in the shared trauma that was bringing them together.

Sophie felt trust—something she found very hard after what had just happened to her.

Olivia felt that they could both help each other through the coming journey. It would not be easy. They were both sad, angry, and confused. The hold this man had on them both had not just disappeared.

Sophie walked out to the car with Olivia. She was very impressed by the big new Jaguar and felt slightly inferior. They agreed to stay closely in touch. Sophie remarked, "I just feel that he'll lie about me, and lie viciously. He has nothing to lose now. He wants you. I was expendable—but what the hell! I don't care any longer." She waved Olivia goodbye and watched the big, sleek car purr almost noiselessly away and around the corner. She was angry and very hurt, but she was glad she had met Olivia. As for Ty, she would get that bastard out of her head. But she knew that it would be a fight, because despite all that had happened, she still loved this man. She had to break his hold on her being.

Olivia drove fast. She was angry too—for both of them. And she was afraid as well, afraid of what was to come. Ty would fight to keep her. She would fight to get away from him. She knew that she still loved him very deeply indeed, and this angered her more. At least now she had an ally in Sophie. The woman was financially poor and weak in some ways; she was bearing tremendous burdens of grief and trauma. But she had spirit, great humour, dignity, and a quiet strength. They shared a problem, the experience called Ty. They would need each other.

That night, just before Sophie fell asleep, her mobile rang. It was Olivia. "Hi, Sophie, I just had to call and say thanks."

"Thanks—for what?"

The Sixth of September

"Probably for saving my life. Ty's temper is terrifying and uncontrollable. If this hadn't happened and forced me to kick him out once and for all, I really believe he would have killed me in a fit of temper. When you picked up that phone, it did a hell of a lot of good."

"For both of us, Olivia. I was at the end of my tether. The stress of finding cash non-stop was making me ill—that and the emotional strain of that man. I nearly didn't make that call. I walked past the phone twice, and then, well, something seemed to tell me—it sounds strange, I know—to pick up and call. So I did."

"No, it doesn't sound strange to me, Sophie—not strange at all. You were told. But that's for another time. Thanks again. Goodnight, and sleep well."

"Goodnight. I'm glad you came. Speak soon."

The same great, cold moon hung in the night sky over the two of them. There was power in their unity. They would need it in the coming days.

The next morning Sophie's mobile rang twice. She didn't bother to pick it up. She knew it was Ty. She had blocked his number, so it would go straight to reject and he would get the message. Then he tried her landline. She let it ring until it stopped; then she picked it up and keyed in the code to block it. The system on her phone was such that it was not possible to block a number until it had actually rung her. That should keep him away for now. She got on with her day's work. She was still shaken, but she tried hard to cope.

Olivia was at home. She had slept in and didn't feel like going to the office that day. Since she was the boss, she could generally do as she pleased. She showered and sat drinking her coffee, still thinking about the previous days. She did not relish going outside to the stares and whispers of her neighbours who had witnessed the recent drama. They would notice that Ty's car, and Ty, had disappeared. He had managed to sneak back and drive the car away on that fateful night. She had texted him to demand its return. As she was paying the credit instalments, it was hers. He called her and begged her to give him the car. "I'll make the payments. I need the bloody car—let me have it." She gave him two weeks to return it. After that she would inform the police that it was stolen. As she sat thinking, her mobile rang. It was Ty. "Hi, baby."

"Sorry. I'm not your baby."

"Aw c'mon, hun. You're too intelligent a woman to let that bitch fool you—"

"What bitch would that be, Ty?"

"That bloody Sophie. She's nothing to me, baby. I only ever slept with her twice. She was coming on to me. I didn't want the silly cow. I couldn't get rid of her—"

"So how did she keep finding you, Ty? Nobody else ever can."

"Very funny. Look, she tried to buy me; she kept giving me money. I didn't ask for it. I had to keep getting my mates to sleep with her. She wanted sex all the time—I got bloody fed up with it. She wanted me to do these foursomes—kept wanting to be taken up to my friends for sex. She never was anything to me and isn't now."

"So she forced money on you, Ty? You never actually asked her for it—is that right?"

"Yes, baby, that's it exactly. She just kept paying it into my account and bothering me to get my friends to fuck her—we were all fed up with her. The guys just pocketed the cash, got drunk, and laughed one hell of a lot. It was crazy. You can't imagine just how—"

"Well now, that's very funny, Ty, because I sat down on her settee with her—the one you used to sit on, Ty. Oh, and I parked my car outside, on that wide pavement just past the garage, where you always used to park. We sat on that throw with the stars and stripes on it, and I read all those WhatsApp messages from you, Ty, all those begging texts, asking her for money. Even when she told you that she was broke, you kept demanding more and more. All those stories about your father dying and asking her for more money for airfares back, when you were flying premier class with me, and staying in the best hotels in luxury. You squeezed every penny you could from that poor woman. She lost her kids so tragically, and she's bringing up her grandson alone, and she's in her seventies. I heard what you said to her on the phone last week. It was despicable. I wanted to tear out your eyes, you bastard!"

"But baby, I didn't love her. I don't know, I told you—"

"Oh yes, I saw all those texts, too. How much you loved her and wanted sex with her. It wasn't her asking you to buy men for her—it was you telling her in graphic terms what you wanted to do to her."

"Livvy—I love you. I didn't know I was going to fall in love with you like this. I must get back with you! I will change, baby. I can change. I'm gonna spend the rest of my life getting you back. Why do you let that poisonous bitch dictate to you, pull your strings like this! I hardly knew the lying cow. She wanted me, but I didn't want her. I was trying to get rid of her, baby. I hardly saw her; I was trying to dump her—"

"I don't need anyone to pull my strings, Ty. I can see exactly what's been going on. And as for dumping her, well, I read all the recent texts. It didn't look to me as if you were dumping her—asking her for sex, telling her you loved her. The last thing you did was to beg money off her, and not to buy men with—it was for clothes for your son. So cut out all the lies, Ty."

"If you listen to that liar—"

"Oh no, Ty, she isn't a liar. I sat down with her for some time. I'm good at sizing people up, and she's as straight as a die. You took advantage of her vulnerability, of her grief. You just used her. For that I hate you even more. You treated me badly enough, but you treated her more than badly—unforgivably. Now get off my phone. I have a business to run." Olivia cut off the call.

Later that day Olivia called Sophie, and they agreed to meet at the weekend again. Olivia would drive down there, she was going to that area anyway, to visit her father—the man who had been her real father after her childhood horrors. She had never forgotten his kindness to her, her siblings, and her mother. Her mother had lived at the house and had passed on there. Olivia could feel her everywhere. Her father had not allowed her mother's room to be disturbed, and it was there that Olivia found her mother's soothing and beloved presence.

On the Saturday, Olivia rolled up at the tiny cottage again, and again she clutched a box of cream cakes. Sophie greeted her warmly. A friendship had sprung up quickly between the two women, based on their shared experiences and hurts. They needed each other to talk their separate ways through the pain and confusion. But they felt a closeness after a very short acquaintance. They sat down with coffee. Already Sophie knew Olivia's taste in that area—two heaped teaspoonfuls of Americano Intense, two sugars, and add a little cold water. They each tucked into their cream cake, and then they launched into another session of "recovering from Ty" therapy. Inevitably the subject of sex and Ty—in particular Ty's size—was raised. Olivia said, "But that cock! Did you manage to take it without any pain at all?"

Sophie wrinkled up her nose and half-grinned. "Omigod, no—not that python, that black mamba! At times I could have screamed, especially when he pushed my knees up to my shoulders. It hit my cervix, and that was too much to take. I used to tell him that it was painful, and at first he took some notice and even said sorry, but after a while he just seemed to enjoy the fact that it was painful. Probably good for his ego."

"God, he made me bleed every single time we had sex, not heavily, but it always happened. And yes, he used to push my knees up like that too, and it bloody well hurt."

"The first couple of times we had sex, I bled like a goddamned road accident." Sophie made a face. "After that I had to tell him to be careful when he went in; he always put it in too low. I used to put my hand down and try to guide it and slow it, but he hated that and used to get really cross. He would say—and Sophie mimicked Ty's Jamaican American accent— 'No, leave it! It's mine, not yours.'" They laughed. Sophie continued, "But if he got rough, it was awful, especially when he did it rear-entry position. That was agony if he went in at the wrong angle."

"Actually I never let him do that; I don't like that doggy-style stuff. I know what you mean by him being rough. I had rows with him and made him stop if he did get too much, but when he was really worked up, and just as he was coming, he really thrust like hell, and it was painful." Olivia sipped her coffee.

"If I was coming at the same time it wasn't too bad. In fact, his size made it a hell of a lot better. It was just the soreness after each session, or if he didn't let me put enough lube on. He hated the lube I used—preferred the gel stuff—but he just got stroppy if I tried to get plenty on him before he rammed that weapon in," said Sophie. They both grinned at the memories.

"But he did know what he was doing, didn't he?" said Olivia. "He was very experienced and knew just exactly what to do to make me desperate for him."

Sophie felt puzzled—and a little hurt. "I wouldn't have said that exactly. He could be good and I know he was very experienced, but after a while he just wasn't marvellous at foreplay, and he didn't do oral— not after the first few times anyway. He just stopped doing it and told me Jamaicans don't do that sort of thing." Olivia put down her coffee mug.

"Hell no! He's a liar, Sophie. He spent ages doing oral on me, knew just what to do, perfection; foreplay was always terrific. He could get me going even when I didn't start off wanting anything at all. He would go on for half an hour or more before actually going into me. He was a very skilled lover." She looked at Sophie's face. "Seems as if we knew two different men—am I right?"

Sophie sighed and grinned weakly. "I seem to have had all the rough stuff. At first I did get a little of that good treatment, but it very quickly turned into wham, bam, thank you ma'am—in, fuck hard, come, and out again. Then look at the phone, and off he goes. He did tell me that he didn't like oral sex, although he seemed to have forgotten that he used it on me to start with."

"Huh," said Olivia. "He was fucking so many women at the same time that he forgot just what he did with, and to, them all. Should have kept a bloody diary. Arsehole." Again Sophie managed a faint smile, but in her heart she was weeping. Olivia had been the one who got the real lovemaking, the foreplay, the tenderness, the holding, the sleeping close to his body after it was over. Sophie felt unwanted, abandoned, and useless. She was the ugly, undesirable child her mother had told her she was all those years ago. She had felt as if she had something special with Ty. But now she realised that she had been nothing to him—she had just been an alternative to masturbation. Olivia was the one he really loved, the one who mattered.

Olivia knew she still loved Ty, and she did really miss his body, his skill and the sometimes-patient gentleness so at odds with the rest of his character. But she was angry, angry because he had needed this other woman. Why? Clearly he had not treated Sophie in the same way; he had used and abused her for his own dark wants and needs. What had he not got from Olivia that he had found in Sophie? It must be something sleazy, something he knew Olivia would have refused to give him. She felt sorry for Sophie. She had watched her face as they spoke, and she realised that Sophie was finding out just how cruelly and coldly she had been used.

Sophie stiffened her back. "So, what the hell. We need to get an STD check. Although I've had nothing so far, I'm a bit worried because he seems to have slept with the entire female population of the Western world." Sophie bit into her cake. "Thank God my ovaries have gone into a retirement home, Livvy."

Olivia chuckled. "Mine too. Imagine finding yourself pregnant by him. I'd have it aborted pronto—"

Sophie thought sadly, *I did wish that I were younger and able to be impregnated by him. I did wish to carry and give birth to a beautiful, mixed race child of his body. I loved him so much. I was that much of a fool.* Outwardly she laughed and agreed with Olivia. "Too damned right I would. How many kids has that man got? I know of two in Antigua, who are supposed to be his only legitimate kids, a son and a daughter. He's got a mixed-race daughter by Shirley, another daughter by a Spanish woman in Florida, a son in London—who was, get this, born only weeks before the legitimate son—that poor little girl in Jamaica, and there was a rumour of a mixed-race girl who lives near Shirley, by one of the teachers at his other daughter's school. It's a real scandal on wheels. That's seven kids spread around, the poor creatures."

"Well, get *this*, Sophie. I spoke to someone in London, some woman who knows Ty's first wife, and who hates him. She says he's the biggest liar ever born; liar is his middle name. She told me that he has *fourteen* kids, and those are the ones she actually knows. Told me there could be more in the States, and in Jamaica, and Antigua, and England. He never uses a condom. Just doesn't care. Disappears, and sometimes they find him when the baby arrives. He told me that Shirley met him on holiday in New York, in a bar. They slept together just hours after they met, and she got knocked up by him that first time."

"They did stay in touch, though. I'm not sure what to believe about their relationship," Sophie said. "He told me that he always runs back to her because he doesn't know where else to go. He's been with her for a lot of years. Seems they don't sleep together—or so he told me."

"And you believe a word he says?" Olivia snorted. "He told me that he's married to Shirley and told you he's married to his daughter's godmother. What the hell do we believe?"

"Yes." Sophie cocked her head to one side thoughtfully. "It is a very weird relationship. Who holds the power there? Does she have him back each time he screws up? Does she see this as power and control? Does she still love him, and this is the only way she can have him, when he's down and needy? He says he hates her and their life together is total misery, yet still he goes back. Why? Does he still love her—in the way he seems to interpret love? What does she know about him that gives her a hold? What forces him to return to someone he hates? They seem to have a sort of toxic symbiosis. The biggest hate affair of the century. And where did Shirley think Ty was all these months he's been with you?"

"Ah, now you remember the names I told you about on the bank statement he tried to burn? Well, one of those women lives in Hertfordshire, where he told me his friends lived, the ones he was supposed to keep going to see. Well, when we came back from Jamaica this last trip, he asked me for a lift, just before I was a bloody fool enough to take him back again. He gave me the postcode, and I put it into the satnav. Well, we never went there. But I got suspicious, and so the other day I drove there. I saw her. Pretty, red hair, about 38. Didn't let her see me, of course. I tackled him about it when he called me the day before yesterday about the car—and all the weeping and begging. He says she's a very old friend, known her for fifteen years; she's apparently married to some bloke in the nursing world. Says they're only friends, and he's always been able to sleep there if he needs a bed while he's passing that way. Well, apparently Shirley knows about her—God alone knows what—but Shirley thinks that he's been there all this time."

Sophie frowned. "How did you know that?"

"Remember when Ty was supposed to take Jamari to see you?"

"Oh yes, and they didn't turn up, and he wouldn't answer my texts."

"They left before I got home, and Ty told me he had to take Jamari back to London. Well, he didn't. He took him down to see Shirley. Remember that Jamari is half-brother to Shirley's daughter, so it's natural that they'd want to see each other. Poor Jamari had been expecting to meet you, Sophie. When he and Ty rolled up here, he looked totally confused. Especially when Ty called me Olivia. Then, when Jamari was stuck, unable to get to Gatwick and fly back to Antigua because his father had been kicked out and had let him down, he called you, and you called me, and I sorted out taxi money for him. He told me he was really sorry, but if he had said a word to me about you, Ty would have just dumped him, and he wouldn't have even got back to London. He was going to try and have a private word with me, but Ty whisked him away before I left the office— obviously to prevent that happening. Well, Jamari told me that Ty parked his car around the corner in a side street, not on Shirley's forecourt. He used to do that a lot when he realised I went down to see Dad and was able to check whether he was with Shirley. And then I asked Jamari where he slept, and he told me on the settee. So of course I asked him where Ty slept, and he said his father slept with Shirley—after all the lies and denials. We were right, Sophie. And that's when Jamari found out that Shirley thought Ty was with that redhead all the time he was with me."

"We really need to chat with Shirley. I wonder how much of this she knows. He isn't going to just stroll in with his carful of bin bags and just say, "I'm home, honey." I wonder if we'll be hearing from her, Livvy!"

"Maybe we should have a word with her, Soph. What say you?"

They finished their coffee and cakes. They talked a little more, and then Sophie waved Olivia goodbye. The Shirley question was going to sort itself out, but neither of them yet knew that.

The following day Sophie was at work when a message flashed up on her phone. "Please ring me." She didn't recognise the number, and she never replied to unknown numbers.

She texted back. "Who are you?"

Again a text came asking her to ring, and again she asked who it was.

Then the reply came. "Shirley Benton, Ty's wife."

Sophie replied that she was at work and so unable to call until later. When she got back to the cottage she decided that perhaps she should call Olivia, but many texts and calls proved fruitless. Obviously Olivia was in one of her many meetings. Sophie dialled the number Shirley had given her.

It rang for a while, and then a voice said, "Hello. Yes?"

"This is Sophie. You texted me and asked me to call you. What do you want, exactly?"

"I just wanted to find out what's going on—if you are who he says you are."

"And who does he say I am? *He* means Ty, I suppose?" Sophie found the woman's voice strangely different to what she would have imagined a woman in Shirley's high-ranking position would have. It was flat, monotonous, a one-note song with no hint of character, or intelligence even. She sounded as if she were reading, badly, off a script. She almost sounded drugged, Sophie thought.

"He says you're called Sophie, and he's been with you and that other woman. I just want to find out if it's true—"

"I am called Sophie, and you seem to know what's been going on, so why don't you ask your husband, Shirley? If he's told you this much, then ask him for all the stuff you want to know."

"Ask that bloody liar? Are you joking? He never told the truth in his entire life—"

"Well, I hope so," Sophie cut in. "He said you'd given him total misery for twenty years or more. He seems to hate you. Why has he run back to you? Why does he always keep running back to you?"

The woman ignored her question. "I can get that bastard deported if I want to—and I do want to! You just tell me what's been going on, and I'll get him run out of England."

"How, exactly? Committing adultery isn't grounds for deportation as far as I'm aware."

"He got kicked out once after he did a sentence over here. I met him in the States. He wanted to come back here, so I married him to get him back here. I hold the power. I can get him deported—you'd better believe it. What about this other woman? Do you know her? Have you spoken to her?"

Sophie's mind suddenly saw a faint red light flashing. "Why don't you speak to her yourself? I don't know her—I don't exactly want to, do I? She's the other woman, for Christ's sake. You got my number from Ty no doubt, so get hers and ask her whatever you want to. It's nothing to do with me. I've known about you for three years. But you have to realise that he told me he was married to your daughter's godmother; he owes her five grand, apparently, for doing this. You're just his ex, the mother of his daughter, and he lives in your house and helps you because you have a big, responsible job."

The woman snorted. "Bloody liar! He's my husband."

"Anyway." Sophie wanted rid of this woman. She was getting suspicious of her identity and her motives. "I think this call will end here. Ask your husband, as you call him, anything you want to know. I don't want to be involved in any more of this horrible mess. He's caused a great deal of hurt and unhappiness to a lot of people. I hope you will be dealing with him—in what way I don't really care. You obviously know him well, so it does beg the question Why are you still with him? And why does he always run back to you? He's been running back for the three years I've known him, so I don't think I really believe a word you've said to me. You two seem to be in a very bizarre relationship, and you're probably as crooked as he is, even protecting him in some weird way. Now, I have a life to get on with. You pick up the pieces. I'm done with him." Sophie didn't wait for a reply. She switched off her phone.

She sat with her cup of tea, thinking hard. Had that really been Shirley? Ty was such a con man; it could have been anyone. Still, if the woman did have some sort of power to get the bastard deported—but what could she possibly have on him.? Did she know something about him? Was that the hold she had on him? Sophie wanted to hurt Ty and hurt him badly. The thought of him being thrown onto a plane and sent back to the slums of Jamaica was one she really liked. He would hate it if that happened.

Then the texts started coming from Shirley. They were long, rambling hate texts about how she had washed her hands of that man now, how he lied all the time, how she had had enough of his dirty washing being dumped on her doorstep.

Sophie briefly wondered, with a smile, whether that washing was comprised of large black bin bags full of his dirty clothes. Then she decided it was probably all his affairs, his wild lifestyle mistakes, his debts, and his illegitimate children.

Shirley continued hotly.

Sophie interjected with brief comments.

Shirley asked questions about Sophie's sex life with Ty. He had apparently denied having slept with Sophie more than once, yet a few texts later, he was telling Shirley that they had had wild foursomes and threesomes. Sophie simply screenshot all the relevant WhatsApp texts and sent them to Shirley. Shirley made a comment about sending all the texts to "her"—this, Sophie supposed, was Olivia.

Then Sophie asked Shirley how she knew her phone number. According to Shirley, she had been able to get into Ty's phone and past his password.

Sophie somehow doubted that anyone could even get a look at Ty's phone. The fact that she had been able to call it when it was away from him had been caused by an extraordinary set of coincidences. Normally it was unreachable.

Shirley said that she knew of a lot of his women, as she had seen their names often.

Sophie replied that she found it strange that Shirley hadn't got in touch much sooner then, as Shirley had mentioned a woman in a nearby town she had known of since the previous October. Why, Sophie asked, hadn't she rung her as soon as she found her number and her name?

Shirley replied that "knowing and having phone numbers is a different thing." She implied that Ty had women just everywhere. She also said that he was still on the dating sites chasing women. Then she asked Sophie whether she knew where Ty was. Apparently, in order to get him deported, she needed to know an address. She mentioned many of the places that Sophie knew were Ty's boltholes of choice. Then Shirley used a phrase that caused a bell to ring in Sophie's head and clearly told Sophie that Ty was there. She had texted, "There you go, then." That was Ty—pure Ty. Shirley rambled on about how she wasn't having him back. She was adamant that she hadn't slept with him for ages. "I'm fussy who I sleep with. Sleep with him and you're sleeping with the rest of the world."

It was almost what Sophie herself had said the other day, that Ty wanted to kid them both about sleeping with Shirley. Shirley had revealed that Ty had an American as well as a Jamaican passport. What for? Why did they need to know that? And Sophie had noticed that every text had the expression LOL somewhere it—inappropriately—another Ty marker. Sophie suggested that she and Shirley should get together to chat about the situation.

Immediately Shirley came back with, "We don't need to get together. He is a problem we have, but at the end of the day, you slept with my husband, so I don't think we will ever be friends, do you?"

Sophie smiled and looked at the screen of her phone. "Nice quick thinking there, Ty—or Shirley, or Ty *and* Shirley. Who cares?" she said. She quickly texted back. "Well, it's been nice chatting to you. I realise that every word I said has been related to or read by Ty. I'm not quite the moron he depicts me as. I knew he would select me when he ran to you with his dirty tale—or simply invented you and all this, as I suspect he has. He knows I am the far weaker of his two victims. But he also thought I would believe this crap. I wish you luck, Shirley, or Ty, or both of you. The mills of God grind very slowly but very small. I wish Shirley much luck—but that will not change the creature she loves into any semblance of a normal human with normal feelings." Sophie sent the missile. Then she blocked the number. She called Olivia again and told her of the afternoon's story. Olivia was convinced it had been Shirley Sophie had spoken to. Sophie half believed it was but felt that there were too many clues to Ty's sticky fingers in the mix. They talked about it for some time.

"Why did she call you and not me?"

"I don't really know. Maybe because he told her I'm the weaker one and will easily tell her things. Or it's him and his friends and not her, so again, he's picking the weaker one so he can get her to believe his fabrications more easily. But it didn't exactly work, did it? I think he's just fishing to find out if we three are in touch already and to stop us from contacting Shirley. I could be very wrong, but I believe he was next to her when she wrote all that, and I told her—or them—as much. I've blocked them now anyway. I told her to call you if she wants to find out anything, but I doubt she will, if it is her—and she won't if it's him playing silly buggers."

"Hmm, you might be right. But I've had quite an afternoon of it too. That moron has been sending me YouTube tunes non-stop—sickly, smoochy, lurv stuff. I kept my phone open because I want my damned car back, and I want to find out what he's up to. He might get into a drunken rage if he's cut off, and God knows what he could do. I'm stuck out there by myself. I know I've got neighbours, but after what they've all seen, I doubt if they'll want to intervene."

"Oh hell, Livvy, poor old you. At least I haven't got that problem, yet. He might come gunning for me, but I honestly doubt it. He's only interested in what he can gain from us. What have I got, for goodness' sake? Sweet FA—no house, no car, no business, no money, no investments, no jewellery, no young body, no pretty face—"

"Stop, Sophie, stop. You're always putting yourself down so much! If that's all he wants from a woman, he's not worth a brass farthing. He took from you with both hands, mercilessly, knowing exactly what he was doing to you. He exploited your frailty so cruelly. Don't let him grind you down any more."

"Yes, I know that you're right, Livvy, but I still love the bloody man. You can't just switch it off like a light. I really thought I was helping him, getting involved with his life, but in reality he was holding me firmly away whilst he let you give him everything and shared it all with you—all his life, I mean. I had nothing. He wouldn't spend a night with me. Not a minute longer than he had to. I wish I could just forget the bastard."

"Well, so do I, but I have to get my car back from him. When I do, then I can block him off everything and stop having to listen to all his musical crap. All this "I lurve you" stuff. He wouldn't know love if it kicked him in his outsize balls." They giggled.

"We have to pay this pig back for what he's done to us." Sophie was angry again. "He's trying to get back with you after all that he's done to you. It's so obvious that it's just the lifestyle and the trimmings he wants. He may have fallen in love with you without meaning or wanting to, but that's bloody tough. Hope it hurts him a hell of a lot. Karma's a bitch, so they say. Hope it bites him in the bum really hard."

"Perhaps that's the way he'll get punished in the very end. I won't take him back, ever, so he can be broke and have a broken heart as well. The swine!" Sophie heard Olivia draw hard on her cigarette. Ty's presence and behaviour had pushed Olivia back into a habit she had nearly kicked. Now the aftermath was stressing her badly. The embolisms the bad sunburn had caused were still in Olivia's bloodstream, despite medication, and the smoking was not helping at all. Sophie, too, had started to smoke quite heavily, for her. She was concerned because her chest was wheezy and she panted a little when she climbed hills. She was, however, seeing a good result of the affair—a pleasant difference in her bank balance. Unused to spending money on herself, she felt almost guilty at buying a new, much-needed pair of quite expensive shoes. They had been on sale. That made her feel better.

The following weekend was not a good one for Olivia. She was at home after a stressful week in her office and after having to waste many angry hours deleting all the sugary songs Ty kept sending her. Because she was keeping channels open, mainly to ensure the return of her car, Olivia also had to endure a barrage of texts from Ty. It was a mixture of messages as before. Ty loved her more than his own life. They were made for each other. There was no life without her. He would spend the rest of his life trying to get her back, and, having done so, would spend every waking minute making her life wonderful. *He could do that by dropping dead of a heart attack*, thought Olivia. The texts continued. He was so sorry. It was all a misunderstanding. She was listening to that woman, that bitch, and her lies. She was not using her intelligence. That woman had tried to destroy them all. She had canned Olivia. *Canned?* thought Olivia. *Conned* maybe. It went on and on, like a second-rate film that wouldn't stop playing. He seemed to live in another universe, one where everything happened differently.

Olivia remembered Ty's brother telling her that Ty lived his life as if he were the lead in a film that was all about him. He loved dramas—creating them, starring in them, dragging other people into them, and then stepping out of them and looking at the aftermath, saying, "What's the problem with you people? Why are you all being so dramatic over nothing?" Olivia and Sophie had discussed this and decided that Ty ticked all the boxes for the role of psychopath. When the police psychologist had said that she could find nothing wrong with him after the gun incident that had triggered the crisis, he had been chatting and laughing with the police officers. Then he had told Olivia on the phone that it was all rubbish; there had been no need for them to be there; it had all been cooked up by someone else! Olivia and Sophie decided he was a psychopath, a sociopath, an alcoholic, suicidal, a serial sex maniac, a con man, and the biggest liar in the universe. Apart from that, he was handsome and could be good in bed when he wasn't spearing your cervix or splitting your perineum with his fascinatingly, yet frighteningly, huge penis.

Olivia sank onto the settee with a brandy. Her daughter and grandson were with her, and she was glad for the diversion of their company. Suddenly there was a loud banging on the door. Olivia spilt her brandy as her hand jerked upwards with shock. Immediately she knew it was him, Ty. Her small grandson ran towards the door. He loved to open the door to people. Olivia rushed over and stopped him, taking him back to his mother.

"Here, hang on to him, love, I'm going out to see what's going on." Olivia opened the door and looked around the road outside the house. All was quiet; she saw nothing. She stood there for some while, then went back in again. Her daughter was far from happy, and she went out to look again. As she went out, a small car pulled away very quickly and sped down the road. Olivia's daughter leapt into her four-by-four and accelerated after the car. Her car had a big, powerful engine, and she soon caught up with it. Whoever was driving didn't know the area, because the small car was driven into a cul de sac. The driver made frantic efforts to turn round, almost demolishing a gatepost in the process. As Olivia's daughter was high up in the larger SUV, she could look down into the smaller vehicle as it attempted to get past. There, crouching in the passenger seat and trying to hide his face, was a black male. Olivia's daughter knew Ty, and this was him all right. The driver was a young white female, possibly in her twenties. The car roared angrily and sped off in the direction of the main road. Olivia and her daughter worked it out that Ty had knocked on her door, jumped back and hidden in the darkness of the driveway next to the house, and then run back to the car and tried to escape quickly.

Olivia's daughter was furious. "Stupid, bloody idiot! What the hell does he think he's playing at? Coming here like that and playing silly buggers. Banging on your door and running off like some 5-year-old!"

Meanwhile, Olivia was working out just how long it would take the local police—local being some six miles away—to get to her if she needed them. After her daughter had left, Olivia went to bed and pulled the heavy chair across the bedroom door. She had checked the door locks three times. She fell asleep soundly, but at three in the morning the YouTube songs began again. She was almost mesmerised by them and sat there looking at them. After a good fifteen minutes of it, she switched her phone off and tried to sleep. She tossed and turned until the dawn limped through with high winds and muddy skies. The assault had begun. The war was on.

Olivia kept Sophie informed of the situation by frequent texts and calls. Olivia dropped by at weekends, and together they built up a picture of what had been going on.

"He sent me this song after that row we had."

"No—hang on—look! He sent me exactly the same song from YouTube, just six minutes afterwards!"

"I sent him this quotation. It said exactly how I felt."

"Bloody hell! He sent it to me—not then, but when we were in Jamaica. The bastard wasn't happy at just taking your money; he had to steal your postings as well." They sat comparing notes and texts once again. It was clear that there was a pattern to the relationships, a thread running through them that defined Ty and his attitudes and outlook on life and on women. Always the women were asking him to stop disappearing, to text or answer texts, to call and pick up calls, but when they didn't answer texts or calls from Ty almost immediately, there were insinuations and outright accusations of infidelity. The terms used were similar. "So I see you're fucking another man."

"No, Ty. I was on the toilet. I do have to go sometimes."

But it wasn't always so funny to have to tolerate his abuse and insults based on suspicion. And always there were excuses and the refusal to actually answer anything they asked him. The answers were stock ones. Sophie said jokingly that she felt he had an app on his phone which supplied the appropriate meaningless and annoying answers, so Ty could go offline and disappear yet again.

"It will be better, baby, I promise."

"I'll come see you all the time when I get back from the States/ Jamaica. Fill in country of choice."

"I know, baby."

"I'll be there soon."

"I'll come see you tomorrow."

"We'll be fine, baby."

"I'm sorry. Something came up."

"I'll bet it did!" The women said in unison.

"You know I love you, baby."

"I love you so very much, hun."

"OMG."

"Are you serious?"

"Do you read what you write, baby?"

"I was coming to see you, but I have no gas for the car, baby."

"It's OK. I respect your decision. You're leaving me. I'm gonna go home now."

"Why do you always lay down ultimatums? I don't like this."

"I would stay, baby, but I just have so much to do."

So it went on, and Sophie and Olivia laughed as they picked out the non-stop Ty-isms. The most familiar ones were the daily "Morning baby.", "You OK, baby?", and "What you doing, hun?". Usually a barrage of these, after silence, would be the forerunner to a request for money or something that was going to cost one of them an awful lot of it. They sat drinking their coffee and eating custard tarts, one of the many types of cake that Olivia always brought with her. They discussed Ty, and Shirley, and all the things that they had both experienced and suffered whilst with the man. They were clear on one thing: both of them had actually loved Ty very deeply. They couldn't actually express the reason why. Was it his physical size? No— but actually, yes. His beautiful deep-brown eyes that narrowed when he was wanting sex, his full lips and the gentle way they kissed your mouth, his dark skin that looked as if it were oiled and polished, his almost childlike pout when he wasn't getting his own way, the way he shaved his beard around his handsome jaw, and that thick, springy, curly black hair that he sometimes had shaped into patterns over his scalp. His soft, deep, dark accent was another thing—oh yes. The women sighed as they remembered.

But there were so many other things that were not very good to think about. Olivia had seen too much of the drunken, nasty Ty. There was the Ty who peed with the door open and didn't wash his hands, who broke wind loudly without apologising or caring, who lay on his back, snoring loudly, with saliva trickling from his mouth. He was the man who kicked doors down, who screamed abuse, who'd accused her of infidelity in front of hordes of curious hotel guests, who had embarrassed her in front of the staff, made horrifically racist remarks, and who expected total commitment when he wanted to go off and do his own thing without bothering to keep in touch.

But at least, thought Sophie. *At least he was there, with you, for all this to happen. You had some very bad times, but you had some very good ones, and he was there, in your life, and your bed, and your body, night after night. I was just the idiot who supplied him with money and believed his lies and thought that he loved me, even though I really knew he was lying and didn't really love me.*

They discussed whether or not it was harder for Sophie to be completely cut off from Ty, unlike Olivia, who had to remain in contact for the return of her car, if nothing else.

"I have to stay online. I may just completely block the bastard later, but I know him too well. If I do it now and he can't get at me and to me, he'll start thinking that I may just have another man, and he'll stew over it, and he'll do something—something stupid and nasty," Olivia said.

"At least I can cut him right off," Sophie said. "But we don't know whether or not he's going to come and get nasty with me. He's doing a good job of blaming me for all this instead of realising exactly what he's done and acknowledging it. Either he's going to stew over that and try to hurt me in some way, or he's going to carry on the act of not knowing me, blaming me, and trying to make you believe that I'm influencing your actions. That way, I'll be a bitter enemy, and he won't want to come anywhere near me. Suits me." But even as she said it, hurt welled up at the thought of never seeing Ty again and the thought that he could blame her for this tragic mess. Part of her realised that he was doing it to try and get back with Olivia, and this hurt even more, but it helped Sophie develop a healthy hatred for the man.

They discussed the recent scare Olivia had been subjected to. What would have happened if her daughter hadn't been with her? Would Ty have come back again? Would he have tried to get in again, perhaps harmed Olivia? Sophie said that Ty might have thought that Sophie's daughter's SUV belonged to some man. Maybe he was checking up on her, jealously wanting to claim her. Olivia tended to agree; she knew Ty was desperately and insanely jealous over her.

"That's why I'm so afraid of what he might do next. This is only the beginning, Sophie. He's cunning and violent." They talked of what he might do and what Olivia would have to do to protect herself. The day wore on, and Olivia had to leave to visit her father. They kissed goodbye on the doorstep and arranged their next meeting. Another week without Ty—and both were already missing him.

Olivia had been subjected to a barrage of Ty's music after she had returned home from visiting Sophie and her father. It had gone on most of the night. There had been texts from him too, in which he pleaded and begged, vowing to change, to make her life wonderful, to spend eternity making her happy. Olivia looked at the screen with a slightly curled lip. "Bloody two-faced, lying, oversexed, cheating bastard!" she said before switching the phone off.

When she arrived at work on the Monday morning, Olivia sat with a strong coffee, checking the mail, throwing that which her secretary could handle into a basket, tossing a lot straight into the wastebasket, and keeping those which required her immediate attention. She worked on them attentively. About eleven it was time to stop for more coffee. As Olivia pushed her chair back, and was about to go outside for a cigarette, her phone rang. It was one of the receptionists.

"It's a Mister Jonathan Purdy for you. He says it's urgent."

"What's it about?"

"He won't say. Just says it's urgent, and says you know him."

Oliva frowned. The name meant nothing to her. Perhaps she had actually spoken to him and forgotten, or maybe somebody else had arranged this and had told her, and she had forgotten that too. With the business growing at such a rate, she often overlooked or forgot things, although not usually the important ones. She picked up the phone. "Hello."

"Olivia."

Her heart leapt painfully. It was Ty.

"What the hell are you doing calling my office like this? How dare you! And giving a false name, and saying it's important."

"I just need to speak to you, baby."

"Don't 'baby' me! I have nothing to say to you now or any other time, Ty. I told you. It's over, finished. All I want is my car back. Just leave it in the driveway and post the key through the letterbox. Apart from that, leave me well alone. I know it was you the other night. Banging on my front door. My daughter chased your car, that car with the girl driving it. What the bloody hell were you up to—"

"What car, baby? It wasn't me. I don't know what you're talking about. I can prove where I was any night. I don't go anywhere, hun—"

"Curled up with Shirley, were you? And stop calling me hun and baby. Just leave me alone. Stop sending me all that musical crap. It won't change anything. You got caught out, and you're not coming back. Do not disturb me at work. Do you understand, Ty?"

"Don't hang up on me baby, please. It's my baby daughter in Jamaica, hun. You know you wanted to bring her back and adopt her. She really needs help badly. Her mother is in an asylum—drugs and drink—and so is that scraggy little junkie that she's pregnant by. The kid's with her grandmother, and she's being treated real bad. My brother called me, baby. I really need you to help her. I know you really loved her, and you were going to bring her back and look after her, and your daughter was going to live in and be her nanny—"

"Ty!" Olivia almost screamed at him. "We are separated now. Don't try and force your family on me again. Of course I loved her—I still do. But when I went to a lot of trouble to get her brought back here, you suddenly decided that looking after her—the responsibility, everything—was too much for you. You said to forget it, and I did. I'm not being emotionally blackmailed for all that again. Just go away. Get it into your thick head that this milch cow has dried up; we're finished. I have a business to run. Now bugger off." She slammed the phone down and went outside for a much-needed cigarette. On the way back to her office, she called on the receptionists and told them not to let that caller in again and to filter all callers carefully.

After work she called Sophie and they talked about it. Olivia was very upset. "He knows damned well that I'll react to anything about the child. How dare he! I feel dreadful—her mother, and that boyfriend—the poor little scrap!"

"Yes, Livvy, I hear you. I'd feel exactly the same, but he's just using emotional blackmail, isn't he. Think of the implications. In Jamaica they have the same, or similar, laws. He'd have parental responsibility, or something equivalent, wouldn't he. When she got here you wouldn't be able to keep him away, would you, and he'd become, very suddenly, the most attentive and caring father on the bloody planet."

"Yes, I know; I'd thought it out. There's no way I could get around that, but thinking about that little girl is killing me."

"But isn't that just what that dog wants, Livvy? For you to think about having the child, having her, and then—whoopee—he's back in and in charge. Or you think it over like this, and you realise that you can't allow it, and you suffer. Either way, he thinks that you can't win this one. You've got to try and put her out of your head. I know it's too damned easy to say and bloody hard to do, but you can't let him win this round. Stand your ground. Show him you can take it or leave it. It's not your responsibility; it's his child, and it's his problem—not a means to blackmail you emotionally."

"I know all this; I know it too well. I keep telling myself to be strong and put him down, but you know how he can talk his way into anything—"

"Well, just don't let him! Keep remembering what he's done to you—to us. He just wants to be back in your house, your purse, and your body."

"He can sodding well keep wanting," Olivia said firmly.

That night she received another round of smoochy, yearning love songs and another round of texts, predictable and boring. *Keep going, Ty, keep going*, she thought. *You won't win.*

The following day Olivia was sitting, surrounded by paperwork. The phone was ringing non-stop. Then her secretary put her head around the door.

"Yes?" said Olivia.

"These just arrived for you." The girl thrust a huge bunch of flowers around the door.

"Who brought them?" Olivia asked. They looked quite expensive.

"They were delivered by Interflora." The girl looked at them. "Shall I put them in a vase?"

"Wait a minute."

Olivia opened the small envelope and read it. "I love you, have always loved you, will never stop loving you. You know we should be together, baby. You know you're mine. You know you miss me. Come back to me. We can make this all right. Your husband, Ty."

Olivia stared at the note for a moment or two. Then she ripped it into tiny pieces and threw it into the bin. She was about to do the same with the flowers, but she stopped and handed them to her secretary. "Put these in a couple of vases and put them somewhere—but not in here." The girl raised an eyebrow, shrugged, and then left, sniffing at the blooms. Olivia went outside and lit a cigarette. She puffed furiously. Would he never stop harassing her? Would he never stop acting as if nothing had happened, as if she was just being childish and sulky over some minor disagreement? She hurled the butt into the grass and went back into her office. She wished she could have driven down to wherever Ty was, told him what she thought of him, and stuck the flowers, forcefully, where he would be extremely aware of them.

I hope he's missing me, she thought. *Missing me like hell, like I really miss him. I hope he hurts badly too.* Then she switched her mind back to business and got on with her day.

That evening brought more music along with more texts. Olivia ignored them.

Sophie was getting through her days. She alternated between deep sadness and longing to hear his voice or just get a text from him and a raging fury, during which she wanted to hurt him deeply, demolish him, destroy him and everything he loved. He had done this to her, even after she had sacrificed so much for him. She thought of the long, cold winter days when she'd huddled up on the settee with her hot water bottle, wrapped in a blanket. She'd been afraid to put the heating on because the gas was so costly. It had all been to help Ty, to help him to get to Jamaica and see his dying father. She thought of the times she had given him her last twenty pounds because he had said he was so hungry—and all that time he'd been living in the lap of total luxury, with everything provided. Olivia had been paying the instalments on his costly car while she, Sophie, had been scraping up the cost of the insurance. She had been so emotionally vulnerable and naïve, and like a wild animal on the prowl, he had scented blood and moved in. She shuddered as she thought of him taking her body. He had just been abusing her, taking her money, and then using her body, without love, or emotion, or any feelings except lust and possessiveness. She sat crying quietly, and then slowly her anger dissipated, and she began to miss him again. She yearned for all those things that she had been denied, all those things that he had given to Olivia whilst she sat alone, missing him and worrying about him. This was the pattern of her life now. The blackness was filling her up, threatening to engulf her. She fought, but her strength was ebbing fast. Life had taken so much away already.

She was sliding into an abyss of loneliness, depression, and total fear.

In her own house, Olivia closed her eyes. She was feeling this emotion from Sophie. She understood. She knew. But Sophie did not yet know. "Soon," Olivia whispered. "Soon." And again they slept under the same cloudy, constant moon.

Olivia and Sophie decided to go on a holiday together. They needed one. Sophie hadn't had a day's break for years, although Olivia went abroad frequently. They sat and discussed where they should go. Then Sophie remembered that she had been messaged by an old friend, Annabelle, who had lived in the town many years ago. She had known Sophie, Ben, and Ella throughout their life together. She had left England to live and work in Portugal, in the Algarve, and she had invited Sophie to go and stay with her whenever she chose. All Sophie had to do was to sort out her flights. She could stay at Annabelle's little home, with her two dogs, in a secluded location outside Albufeira. The tiny house would not accommodate them all, so Sophie decided that they could find a cheap villa or apartment. Annabelle was in the business of looking after rental properties for their owners, so she would know the lets and their owners well; she would know all the local stuff that was often a problem to work out. Having messaged Annabelle, Sophie worked on the booking for the flight. Annabelle sent her the details of two available lets. As it was nearing the end of October, accommodation was considerably cheaper, and they had the choice of a rather posh villa in the town itself or a smaller apartment in a gated development outside Albufeira, quiet and secure. Olivia and Sophie discussed it and decided that the apartment was the better bet, as the villa was located right in the centre of a walkway of nightclubs and bars and could be very noisy.

"Who wants all those pissed Brits rolling around outside?" said Olivia with a grin.

The most surprising thing was that Annabelle was going to be in England and the town visiting her family at the end of October, and she was leaving to return to Portugal on the Saturday that the girls had booked their flight. Sophie had booked from Southend Airport on Annabelle's advice. Sophie was beginning to be slightly bemused by the string of apparent coincidences that were pushing into and, sometimes, improving her life. When she spoke to Olivia about it, Olivia just smiled knowingly and said little. Both were excited about the coming holiday. Sophie was apologetic about their economy travel, as she realised that Olivia did a lot of flying by premier class, but that was usually long-haul flying, and this was a mere two and a bit hours.

Olivia was quite happy about it. "I've flown easyJet a lot before now. It's pretty good. A bit cramped, but not for too long. I'm perfectly content with it. Don't worry." Sophie too had flown by easyJet on four occasions, and she recalled a touchdown so smooth that she hadn't realised they were actually on the ground. She began packing her suitcase well in advance, wondering if she could keep her necessities under twenty-three kilos of weight. Olivia usually waited until the night before she flew to do anything like that, mainly because she had so much to do. She was very used to travelling like this, so she knew what to fling in in a hurry.

The excitement and uplifted mood was destroyed by Ty. Once again he tricked his way through the defences at the office. The receptionist told Olivia that there was "a man calling about Wayne".

Olivia's heart lurched painfully. Wayne? Her dead brother? "Put the caller on," she said. There was a pause. "Who is this?" she asked.

Then the familiar deep lilt hit her. Ty. "Hi, baby. I'm sorry to do this, and I know it must have upset you, but I just have to talk to you—"

"What the hell do you mean by using my dead brother's name like that! How dare you even breathe his name. Using it to get to me like this after I told you never to call me at my office. What could possibly be so important, Ty?"

"Livvy, I desperately need your help. It's my dad, hunny. He's going, dying, and I must get to him. All the family are gathered there. It's a matter of time. Oh help me, please! I haven't got anyone else to ask." He started to sob, brokenly, convincingly, not the heaving, dramatic sobs he kept for his attention-seeking acts but quiet, heartbroken, real-sounding grief.

Olivia was confused. She wanted to be very angry with him, but something inside her was reacting to his despair. She could not say what she wanted to. She thought with lightning speed. "Ty, I just have to do something. Stay on the line."

She grabbed her mobile and texted Sophie quickly. "He's called me at my work again. He needs help to get to Jamaica. It's his dad. I think this is the end. He's really upset. I don't know what to do. Help!"

Sophie texted back immediately. "Is this the real thing or just another of his tricks? Be careful. You know what a brilliant con artist and emotional blackmailer he is."

"Yes, I know that you're right, but he really is sobbing, and it's real grief, I just know it. I don't know what to do. I can't just turn my back on him if he needs to get to Jamaica to say goodbye to his father and bury him."

Olivia was biting the side of her hand. She picked up the phone from her desk again. She heard Ty sobbing very quietly. "I promise, baby, I won't ask you for anything ever again. I know it's a hell of a cheek and I don't deserve it, but please, for all the good times we had together, hun, for the fact that you love my dad and mum, for the love we once had—"

Olivia was wavering; something inside of her was giving way. She texted erratically, with one finger, to Sophie. "I can't bear this. I know I should tell him to sod off, and you'll tell me what I always tell you—he's breathing, so he must be lying—but Sophie, I feel terrible. I just can't refuse to help him at a time like this."

"Tell him you'll call him after work or something. You mustn't weaken now; you can't! If you do, he'll be back in your house within a week. I know how you feel, but don't weaken!"

Olivia took a deep breath. "Ty, I can't give you any more money. I'll try to help in some way. This is not really very fair of you. I understand what you say and what you feel, but no, no more bankrolling. I have to work now. Call me this evening, just after seven." She rang off quickly and then went outside. She needed a cigarette. Her hands were shaking. She was in turmoil. His weak, sad voice had crept past her defences. She still loved this man, for God's sake. She couldn't actually bear to think of him in this sort of pain, although with her next thought she wished him all the misery that he had inflicted on her and on Sophie. She smoked and thought. She knew what to do. She called Ty's sister Carol Ann in Jamaica and asked her if the news was true. Was Sebastian really at the end of his struggle? Carol Ann told Olivia that, sadly, this was true. Sebastian was now paralysed. The cancer had spread throughout his thin, ravaged body, and time was running out for him. Olivia knew now what she must do.

That evening when Ty called, Olivia was sitting in the big red chair that had been their love nest. She had rearranged the furniture to try and remove his taint from the house. She had stripped the bed and washed the mattress cover, all the pillows, and the duvet. Everything had been scrubbed and sanitised to dispel his shadow. She picked up the phone.

"Hi." Ty was quiet and nervous.

"Hello, Ty. I need you to listen to me carefully. I have no obligation whatsoever to help you in any way, after what you did to me and to Sophie." Every time she spoke to Ty she included Sophie. He had to know that she was part of this, another victim, not the cause of the problem. She was not going to let him forget the reality of his crimes.

"Don't imagine that this is setting some sort of precedent, Ty. I love your father, as you well know, and Mary, and the rest of them in Jamaica. I will give you the airfare, but not for you, for the sake of your family, so that they are not upset that you can't be with them at such an important and sad time. Your mother will need you—they all will. So I will transfer the money. But I don't want any more stupid love songs, and texts about you loving me, and all of that shit, please, Ty. It's all over between us. Finished and done. Go and say goodbye to Sebastian and kiss him for me, and bury him, and grieve with your family. But we are through. Finished. I'll transfer the money now. No more texts, please."

"Baby, thank you, thank you so very much. I will always love you. My family loves you too. If that fucking bitch hadn't schemed to split us up—"

Olivia cut in on Ty. "I said it's over. I don't want to hear you telling lies about Sophie. Stop while you're winning, or I might just change my mind."

Ty sounded resigned. "Thank you again, baby."

"Stop all this *baby* and *hun* stuff, Ty. I'm not either. Just get over there—and leave me alone. Goodbye." She put the phone down hard, went into the garden, and lit up a cigarette. Inside she was crying for him. She cried for his grief, for his coming loss, for the love they had once shared, for the love he had pretended to share, and the lies, disappearances, and pretences. Her mind was on the merry-go-round again. She mentally picked daisy petals. *I love him; I hate him; I love him.* She finished the cigarette and went back into the living room. She picked up her phone and transferred £1,000 to Ty's account. What was she going to say to Sophie? She had nearly given way completely and told Ty to come back. And she would have gone with him to Jamaica to support him, as she knew he was going to be deeply affected by this coming trauma. She sat staring at the phone; then she lifted it and dialled Sophie.

"Hi, Sophie. Thanks for telling me not to weaken today. I was very wobbly, I have to be honest. It was very hard, but I managed not to give in."

"Good! You told him nothing doing, did you? Well done. I was really worried about you."

"Well, I nearly gave in altogether and asked him to come back."

"You *what!*"

"Hang on, I said 'nearly'. But I managed not to. It was so hard, Sophie. He was really crying, not all this dramatic sobbing but real, quiet, heartbreaking tears. If you'd heard him you would have been moved, honestly you would."

"Well, I do understand, but don't let that king of con men get back into your life, Livvy. He's caused us both enough grief. You've still got the bruised arms, and the embolisms, and your car's still missing, and he keeps harassing you. What more do you want, the same as before? Only it'll be much worse if he knows he's forced you to take him back—he's won. You said it was a war. You won't win it by giving in to the first bit of squishiness on his part."

"But I didn't give in. I told him he could whistle for the money. I'm not bankrolling him any more Sophie, he can look after himself now. He had everything when he was here. He lived in total luxury. He had champagne tastes on beer money. He paid for nothing. I told him nothing doing. It was hard, but I told him."

"Well, thank Christ you didn't weaken. I know I would have wavered a bit, to be quite honest, but I wouldn't have given in, Livvy. You can't. Look, I have to leave for work now. Talk later. Keep me updated if you hear any more."

Olivia rang off. She felt guilty. She hadn't been honest, and she felt as if she had betrayed Sophie. She would have to tell her, somehow.

When Sophie arrived at work, she got on with her job but thought deeply about the matter. If she were to be totally honest, she knew she would have given way quite shortly; she knew that she would have given Ty the money if she had money like that at her disposal. She was gutted at the thought of him alone, desperate, and needing to get to his family. Her soft heart melted into love and forgiveness—only to be instantly replaced by hot anger as she remembered what he had said about her and done to her, the pain he had caused her. But despite this, she knew with certainty that she would have given him that money. When she returned home after work, she took her night medication and was making herself a cup of tea. The phone shrilled. It was Olivia.

"Hi, Soph. Look, I was doing a lot of thinking, and—"

"And you decided to give him the money for his fare."

Olivia was surprised. "Well, yes, actually I did. You don't sound at all surprised."

"I'm not really. I did a lot of thinking too. If it were me he came to, I'd have to give him the money. I don't think I could bear to see him so upset and know I could have done something to help. I still love him, just as I know you do, Livvy. It's bloody hard. It's easy to say but hard to do. I don't advocate doing much more, or he'll be back in your bed in no time at all."

"The hell he will! This is just for this one event because it's so important. But I told him it's not for him; it's for the family, and it is." Olivia said this last thing firmly, to convince herself as well as Sophie.

"Well, as long as you told him that and he takes it on board, that's OK for this time, but don't weaken again, Livvy. I was worried about you." They said their goodnights and rang off.

Olivia could not sleep. *How will I ever get rid of this man from my life?* she thought. *I cannot just ignore his plight. I still love him, but I will not take him back into my life. He has betrayed me totally and done the same despicable thing to Sophie. Let me just get over him, wipe him from my heart.* She fell asleep at last.

Sophie lay awake. She was worried. She knew that Olivia was weakening because she was so accessible to Ty. He could wear down her defences with all his cunning, charm, and drama. Olivia still loved him deeply, as Sophie did. Sophie was isolated from his tricks and pressure, but she understood just how Olivia felt. She could not guarantee that, subjected to his campaign, she would not eventually give in and allow him access to her life and, inevitably, her bank account. But even as she thought this, she clenched her fists angrily and vowed that he would never again abuse her tenderness and caring. He would never again use her feelings and her body so cruelly and carelessly as he had done. She wanted him to disappear from her mind. He had effectively done so from her life already, but she could not escape him whilst he stalked Olivia so cunningly. He had made a good case for this day's pay-out, but what would the next day bring? Sophie fell into a troubled sleep.

The following morning, Olivia was taking her coffee break when her phone rang. It was Ty. She was tempted momentarily to reject the call, but she took it anyway. "Yes, what do you want now, Ty? I transferred the cash. You must have got it by now." "Well yes, baby, and thank you so much for helping me like this." Olivia knew that Ty was leading up to something else, a request for more help, and she knew what it was.

"I'm very busy, Ty. I must get on with training in a minute. Just let me know about Sebastian when you get there—"

"Baby, I kinda hoped that you'd come with me. I'm gonna be so stressed and upset when my dad does go. I really will need you then, hun."

"But you have a family, Ty. People cope. Sophie had to cope with the deaths of two of her children. What help did you give her when her son was dying? She asked for a lift to the hospital, and you couldn't get away quickly enough after dumping her there. And you moaned the whole time about it making you late. Then she asked you to go to the funeral to support her, and all you could say was that you "don't like funerals"—you selfish bastard! No, you have a huge family and lots of friends over there. You don't need me. I know you want me, though, Ty. You want me because you don't want to have to stay at your family house. What you want is for me to fly over with you, upgrade you to premier class, and book us both into a five-star hotel. Well, you can forget all that, Ty, because it's not going to happen. Stop while you're winning. You got the money out of me, but I told you already—it's not for you; it's for your family. Now get off the line and don't harass me again." She slammed the phone down hard and again went outside for a cigarette.

"Bloody cheeky bastard," she muttered to herself. She had known that he would push and push to get all he could from her. He still sincerely believed that he was entitled to everything that he could possibly relieve Olivia of. She had fallen for his needs this time, but this would be the last time. Olivia went back into her office and called Sophie. "Hi there. Guess who's just been on the phone again?"

"I would guess it was probably Ty, and I would also guess that he wanted you to go to Jamaica with him and you to upgrade him to premier class on the way. Most importantly, I would guess that he wanted you to go with him so that his grief would overwhelm your defences, and you would be obliged to fall into bed with him. Am I right?"

"Spot on, Sophie. He seems to think the world should run around when he snaps his fingers. Not just satisfied with being given the money to get there—not premier class, but normal class—he's ignoring the fact that it's been given for the sake of his family, quite definitely not for his wants. I told him where he could go, but tonight he's supposed to be bringing the car back. He just texted me."

"He must have someone to drive him to Gatwick, then. Wonder who."

"He has a big bunch of friends, some of them rather dodgy. One of them may be taking him. Maybe it's a woman, and she's flying with him. Great—I may have paid for him to go on a holiday with another of his harem! Anyway, I'll be glad to get my car back again. Must get back to work now. I'll call you after he's been. Bye."

That evening Olivia paced nervously, waiting for Ty's arrival. She didn't really want to have to see him, yet she yearned, with her whole being, to see him again. She stood out in the garden, smoking endlessly. Then she heard the car being driven into the driveway and up next to her Jaguar. Her heart was pounding. She felt as if she would stop breathing. He opened the gate and came in. They looked at each other for several seconds; to Olivia it seemed like hours. Ty looked tired and stressed. He was untidy. Her heart began to soften; she longed to reach her hand towards him and stroke his face.

She pulled herself together sharply. "Right, I have all the paperwork for the car. I'll just check that you haven't damaged it before you go." She went out into the driveway quickly and looked over the car. It was well polished and clean inside and out. There was no evidence of dents or scratches—or of the original wheels being removed so that Ty could sell them. Olivia didn't trust him. He and the circles he moved in were shadowy and suspect. She went back into the garden. Ty was sitting in a garden chair and had lit up a cigarette.

Olivia raised an eyebrow. "You were supposed to bring back the car, Ty. You've done that, so you can go now."

"Baby, can't we talk for a little, please? You know you really want me back again. We were fine until that bitch called you and told you all those lies. She's controlling you. Think for yourself, hun. You're an intelligent woman."

"Yes, Ty, I am, and if you had an ounce of intelligence you'd realise that she didn't know I existed—or my phone number. In any case, she called your phone, not mine. Are you really suggesting that she knew I would pick it up?" Olivia laughed mirthlessly.

"Shirley's behind it all; she set it up! She—"

"Oh, for Christ's sake, Ty! Stop right now. I don't want to hear any more of your bloody lies. All this is your fault, your doing. You ran a bunch of women like a stable of mares. You got too much going and you couldn't handle it all. You were sleeping with at least three women, probably more, and taking money from a whole bunch of them. And at the same time you were living with me—off me—in luxury. You had everything provided;

you hadn't a thing to buy for yourself. You had two top-class holidays in Jamaica paid for by me, but you still kept lying to that poor woman to get more money out of her. Lie after lie! You lied to all of us, over and over again. I don't know how you can live with yourself, Ty. Anyway, you were already finished, as far as I was concerned. Your bags were thrown out. You were a done deal. Her calling just made it easier, because I knew I had a very good reason to never have you back again."

"Baby, you know how much I love you. You know you love me too. Let me back into your life, hun. Let's start again. I'll be the perfect guy—you'll see, baby! I'm gonna spend the rest of my life showing you how much I love you. Don't let that lying bitch spoil what we had. I didn't sleep with her, baby. I hardly knew her. I told you, she had this thing about me and I had no feeling for her. I only met her at this swingers' do. She latched onto me, and I couldn't get rid of her. I tried everything to get shot of her. She kept sending me money to buy her younger men to fuck her all the time. I hated it, baby!"

"But she knew your bank account details, despite the fact that she didn't really know you, Ty? You must think I came off the last banana boat. I've sat down beside her and read her WhatsApp texts to you and from you. You asked the woman to marry you, for God's sake! You had everything you needed and wanted here. Why did you need her, Ty? She's older than your own mother, not at all good-looking or special, and she's scruffy and poor. You refused to even spend a night at her home, so you must have thought the same. You just used her for money ... and for sex. Just pretended to love her so that you could have the odd session of quick, rough, meaningless sex. You told her the lies she wanted to hear and then took every penny you could get out of her by playing on her weakness and her shattered emotions. You didn't need her for anything—you had it all here. But you two-timed me, Ty! I asked only one thing of you, to be faithful, and you lied to me. I could have just about understood your finding a younger woman, Ty. The difference in our ages has always concerned me, although I've always preferred younger men, and I've usually always had them. If you had found yourself a younger, more attractive woman, well, I could have taken that and even understood it a little. But to cheat on me with that ..." Olivia clenched her fists and pressed them to her face.

Ty stepped forward and put his hand out to her.

Olivia stepped back. "Just get out, now! Your father is dying, so you need to go to Jamaica immediately. I ask only for a short text to tell me about Sebastian's state—nothing else."

"You love him, baby, I know. He'll be so disappointed that you're not—"

"Out, Ty—now. Just go." She pointed to the gate. He hesitated, stood looking with yearning and desperation in his eyes, handed the car keys to Olivia, and then walked slowly out of the garden. He took his small case on wheels out of the car, shut the car door, and crossed the road. Olivia went quickly into the house and looked out of the kitchen window. She saw Ty getting into a BMW sports car, a smart new model. It was parked opposite the house, and Olivia could see that the driver was a very attractive female, a brunette, suntanned, expensively made up, with jewellery on her fingers and wrists. The woman ran her fingers over Ty's face and then leaned over and kissed him on the lips. She whispered something, and they both laughed and looked at the house. Then the car pulled away rapidly.

Olivia was left, angry, hurt, and confused. For a second out there in the garden, she could have weakened and taken him back, told him that she would give him yet another last chance. She was hurt, but deep inside she suspected that the woman was just another weapon in Ty's armoury. Had Olivia taken him back, Ty would have brought his bag in from the car, sent a quick text on his phone, and the woman and the car would have disappeared, unseen by Olivia, no longer needed in Ty's elaborate, vicious games. Olivia huddled up on the settee. She wished that she had never met him and that she could forget him and get on with her life. But deep inside her she knew that he still had a stranglehold on her soul and her feelings. She must do some positive thing to try and rid her body of his taint. She thought for a while, and then she lifted the phone and pressed in the number. A male voice answered in a deep American drawl. Olivia smiled and relaxed down into the cushions. "Hello there, Billy."

Next Olivia phoned Sophie. "I've decided I need to wash Ty out of my womb, Sophie. I know this lovely black guy from the American camp—not very handsome or anything, but really nice. I think he may be well hung. I'm going to invite him over for supper, cook him a nice meal, and then tell him it's his lucky day."

"Hell, girl, you go for it. Give me a blow-by-blow account afterwards," Sophie said and grinned. She wished that she could find the momentum to do the same, but she hadn't recovered from Ty yet. Nothing and nobody would ever be the same for her.

Olivia left the office early and bustled about cooking steak, thick chips, sweet corn and onions. She tossed together a crisp salad and put some cans of beer to chill in the fridge. Then she went up; showered; shaved her pubic area; put on a revealing dress, make-up, and jewellery; and sprayed herself liberally with Chanel No 5. Billy arrived at six clutching a bunch of flowers, which Olivia put in a vase. They ate, drank beer, smoked, and chatted. Ty knew a lot of people from the American base, and he probably knew Billy. Olivia didn't know, but she didn't talk about Ty. She wanted to forget him. It didn't take too much effort to seduce Billy. He was tall and skinny, not desperately good-looking, but he had a satisfying set of genitals which she would put to very good use. Soon they were climbing the stairs, hand in hand, and he was kissing her and stroking her ample breasts. Olivia had missed the lovemaking at which Ty was so skilled and for which he was so well equipped. She wanted the release of orgasm. She responded eagerly to Billy's expert handling of her body. Soon they were on the bed and he was employing everything in his repertoire to pleasure Olivia. He was nowhere near the size of Ty, something which afforded Olivia great relief, but he was adequately equipped, and he knew how to use what he had. Twenty-five minutes later, gasping and panting, Olivia reached a very sweet orgasm. Billy lay breathing heavily, a smile on his face. They curled around each other and slept briefly. Then Olivia got up.

"Sorry, love. I have to go back into the office for a meeting at seven. That's my life. It was really lovely having you here. Sorry I have to rush you away."

"We'll have to do this again another time," Billy said. Olivia just smiled. She had used him for her own purposes and enjoyed it all. There would be no other time. She had a very quick shower, dressed, and then hurried Billy downstairs and out to his car.

They kissed briefly, and she waved as he drove away. When he was out of sight and well gone, Olivia walked back into the house, went upstairs, undressed, put on a loose housecoat and slippers, and went down to lounge on the big red chair. She picked up her phone and called Sophie.

"Hi—it's done. He's just left. I've washed Ty out of my womb, good and proper."

"Was it really good?"

"Hell, yes, really hard and satisfying. He knows what to do and how to do it. But I shan't be seeing him again. He served his purpose, but he's not quite my type. Not a looker and far too skinny for my tastes. But it was good. I shall sleep well tonight."

Sophie began to think that she might surf the dating sites once again, but she felt less than enthusiastic. Her knowledge and experience of them had been pretty awful so far. She missed Ty's body, his solid, dark body, the smell and feel of his ebony skin, the soft lilt when he spoke, the firm mouth he kissed her with—when he kissed her. She sat thinking, hurting, and wishing, and eventually she cried a little. Then she went up to bed, where she lay still thinking of Ty. She was missing him and hating him and all the malevolent things he had said to her and about her. It all tumbled about wildly in her head. She wished him all the worst things in the world, and in the same thought she wanted him there, next to her, holding her tightly. *But*, she told herself, *he never stayed. He always ran away, to Shirley, and to Olivia, and to God knows who else.* He had used her, coldly and knowingly. She slid into sleep. The next morning would be the same, a mixture of conflicting emotions and wants. She had to heal. She had to survive. She had survived so much—she would survive Ty.

The holiday drew near, and both Olivia and Sophie were becoming very excited. Sophie had not had a break since flying to Fuerteventura with the nasty Enrico. She had barely come to terms with the death of her son before this trauma over the discovery of Ty's real life had rocked her emotionally. She was tired and longed to escape. Olivia's business life was tough and draining, and she, too, had had to face the revelation that her fiancée was a serial prostitute, liar, con man, and thief. They both needed this getaway. So far there had been no indication from Ty that he had even arrived in Jamaica, let alone a message about his father's welfare and/or demise. Both of them began to suspect that he had simply lied to get money from Olivia. Sophie recalled how Ty had over and over again conned her out of money to take him to Sebastian's deathbed. It seemed his father was still hanging on, terminally ill but not in the condition that Ty would have his victims believe he was. Sophie packed her case for the holiday well in advance. She had to work up until the evening before the flight.

Olivia packed a few pairs of shoes and a huge box full of jewellery; everything else she left until the last minute.

Sophie's step was lighter as she thought of the Algarve, the coast of Southern Portugal, the isolated complex where the apartment was, the peace, the escape. She was slightly happier, but still the darkness within her weighed her down. It was like a huge mass crushing her heart and soul. Friday came, the last day of work before the holiday. Sophie popped into the toilet just before she prepared lunch for her clients. As she was washing her hands, she glanced into the mirror above the sink. She could not see herself clearly. She looked again. Perhaps her glasses were smeared with something. She took them off, ran the lenses under warm water, and then wiped them with toilet paper. She put them on again, but still something was wrong. She took her glasses off again and peered into the mirror. There was something stopping her vision. She was unable to see properly out of her right eye. Her heart trembled. Nothing must be wrong! Nothing must spoil this holiday. Please let it just pass.

Sophie completed her work and rushed home, worried. Could this be a minor stroke? No, there were no other presenting symptoms. Maybe a retinal detachment? But there was no "curtain effect" over her vision, just a loss of sight. She didn't think that it could be sudden glaucoma. She phoned a taxi and went up to the doctor's surgery, where she saw the nurse practitioner. The nurse practitioner could not give her a definitive answer, but she was worried too and advised Sophie to go to the main hospital, which was some ten miles away. Sophie was getting stressed and desperate. How would she get there? She texted her work partner, explained the emergency, and asked her to cover her evening shift. Then she called Olivia and told her the bad news. She explained that she was unable to get to the hospital except by taking two buses, and that she was not able to see well enough to do this.

"Get a taxi back to your house," Olivia commanded. Sophie did, and some forty-five minutes later Olivia appeared. Sophie had worked herself up into a state of great agitation, and Olivia calmed her gently. "Don't worry. It will be OK. I know this."

"How can you possibly know, Livvy? I'm spoiling your holiday. Maybe I won't be able to fly—"

"I told you, Sophie—it will be fine. I promise you."

Olivia drove to the hospital, and very soon they were in the A and E department. They didn't have to wait more than a half hour before they were called in. An extremely good-looking young Australian examined Sophie's eye. In order to do so, he had to come into contact with her, very closely. Sophie's spirits rose. When he left the cubicle briefly, Sophie said to Olivia, "Wow, he can keep doing that all night long." Olivia laughed.

The young and attractive doctor made a very thorough survey of the eye but was puzzled.

"The eye looks very healthy, actually," he said, frowning. "I'll go and have a word with my boss." Soon he returned, followed by the senior eye consultant. That man briefly peered into Sophie's eye, pursed his lips, and agreed with the dishy Aussie that the eye was, indeed, healthy.

Sophie told them, "I've had cataracts done on both eyes, and so both lenses are implants."

The consultant looked at her, raised his eyebrows, and then looked not into her eye but down over the top of it.

"I know what it is!" Sophie said triumphantly.

"What is it then?" asked the consultant, a tall, dark Indian man with a perpetual half smile.

"I think my lens may have slipped."

The consultant smiled. "Yes, you're right. It has dropped backwards. You'll need an operation to correct it soon."

"Please, please tell me that I can fly tomorrow," pleaded Sophie.

The consultant pursed his lips. "Yes, that should be OK. Where are you going. Far?"

"Only to Portugal."

"That will be fine. Just treat your eye with care. I'll get an appointment for you as soon as I can."

"Oh, thank you so very much." Sophie was ecstatic. "I love you and I want to have your babies!" The two men dissolved into laughter.

Olivia grinned and said teasingly, "Come on. I can't take you anywhere where there are men!" They left the building and walked back to the car.

Sophie stopped and looked at Olivia. "Thank you so much for rushing over to help me like this. You were so sure that everything was going to be OK—as if you knew."

"I did know. I was told, but you'll find out eventually. Let's just get you sorted out now. You might as well come back to my house tonight so you won't have to rush about tomorrow. Text Annabelle and tell her. She can drive straight here." Annabelle's brother was to have picked Sophie up and taken her and Annabelle to Olivia's home, where Olivia would drive them all to Southend Airport. Now, Annabelle and Gavin could drive straight to Shrewsham next day, and the girls could meet up and set off. Olivia drove Sophie to her home and last-minute packing was completed. Fortunately Sophie had only a few items to put into her case. Freddie lifted the case and hooked it onto the digital mini scale. It was well below the twenty-three kilo allowance.

"Good." Olivia said, grinning wickedly. "I can take a lot of stuff home with me and pack it all in your case, Sophie—well done, gal."

Sophie was not happy at leaving Freddie. He was now seventeen and eminently capable of taking care of himself. He was able to cook, if not always willing to wash up immediately; he had a good neighbour next door and his father was not far away. But Sophie was worried. Since she had lost her two children she always feared the worst in every situation. Freddie was very precious to her. She had an enormous responsibility to him—and to his dead mother—and she took it very seriously. She transferred £70 to Freddie's bank account to ensure that he was not hungry or cold. Their gas and electricity was prepaid, and this was the end of October, so whilst not yet cold, it was getting quite chilly at night-time.

"Will that be enough?" Sophie asked Freddie.

"Good God, Nan, that's loads! The kitchen cupboards and the freezer are full already." Freddie smiled at Olivia. "She seems to think I'm going to have to exist for the next six months."

"Well, darling, you do eat a lot, despite the fact that you're so thin." Sophie was looking around frantically and talking to herself as she tried not to forget what she should remember. The eye incident had thrown her out of her planned routine.

"Come on, Soph." Olivia picked up Sophie's case, which Freddie had brought downstairs.

"No, leave it. I'll take it." Freddie lifted the case easily with one swing of his arm and carried it out to the car.

Before she got in, Sophie hugged Freddie. "Take care, my darling. Don't forget to lock the front door at—"

"Yes, Nan! I won't forget anything. Now, get in and go, and have a really great holiday."

The Jaguar purred off while Freddie waved them goodbye. Sophie sank back into the heated seat, which also massaged her back and helped to relax her. The day's events suddenly caught up with her, and she felt very tired. She was so grateful to Olivia for rushing all that way to help her. She dreaded to think how she would have managed otherwise. She was very used to being alone, without money and possessions, and having to cope with what life threw at her, but she was also beginning to get very tired. The darkness inside her was pulling her down, and she was losing the fight. This holiday must help her to battle back again. They glided through the Suffolk countryside and Sophie almost fell asleep, but she was also feeling very excited about the trip, and she and Olivia discussed it happily. When they reached Olivia's house and pulled into the driveway beside the house, they were both tired and longing for bed. Sophie followed Olivia into the house. It was a very modern house, with a large living room, a nice sized kitchen, a downstairs toilet, and two upstairs floors with another bathroom and three bedrooms, one with an en-suite shower. It was beautifully and expensively furnished—as Sophie had expected it would be. It made her feel just a little more inferior and poor. She saw the big red chair in which Ty and Olivia had sat, arms around each other, and the matching stool on which Ty had made frantic love to Olivia. Sophie was near to tears. He had had all this—she had been nothing to him—just someone to lie to for a financial reward—just another female body to penetrate, to keep happy and captive. Olivia was right. He was just a prostitute. He had sold his body to Sophie for money. Sophie shuddered a little. She felt sadness, but she also felt instant anger that Ty could have used her so cruelly and selfishly. *Fuck him!* she thought. *I'm going to Portugal for a break. He can go to hell! I hope his life is a miserable mess. He didn't love me or give a damn about me. He just used me, so now he can experience the kind of misery he's brought on me and on Olivia.*

They drank tea and ate sandwiches. Neither of them had much appetite. Then Sophie took her medication, kissed Olivia goodnight, climbed the stairs, washed, and cleaned her teeth. She fell into the large and extremely comfortable bed. She slept deeply and peacefully until the early hours of the next day, when she started dreaming that Ty was chasing her and Olivia. They were running frenziedly, terrified, and Ty was a huge animal, snarling as he pursued them both. Sophie was growing weak and tired. A large black cloud was lowering itself onto her, threatening to engulf her. She cried out as she felt herself falling. Turning, she saw Ty, a huge creature with fangs and red eyes, nearly on top of her. Then Olivia had her hand, and she was pulling her up and away from the approaching danger and the black fog. They both soared up into the air, above the darkness and into the sunlight. Silently they floated in the blue, clear air, and a feeling of all-embracing peace enfolded Sophie. Olivia turned to her and smiled. "Soon you will know," she told her. "There is a reason and a purpose in everything. Everything unfolds as it must." They soared through the sun's beams—and then the dream was shattered by the shrill tones of Sophie's alarm on her mobile. Disoriented, she sat up. Today was the start of her holiday.

She padded down to the kitchen and made a cup of tea for Olivia and a cup of coffee for herself. She carried her coffee up to her room and then went up to the next floor with Olivia's tea. She tapped gently on the door. There was a muffled grunt from the room. Sophie tapped again. Another grunt. She entered the room. In it was the biggest bed she had ever seen. Not super king size, it was more like empire size—or Europe size—or Russian Steppes size. And in this monstrous bed Olivia was dwarfed. She lay like a tiny pea in a very large saucepan. She grunted once more. Sophie put the tea beside the bed and tiptoed out again. She went downstairs and had a shower, dressed, and put on some make-up. She checked all the things she would need for the trip, closed and locked her case, and then went down and took her daily medication. It was a pleasant day. It was the end of October, and the year was closing down, but the garden was still a blaze of colour. Yellow and red leaves were piling up, and the sun's angle was more extreme, but it was still quite warm. Soon Olivia came down, yawning and tousled.

"Morning. Sleep well?"

"Oh, yes, I certainly did. Had a bit of a funny dream, though—"

"Tell me later—I'm not awake yet."

"Gosh, that bed of yours is huge—do you use a satnav to find your way around it!"

"Funny girl—but, yes, it is big. I had it specially made. Can't stand small beds. I like to disappear into it, and I like to be in total darkness all night. I'm a fussy sleeper, I am."

Sophie made herself another coffee. Olivia disappeared upstairs and soon emerged, meticulously dressed and made up, with her fine blonde hair carefully pulled back in a ponytail. She went around the house checking, locking up, and turning off. Then she dragged her suitcase down to the front hall. Sophie went up to get hers, but Olivia refused to allow her to do this; she was concerned about the effect on her eye. Soon all their luggage was packed into the Jaguar, and they went out into the garden for a soothing smoke. Olivia looked at her phone. "Oh God, no—not him again!"

"What is it? Ty?"

"Yes, that arsehole. Listen to this." Olivia showed Sophie her phone, on which Ty had posted a plethora of songs beseeching Olivia to come back, think again, give him another chance, not break his heart, and more treacly sentiments. Then she looked hard at her messages. She sighed and looked pale. She handed the phone to Sophie again. Sophie looked at the text. "I will get you back again. You might as well give in now. I won't stop until I have you back in my arms and my life. Stop mixing with that bitch. Think for yourself. If she causes any more trouble in our lives, I'll make her sorry. Stop running away from me. I'm going to have you, baby."

The two women looked at each other. Olivia looked grim. "I told you he wouldn't stop until he's got his own way."

"Those are just words, Olivia."

"But you don't know what he's like, Sophie, the sort of people he mixes with! And he's threatening you. Don't, for God's sake, ever let him know that we're friends. Or that we're going on holiday together. That'll really stir him up, and I don't want you in danger. I'm quite able to defend myself—if he doesn't point a gun at me—but you're defenceless."

"OK then, we won't let him know. I have absolutely no contact with him any more now, so that's no problem. Does he know you'll be away?"

"He thinks I'm going to Turkey for a week's break."

"OK, fine. So nobody send him a postcard. Don't let him spoil our holiday."

"Oh, he won't, I assure you." Olivia felt protective towards Sophie. She realised that Sophie had really loved Ty, and she now saw just what Ty had been doing for the last three years, and how he had maintained his lifestyle by using more than one woman. But this woman had been the weakest, the most vulnerable. Her hurt was the worst, because now that all was coming to the surface, like scum on a drain, she was the one who was least loved, cared for, wanted, or needed. Olivia felt, without knowing why, that they must go away together, talk together, work their respective ways through the hurt and the shock. They must try to understand the depths of depravity to which Ty had sunk. She thought that the escape and rest would be good for both of them. They could help each other. It would not be a counselling situation—just an attempt to piece together the years, to discuss the experiences, the motivations, the emotions, the blackness of this man.

Olivia knew that there was a reason for all this. The amazing coincidence that had led Sophie to call Ty's mobile on September 6 had been for a very good reason. It was a coincidence that Sophie knew Annabelle and that Annabelle would be in England at precisely the time that they had booked their flights and would be returning to Portugal the same day. Annabelle would be able to drive them from Faro to Albufeira, would arrange for food to be delivered and put in their fridge at the apartment, would be able to tell them everything they wanted to know locally, and would be there to help if they ran into problems. Olivia had always had this spiritual gift of knowing. She had picked up Sophie's aura, finding it thick, muddy, depressing, and destructive. It was threatening to attack Sophie's body, probably her heart. Olivia did not know exactly why going to Portugal was necessary, but the mass of coincidental happenings was telling her that something was about to happen, something that had been planned. All her life she had been guided by spirit. It was leading her now, and she had to follow.

Their flight was a pleasant one. Southend Airport was small, informal, and not at all overcrowded. Olivia was, as ever, stopped and searched by security. "It always happens to me." She grinned resignedly. There were sixty or more people on the plane and, amazingly, because they had booked their two seats with a different agent, on a different day, at a different time than Annabelle, she was on the third seat, next to them. Olivia knew then that the spirit was taking her to Portugal for a very good reason.

The flight only took barely over three hours, and they touched down at Faro just before nine that evening. They soon cleared customs and passport control, and Annabelle drove them along the motorway and then off on country roads and outside of Albufeira to a remote area where the little apartment was located. It was a pleasant surprise, quite large, with a well-fitted kitchen, a downstairs bathroom and shower, and two upstairs bedrooms with another bath and shower room. It seemed welcoming and peaceful. The food had been put into the fridge for them, and they were able to concoct a meal after unpacking and settling into their bedrooms. They sat up, talking and discussing the edges of their shared problem, and were in bed by midnight. The following day dawned with sunshine and mild weather. Although it was the very last days of October, the temperature was still in the twenties. They sat outside on the small terrace, drinking coffee and watching the life of the small road unfold. Annabelle had arranged car hire for them, yet another problem that they hadn't been obliged to tackle, another wrinkle smoothed for them. The hire car arrived that afternoon, a minute automatic Citroën. Olivia was more used to very large luxury cars, and she looked quite comical huddled in the tiny vehicle with her knees nearly reaching her chin. They went for a test run in the little creature. The gearbox sounded worryingly noisy, and Sophie was concerned that Olivia seemed to get far too close to the wing mirrors of parked cars on the right. They had a satnav—or so it claimed to be—which on occasions seemed to want to take them on a guided tour of the whole of Portugal when it had merely been asked to take them back to the apartment. But it got them around and provided entertainment. They sat and talked—and talked. They both smoked too much. But they were, very slowly, beginning to push off the load of those years with Ty.

On the second evening, after they had eaten a good meal at the apartment, they sat facing each other on the comfortable settees. They had been chatting—Sophie talking about Ella—and were both relaxed. That was when Olivia looked up and saw Sophie's dead daughter, Ella, come into the room. Ella stood behind Sophie, with her hand on her mother's shoulder. Olivia felt the strong messages from Ella. The messages were of pain, despair, grief, hurt, heartbreak, and loss—all the things Sophie had suffered and borne in the loss of her beloved children, Ella and Sean, and of Ben, too. And now she had suffered the loss of Ty. Then, silently, Sean entered too, and he was followed by Ben. Olivia was shaken by the good looks of the young, blond, blue-eyed man who walked in and stood behind Sophie. He also put his hand on her shoulder, gazing at her with concern and deep love.

Olivia felt an enormous surge of energy from them all. She would need this energy to do what she now knew she had been brought to Portugal to enact and fulfil. She knew that what was about to happen was going to be a life-changer. Gently she told Sophie that her children were with her always—not just in her memories and her feelings but really there, in spirit. She continued to reassure Sophie, quietly and slowly. This woman carried so much blackness in her being. Olivia could see the blackness; it was a huge ball of thick, choking misery which was filling Sophie and was on the point of taking her. Sophie's heart was badly affected, and Olivia could see that she was in a desperate plight. She must remove this terrible burden and send back the pain and misery to its current source. This would take enormous energy and power. Olivia steeled herself for the ordeal ahead.

Sophie sat looking at Olivia. Something was happening to her friend—something quite amazing but almost frightening. Olivia appeared to be covered in a myriad of tiny, twinkling lights, like stars in a galaxy. Her skin glowed. Sophie looked about her. Everything else in the room appeared to be normal—there were no lights anywhere else. It wasn't her eye. Neither she nor Olivia, then, were drinkers; they hadn't touched a drop of alcohol for months. They did not touch substances, except for normal tobacco. Sophie turned back to Olivia. The lights had become even brighter; they spread out around Olivia's body, and Olivia's face was alight with a kind of energy. Then she appeared to be floating just above the settee.

Sophie felt some sort of power entering her body, pulling at her whole system, lightening her and freeing her. Then the wall behind Olivia and to her left began to dissolve as if it were liquid. Sophie sat staring in amazement as a long, high room appeared. It had marble floors and pillars and huge shelves filled with books—so very many books. She knew, somehow, that these books were filled with a great wisdom and that she was being shown something wonderful, something very real. She turned yet again, to try and balance her perception of what was happening, and the room appeared just as it had been before. She did not really remember exactly what they talked about. She recalled only that Olivia floated, sparkling like the night sky, and talked softly of the spirit world, with the great room behind and beside her. Her eyes seemed to emanate an unearthly radiance. At one point a huge wave of energy seemed to come out of Olivia, washing her and her surroundings in the beautiful stardust.

At that precise moment Sophie felt her body lighten, her soul become free, her heart warm and escape from the weight, the pain, the loss, and despair of the past. Sophie felt suddenly beautiful and desirable. She felt free and empowered. She looked again at Olivia, and instead of Olivia's face, she saw the face of an older woman, a very beautiful woman, like Olivia, perfectly made up and with what appeared to be a grey veil over her soft, well-coiffed hair. Olivia told Sophie that this was her mother, who had come to help her, as the process was draining Olivia's body. She told Sophie of her mother's powers and her fame, her strong connections with the spirit world, and the way Olivia had inherited this wonderful gift. She also told Sophie that the huge room she was seeing was one of the halls of learning, one of the things that gave Olivia the power and ability to do what she was doing. Sophie sat there in wonderment. Now she understood just why Olivia had always seemed to know how things would go. She had known, calmly and assuredly, that Sophie's eye would be fine. She knew how all the "coincidences" of the past weeks had occurred, and why. Why the police had been to Olivia's home, why Ty had been in that car in handcuffs, why his phone had been on that table, why she had hesitated to call him that evening, and why something had told her to pick up her phone and go ahead. Why Olivia had come in from the garden at that precise second and seen Sophie's name on the screen, why she had found the half-burnt bank statements and seen Sophie's name on them, made the connection, lifted the phone—and triggered the events that had led them both here for this night. She should feel afraid and worried about all this talk of spirits, all the things she had without doubt seen and heard. But inside her a light was rising. She was experiencing a freedom of spirit, a knowledge that her lost loves were really with her—and it was not because somebody had told her so and she'd chosen to go along with their beliefs. No, it was because she knew! She knew and felt the reality of their presence in that room that night. And she knew also that she would not go to bed on a high and waken the next day back in her darkness and misery. She knew that this cleansing had lifted a lifetime of painful experiences and burdens. Sophie looked at the clock. It was nearly five in the morning.

"Good grief, Olivia, look at the time—it's almost five!" It had felt to Sophie as if minutes, yet years, had passed. Olivia looked drained. She was sounding her normal self again, but she was exhausted. She had given a great deal of herself in this healing ritual, and it showed. The energy she had sacrificed to help Sophie was coursing through Sophie's being. She felt as if she was giving out a beam like a lighthouse on a rock. She looked at Olivia with concern.

Olivia slowly came to herself. She had expended enormous energy to help Sophie; she knew it could take her days to recover. But she saw Sophie's new aura, the sweet lightness and joy, the freedom of a healed spirit. She had watched as Sophie's bewilderment, disbelief, and amazement had turned to a wondering acceptance as her scientific mind realised that this was indeed truth, that they were not drunk or drugged or in a state of anything abnormal. She had watched Sophie being freed of the miserable captivity of the past, of those searing losses, of the vicious pain of Ty's betrayal and his treacherous words that Sophie was nothing to him. All that malevolence had been pulled away from Sophie's mind and body. Olivia watched as Ella, Sean, and Ben quietly withdrew, smiling at her as they went.

The two women were tired beyond anything they had been in a very long time. Sophie made them tea, and very soon they went to their beds. Olivia was asleep in seconds.

Sophie whispered, "Night, all of you. Don't leave me—ever."

Just as she lost consciousness, she heard them all whisper in unison, "Goodnight, darling Sophie." And she felt a soft kiss on her forehead.

Next to Olivia's bed, the shadowy form of her mother leaned over her and gently stroked her daughter's face. Silence and the misty October moon hung over the little street, and a million stars twinkled in the black, velvet sky. There had been an end tonight—and a beginning.

The following day found them both weary, but Sophie was a different person. Olivia was delighted to see the change. Sophie was concerned about Olivia's tiredness, but Olivia assured her that it was normal and she would recover in time. They drove in the little Citroën to Albufeira, parked near the museum, and went for a walk around the town. They went into a shop and tried on the locally made straw hats, giggling like schoolgirls. Olivia looked lovely in a wide-brimmed hat. She didn't buy it and regretted that afterwards. Sophie purchased a small straw hat with two pink flowers on the front, which she wore as they continued their walk. At another shop Olivia bought jewellery, and Sophie bought two pairs of sandals. Suddenly she wanted to look good, to care about herself again. They stopped at a café, where Olivia had a coffee. Sophie had a freshly squeezed orange juice, a drink she became so fond of that she had it again and again on their visit. They walked down to the beach and looked at the blue sea, the boats, and the brightly painted houses. Then they bought themselves a delicious ice cream lolly each and strolled along, licking the fruity treats.

They decided to go for a jaunt in a *tuk-tuk*, a tiny three-wheeler taxi. The engine seemed too small to even move it, but it flew around at breath-taking speed. Their driver was a charming swarthy-skinned, black-haired young man. He spoke good English and, as Sophie discovered, quite passable French, too. Olivia handed him €20 and asked him to drive them all around, including the old town, built by the invading Moors. They went up and down steep hills, with the young driver, Edwin, pointing out landmarks and explaining the history of the area. He stopped near the beach to let them out so that they could take pictures, and he posed, his arm around Sophie, so that Olivia could take a picture of them—Edwin and the new, radiant, smiling Sophie. They were so relaxed. The weather was kind; the sun was out. They had invited Annette to have supper with them in the main square that evening. They drove home and sat drinking tea and discussing Ty for some time. There was so much to talk about, comparisons to be made and incidents to recount. Olivia was still afraid that Ty was hatching some unpleasant plan to further harass her and disrupt her life.

"I know him a lot better than you do, Sophie. He has to have exactly what he wants, and if he can't, he has a terrible temper. If he knew we were on holiday together he'd be incandescent with rage. I just worry about his jealousy. If he thought I had another man, he'd go crazy."

"Well, you're very aware of all this, so you'll just have to be on your guard. Wouldn't it be better if you blocked him completely from your phone—I mean everything, all means of contacting you?"

"No, actually, that's not a good idea. If he can contact me it gives him some sort of security, and that will stop him from going over the top. If he was totally cut off, and I couldn't merely fob him off, he'd be driving up to stalk me, quite literally. He has to feel in charge of my life. I won't let him be, of course, but if he has the illusion of control, it will hold him at bay while I get it into his stupid, thick head that we're over. He will take a very long while to understand that." Olivia lit up another cigarette.

"I suppose it's a cultural thing with Ty. Jamaicans have their own take on relationships, even on marriage, don't they? I've heard Ty say things that made me realise this. And his attitude—his amazement that we should actually want to know where he was and what he was doing, that we should be annoyed at his disappearances and failure to contact us."

"Oh boy, yes, Sophie. Sebastian wasn't exactly a role model for that. He had five children with Mary; two that he had with other women were brought into the family and raised by Mary; and he had another five—at least, maybe even more—that were raised outside the family. Ty and his brothers and sisters knew all this, so they grew up with it and thought it was normal, what you did. Then there's his oldest brother, Michael. He flies back to the States regularly from Jamaica, and his wife puts contraceptives in his luggage, and she tells him to be sure to use them."

"I suppose that's an intelligent way to behave if you can't change things." Sophie sipped her orange juice.

"I think I told you about Carol Ann's husband. He was sacked from his job at a local five-star hotel because he was found there after a weekend in bed with a guest. Carol Ann took him back and forgave him. But that's what they do, Sophie, accept it and have them back. What they really feel doesn't matter. They're conditioned to expect their men to sleep around, and if they want to keep them they have to shut up and put up. The men wouldn't be too happy if their women kicked back. So our darling Ty expects us to accept and forgive. Can't quite understand our anger and hurt—or mine, at least."

"Yep." Sophie looked sad. "He decided to just disown me to keep you. He never read Shakespeare, obviously." The women looked at each other and laughed. "He can hardly read a text, can he? But he should have read that quotation: "Love is not love that alters when it alteration finds." The bard meant that we all lose our looks, and nobody is perfect, and you don't just dump someone you claim to love when they show signs of not being what you want them to be. Ty wanted you and all he could get out of you and your lifestyle, so he altered when his life seemed about to alter. He just dumped and disowned me because he was terrified of losing all you supplied. The quote means that you don't stop loving somebody when something about them alters of course but the alteration he found was in the setup. His love wasn't love, anyway. Funnily enough, I used to tell him over and over that I was too old for him, that my looks were long gone, but he said that you don't love someone just for looks. Now that could have been a profound pronouncement for him if it were true, but he only 'loved' me for my stupidity and my willingness to give him money. I daresay my lack of looks and everything else must have infuriated you."

Olivia looked puzzled. "What does that mean, Sophie?"

"Well, look at me. I'm damned certain that you must have thought, How could he want her when he has me, with my looks, jewellery, clothes, lifestyle—everything. Maybe you even asked him. If the situation were reversed, I know I'd have thought it—and said it. We both know that he was only exploiting me."

"There must have been something there to keep him with you for three years. We were separated when he met you, but we got back together, and he still didn't drop you, did he? There must have been something that he didn't get from me."

"Rough sex, his dark fantasies, a beaten-down, tame possession?"

"Don't keep running yourself down like that, Sophie. For your age you're a good-looking woman. I'm soon going to lose my looks too. You have intelligence, an ability to survive tragedies, a great sense of humour, and a terrific personality. We're both cougars, and you're proud of it, as I am. You enjoy life because of that, and you're not old. You don't sound it, or behave like it, or think it, or even look it—"

"Not with lots of make-up and in a dim light," Sophie quipped. They laughed again.

That evening they showered and dressed in their glad rags to go and have supper with Annabelle. Olivia had insisted that they dress up, although Sophie felt sure that they would stick out like turnips in a rose bed. Olivia put on a beautiful dark-blue dress. It had been Ty's favourite, and she had worn it on the night of the proposal, at Ty's command. She wore her fabulous gold jewellery, and with her flawless make-up, and her long artificial nails studded with tiny jewels, she looked like something out of a Hollywood premiere. Sophie only had one item that resembled a formal dress. It was a long black kaftan embroidered with silver thread, which she had bought herself in the Canaries. She had little jewellery, save for a silver chain she wore around her neck with a locket containing Ella's photo and a pair of silver hoop earrings.

Olivia came into Sophie's room. She looked appraisingly at her. "Yes, you look good. I've laid my jewellery out on my bed. Help yourself."

Sophie was happily surprised. She went into Olivia's room and stood looking at the cornucopia of goodies in front of her. She picked up one lovely thing after another, turning them around in her hands, seeing the glint of the gems and feeling the weight of the gold. Eventually she chose a heavy gold-and-diamond necklace, a pair of gold-and-diamond earrings, and a matching bracelet. She put them on and looked at herself in the mirror.

With her carefully applied make-up, her well-cut and tinted hair, her black dress, and now this bling, she felt attractive, desirable, smart—and normal. The disapproving voice of her mother began in her head, but Sophie dismissed the voice, and her mother, from her mind and being. That was the past. That had gone. This was now. The few years that were left— she was going to live them. She would have to work hard and worry about money still, but she was going to love herself and love the life she had. She could no longer teeter around on heels, as Olivia could, in her many pairs of beautiful shoes. But Sophie slipped on a pair of the sandals she had bought in the town; they were nice looking and comfortable. She picked up her black-and-silver evening bag and descended to where Olivia was waiting. They had ordered a taxi, as they intended to have a few glasses of wine, so they would not be taking the noisy little Citroën. They climbed in and were soon at the centre square of Albufeira.

Annabelle was there to greet them. Sophie felt extremely overdressed when she saw Annabelle wearing jeans and a shirt. But *What the hell!* she thought. *I feel fabulous!* They went down the steep hill and wandered through the open area of shops and restaurants, eventually settling on a tiny place in an attractively shabby back alleyway. The table was impeccably laid. The service was excellent, and the food was delicious. Sophie chose a good wine, and soon the girls were chatting and laughing happily. The evening passed by. Full of a memorable meal and wine, they parted company, and Sophie and Olivia took another taxi back to the apartment. They sat outside on the terrace in the washy light of the rising moon, smoking and drinking tea. Olivia had recovered a little of her sparkle, which satisfied Sophie, who had been very concerned about her friend's pallor and weakness.

"I can't get over all that coincidence, all that working together towards this. As if it were all planned long, long ago." Sophie gazed up at the moon and blew out a cloud of smoke.

"It was, Sophie. Neither of us knew, but the spirit world did. That's what it's like, what it's all about. They're with you always. Ella, and Ben, and Sean. They never went away. They stay with the people they love. Know that, and be happy because of it." They sat in silence.

Later, after they had said their goodnights and gone to their rooms, Sophie sat on her bed in her lacy underwear—she had bought it for Ty's benefit but decided that she would wear it for herself. Suddenly she was aware of a presence next to her. Without even looking, she knew that it was Ben. She looked up to see him there beside her. Still only thirty. Still devastatingly handsome. His blond hair was in a plait—just as he had been in his coffin after she had plaited it. Around his neck was the gold chain and on it was her engagement ring, which she had hung there. His blue eyes were even bluer. He looked appraisingly at her black underwear. Sophie was suddenly aware of her ageing body, and she tried to cover herself with her dressing gown that was at the bottom of the bed.

"No." Ben grinned and spoke softly. "You don't have to do that, my lovely. You're still young and beautiful to me." When Ben called her "my lovely", it brought tears to Sophie's eyes. Ben wiped them away gently. "Don't cry—not any more, my lovely. I'm here. I've always been here with you. You're still my love and my life. I'm looking after Ella. We're all here for you, me and Ella and Sean. Now go to sleep and rest. I shan't be far away, ever." Ben leaned towards her, and Sophie was shocked to feel the warm pressure of his lips on her mouth. She closed her eyes. When she opened them he was gone, and a shaft of cold, unearthly moonlight lit up the place where he had been. She put her hand to her lips where she had known him again. She smiled, put on her nightie, slipped under the covers and fell instantly into a deep sleep.

Olivia stirred in her sleep, and she smiled. The healing had begun. The years the locusts had taken away were slowly being restored.

Olivia's peace was soon shattered by another outburst of Ty's texts. First came a barrage of music, the usual sickly type, entreating Olivia to reconsider, to realise, to forgive, to look into her heart. Then the drip-feed of hate towards Sophie. Sophie was pulling Olivia's strings. Sophie was working with Shirley now. She was jealous and angry because she wanted Ty—but Ty didn't want her. He had only had sex with her twice in three years. She just wanted to break up Ty and Olivia's beautiful relationship. Olivia was too intelligent to accept the lies. She retaliated by sending screenshots of the texts Ty had sent to Sophie. The texts told Sophie how much he loved and wanted her and described what he wanted to do to her. They begged her not to leave him, when she'd had enough of being used and had threatened to end the non-existent relationship. The messages continued to disturb Olivia's peace. Sophie was seeing signs of stress in Olivia, although they laughed at most of the messages and at the replies Olivia sent back.

Then Ty texted, "Don't think you can get away from me. You're mine, and no other man is having you. I know what you're doing. I love you so very much. More than I've ever loved another woman. I won't let you go."

Olivia bit her lip. "He means it, Sophie! He has friends just about everywhere. I think I may have made a big mistake having that quickie with Billy. Ty knows a hell of a lot of people from the air base. He'll find out one way or another."

"So what? He cheated on you and treated you very, very badly. You spent more time chucking him out than doing anything else. He doesn't own you, and he needs to know that. If you show him you're afraid, he'll go for the kill. What's the worst he's going to do? Ring your doorbell and run away? Play every recording on YouTube?"

"OK, Sophie—that's funny! But you really have never seen Ty when he's drunk, and angry, and upset. He has no override, no safety cut-out, no social restraints. You barely even saw him. I lived with him for nine months. In Jamaica I couldn't escape him. He's obsessed with me—or should I say with my bank account, and lifestyle, and the premier-class flights, and the five-star hotels, and the clothes, and the hair products and grooming and, of course, the vodka." Olivia slumped in her chair. She was badly affected by all this.

Sophie thought for a minute. "Why don't you call him and ask him if he went to Jamaica? His father was supposed to be dying, wasn't he? Funny that there's no poor-old-me text from him. No scraping for sympathy. No demands for more money to help with the funeral or clothes to wear at the funeral or anything. Call him. Find out."

Olivia picked up her phone and selected Ty's number. The phone rang for some time. Olivia was about to hang up when the familiar deep voice answered. "Hi, hun. I was hoping you'd come to your senses and ring me. I expect you miss me, don't you, baby."

"Oh yes, Ty. Like a bad migraine—or a bout of piles. I just wanted to know about Sebastian. Did he pass away peacefully? Did you get there in time?"

"I thought I told you, baby. Are you still in Turkey? We can meet up when you land and talk all this over, can't we baby—"

"When hell freezes over, we can!" Olivia disconnected the call sharply. "Bastard! Lying bastard! His father wasn't at death's door. He just wanted to con another holiday out of me—and I bloody well fell for it again! And he made me so bloody angry that I hung up. And I still don't know. I just feel that he's conned me again. Then again, he might just be totally truthful this time. " Olivia's nostrils were flared. She lit up a cigarette and inhaled deeply.

"Whoops—and me, too. He would have got that money out of me, too, Olivia. He has no morals, no principles, nothing. He uses his father, his kids, everybody, to steal from people. He seems to think he can still laugh at you and abuse and exploit your emotions. I hate him. I just bloody hate him!"

"Well, it's the last time I'll do that for him. He can starve in the gutter; I don't care! He knows I still love him."

"Of course he does, Livvy, and he'll go on using that as long as you allow him to. He also knows—he must know—that you're scared of him and what he might do and of the people he mixes with. You have to stand up to him. If he harasses and stalks you, then you must tell the police. There are laws against it nowadays. Show him that you won't tolerate any of this crap. As long as you keep letting him in, giving in, and just-this-timing him, then he's got you by the earlobes. He's cunning. He knows how to play you and land you. You have to convince him that you don't love him any longer—that your love altered when it alteration found. Then he's got nothing to blackmail you with emotionally."

"I know you're just too right, Sophie, but the trouble is that I do still love the crooked pig. I sometimes work up a healthy hatred, and then it just goes, and I love him again, and I really want him and miss him. It's not bloody fair."

No, thought Sophie. *No, it's not fair at all. I love and miss him too, and I hate him too, but he doesn't want me. He's had all the money he could get, along with all the dirty, sneaky, unfeeling sex he could bully me into, and now he's denying my very existence.* At least he wouldn't be texting and harassing her. But sometimes she would have given anything just to see his "Morning, baby" on her phone.

Olivia put her phone away. She was unable to completely switch it off, as she had to stay in touch with her business. But for now she could stay away from it and give herself a break from Ty and his psychotic behaviour. They decided to go out for a drive and do some shopping. They stopped for a coffee, glancing sideways at some good-looking young locals. Then they browsed the shops and bought jewellery and some ornaments for the house. Olivia bought a really unusual and expensive handbag. When Sophie admired another one, Olivia offered to buy it for her. Sophie immediately thanked her but refused her kind offer. Sophie was fiercely proud and independent, and nothing and nobody was going to change that.

The sky became cloudy. Light rain began to fall, and soon the early November day merged into twilight. They returned to the car park. The satnav was in a bad mood again, and soon they became hopelessly lost. The woman who lived inside the satnav kept insisting that they turn right, but the road signs said a clear No Entry. Olivia was obliged to chase around tiny one-way roads until they seemed to be going in the right direction. By now it was dark and still raining. As they drove up a narrow hill there was a *whack*, and Sophie realised that Olivia had driven too close to a car and hit its wing mirror. The Citroën did not appear to have suffered any damage, so she breathed a sigh of relief and warned Olivia not to get too close again. Then they were in another narrow road, with a stream of oncoming traffic. Sophie saw that, again, they were much too close to the parked cars. She heard another bang. "Oh shit, Livvy, you've hit another mirror." All of a sudden they realised that they were being chased. It was a taxi, and the driver was not happy. He screamed at them in Portuguese and waved his hands furiously. Then, worse than this, a police car pulled up between them and the taxi.

"Oh God, Livvy. We'll be arrested! They'll take our passports, handcuff us, torture us. You know they carry guns over here. They shoot you if your lipstick's the wrong colour. We'll never get home again!" Sophie did not know whether to laugh or cry.

"Shut up, Soph." Olivia wound the window down. She put on her most appealing dumb-blonde expression. The good-looking police officer began waving his arms around and rattling away in Portuguese.

Olivia said, sexily and sweetly, "I am *so* sorry. We are English. I was lost.I am having to drive on the wrong side of the road. I am not used to this car." She held up her well-manicured hands in an expression of despair and penitence. The police officer stopped babbling. Looked Olivia up and down appreciatively, he appeared to be thinking, *Nice blonde, but I don't think much of her mother.* Then he waved his hand imperiously and dismissed the shaking women. The taxi driver started complaining loudly, but the police officer turned to him and disposed of him with an abrupt hand gesture. Olivia pulled away carefully, avoiding the parked cars very markedly. The police car appeared to be following them, but soon it turned off, and they let out a combined sigh of relief.

"God in heaven! I need a fag," Olivia said. Quite soon they were out of the town and in a country lane. Olivia pulled off the road, and they both got out and lit up.

"Thank God you're a dumb blonde, Livvy." Sophie grinned at Olivia, and they both burst out laughing. "That poor taxi driver. The policeman just waved him away."

"You and your 'They're going to lock us up!'"

"But I honestly thought they'd arrest us. Just watch those damned wing mirrors in future."

"It's actually easier in a bigger car. I hate these little baked-bean tins. I've driven in Germany for eight years, so I'm quite used to it." They laughed again, finished their cigarettes, got back in the tiny car, and drove home.

Ty started his assault almost as soon as they entered the apartment, treating Olivia to more songs and texts. There was a slightly more threatening note creeping into his messages. Olivia was worried, but she chose to block out the worry and enjoy her break. They went out for meals again and sat talking again—about their mutual enemy. Always the conversation drifted to Ty's size, his terrifyingly huge penis and his sexual techniques. Olivia had known everything from the gentlest of lovemaking, to a frantic minute-long quickie with their clothes still on, to a steamy session in a Jamaican swimming pool. Sophie had briefly known really sweet, genuine lovemaking, but mostly it had been hurried, selfish stuff and at worst really painful, brutal, and emotionless fucking. Olivia still spoke of Ty's obvious experience and knowledge, of the way he knew exactly what he was doing. Apparently he knew how to excite and stimulate Olivia to a frenzy. Sophie listened, crying inside. If Ty did indeed know what he was doing, then he must have realised just how cruel and contemptuous he was being towards Sophie. Was it because of Sophie's low self-image that Ty had felt at liberty to almost abuse her? But had she actually felt abused? She thought about it honestly. No, she had liked the slightly rough sex sometimes, but she just wished that Ty would have spent more time with her and shown her real love. Then the rougher times would not have felt so vicious and degrading. She wished that she could have had a few hours more of his expertise and gentleness. Why worry any more? She would never find out. She had been discarded.

Olivia sat drinking a mug of tea, glancing at Ty's verbal barrage from time to time. She pushed her mobile in front of Sophie. "Hey, just look at this, will you?"

Sophie read the text from Ty. "I suppose you're on holiday with some man. You're still my fiancé, remember. I'm the man who makes love to you, not anyone else. Just because that bitch is controlling you makes no difference. When you come to your senses, you'll come back to me. Don't sleep around."

"Cheeky bastard," said Sophie. "You belong to him—really? He sleeps around with God knows how many women, actually lives with Shirley, or at least goes to her for periods of time, and he thinks he has a right to tell you what to do and not to do.

He can't accept that he's done a damned thing wrong. This is all *my* fault, of course. And he seems to think that you'll phone him one day and ask him to come back. Tell him to get lost."

"I do keep telling him, all the bloody time, but he can't accept reality. He expects me to accept his sleeping around as if it's normal and I've just got to put up with it. Doesn't understand why I—we—are so angry and so hurt. He really does believe, however, that I belong to him, and that I can't tell him goodbye and don't come back. He would explode, literally, if he thought I was with another man. That's why I'm so scared, Sophie. You've seen a little of his temper, but believe me, he's a lot worse than you can possibly imagine. His temper when mixed with alcohol is a recipe for a nightmare!"

"But surely if you just ignore him, Livvy—just block him off everything and make sure he can't call, or text, or WhatsApp, or even email you—he'll eventually just get fed up with trying and take the hint?"

"No, Sophie, it's not that simple. If he has some sort of contact with me, it gives him a sense of control, and that will stop him from doing anything too scary. If I completely cut him off, he would be frantic, imagining me with another man and getting himself into a state of fury. Then he would do something really stupid. Remember, he's reactive—he just responds to what's happening at the minute. He doesn't think anything out. His life is a total mess because he lives from day to day, from hour to hour, from drink to drink. I have to give him a certain amount of window into my life—or let him imagine he has that—and it keeps him quiet, or quieter anyway."

"But just how long do you have to go on letting him have this control, Olivia? You haven't really got your own life back, have you? Not if you have to be scared to come home from the office in case he's waiting outside. Or if he's going to turn up at your office—"

Olivia cut in. "He wouldn't dare do that. My partner's husband would take him apart limb from limb. The worst he can do is to fool my receptionists into letting his calls get through to me, but they're getting good at recognising him now. Mind you, he's got a couple of his dodgy mates to try and get past. The first one got by, and then Ty tried to speak to me, but I slammed the phone down. The second one had a slight Caribbean accent, and my receptionist picked it up. She cut him off quickly. No, I'm more afraid of him hanging around waiting for me, trying to spy on me and find out what's going on, see if I've got another man, that sort of thing. The police will take a hell of a long time to get out to me if I call them. He knows that, and he'll make damned sure to do whatever he's planned to do and be long gone when the boys in blue come chugging around the corner. I'm also a bit concerned about how safe you are, Sophie. You're there alone—with Freddie, I know—but what could he do against someone the size of Ty? And he might be out at college. It really does worry me."

"Oh, I think that I'm the last person on earth that our Jamaican will be bothering about. Remember, I have nothing he wants— he won't get any more money out of me, will he? I have no house, car, money, or lifestyle that he wants to retain. He's written me into the script of his ongoing film as the jealous unwanted interloper who's hatched up this diabolical plot to break up your fairy-tale romance. He's not going to waste time on me. He could be spending it better by trying to get you to

take him back, surely? He's finished with me. I'm past now—
nothing and nobody."

"Yes, but you don't know how he's convinced himself that you
really did cause this, Sophie, and what he said. He said you
were truly evil and destructive, and if you were in Jamaica he'd
get you killed—" Olivia stopped. It had all come out in a rush.
She looked guilty. "Perhaps I shouldn't have said that. I don't
want to upset you even more. You've had to take more than
enough already. But I had to let you know why I'm so worried.
You know that he and his friends aren't exactly the nicest of
people; they move in nasty, dirty underworlds, and they all
have guns, Sophie—they do!" She put her hand on Sophie's
arm, seeing the fear in her friend's eyes. "You know about his
drug connections already, but I don't think you realise just how
deep into that world he is. He could shoot you, or get you shot,
if he wanted to. In Jamaica, when I went to the cashpoint to get
money, he and his brother always went with me. They stayed
very close to me, one on each side, and they were armed. The
crime is terrible out there. People will shoot you for money—not
just grab it and run—so they had to bodyguard me everywhere
I went. Ty was always armed. His family knows the head of
the police set-up out there. Once Sebastian was driving while
he was drunk, driving a people carrier, and he crashed it, and
he killed eight people—eight people! But he got away with it
because of his connections with the police chief. Ty wasn't just
making an idle threat, Sophie! He meant it, and he could do it.
If you went out there he could get you shot, and they'd never
find the killer. They'd just say it was another tourist robbed and
killed."

"So I'd better make sure I never go out there then, hadn't I?" Sophie was grinning, but inside she was weeping. She felt fear and hurt that the man she had sacrificed so much for could think about her in this way. "We'd better hope he has gone back to Jamaica and that he bloody well stays there." They went indoors and made themselves another cup of tea.

Sophie was curious. "Your phone's working overtime, Olivia. Is the Jamaican still sending you crap to listen to?"

"Yes, I keep getting these silly songs and texts reminding me that I 'belong' to him."

"And I can see that you're not just annoyed—you're upset, because you still really do love him, don't you, Livvy." Sophie looked at her sympathetically.

Olivia looked back at her. "Yes. Yes, Sophie, I do, and so do you."

"Yep—it's like a disease he's left us with, a reminder we don't need, hurtful and damaging. We have to get that Jamaican out of our lives and our systems. Whatever it was that held us to him all this time has to go. There are other men in this world, other men with decency, respect, honesty, and real love, and we'll find them, eventually—when we've forgotten that bloody Jamaican.

But both of them were thinking of Ty, and his soft brown-sugar voice, and his huge body, and his handsome face, and the touch of his hand on their skin. And both of them wanted to be with him then, and forever. From then on the two of them called him not Ty but "the Jamaican". Because the word *Ty* was too painful, too personal.

Olivia snapped out of her mood. "OK, what shall we do tomorrow, Sophie?"

"How about going out in the tin can and smacking up a few more wing mirrors? We may just get arrested and sexually molested by a couple of handsome Portuguese policemen!"

"Oh, very funny!" Olivia laughed. "Yes, why not? I think that tomorrow we should think about going back on the dating sites, just to give ourselves a laugh. Treat 'em like the buggers treat us." Sophie was heading up the stairs to bed.

"Why not, Livvy? Could be fun." They washed, and creamed, and settled down. Soon the two of them were soundly asleep. Both had thought, briefly and with a hot pang of hurt, of the Jamaican, and of how they wished he were there. And then they'd thought of how they hated him for what he had done. It would be a hard, long road for them both.

The holiday flew by too quickly. Olivia and Sophie spent hours out in the little car, ate out in local cafes, browsed the shops, and sat through the evenings and into the nights talking of their Jamaican; there was so much they had to tell each other about him. Soon they were packing to go back to gloomy, cold England and their work, their stresses, and pain.

Sophie knew that her life could never be the same again. She was very aware that her lost loved ones were with her. She could feel and hear them, and sometimes she could see them. Her contact with Ben had given her back so much joy and love. Also, she had spoken with Ella one night. Sophie had woken up quite suddenly. She'd turned to look at the moonlight spilling over the floor and the edge of the bed and seen—her lovely, wavy, red-blonde hair over her shoulders, her cornflower-blue eyes tilted with smiling—her darling child Ella. They'd looked at each other for some time, and then Ella had been beside her,

Sophie's arms tight around her baby girl. She'd rocked back and forth, tears running down her face. "Oh, my darling, I have missed you so much! I love you, my baby. Why did you go?"

"I'm so sorry, Mum. I didn't mean to hurt you—and Freddie—so much. I saw you both and felt your pain. I was very ill; I wasn't going to get better, Mum. I couldn't bear Freddie to have to grow up seeing me as ill as I was. He is so happy with you, Mum—and you look after him so well. I can see him growing up into a beautiful young man, and you are so good with him." They held each other closely. "I'm always here—always." Ella's voice grew faint, and Sophie felt her slipping away. She remained sitting on the bed in the moonlight, alone but happy. She had seen Sean just as she was falling asleep on another night. He'd stood quietly by the bed. Then he'd sat down next to her and held her hand. Sophie had looked at her troubled, addicted son, who now looked young, peaceful, and handsome.

"Are you at peace now, darling? Are you well?" Sean leaned down and kissed Sophie's cheek.

"Yes, I am, Mum. It's all over now. No more pain. No struggle. I watch you always. I love you so very much." Slowly he faded away—smiling. Sophie lay there crying for her only son's addiction and terrible death, but crying also with relief for his release and peace. For her, life was very different now, and she understood why she had been through the things she had. It was so that she could meet Olivia, with her powerful spiritual connections, and be healed of her grief. It was so she could know that her beloved lost ones were safe and with her forever. Olivia, too, knew why all these things had had to occur to her and Sophie. She understood that all the coincidences had had to come together, like a jigsaw in the cosmos, to fulfil the spirit destiny of both their lives. She had been brought up with this, lived with it, known it for a very long time. The cleansing of the deep and destructive blackness inside Sophie's being had exhausted Olivia, but she felt happy that she had brought such healing and knowledge to her. Now they had to fight the shadow of the Jamaican together.

It was time to fly home. Annabelle drove them to Faro, and they had a short, uneventful flight back to Southend. They cleared customs quickly, Olivia collected her car from the secure parking, and they were soon on the way back to Sophie's home. They said their goodbyes, and Olivia drove to her home, tired and worrying about what the Jamaican would do next. She ate a small supper, showered, and settled into bed gratefully. She had just started to slip into sleep when her mobile rang. She looked at the caller identity. It was him. She took the call.

"Yes, Ty, what is it? You woke me up."

"You back from Turkey, baby?"

"Yes, why?"

"Nothing, just asking. You OK?"

"Of course I am, just fine. You didn't bother to tell me how Sebastian was. Is he still alive? How did the funeral go? You didn't send me a single text—and after all that pleading, and all that grief."

"Sorry, baby, you said you'd be away on holiday. I did try to tell you when you called, but you hung up on me. I didn't want to disturb you. My dad's still in hospital, but he's fine—still very ill, of course. I had a good time with my brother. We went fishing, and then we cooked the fish together; it was great. Haven't spent time with him like that for ages."

"So your father wasn't dying, and there wasn't a funeral, Ty?"

"Well, I didn't know that, hun. I was told he was going, and I was frantic. All I could think of was getting to him—"

"Well, you'd better not have any more false alarms, Ty. I shan't be dishing out airfares like Smarties any more. You could at least have let me know what was going on. You know how much I love Sebastian and Mary."

"Yes hun, I do know. Like I said, I didn't want to disturb your holiday. The family really missed you, baby. Let's stop all this silliness and get back together. It's only because of that evil bitch that all this shit is happening. She and Shirley cooked this all up. She's so jealous, and she wanted to ruin our life together. Let me come back, baby. It'll all be good from now on. I've got help with my drinking—I've stopped smoking. We can have—"

"Ty, are you deaf or totally stupid! You were sleeping around with a whole bunch of women, and you were living the good life at my expense; you were lying and cheating. You slept with Sophie just to get money—that makes you a prostitute, Ty. Had you ever thought of that? You had no need to steal Sophie's earnings, had you? You had everything from me—everything. You flew premier class twice at my expense, and you stayed in the best hotels in Jamaica, ate the best food, drove hire cars, and wore over £600 worth of clothes at the wedding. Why did you need to take her earnings? Why? That poor woman, bringing up her dead daughter's son, sitting with a hot-water bottle on the settee with a blanket around her and the heating off to save money—so that she could feed that boy. Why? How could you do that?"

"Baby, I needed that money. I had to show you that I was a man, and I could get money for things—"

"A man! A bloody man, Ty? Stealing and lying and prostitution made you a man, did it? You thought it was fine to get money that way to make me admire you? And then you bloody well proposed to me. What were you going to tell that poor woman— nothing?—and just keep on taking her earnings and telling her you loved her? How the hell did you think she felt when she found out I was your fiancée? You didn't cheat and lie only to me, Ty—you did it to her, too. And you were living with me and running back to Shirley at the same time. Stop blaming Sophie for your wickedness. She did nothing."

"But she called you and told you lies—"

"No, she bloody didn't! She was worried about you and she called your phone—not mine, you idiot. You tell me you had nothing to do with her—really? That very morning you spoke to her and told her you were in a terrible way. And you got over £100 out of her for clothes for Jamari. I saw all the texts. Stop lying so much. That woman lost two of her children—two—and you said that wicked thing to her over the phone. Yes, I was listening. You keep forgetting. She can prove everything she says—everything."

"But, baby. We have this thing between us. You know you love me still—"

Olivia thought, *He sounds just like one of his cheesy love songs.*

"I am different. Give me another chance, hun. We all make mistakes, baby."

"And you make the biggest ones of all, Ty. Don't think for one minute that it's ever going to happen again. This milch cow has run dry; the bank of Olivia is closed. If I give you the ghost of a chance I'll get badly hurt and used again. I don't trust you an inch. I always knew you lied, and I knew, deep inside me, that you had other women, but I tried to ignore it. I just hoped that you'd leave it all for me. What a fool I was. And you haven't just hurt me. You've done the same thing to Sophie. You want me to take back someone who thinks that proving he's a man involves destroying another human being like that? Just get off the line and leave me alone." Olivia disconnected the call and threw her phone across the bed. It took her a very long time to settle to sleep.

The next time the girls were performing the coffee and cakes ritual, they were discussing the number of times they had tried to get rid of Ty. Both of them had sent inevitably long texts, giving him the reasons that they could no longer tolerate his behaviour. They had also given deadlines and ultimatums. He had not liked any of this. And he hadn't liked texts that contained other than the information that the money was in his account, or that they loved him too—or anything that involved the effort of reading more than a dozen words—and simple ones at that. Sophie showed Olivia numerous heartfelt messages that she had sent Ty when she had tried to make him see how hurt and neglected she felt. Olivia showed Sophie very similar ones that she had sent. Ty had typically reacted by agreeing with them and then saying that he was sorry, he would try hard to change, he had heard them, he knew where they were coming from, and he would do his best to make it all up. Things would change when he came back from Jamaica/the States/Florida— or wherever he was supposed to have been right then. He had a plan to make it all different when he got back. "Just wait, baby." "Just trust me." "Work with me." Alternately, there would be the angry, hurt response. "So you're leaving me. I don't blame you. I respect your reasons. I'm leaving now. I'm going home." If he was in a weepy mood, he was always going home, or wanted to go home. They suspected that it was a euphemism for yet another suicide threat. Sophie told Olivia about one of these exchanges. Ty had tried another tactic—he'd actually told her that he was dying. There had never been a diagnosis of the possible cause, but there was a veiled suggestion of cancer. Ty had looked on the Internet for a list of believable symptoms, realising that his chosen harem of victims was knowledgeable where things medical were concerned.

Olivia was horrified. "That bastard told you he was *dying*?"

"Yep—really convinced and upset me. I was at the stage where I think I could have walked away. It would have hurt for quite a while, but I know I could have done it—and he knew it too. He thought that one up to keep me dancing on his string. Cruel, wasn't it—nasty and selfish. He knew the losses I'd suffered and how I feared losing anyone else I loved—so he went for the jugular with that one. How could I leave him dying, alone?— or as I thought, alone except for Shirley, who hated him, and whom he hated too."

"Selfish, conniving pig! Couldn't afford to lose his pocket money, so he caused you even more pain by playing on your vulnerability."

"Yep, and when he thought he was losing his main income, he just dismissed me. Claimed he'd never known me. I was nothing. He really is a cunning, unfeeling crook."

They finished their eclairs, bursting with fresh cream and heavy with chocolate. Olivia wiped a tiny spot of cream from her nose. "He's still harassing me. Flowers sent to the office, and home. Stupid messages with them. My God, what trite rubbish. And texts and emails all the bloody time. Still just a bit too threatening—"

"Threatening—how threatening?" Sophie was worried.

"Oh, stuff like 'I know what you're doing and who you're with.' All the 'You're mine and nobody else can have you' threats again and again. It's really getting to me. I have a business to run. I don't need this. Sometimes I feel I want to call him and offer him a substantial sum of money to get out of England and never come back." Olivia picked up her second eclair. The stress was getting bad, thought Sophie. Two eclairs was a bad sign.

"But if you did, what would happen, Livvy? You can't guarantee that he'd go. He might go and actually stay there—or he might stay for a few years and then return to cause more nuisance. He might just take a holiday in style, or buy himself a fast, expensive convertible and stay here, or set up home with another victim, near here—near you and near me!"

"Yes, I know all this. That's the precise reason I haven't done it. But I was working on other things."

"What things, Livvy? Fixing the brakes on his car? Has he got another car now? Or putting a bomb under it, maybe?"

"Yes, he has got another, older car. An expensive one originally but nothing like the one I paid for. Actually the brakes and the bomb are possibilities." She smiled and wiped yet more cream from her shiny red lips. "But I had thought of something even better."

Sophie was interested. "And that is?"

"Well, you know how he suffers from claustrophobia, and a fear of being confined, unable to escape—"

"Yes!"

"Well, I thought that you could go to the police, show them the videos and stuff he took of you two doing it doggy style, the ones you didn't know about, and tell them—and tell them that he raped you."

"*Raped* me!" Sophie was horrified. "But he didn't rape me, Olivia. And how can I prove that I didn't agree to those photos and videos? He used to make me say, in texts, that I really loved all the stuff we did. It gave him sexual satisfaction. Remember, he told me he was alone, had a miserable little room with all these drunks, was away from me for ages, and needed help with his sexual stuff. As we couldn't be together, I had to help him that way. I really did think I was doing it to be loving towards him and to help him. I know you wouldn't have done it—you had no need to do anything like that. You and he lived together. I didn't see him for months on end. My common-sense part realised that he was too young and good-looking to be without a fuck when he needed one, but the other part, the idiotic, emotionally squishy part, just wanted and needed to do anything to show my love—and to keep him. Nothing I said to the police would stick. It would be ridiculous. He's had years of dealing with the police. He'd walk all over me. No, it can't be done."

"And even if it could, you wouldn't do it, would you?" Olivia raised a questioning eyebrow.

""Yes, something like that. You wouldn't do it either, Livvy. You still love him, just as I do. You'd talk about it, plan it, get excited about it, but you'd pull out at the last minute. You'd find some reason why it was impossible. Anyway. You seem to think that I hated every minute of what he did to me. I hated the way he was always in a hurry, the way he would take calls and texts on his phone while he was in the middle of fucking me. I hated the fact that I rarely saw him, that we had so little time together. Deep inside me I really knew that I was a poor second to at least one other woman and maybe more. But I didn't totally hate the rough sex. I much prefer the gentle, unhurried, real lovemaking we used to have three years ago, but I can't and won't use any of this stuff as an accusation of rape. It is a form of sexual abuse in a way—but I let it happen. I agreed to it. Sorry, Livvy. That's the way it is." Olivia shrugged.

"OK, Sophie. I understand. I get angry and want to lash out at him. Then I work off my rage a while later and realise that I couldn't possibly go through with any of the stuff I think out."

"Thanks. I knew you'd understand. Anyway, why bother about any of this stuff? You said he sounds really unhappy at times and that lately he's been very down and depressed. If he's in that state, then why do we need to do anything else? He's lost everything, hasn't he? You, his lifestyle, his home, his car, his trips to Jamaica by premier class and staying at the top hotels. All those expensive clothes. The vodka all paid for. Now he has zilch. He has to do drug runs to survive, and from what he told me, that's not too profitable."

"He told me he gets—what was it? A hundred for every year he'd get if he got caught. I don't believe that, actually. I think it's a lot more."

"And you said he has no friends left now, since this blew up. Why? What real friends just turn their backs on you for something like this? A real friend would be sympathetic, would support you in every way. He or she would give you a home and a meal. I think Ty does have an alternative to Shirley and her so-called settee. He chooses to be where he is. He has a hell of a lot of friends—not all of them nice. A bit shady, just like our Jamaican. I really think he may be very depressed because he's got a serious drink problem, and he needs help with that. It's all part of the same thing—this all fell on him suddenly. You threw him out for the umpteenth time and said you wouldn't have him back. Just turn back the clock, Livvy. If the doctor had called at the house, left him a script for some antidepressant meds and arranged treatment, would you have said "Get out, Ty."? I really think not. I think you would have put your arms around him, comforted him, seen that he took those meds and got that treatment, and helped him as much as you could to beat his alcohol problem. You loved him—still love him. Am I right?"

"Yes, you are right. I would have done all those things, Soph. Because I would have known nothing about all this, about you. I would have loved him deeply enough to help him."

"We would both have done anything to help him. But the problem now is that we both do know about all this—about each other—and it's all a bloody great mess. We love him one minute and totally detest him the next. Hate is the other face of love. Indifference is the opposite. But we can't be indifferent to anything connected with our Jamaican. We're stuck with all this pain and all this anger. We want to make him pay for it all, but there's nothing we can do that won't actually hurt us as well. Maybe we have to leave it to fate—to spirit—to work out his destiny and any revenge that awaits him. Maybe our role is just to stand by and wait."

"Maybe. Maybe you're right." Olivia shrugged.

They said their goodbyes, and Sophie watched the big Jaguar purring away.

Olivia drove quickly; the road was almost deserted on this Sunday evening. She listened to a collection of her favourite music as she drove, singing along with the lyrics she loved. As she approached a roundabout, she automatically looked into her mirror to gauge the traffic situation behind her. She caught her breath sharply. That was Ty's car—she was sure! She slowed, still glancing into the mirror. As the car got nearer to her, Olivia saw that it was indeed the Jamaican. She tried to nip across the roundabout without having to stop, but several cars were approaching quickly from her right, and she was forced to pull up and wait. She looked in the mirror yet again— and saw him grinning at her. He raised his hand and blew her a kiss. At that moment there was an opportunity to pull away, and Olivia did that, fast. The Jamaican tried to follow her, but another car was hurtling towards him from the right, and he had to stop. Olivia took advantage of the break to accelerate to almost seventy; she drove determinedly. What he was up to she neither knew nor particularly cared at that moment, but she was afraid. She knew it was not going to be anything good if he caught her.

She thought quickly. He knew her normal route home. She must get far enough ahead of him so that he could not see what she was doing, and then she must get off this main road onto a side road and take a diversionary route home. The Jamaican did not know this part of the country as Olivia did. If he lost sight of her he would not be able to work out where she had gone. Olivia glanced in her mirror. No sign of his silver convertible. She went through Owlsbrook village and then swerved off to her right. She took the narrow, twisting lanes that would lead her eastwards, around the main route, under the motorway, and eventually to home and safety. Olivia still drove quickly, but she had to match her speed to the nature of the narrow road. She put her music on more loudly and started to sing again, to comfort herself.

There was a straight part of the road, and she picked up speed. She glanced in the mirror almost automatically, and again she saw the silver sports car—his car—rounding the corner behind her. She was aghast. How had he found her? How did he know this way? This was a secluded and lonely place, and she was exposed. If he caught her, there was nobody to call to. He might have his gun, and she would be trapped in the car. If only she had stayed on the main road; at least there would have been other people around! Her mind whirled desperately. She must outrun him, outsmart him. She put her foot down hard, and the big Jaguar roared and leapt forward. She kept looking briefly into the mirror. He was keeping up with her. She cursed the fact that he was a very experienced driver. She could not shake him off. She thought furiously and fast. There was a tiny turning up ahead to her right. If she could get into it and divert, she could escape him. She drove relentlessly and very dangerously, and then she was out of sight. She had a chance—one small chance. She threw the big car to the right and it skidded. Its rear end slewed as it threw up dust and pebbles and bounced off the hedge. She was sweating, and her heart was thumping so loudly that she could almost hear it. She wrestled the machine back onto the road and roared away. Again and again she glanced into that damned mirror. She was biting her lip so hard that she could taste blood. So far he seemed to have been fooled. She went another mile; she was forced to slow down as the road narrowed even more, but she had started to feel safer. She only had about another quarter of a mile to go, and then she could join the bigger road that took her underneath the motorway. After that she could drive like hell and soon be back home, safe from the threat of that Jamaican.

Olivia slowed down to round a sneakily sharp bend—and gasped with horror. At the end of the lane was the silver car, standing like some silent animal of prey, facing her, threatening her. Olivia slowed, shaking and sobbing. "Oh God—spirit—help me!" she begged. For a few seconds they were frozen in time, Oliva's big black jaguar and the Jamaican's sleek silver convertible. Then she heard a sound, the sound of a tractor as it approached. And there was her saviour, a huge tractor with a large trailer attached coming out of a gateway to her left. It swung to its left and blocked the lane completely. To Olivia's right was another gateway. She drove into it and into the field, ignoring the damage she might be doing to her car. Frenziedly she threw the car into a series of turns until she could drive out of the gateway and onto the lane and escape. Then she felt the wheels spinning—the car was stuck! Olivia was screaming with frustration and terror. Then into her head came something Sophie had told her about getting stuck and spinning the wheels, something from her days of running a haulage. Olivia "bounced" the expensive car on the clutch. Slowly, so slowly, it found some traction, and then it was pulling away, out of the gateway and out of the field. Then she swerved to her left and was screeching madly up the lane. She looked in her mirror and saw the Jamaican waving his arms furiously and yelling at the tractor driver. Through the tears running down her face and destroying her meticulous make-up, Olivia laughed. She laughed with sheer relief, and at the sight of him, angry and foiled. But even as she laughed, she realised that his defeat would enrage him. She drove steadily, until at last she was pulling up the hill towards her home. She grabbed her briefcase and handbag, ran into the house, and locked and bolted the front door. She collapsed, breathing heavily, onto the settee. She opened the French windows and lit up a cigarette, which she demolished in three drags, thinking as she did so that she really must give it up. She quickly relocked the doors, closed the curtains, and poured herself a brandy and Coke. The warmth of the alcohol hit her stomach and relaxed her. She was not a drinker, but this was somewhat different. Not every day was she expected to act out a scene from a Bond movie. But it wasn't actually that funny. Her hands were shaking uncontrollably. She dialled Sophie's number and poured out a stammering account of what had just happened. She managed to laugh at the memory of Ty's furious reaction to the tractor blocking his way, but she was almost in tears.

Sophie listened in horror. "Poor Livvy! You must be badly shaken up. What are you going to do about it? I know you'll think of calling the police, but you know as well as I do that he'll have a really good alibi waiting, and a bunch of friends—that he doesn't have—ready to make and sign statements that they were all at knitting club together before they baked cakes for the needy."

"Yes, I had thought of calling the police, and yes, I had thought that it would be a bloody big waste of police time—and mine. He's dealt with them so much that he can play them with ease. So somebody follows me in a car. How can I even prove it? Then the tractor driver sees us—but what does he see? He sees two cars going in opposite directions, facing each other, stopped because they can't move, as the road is too narrow. He pulls out. The second car goes into a field and turns and drives away. The other car is stuck, and the driver gets out and yells at him. Even if I say I can describe this guy—well, I saw him get out of his car and shout at the tractor driver, so I'd be blind not to notice that he was black. I got a good description of the car from actually seeing it."

"You know the registration of the Jamaican's car, though?"

"No, not this one. He got it after he returned my car, remember?"

"I think you're right—and so am I. If you keep on going to the police after every incident, and he can prove very definitively that he wasn't there, or explain it away very cleverly, then he's going to make you look like a cheated woman who's trying to pin something on him for revenge. And the police will eventually get just a little tired of you—and he'll win. It's not at all fair, I agree. But you'll be playing into his hands Livvy, won't you."

"Bloody hell, it's so damned unfair! I want to go to the police, but you're right. What the hell is he hoping to achieve with all this bloody nonsense?"

"He's hunting you down—hoping you'll roll over, give in, take him back. Or that you'll pay him a large sum to disappear into the sunset. Problem with both those is that he'll come back, fuck you like crazy for a few weeks, be a very good boy for the same length of time, and then one morning he'll wheel his little case out and kiss you goodbye. He'll not text you for ages, and he'll then roll in, drunk, wanting sex, and money—lots of both— and you'll be fighting again within weeks. And you'll pack up his belongings or burn them, and throw him out, and then he'll be back again in weeks. Round and round goes the roundabout, the carousel of love and hate, the Jamaican roundabout. You know it's true, Livvy. So say you pay him a considerable sum of money. For his premier-class flight; for the rent on a house for a year; to buy a business, or a share in one; to buy himself an impressive car; to buy him the clothes he wants to be seen in; to replace that thick gold chain around his neck—"

"But he's already got one—he's always worn it—it's his prized possession."

"Yep, I know, Livvy, but I can guarantee you that he's had to sell or pawn it to survive. It's worth a hell of a lot, and he'll want to replace it. Can't imagine the guy without it." As she spoke, Sophie saw herself lying beside Ty, stroking his face and twisting his gold chain around her finger. She could smell his skin too and feel the warmth of his body .... She pulled herself away sharply from this painfully beautiful memory. Olivia, too, was remembering that chain, next to her blonde hair as she lay on Ty's chest, spent, glowing, and loving the man she now hated.

"Anyway, after you'd paid out all that, and maybe even thought of going, with me, to wave his plane off ..." They both sniggered. "There would be that day when you got some sort of clue that (a) he hadn't even gone and was shacked up nearby with a female; (b) he had gone there, started his business, and lost the lot; or (c) said business was wavering, and he needed cash for bills, cars, or medical costs for pregnant girlfriends—tick your own box. With him it all seems so sorted, so believable! But the reality is usually completely different. If this happened— and I'd bet a tidy sum it would—you'd be stuck with him. He'd have proved that he can still squeeze cash out of you, and he'd interpret your giving as a sign of your love rather than an attempt to get rid of him finally. It isn't a viable solution,

Livvy. You can't trust him any further than you can throw him. Remember, if he's breathing, he's lying. I can see having him assassinated as the only way to be rid of him forever."

"Hah! Don't think I haven't thought of that, more than once. It just goes on and bloody on. I decide to completely block all his access on my phones, and then I panic, because I know if he's thwarted, he gets nasty—very nasty. If he harasses me at my office, then I will call the police. He can't creep up on me then; I will have all my staff as witnesses. But he's sneaky when he does other things. I don't bloody well know how to get it into his stupid head that we're finished. I shall just have to hold out until he actually gets the message.

"But he's called me once or twice when he's been very drunk, and he's scared me, Sophie—really scared me. He seems to think he owns me. Can't grasp the reality of all this. Insists you broke it up out of spite—that he and I were the world's most wonderful couple and the two Jamaican trips didn't happen the way I remember. They were a paradise on earth. The times I kicked him out didn't exist, apparently. And he still keeps threatening you; it does worry me, Sophie. I know you say he's finished with you, but when he starts to realise that he's lost me, he just might turn on you. Oh, what the fuck do we do! All we both did was to love this sodding Jamaican, and he cheated, and lied, and stole, and hurt us. We seem to be paying the price, not just in hurt, loss, and grief but also in the worry of constantly having to look behind us. Anyway, it's getting late. I've got a few calls to make concerning work. Then I have to try and sleep before another week begins. Night, Sophie. Sleep tight."

"You too, Livvy. Try not to worry too much. Night."

Olivia hung up and then sat thinking. She made her work-related calls and sorted some paperwork. Then she climbed the stairs to her bed, having double-checked the doors and locks. She slept fitfully. At three the next morning her phone chirruped—the sign that the Jamaican was messaging her. She rolled over and picked up her phone. It was another onslaught of syrupy love-and-loss songs. Olivia sighed and was about to put her phone down when a text came in. It was from Ty. "You will come back to me. She caused this, and I can hurt her. You can prevent this if you come back where you belong."

Olivia frowned. Her heart lurched painfully. He was threatening Sophie! This would not happen. She lay thinking frantically. She would not tell Sophie about this; she could not frighten and distress her after all the woman had borne in the past few years. There must be something she could do to protect Sophie, to protect both of them. She lay awake, thinking, into the misty-white creeping hours of dawn. Outside, he prowled, waiting to rip both their lives apart again.

The Jamaican did not contact Olivia again for some weeks. This worried Olivia more than if he had done so. What was he plotting? She took different routes each time she drove to or from one of her three offices. It made her feel a little safer. She was still waiting, on edge, for his next move.

Sophie was checking her phone. She had blocked the Jamaican on every possible way he might try to contact her. Then she remembered her email. She had three addresses, and she checked them all so that she could block them. When she came to the one that she rarely used, she was surprised to see that he had sent her a message. She had not been aware that he knew this address. The date showed that the email had come in about a week ago. She usually simply cleared the screen of all incoming mail and checked it by going into the address later, when she had time to read it. Ty's message had gone to the third address, and she hadn't seen it as she so seldom looked at that one. She opened the message now. "I just wondered how you were. I am in a very bad way. You did this to me. Why did you do it? You are evil." Sophie sat looking at the message. Mixed emotions rose, hotly, in her throat. She felt a surge of love, and loss, and hurt, and terrible grief. But she also felt anger, hatred, and a burning wish to hurt him back. She wrote several replies but quickly deleted them. Then, after some thought, she wrote, "I did nothing to you except love you and help you. You were living with a woman you were going to marry. I paid for her engagement supper while I was sick with worry about paying my own bills. When did you plan to tell me about all this? I am not the evil one, Ty. You have caused hurt and anger to two women who loved you. You have crushed me and lied about me. You even said you never knew me after all the sacrifices I made to help you. You lied so much and so deliberately. I did nothing, and you know this."

Sophie sent the email. She decided not to tell Olivia. She would not get a reply, so what did it matter? How dare he accuse her of causing all this trauma and pain! He could go to hell. But her heart wept for him. Even as his fangs were sinking into her neck, she put out her arms to embrace him. She wished she could forget him totally. But she walked in his shadow, and part of her was a part of him.

The year slid into winter, and the days were short and dark, and cold sneaked into bodies and souls. This was the first winter that Sophie hadn't totally dreaded because of the cost of heating her small cottage. At night she turned the heating off. Freddie had two big, thick duvets and was snuggled up like a chick into a brooding hen. Sophie had two hot-water bottles and a winter-weight duvet which she wrapped around her; these kept her comfortable and warm throughout the night hours. As Christmas approached temperatures dropped, and the night air crackled with frost. Sophie's breath streamed in a cloud before her as she walked home from work late each night, wrapped up in a thick coat, scarf, fur gloves, boots, and a woolly hat.

She sat up and finished writing out her few Christmas cards. Most of what she sent were e-cards; they were easy and cheap to organise as well as very pretty and festive, with music adding to their appeal. As she wrote them, she felt a very strong urge to contact the Jamaican. She felt that he was desperately lonely and in need of someone to talk to. But why should she care? Had he ever thought of what she felt or what she had given to help him? Why should she bother with this man who had even denied knowing her in order to wriggle his way back into a life of luxury supplied by another woman? He had told the vilest of lies about her. She put him to the back of her mind and went to make herself and Freddie a cup of hot chocolate. She forgot his email after a few weeks.

Christmas was fast approaching. Sophie would spend it alone again, from choice. Her remaining children spent it with various relatives, and there was no place or time for her. She preferred to be alone, as she did not want to have to relive past Christmases in the company of people who could not possibly understand her feelings and reactions. Freddie went to his father, with the father's girlfriend and her children, for his Christmas. He got on well with the other children, so the whole arrangement suited everybody. Sophie wrapped the few gifts she had bought. In previous years she had gone without to buy Ty the gifts he'd wanted—and expected. Twice he had left them in her house and had to be reminded to take them with him some months later. Clearly they had been meaningless to him. Sophie went to the kitchen to make herself a cup of tea, and as she took it back to the living room, she heard the tinkle of her incoming email. She was going to ignore it, but something made her pick it up. It was an email from the Jamaican. Her hands shook as she read it. "Why did you send this to me?"

Sophie was puzzled. She scrolled back and saw that she had sent a general Christmas greeting to all her email addresses. She had pressed Send to All without thinking. This had resulted in people she didn't even care about receiving this wish. Sophie had found this amusing at the time but had forgotten that Ty would be a recipient. She replied, "Sorry. It was something you send to a lot of people. You know. You just press Send. I sent it and forgot you were on that address. Lots of other people got it too, and I didn't mean them to get it."

There was a pause. Sophie drank her tea and turned on the television. Then another email came in. It was from Ty again. "Can you open up WhatsApp and let me message you. Please." Sophie thought very hard. Her heart was tripping along frenziedly. She wanted to contact the Jamaican, but she also wanted to delete him entirely from her life. She sat for a while, biting her lip and clenching her hands. Then she picked up her phone, unblocked Ty from the site, and sent a message. "You are unblocked. What do you want?"

"I'm in my car outside her house. I'm very cold and hungry."

Sophie was almost in tears but she tried to think coolly and logically. "How do I know this is true? You lied so much to both of us in the last few years. And if it is true, then it's your own fault. Why are you outside in the car? Outside where?"

"Well, you can gloat now, can't you? I'm chucked out for Christmas. Got nowhere to go. Will have to go into a hostel. Freezing in this car."

"I asked you why you were outside and cold—and who had thrown you out." But Ty was, as ever, not going to answer her questions. She waited, but there was no more from him. He was deliberately baiting her. Upsetting her. Working on her soft, easily persuaded nature. Sophie knew this. Yet she could not fight it completely. She longed to be able to drive over to him and bring him back into her humble but warm cottage. To feed him. To show him the qualities he scorned and which he had used to exploit Sophie. She knew what was happening, what he was doing. She must harden her heart. She would not play his cruel games any longer.

Olivia was relaxing after a long and busy day. Then she heard the sound her phone used to identify the Jamaican's messages. She picked up her phone and opened the message. "Hi, baby. I want you for Christmas. You know you can't hold out without me for much longer. She's all alone there. Weak and helpless and poor. Not like you, hun. You really do need to think about her. Just say the word and she's safe. That stuff about the revenge wasn't bullshit. It was very real. I can't wait to be back with you."

Olivia dropped her phone on the settee. This revenge business! The Jamaican had told her about a white woman who had married a family friend. Ty had said that the marriage was perfect. Olivia suspected that the woman had escaped for the same reasons she had for escaping Ty. It sounded as if the reason for the marriage had just been money and possessions. The woman had run. A friend had helped her, offering to drive her to the airport at Montego Bay Sangster Airport. They never arrived. They were found in the car, just off the road. Both had been shot in the head. The killers were never found, and robbery of white tourists was spoken of, although neither had been tourists. Other family members had mentioned things that had assured Olivia the story was true. The victim's husband had been the Jamaican's closest friend. Ty had always called it "the revenge".

Olivia shivered. Sophie seemed so sure that she was immune to the Jamaican's violence, that she was of no importance to him. Sophie didn't realise quite how devious and cunning this man was and how cleverly he exploited human nature and feelings. Olivia needed to keep close watch. She did not reply to the email, and she tried to forget it, but she was deeply worried. Ty was erratic, unreliable, and a heavy drinker. He had a streak of violence, and he had violent and unpleasant friends. The emails continued. "Christmas would be so nice if we were together, baby. You know you want me back. Just talk to me, hun. We can sort this mess your friend caused."

"I think you should talk to me, baby. You owe me. We had such a good thing going until you listened to that bitch. I could make her pay for this, but I love you and I might upset you."

"I shall spend the rest of my life making up to you for all the mistakes I made. Don't ruin our life together by listening to that jealous, dried-up, lying, evil bitch. I'm laying off her for your sake, but I won't wait forever."

Finally Olivia cracked and replied. She was sick of this constant verbal attack and the Jamaican's arrogant assumption that she somehow belonged to him.

"Just get this straight, Ty. I am not your baby, or your hun, or your anything else. I don't want you back, ever, and we're finished. Not because of anything Sophie said or did but because of the way you cheated on and lied to both of us. You were running a whole bunch of women and taking money from quite a few of them. You lived a very good life at my expense and treated me without respect, let alone love. I am not going to put myself in the position ever again of being your victim. I loved you a hell of a lot, and I did everything I could to help you. Love can't just die, but it starts to fade away quickly when someone like you kills it. I could never take you back and not imagine you in another woman's bed and body every time you were away. And I can't see you not wanting to run off every five minutes—after all, you'd need to keep another bunch of women to finance you. Just forget me and Christmas, and stop harassing and stalking me. I'm growing very sick of it. We are FINISHED, Ty—you are not coming back into my life. Leave me alone and leave Sophie alone. She's innocent and harmless and weak. Stop threatening her and screwing up my life, or I will go to the police."

Olivia sent the email and waited. There was silence. She told Sophie the whole story at their next meeting and cake ritual—except for the threats the Jamaican had made against her—and Sophie's eyes filled with tears. Olivia put down her coffee cup. "Soph, whatever's the matter?"

Sophie wiped her eyes, sniffed, and looked at Olivia. "I just can't bear to think of him out there in the cold, in his car, in this weather—and on his own for Christmas. Whatever he's done, I can't bear the thought—" She continued to sob.

Olivia passed her another tissue. "OK, so what's been going on? What's all this 'in his car in the cold' stuff about? And how do you know, Soph?"

Haltingly, Sophie told Olivia what had happened and showed her the messages and emails.

Olivia snorted. "Serve the bastard right! He didn't care a fuck when you had to go cold so that he could steal your income for his pocket money! Stop feeling sorry for him. He didn't sound exactly cold and homeless when he was telling me to take him back. He thinks we don't communicate as much as we do; he believes that we keep in touch very sketchily and don't tell each other all that really goes on. He knows exactly how to make you feel sorry for him, Soph. And he won't take up your offer of a bed for the night, oh no! He'll just accept all cash donations—dollars or sterling will do nicely, folks. No! Stop contacting him. He doesn't care a damn about your welfare. He just wants to use you to get money. Just stop, Sophie. I don't think you're as weak as he thinks you are, but he can run rings even around someone as street hard as me, so you haven't a snowflake's chance in hell. Forget that Jamaican. Get on with your life. Just forget him."

"Yes, you're right, Livvy. I know it, but I can't help reacting like this. I still love him—you still love him too. Whatever's happened doesn't stop me from wanting to help him. I can't bear the thought of him out there in—"

"Sophie, *stop*—just bloody well stop! That's just exactly how he wants you to feel. So don't. Just remember what he did to you—what he said to you and about you. And what about the things he said about your kids, Sophie. He hasn't a feeling bone in his selfish body. He lives in his own world, where he's king of all he surveys, and everyone must jump to supply his needs and be the supporting cast in his stupid dramas. Walk off the film set, Sophie. Let him play out the scenes to an empty theatre. I do know how you feel, really I do." Olivia put her hand on Sophie's hand. "I still love the bastard too. At least I have a few good memories of my years with him, but what did he leave you? Debt, heartbreak, and hurt. I got the two last things as well, but at least I had more of him in my life than you did. He asked me to bloody well *marry* him, Sophie—and you paid for the dinner on the beach. When we flew back, I had finished with him for the umpteenth time, but if the armed police thing hadn't happened—well, you were right—I would have taken him back yet again, tried to help him dry out and get help with his demons. But then what would he have told you? Would he have said, 'Oh by the way, baby, I got engaged in Jamaica. You paid for the dinner where I proposed, thanks so much, and can you give me something towards the wedding.'? Let's face it, Sophie, he might never have told you *or* me. It might have gone on for a very long time. But what would have happened if one of us had found out after we were married—if we ever were? All that deception, and lying, and stealing. No, my girl, you're well out of all that now. I took away the blackness from your soul, and he's not going to drag you down again—nor me, neither."

"OK, yes, you are right—very right." Sophie bit into the remains of her cake and chewed it frantically, tears still dribbled down her cheeks. "He told me he was dying in order to stop me leaving him. He told me that not because he loved me and didn't want to lose me—he told me that bloody awful lie just to keep me giving him my last penny." She was almost talking to herself.

"Exactly, Soph. He's told so many dramatic lies. The poor-little-me type lies. Any old lies, just to hold onto a good thing. Living in luxury with me, top-of-the-range sports convertible; he had all the perks and didn't pay for sod all. Food, booze, clothes, premier-class flights—you name it, that bastard took it. And then there was you. Just a cash machine for his pocket money and his debts. A bit of nasty on the side to make it even more enjoyable. Sorry about the word *nasty*, but there was no love involved. He was sex obsessed. Do you suppose that he is a sex addict, Soph?"

"I would imagine you could call him that, but psychiatrists don't agree on the definition or even on the reality of the term. Certainly Ty wanted sex non-stop—all that texting me and asking me to text back and live in his dirty fantasies. Do you know that he told me he usually masturbated at least three times a day—*every day*! It's mind-blowing! Certainly he fulfilled some of the things written about sex addiction. People who are like this screw up their lives because they're so busy galloping after the next receptacle for their dicks; they lose jobs, have endless problems with relationships, run too many females at once—as we know all too well—have a messy working record, and are often in debt. They also have unpleasant side effects, like STDs and unwanted children. Lots of guys cause unplanned pregnancies—but not the numbers the Jamaican caused. The evidence shows that he had three sons and two daughters in one year alone, when he was only twenty-two! Do you know, Livvy, he told me he was called 'Supersperm'? Even seemed proud of it. Told him I didn't think that it was all that funny that he just deposited some semen and then walked away and left the mothers to bring up the result. But he was so bloody proud. His idea of being a man, I suppose."

"Yes, typical. He favours some of them and just rejects the others. That poor little scrap in Jamaica. I would have brought her up—but he just changed his mind and decided she would be too much bother. I'm really beginning to think that it was simply a very nasty, underhanded way of trapping me. First he wanted to marry me, and even if we didn't get married, he was going to make bloody sure that I fell in love with that beautiful little girl and wanted to look after her—at my expense, of course. Then, naturally, he would have parental responsibility, so he would have the perfect excuse to be in my life whenever he wanted to be, and legally I couldn't oppose that. He idolises most of his sons. Rejects a couple of daughters, has a few daddy's-girl pets, and generally fails to be a father to any of them. The mixed-race ones are stunning, handsome and beautiful. He's proud of them in that they make him look good, but he doesn't bother with them in the least. They are just collateral damage in his selfish, messy, greedy, sex-and-money-obsessed life. I wonder if there are some of the poor little things who have never ever seen their daddy, just a picture of him on Mummy's phone. And he flashes their pictures around and glories in the comments about how beautiful his kids are. Tosser!"

Sophie wiped her finger around the plate and picked up every crumb. Stress made her hungry. She was very hungry right now. The women decided that there were two things to worry about at that point, Ty's stalking of Olivia and his attempts to convince them that he was sleeping in his car, alone and freezing. Olivia had decided not to remind Sophie of Ty's threats towards her safety, but she was very worried about that. She reminded her to be sure to lock her door and bolt it whenever she and Freddie were alone. Olivia knew that Freddie very often neglected to lock the door, sometimes at night, and that Sophie often fell asleep before she checked it. She also knew that, whilst Sophie was aware of these threats, she was so deeply convinced that Ty regarded her as non-existent that she pushed the facts out of her mind.

Olivia looked at Sophie sternly. "Don't answer any emails, and block him on WhatsApp. He's only using your kind nature to upset you. He just wants money. Let him suffer, if it's really true. He needs to find out what it's like to have to go cold, as you had to for his demands, Sophie. Shut him out of your head, and your life. If you let him anywhere near you, he'll be on you like a great white on a diver."

They said their goodbyes, kissed, and parted. Sophie waved the big Jaguar off down the hill and went back into the cottage. She curled up on the settee and thought hard. She missed the Jamaican so very much. She tried hard to hate him for the appalling things he had done to her and said about her, but there was something—that indefinable something. Like gentle fingers stroking her neck, it was something that made itself real in her being. There was a voice that whispered "but …" each time she tried to kill her feelings for the big, beautiful man. She must fight back and fight on. She had fought back so often, after so much grief and hurt. It would be better if he were dead, because she would not think of him as being out there somewhere,—so close, so elusive, so wanted, so dangerous, and so evil.

Sophie went up to bed after locking and bolting the door. She slept fitfully and dreamt of seeing him ahead of her, out of reach, always out of reach. Then he turned, looked at her, and slowly merged with the landscape of palm trees, exotic flowers, dried grasses, and brilliant birds. She was left looking at the essence and the spirit of him.

Olivia left Sophie and drove back to her home. She made good time on the main road as it was nearly empty at this time of the year, and it was a Sunday evening. As she reached a large roundabout at which she took a left and joined another road, she glanced into her mirror. There was a sleek, dark sports car behind her. It was not the one that she knew the Jamaican drove, but there was something about the long, feline lines of the expensive vehicle that stirred slight worry in her. The road was twisting and narrow, governed by constant speed restrictions. It was impossible to overtake, so Olivia was not unduly alarmed when the car sat behind her at a sensible, safe distance. Still she felt uneasy. She decided, once again, to divert. This time she turned onto a not-too-narrow complex of roads, where she would not be trapped if she were being followed. She knew she was breaking the speed limit, but she knew this road very well. She suddenly sped ahead, leaving the convertible far behind. When she was out of sight, she swung left into a minor, but well made up and straight, road and drove as fast as the conditions would allow. She kept glancing in the mirror, but there was no sign of any car. She reached the junction with the main road and rejoined it. The road was empty save for a couple of LGVs lumbering towards London. She turned into the close, stopped, and looked both ways. Still nothing. She turned into her driveway, grabbed her handbag, and ran into the house through the French windows at the back. She pulled all the heavy curtains after bolting the French windows and sat, breathing heavily, on the settee. She kicked her shoes off, put her feet up, and sank back with a sigh of relief. That car had been just another car. She was getting too jumpy. She picked up the hand controls to turn on the television. Just then her phone rang out sharply. She dropped the controls and picked up the phone. It was the Jamaican. She allowed the call.

There was a short silence. Then he spoke. "Hello, baby." It was a soft, purring, leonine drawl.

"Yes. What do you want, Ty?"

"There was no need to divert, baby. I knew where you were going—and where you'd been."

"What the hell is this, Ty! Are you stalking me again? I told you—"

"But hun, I'm not stalking you. Just protecting you. Just making sure that my woman isn't bothered by other men. You are just so beautiful, baby. Those breasts—so many men want to hold them and suck them. But they're mine, sweetheart, mine—and no other man must touch them or any other part of your beautiful body. So I'm looking after you, guarding what is mine. Soon you'll tire of this silly game—all that crap that bitch has filled your head with—and you'll want my body again. You know I'm the best you've ever had in your life, baby. You must be missing my dick, the length and the width of it used to send you crazy, baby. Oh, how you used to scream when you came, my hunny. I can wait until you come to your senses. But I'm gonna keep an eye on you—"

"Just shut up, Ty!" Olivia had gone into the kitchen without turning on the light. She pulled back the blinds and scanned the street from end to end. And there it was, the big sports car, an Audi, sitting beneath the streetlight. Olivia dropped the blinds. "You're stalking me again. If you don't piss off and leave me alone, and stop talking all that filthy shit, Ty, I'll call the police! I've warned you again and again. We're finished. What don't you understand about that word? *Finished.* Not together. Completely apart. Out of each other's lives for good. You were whoring around, using me and Sophie to live off, to get money from. Lying and two-timing us both. You got found out by sheer accident. A very fortunate accident, as it happens, or I might have been stupid enough to take you back for the millionth time. Sophie just happened to call, that's all."

"Baby, you are such an intelligent woman, yet you allow that jealous, conniving bitch to tell you a pack of lies, just to break us up. She wants me but can't have me. So she tries to break us up. I told you I only slept with her twice—just to shut her up. She tried to buy me, gave me money non-stop to get my friends to fuck her. I was glad to be shot of the bloody woman. Use your intelligence, baby. I was trying to get rid of her when all this blew up—"

"The hell you were, Ty! Hours before you were found out, you were telling her you loved her and begging her for money. You sent a text thanking her for the money and telling her again how much you loved her. And why the hell would she call your bloody phone to tell me about all this, Ty? You aren't using too much intelligence, are you? We've been through all this. I've seen the evidence for everything she says. She bears no blame at all. She's just another victim. Anyway, I've been through all this with you already. Just stop calling me, and stop following me, and mind your own sodding business about my life. We're finished. I belong to nobody but me, now. I have no other man—not that it's any business of yours. I have had nobody since I met you over four years ago. You've had just about anybody who was bowled over by your lies, charm, and big dick. Just bugger off—or I really am calling the police. Understand, Ty?"

"Perfectly, baby. But just understand me. I couldn't give a fuck about your stupid, evil friend. Remember, if she was in Jamaica, I would have her despatched very quickly and efficiently. I never want to see that bitch again, ever. But if you go to the police, then I will be seeing her—and so will my friends. Keep talking to me and humouring me, baby, and she's safe. Before the police can do anything, she'll be in serious danger of harm. If I get taken in—well, my friends are everywhere. They know where to find that scheming little ho, and her grandson—"

"You keep them both out of it! She did nothing. This is all because of your evil wickedness!" Olivia was shouting into the phone. "Leave her well alone—"

"Of course I will, baby. And you leave the police well alone, like a good girl. Daddy's girl." Olivia could hear his breathing getting deeper. "I just can't wait to suck those huge breasts again—and to fuck you so slow, and so deep. You know you can't wait either."

"Leave me alone, you vile bastard! I don't want you near me!" Olivia cut the call off abruptly. She was shaking and crying. She wanted to call the police, but she believed Ty's threats. She knew he had spoken the truth for once. He would use poor Sophie and her grandson; he would hurt her. Olivia's mind was racing. If she let this go on, he would force his way back into her life. Part of her wanted him back; when he had spoken to her about her breasts it had made her nipples go hard; she had quivered and closed her eyes. But the sensible, world-wise part of her knew that it would take only days for the fucking to stop and the fighting to start. He would disappear again. And she would get angry. And he would drink heavily. And he would want money—and they would fight, furiously. And always she would be suspicious of him, and his whereabouts, and what he did. No, she would never forgive him for what he had done. Somehow she and Sophie must fight back. But how could she prevent Sophie from being harmed? And Freddie? Olivia went into the kitchen and looked through the blinds. The street was empty. The Jamaican had gone, for now. She opened the French windows and went into the garden to smoke. Her breath streamed into the cold air. She pulled her jacket around her. She would not let that man threaten her existence any more— or Sophie's and Freddie's. She had to win this. She had to.

Christmas was approaching. Olivia would have her family around her, as ever. But Sophie would be alone, and Freddie would be with his father. Olivia busied herself with decorating the house, wrapping presents, and making huge shopping lists. Sophie had bought a few gifts for Freddie and her other grandson James—the son of her dead Sean—and his sweet little girlfriend. As she wrapped them, she recalled wrapping presents for Ty. He would open them, always after Christmas— he never turned up even though he promised to do so for three years—and then leave them behind for months. It made Sophie feel that these gifts, like her little humble cottage and herself, were never good enough for him. She had bought herself a frozen turkey dinner. It sat in the freezer, awaiting the festive, and lonely, day.

Christmas day dawned and Olivia's family descended, a large crowd of happy, loving, excited, noisy children and grandchildren. Presents were unwrapped and paper piled up in every room. A huge meal spread tempting odours throughout the house, and soon they were all sitting down to a feast. Olivia was a brilliant cook. Crackers were pulled, hats put on, mottos and jokes read out, and gifts examined. The winter afternoon started to die into darkness. Olivia went outside to smoke and looked up into the puffy, looming clouds. Tiny snowflakes suddenly appeared, which rapidly picked up speed and grew larger. Suddenly the snow was settling, sweeping silently and coldly across the houses, gardens, roads, and trees, covering everything it touched with an unearthly beauty. Olivia stood for some time watching the scene. She thought of the Jamaican. He might be out in his car, alone, cold, without a Christmas meal, feeling hopeless and depressed. Her heart was torn. She longed to call him, to tell him to come up to her when the family had left. To eat some festive food. To drink wine. To sit in the big red chair with her, holding hands and listening to their music. To dance, closely. To climb the stairs to the huge bed.

To lie back and accept his mouth, and his hands, and his huge maleness, and to writhe, and to move with his body, and to dig her long nails into his buttocks as she climaxed, screaming. The snow fell on her blonde hair, her long eyelashes, and her nose; it melted and mingled with the tears that the memory had provoked. She left that image of her love—sadly. She hated him, but she missed him, and she loved him, and she wanted him not to be cold and lonely. The children spilled out into the garden and began to make snowballs and hurl them at each other, shrieking with sheer joy. Olivia joined in for a while; then she went back inside. Christmas day was closing.

Sophie stayed in bed with a cup of coffee, watching television. There seemed nothing to get up for. She showered and dressed just before eleven. Then her daughters called her from France, and she chatted happily with her family. Her older grandson James and his little lady called too, and Sophie chatted with them. Then there was silence. Hardly a car passed outside in the road. She watched more television but grew rapidly bored. She went into the kitchen and pulled everything off the work surfaces and washed them down. She cleaned out the fridge and then she baked some cakes and biscuits. The afternoon was marching on. Sophie was tempted to have a cigarette. She had made a very big effort to give them up. Ty had pulled her into the habit, and all the tension and stress after the sixth of September had made her habit worse. She rarely touched them now. She opened the door to the little garden, stood outside, and lit the cigarette. She blew out a plume of smoke, which seemed enormous in the cold air. There was a stillness in the darkening day, and the heavy clouds were both purple and pale, like a bowl of plums and cream. Then the snow came, minute flakes at first and then quickly thickening. Sophie stood outside in it, holding out her hands to the falling jewels, which melted on hitting her palms. She was entranced. However old one grew, there were things that always held wonder and beauty; this was one of them. She stood there for some time, and then she felt chilled. She didn't have a coat on, and it was really cold. She thought suddenly of Ty. Was he outside in this snow, huddled inside his car, hungry and lonely because Shirley had thrown him out? Sophie's tender heart could not bear to think of this being Ty's fate on Christmas day. Whatever he had done to her, her love for him swelled through her being. She went back inside and picked up her phone. She stared at it for some time, and then she started to WhatsApp him. She hesitated and deleted the message. She made herself a cup of tea and sat on the settee drinking it. She screen-imaged her mobile to the television and played her music. She closed her eyes, listening. Then the song came on, the one Ty had put on her phone. It was like a knife through her chest. It hurt badly. The tears welled up, hot and huge. She wept and cried out his name. If only he had had just one tiny bit of love for her. She had adored him. The song finished, and Sophie sat there sobbing gently. Then she turned off the music, picked up her phone, and texted Ty.

"This is just to say Happy Christmas. I hate to think of you alone and outside in your car with no Christmas dinner and no company. I would ask you here, but I know you hate me, and after all the things you said about me and the way you have lied to me and cheated on me, I think that would not be appropriate, really. Despite all that, I still thought of you." She read the message and then sent it.

She did not expect a reply, and was surprised when her phone announced a message. She opened it. "I am with someone. The friend of an old friend."

Sophie replied. "A woman, no doubt."

"I wish," Ty replied.

"Well, I'm glad you are inside and with someone, anyway." Sophie turned her phone off and sat, thinking of Ty and the early part of their relationship, when he had lain above her, looking into her eyes as he climaxed, and told her that he loved her. How cruel he must be to do that to someone so helpless—to show what seemed to be love, to use her, and then to denounce and revile her in order to save his lifestyle. And yet she could not condemn him to cold and loneliness on Christmas day. He was probably surrounded by friends, drinking vodka, with his arm around a woman. That's what Olivia would tell her, to stop her concerning herself about someone who didn't give a fish's tit about her or what she was doing on this day. She tried to forget him. She watched boring, meaningless television long into the night before she slid into sleep. As she lost her contact with the world, she whispered goodnight to the Jamaican. She wished him a warm night and at least one human for company.

The New Year came in with fireworks and alcoholic overindulgence. Both Sophie and Olivia spent it alone and in bed. Olivia, too, had been upset by the thought of Ty outside in his car, although she knew it might have been just another sympathy drama. One night he called Olivia and told her he was so very cold outside. He said that Shirley had complained because he was running the car engine in the early hours of the morning to keep warm. She had shouted down to him to shut up, and then she had thrown him a blanket, in which he was huddled, still freezing and sleepless. Olivia was saddened by this. Whatever she felt about his betrayals and manipulation, this was the man she had loved—still did love. Despite her intense anger and her desire for revenge, she was moved by his plight. She was also torn in half mentally. Ty was such a manipulator of emotions, such a clever con artist. She thought it out. Probably Shirley was making him pay for what had happened by making his existence a living hell. But he had a choice; he didn't have to live there. Despite what he had said about having nowhere to go—it seemed his friends had mysteriously all dissolved into the woodwork overnight—Olivia believed that Ty did have alternative places to live for a while, women who would happily put him up. But she also strongly believed that he wanted a place of his own, a retreat where he could escape and live his own life in peace and the style he wanted to live in. He probably wanted women all over the place, women he could use for sex, and for income, and whom he could keep at arm's length, who would not invade his private world, or make demands, or impose rules. He wanted women who were too old to produce any more babies but still sexually very active—cougars—and preferably with a good income or money inherited from a dead husband. Olivia was waiting for him to work his way in far enough to ask for money to get a flat or house. She suspected that he might even blackmail her by demanding a good lump sum as the price of her freedom from his possessiveness and Sophie's and Freddie's safety. She had heard nothing from him for some weeks after the New Year.

Then, one Tuesday at the office, she was just about to have her lunch at her desk when he texted. "I need to speak to you urgently. It really is important."

Olivia texted back. "Call me at eight this evening. On the dot. Any later and I won't pick up."

Ty replied. "OK."

That evening Olivia ate her supper, showered, and sat in her bath gown on the settee. At two minutes past eight her phone rang.

"Yes." There was a pause.

"It's me, baby. Ty. Look, I really need to speak to you—"

"You're doing that right now, aren't you Ty?"

"Properly, baby, face to face. I need you to really listen to me."

"I always listen to you, Ty."

"I know, but this is very important. I need you to hear me out. So you can't hang up on me. I need to see you—"

"I don't know about this, Ty. After what's happened, I don't trust you an inch—you must know that. After all the threats you've made to me and against Sophie—and Freddie. Don't imagine for one minute that you're going to talk me into taking you back yet again; it's not going to happen. You're not coming to my house, and we're not going to go for a ride in my car or in yours. It will be somewhere very public indeed. Meet me at the big McDonalds just off the roundabout going out of town."

Olivia knew too well that Ty hated McDonalds and everything that issued from it. It would be a fitting place to force him to go. It was always crowded. There would be plenty of witnesses.

"But I don't like this one little bit. Just don't get any stupid ideas. Oh, and don't ask me for more money. The last lot was for your dying father. He's still very much alive, and you were happy to tell me about your lovely fishing holiday. The bank's closed. If it is important and involves you disappearing and leaving Sophie and me well alone, then I'm all ears. I'm free on Friday after two, so we'll meet at two thirty." She waited for him to argue, to wheedle, to protest. But he simply said OK. Olivia hung up. She was thoughtful for some minutes. Then she called Sophie and told her what had happened and what she thought the Jamaican was really after. Sophie said she tended to agree and asked Olivia to report immediately after the meeting.

Friday came. It was a hectic day at the office. Olivia had to drive to her other local office some forty miles away to sack the manager for some quite serious misdemeanours. She was not in a good mood when she returned and had had no time to eat lunch. She drove to the McDonalds she had specified, parked the car, and went inside. She did not want to remain in her car and give Ty an excuse to open the door and get in, thereby trapping her. She did not trust the man. She ordered a coffee and sat by the far window, which gave her a panoramic view of incoming cars and people. The time slid by. Soon it was five past three. Olivia was annoyed. Ty was always late for everything, but he had demanded this meeting. She took her phone from her bag and texted him.

"Where are you? You were supposed to meet me at 2.30." She sat drinking her coffee. There was no reply. Olivia sent three more texts, and the time reached ten past four. Olivia was furious. He had stood her up, made her go there and wait for him, forced her to text. The arrogant sod! He was playing with her again, laughing at her. Well, if he had had a single thought that she would help him ever again, he could forget it! This was what Olivia called a done deal. When she used that term it was just that. There was no comeback, no last lingering hope or chance. She drove away angry and humiliated. She had no appetite for her supper and threw it in the bin. She went into the kitchen and made herself a cup of tea. She turned off the light and then, almost unconsciously and instinctively, she lifted the blinds and looked down the road. The car was there, parked underneath the lamppost, gleaming like some ebony beast of prey. She dropped the blind.

Sod him! He can damned well get on with it. I hope he does sleep in the car, and I hope he freezes every bloody night! she thought as she climbed the stairs to bed. She did not sleep well and dreamt of being chased up country lanes by a sleek, black crouching animal, which snarled at her when she stopped and turned to look at it. Then she stopped running and walked towards the animal. She slowly stroked its head, and the creature gave out a deep, throaty purr and closed its huge yellow eyes. Then it suddenly growled and ran away from her into a field. She followed and saw the beast came out of the field; in its enormous jaws was Sophie, bleeding and screaming and begging for help. Olivia ran, but the thing was too fast for her and loped ahead, taking Sophie further and further away. Somehow she knew that she was the only one who could help, and she must help, so she quickened her pace and soon caught the animal. Just as she began to prise the great jaws from Sophie's body, her alarm woke her, and she lay there, confused and concerned. Spirit was warning her. She knew something dark was in the offing. She must be on her guard, on the defensive—always.

Sophie lay in bed, listening to the rain falling gently with that soft, comforting sound that always made her feel safe and protected when she was snuggled down and on the verge of sleep. She remembered lying close to Ben, when they were over in France, and listening to the rain pouring over the tiled roof, sliding and gurgling down the gutters and onto the waiting soil below. She recalled the warm, earthy smell of the grateful garden. Ben had said, "I love it when it rains at night. It makes me feel so safe and secure ... and so sleepy." And he had kissed her long auburn plait and curled into her warm skin, and they had both sunk into a deep, forgetful sleep. Sophie knew many people who felt this way. She just assumed it was some inbuilt primal reaction from the time of the primitive human— safe in his cave, out of the rain, wind, and cold, with his fire burning and his skin rugs over him. It must be that, she thought, as she dug herself even deeper into the duvet and pulled the hot water bottle into her back. She was sliding slowly and deliciously into sleep when her phone flashed brightly in the dark silence. It was usually to denote an incoming call. Sophie turned off her phone's sound at night and sometimes during the day. She needed to be in touch but resented the feeling of being a prisoner to the robotic brain. She stirred and then went back to sleep. The rain whispered down, while again and again the screen on her phone flashed.

In the morning, Sophie checked her phone and was surprised to find six missed calls. She checked them and found the caller's identity. It was him, the Jamaican. She sat looking at the screen for some time; then she called his number. The first call rang out and then went to voicemail. The next two were cut off rather quickly. Sophie shrugged. *Damn him.* Typical. Calling someone in the middle of the night when most normal people were asleep. Let him get on with his nonsense. She wanted no more of his silly dramas and stresses. She got on with her day, and then there was a text from Ty.

"Why did you call me?"

"You called me six times last night. I'm replying. Why did *you* call *me*?"

"I didn't call you, you sick fuck. Leave me well alone, or it will get ugly."

Sophie glared angrily at the screen. *Troublemaking bastard!* She should have ignored his calls. She knew what he was up to. It was not long before Olivia called her.

"Ty called me. He said you'd been calling him all night and—"

"Go no further, Livvy. *He* called *me* all night, but my phone was turned onto silent, and there were *six* calls on it this morning. I simply called him back to know what the hell he was doing it for, and he accused me of, well, of lying. He said he hadn't called, and he called me a sick fuck. I'll screenshot everything and forward it. You know what he's up to. Trying to make me look like the fruitcake he's painted me as, chasing him. He wants to convince you I'm mad as well as bad, to get you back."

"Well, he can save his efforts. I know it's all cooked up. He is so incredibly cunning, yet so stupid at the same time. He forgets it's all recorded on our phones, all dates and times, and that we can send it to each other by screenshots and forwarding. He actually really believes that we have little contact, at least a lot less than we do, and he doesn't realise that intelligent women aren't going to fight over an arsehole like him, especially when neither has wronged the other." *But*, she thought to herself, *he does realise that he can worry me by threatening Sophie and*

Freddie. He's using the threats to sound out just how close we are and where our loyalties lie.

Olivia and Sophie met again at the weekend, and this time it was frangipane tarts with whipped cream. Olivia complained that she was putting on weight. Sophie snorted. "You, putting on weight! Ha, bloody, ha. You're only a size twelve, like a little doll. Tiny little legs, super big boobs—stop complaining." They both laughed and tucked in. They talked about the Jamaican. Olivia did not want to alarm or frighten Sophie, but she had to make her realise just how violent and dangerous the man could be when things weren't going as he wanted them to—if he weren't in control. He would throw away anyone he no longer needed, without caring a damn how much hurt and damage he did. If he wanted someone, she was not free to go; he had to *allow* her to go. Otherwise she was his, his possession. To try and escape was an unthinkable idea. She had told Sophie about her life with Ty in the utmost detail, trying to show her just what they were both up against.

Sophie still believed that Ty had finished with her; she was meaningless in his life, and that this made her immune to his schemes and revenge. After all, she had nothing he wanted any longer. He had only wanted money; the sex had been meaningless to Ty. Why should she worry?

Olivia just wished that something would happen to firmly convince Sophie of this danger that she seemed unable to acknowledge. They ate cake, drank coffee, and chatted more about life with Ty and about life in general.

"I just have to tell you this—it's so funny, Livvy. This person I know has twins—a boy and a girl—who don't look remotely like each other, not even like brother and sister. Well, they're at this bunfight, and this woman comes up to them, has heard they're twins, and starts gushing on about how fantastic it is that they're so different and yet they're identical. Well, the girl twin starts to try and explain that they are most definitely *not* identical twins, and this stupid woman just ignores her and burbles on. Eventually the twin gets bored and gives up. She says, 'No, we aren't identical—but we used to be.' Sophie and Olivia laughed loudly.

"Oh, that's priceless," said Olivia. Must tell that one in the office." Then her phone chirruped, and she looked at it, no longer laughing. "That's the tone I keep for the Jamaican's texts and calls. What the hell does he want now?"

She picked her phone up and read the incoming message. Her face screwed up with anger. "Bloody hell—the bastard! Who the hell does he think he is?" She handed the phone to Sophie. Sophie read the message. "You're nothing but a bloody slut. My friend from the airbase told me that you were whoring with him. Can't you behave like a bitch in heat away from my friends!"

Sophie's mouth dropped open. "But you and Ty had broken up weeks before that, and you certainly weren't going back to him. Anyway, he sleeps with anything that has a pulse—and yet he dares to call you these filthy names!" She was disgusted. She handed the phone back to Olivia, and, as she did so, the phone announced yet another Ty message.

Olivia hastily opened it. "You are a dirty slag. I told you that mixing with that filthy, corrupt, scheming little bitch was going to cause you trouble. She is turning you into the whore that she is. I will give you a chance to come back to me and make amends for the wrongs you have done to me. You are my fiancée, and you have slept with another man, and listened to that evil woman, and left me. You will come back to me or I will punish you and her. You may escape with just a beating, but she will pay the price of daring to take away my life and my woman." Olivia stared at the screen, pale, wide-eyed, and shaking.

Sophie asked, "What is it Livvy? What's he said now?" Wordlessly Olivia passed her the phone and Sophie read the message. They both sat in silence, and then Sophie said in a tiny, frightened voice, "What does he mean, Livvy? Is this a joke or something, just a silly threat? You have to go to the police this time—you have to! He can't just threaten us like this."

"No—no, Soph, I can't! I mean, I know how to handle him. Going to the police would only—he's obviously very drunk anyway." She was struggling to prevent Sophie from triggering the worst reaction from the Jamaican. She knew that Ty would manage to convince the police that it was something else entirely. He would play along with them and lie to them. And then he would know that she had reported him—and she and Sophie would both be in real danger. To stop what she knew Ty would do, Olivia had to spin him along, play a game. She had to protect Sophie and Freddie. There would be no police. She took a deep breath.

"Don't worry about this. I can handle the bastard. You know he's all wind and puff. Shouts a lot, bad temper—but you leave it all to me. I'll sort the idiot out." She said it with a lot more confidence than she felt. She told Sophie that she had to fly—work the next day, miles to drive—and not to worry. She would be in touch.

Sophie waved her goodbye at the gate and went back indoors. She had sensed Olivia's tension and fear. She felt Ben, Sean, and Ella around her, protecting her and warning her—but of what?

Olivia hurtled along the main road. She pulled off the road into a lay-by and picked up her phone. Ty had sent more unpleasant messages. She called his number. Her hand was shaking as it rang out.

"Hello. So you came to your senses, baby. You've been fucking a nigger from the airbase, hunny. That sweet little pussy of yours belongs to me, darling, and I want it back. If you're a good girl and come back to Daddy, then I'll just punish you a little to teach you to be good. If not, then that evil bitch will suffer, really suffer. You have a choice. You're my fiancée, and you don't go whoring with my mates. OK, you've been a silly girl, but stop it all now. Just say the word—just let me back where I belong—and all you have to worry about is being fucked every hour on the hour to keep you in your place." He laughed mirthlessly.

"Ty, I *was* your fiancée, but I didn't know that you were whoring around, as you put it, whilst I was faithful to you for the time we were together. You promised never to cheat on me—promised it twice—but you had more than one other woman all the time. And you used money you conned from one of those victims to pay for our engagement dinner. You have done so many dreadful things, told so many lies, hurt so many people. I have done nothing, Ty—nothing in the least wrong. I do *not* belong to you. There is nothing between us any more. Yes, I still love you a bit, but what you did has successfully killed that love, and everything you're doing now is ensuring that any love that exists will disappear." Olivia thought quickly. "I have to be away on business next week, and I'm going to be very tied up. I really will be unable to do anything except business. When I get back we'll talk some more." This might buy her some time. He might believe that she was going to listen to him when she returned. She held her breath.

"OK, baby. You go make lots more money. Call me when you get back, OK?"

"And before that, you leave Sophie well alone—or we won't be speaking, and the police might just be involved."

Ty laughed. "You and your policemen, baby! Been sleeping with a few lately, have you—whoring around with the big men in blue? Your pussy is crying for my big boy, hun, I know it, so you go out looking for something to replace it, and you can't find it, so—"

"Ty, just stop there. I won't listen to any more of your filthy insults. I'll call you in a week's time. Leave me alone until then, and leave Sophie well alone." She cut the call off, went out into the garden, and lit a cigarette.

Oh God! she thought. *What do I do? I won't go back to him, and I won't let him hurt Sophie and Freddie. If I call the police and they arrest him, I know he'll wriggle his way into being released, and then we're both vulnerable.* She closed her eyes and pleaded with spirit to help her. She felt her mother's gentle hand on her head and heard the faintly whispered word *Trust.* She took a deep breath, stood up straight, and went up to pack her case for the journeys—the known one and the unknown one.

Sophie picked up the mail. Most of it was boring leaflets and offers, and they all went straight into the bin. The bank statement she knew off by heart—every minus amount. Then there was an interesting envelope with the name Beardsley and Tope, Solicitors at the top left hand of the envelope. Something stirred in her brain. She knew that name. Some years before a genealogist had traced her and her sister to inform them that their great-aunt had died, alone, in a large house in London. She had been found days later in front of an electric fire. She had died intestate and the family was being traced for the purposes of the distribution of the estate. There were dozens of descendants, and by the time they had all been paid out, the three quarters of a million pounds had dwindled to almost nothing, especially after the solicitors and the genealogist had taken their cuts. Then the great-aunt's mother, who was not related to them, had been found to have a great-nephew in Australia, so yet more money disappeared. The eventual amount had been pathetic, but very welcome at the time.

Intrigued, Sophie opened the letter. How had they found her? She had moved often since the previous matter. It was probably through Rachael—so why hadn't Rachael told her? It was because they had no real family relationship, Sophie told herself. She read the letter with growing excitement. Apparently, a will had been found—how, she was not told—and the great-aunt had left everything she possessed to Sophie's father—an only child—and thus to Sophie and Rachael. As well as the original house, investments, and cash deposits, there was now more money, more stocks and shares, and more property. Sophie sat down. She was numb. Her money troubles were at an end. She laughed out loud, and then she burst into tears of pure relief and joy.

Sophie quickly dialled the firm and asked for the extension given. One Guy Tope came on the other end of the line. He was unctuous and deferential. He regretted that they could not get any money to her for at least a week, probably longer. He took the details of Sophie's bank account and promised he would pay her something as soon as he could. Sophie put the phone down. She was ecstatic. She felt Ben, Sean, and Ella around her, sharing in her joy. Usually she had to count every penny, but today she went up to Tescos on the bus and got two large, juicy sirloin steaks for herself and Freddie. She took them home triumphantly and cooked them for supper. Freddie enjoyed his immensely. Sophie had decided not to tell him about the money. She merely told him that she was leaving her job. Freddie knew how much she hated her post with a toxic, snobbish widow. The woman was a self-indulgent, selfish, attention-seeker who delighted in telling appalling, vicious lies about people to cause maximum hurt. She was also rude and a bigot. She was a complete nobody who had married a rich, common man, as unpleasant as she was. The man had spoilt her and made her believe she was a somebody and too good for everybody else. Sophie's work partner, Isabelle, was this woman's pet; she was unable to do or say a thing wrong. Any good Sophie did was attributed to this partner; anything that went wrong was blamed on the beaten-down Sophie. Lies were told about her daily. The hypocritical tyrant said vile things to and about her, and Sophie was forced to endure it in order to keep a roof over her head and Freddie's and food on the table Now she could do what she had wanted to do for so very long! She could have left the post, had she been driven to illness— which was looming—but it was near her, just a bus ride away, and so she had struggled on, hating every second that she had to endure. The colleague who was the pet was always happy to tell Sophie of how, when told that Sophie would be working next week, the client had groaned and said, "Oh no, not her for a whole week."

Sophie had done this job for many years, when circumstance had prevented her from returning to teaching and nursing. Over the years she had encountered clients of many types. The aristocrats she loved for their impeccable manners, good humour, and humanity. The nouveaux riches she found to have appalling manners, ignorance, and crass stupidity. She had cared for the famous artists and sculptors in beautiful environments. She had encountered faded, pretentious, would-be intellectuals who knew it all and represented the worst of the past British Empire. Sophie's current client had embodied the very worst attributes of all her past clientele.

Sophie went in, cheerful and smiling. Performing her duties flawlessly, as ever, she then went to say goodnight to the hated female. Sophie stood in the door of the bedroom. "Good night, Freda."

"Good night. I'll see you next week."

"No, you won't, actually. You won't have to tell Isabelle how you're going to hate having to bear me for a whole week—not ever again. And I won't have to put up with your rudeness, lies, dirty habits, bigotry, and bloody ignorance for a minute longer, thank God!"

"What? You're leaving? I wasn't told. You won't get your wages then! Who's going to look after me?"

"I care little about that. You just sit and count the cash you saved. Money's all you care about anyway. Now, I'm going back to the normal world of normal people—and you can just wallow around in your depressive cloud of negative hypocrisy, and rudeness, and ignorance, and tell lies about everybody and everything. Bye!" Sophie swept out and downstairs, laughing joyfully. How she had dreamed of this day, this minute. She heard Freda babbling loudly to herself upstairs, and she laughed even more. She was free of the hated Isabelle, the self-righteous, domineering know-it-all whose inferiority complex obliged her to rant bitterly at anyone who knew more than she did—who delighted in tattling behind other employees' backs, undermining and slandering them. How had Sophie endured this pair of bitches? She locked the door and put the key in the key safe. Then she danced down to the bus stop, away from the misery and servitude she had endured for over two depressing years. She went into the cottage, put her feet up on the settee, and watched Amazon Prime movies. She even opened a bottle of wine from the case she'd treated herself to with her savings now she would soon have her inheritance. She toasted the future. She expected frenzied calls from the client, the family, and Isabelle. She went through her mobile and blocked all the relevant numbers. Let them get on with it. She had suffered more than enough in the past few years. They had been part of that suffering, so they could just disappear and leave her and Freddie in the peace they needed and had earned. The night rolled on.

Sophie had a call from Olivia. She seemed very edgy and a little concerned about Sophie. Sophie told her that she had walked out on her hated post. Olivia knew how traumatic her time there had been and was relieved for her. Sophie decided to keep news of the inheritance to herself for the time being, even from Freddie and Olivia. She calmly lied and said that she had a possible job lined up for the future and that she was going to take a badly needed break; she had been able to save enough money to tide her over. She didn't feel too bad about it, as it wasn't a very big lie. She would be able to tell them the truth by and by. They chatted, and Olivia said, as she always did, "Make sure you lock and bolt that door, Soph."

"Yep, yep, of course I will. It's locked right now. Freddie's gone to his dad for a week or more. Stop worrying so much." They wished each other goodnight and sweet dreams. Sophie settled down to watch a good sci-fi film and sink a few more wines. She drifted off to bed happily. The money was beckoning; if only it would arrive. Never mind. Only days now and she could plan a future—at last.

Olivia was away up north on business. There were endless meetings, staff interviews, training sessions, and demonstrations of new products and techniques. Olivia was exhausted. She was stressed out with worry about what Ty might do next. She got back to her hotel about eleven that evening, and sank gratefully onto the comfortable bed. No bed in the world could equal her custom-made bed back at home, but this one was pretty damned good. She made herself a cup of coffee and was in the middle of studying notes for the next day's agenda when her mobile bleeped. It was the tone for Ty. She picked up the phone.

"Ty, I'm very busy up here. I told you I was away on business. It's late. I need to sleep. This had better be something sensible. I did tell you to leave me well alone for this week."

"Baby ... baby ..." Ty's voice was slurred, his Jamaican accent more pronounced, and he was barely intelligible. He was very drunk. "Just wanna hear your voice. I ... I gotta do it ... no other way. You won't help me. She can't ... have to ... but if they—"

"Ty? What on earth are you talking about! I don't understand you. Are you in some sort of trouble? How am I supposed to help you, for God's sake? We aren't together any more, and I'm not being conned out of any more cash. Don't try and blackmail me with any more suicide threats. You've been drinking a lot by the sound of it. Sleep it off. Leave me alone. It'll sort itself out in the morning—whatever it is." Olivia was annoyed. She had had her fair share of his drunken dramas. They were not together any more, and it was just one aspect of Ty that she was happy to put behind her.

"Yes, sleep, baby. Sleep. Gotta do it. Sleep now." The call ended abruptly, cut off by Ty. Olivia sat thinking. Ty's arrogant manner had changed very suddenly. What was going on? But then she wondered why she was really bothering. After everything that had happened before and after September the sixth—his lies, his threats, his arrogance, his stalking her, and his conning her out of yet more money—part of her yearned to see and hear him again. She yearned for their passionate lovemaking, the few good times they had shared, the life Olivia had dreamed might be theirs. But then she remembered what he had done to her and to Sophie, and she was angry, coldly angry. If he was in some sort of trouble, then sod him. He mixed with some very dodgy people, sliding through the scum of the drugs underworld. Let him sort out his own stuff now. He was trying to get her back by threatening Sophie and Freddie. She had just days to think of a way to beat him before her life—or Sophie's life—was crushed and ruined yet again. She took two diazepam, cleaned her teeth, rolled into bed, and lay there reading the agenda until she slipped into sleep. The rest of her working week flew by. She called Sophie every night, just to assure herself that Sophie and Freddie were safe. She was too occupied with her business, Diamond Lady, to think much more about the serious problem Ty was causing her.

Olivia drove back on the Saturday. The motorways were crowded, and there were frequent holdups due to accidents and roadworks. Olivia was exhausted when she swung into the close and up the hill to her home. She parked in the driveway, took her luggage from the boot, and went into the house. Before she did so, she glanced at both ends of the road to make sure his car was not there. No sign of him, thank God. She went in, kicked off her shoes, and poured herself a brandy. She was about to drink it when a voice in her head whispered, "No! Keep a clear head—you must! Don't touch that drink." Olivia was used to spirit giving her puzzling instructions and warnings, so she put the glass down obediently. She was curious about why she should not drink it, but she made herself a cup of tea instead, took it into the living room, and curled up on the settee. She dozed. The evening wore on.

Sophie was bored. She was used to working, and cleaning the house frenziedly did not fill her time well. Freddie was with his dad, and she missed him a lot. She had cooked herself a macaroni cheese, eaten a little, and then put it away in the fridge for later. She went upstairs to clean out her wardrobe. Whilst there, she noticed that her mobile was nearly out of charge, so she connected it to the charger and left it by her bed. Then, bored again, she went back downstairs. She remembered she had left her mobile up there but decided it didn't matter, as she wasn't going to need it any more that day. She watched Amazon Prime movies and became engrossed in another of her sci-fi favourites. Then someone knocked at the door. It was not knocking but heavy pounding, and it startled Sophie. She jumped up and went to the door.

"Who's there?" she asked nervously. "Who is it?" There was silence. Without thinking, she unlocked the door. The minute she turned the key, someone pushed the door hard, and Sophie was propelled backwards by the force. She was stunned to see Ty, his face covered in blood. His eyes were almost closed, cut and bleeding. His face was grossly swollen, his handsome features twisted and spoiled. Despite his dark skin, she could see the bruising that was appearing rapidly. His hands were bruised and bleeding too. Sophie gasped in horror, and her soft heart immediately leapt to his protection.

"Who did this to you, Ty? We must get you to a hospital—"

"Shut up! Just shut up and get over there." It was then that Sophie realised that Ty had a gun in his hand. Big and frightening and ugly. Sophie had never seen a gun before. She was terrified.

"Ty," she whispered. "Don't harm me. Freddie has nobody but me. I did nothing to hurt you—you know that. Please, Ty."

He stared at Sophie blankly as if he didn't recognise her. Then he gestured with the gun. "Get me a drink."

Sophie swallowed. "I've only got a bottle of wine, Ty—I don't touch spirits. Will that do?" She stood there, afraid to move.

"Go on, get it. Hurry up!" Sophie went into the kitchen quickly and came back with a large glass of red wine. She had a good store of wine now that she could afford it. Her money still hadn't come through, but she was spending her meagre savings on a few luxuries. Ty snatched the glass and downed almost all of it in one gulp. He wiped his mouth with the back of his hand, wincing as he touched the cuts and bruises there.

Sophie wanted to help him but was afraid to move in case Ty used the gun on her. She spoke hesitantly. "Wh—what happened to you? Who did this? Was it a car accident or something?"

Ty again looked at her blankly. Then he finished the wine and went to sit on the settee. He put the gun on his lap, took out a cigarette, and lit it. Sophie, quite automatically, went to open the door, and Ty swung round with the gun in his hand. "Leave that fucking door. Just come over here, and don't do anything stupid."

Sophie's heart was thundering. She felt unwell and dizzy. She walked slowly to the settee and sat down beside Ty. "I can sort out your wounds, Ty. You know I'm trained and qualified. Let me do something to help you, please."

Ty shrugged. "Get me more wine," he snapped, holding out the glass. Sophie did so, returning with the glass full of red wine and the bottle. Ty drank this quickly. When he had first come in Sophie had noticed that he smelt strongly of vodka. She was very concerned that he would get into one of his rages when she was there alone and defenceless. She sat beside him, stiff and shaking, breathless with terror. Then he turned to her.

"They did this to me, baby. I took that money, but they found me. I got away but they beat me up real bad and they're after me now. I need that money—I have to get back to Jamaica. The bastards got me and beat me up."

Sophie thought rapidly. She asked him, "Was it those drugs people you stole from, Ty? You told me you handle a lot of their money and know where it's kept—did you take that—and you hoped to get to Jamaica and outrun them?" Ty looked at her with tears in his puffy, bloodied eyes, and he took her hand. Sophie was still frightened of him and what he might do. She sat very, very still.

"I just need money to get to Jamaica, baby. Money for my fare, and money for a car, and to rent a place, and to set up a little business. That cash was going to get all that for me. Now I just need to get out. They'll chase me. I escaped them, but they'll be after me. They're ugly people, baby. They'll kill me." He dropped her hand. His face changed. Suddenly he pulled Sophie's hair hard and yanked her head backwards. He held the gun to her cheek. She was gasping and panting. Sweat ran down her face. What was he going to do to her?

"I need that fucking money—just enough to get out. I've gotta beat them. How much have you got?" Sophie was really afraid. She tried to speak but nothing but squeaking noises emerged from her dry throat.

"What? Fucking well answer me!"

"Hardly anything, Ty," she whispered.

"Like what? £100? £200? What?"

"Only about £80, Ty. I'm sorry. I don't have much this week. I've had to pay my—"

"OK, OK, just fucking well shut up! I need more than that." Still he was pushing the gun into Sophie's cheek. Then he took it away and threw her onto the settee. He sat back, almost asleep. He was very drunk and suffering the effects of the beating.

Sophie tried again. "Ty, please let me clean up your injuries—I won't do anything, I promise. Just let me, please."

He looked at her for a while and then shrugged. "OK—I know you know what you're doing."

Sophie went to the cupboard and took out her bag of medical supplies. She asked Ty if she could go into the kitchen to get the saline solution she kept in the fridge. He nodded. Sophie came back with it and set to work cleaning, swabbing, and applying dressings. Touching Ty's skin was difficult for Sophie. She felt an almost electrical sensation in her fingertips. She still loved this man, and her heart was broken at the sight of him beaten and desperate—but she was also aware of his dangerous volatile nature. But along with the love and tenderness came feelings of anger and revulsion at what he had said and done to her—the bitter hurt and rejection he had caused her, the callous way in which he had blatantly used her, and all those cunning lies.

Sophie shuddered slightly as she finished the majority of the dressings. She lifted his hand and examined a nasty tear on the back of it. "That's going to need a few stitches to hold it; otherwise it'll keep opening up and bleeding badly. You'll not be able to drive—or anything, really—and the wound won't heal. I'll need to stitch it."

"Can't you put those steri things on it?" He pulled his hand away angrily. "I don't want a lot of messing about. Anyway, it'll hurt."

"Well, yes. I can't give you anything for the discomfort, but it won't take long if you cooperate."

It all seemed surreal to Sophie. The big gun was lying next to her on the settee. She couldn't, somehow, equate it with Ty, the Ty she had thought she knew. She waited quietly whilst he bit his lip, and sighed deeply.

"OK, stitch the damned thing up, but make it quick, and don't hurt me too much." Sophie cleaned the area and then sterilised the needle and cotton in boiling water. Ty took a swig from the wine bottle and turned his head away. Sophie carefully inserted four sutures, which she tied off professionally and knotted firmly. Her hands were shaking, but she bit her lip very hard to control them. Ty winced a few times, but at last Sophie was done. She put a dressing over the stitched wound.

"Keep it dry—and just be careful." She cleared away the mess she had made doing the dressings, took the remains into the kitchen, and put them in the bin. Ty seemed to have calmed down. His eyes were closing, and Sophie thought with relief that he might fall asleep. But then he suddenly sat up and looked at her wildly.

"I need some fucking money—I must get out and away from them! They're after me. You must have some more money somewhere. You must have your rent money put away—something—anything!

"I only have the £80, Ty; I'm not lying. You need several thousand to get out and fly to Jamaica, and you'll need money for a small business, and rent for a house, and cash for a car. I don't have that sort of money, and you know it. After all, that was why you turned on me, wasn't it? When you were caught out you turned on me and denied you even knew me. You wanted Olivia and her money, and her lifestyle, and cars, and premier flights, and expensive holidays—everything you thought you deserved. You took over £40,000 from me—and you never as much as bought me a cup of coffee."

Ty looked hurt. "But that's not true. I did love you."

Sophie's anger mounted. She squared up to the big Jamaican. "Love! Don't use that word on me, you bastard! You don't know the meaning of it. I really loved you, and you knew it, and you lied to me over and over again, and you used me so badly. But now I'm back and fighting, and I don't want to hear that word in your mouth—d'you hear me? Not that *love* word—it's meaningless now. And as for demanding that I help you, Ty, when did you ever help me? When my son was dying you were chasing me for my last penny, even on the day of his death *and* the day of his funeral. You want money from me because you've been bloody stupid enough to steal from the local drug lords. You're a damned fool, Ty. Even if I had the money I wouldn't help you. You turned my whole life upside down. I gave you unconditional love, but you lied and conned me out of everything I'd worked so hard for, and all that time you were living with—" Sophie stopped. She saw Ty's face was contorted with anger. He picked up the gun and pointed it at her.

"Shut the fuck up, you stupid, mouthy bitch. Yes, you gave me money to help me exist, and I got a bit of fun out of fucking you when there wasn't anything else much around to fuck. Just don't give me all this *love* stuff, and stop telling me what to do and to think. You were one of my women—I've had over a hundred—and you're finished with, so shut your bloody mouth and help me. You keep telling me you still love me, so help me." He stopped and stood, still pointing the gun at Sophie. For several minutes they stood in silence. Sophie was shaking, and she had to dig her nails into her palms to stop herself from fainting. Then he stepped forward. He put the gun on the table, lifted his arms, and put them around Sophie. He hugged her very, very hard, and Sophie was unable to breathe properly. He stroked her hair gently.

"Sophie—my little Soph. I need help. They're really nasty guys, baby. Really nasty. They'll kill me, baby. Kill your Ty—and it won't be a clean shot to the head, hun. They'll beat me to death, torture me." He held her close and kissed her hair.

Sophie wanted to escape. She felt suffocated and angry, and her love for him was fighting a battle with her desire to hurt him for what he had done and was still doing to her. Ty let her go so suddenly that Sophie nearly fell over again. He sat down on the settee again, poured himself more wine, and drank half the glass at one gulp. He turned to Sophie, his face again angry and scowling.

Sophie swallowed hard. Her mouth was dry, she was terrified, and she felt nauseous. How could she do something— anything—to end this nightmare?

Then Ty began again. "But I had her—my love, Olivia—and we were really happy, really good together, and you finished that. Yes, it was you. You called her and told her a lot of lies, and Shirley was with you, wasn't she? Why? Why did you do that to me—why? You wanted me, and I had her, and you were going to get your revenge on me, you fucking bitch. I should kill you for that." He poured more wine and drank it.

Sophie was becoming totally desperate. Her brain was working overtime. She must try and contact Olivia—but how? Then she remembered the mobile phone she had left on charge in her bedroom. She must get to it somehow. Ty had stopped ranting. He had put the gun down beside him and was slumped forward, muttering to himself. Sophie thought rapidly. She coughed to clear her very dry throat. Ty looked up.

"I have to go upstairs to the toilet, Ty—please."

"What the hell for?"

"I really do need to pee, Ty. Sorry, but I can't hold myself any longer." She waited, holding her breath.

He frowned again. There was a long pause. "Oh well, I suppose you have to. Go on and be quick, and no fucking nonsense."

Sophie fled upstairs. She usually found the twisting staircase hard to climb, but now she scaled it like a mountain goat. She crept into her bedroom, trying not to alert Ty to the fact that she was in there. He knew the layout of her house all too well and knew that the bathroom was to the left of the top of the stairs, not to the right and directly overhead where he was. She tried not to make a sound, but a board creaked, and Ty called up to her, "Why are you in the bedroom? Are you gonna piss in the bed, then?"

"I need my migraine tablets—" Sophie called back. She had thought of this in case Ty sussed her. He was aware that she suffered from very acute migraine. She had a pack of her medication in her bedside drawer, and she grabbed this as she pulled her phone off its charger. She went to the bathroom and sat on the toilet, trying to pee as noisily as she was able to. Meanwhile, she texted furiously to Olivia.

"He's here in the house. Got a gun. Come quickly. Desperate. Don't contact me." She sent off the text and heaved a sigh of relief as it left her phone. Then she quickly got up and flushed the toilet. She turned off her phone and stuffed it under a pile of clean flannels kept in a basket under the washbasin. She went back down and showed Ty the strip of tablets.

"I need to take some. I'll have to get some water." She waited for him to allow her to go and then swallowed them gratefully, as she actually did have the first flashings of an attack coming on. Ty ordered her to sit by him again. She sat down, still shaking and wondering what was going to happen.

Ty sat, staring into space, and then lit a cigarette. A car pulled up near the cottages and he jumped up. "Who's that?"

Sophie tried to calm him. She knew it wasn't possible for Olivia to get to her that quickly.

"Just someone parking outside, I expect. Several people live in the lane." Ty grabbed her by the arm.

"Go to the gate and tell me what you can see—and don't go out of my sight." Obediently Sophie went to the gate and looked over it and into the main road. She turned to see Ty beckoning her back furiously. She went to the doorway.

"Well, what did you see?"

"Just your car and a small Citroën." Ty let his breath out sharply. "They might find me here—they don't know her, though." He was muttering to himself. He paced up and down, ignoring Sophie. Then he grabbed her by the arm. "You must know someone with money. You've got a sister—yes! Call her."

Sophie thought fast yet again. "She's on a world cruise. The other side of the world now. I can't get hold of her."

"Well, try someone else in your fucking family then!"

"Ty, don't be insane. If I tell them I'm being held at gunpoint, then they'll just call the police. Anyway, nobody's just going to give me money like that—full stop. You always think money grows on trees, that everybody's swimming in it. You took enough off me, Ty—enough to get you all you wanted. You were living in total luxury with Olivia, but still you needed thousands more. I can't get any money. I haven't got any, so just leave me alone."

Sophie was terrified that she had said too much.

847

Ty stood looking at her for a few minutes. He sat down again and poured the remains of the wine into his glass. He downed it and wiped his mouth. He was muttering again. Sophie couldn't catch anything he said. She could see that his eyes were slowly closing, and then his head drooped, and he fell back against the cushions. The gun was to his left, and his hand was on it. Sophie couldn't reach it without waking him, and she stood, not moving a muscle, trying to think of a way to escape. She had left her phone upstairs under the flannels, and she would rouse Ty if she climbed up to get it. Without it she couldn't contact Olivia and tell her what had happened if she did manage to get out of the house. She didn't want Olivia to walk into this alone. She couldn't just wait outside, or Ty might wake up, find her gone, and come out to look for her. What the hell could she do? She stood immobile, watching Ty's mouth drop open, and listening as he began to snore gently. She made up her mind then. She moved very slowly and quietly towards him and leaned over him. His hand was on the gun, but he wasn't holding it. She could, if she was very careful, slide it out from under his hand. She grasped the cold, deadly thing, and with painful slowness inched it away from Ty. He mumbled and stirred, and Sophie froze. She stayed still, and soon Ty had settled back into his deep sleep. After what seemed a lifetime, the gun was free, and she picked it up carefully and nervously. She would hold him with the gun whilst she called the police. She had it in her hand now. She felt safer. She glanced at Ty. He was snoring loudly, deep in sleep. She picked up her landline phone and went into the kitchen, where she called the police. It did not go straight through to the local police as it had done when she'd last used the service but through an interminable press-one-for-this-press-two-for-that series, and when it had reached two, there was another list of choices. At last she reached the number she needed to press. Her heart was thudding so hard that she was sure it could be heard all over the area. Just as she was about to press the number, a hand gripped her wrist and a finger cancelled the call. She knew that it was Ty and that she must hang onto the gun at all costs. She dropped the phone, ducked down under his arm, and ran out of the kitchen. Ty ran too, faster than she could, and grabbed her wrist hard. Sophie fought back in terror and primal defensiveness. She bit his arm hard, and he dropped her wrist. He grabbed again, this time at the gun. Sophie dropped the evil thing and then kicked it across the room. She rushed to the door and grabbed the handle, opened the door. She was almost out when Ty grasped her by her hair and pulled her back. He put his arm around her neck and dragged her backwards. Sophie struggled and kicked with all the strength her frail elderly body could call up. They whirled around the small room, knocking over the table and plants from the sideboard onto the floor. Sophie was tiring. Ty was huge, and very strong; she felt herself fading. She must not give in—she must not! And then, just as she felt herself at the end of her strength, there was a crash, and the front door was flung open. Ty whirled round. He bent down and picked up the gun. There was Olivia. Sophie took her chance to pull away from Ty and duck behind him.

Ty snorted derisively. "Oh, so the fucking cavalry's come, has it? Brought my money, have you baby?"

Olivia glared at him menacingly. "You can put that gun down—now! If you think you can frighten and bully me, you can think again!" She looked at Sophie and the bruises appearing on her arms and face. "Are you OK? What the hell is this all about, Ty—I warned you to stay away from both of us." Then Olivia registered the state of Ty's face. "What happened to you?"

Ty dropped his hand, with the gun still in it, to his side. "They beat me up bad, baby. I need the money to get out and go home—"

"*They?* I get it. You stole money from the druggy big boys you work for, and they caught you and beat you up, did they? I guess they took the cash back again. Tough."

Ty's lips curled angrily. "This isn't a fucking pea shooter. If I need to, I can make a very big hole in you."

"Put the bloody thing down, Ty. Where will it get you? In a prison, where you'll be in your nightmare—confined, claustrophobic, raped, beaten up for being black—you know it. Just stop now—"

"Don't tell me what to do. Both of you have got me to this. You both deserve to be wasted. I don't care any more. I'll kill you both and then finish myself." He raised his arm and pointed the gun at Olivia. She took a step forward.

"Put it down—now—and leave. Get away while you can." She inched forward. Sophie's heart raced so hard that she was sure she would faint. Olivia continued to get closer, and then Sophie saw Ty's muscles tensing and his hand going up. Certain that he was going to shoot Olivia, she brought her knee up very hard to hit his elbow, causing his arm to swing up. The gun went off with a loud report, and a hole appeared in the ceiling. Plaster showered down over them. The gun fell from Ty's hand and slid over the carpet. Olivia grabbed it up.

"Come here, Sophie," she ordered. Sophie walked around Ty and stood next to Olivia. Olivia put the gun in her hand. "Don't pull the trigger unless I tell you to," she said. "I don't even know if it's the right way round." Sophie said in a shaking whisper. Then Olivia walked up to Ty, pulled her arm back as far as she could, and slapped him, very hard, across the face. Ty reeled and staggered. Olivia folded her arms. "That's for all the lies, all the broken promises, all the deception, all the sleeping around, all the stealing of hard-earned money, all the smooth conning just to get the lifestyle you thought you deserved, at someone else's expense. I hope that hurt, just as I hope the beating you got damned well hurt. That's what it's like to hurt when you're hurt as badly as we were! That's what it feels like to know that the man who asked you to marry him was sleeping with other women all the time and telling them he loved them. How it is for Sophie to find out that the man she was giving so much money to had spent it on a top-of-the-range engagement dinner, and that while she was skimping and going without he was living in utter luxury with another woman, as well as visiting his so-called ex. Oh yes—that hurt all right. You total bastard—you need to be really hurt!"

Ty went to the settee and slumped down. He put his head in his hands and began sobbing. "I only need enough cash to get out of the country … to outrun them … to get to Jamaica … to go home." He was whimpering like a baby. He looked up at Olivia. "Baby, you know what love we had for each other. Just help me now. I did a lot of bad things in my life, but I never did you wrong, hunny."

"Never did me wrong, Ty? Oh, that's really funny. You did a lot of things wrong. They may have seemed right at the time—sometimes—but all the time you were sleeping around, and taking money off a bunch of women, and two-timing me. You were just a bloody prostitute, Ty—a prostitute—because you slept with Sophie just for one thing, money. You were living with me all the time you were conning her for money. You told her you were living in a miserable little room, with a bunch of drunks, and you hardly had money enough to eat, and you were taking the last penny she could scrape up, and the poor woman really believed that you were starving and cold. She didn't know the real truth, did she, Ty? That you were living with me in real luxury. You had everything provided, the very best of everything. You were flown to Jamaica twice on premier class, because Ty Benton doesn't do normal class like all the other poor people, does he? You stayed, twice, in the best hotels on the island, spending all day in the bars and drinking yourself into a vile, spiteful mood. And it was all free, all on me, every damned thing on me. You took cash out on my credit and debit cards to flash in front of your family—and when when I got serious burns on my legs, what did you do? Treated me like a bloody nuisance! And when we eventually got back to England, I had to drive you home, although I'd kicked you out yet again. And because you can't go through tunnels, I had to drive you the long way home, with my legs in agony. But it didn't stop there, did it? I had serious embolisms, and you didn't even turn up at the hospital. When you did, you were more concerned about your sodding friend at the American base than about me. Then, when I told you that it was clear to me that there was no love from you, you tried to drive the car into the back of a lorry. I really needed that, didn't I, Ty? And then you just dumped me at home, dumped me on the doorstep, and left me to pass out, alone. I could have damned well died, but you didn't care! If it had been the other way round, I'd have stuck by you through thick and thin—that's what love is. Both of us gave you total and unconditional love, and you betrayed us both; you cheated, and lied, and conned, and demeaned, and used us—you hurt us badly. Well, now it's your turn, Ty Benton, your turn to hurt really badly!" Olivia's voice rose. Her cheeks were flushed, and her fists were clenched.

Ty looked at her, pleadingly, desperate. "Please baby, please. Just enough to get me the fare over there. If they find me, they'll kill me. I have to get out tonight. Please, please, baby, help me." He held out his hands. He was sobbing and shaking. Olivia folded her arms again and held her head up high.

"No, I won't help you, Ty. You didn't help me when I nearly died. As soon as you were found out, you dumped Sophie, said you hardly knew her, and told filthy lies about her. You can get caught for all I care. I hope they torture you until you scream for death."

Olivia turned and looked at Sophie. She was still holding the gun in shaky hands, and her face was a study in misery. There was the faintest glint of tears in her eyes. *Bloody Sophie!* thought Olivia. *She's feeling sorry for the bastard.* She spoke softly. "Soph, just remember all the bad times you had because of this excuse for a human. Remember what he did to you, what he said about you and your children, how he hurt you and lied to you. Don't feel one bit sorry for him. You're too soft, too forgiving. He's hurt and used women all his damned life; there's nothing soft or forgiving about this pig. He needs a lesson, and he's going to get it. Hurt is what he freely dished out, and hurt is what he's going to get."

Ty stared at them both. Sophie lowered her eyes; she didn't want to look at him. But then she raised her head and looked at him unwaveringly, and she saw not the man she had adored and sacrificed for but the cunning, cruel, selfish, lying, thieving parasite that Ty really was.

Olivia turned to Ty. "Get out now. Go on—just get out."

"But where will I go? What will I do? I must have cash to get out of this country! Please, baby, please ..." Ty was sobbing again.

Olivia sneered. "Find another couple of victims from the dating site, and bleed them dry." She laughed mirthlessly and coldly. "Go on—out." Ty put his hand out to Sophie for his gun, but Sophie quickly handed it to Olivia.

Ty turned once more and looked at them both with a sort of yearning in his eyes. Then he shrugged and went out of the cottage and through the gate. They heard the powerful engine start up and the car pull away. They stood outside in the garden for a while, but there was just silence. They went inside, where Olivia locked the door and went to make tea. She came back with two mugs and put them on the table. She looked at Sophie. "You OK? What did he do to you? Those bruises?"

Sophie smiled wryly. "We had a bit of a scuffle over the gun just before you came in. I'm OK, really."

"But your hands are shaking like jellies, and you're pale, and you're bruised. Here, sit down and drink this tea. Tell me all about it."

Sophie slowly recounted the night's events, remembering her mobile phone nestled amongst the flannels in the bathroom. This made them both laugh. They also laughed over the snowdrift of plaster that had descended from the ceiling when Ty's gun had gone off. Sophie said she would clear it all up the next day.

Olivia looked at her thoughtfully. "So, you tended to his injuries— even sewed his hand up. Why?"

"Well, he had a gun. But truthfully, I can't bear to see anyone injured and not help them. You're exactly the same—don't deny it, Livvy."

Olivia shrugged. "Yep, I suppose you're right. But you went all soppy on me! God, woman, you have a short memory. You were devastated when he treated you like shit. Try to remember all that and stop drooling over his handsome face and his ability to act like a hurt child. That's how he always gets what he wants from every woman he meets. But not this woman—oh no! He can die a horrible death and burn in hell for eternity for all I care. What he did to us both was unforgivable—wicked, immoral! He's on the run because he stole, anyway."

"But he stole from real criminals," Sophie said quietly.

"And he used to drug run for them, didn't he, Soph, so he's as much a criminal as they are. You just forget him. He's getting what he deserves, at last. And if you still can't feel good about what he's facing, just remember all the kids he's so happily sired and left with their mothers to face life without a father. There's something like twenty-odd out there. Most of the older ones wish he would get what's coming to him."

Sophie did think of them, deserted and fatherless. They'd been left behind because he didn't want his life disrupted by responsibility. She became very angry on their behalf. Now the hurt she had felt at the beginning began to resurface, hot and painful. She drank her tea and suddenly felt very tired.

Olivia stayed for just over an hour to ensure that Ty was not going to return. She and Sophie took torches and went up and down the silent, empty street, checking to see that Ty had not pulled in somewhere to wait. When she was satisfied, Olivia left, after stressing to Sophie that she must lock and latch her door. She took the big gun with her. She would lose it; she knew how to. They kissed goodbye and hugged. Olivia stood outside whilst Sophie secured the door, and then she drove away.

Sophie stood for some while, just staring at the wall; then she flopped down onto the settee and curled up in a foetal huddle. She was shaking still, her mouth was dry, and her heart was racing. She felt numb, unable to comprehend exactly what had happened to her. She could not forget the cold, hard feel of the gun pressing against her face, Ty's snarling voice and vicious orders, his drunken ramblings, and his threats. But she also could not forget the sight of his face so beaten and bloodied or his tearful desperation. Whatever he had done to her, he was a human being. He was the man she had loved—still loved. If only she had been able to help him. Would she have given him the money to flee and set up a new life? She knew that the answer was yes; she would have done just that. And she would not have told Olivia about anything that had happened, explained her bruises by saying she'd fallen on the stairs. They were dangerous and twisty, and the probability of such an accident was logical. She would have told the Jamaican to send Olivia a text telling her that he had managed to raise the money and had gone back to his island, where he would stay out of her life. If only she had that sort of money. In her shocked and stressed state, Sophie had completely forgotten that she now did have money, even though it still hadn't reached her bank account. She opened a bottle of wine and poured herself a glass. The red wine hit her stomach and then her brain, with the impact of a crashing train. She went up to the toilet and then lay down on the bed, exhausted but unable to sleep.

Every time a car came down the hill she startled and lay tense and uncertain, waiting for it to pass. Olivia rang from her car to check that Sophie was OK. Sophie told her that she was fine, nearly asleep, and would talk to her in the morning. This wasn't totally true, but Sophie had had her fill for today, and she wanted to be left alone. Slowly she relaxed and stopped listening to the drone of approaching vehicles. Her eyes closed, and soon she slept.

Two hours later Sophie woke. Her head was aching and she was extremely thirsty. She had a bottle of water by her bed, and she drank all of it. She sat up and began thinking of the Jamaican again. If only she had something to help him! Then she remembered the tiny savings account she had. Her "desperation fund" she called it. She opened her phone and logged onto her banking site. She opened the small account and looked at what was there. She had exactly three hundred pounds and six pence. Maybe that would help him. She returned to her current account to see if she could scrape up any extra— and then it hit her full in the face. There was a deposit of £30,000, and beside it the words "Beardsley and Tope. Client account." Her inheritance—that money! That plum-in-the-gob creep had promised her a "small amount to be going on with" and this was it. It had arrived at such a providential time. Sophie thought hard. Ty would need his plane fare, cash to buy a small business, maybe a bar or restaurant or shop. He would need a car, clothes, the rental of a house …. Sophie reckoned it all up. She thought that £7,000 sounded about right. She thought for a while longer but then realised that every second was putting the Jamaican in more danger. Hastily she transferred the amount over to Ty's account. Then a message came up on the screen that bank security wanted confirmation that she really did mean to transfer such a large amount.

Oh, sod them—it's my bloody money! Sophie thought angrily. She waited for the email that they sent her. It seemed to take hours. Finally it came, and Sophie pressed Yes, she did mean to send this amount. Another century seemed to pass, and then the message flashed onto the screen. "Your transfer has been successful." Sophie was overjoyed. She rang Ty's number, but her call was not picked up. She called another three times with the same result.

Damn! she thought and sent him a text, hoping that this would reach him and be read. She wrote,

> Ty, I know how you feel about me, and you are so wrong—and you know it. You treated me so very badly, but I still have feelings for you, and I can't bear to think of you hurt any more. You asked for the trouble you're in, but I have put £7,000 in your account to get you to Jamaica and set you up. I really didn't know I had it when you asked me for cash earlier. It's a long story. I will just wish you the very best of luck. Make something of your life now. God guard you, and take care. Please never breathe a word of this to Olivia.

She read and reread the text and then pressed Send. She prayed he would look at it. She could not settle after this, so she went downstairs and made herself a cup of tea. She found a dried-up cigarette and went outside and smoked it. She stood looking at the moon and wondering where the Jamaican was and what he was doing. Then her phone chirruped. She went back into the little room, picked up the phone, and read the text he had sent.

Thank you so, so much. I don't deserve anything from you after what I did to you. I did sacrifice you for my own selfish wants, but that's life, baby. You have to take what you can when you can and the weak go down. You take care.

Sophie read it a few times. The bastard was still a bastard. He was admitting it even as he thanked her. Well, what else did she expect from that— Sophie stopped. She wasn't going down that road. He hadn't escaped yet, but she wasn't going to stress over him any more. This was her last act of love. She went up to bed and slept.

Olivia drove home very quickly. The roads were deserted. The moon was brilliant. She parked the car and ran into the house. She locked the gun in a safe box after removing the bullets; tomorrow she would make a phone call and it would disappear from existence. She was on edge and stressed. She poured herself a brandy and added Coke to the glass. She downed half of it quickly and sat on the settee, thinking. She went into the garden for a cigarette and thought very hard about the Jamaican. She was not at all contrite about hitting him or about what she had said to him. He was all the things she had told him he was. But she loved him still. She would never take him back again—never—but she could not bear to think of what she knew they would do to him if they caught him. They would spin his death out, torture and hurt him until he died, slowly, in total agony. She found her eyes getting hot and tears welling up. She swallowed hard. No, not that, she could not let that happen to Ty! Whatever he had done, they had been lovers, they had shared a bed, and a home, and a life. She would not be able to live knowing that she hadn't helped him to escape this awful fate.

Olivia lifted her phone and called her phone banking service. She had thought out the Jamaican's needs. Air fare, a house, a car, furniture maybe, clothes—and most importantly, a small business, a bar or a shop or the two combined. She remembered Ty being offered a shop which was also a bar. It was a busy place on the waterfront, a thriving little set-up called Errol's Bar. Olivia calculated in her head what the Jamaican would need and decided to give him £10,000—she had added extra for the stock for the business. She made the transaction and then texted Ty.

Nothing has changed. I meant everything I said and did. You are what I said you are. Love doesn't just disappear. Not when it's been so real and so true and so strong. I gave you everything, but you couldn't be honest, or loyal, or faithful. You couldn't breathe without lying. We could have had such a good life, but you didn't want it. I have transferred £10,000 into your account. Just get out of England, set up in business, and settle over there. Don't come back. And try not to hurt and destroy more lives. And use condoms—you've left too many fatherless and damaged kids all over the place. Do not tell Sophie about this. I know you have no contact with her—not much anyway—and that you blame the poor woman for your crimes. Anyway, please do not tell her this. It won't help anyone. You made her feel unwanted and rejected enough already, and I don't want to hurt her even more. Take care.

Olivia pressed Send, and the message sped to Ty. She sat drinking her brandy and Coke, curled up on the settee and thinking of the Jamaican. She would never see his handsome face again, or hear his seductive Jamaican/Yankee accent, or smell his musky skin, or— *Stop this!* Olivia told herself. *He was a total crook, a first-class bastard and con man. He needs to be taught a lesson!* But not the appalling violence he faced if she didn't help him. She sat in thought for some time, until her phone gave the sound that announced Ty. Olivia picked up her phone and opened his text.

Baby I can't thank you enough. I knew you still loved me. This means so much to me. I will get you back when I'm sorted out over there. You are my life. I love you so much. I'll let you know when I get there. Take good care of yourself. You belong to me, my baby.

Olivia curled her lip. Still the same Jamaican—still unable to see the reality of anything. But she wished him godspeed in her heart. She finished her brandy, checked all the doors, and then climbed upstairs to her massive bed. The traumatic day was over—the second-most dreadful day in the last few months. She hoped it would only improve.

The following day Olivia called Sophie first thing in the morning. "Are you OK? Did he come back? Did you hear anything?"

"Yes, no, and no. I was a bit jumpy every time I heard a car, but I was so knackered that I soon fell asleep. How about you? Has he been in touch?"

"No, thank the Lord. Not a peep. All quiet on the Western front so far." Both of them felt slightly guilty at not exactly telling the truth, but they rationalised it by thinking that there was no need to reveal what they had done. The Jamaican was only too glad to run for safety. He wasn't going to tell. Each clung to her little secret.

"Well, I suppose that's it. I wonder if he'll tell you when he gets there—if he gets there," Sophie said.

"He might tell you," Olivia said.

"Hmm, I doubt it very much. You're the love of his life. I'm just an evil bitch who parted you. The fact that he's on the run because he was stupid enough to steal from the rough crowd will probably also be my fault, not his. We'll just have to wait and find out. I really hope he made it, actually. Whatever and whoever he is, and whatever he did, I can't bear the thought of him being cruelly treated by rough thugs like that."

"But he treated you cruelly, Sophie! Don't you think he deserves a bit of his own medicine?"

"Well, yes and no. He deserves it, yes, but I still feel for him, and anyway, I can't tolerate violence and physical torment. He may get his punishment one day, in some other way we haven't thought of. God will have planned it all. I just want to know he's managed to get out and fly to Jamaica. He always said he wanted to go home, and I hope he gets there."

They agreed to meet on the following Sunday. Sophie hadn't yet told Olivia of her good fortune, and she wanted to tell her the truth. Anyway, she wanted plan another holiday, somewhere exotic and warm. She was getting excited about the future.

On the Sunday, Olivia rolled up laden with a coffee-and-walnut cake. Sophie made the coffee for them both, cut two enormous slices of the buttercream-laden cake, brought them through, and sat on the settee next to Olivia. "Well, what a week. Thank God we've survived it all. I was so glad to see you crashing through that door!" They laughed. "Just another spirit-inspired act—me putting my phone on charge in the bedroom," said Sophie, taking a large bite of the delicious concoction.

"And putting it in the flannels basket!" They laughed again. "What about that kick! It was epic, my girl, epic—except for the hole in the ceiling." They both looked up at the mess above them. "Your house insurance will cover that, of course."

"Actually, no. I won't be telling them, Livvy. How on earth do I explain it all! They will expect me to have involved the police. I'll pay for repairs myself."

"Have you suddenly become rich, Soph? It'll cost an arm and a leg to make that good and redecorate it all—"

"Actually, Livvy, you've hit the nail on the head." Sophie explained her windfall to Olivia and told her how she had walked out on her hated job.

"So, wow, wonderful! What are you going to do, then? Buy a house for you and Freddie?"

"But of course. Out in the country, just outside the town here probably. Lots of garden. Might keep a couple of Labradors again. Must get a Jeep, my dream vehicle. I can't wait to get viewing! You must come with me, Livvy. There's also something else I wanted to discuss."

"Mmmmm?" Olivia's mouth was stuffed with cake.

"I want to invest some cash in Diamond Lady. To work in it with you. I had an idea you might like."

"Which is?"

"Well, there's a lot of emphasis on older women and guys these days, mainly because we have such a large over-sixty population, and they have money to spend. Now, if I get made over—facelift, good hairdos, dental implant treatment, all that stuff—I could be a sort of spokesperson or model, whatever you will, for that sector. You don't have a huge range at present to cover their special needs, so we could develop several—"

"Sophie, that's brilliant—just brilliant!" Olivia swallowed the last piece of her cake. "We really must discuss this with my team. Let's make an appointment to do it all. When are you free?"

"All the time now, Livvy. Make the appointment to suit your movements." They munched cake and swallowed coffee.

Then Olivia said, "Soph—"

"Yep, I know that tone. What is it now?" Sophie was grinning.

"Well, I'm getting kinda restless. Need to surf the sites again and have a little fun."

"Great, but ..."

"But what, Soph? I know you're feeling the same. What's the 'but' for?"

"Well, it's almost impossible to find a man who's any bloody use, really. They look good, but they have the intellect of a whelk. They have so much baggage that they come with six bearers carrying it all. They have the sexual technique of a rocking horse, and even if they have the abilities of Casanova, their equipment is, well ..."

"The size of a walnut whip?" Olivia suggested with a wicked grin. "I think we may have been ruined by the Jamaican. I remember him telling me that when he worked in a store in New Jersey, when he was only about 17, the middle-aged woman who worked with him used to have sex with him in the back storage room. She told him that he'd always have problems, because women would become addicted to his huge cock."

"Yep, she was not wrong. We keep saying that we'd be relieved to have guys who are normally sized, but the truth is that I can't imagine anything smaller than that, and I can't imagine getting satisfaction from anything that's not that massive. Can you?" She grinned at Olivia, who grinned back.

"Well, size isn't supposed to be everything, is it? Technique counts a lot, and the Jamaican had that too, so he'll be hard to replace."

"Sort of not the size of the car but the way you drive it. And he had the biggest car going, and he certainly knew how to drive. I do miss him that way, I have to confess." Sophie sighed. "But where is this elusive guy who has exquisite manners, no past, pots of money, a brain, wonderful taste in everything, an upmarket car that he drives with enormous skill, an understanding of the female sex, a large dick, fantastic sexual technique, sweet breath, floral armpits, and considerable taste in clothes? Yep, there he is Livvy—coming out of that forest, with four legs, and hooves, and a very big horn on his head, and preferably with a black coat—it's a unicorn. A red-hot unicorn!"

Olivia hooted with amusement. "A sort of hotti-corn—a fabled, non-existent, much pursued creature. We need to get ourselves a unicorn each—when we have time."

"It would be nice to find a suitable unicorn." Sophie sighed. "I really want to have a fling with no love stuff and no strings, just lusty, rollicking sex, and a bloody good time. She grew serious.

"I wonder how our Jamaican's doing, Livvy. I really can't stop thinking about him and if he got away. Until I know, I shall really worry about him."

Olivia pursed her lips. "Don't worry too much, Soph; he's a survivor. He'll get where he needs to be."

"Yes, probably, but I would just like to know." They sat in silence for a minute, then Olivia's phone tweeted with the tone she always reserved for Ty's calls and texts. She snatched her phone and opened the text. She looked at Sophie, then began to read the message out loud.

"Hi, hun. Just thought I'd let you know, although I know you no longer want me, I've arrived in Jamaica. I'm safe, and I've taken over Errol's bar and shop. The only thing that is missing out of my life is you. Please come over here. I love you so much. Ty."

They looked at each other. Sophie breathed deeply. "Thank God he's safe. I wonder how he got over there and got a bar and shop to run. It sounds as if he's fallen on his feet."

"Yes, I wonder too. Maybe he's got more women bankrolling him than we were aware of," Olivia said hastily. "At least we know now. Hopefully he'll stay there and leave us in peace—that's if he really is there," she said grimly.

"Why?" Sophie asked." Do you really think he's just lying to you again and he's holed up somewhere in England still?"

"Dunno—I just can't trust the bastard. You know, Sophie, we need another holiday."

"Do we? Sounds good. Where?"

"Oh, I think somewhere far away and fairly exotic—the Caribbean, I think. A premier-class flight, and the best hotel on the island. You can afford it all now, Sophie. And we can do some snooping while we're there—"

"No, Livvy, better than that! We can pay a professional to do the snooping and stay hidden in our luxury hotel, sizing up the talent."

"Sophie, you're a genius—we'll do that! I'll do all the bookings and stuff. You can house-hunt when we return. Why don't you bring Freddie along, too? He deserves a holiday. I'll do all the bookings and text you the cost, and you can just put it in my bank account."

"Whoopee!" Sophie was overjoyed. She really needed this trip and the excitement of finding out if their Jamaican was really over there—if he had, indeed, gone home.

They chatted more about Diamond Lady and Sophie's ideas, and then Olivia left to drive home. Sophie washed up. She was tired. She went to bed early and watched television. Only half her mind was on the programme, a documentary about dinosaurs. She was thinking, sadly, that Ty hadn't bothered to let her know that he was safe. She kept falling asleep, so she eventually turned off the television and settled down. She realised that she had forgotten to set the alarm on her phone, so she rolled over and picked it up. Just as she was putting the phone back on her bedside cabinet, a message came through. It was from Ty.

"Hi, Sophie, thanks for your help. I know you didn't need to do it after all that's happened. I'm safely in Jamaica. I'm sorry I hurt you. Take care. Ty."

Sophie read it several times. She sighed. At least she knew he had remembered her and bothered to let her know what was happening. She decided not to show Olivia the text. After all, Ty had actually given away the fact that Sophie had helped him in the message. She would just pretend that only Olivia had been informed of Ty's situation and leave it at that.

"Forget him," her loved ones whispered as they gathered around her bed. "Leave him to fate." Sophie slipped into sleep. Soon she would be in Jamaica, Ty's home. Soon they would both know whether he really had gone home. For now they knew he was safe, and that was all Sophie really cared about.

The next few months were frantic. The girls could not leave for Jamaica immediately, as Olivia had heavy business commitments and Sophie was wavering between buying one of the many houses she'd viewed or waiting until she returned from the trip to sort the whole matter out. Olivia zoomed around England in her Jaguar, sorting, training, discussing, demonstrating, interviewing, reprimanding, and generally doing the work required to build her company and its high reputation. Sophie sat knee deep in details of houses, reading and rereading. They all looked so terrific. She looked at many of them, wanting them all. Eventually she had shortlisted four and informed the estate agency that she would be viewing them on her return from Jamaica.

She went shopping one Saturday with Olivia and Freddie, and they all went crazy, buying holiday clothes, cosmetics, sunscreen products, and shoes. Sophie bought Freddie two smart navy blue leather suitcases, one small and one large, for the trip. She got herself a red-and-white matching set and a very smart designer leather handbag. She had her nails done like Olivia's beautiful nails. She had long been in awe of the brightly coloured false nails set with jewelled designs. She had some deep-red ones attached, with red and champagne coloured jewels spread across them diagonally. At first she felt uncomfortable and awkward with them, but very soon she grew accustomed to them and was quite proud of them. She had grown her hair in the last few months; she had been too depressed recently to bother with the hairdresser. Now she had her hair coloured in two tones and pinned up as she used to have it when she was younger. She and Freddie had packed their cases well in advance and were really longing for their trip. Sophie had never flown a long-haul flight on a large aircraft, and she was nervous. Olivia told her to relax. She would bring along some diazepam. Sophie could pop twenty milligrams before take-off and all would be well. They were flying premier class on Virgin Atlantic, so Freddie's long legs would have somewhere to rest comfortably.

At last the day dawned. Sophie and Freddie had left the house secure. They informed their next-door neighbours, who happily agreed to keep an eye on the cottage. Olivia picked them up the day before, and they slept at her house, going to bed very early, as they had an early start. They drank coffee and ate toast, bleary eyed and excited. Olivia drove them to Gatwick and left her car with the man from the secure parking firm. They dragged their luggage to the check-out and went through the formalities, stood in a very long line to have their hand baggage inspected by security, and at last were through and sitting down to more coffee. Freddie was tucking into a plate of bacon, eggs, sausages, tomatoes, and fried bread. Olivia and Sophie ate sandwiches and swallowed their diazepam. Freddie had declined Olivia's offer of one or two. He said he was fine, not worried about a thing.

Then they were at the departure gate and following what seemed to Sophie like the entire population of London, as they went down escalators, round corners, and along miles of corridors to the waiting aircraft. It was a massive 747, incredibly large compared to the small aircraft that Sophie had flown in to the Canaries, Portugal, and Greece. Olivia had flown all over the world and often; she was used to these giants of the air. They were shown to their upmarket seating, put their hand luggage away in the overhead compartments, sorted out that Freddie would sit next to the window, as it was his first flight, and were soon settled, awaiting the start of the adventure. The big aircraft was soon taxiing out, ready for take-off. The huge engines roared as they picked up power for the ascent. Then they were hurtling down the runway, and the engines screamed as the 747 lifted and pulled up and away into the blue sky. Sophie grabbed Olivia's hand as the force of the lift-off pushed her back into her seat. Freddie was amused by how quickly the ground, the buildings, and the cars became like tiny toys. They sank back in their comfortable seats as the giant craft turned and set course for the long flight. Soon the stewardesses came round and offered them drinks—glasses of champagne, small bottles of spirits and mixers, and wine. Freddie decided to try the champagne. He was now old enough to drink legally, so they all toasted their holiday, clinking the champagne glasses together musically. Freddie liked the bubbly a lot. "Could get very used to this stuff." He grinned and toasted them all again. Sophie was happy to see Freddie so relaxed and happy. The diazepam and the alcohol were beginning to induce a happy state of sleepiness in her, and soon she was out for the count. Olivia and Freddie chatted away happily. Olivia was telling

Freddie all about Jamaica and the many other places in the world that she had been to. Soon they too dozed. Freddie woke and ordered himself some food, which he ate accompanied by a cold beer whilst Olivia and Sophie slept. It was a long journey. Olivia was used to a maximum flight time of four hours, so when she woke up she was a little disconcerted to see that they still had five hours to go. She was terrified when they ran into some bumpy patches, but Olivia calmed her down. They both had a couple of brandy and Cokes to help the situation. Freddie found the bumping entertaining; he laughed at it all. He was beginning to show interest in one of the stewardesses, which amused the women a lot. He chatted to her about technology and the computers which were his passion. He was a real technology geek, highly gifted, and this was his life.

Time crept past. Olivia and Sophie got up to visit the toilet and to stretch their legs. They listened to music on their headphones for a while. Then they began to discuss the arrangements Olivia had made to check whether the Jamaican really was doing what he said he was doing and where he said he was doing it. Olivia brought up the emails on her phone. They were from the man she had retained to do the surveillance on the Jamaican. He was an Australian, a hardened ex-army, worldly wise and seemingly trustworthy type of man. Sophie liked the well-written, well-spelt and grammatically correct emails that he sent. He was to check out everything he could to do with their Jamaican. They would remain in the hotel complex, and he would report back to them. As well as his security service of observing Ty, he had hired them a car in advance and arranged for it to meet them at the airport. It had tinted windows so that they could avoid any possibility of being recognised by members of Ty's family, who knew Olivia. If they felt unsafe, their dependable Aussie would accompany them in the car.

Jamaica was a country in turmoil. The government and security forces were failing to control the rising tide of crime, and murders of tourists and nationals were occurring daily. It had always been a country where you didn't wander off the places you were told to stay in, or stray away on your own, or trust strangers, or take money from an ATM without a guard—of late that meant an armed guard. Their Aussie angel would protect them from all this, they hoped. His name was Kieran McCarthy.

"But call me Plug," he wrote.

"Why Plug?" Sophie laughed.

"Maybe an old army nickname?" Olivia was amused too. They talked about the coming adventure.

"You'll see some pretty gorgeous specimens of beautiful black manhood there, Soph. Just try to keep your cougar claws in, and try to eat toast for breakfast—not the waiter on room service!" Sophie ran her tongue over her pink lipsticked mouth.

"Grrrrrr—" They both roared with laughter.

"Bring 'em on," Sophie murmured.

Soon they were nearing their destination, and the big aircraft dropped down and changed course for Sangster Airport. The stewardesses came around to ensure that all seatbelts were fastened and all handbags and other items that could cause injury were safely out of the way. As they dropped down, Freddie, who had come out of his trance of sleeping and then ogling the young stewardess, exclaimed with awe about the first sight of the coast of Cuba as the huge Boeing passed over it en route to Jamaica. Very soon they were slowing and circling over Sangster. Then they had landed, and were walking from the plane and down the steps to the tarmac. The heat hit them all with force. It was like opening an oven door. They crossed the area to customs and passport control, where they were kept some while. Then they had to queue around the luggage carousel for what seemed like a fortnight before their cases came whizzing past. They were stiff and tired and all dying for a shower and a drink.

They walked out to search for Plug, who was hard to miss. He was tall, suntanned, blond, and blue eyed, and he was holding up a card which read Olivia, Sophie, and Freddie. It could not have been clearer. Olivia smiled at him, went over to shake his hand, and introduced them all. Plug had been in Jamaica for some years and had a curious accent, a mixture of Australian and a slight twang of patois.

"I'll take the baggage for you all, take you to the hire car, and then I'll drive ahead of you to the hotel," Plug informed them. He and Freddie managed the cases between them, and they stepped outside into the merciless sunshine and the noisy world. Sophie was entranced. She didn't much like too much heat, but she knew that the hotel would have air conditioning. The car was outside with a rep from the hire company, a tall, very attractive Jamaican woman. She smiled at Olivia, and they went quickly through the paperwork and showing of ID. The agreement was signed, the keys handed over with a satnav, and the luggage piled into the boot.

Plug drove ahead of them in his Land Rover. They followed him through the streets and out into dusty roads that crossed vast grassy areas. Olivia pointed out a deserted house that looked as if it dated to the early 1800s. "Look, Freddie. That was an old plantation house where slaves were used to grow sugarcane."

"I hope they've stopped doing that," Freddie said mischievously.

"Of course they have, Freddie. Don't be so sarcastic. It was a nasty slice of this island's history. Slavery goes on all over the world, all the time, but this was terrible—especially as it made other people rich on the results of these peoples' miserable torture." Sophie looked at Freddie sternly. *Slavery is not just about sugar and cotton plantations*, she thought. *Slavery can be the effect of some other human being on your life.* She was thinking of Ty.

Olivia was telling Freddie about the hotel, the swimming pools, and the beach, and Freddie was whooping with happy expectation. "I want to go in the pool as soon as we get there," he told Olivia.

"I'll join you, if I don't go to sleep first." Olivia said with a grin.

"Nan won't come—she can't swim," he informed her. "And she's scared shitless by water. She showers and bathes, of course— thank goodness—but pool or sea, and she's off."

"Shut up, Freddie! I'm not the first person in the world who's afraid of water and who can't swim." Sophie had always longed to be able to swim. She often dreamed about swimming, expertly and confidently in the sea. An early life experience had traumatised her, and try as she might, she was unable to cope with her phobia.

"You just come with us. We'll try and teach you, won't we Freddie?" Olivia was laughing.

Sophie looked sad. "Dream on. The universe has tried to teach me—and failed."

"Well, watch this space," said Olivia. "We will do this thing."

They arrived at the hotel, a very luxurious and imposing complex, with security guards in evidence everywhere. Freddie was impressed by the guns they wore. Sophie wasn't. Olivia told them that it was an absolute necessity and to get used to it. They drew up at the entrance. Plug had already got out and waved to the staff members on the steps for help with the luggage. Three young guys came and smilingly took their belongings in. They went to the reception and signed in. Olivia was cool and knowing. She had stayed there often. Sophie had been raised in this environment, and she was not at all overwhelmed by it. The foyer was air conditioned and beautifully furnished. They were taken up in the lift to the suite of rooms they had booked. Two staff members went with them, carrying their luggage.

"Your floor, madam." The lift attendant smiled warmly, and Olivia tipped him. Sophie already knew of the system of tipping, but she realised that in this country, beautiful as it was, poverty was the creeping enemy. It was essential to ensure that they showed their gratitude appropriately. The cream-and-gold door was opened, and they entered. There was a long corridor carpeted in sage green. To the right were three cream-and-gold doors leading to three bedrooms, each with a double bed and en-suite shower and bathroom. The rooms led out into a large lounge, and this led out, through sliding glass doors, onto a long balcony. There were huge armchairs that a person could get lost in, potted palms, and tables.

Freddie threw his cases across the room and bounced on the huge bed. "Gosh, this is super! Where's the pool, Livvy? I want a swim—like now."

"Oh, hang on, Freddie. I need to unpack, shower, and relax for a while. Be patient." She and Sophie settled in their rooms after Sophie had tipped the two staff members, who thanked her with genuine smiles.

"If you need anything, madam, just call room service. It's open 24/7," the taller and better looking of the two said.

"I will—and thank you." They left, and the girls wandered around and unpacked. Sophie poured herself a gin and ice-cold tonic, wandering into Olivia's room with it.

Olivia, unpacking enough clothes to last a year, looked up and grinned. "I think I'll join you, Soph." She poured her own drink, and they went outside onto the terrace, sat with their drinks, and lit up. Despite Sophie's commendable withdrawal from the habit of smoking the fact that she could actually afford the wretched things and Olivia's chain smoking had pulled her back. The view was breath-taking. The complex had a huge swimming pool and grassy areas that led down to a stunningly white beach. Palm trees grew everywhere, and hibiscus, jacaranda, and bougainvillea climbed walls and trellises, bright with their riotous beauty. The heat could almost be heard, and the shrilling and clattering of many exotic birds was deafening but pleasing.

Freddie came out to join them, carrying a can of cold beer. He sat down with them and surveyed the scene. "Wow, this really is something! I can't wait to look round!"

"Right, young man." Olivia winked at Sophie. "This is the lecture bit—we'll get it over quickly. First of all, you have skin as white as a soap powder advert. So sun blocker—always! Never forget it, or you'll land up in hospital in agony. Secondly, remember that this is not a safe place to roam alone, not like back home.

So never, never go out alone—never! D'you hear me? Thirdly, there are some very pretty girls around here. Just be careful, Freddie. This is all new ground for you—you could catch something nasty." Olivia held up her hand as Freddie's mouth opened. "Hear me out, Freddie. You need to use condoms, my man. No pregnancies and nasties, OK? Did you bring any?" Freddie shook his head. Sophie and Olivia reached into their handbags simultaneously and each brought out a small box of Durex. They all looked at each other and burst out laughing. Freddie took the proffered boxes. "I shall be giving these back to you unused—you know that."

"OK, but if you don't, then we'll fine you a tenner!" They all chortled again, and then they settled back to drinking and relaxing. After a bit, Freddie went with Olivia to the pool, and Sophie had a much needed lie-down. She was soon asleep.

Olivia took Freddie to the large pool with its swim-up bar and lifeguards on their high perches. Freddie ran and bombed in, splashing two pretty black girls, who turned and laughed at him. Soon they were all swimming and chatting together. Olivia swam around at a more dignified pace, keeping an eye on Freddie. She was remembering this very pool, Ty pulling her body onto his, and the fierce and satisfying lovemaking they had had. But, in the same second, she remembered the horrors that had followed, day after terrible day. She shook her mind free of these shackles, and called to Freddie to swim up to the bar. They sat on the concrete seats, and Olivia ordered a cold fresh pineapple juice. Freddie wanted another beer, so Olivia asked the barman for one with very little alcohol—none, if possible. They sat drinking and relaxing in the warm, soothing water, while the island magic washed over them.

"This is the life," Freddie said, watching another bunch of pretty, giggling girls go past in their skimpy, revealing bikinis.

"Yep," said Olivia. "If you're a tourist. It's not so pretty if you live here and don't have a business or a decent job. But yes, it's a sort of paradise. Just watch that you use that sun blocker all the time." Drinks downed, they swam some more and then gathered up their belongings and returned to their suite. Sophie was still deeply asleep.

Olivia showered again and dressed in a cool shift. She went out onto the balcony and called Plug. She wanted to know his plan of action. "Hi, Plug, it's Olivia. What's the brief, then?"

"Hi, Olivia. I'm going to Errol's Bar this evening to hang around and have a beer or three and, if it's essential, stay and eat there to give me time to pick up facts. I may follow said Jamaican back to wherever he lives and check that out too. It all depends. As soon as I have anything I'll let you both know."

"Fine. OK, thanks Plug. Look forward to hearing from you soon. Don't get too drunk at Errol's!"

"Don't you worry about that, girl—I can outdrink most guys around here. Can still be sober when they're pissed and telling me what I want to hear. You enjoy your evening, both of you—all of you. Talk later." Olivia sank back into the cushions of the large armchair.

Freddie, having showered and dressed in jeans and a T-shirt, joined her. "I'm hungry—really starving," he said.

Olivia sat up. "I could murder something edible too. What do you fancy?"

"Dunno. What's on offer?"

"Just call room service and ask for whatever you want. Go get me the phone; I'll do it. I want some food too. Thought of anything yet?"

"I think I want a large, medium-rare sirloin steak, with a small salad, mayonnaise, and chips—oh, and a cold beer, too."

"OK." Olivia went into the lounge, picked up the phone, and ordered Freddie's desired meal. She also ordered herself a steak, salad with French dressing, and a jacket potato. Just as she was finishing the order, Sophie wandered into the lounge, yawning and tousled. Olivia looked up. "I'm ordering us some dinner—want anything?" She asked room service to hang on for a minute.

"Actually, I fancy some salmon, cold, with mayonnaise and salad, and a few sauté potatoes." Sophie yawned again and stretched. Olivia relayed Sophie's order; then they went back out onto the balcony. Sophie saw Freddie's cold beer and fancied one herself. Freddie got her one from the well-stocked fridge in the lounge, and they sat, quiet and happy, awaiting their food. Room service arrived with a laden trolley, linen napkins, and silver cutlery, and took it out onto the balcony at Olivia's request. They put their plates on the table and sat enjoying the excellent meal. Sophie's salmon was delectable. She held out forkfuls for Olivia and Freddie to try, and they, in turn, gave her portions of their steak. They sat, talking and sipping at their drinks, as the night fell and lights started to bejewel the complex. Room service came in to clear away the trolley and to ask whether they required anything else. Sophie said a smiling "No, thanks. That was lovely." She tipped generously and the smile she got was heartfelt.

They were all exhausted and soon turned in for the night. Olivia had texted Plug that they were going to bed. Had he anything to tell her yet? But he told her that the night was yet young, and he would contact her first thing the next day. The sounds of the night birds lulled them all to sleep, and the soft, warm breeze brought in the smells of unknown night-blooming flowers.

Olivia was up first the next morning. She was anxious to hear from Plug. She went out onto the balcony with a strong coffee in her hand, and sat, smoking and waiting. Soon Sophie joined her, and she, too, hugged a strong coffee. Freddie was comatose as ever. His autism had gifted him with a curiously irregular sleep pattern. If he needed to get up early in the morning he could manage it but, normally, he slept deeply until about lunchtime if his presence wasn't required anywhere.They sat listening to the birds and the buzz of the wakening complex while they ingested their daily dose of caffeine.

Olivia told Sophie about her chat with Plug. They waited expectantly. Then Olivia's phone tinkled. She picked it up quickly. "Hello—Plug?"

"Morning, darling. Well, I had to stay some time, as the man in question was out somewhere. He eventually rocked up late, with a woman in tow." Olivia snorted and raised an eyebrow at Sophie. The speaker on Olivia's phone was on, and Sophie could hear the conversation.

"He does own the bar—I mean actually own it. I found out that he had originally just rented it; he bought all the stock there and paid a rent for the store and the bar. Only weeks later he made an offer, and it was accepted, and he became the owner. About the time of the offer, this female came on the scene.

White, expensive looking. Locals say she's been over here on holiday a few times in the last five or so years. No man in tow ever—alone. Some think that she and your guy already knew each other. Did hear that they were seeing each other about the time you were last here with him. You did tell me he kept disappearing, yes? Well, there's a strong reason to believe that he was with her then—doesn't get better, does it, sweetheart? Well, this guy can drink. He was swilling back vodka nearly all night. She can sink it too. I crept out at dawn. Don't want him to get too used to my face, or he might get suspicious. He strikes me as very streetwise, and paranoid, and wary. Anyway, I'll be on the trail again just as soon as I get more info. Hope you two girls are having fun—and that lad. Keep an eye on him! I'll call you again ASAP. If you need me for anything—to go anywhere or whatever—just holler. G'day." He had rung off before Olivia had a chance to say a word. They looked at each other.

"Well, she must have cash. That's how he managed to buy the business—bastard!" Olivia said with a frown. Both of them instantly thought of the money they had given Ty but just as instantly tried to forget it. "He's just the bloody same. Drinking and womanising. It never changes—"

"But it always ends, doesn't it." Sophie was thoughtful. "He's had business after business. Bar after bar. Store after store. Woman after woman. They never last—none of them. The businesses fold, the women disappear or are dumped after they're used. This will go tits up too, and what will he do then?" Olivia sneered. "Find yet another besotted victim. How does he do it each time? If he screws up this business, then she won't hang around if he burns all her money. The fucking will lose its fascination after her cervix gets fed up!" They grinned in unison.

"Then what will he do, if he can't catch another tourist with money and an appetite for sex?" Sophie finished her coffee and got up to fetch another one. "We'll just have to see what Plug can dig up, won't we?"

Later in the day, Freddie surfaced, drank a large coffee, and then went with Olivia to the pool for more water sports. The two attractive Jamaican girls were there again, and Olivia smiled to herself as they homed in on Freddie. He was slightly uncomfortable but learning. They all lunched at one of the restaurants, where there was a huge buffet spread out. Freddie's eyes widened. He didn't know where to begin. He settled for jerk chicken, as it was a new dish for him. Although it was so hot, Sophie decided she really wanted stewed oxtail, and it was worth the wanting. Olivia settled for chicken salad. They all had fresh fruit for dessert; the pineapple, mango, and papaya were local and mouth-watering.

They went back to their suite for a sleep, and while they were there, Plug called Olivia. "Could I have dinner with you tonight, darling—all of you? I have more to tell you. " Olivia was amused by the cheeky, charming colonial boy.

"Yes, of course you can, Plug. I know Sophie and Freddie will be very pleased to have your company. Can we say eight this evening, at the big restaurant next to the pool?"

"Super, my love. Are we dressing for dinner—or shall I come naked!"

"Cheeky sod! Yes, strict dress code. We're all dressing up. See you at eight."

Sophie had bought Freddie a dress suit for such occasions. He had looked at it and groaned. "I'm not wearing that thing—it's old fashioned."

"No, it's not. It's the latest thing out. You look really smart in it. You'll wear it and be civilised or not come with us." But she was laughing and didn't care too much. However, Freddie relented and soon became interested in the hated outfit. That evening he showered, waxed down his thick, curly hair, and put on the suit. It had a black satin cummerbund and was piped with black satin. He had a pair of shiny black leather shoes which he rather liked, and he put in his diamond ear stud for the finishing touch.

Olivia was in a gorgeous green number which set off her amazing breasts. She wore emerald and diamond jewellery everywhere and emerald combs in her upswept hair. Her shoes were of matching green satin, with emerald and diamante stones in flower motifs. Sophie wore an empire-line red dress that reached her ankles. Her legs offended her greatly, so they were best covered. She put her hair up and wore ruby and diamond jewellery with matching hair ornaments. She had a pair of matching satin shoes with tiny, low kitten heels. Anything higher made her airsick. Both of them carried matching clutch bags.

"Well now, just look at us, will you?" said Olivia approvingly as Freddie paraded his finery. "Love your ear stud, Freddie."

"Thought I might put some combs in my hair, but I might make you look bad," Freddie quipped, grinning at Olivia.

They arrived at the restaurant, sat at their table, and had a couple of dry martinis. Freddie stuck to fresh orange juice.

Then Plug appeared, looking quite fetching in his evening suit. Olivia raised an approving eyebrow and smiled faintly.

"Yes, I do scrub up well." Plug smiled back at her. He sat down and ordered a scotch on the rocks. They dived into the enormous menu and chose a starter each. The waiter took the order and brought another round of drinks. Plug folded his arms and tipped his chair back ever so slightly. "Well, ladies, and gentleman!" He turned and grinned at Freddie. "Pin back your ears. Listen well. I followed the target around and found that he rents quite a decent garden shed. By that I mean a pretty substantial dwelling, in good nick, and well furnished. He drives a brand new Merc—"

"Probably hers!" Olivia cut in.

"No. Surprisingly, it's definitely his vehicle. He seems to live in some style, with expensive clothes. Eats very well. Staff in the house, too."

"What? She lets him have other females where he has access to them?" Olivia's face was a study in disbelief.

"Actually, my darling, they're all male. Even the cleaning lady is a man. Clearly the girlfriend knows him too well. Anyway, that's the picture. He seems to pay his bills on time. He pays his staff in the house and the place—Errol's—not just on time but pretty well, too. He totes a gun and has a couple of hefty bodyguards, armed as well. It's hard to get too close to him, and people seem to respect him—or are maybe a little bit scared of him. I found out that he likes his game of cards, so I got myself into an all-night session. Didn't do too well, I'm afraid—sorry, but it will have to go on the bill." Plug grinned bashfully.

Olivia looked at Sophie sternly. "Can we allow this expense, Sophie?" Sophie knew this tone. Olivia was playing with poor Plug.

"I don't really think so, Olivia. After all, we work damned hard for our pittance; this guy should pay for his own gambling losses. He sounds like the Jamaican, I fear. 'Darling,' she drawled, mimicking Ty's accent, "I just lost a fortune on cards; you don't happen to have it lying around, do you, baby?" They managed to keep straight faces while Plug looked from one to the other, getting more uncomfortable by the second.

Then Freddie cut in. "Ignore them. They're like a couple of bullies in the playground, Plug. They're just winding you up. It means they like you."

Plug beamed and looked relieved.

"Of course that goes on expenses." Olivia had to laugh. "Now, get on with it."

Their starters arrived, and they tucked in to a creamy seafood salad. Plug swallowed a large mouthful. "Anyway, I followed him around very discreetly. I was sitting, nursing a cold beer and pretending to read a paper, and I heard him tell the current woman that he had to go out that night 'on business.'"

Sophie and Olivia exchanged glances. They knew Ty and his business trips, both local and overseas.

"Well, I sat across the road, out of sight—easy to do, as there are so many tourists blocking out the skyline. About nine thirty that evening he slips out with the bodyguards and whizzes off in his Merc. I didn't have to keep too close to him, because I had sneaked up on the car when nobody was around and put a tracker on it. Eventually I traced him to a bit of a dump on the edge of the shanty town area just outside here. The bodyguards lolled around outside and rolled spliffs, and your man went inside. I went around the back, where the two goons couldn't see me. The ground rises there, and I could get to the ridge and look down on the windows at the back. The house was very small so easy to get sight of any movement." Plug stopped and ate more of his starter. "Mmm, nice this. Well, I used my powerful binoculars, and what did I see! This pretty damned gorgeous woman. Local, beautifully put together, plump everywhere. Well, they aren't there for a Bible class, that's for sure." Again he ate, wiped his mouth with the linen serviette, and continued. "Well, I was there all night, knackered, and so must he have been. The so-called bodyguards were wasted. Been smoking weed and drinking rum all the night long, so out cold. Your Jamaican had been at it nearly all night long—boy he's one virile guy!"

The girls grinned at each other. Freddie raised his eyebrows beseechingly and spooned salad into his mouth.

"It gets better—or worse. As dawn comes up, he stops coming up and goes to the door, followed by the object of his very considerable desires. She follows him out onto the porch, kisses him and snuggles up and all that crap, whilst the two idiots struggle up off the ground and pretend to be on duty. It's then, as she turns to kiss him goodbye, that I see him patting her belly. And it's a pretty big belly. Full of a little Jamaican, I suspect." Plug finished his food and took a swig of his second scotch.

Olivia's face was thunderous. "She's pregnant, and he's still at her, and all night! Bloody hell! The animal. I feel sick, really sick."

Sophie looked quite horrified too. She thought for a minute. "It's not totally unusual for couples to keep having sex right up to birth, to be honest. But all night, and … was it rough? I mean, what positions was it in?"

"Oh, he wasn't squashing her, if that's what you mean. Spoons, him behind her, all the gentler positions—"

Freddie coughed. Plug grinned. "We must have a talk later, young Freddie."

"Kill me now," said Freddie, winking at Olivia.

"So, what we have is the Jamaican shacked up with a rich woman, doing well it seems, but with a very pregnant bit of stuff hidden away outside town. I wonder if he has to pay those useless goons of his to keep their mouths shut."

"Probably threatens them," Olivia remarked grimly.

They took a minute to look at their next choice of food courses.

"Freddie," said Plug, "I'll order one of their giant steaks, and we'll see if we can't murder it between us, OK?"

"Right on," agreed the boy.

Sophie wanted jerk chicken, as she hadn't had too much of it in her lifetime, and Olivia had assured her that Ty's version was total crap. Olivia decided on a steak too, but a very much smaller one than the men intended to do battle with. They ordered, and then Sophie asked for the wine list and sorted that; she was the connoisseur in that field.

After that was done, Sophie turned to Plug.

"Can you get us a sleeper phone, Plug?"

"Yep, my love, no problem." He grinned. "I know what you're thinking."

"And exactly what is she thinking?" Olivia asked him.

"Get a sleeper phone—a very cheap thing—with a new SIM card, a number your target doesn't know. Do your calls or texts or whatever, and then chuck the lot away."

"But what—" Olivia stopped, and a smile spread across her face. "OK, I get it. We send a message to the main woman, and tell her about her baby's baby's baby, if you get my drift—" They all smiled.

"Ouch!" said Sophie. "I just hope it doesn't backfire."

"Meaning what?" asked Olivia.

"That the main woman doesn't shoot him or something. I would hate to be responsible for a murder."

"Oh, for heaven's sake, Soph! Stop being so soft and sloppy. The bastard deserves whatever he's got coming. I wouldn't pee on him if he burst into flames." Even as she spoke, Olivia was remembering that Ty was probably where he was because she had put him there. She hastily dismissed the thought. "Perhaps he'll get away with being castrated with a blunt penknife." They all raised their glasses and laughed.

Then the food arrived, huge platters piled with first-class cuisine. Plug and Freddie attacked the steak, which appeared to have originated from a dinosaur. The wine waiter poured for them, and soon they were all enjoying the gourmet meal. The payback was on hold until the next day, at least. Two hours later, after fresh fruit, a selection of good cheeses, and really good coffee, they were sitting down by the edge of the sea on the recliners that were there for hotel clients. Plug, Olivia, and Sophie were savouring Remy Martin cognac to round off their evening. Freddie was lying back and looking at the stars.

Afterwards, Plug walked them all back to their room, wished them a very good night, and went away to his Land Rover.

Sophie was concerned that he was sober enough to drive. Olivia assured her that he was drink-proof, whatever that was. They were both pleasantly fuzzy, too tired to plot anything until the morrow. Soon they had all settled in their beds and were lulled to sleep by the soft breeze and the distant calls of night birds, the sounds of the exotic island.

In the morning Sophie and Olivia were both up early, out on the balcony, drinking coffee. The day was opening into fierce, bright heat and showcasing the beauty of their surroundings. Freddie was still semiconscious and recovering. They sat in silence for some time. Then Olivia said, "We'll send that text as soon as Plug brings the sleeper phone. We've only got one more day here. I'd like to leave behind maximum damage to that arrogant bastard."

Sophie agreed, as she sat sipping coffee and yawning. They showered, dressed in loose, comfortable dresses, and sank into the deep cushions of the balcony chairs.

Plug arrived about eleven, no longer a fashion plate but casually comfortable. He joined them for another coffee, and then he produced the sleeper phone. The SIM card was already inserted, and Plug handed it to Olivia. He laid his hand on her arm. "Look, before you send that killer, I heard something this morning at Errol's bar. I dropped in just to update myself. It's always good to keep an eye and an ear on the situation. Last night was a bit of a revelation, but it gets better—or worse. Depends who you are."

Olivia was growing impatient. "Well spit it out, Plug—"

"OK. Tonight your man intends to propose to the main woman."

Olivia and Sophie sat up as if connected to the mains electricity. They stared at each other. "Oh my giddy aunt, it's all happening again—all over again! The lousy, whoring, selfish, lying, two-faced, thieving—" Olivia stopped for breath.

"Do I gather that he's in the habit of doing this?" asked Plug, with a smile.

"You could say that," replied Sophie.

"Oh hell! I hope he's not coming here to do it." Olivia looked worried.

"No, don't stress, my love. He's going to throw a party at Errol's. Just for the tourists, he's told her, but it's more for friends and family, and then he's going to pop the question, put the ring on her finger—"

"And a collar and lead round her neck!" added Olivia sarcastically.

"So, ladies, that seems to be the time to make your move. I'll be hanging around, and I'll text you when to do it, OK?"

The ladies agreed. Plug stayed, chatting with them for hours. He told them about his nomadic life, his adventures, his scrapes with the law, and the countries he had been too. They were many, and Olivia had been to most of them, so she could happily swap experiences with him. Watching them as they laughed and swapped memories, Sophie saw a relaxation in Olivia, a softening and sweetening of her nature, a dropping of her tight guard. This pleased Sophie a lot. She was growing very fond of Olivia and was concerned at how their life collisions with the Jamaican had affected this kind, caring woman. At times she felt almost guilty, but why? She hadn't spoilt Olivia's life; she had transformed it or even saved it.

Lunchtime approached, and they invited Plug to the pool. Freddie was up and crawling about in a daze by then. He brightened up when the pool was mentioned. He turned to Sophie. "Come on, Nan—you're coming too. You've got to learn to swim. You'll be dead soon, so get on with it!"

"You charming little brat!" Sophie retorted. "I'll just sit and watch all of you."

"Oh, no you won't," Olivia said. "You're going to try, so get your cozzie and towels and follow us fishes."

Sophie was dismayed. Apart from her fear of water, she dreaded the thought of displaying her ample thighs, belly, and upper arms to the public gaze. She felt like a hippopotamus in her costume. Reluctantly she went to her bedroom to change for the ordeal. Behind her she heard a gentle whisper. It was Ben's voice. "You're beautiful—in every way. Go out there and show them, my lovely." She swung round, but the room was empty. She smiled to herself. Then she stripped and put on her red-and-black costume with its special panels which claimed they would "flatten and reduce the stomach." She wondered vaguely what these panels would actually do with her large belly—push it round to her buttocks, perhaps, and make them even bigger? She laughed as she picked up her towels. Then she slipped on a loose, comfortable kaftan and a pair of flip-flop sandals. She gathered up her life support system into a large tote bag and joined the others to walk down to the pool. Sophie's heart was galloping with fright.

Everyone jumped in and swam around for a while. Then they turned to Sophie, held their arms out, and encouraged her to join them. She sat, petrified, but then, remembering Ben's voice, she took off her kaftan and walked self-consciously to the steps. She slowly lowered herself into the warm water. She splashed around, dipped her head under the water, and tried to relax. She watched Olivia and Plug swimming together confidently and expertly. Freddie was showing off to the young girl he had met there a few days ago. He was diving in and looping around underwater like a fish. Oh, how Sophie wished she could just do that. She tried again and again to let her feet leave the bottom of the pool, to just kick off and glide through the turquoise water, but again and again she panicked and failed.

Sophie was about to give up and climb out when she saw him. He was sitting at the side of the pool, smiling at her. He was, she assumed, Jamaican—about sixtyish, muscular, with greying hair and that goatee-type of beard that Ty had and which Sophie loved. The man had a tiny diamond stud in his ear and a thick gold chain around his neck. He was wearing only very smart Bermuda shorts, and greying curls covered his large, firm chest. He had a discreet tattoo on one forearm. Everything about him sang to Sophie's soul. Suddenly she felt a hot surge of courage. She launched herself forward strongly, kicked her feet away from the bottom of the pool, and did what she hoped was a crawl stroke—and she was swimming! Sophie was swimming, awkwardly but determinedly—not splashing about frenziedly and unhappily but with growing confidence. She went past Olivia and Plug, who stopped swimming, trod water, and cheered her on. Freddie jumped up and down and shouted, "Go Nan, go!" Sophie was exhilarated. She turned, kicking against the side of the pool as she had seen Olympic swimmers do, nearly sank, but ploughed upwards and onwards, eventually coming to rest by the steps, right next to the desirable guy she had, apparently, done this for. She climbed out onto the steps, and the gorgeous guy stood up and applauded her. He then put out his hand and helped her out. Olivia, Plug, and Freddie were applauding her too. Sophie could have floated up to heaven at that minute. The vision asked her to sit down with him. Sophie went to get her kaftan and tote bag and sat. She was about to pull her kaftan over her hated body, when the guy said quietly. "Don't cover up. The view is stunning from where I am."

Sophie felt herself blushing.

He smiled. "Can I offer you a drink of something?"

Sophie felt daring. "Yes, please. I'd love a rum and pineapple juice."

As well as the pool bar there was waiter service, and the dream called one over and ordered two rum and pineapple juices. He smiled at her. "Are you on holiday? Is that your family—I mean the support group?"

"Oh, well, Freddie's my grandson, but the others are my friend Olivia and, well, a business associate, Plug." The dream seemed amused by the name. "We're on holiday—at least Freddie and Olivia and I are. Plug lives here. Oh, I'm Sophie."

He put out his large hand. "I'm Gayelord. I'm here on business with my cousin Otis. He's sleeping off a rather too-good night. When do you two ladies return to your husbands?"

Sophie smiled. "There are no husbands, or partners, or anyone of that kind. We're sort of recovering just now."

Gayelord smiled. "Yes, I know that situation. Was that the first time you ever swam, Sophie?"

"Yes, did it show that much?"

"Not really. I could see how nervous you were. I was willing you to let go and just do it. I felt really happy for you when you took off."

"Thanks." Sophie was feeling relaxed and actually happy. Just then Olivia came up with Plug. They towelled themselves down and then came over to the table where Gayelord and Sophie were sitting. Introductions were made, and then Plug excused himself to get on with business.

"I have to be somewhere important tonight," he said, looking meaningfully at Olivia and Sophie. They said their goodbyes to him and turned to chat with Gayelord. Just then another very good-looking, slightly younger, man arrived. He was introduced as Otis, Gayelord's cousin. They all drank, chatted, and had a really pleasant hour and a bit. The men were indeed Jamaican but had homes in London, too. Hints told Sophie and Olivia that the men could be free of other women and available. But then Gayelord informed them that, regretfully, he and Otis had a business meeting of some importance. They had to leave but really hoped that they might see the ladies again. No meeting was arranged, and Sophie was slightly disappointed, as was Olivia. Ah well, they were leaving for England the next day. It had been very pleasant, but … The girls remained, smothered in sun blocker and soaking up the sun, watching Freddie with his lovely little Jamaican girlfriend. This night there would be payback for the Jamaican. For now they would relax and contemplate what they would inflict on the man who had dragged them through hell. They closed their eyes and soaked up the expensive sun. Both were beginning to go a healthily dark colour. Sophie was smothered in freckles, but she was beginning to accept and even love all of her imperfections. Olivia was a gentle shade of dark sand, and her blonde hair had become even blonder.

The day rolled by. Freddie, tired and content, came to join them, and soon they were all back in their suite, showering and ordering room service lunch. It was a rather late lunch, but Freddie was ravenous, and he ate enough food to fill a horse. They sunbathed some more, and Freddie disappeared with his girl, Mahalia, and her parents, who appeared to like him a lot. Mahalia's father asked Sophie if Freddie could stay with them and have dinner, and Sophie happily agreed. She and Olivia returned to the suite. The plot was unwinding. They took out the sleeper phone, waiting for Plug to call and tell them what was happening. As the evening wore on, they felt nervous and impatient. Then Olivia's phone shrilled. It was Plug.

"OK, I've got the woman's number and other information you'll need. I'll text it to you in a minute. Wait until I tell you when to do it. Good luck." He disappeared. The text with the number arrived, along with the name of the other woman and her address. Olivia and Sophie were on edge. Sophie mixed up two gin and tonics with plenty of ice and slices of lime. They sipped at them—and they waited. Then the text came from Plug.

"OK. Send it right now. See ya both." They looked at each other. They had decided on the message. Olivia typed it, retyped it, corrected it, edited it, and finally it was ready to send. They read it once again before the Send button was pressed, just to be sure it would have the impact they needed it to have.

Congratulations, my dear. So you're marrying Ty Benton. Before you plan your big day, you might just want to pop down to Anderson Drive. Number 10. Have a word with Lorna who lives there. She might just be a bit surprised when you tell her that you're marrying Ty, because she's been sleeping with him for some time now and he's been telling her how much he loves her. Oh, and just one other small detail—she's expecting Ty's baby in a few months. He must have forgotten to tell her about you when he was staying overnight with her a couple of days ago. I know you've probably parted with quite a lot of your cash since you met him, but it was two other women who paid for most of what he's got. They've got off the gravy train now, and in any case, you'll grow tired, as they did, of that outsized dick. Watering eyes and ripped cervixes can get boring after a while—and in any case the drinking, violence, disappearances, lies, and constant pleading for money for everything he can invent will kill any feelings you imagined you had. Enjoy your engagement party.

It was sent, and they waited for the fallout. Just over half an hour later, Plug texted Olivia. "Bullseye, ladies! Spot on. The shit has hit the fan, and boy, what a performance is going on right now—you'd love it! I'll be over in about twenty mins to settle, as you're all flying home tomorrow. Plug."

They looked at each other for a moment. Olivia laughed heartily. "Serves the bastard right. He didn't learn from the first time he did this. Hope she gives him total and utter hell."

Sophie felt momentary sadness. She was sad that the Jamaican had not learned a thing from the trauma of September the sixth and also because her faint, undying hopes that he was basically decent and redeemable were all in vain. But he deserved this. He deserved to suffer for what he had done to them both. She recalled the pain she had felt when he'd denied even knowing her, when he'd lied about her so disgustingly after all the sacrifices she had made to help him.

Olivia recalled her shock and deep hurt when she'd discovered that her so called fiancé was texting with another woman even while he was proposing to her, that he was sleeping with her when he disappeared, and that he was sleeping with the ex he denied having anything to do with. The hurt of finding all this out after she had given him a home and indulged his demands for cars, clothes, travel and accommodation, and food—and a great deal of alcohol.

The two ladies topped up their glasses and lifted them. "To karma—may she bite the Jamaican hard where it hurts the most." Then they started packing for the next day.

Sophie called Freddie's phone and told him that he needed to return very soon, as he had to pack too. The girl's father chatted with Sophie. "Your grandson is a lovely young man, a gentleman. I am very particular about who Mahalia mixes with. It is very sad that Freddie has to return to England tomorrow, but maybe he could return one day. We may be going over there soon, and I would love to have your address so that Mahalia may visit you with us, if that is agreeable with you."

"Thank you so much. Of course you may visit us, at any time. I'll text you our address."

"I'll bring Freddie back to the hotel right away."

"Thanks. He needs to pack for tomorrow. Thank you for having him this evening."

Freddie returned and watched sadly as Mahalia waved goodbye from her father's smart red convertible. Sophie and Olivia comforted him, telling him that they could Skype frequently, and he cheered up. He told them of the really fantastic meal they eaten at a large restaurant in Kingston. Then he went to sort out his luggage.

Later Plug arrived, and Olivia and Sophie each paid half of his considerable fee. They thought it well worth the money. He sat and described the chaos that their text had unleashed. The female had screamed at Ty and thrown nearly every plate and bottle in the place at him. He had accused yet another woman of manufacturing the accusations "because she was jealous, baby." To Olivia and Sophie that sounded sort of familiar, and they laughed heartily.

"Well, ladies, it seems as if you might have got your own back and seen the last of him," Plug said.

Olivia frowned. "No, I wish it were true, but he's the comeback kid. I fear we may yet see him again, when we least want and need to. I'm really grateful to you for all your help, Plug, and so is Sophie. We really hope he gets his payback in full measure over this. He's had it coming for years now."

"OK, you two lovely ladies, I must go home and sleep now. I'll be here to drive ahead of you to the airport and hand the car over to the hire firm. Sleep tight, and don't be late."

They wished him a good night and resumed their packing. Later they had a light supper brought up by room service, after which they went to shower and sleep. Freddie was already stuffed with good food. He had packed and was settled down to sleep. Soon all was still.

Olivia

I loved you so much Ty. I would have given you the world. You lived like a king anyway. You had all of me— my soul, my heart, my love. Most certainly you had my body, often and passionately. What did I not give you, do for you, sacrifice for you? I gave you almost all the freedom you demanded—and a lot you just took without caring about my feelings. And all the time you were in other womens' beds and bodies. Whoring, Ty—yes, whoring. Stealing from that poor, struggling woman who had so little, just to prove to me what a 'man' you were. Sleeping with her to get money. The only thing I asked of you was to stay faithful to me. I endured all the rest because I loved you and adored you. You were my everything. In this country—your country—I saw a dark and terrible side to your nature. Despite all the horrors of those two holidays, despite my reaching the end of my emotional tether, I took you back yet again. And you repaid me with that evening of September the sixth. Part of me still wants your body next to me here. I can never totally stop loving you—and this you know and will try to exploit, if ever there is another time for us. But if there is, you will not do this to me again—ever. You will live to my rules, be my man, be what I want you to be. You will do this, and again, you will live the life you aspire to. But the other half of me—the badly hurt part—will never have you back, never, ever forgive you. I only want to hurt you as you have hurt me—badly and never-endingly. In the deepest recesses of my being you will always exist, something I want so badly that it burns me like acid. But something I can never have, because I will no longer be yours now that you have betrayed me. I listen to the sounds of the oncoming night. You are hearing them too. We did everything together once. Now that is over. We are finished, and the pain will be there—always.

Sophie

I cannot bear the thought of you being hurt now, as I could not bear it before. I am always the weakest one— easy to use and reject, easy to hurt and exploit. I had so little, but whatever I had was yours when you begged me for help. I happily huddled in a blanket in my cold cottage when the icy winds howled outside, because I believed that you were cold and hungry, and I could not bear to have if you had not. I accepted your indifference to my suffering and tragedies. I had to respond to yours. I had so little. No beauty or shapeliness. No house, or possessions, or savings. Just my stubborn ability to work, when I was exhausted and unwell. And you grew greedy, and demanding, and cruel. You used my body for your needs, with no concern for mine. You pretended to love me, and I believed you because I wanted to—needed to—because my love for you was so deep, so true, so unconditional. You were my world, my life, my everything. My intelligence told me that I had nothing to offer you, that you had other women who were younger, richer, and more attractive, but my stubborn heart refused to acknowledge the painful truth. The hurt you caused me was beyond describing. You denied me, as Peter denied Christ. You denied even knowledge of me. You told lies that tore my heart to shreds. I was vulnerable, fragile, easy to hurt and to use, and you homed in on me like a raptor. I will not stop loving you. I cannot. But part of me is hardening, and hatred of you, which is only another face of love, is very, very slowly turning to indifference. I have flashes of tenderness and distress at your comedown, but I cannot forget what you did to me when you were found out. You sacrificed me, without mercy. Life will pay my debts for me. I know, with a deep knowledge, that you will never stop trying to get back to her and to get her back. And I know that, whatever she says and professes to think, she will never stop doing the same. But she has you at her mercy, because she found you out. I would never stand in the way of either of you; I would just quietly disappear. I love you enough to want any chance of happiness you may grasp at to work, even if it breaks my heart. You used me cruelly, but the love I still have for you will not allow me to wish you ill.

I made my last gesture of love some months ago. Now I am turning away. Remember me.

The hot, beautiful day dawned and found them all up early and checking everything. Freddie couldn't find his passport, and there was a minor panic, but that resolved itself when he found it packed with his laptop. Plug rolled in, and soon their luggage was being taken downstairs to the waiting car. They thanked the staff warmly, left a substantial amount to be shared between them, thanked the manager on duty, and left sadly. Olivia drove the hire car behind Plug's car to Sangster. As she drove, Sophie remarked, "I don't really know why we bothered to hire the car, do you? We only went out in it once. Plug could have taken us, couldn't he?"

"Yep, I suppose you're right. But we didn't know what we were going to do really, so it was there if we had needed it.

Expensive, though." They drove through the open scrubland and woodlands and were soon at Sangster. They hadn't eaten breakfast and so were all hungry. As they had plenty of time, they went into the restaurant after they had cleared customs and checked their luggage. Plug wished them all good luck and goodbye and kissed the two women on the cheek. He waved them off and left them to eat. They had quite a while to kill and chatted about their days with the dating sites. Sophie was adamant that she had had quite enough of the cattle market called online dating. Olivia was willing to give it another try. After all, they had encountered quite a few nasty specimens and knew now what to avoid. Forewarned was forearmed, surely? Sophie was still reluctant, although she conceded that if—and it was a very big if—she found a man with the slightest spark of what she wanted, she might just give it all another try. They tucked into their food and were just considering a dessert when a voice behind them said, "Well, hello ladies. Olivia and Sophie, isn't it?" They both turned. There were Gayelord and Otis—smart, handsome, tall, and rather appealing. "We're on the noon plane to Gatwick. Are you on it too?"

"Yes, we're in premier class," Olivia told them.

"Well, how about that. So are we." Gayelord smiled. "May we sit down with you?

"Yes, of course," the girls chorused, moving their hand luggage off the chairs. Gayelord and Otis ordered coffee and sandwiches, and soon they were all chatting happily. The two cousins were involved in exporting Jamaican foodstuffs to European and other markets; they had a thriving business set up.

As Gayelord spoke to Sophie in his deep, sexy drawl, she found herself looking into his eyes with a steady gaze. *I like you*, she thought. *Just like—that's quite enough! I feel so comfortable here, so natural.* Olivia was interacting well with Otis too. They were deep in business discussions, which lasted until the tannoy announced that their flight was boarding. They all filed onto the plane, and the girls were delighted to find that Gayelord and Otis were seated opposite them.

The formalities were gone through. The stewardess waved her arms about and told them what to do and how to do it if the plane crashed. "Just what we need to hear," Freddie muttered sardonically. Then the huge aircraft revved up, shuddered, roared loudly, gathered speed, and took off. Sophie clutched at Olivia's hand as they climbed quickly into the Caribbean skies. Soon drinks were being dished out.

The girls sat, champagne glasses in their hands, watching Jamaica disappear. Sophie, looking a little sad, said, "Ah well, and now it ends."

Olivia glanced across the gangway to the two men, who smiled back. She raised a well-manicured eyebrow, raised her glass, and replied, "No, Sophie—and now it begins."

The big aircraft banked and turned towards the coast of Cuba. Life was all out there, waiting.

CPSIA information can be obtained
at www.ICGtesting.com
Printed in the USA
BVHW030214110320
574716BV00001B/2

9 781728 385150